U0107604

张 巍◎主编

荷马与赫西奥德的竞赛

The Contest of Homer and Hesiod

复旦大学历史学系主办

西方古典学辑刊
Museum Sinicum

第五辑

复旦大學 出版社

目　录

编者引言

柏拉图在《理想国》的末尾提起一场"哲学与诗之间的古老纷争",并让他笔下的苏格拉底站在哲学的一方将这场"纷争"推向前所未有的高度。所谓"哲学与诗之间的古老纷争",实质上是一场"建设性的竞争"(agōn),而非"破坏性的斗争"(关于这一区分,参见尼采《荷马的竞赛》一文)——这是哲学要超越并取代诗成为古希腊最高智慧的"竞争"。如果说"哲学与诗之间的古老纷争"本质性地决定了柏拉图所创设的"哲学",那么在此之前,还存在着一番"诗人与诗人之间的竞争",同样本质性地决定了"哲学与诗之间的古老纷争",因为只有首先明确与"哲学"发生"纷争"的"诗"本身的性质,才可能真正理解这场"纷争"的意义所在,而要明确"诗"本身的性质,又必须透过"诗人与诗人之间的竞争"。

我们知道,"竞争"精神早就洋溢于古希腊文化的方方面面,例如宗教庆典或葬礼仪式上举行的体育竞技、城邦生活里展开的政治角逐和法庭诉讼,私人空间里进行的会饮游戏,等等(参见布克哈特《希腊文化史》论"争胜时代",1872年德文本卷四,第82—159页,或1998年Sheila Stern英译本,第160—213页);而在智识领域,则最早见诸"诗人之间的竞争"(同样早期,甚至更早的"先知之间的竞争",如赫西奥德残篇278M-W所载的先知卡尔卡斯与墨普索斯之间的竞赛,因材料不足征而难以考索)。正是"诗人之争"为古希腊智识领域里的竞争抹上了底色,影响了后起的智识之士如哲学家、智术师和史学家相互之间的竞争,以及他们挑战诗人的竞争(柏拉图的"哲学与诗之间的古老纷争"便是其中的显例)。**诗人之间的竞争之**

所以至关重要，**既在于它规定了诗的本质**（正如哲学、智术和史学也是在与诗的竞争中规定了自身的本质），**亦在于它奠定了古希腊"争胜文化"的精神根基**。

早期希腊的"诗人之争"最典范地体现于"荷马与赫西奥德的竞赛"。荷马是古希腊首位也是最伟大的诗人，被誉为"（独一无二的）诗人"（the poet），而赫西奥德则是仅次于荷马的"另一位诗人"（the other poet），他们之间的竞赛自赫西奥德的时代以降就在希腊广为流传，载录于后来的诗人传记。不过，存世文献所见版本，从年代上看，都不早于罗马帝国时期，比如普鲁塔克（1世纪）的"七哲宴谈"（《道德论丛》153F—154A），金口迪翁（1—2世纪）的《论王权演说辞之二》（2.9—12），还有其他几个版本如路吉阿诺斯（2世纪）的《真实的故事》（2.22）以及菲罗斯特拉托斯（2—3世纪）的《论英雄》（43.7）则更为晚出。相比之下，同样来自2世纪的匿名文章《荷马与赫西奥德的竞赛》（以下简称《竞赛》）算是最完整的版本。该文全名《论荷马与赫西奥德及其世系与他们的竞赛》，体裁上属于荷马传记，往往与其他数种传世的荷马传记归为一类，且被置于首位。自1870年尼采首开先河，学界对这篇传记的作者归属、创作年代和材料来源已展开深入的研讨（详见本辑韦斯特和理查森两文，后者对前者多有回应和辩难，颇可对读）。目前学界公认，该传记的主体部分最晚来源于前4世纪的智术师阿尔基达马斯的作品《缪斯集》（韦斯特所持观点），很有可能源于前5世纪甚至前6世纪（理查森所持观点）。无论前6、前5还是前4世纪，《竞赛》都反映了更早时期的书面及口述传统，无疑是我们考察早期希腊"诗人之争"最为详尽而全面的文本（另一个完整且详尽的文本，即阿里斯托芬的喜剧《蛙》，延续了早期的"诗人之争"，将之展演于两位悲剧家埃斯库罗斯和欧里庇得斯身上，并与"荷马与赫西奥德的竞赛"构成巧妙的互文关系，详见本辑罗森一文）。

据《竞赛》所言，荷马与赫西奥德之间展开的是一场"智慧"（sophia，见第六节）的竞赛（agōn），这里的"智慧"指的是古希腊两位最伟大的诗人所代表的"诗性智慧"，因而是一场关乎"诗性智慧"之本质的"建设性竞争"。这场"竞赛"共六个回合，可分两个阶段，每个阶段有着不同的竞赛模式(参见本辑格拉齐奥西一文)。第一个阶段由赫西奥德发问,荷马回答,一问一答围绕不同的主题,凡五个回合。引人注目的是,最重大的"哲学"问题构成了一首一尾的框架(第一、五回合),而中间三个回合系展示诗艺的各种"谜题"(第二、三、四回合)。在这个阶段,表面的竞争之下,两位诗人实质上完成了一种合作:赫西奥德通过发问,让荷马的回答涵括了他们各自所代表的"诗性智慧",熔铸成浑然一体的最高智慧。缘此,第一个阶段的竞赛首先在"最高义谛"的层面展开,即关于"最好、最善、最美之物"(phertaton, ariston, kalliston)的问答(见第七节)。人类此在的"最高义谛"必定从"最好、最善、最美之物"当中探寻,因此赫西奥德向荷马首发此问,而荷马的回答突出了人类此在的"悲观主义"基调。正是在这一基调上,"诗性智慧"才能充分施展,于是赫西奥德所发第二问关于"最美之物",荷马的回答便突出了诗歌的优先性。概言之,"诗"乃人生此在的悲观境地里的"最美之物"——即此便是"诗性智慧"的"最高义谛"。倘若比较其他古代文明,鲜有例外地皆从道德标准出发回答"最好、最善、最美之物"之问,只有早期希腊文明里的"诗性智慧"不从道德标准衡量人类此在的最高价值,而是从丰沛的生命力及其带来的生命之乐;与之相比,共同体的良好秩序及其带来的富足安康并非最终目的,那只是"诗歌"创作、表演和观赏的前提,诗歌作为"最美之物"赋予个体的美名才是最终目的。

竞赛的第二个阶段只有一个回合(即第六回合),此时荷马与赫西奥德被要求吟诵自己诗作中最出色的篇章,并由第三方担任裁判(见第十二节)。在场的希腊人要求将胜利授予荷马,而国王帕诺伊德斯却主张,公正的评判是让歌颂劳作与和平而非战争与杀戮的诗人获胜。这个出人意料的结果引来了众说纷纭的解释(参阅本辑格拉齐奥西、巴西诺及罗森诸文)。问题的关键在于,这里的竞赛模式发生了变化:由最后这个回合构成的第二个阶段从"竞争性的合作"转向了"竞争性的对立",意在彰显两位诗人之别——竞赛的对手是荷马与赫西奥德,更准确地说,是荷马与赫西奥德所代表的两种史诗传统。他们的竞争关乎这两种史诗传统的"诗性智慧",可视作"诗性智慧"的内部竞赛。那么,荷马的"诗性智慧"与赫西奥德的"诗性智慧"差异何在？两者通过"竞争性的对立"又形成何种关系？

在早期希腊，归于荷马名下的主要是英雄史诗，尤以《伊利亚特》和《奥德赛》为代表；而归于赫西奥德名下的主要是神谱史诗和教谕史诗，前者以《神谱》，后者以《劳作与时日》为代表。两部荷马史诗当中，《伊利亚特》通过对"英雄之死"的肯定与颂扬，生成了一幅悲剧性的世界图景：悲剧性乃英雄存在的根本基调，只有饱受苦难，直至经历终极的苦难——死亡——英雄才能证成自己；因此，死亡具有优先的此在意义，而人类此在的最高意义正由悲剧性的"英雄之死"成就。《伊利亚特》的主题"阿基琉斯的忿怒"突出了人类此在的悲剧性，"忿怒"带来的"无数苦难"导致阿基琉斯的战友和他自己的"死亡"，而《奥德赛》的主题"奥德修斯的归家"，也强调奥德修斯在归家途中"饱受苦难"，但他终究得以生还。《奥德赛》序诗里的"饱受苦难"(polla algea)与《伊利亚特》序诗里的"无数苦难"(muria algea)正相呼应，可见两部史诗的主题通过人类此在的悲剧性，巧妙地交织了"英雄之死"与"英雄之生"。

正如《伊利亚特》这部"英雄之死"的史诗必然优先于《奥德赛》这部"英雄之生"的史诗，且构成一种先后等级的互文关系，《神谱》这部"宇宙秩序"的史诗也必然优先于《劳作与时日》这部"社会秩序"的史诗，且同样构成一种先后等级的互文关系。《神谱》从宇宙创化的宏观层面上，叙述宙斯及奥林坡斯诸神如何用"公平分配"原则(dasmos)取代了克罗诺斯及提坦诸神的"一报还一报"原则(tisis)，建立了公平正义(dikē)的宇宙秩序(kosmos)，整个宇宙的演化进程得以从"毁灭性的斗争"向"建设性的竞争"转化。《劳作与时日》的开篇(第11—26行)将"毁灭性的斗争"和"建设性的竞争"表述为两位不和女神之间的差异和高低之分，并从人类社会的中观层面以及单个个体的微观层面上，叙述人类生活同样基于"毁灭性的斗争"向"建设性的竞争"的转化，如同"青铜种族"到"英雄种族"的"历史"所显示的那样，而在人类目前所处的"黑铁种族"的境遇中，每个个体都应当抛弃"毁灭性的斗争"，取法"建设性的竞争"。

从整体性的眼光来看，荷马史诗聚焦于人类历史的英雄阶段，而赫西奥德史诗则指向英雄史诗之前的宇宙创生和演化阶段,以及之后的人类历史的黑铁阶段。两部赫西奥德史诗从而与两部荷马史诗构成先后等级的互文关系,即《神谱》被置于英雄世界之前,《劳作与时日》被置于其后,用这样的一前一后的框架设计将整个英雄世界置入后景的相对性当中。作为"荷马与赫西奥德的竞赛"故事的最终来源,《劳作与时日》第648—662行叙述的诗人参加安菲达马斯的葬礼竞赛并获胜一事,是这一层互文关系的枢纽。两位诗人的"竞赛"故而也是两种史诗传统的较量,但这种较量恰恰实践了赫西奥德所昭示的"建设性的竞争",用赫西奥德史诗的"诗性智慧"来融摄荷马史诗的"诗性智慧",以一种超胜的方式将之纳入自己更加宏阔的终极视野,并共同成就古希腊最高的"诗性智慧"。

因此,当帕诺伊德斯着眼于"公正"或"正义"(dikaion, dikē 的形容词),做出那个"出人意料"的评判之时,恰恰确证了由《劳作与时日》开篇里的两位不和女神所代表的"毁灭性斗争"向"建设性竞争"的转化实乃"正义"("公正")的本质——从宇宙创化到人类社会,再到单个个体,莫不如此——而赫西奥德的胜出,也就意味着赫西奥德史诗所代表的"诗性智慧"通过"建设性竞争"对荷马史诗所代表的"诗性智慧"的涵纳。

张 巍

二零二二年十一月

经典译解

Classical Text: Translation & Studies

《论荷马与赫西奥德及其世系与他们的竞赛》汉译简注[*]

古希腊语原著研读班 译注

一[1]、所有人都希望最神圣的诗人荷马和赫西奥德被称作自己的公民同胞。但赫西奥德曾提及自己家乡的名字，这就平息了一切争论，因为他说他自己的父亲

> 定居在赫利孔山附近的凄凉村庄
> 阿斯克拉，凛冬苦夏，没有好年光。[2]

---

[*] 下文简称《竞赛》。译者使用的古希腊文底本为 P. Bassino, *The Certamen Homeri et Hesiodi: A Commentary*, Berlin; Boston: de Gruyter, 2018, pp. 86–113, 部分读法有改动，同时也参考了巴西诺的评注（即前引底本），并参考了以下的英译本：H. G. Evelyn-White ed., *Hesiod, the Homeric Hymns and Homerica*, Cambridge, Mass.: Harvard University Press, 1936; M. L. West ed., *Homeric Hymns. Homeric Apocrypha. Lives of Homer*, Cambridge, Mass.: Harvard University Press, 2003. 翻译与注释工作在张巍教授指导下由段盛雅、何炜、姜宏宇、彭川、孙东生、杨勤杰、于明睿共同完成，何炜、彭川负责统合工作。国内现有吴雅凌的《竞赛》中译本（赫西奥德著，吴雅凌译：《神谱［笺注本］》，华夏出版社，2022 年，第 395—410 页），但注释较少，部分细节与原文有一定出入。译者希望新的译本能为国内读者更忠实地展现《竞赛》的原貌。

[1] 《竞赛》抄本并无分节，本文使用巴西诺对《竞赛》的分节（源自维拉莫维茨编订的版本，见 U. von Wilamowitz-Moellendorff, *Vitae Homeri et Hesiodi in usum scholarum*, Bonn, 1916）。第一节通过探寻荷马和赫西奥德的家乡来展开主题，首先从赫西奥德的家乡开始。从《竞赛》编者的"传记式"解读法看来，赫西奥德的家乡已经由他本人的诗歌清楚地揭示了。

[2] Hes. *Op.* 639–640. 文中所有来自其他古典文献的诗文皆为此次新译。

二[3]、至于荷马，几乎所有的城邦及其居民都宣称他出生在他们当中。首先，士麦拿人说他是当地的河神墨勒斯（Meles）和宁芙克瑞伊提斯（Creithis）[4]所生，起初被称为墨勒西格涅斯（Melesigenes）[5]。后来，他因双目失明被更名为荷马，因为在他们当中这个名字是惯用于这样的人身上的。继而，基俄斯人拿出证据证明荷马是他们自己的公民，声称甚至有一些源自荷马血脉的人在他们中间绵延下来，这些人被称为"荷马裔代"（Homeridae）[6]。而克罗丰人甚至指出了当地的一个地方，他们说荷马教授文法时在那里开始了诗歌创作，并首先创作了《马尔吉特斯》（Margites）[7]。

三[8]、关于他的父母同样是众说纷纭。赫拉尼科斯（Hellanicus）[9]和克勒安特斯（Cleanthes）[10]说［他的父亲］是迈翁（Maeon），欧盖昂（Eugaeon）[11]说是墨勒斯，卡利克勒斯（Callicles）[12]说是马萨戈拉斯（Masagoras）[13]，特洛曾的德谟克利特[14]说是商人戴蒙（Daemon），一些人说是塔米拉斯（Thamyras）[15]，埃及人说是书吏（hierogrammateus）[16]墨

3　第二节围绕希腊世界对荷马家乡的争执展开，列举了三座城市对荷马家乡的主张。这三座城市都位于小亚细亚西部的伊奥尼亚地区。

4　抄本原文如此，与下文（第三节）"克瑞特伊斯"（Cretheis）不一致，可能是抄本有误，但巴西诺认为这可能是变体而没有改正。

5　即"墨勒斯的后裔"，尽管这并不符合构词法，详见Bassino 2018, pp. 120–121。

6　许多古典作家曾提及这一诗人群体，如品达（Nem. 2.1）、柏拉图（Phdr. 252b, Resp. 599e）、伊索克拉底（10.65）等。关于荷马裔代、荷马及基俄斯的关系，详见Bassino 2018, pp. 121–122。

7　谐拟史诗《马尔吉特斯》曾被亚里士多德（Poet. 1448b24）和金口狄翁（53.4）等人看作荷马的作品，但后来被判为伪作。该诗仅存少量残篇，其中一段提到一位神样的老诗人来到克罗丰（fr. 1 West）。

8　第三节列举了希腊世界对荷马父母的数种不同说法，最后叙述了哈德良求问德尔斐神谕的故事，并吁请读者相信德尔斐神谕对荷马家乡世系的权威答复。

9　公元前5世纪末来自米提列涅（Mytilene）的散文纪事家。

10　公元前4—前3世纪来自阿索斯（Assus）的哲学家，廊下派的第二任主持。

11　大概是萨摩斯的欧瓦贡（Euagon，也拼作Eugaeon或Eugeon），公元前5世纪的散文纪事家。

12　可能是生活在公元前3世纪的史家、语法学家。

13　在其他文献中此人名为马萨戈拉斯（Massagoras，见Tzetzes Alleg. Prol. 62），或者德梅萨戈拉斯（Dmesagoras，见AP 7.5）、德马萨戈拉斯（Dmasagoras，见Eust. ad Od. 1713.18），但后二者来自一个宣称荷马是塞浦路斯的萨拉米斯人的传统。

14　公元前1世纪的一位作家，其残篇涉及诗人和哲学家。

15　应指塔米利斯（Thamyris），传说这位诗人挑战缪斯而遭到惩罚（Il. 2.591–600），变成盲人（Hes. fr. 65 MW; Paus. 4.33.7; Dio Chrys.13.21）。

16　指埃及书写圣书体的书吏。

涅马科斯(Menemachus),还有些人说是奥德修斯之子特勒马科斯。

与此同时,有的人说他的母亲是墨提斯(Metis)[17],而有的人说是克瑞特伊斯(Cretheis),有的说是特弥斯特(Themiste)[18],有的说是欧格涅托(Eugnetho),一些人说是某个被腓尼基人卖掉的伊塔卡妇女[19],有的说是缪斯卡利奥佩(Calliope),有的说是涅斯托尔之女波吕卡斯特(Polycaste)[20]。

他被称作墨勒斯,而某些人称他为墨勒西格涅斯,一些人则称之为奥勒特斯(Auletes)。[21]某些人说他得名荷马是因为他的父亲被塞浦路斯人当作人质交给了波斯人[22],有的人则说是因为双眼的残疾,因为在埃奥利斯人中间残疾人被这样称呼。

我们将要阐述[23]的是我们在最神圣的皇帝哈德良的时代从皮提亚女祭司那里听说的关于荷马的语句[24]。当皇帝询问荷马的家乡和父母时,她用六音步诗句这般吟咏神言:

> 你问我不朽塞壬[25]的鲜为人知的世系
> 及故土。依住处他是伊塔卡人,
> 特勒马科斯为其父,涅斯托尔之女厄皮卡斯特

---

17 《苏达》辞书(s.v. 'Homer' 1)给出的名字是欧墨提斯(Eumetis)。

18 保萨尼亚斯(10.24.3)给出的形式是特弥斯托(Themisto)。

19 《奥德赛》中的伊塔卡牧猪奴也是被家乡的西顿女奴伙同腓尼基人拐走(Od. 15.415–484)。

20 《奥德赛》提到波吕卡斯特为特勒马科斯沐浴更衣(Od. 3.464–469),赫西奥德《名媛录》残篇(Hes. fr. 221 MW)说波吕卡斯特为特勒马科斯生下佩尔塞波利斯(Persepolis),但下文(本节)中特勒马科斯的配偶却名为厄皮卡斯特(Epicaste)。

21 除了巴西诺,其他学者都根据古注(Schol. T Il. 22.51)改为阿尔特斯(Altes),这是《伊利亚特》中的一个角色(Il. 21.85–86, 22.51)。但巴西诺认为这也可能是一个揭示身份职业的名字或诨号(speaking name),即“吹管者”(来自 aulos),这类名字在《竞赛》中十分常见,详见 Bassino 2018, pp. 129–130。

22 希腊语 ὄμηρος 一词有“人质”的含义。

23 ἐκτίθημι 也可译作“揭晓”。

24 此事大概发生在公元 125 年哈德良访问德尔斐时。

25 将荷马比作塞壬,也许是因为诗人诗歌的魅力堪比塞壬的蛊惑力;或是体现诗人具有塞壬般的见闻(Od. 12.188–191;西塞罗也说塞壬们提供知识,见 Cic. Fin. 5.48.18),呼应诗句末尾对荷马智慧的赞颂;或是为后文荷马的落殁埋下伏笔,因为神话中有塞壬与缪斯竞赛落败的故事(Paus. 9.34.3);或是作为缪斯女神后代的一种代称,一说塞壬为缪斯忒耳普西科瑞(Terpsichore)与河神阿克罗俄斯(Achelous)的后代(Ap. Rhod. 4.895ff.),而文中提及荷马生母的一种说法是缪斯卡利奥佩。

为其母,她生下了这位凡人中最富智慧的男子。

鉴于询问者和回答者[的身份],特别是因为诗人曾以极高的天分用诗歌颂扬了他的祖先[26],对此我们必须完全相信[27]。

四[28]、一些人说他比赫西奥德更早出生,而另一些人说他[比赫西奥德]更年轻且是近亲[29]。他们这样描述〈他们的〉谱系:据说阿波罗和波塞冬之女托奥萨(Thoosa)生了利诺斯(Linus)[30],而利诺斯生了皮埃洛斯(Pierus)[31],皮埃洛斯和宁芙墨托涅(Methone)[32]又生了俄阿格洛斯(Oeagrus)[33];俄阿格洛斯和卡利奥佩生了俄耳甫斯,俄耳甫斯生了奥尔特斯(Ortes),奥尔特斯生了哈尔蒙尼德斯(Harmonides),哈尔蒙尼德斯生了菲洛特尔佩斯(Philoterpes),菲洛特尔佩斯生了欧菲莫斯(Euphemus),欧菲莫斯生了埃皮弗拉德斯(Epiphrades),埃皮弗拉德斯生了墨兰诺珀斯(Melanopus)[34]。狄奥斯和阿佩莱奥斯

26　应当主要指奥德修斯。荷马史诗对奥德修斯的品德和智慧不吝赞美之词,雅典娜甚至将奥德修斯的智慧与她自己的智慧相媲美。在《奥德赛》的主要故事情节中,奥德修斯是正面的、光辉的主人公形象,荷马刻意淡化其缺点。

27　但在后文中,《竞赛》的编订者并未将神谕给出的伊塔卡出身说奉为唯一正统。乌登(James Uden)提出,《竞赛》中哈德良求问神谕的段落为编订者添加,主要是为了表达对当时"行政干预学术"现象的不满,动词"必须"(δεῖ)充满了对企图控制希腊精英圈、号称在希腊文化上"全知全能"的皇帝哈德良的讽刺,并暗示他与字面意为"全知"的帕诺伊德斯国王相似,后者的决定往往被认为是愚蠢的、不中肯的,因此哈德良求得的神谕及决定也拥有类似的性质。详见 James Uden, "The *Contest of Homer and Hesiod* and the Ambitions of Hadrian", *Journal of Hellenic Studies* 130 (2010), pp. 121–135。

28　第四节列举了**一份赫西奥德和荷马的谱系**,在这一谱系中,两位诗人都是阿波罗的后裔,而且荷马是赫西奥德的晚辈亲戚。这份谱系并不符合上一节中的德尔斐神谕。

29　原文采用了"μὲν οὖν...δὲ"的结构表达过渡到更相关、更切题的部分,强调荷马比赫西奥德更年轻,暗示了竞赛的结局。

30　荷马和赫西奥德都提到过以他命名的古老哀歌: *Il.* 18.569–570; Hes. fr. 305–306 MW。神话中利诺斯以其音乐造诣而知名,关于他的父母有非常多的不同版本。

31　马其顿的皮埃里亚(Pieria)的王和名祖,传说他在特斯皮亚(Thespia)建立了缪斯崇拜,他的九个女儿(Pierides)也和缪斯同名(Paus. 9.29.3–4)。

32　巨灵(Gigas)阿尔库奥涅(Alcyone)所生的宁芙七姐妹(Alcyonids)之一就叫墨托涅,据说她们在父亲被赫拉克勒斯杀死后投海化为翠鸟(Eust. ad *Il.* 9,558)。

33　关于此人的统治区域和谱系有许多不同的神话版本,唯一相同之处是他成为俄耳甫斯的父亲。

34　此人常以不同身份出现在荷马和赫西奥德的谱系中,也许是保萨尼亚斯提到的一位同名库迈诗人(Paus. 5.7.8)。《竞赛》在他和俄耳甫斯之间插入了数位不知名的角色,且他们的名字大都适宜作诗人的诨号。

（Apellaius）[35]生自此人，而狄奥斯和阿波罗的女儿毕基墨德（Pycimede）生了赫西奥德和佩耳塞斯[36]。佩耳塞斯生了迈翁，而迈翁的女儿与河神墨勒斯生了荷马。[37]

　　五[38]、然而，有些人说他们活跃于同一时期，甚至共赴彼奥提亚（Boeotia）的奥利斯（Aulis）进行竞赛[39]。荷马在创作了《马尔吉特斯》后周游各城邦吟诵诗歌，当他去到德尔斐时，他就自己的家乡何在发出询问，皮提亚说道：

> 有座岛屿伊奥斯，你母亲的家乡，死后的你
> 会得到它的接纳，但要提防年幼孩童的谜语。

　　听了这话，他便避免前往伊奥斯，并在周边地区消磨时间。

35　狄奥斯来自对赫西奥德诗行（Πέρση, δῖον γένος, "佩耳塞斯，神/狄奥斯的血裔"，Hes. *Op.* 299）的字面理解。阿佩莱奥斯也许来自阿波罗（阿波罗的多里斯方言形式为 Apellon，但 Apellon 应该衍生出 Apellonios；Apellaios 也可以理解为来自多里斯方言的集会一词 "Apella"），名字相近的阿佩莱斯（Apelles）也出现在其他荷马传记中。

36　赫西奥德没有在诗作里提及父母的名字，但各种传记都把赫西奥德两兄弟的父母定为狄奥斯和毕基墨德，其中一则（Ps.-Plu. *Vit. Hom.* 1.2）将这一谱系上溯至公元前4世纪的史家埃福洛斯（Ephorus）。

37　此处对荷马世系的叙述不按照伪普鲁塔克（Ps-Plutarch）《荷马传（其一）》（*On Homer I*）第二节所陈述的荷马私生子的身份，而是有意突出了荷马自身世系的神圣性，从而为后文中六步格诗歌的韵律比按照荷马的创作风格奠定基调。而作为私生子意象的荷马，往往有超越荷马及其诗歌传统的意图，这方面最为显著的代表是农努斯（Nonnus of Panopolis）的《酒神纪事》（*Dionysiaca*）第25卷第253—260行，相关研究见 Marissa Henry, "Epic's Bastard Son: The Importance of Being Nothos in the *Dionysiaca* of Nonnus", *American Journal of Philology* 141 (2020), pp. 448–449。

38　第五节提出了**与上一节不同的世系说法**，即荷马与赫西奥德生活在同一时期，这一说法是两位诗人展开竞赛的基础。在进入对竞赛的叙述之前，《竞赛》首先记载了**荷马求问德尔斐神谕**的故事，这则神谕预示了荷马之死。

39　赫西奥德自述他唯一的航海经历便是从奥利斯（特洛伊战争中希腊联军的集结点）前往优卑亚的卡尔基斯参加安菲达玛斯的葬礼竞赛，凭一首颂诗获奖，随后他把奖品三足鼎献给了赫利孔山的缪斯（*Op.* 648—662），这段故事显然是荷马和赫西奥德诗歌竞赛故事的原型。抄本原文作 ἐν Αὐλίδι τῆς Βοιωτίας；称两位诗人在奥利斯展开竞赛，但这与《劳作与时日》及《竞赛》下文不符。尼采和伊夫林-怀特等校改为 ἐξ Αὐλίδος τῆς Βοιωτίας【从彼奥提亚的奥利斯出发】，维拉莫维茨和韦斯特直接改为 ἐν Χαλκίδι τῆς Εὐβοίας【在优卑亚的卡尔基斯】，巴西诺则采纳布塞（Busse）的读法补上 γενομένους 一词，即两位诗人先是在奥利斯碰面（见下文第六节），言下之意是，随后再一起航行至卡尔基斯参加竞赛。据此，译文中补上"共赴"二字。

六[40]、在那时，伽尼克托尔（Gannyctor）正在举办他的父亲、优卑亚（Euboea）王安菲达马斯（Amphidamas）[41]的葬礼，他邀请所有不仅在力量和速度上出众，还在智慧上出众的人参加竞赛，并用厚礼予以参赛者尊荣。于是，据他们说，这两人[42]在偶然的晤面之后前往卡尔基斯。一些显赫的卡尔基斯人作为竞赛的裁判出席，死者的兄弟帕诺伊德斯（Panoides）[43]也在他们之中。

虽然两位诗人都以非凡技艺参赛，但据说赫西奥德是这样取胜的：他走上［赛场］中央，向荷马提出一个个问题，荷马则逐一作答。

七[44]、赫西奥德说道：

> 墨勒斯之子荷马啊，知晓诸神计划之人，
> 请首先告诉我：什么对凡人来说最佳？

荷马道：

> 对地上的人来说，最好是一开始就不要出生，
> 抑或出生后不论如何尽快跨越哈德斯的门扉。[45]

40　第六节介绍了荷马和赫西奥德在卡尔基斯展开诗歌竞赛的背景。竞赛最终的裁判帕诺伊德斯在此也加以介绍，但和后文不同的是，此处他只是裁判中的一员，也并不具备国王的头衔。

41　普鲁塔克（Plut. fr. 84 Sandbach, *sept. sap.* 153f-154b）声称他是卡尔基斯公民，在公元前8世纪至前7世纪的勒兰托斯战争（Lelantine War）中战死。

42　荷马和赫西奥德。

43　在其他文献中也拼作 Πανίδης，意为"全知的"，但阿尔基达马斯作品的出土纸草（coll. P. Petr. I 25 (1), l. 4）拼作 Πανήδης，意为"享受一切者"。阿尔基达马斯（Alcidamas）是公元前4世纪的一位智术师，师从高尔吉亚，《竞赛》的主要内容一般认为出自他的著作《缪斯集》（*Mouseion*）。

44　第七节是荷马和赫西奥德诗歌竞赛的第一回合，赫西奥德询问荷马，对凡人而言何为最佳（φέρτατον）和最美（κάλλιστον）的事。

45　同样的主题最早见于特奥格尼斯的四行挽歌对句（Thgn. 425–428），也在各种文献乃至神话中反复出现。智慧竞赛的背景是葬礼，所以荷马回答说，次好的事情是快快地穿过冥府的大门，也让这些权贵、逝者的亲戚得到心理上的安慰。从这个角度来看，这两行诗不仅没有体现出古希腊人的悲观主义，反而是乐观的一面：每个人都应该为此感到开心，为逝者开心。这样的话，第二个回答中的场景，即他们当时所处的环境（宴饮、美酒、诗人的吟唱），荷马赞颂的就是当下，就是此刻。所以荷马的回答不仅无懈可击，还能够起到劝慰的作用，更能够引起在场者的共鸣。尼采在《查拉图斯特拉如是说》中提出"相同者的永恒轮回"，提示我们关注此刻、关注瞬间，时间在瞬间上是圆的。然而这些（转下页）

赫西奥德第二回问道：

> 再告诉我这个吧，神样的荷马啊，
> 在你心中什么对凡人来说最美？

他便答道：

> 每当欢乐传遍了全体人民，
> 宾客们在厅堂中挨次安坐后倾听
> 游吟诗人，一旁的餐桌摆满了
> 面包和肉食，司酒从混酒钵舀出
> 酒水并用来斟满大家的酒杯[46]；
> 在我心中这似乎就是最美的。

八[47]、据说，当这些诗句得到吟咏后，它们是如此令希腊人惊异，以至于被称为"黄金的"，而且甚至今天[48]所有人在公共献祭时也还要于进餐和奠酒前念诵。

赫西奥德对荷马的成功感到不快，他开始提出难解的谜题，并说出如下诗行：

> 缪斯啊，那些当下在、将在或曾在的事物
> 不要对我歌咏它们；请你回想其他的诗篇。[49]

（接上页）都是对于有死的凡人来说的，时间不管呈现什么样的状态，对于诸神来说都是同一永恒的。下一回合的问题开始与神产生联系。

46　这五行出自《奥德赛》中奥德修斯在腓埃基亚（Phaeacia）回答自己为何悲伤的自白（*Od.* 9.6–11）。

47　第八节首先描绘了荷马在第一回合中的巨大成功，然后**转入第二回合的较量**。面对赫西奥德提出的永远不可能发生的谜题，荷马巧妙地以描绘宙斯的葬礼竞赛的诗句作答。

48　καὶ ἔτι καὶ νῦν 这四个词在阿尔基比阿德斯作品的纸草里没有出现，可能是后来添入传世的《竞赛》抄本的。

49　赫西奥德在《神谱》里称缪斯们能述说现在、将来和过去，而且也正是缪斯让赫西奥德能够歌唱将来和过去：*Th.* 30–34; 38–40。赫西奥德似乎希望检验荷马是否像他自己一样能得到缪斯的青睐，因此他才直呼荷马为"缪斯"，即向降临到诗人身上的缪斯发问（对比 *Il.* 1.1; 2.484–493, *Od.* 1.1–10等）。第一回合的两个问题，荷马的回答（转下页）

荷马有意解开难解的谜题,他相应[50]说道:

> 蹄声响亮的马群从未在宙斯墓旁
> 因努力竞比争胜而损坏车舆。[51]

九[52]、鉴于荷马把这些谜题也解答得十分巧妙,赫西奥德转向模棱两可的主题,他说出更多的诗行,要求荷马逐一恰当地作答。第一行是赫西奥德的,接下来的一行是荷马的,不过赫西奥德有时也用两行诗来创设谜题[53]。

———————

(接上页)是:最好的是不要出生,次好的是死亡,最后是现世的快乐。对于凡人的一生来说,出生就是过去的事情,死亡是未来的事情,第二个回答里描述的场景是现在的事情。所以赫西奥德就说:不要对我歌唱过去、现在和未来的事情,说说其他的事情吧。译者因此认为这三个问题之间存在递进关系,出生、死亡、现世,都是比较具体的,是与凡人相关的东西,其他的事情是否可以认为是与神相关的事?对于凡人来说,获知过去、现在、将来的途径有两种:缪斯与阿波罗。从前文关于两位诗人的世系可知,阿波罗是两位诗人的共同祖先,这是他们相同的条件,而赫西奥德开头就呼唤缪斯,他又认为这道题目对于荷马来说是无解之题。那么,赫西奥德提出这个问题也许是因为他主观上认为荷马无法与缪斯联结。

50　ἀκολούθως 表示荷马对赫西奥德抛来的谜题相应地做出适宜的答复,另一种可能是表达"接着说道"的含义。

51　宙斯永生,因此他的葬礼竞赛永远不会发生。尽管如此,传说在克里特有宙斯墓(如 Euhemerus T 69 A Winiarczyk, Callim. *Jov.* 6–9)。不过,诗行的作者或编者——一般认为是公元前5世纪至前4世纪的智术师阿尔基达马斯——大概并没有想起克里特的宙斯墓,毕竟他的目的只是设计一个不可能的事件。下文表明荷马通过了考验,而且以宙斯不死为谜面的谜题还再次出现。参见 M. Winiarczyk, *The Sacred History of Euhemerus of Messene*, Berlin, Boston: de Gruyter, 2013, p. 36。另外,普鲁塔克的版本(Plut. *sept. sap.* 154a)是荷马发问而赫西奥德作答。

52　第九节描写了**竞赛的第三回合**,在一连串的对句中,荷马将赫西奥德抛来的意义不当的句子统统扭转为正常的含义。B. Graziosi, "Competition in wisdom", in F. Budelmann and P. Michelakis eds., *Homer, tragedy and beyond*: London: Society for the Promotion of Hellenic Studies, p. 72(见本辑第93页)认为这些对句体现了荷马和赫西奥德的合作,他们竞争的目的不是输赢,而是想把智慧展现给观众。

53　下文的"对诗"考验诗人跨行连句(enjambment)的技巧,赫西奥德所出的上句往往存在逻辑矛盾或其他违反古希腊人认知的内容,但荷马总是通过补充下句扭转含义。译者尽量将原文中上句的原意保留在译文中,但为保持两句相连时的意思通顺,有时不得不插入一些标点。"轮流对白"(Στιχομυθία)是诗体戏剧里的一种技巧,即给交替出现的角色以单行、半行或两行台词,而在两位史诗诗人的作品中也有类似的体现,比如莫斯特(Glenn Most)在分析五个种族神话时指出,赫西奥德的语言似乎经过精心设计:通过《劳作与时日》第148—149行描绘青铜种族非凡的身体力量,然后又以"他们……是青铜的"开始下一行,赫西奥德引导他的听众们期待他接下去会说他们的身体某部分是青铜打造的;但他马上纠正了这种预期,加上了"盔甲"一词。参见格兰·莫斯特著,高峰枫等译:《从荷马到古希腊抒情诗》,北京大学出版社,2021年,第179页。

赫：然后他们享用牛肉大餐以及马的脖颈

荷：上汗湿的轭被他们解下，因为疲倦于战争。[54]

赫：弗里吉亚人在所有乘舟男子中最擅长

荷：在海岸上从海盗男子处偷盗晚餐。[55]

赫：控矢射向所有巨灵部族，只用双手

荷：赫拉克勒斯从肩头解开弯弓。[56]

赫：这个男人的父亲高贵而懦弱

荷：的是他母亲，因战争对所有女人来说都艰难。[57]

赫：你的父亲和尊贵的母亲不曾为你结合

荷：他们通过黄金的阿芙洛狄特种出这具身体。[58]

赫：射猎女神阿尔忒弥斯，屈从于婚姻

---

[54] 这两句来自阿里斯托芬的喜剧《和平》(*Pax* 1282–1283)，主角特律盖奥斯(Trygaeus)要求男童歌唱和平饮宴的场景，并以参加宴会、享用牛肉为例，但男童却总是演唱英雄史诗的战争主题。《和平》中这两句是由同一人(男童)吟唱而非对句，尽管阿里斯托芬也可能引用了当时已经存在的对句。如果没有下句，上句可直译为"然后他们享用牛肉和马颈的大餐"，然而吃马肉是野蛮人的习俗(如 Hdt. 4.61 中的斯基泰人)，因此下句通过跨行连句把意思完全扭转。现行的《和平》译本都将 ἔκλυον αὐχένας ἱδρώοντας 理解为"解开汗湿的马颈(上的轭)"，但韦斯特和巴西诺的译文将其理解为"将马颈的汗渍去除"，取 ἐκλύω "被停息"的意义，其依据大概是 5 世纪辞书编纂者海斯基乌斯(Hesychius)词典的第 3699 条。但结合荷马对这一谜题的解答，取 ἐκλύω 的本义"解轭"更有说服力。

[55] 上句赞扬了弗里吉亚人的水性卓越，尽管弗里吉亚并不沿海(但历史上弗里吉亚王国曾扩张至海边)，下句则用他们与海盗的联系贬低了其秉性。对于希腊人来说，弗里吉亚人是懦弱的代名词，参见 West 2003, p. 329; Bassino 2018, p. 150. 译者采用了伊夫林-怀特的译法，而科林斯理解为"在海盗男子中于海岸上享用晚餐"(D. Collins, *Master of the Game: Competition and Performance in Greek Poetry*, Cambridge, Mass.: Harvard University Press, 2004, p. 187)，巴西诺理解为"和海盗男子在海岸上享用晚餐"，维拉莫维茨和韦斯特则在改动动词后理解为"在海岸上为海盗男子准备晚餐"。

[56] 上句形容某个人用双手便能射箭，下句则把意思改为用手解开弯弓，并融入了巨灵战争(Gigantomachia)的主题。这两句在抄本中被错误地放在相反的顺序。

[57] 下句消除了上句中的逻辑矛盾，但似乎并不认为神话中的阿玛宗女战士需要纳入考虑。

[58] 假设下句能够消除上句的矛盾，那么荷马似乎是在表达某种超自然的受孕，类似神话中赫拉生育赫淮斯托斯的情形。但下句中"黄金的阿芙洛狄特"这一饰词和动词 σπείρω 一般都用于表达两性的正常结合，因此存在疑difference。相较于抒情诗，史诗文体对情色内容一般采取回避态度，故此赫西奥德的谜语有意引诱荷马偏离史诗文体的特征。据 Tim Whitmarsh, *Dirty Love: The Genealogy of the Ancient Greek Novel*, New York: Oxford University Press, 2018, p. 6, 文学中的情欲是错置的情欲，赫西奥德欲使荷马陷入情欲错置的陷阱。

荷：的卡利斯托是她用银弓射杀。[59]

赫：他们遂终日大摆筵席，一无所有

荷：的是家中私物，而是由人王阿伽门农提供。

赫：在烟雾缭绕的灰烬间享用宴席后，

　　他们收殓逝者的白骨，它属于宙斯[60]

荷：之子，高傲的、神样的萨耳佩冬。

赫：我们坐在西摩伊斯平原上，这般

　　自船只出发走向道路，肩头所扛[61]

荷：乃带柄的刀剑和长颈投枪。

赫：而那时最优秀的青年们用手从海中

荷：愉快而急切地拖出一条快船。[62]

赫：然后他们带走了科尔基斯女子及埃厄特斯王

荷：他们从他手下逃走，因为觉得他没有炉灶，目无法度。[63]

59　此处赫西奥德把童贞女神阿尔忒弥斯同婚姻相关联，有意营造一个悖于常识的谜题，而荷马的应答则把屈从于婚姻的角色改为失贞的卡利斯托。在最流行的神话版本里，卡利斯托被阿尔忒弥斯、赫拉或宙斯变成了大熊，但也有一些版本认为她被阿尔忒弥斯（Callim. fr. 632）或自己的儿子（Eratosthenes, *Katasterismoi* 1 p. 1 Oliveri）射杀后化为大熊星座。

60　这两句本身也是一个通过下句改变上句意思的对句谜题，因为首句本身描述了在灰烬中饮宴的奇怪情形。韦斯特认为阿尔基达马斯很可能并没有亲自创作这些对句，而是从现存的赛诗诗集中摘取合适的句子，例如上文中与《和平》重合的句子。阿尔基达马斯也许在摘句时摘录了一些用于三人连环斗句或二人互相解谜的诗句，尽管它们并不完全适合《竞赛》文本中赫西奥德单方面发问、荷马单方面回答的语境。M. L. West, "The Contest of Homer and Hesiod", *The Classical Quarterly* 17 (1967), pp. 440–441.（参见本辑第39—40页——译者按）

61　把这两句本身也看作对句谜题存在一些困难，如果认为"坐在平原上"是很奇怪的搭配，而第二句可以把意思改为走向平原，那么ἥμενοι就会失去宾语。两句合起来时，谜题在ἔχοντες的宾语只能是ὁδὸν。西摩伊斯（Simois）是特洛伊的一条河流。

62　很难看出上句要创设何种谜题。巴西诺（Bassino 2018, p. 154）认为上句把海（θάλασσα）进行了人格化，类似于特洛伊战争中的斯卡曼德河（Scamander），但说服力有限。

63　"科尔基斯（Chochis）女子"即美狄亚。上句的谜题在于让阿尔戈英雄们不仅从科尔基斯带走了美狄亚，还把本应派兵追杀英雄们的科尔基斯王埃厄特斯也带走了。没有炉灶（ἀνέστιος）、目无法度（ἀθέμιστος）连用，形容破坏（内部）秩序、引发纷争的人。这一用法曾在《伊利亚特》卷九中出现，第九卷中涅斯托尔说："一个喜欢在自己人中发动可怕战争的人，是一个没有宗族、目无法度、没有炉灶的人。"（ἀφρήτωρ ἀθέμιστος ἀνέστιός ἐστιν ἐκεῖνος ὃς πολέμου ἔραται ἐπιδημίου ὀκρυόεντος, Hom. *Il.* 9.63–64）此处译文保留这一直截的表达，不将ἀνέστιος引申为"残忍的""残酷的"。

赫：而当他们奠酒并饮尽，大海的浪涛[64]

荷：乃他们意欲航行之所，凭借那甲板精良的船只。

赫：阿特柔斯之子郑重祈祷，希望他们全体遇难

荷：永不在海上，并张口说出诗句：

赫："吃吧，客人们，喝吧！愿你们中无人

归返家园回到亲爱的乡土

荷：时负伤，愿你们毫发无损地回归家乡。"

十[65]、鉴于荷马完美地解答了所有的谜题，赫西奥德又说道：

你只需详细回答我问的这个小问题：

多少阿凯亚人曾随阿特柔斯的两子前往伊利昂？

他便以算术问题这般作答：

生火的炉灶有五十座，其中每处有

五十根肉签，在每根签旁有五十块肉；

每块肉边的阿凯亚人有三乘三百个。[66]

但这会得到一个难以置信的数目：若有五十处灶，就有两千五百根签，十二万五千块肉……[67]

64　上句的谜题在于"饮尽大海的浪涛"。

65　第十节是**竞赛的第四回合**，双方围绕着与特洛伊战争中希腊联军人数相关的数字谜题展开较量。

66　*AP* 14.147也有以阿凯亚人的火炉肉签创设的数字谜题，但数目不一样（7×50×50×900）。谜题模仿了史诗中特洛伊人五十人一组围着一千处灶火的情景（*Il.* 8.562–563）。此处荷马给出的总数极其庞大（一亿一千两百五十万），和《伊利亚特》第二卷的舰船名录也无法对应。但谜题的难点并不在于给出真正的数目，而是要在合乎格律的前提下答上一个没有答案的数目问题。这种问题在民俗学中被归类为"数字谜题"（riddle of numbers），在阿尔奈–汤普森分类法（Aarne-Thompson-Uther Index）中编号为H700，如H702"天上有多少星星"等。不仅如此，荷马在《伊利亚特》中表示特洛伊远征的人员、船只数目只有缪斯能给出（2.484–493），因此这道谜题也是在检验荷马和缪斯的联系。

67　在抄本中，本节最后一句话的数字δεκαδύο μυριάδες εὖν【120000+5450】难以解释，存在疑难。由于下文宣称荷马的回答完美，这句话被韦斯特看作窜入的旁批。

十一[68]、因为荷马在所有问题上都占了上风，嫉妒不已的赫西奥德又说道：

> 墨勒斯之子荷马啊，若缪斯们，至高大神
> 宙斯的女儿们当真如传言般敬重你，
> 请你合乎格律地言说[69]：对凡人来说什么
> 最美好又最可憎？我洗耳恭听。

荷马便说道：

> 狄奥斯之子赫西奥德啊，我愿意回应
> 你的要求；我非常乐意答复你。
> 最美好的事情是善人成为自己的
> 尺度，最可憎的是坏人成为自己的尺度；[70]
> 请询问任何其他合你心意的问题。
> 赫：城邦怎样会被治理得最好，要采取何种风俗？
> 荷：倘若他们不愿从可耻丑事中牟利，
> 　　善人得到褒奖，正义追捕不义。
> 赫：万事之中向神祈祷何事最佳？

68　第十一节是**竞赛的第五回合**，赫西奥德在这一回合中向荷马询问了许多哲学式的问题。第七和十一节的问题都围绕凡人世界展开，而第八至十节中的竞赛内容则都以英雄或神为主题，但荷马在这两方面都占据着上风。

69　韦斯特和巴西诺相信这里的 μέτρῳ 系指"合乎格律"而非普罗塔戈拉名言所提到的"尺度"，见 Bassino 2018, pp. 160–161。魏塞尔（Paul Sommer-Weisel）在其为《荷马与赫西奥德的竞赛》第151—163行所作评注中指出，文本来源之一的作者阿尔基达马斯是高尔吉亚的学生，而高尔吉亚对诗歌的理解见于《海伦》第9行的这一观点"我觉得并称所有诗歌为拥有韵律的话语"（τὴν ποίησιν ἅπασαν καὶ νομίζω καὶ ὀνομάζω λόγον ἔχοντα μέτρον）；荷马和赫西奥德之间的竞赛是诗人之间竞赛最为典型的例子，故"韵律"这一理解更为妥帖。参见 Paul Sommer-Weisel, "Kommentar zum *Certamen Homeri et Hesiodi*, 151–163", p. 7（https://www.academia.edu/47776044/Kommentar_zum_Certamen_Homeri_et_Hesiodi_151_163［访问日期：2022年8月16日］）。

70　译者采纳了伊夫林-怀特的译法。巴西诺理解为"最美好的事情是自己成为自己的善的尺度，最可憎的是成为自己恶的尺度"，另一种可能的理解是"好事中最美好的事情是自己成为自己的尺度，坏事中最可憎的是成为自己的尺度"，参见 P. Osorio, "Protagoras' *Homo-Mensura* Doctrine and Literary Interpretation in *Certamen Homeri et Hesiodi*", *Mnemosyne* 71 (2018), p. 5。

荷：由始至终永远善待自己。

赫：你能说什么是在最小处诞生的最好的事物吗？

荷：在我看来，是人躯体中高贵的心灵。[71]

赫：正义和男子气概能做到些什么？

荷：以一己之辛劳带来公共的利益。

赫：在人类之中什么是智慧的标志？

荷：正确判断处境，同时把握良机。

赫：凡人何种情况下值得相互信赖？

荷：当同样的危险也紧随他们的行动时。

赫：人类能把什么事物称为幸福？

荷：死前经受过最少忧愁与最多欢乐。

　　十二[72]、这些诗句被言说之后，所有[在场的]希腊人都要求授予荷马桂冠。但国王帕诺伊德斯要求双方都吟诵自己诗作中最出色的篇章[73]。赫西奥德便首先说道：

阿特拉斯生养的普勒阿得斯在天空升起时
你要开始收割，她们落下时要开始耕种；
她们确实隐藏了四十个日日夜夜。[74]
一年周而复始后，她们再次露面，
那时首先要做的是把铁农具磨砺。

71　类似的问题也见于 Stob. 3.3.45。然而，奥沙利文（N. O'Sullivan）认为"在最小处"（ἐν δ' ἐλαχίστῳ）应理解为"在最短时间内说"，这是高尔吉亚和阿尔基达马斯热衷的修辞学训练，见 Bassino 2018, p. 162。

72　第十二节描绘了**竞赛的第六回合，也是最后一个回合**。在这一回合当中，竞赛的主题是帕诺伊德斯提出的，荷马和赫西奥德分别吟诵了各自诗作中最出色的篇章，这些篇章是从传世的荷马和赫西奥德的诗作中摘取的。

73　在诗歌竞赛中挑选最精彩的片段进行吟诵可以上溯到公元前6世纪诗人科琳娜（Corinna）的残篇（*PMG*645, P. Berol. 284），这一残篇描述了基泰戎山（Cithaeron）和赫利孔山的诗歌竞赛，虽然现存残篇只涉及基泰戎山胜利的结果及其吟诵宙斯诞生后被藏在克里特岛躲避克洛诺斯残害的内容，但也能从中推断出诗人间竞赛的诗歌在古风时代有着明确的依据，也为阿尔达斯马斯或/和本文的编者提供了依据。

74　神话中普勒阿得斯（Pleiades）是阿特拉斯的七个女儿，被认为是天上的昴星团。诗人请听者在昴星团升起时（5月）收割，落下时（10月）播种，即种植冬小麦。"四十个日日夜夜"系指3月至5月之间，参见 Plin. *NH* 17.128, 18.201–202。

> 这是平原的规律,对那些在海洋
> 附近居住者如此,对居住在远离
> 汹涌的海洋、土地肥沃的幽谷者
> 也如此。要光着身子耕耘、播种
> 和收获,每当万物合乎时令之时。[75]

在他之后是荷马:

> 强大的战阵在两个埃阿斯周围布起,
> 哪怕阿瑞斯或催人作战的雅典娜来了
> 也无可挑剔。被选出的最好的战士
> 等待着特洛伊人和神样的赫克托尔,
> 用长矛围着长矛,大盾连着大盾,
> 圆盾抵圆盾,头盔顶头盔,人挨人,
> 只要身子一倾,马鬃战盔的闪耀尖顶
> 便会相触;他们就这样互相依凭而立。[76]
> 令人丧命的战场上长枪林立,
> 这些刺人的尖枪皆由他们手持。
> 耀眼的头盔、新擦的甲胄和闪亮的盾牌
> 发出铜色的光芒,[77]亮光一同发来
> 令人目眩。谁若见此苦战不生哀叹
> 反倒欣喜,那可真是一副铁石心肠。[78]

---

[75] 这一段出自 Hes. *Op.* 383–392,从神灵开始而转入属于黑铁种族的农事。赫西奥德并未选取《神谱》而是《劳作与时日》中的篇章作为其得意之作。此前,赫西奥德在提出具体问题的时候关注点也在凡人,符合他关照现实的诗人身份,或许这也可以说明为什么他会选择《劳作与时日》的内容,而不是《神谱》。

[76] 以上出自 *Il.* 13.126–133,从神灵开始而转入英雄们的争战。

[77] 注意荷马描述的战士的铜器与赫西奥德描述的生产者的铁器之间的对立,参见 Bassino 2017, p. 202。

[78] 以上出自 *Il.* 13.339–344。"铁石心肠",原文直译为"胆大"(θρασυκάρδιος);荷马史诗中也有"铁石之心"的表述(σιδήρεος θυμός,例如 *Il.* 22.357;σιδήρεος ἦτορ,例如 *Il.* 24.205)。杨科(R. Janko)在《伊利亚特》剑桥评注本中也提到:"这个图景结束于一个提醒:这是一场双方的战斗,带着旁观者的哀伤。"(R. Janko, *The Iliad: A Commentary, vol. 4: Books 13–16*, Cambridge: Cambridge University Press, 1991, p. 89)显然,诗人(转下页)

　　十三[79]、希腊人在这一回合感到惊异，他们对荷马赞叹不已，因为这些诗行异乎寻常。他们又要求将胜利授予荷马。国王却授予赫西奥德桂冠，宣称让呼唤劳作与和平之人，而非缕述战争和杀戮之人获胜才是正当的。据说赫西奥德就是这样获胜的。他得到了一只三足铜鼎，随后将其献给缪斯，并刻下这样的铭文：

> 赫西奥德将此物敬献给赫利孔山的缪斯，
> 他在卡尔基斯凭诗歌打败了神样的荷马。[80]

竞赛结束后，赫西奥德渡海航向德尔斐[81]请示神谕，同时也把胜利的初次成果[82]献给神明。当他来到神殿中时，据说女祭司被神明附身后开口讲道：

> 这位前来朝觐吾之居所的男人是有福的，
> 被不朽的缪斯崇敬的赫西奥德，
> 他的荣光无疑将遍及日光照耀之地。
> 但你要小心涅墨亚宙斯的美丽圣林，
> 你死亡的结局已经在那里注定。

　　十四[83]、赫西奥德听到这则神谕后便远离伯罗奔尼撒[84]，他相信

（接上页）荷马看到如此肃杀的战争场景，也为将士们感到不忍，那么后面的判决就显得更加荒谬，这也可以增加文本的戏剧性：由于裁判过于不公正，落败者也就没必要将这判决放在心上。不过，在宴饮时分提及战争一直是被厌恶的行为，也许荷马是输在场合了，参见 N. J. Richardson, "The Contest of Homer and Hesiod and Alcidamas' *Mouseion*", *The Classical Quarterly* 31 (1981), p. 3.

　　79　第十三节叙述了**竞赛的结局**。虽然荷马得到听众的一致支持，但帕诺伊德斯却裁定赫西奥德获胜。然而，在赫西奥德向德尔斐献上奖品后，德尔斐神谕不仅预言了赫西奥德的荣光，还预言了赫西奥德之死。

　　80　这两句也见于 *AP* 7.53, Procl. *Vit. Hom.* 6, Dio Chrys. 2.11 等。在《竞赛》的语境之外，ὕμνος 可以狭义地理解为"颂诗"，即指代《神谱》。这里作广义的诗歌解。

　　81　前已述及，赫西奥德自称只有一次航行经历，这里大概指的是赫西奥德返回奥利斯后从陆路前往德尔斐，而不是绕过整个伯罗奔尼撒半岛驶入科林斯湾。

　　82　ἀπαρχή 指宗教上的初次收获或初熟祭品（primal offering, first-fruits）。

　　83　第十四节叙述了**赫西奥德的结局**：诗人在误解了神谕后遭遇杀身之祸。

　　84　涅墨亚（Nemea）位于伯罗奔尼撒半岛东北，因涅墨亚巨狮和涅墨亚竞技会而闻名。

神祇所说的涅墨亚就在那个地方。当他去到洛克里斯（Locris）的俄诺厄（Oenoe）[85]时，他和菲勾斯（Phegeus）的两个儿子安菲法涅斯（Amphiphanes）及伽尼克托尔（Ganyctor）[86]一块住下休息，因为他没能读懂神谕；其实这整片地区都被称作涅墨亚宙斯的圣地。他在俄诺厄人中间消磨了不少时间，后来一个年轻人怀疑赫西奥德和自己的姐妹私通，便将他杀死并把尸体扔进优卑亚和洛克里斯之间的海域里[87]。在第三日，他的遗体被海豚们带回到陆地上，这时当地正在举行某个纪念阿里阿德涅的节日。所有人都奔向海岸，认出那具遗骸之后，人们在哀悼中为他举行葬礼并寻找凶手。那些凶手害怕公民同胞们的愤怒，便把一条渔船拖下海，随后渡海航向克里特。但宙斯在航行途中用霹雳击打他们，将他们沉入海中，正如阿尔基达马斯在他的《缪斯集》（Mouseion）[88]里说的那样。但埃拉托色尼（Eratosthenes）在《恩涅波多斯》（Enepodos）[89]里说，伽尼克托尔（Gannyctor）的两个儿子克提墨诺斯（Ctimenus）和安提福斯（Antiphus）在因上述缘由杀人后，被先知欧律克勒斯（Eurycles）献祭给了司掌待客之道的诸神[90]。至于那位少女，那个人的姐妹，则在被污辱后自缢而死，她被某个名叫德莫德斯（Demodes）的、和赫西奥德同行的外来人玷污了。他说这个人也被同一伙人杀死

85　希腊本土有两个名为洛克里斯的区域，其中位于西方的奥佐里亚的洛克里斯（Ozolian Locris）有一座名为俄诺厄、俄涅翁（Oeneon）或俄诺亚（Oenoa）的城市。修昔底德提到那里有一座涅墨亚宙斯的神殿，而且也提到了赫西奥德被当地人杀死的神谕和传说（Thuc. 3.96）。

86　和前文（第六节）提到的安菲达马斯之子只差一个字母，从下文埃拉托斯特尼的引文来看，应该只是同一个名字的不同拼写。让赫西奥德在同名的两人身上分别获得荣耀和死亡也许是有意的设计。

87　这里表明诗人遇害的地方在位于东方的奥普恩提亚的洛克里斯（Opuntian Locris），也许阿尔基达马斯弄错了，抑或存在不同的故事版本。

88　这部作品从残篇来看是一部传记和轶事材料的集合。不清楚Μουσεῖον是指缪斯的节日，还是神殿，或者只是纯粹题名为《缪斯集》，抑或雅典一处与缪赛奥斯（Musaeus）相关的地名（Paus. 1.25.8）。

89　抄本读作 ἐν ἐνηπόδῳ，无法解释其含义。一些学者校改为 ἐν Ἡσιόδῳ，但缺少证据表明埃拉托色尼（或译埃拉托斯特尼，公元前3世纪末的著名大学者，亚历山大里亚图书馆馆长）有这样一部作品。

90　虽然此处使用了复数，但"护客者"或"司待客之道者"基本上是宙斯独享的头衔，尽管也存在例外，如基俄斯的护客者阿波罗（Apollo Xenios, CIG 2214e）。

了⁹¹。后来奥尔科墨诺斯人(Orchomenioi)依据神谕移走他的尸体，葬在自己的土地上⁹²，并在他的墓碑上刻下铭文：

田产丰饶的阿斯克拉⁹³是他的故乡，但在他死后
策马的米努阿斯之裔的土地掩盖了
赫西奥德的遗骨；此人的荣光在人类中最伟大，
当人们被智慧的试金石检验之时。⁹⁴

十五⁹⁵、关于赫西奥德的内容就这么多⁹⁶。至于荷马，他在错失胜利以后周游各地吟诵自己的诗作。首先是七千行的《忒拜纪》(Thebaid)，其开头如下：

请歌咏干旱的阿尔戈斯⁹⁷，女神啊，诸英雄在那里

然后是七千行的《后辈英雄纪》(Epigoni)，其开头如下：

91　如果编者前面引用的框架来自阿尔基达马斯，那么在这里增补的埃拉托色尼的材料，正是与前者的不同之处，更能体现编者的意图是在为赫西奥德的名声辩护。

92　奥尔科墨诺斯(Orchomenus)是彼奥提亚北部的大城，传说中以富有闻名的米努阿斯(Minyas)曾统治此地。古注(Schol. Op. 631)援引已佚的亚里士多德的《奥尔科墨诺斯政制》及普鲁塔克的作品，声称阿斯克拉被摧毁后其居民流亡到奥尔科墨诺斯，并依据神谕把赫西奥德的遗骨也移到那里。神谕故事的详细版本见Paus. 9.38.3–4。同样的地点还有赫西奥德的另一方墓志："向你致敬，两次年轻，两次被埋葬；赫西奥德，你为人们提供了智慧的标准。"

93　有关阿斯克拉是否像赫西奥德说的那样糟糕，古代已有争议，参见Strab. 9.2.35。

94　最后这段墓志诗也见于AP 7.54, Paus. 9.38.4等，但有关作者的说法不一。

95　从第十五节开始，《竞赛》转入对荷马周游希腊各地的叙述。在竞赛失败后，荷马创作了忒拜诗系的两首英雄史诗，因此得到了弗里吉亚王室的垂青，并且得以将王室颁发的奖品献给神明，恰与之前竞赛的落败形成对照。

96　结合赫西奥德并未到处游历且因误解神谕导致死亡和后文荷马游历希腊"本土"及其相关岛屿且顺从神谕的内容，不难看出赫西奥德之死同荷马构成一种典型的"对比"(σύγκρισις)。这种对比是以赫西奥德之死展示他代表的道德教谕生前未被希腊人广为接受，进而同荷马游历希腊本土各地吟诵诗歌且大受欢迎进行对比，彰显荷马的泛希腊性。

97　攻打忒拜的七雄从阿尔戈斯出发。关于"干旱的阿尔戈斯"如何解释，参见Strab. 8.6.7。

现在让我们开始歌唱年轻男子,缪斯啊

因为有些人说这些诗行也是荷马的[98]。

听到这些诗行后,弥达斯王之子克珊托斯(Xanthus)和戈尔戈斯(Gorgus)邀请他为自己父亲的坟墓创作墓志诗[99],在那里有一座为弥达斯哀悼的少女的铜像。荷马遂作诗如下:

吾乃青铜少女,立于弥达斯墓之上。
只要水还流动,树木仍繁茂生长,
河流满溢,海浪依然四面冲刷,
升起的太阳和皎洁的明月尚在照耀,
矗立在这充满哀思的坟墓上的我
就将向来客指明:弥达斯于此安葬。[100]

----

[98]　古代对《后辈英雄纪》归属已有疑问,如 Hdt. 4.32。更多忒拜诗系的信息可见: M. Fantuzzi and C. Tsagalis eds., *The Greek Epic Cycle and its Ancient Reception. A Companion*, Cambridge: Cambridge University Press, 2015, pp. 213–260.

[99]　考古学家曾怀疑弥达斯墓在弗里吉亚的古都戈尔迪翁(Gordion)或雅兹勒卡亚(Yazılıkaya),但在伪希罗多德的传记中(Ps.-Hdt. *Vit. Hom.* 11),荷马在小亚细亚的库迈(Cyme)为弥达斯创作墓志诗。弥达斯妻子的父亲是小亚西北部希腊殖民地库迈的国王,这个国王的世系可以追溯到阿伽门农。库迈很可能是弥达斯向德尔斐进献宝座时船队登陆的港口。

[100]　此诗流传甚广,有繁简不一的多个版本,其中数行诗句可按任意顺序排布(Pl. *Phdr.* 264e)。第欧根尼·拉尔修(1.89–90)以西蒙尼德斯的诗为据把这首诗的作者定为七哲之一、林多斯的克勒奥布洛斯(Cleobulus of Lindus),并认为荷马与弥达斯的年代差使荷马不可能作此诗。古希腊人会用雕像和石碑在墓地上作为标志,死者的灵魂和这个墓地标志有着紧密的联系。散文墓志铭在公元前7世纪中叶开始出现,突出的重点在于死者的名字。韦尔南指出:"公元前6世纪开始,墓碑开始承载死者的形象,或是在墓地旁竖起一尊普通的雕像——青年雕像(*kouros*)或是少女雕像(*kore*)。这种墓碑看起来就像是一种有形的替代品,以一种不朽的形式表达了人在短暂的存在中所体现的美和生命的价值。" J. P. Vernant, "Mortals and Immortals: Body of the Divine", in Froma Zeitlin ed. *Mortals and Immortals: Collected Essays*, Princeton: Princeton University Press, 1991, p. 41. 一般来说,男性逝者的墓地旁都竖立着男青年像,弥达斯墓地上的少女形象可能与弗里吉亚地区的母神马塔尔(Matar)崇拜有关,她是弗里吉亚地区唯一以人的形象出现的神,可以追溯到公元前8世纪晚期,也就是弥达斯统治时期,参见 C. B. Rose, "Midas, Matar, and Homer at Gordion and Midas City", *Hesperia* 90 (2021), p. 63;但是母神与处子像也存在矛盾。

从他们那里获赠一只银碗后，荷马在德尔斐把这只银碗献给了阿波罗[101]，并刻上如下铭文：

> 福波斯王啊，荷马送出这件美好的礼物
> 皆因你的智慧。请你永远赐我荣耀。

十六[102]、在这之后，他创作了一万两千行的《奥德赛》，当时他已经创作了一万五千五百行的《伊利亚特》[103]。当他从那里来到雅典时，人们说他受到了雅典人的国王墨冬（Medon）[104]的款待。在议事厅（Bouleuterion）[105]里，由于天气寒冷，点起了火，据说他即兴赋诗如下[106]：

> 儿子是男人的冠冕，有如城墙之于城邦，
> 马匹是平原的装点，恰似船舶之于大海，
> 落座于集会中观看的人民也是这样。[107]
> 火焰被点燃时，房屋在冬日里看起来
> 也更体面，每当克洛诺斯之子送来大雪。

101　荷马的银碗（又译作银杯）对应于赫西奥德的三足鼎，它们都是智慧的象征。这些象征智慧的器具都是由人类颁发的，他们需要一个更高的智慧——阿波罗来检验认证。

102　第十六节叙述了**荷马接下来的诗歌创作——特洛伊诗系的两部伟大史诗**，以及**他周游希腊的下一站——雅典**。

103　刻意调换两首诗的叙述顺序显得非常别扭。巴西诺认为《竞赛》在提到荷马的主要作品时存在一种地位上的递增顺序（Bassino 2018, p. 181），也就是说，从《马尔吉特斯》上升到两首忒拜诗系的史诗，再到两首特洛伊诗系的史诗，最后以致阿波罗的颂诗收尾，诗歌的价值依次递增，其中《伊利亚特》虽然比《奥德赛》创作的时间更早，但其价值更高，故而调换了叙述顺序。《竞赛》引用的荷马诗文，也大多来自《伊利亚特》，特别是上文中"最出色的篇章"。

104　传说他是雅典国王或第一位王者执政官，见 Arist. *Ath. Pol.* 3。

105　雅典在公元前6世纪末为五百人议事会兴建了议事厅，位于市集广场西方，公元前5世纪末又在旁边建立了新的议事厅。

106　在伪希罗多德的版本里，这段故事发生在萨摩斯，见 Ps.-Hdt. *Vit. Hom.* 29–31。

107　伪希罗多德版本和《苏达》辞书用两句诗替换了这一句：χρήματα δ' αὔξει οἶκον· ἀτὰρ γεραροὶ βασιλῆες / ἥμενοι εἰν ἀγορῇ κόσμος τ' ἄλλοισιν ὁρᾶσθαι.【财物为房屋增光；可敬的诸王/坐在广场里，在他人看来也是美好的点缀。】

十七[108]、他从那里前往科林斯并吟诵了自己的诗作。备受推崇的他又来到阿尔戈斯,吟诵了来自《伊利亚特》的这些诗句[109]:

> 那些人占据阿尔戈斯、高墙的提任斯、
> 赫尔弥奥涅、拥有深海湾的阿西涅、
> 特洛曾、埃伊奥奈斯和盛产葡萄的埃皮道罗斯、
> 还有埃吉那岛和马塞斯;阿凯亚的青年们,
> 统领他们的是擅长呐喊的狄奥墨得斯,
> 堤丢斯之子,拥有其父——俄纽斯之子的力量;
> 还有斯特涅洛斯,闻名的卡帕纽斯的爱子。
> 和他们同来的第三人是神样的男子欧律普洛斯[110],
> 他是塔拉奥斯王之子墨基斯透斯的儿子。[111]
> 所有人中擅长呐喊的狄奥墨得斯作统帅,
> 和他们同在的八十艘黑色船只紧紧跟随。
> 船中成排列队着久经沙场的男子、
> 身披亚麻甲的阿尔戈斯人,战争的掀起者。[112]

阿尔戈斯的显贵们欣喜若狂,因为自己的民族得到了诗人中最负盛名者的赞美。他们用贵重的礼物尊崇他,为他竖立铜像,并投票通过决议:每天、每月、每年都要为荷马进行献祭,且每五年要到基

108　第十七节叙述了**荷马游历科林斯和阿尔戈斯**。荷马在科林斯的经历没有任何具体细节,但他在阿尔戈斯得到极高的礼遇。

109　以下的诗行除第6行和最后两行外,都来自《伊利亚特》的舰船名录,见 *Il.* 2.559–568。

110　抄本原文如此,但据史诗原文应为"欧律阿洛斯"(Euryalus)。欧律普洛斯 (Eurypylus)在《伊利亚特》中也屡次出场,作为帖撒利的领袖,他是希腊联军的主要英雄之一。

111　罗念生、王焕生的译本作"墨基斯透斯王之子",但在神话中墨基斯透斯并不是阿尔戈斯王,他的父亲塔拉奥斯把王位传给了墨基斯透斯的兄弟阿德拉斯托斯 (Adrastus),也就是攻打忒拜的七雄的统帅。

112　最后一句也见于一则神谕(*AP* 14.73.6)。κέντρα πτολέμοιο 或许也可译为"战争中的折磨",采用 κέντρον "折磨""磨难""刑具"的比喻义,与前文的"久经沙场"共同显示阿尔戈斯人在战争中的威慑力。

俄斯举行另一场献祭[113]。他们在他的雕像上铭刻道：

> 这是神样的荷马，他用辞藻华丽的智慧[114]
> 　　装点了意气扬扬的整个希腊，
> 特别是阿尔戈斯人，他们把神明筑墙的
> 　　特洛伊城摧毁，为美发海伦的缘故。
> 为了他，伟大城邦的人民将它竖立
> 　　于此，用不朽诸神的荣光崇敬他。

　　十八[115]、在城中消磨了一段时间以后，他渡海航向提洛岛，前往节庆大会[116]。他站在兽角祭坛[117]向阿波罗吟诵了一首颂诗，其开头如下：

> 愿我铭记且不遗忘远射神阿波罗[118]。

颂诗被吟诵完毕后，伊奥尼亚人让他成为自己的公民同胞，而提洛人

　　113　如此频繁的献祭显然是修辞性的夸张。献祭仪式要到基俄斯举行，说明这则故事支持荷马来自基俄斯的说法。另外，在公元前4世纪斯巴达的吕山德（Lysander）以前，为生者组织宗教崇拜性的活动是不可想象的，甚至吕山德也还与希腊化时期的君主崇拜存在时间上的断层，因此这一故事成型的时间应在希腊化时代以后。

　　114　强调荷马善用优美的文辞，并称之为一种智慧。《竞赛》全篇提及并列出的碑铭共六则，其中与赫西奥德有关的两则，分别为第十三节赫西奥德自己敬献给缪斯女神的铭文、第十四节奥尔科墨诺斯人为他撰写的墓志铭；与荷马相关的有四则，分别为第十五节的弥达斯墓志诗、同一节敬献给阿波罗的银碗上的铭文、第十七节阿尔戈斯人在荷马铜像上的铭文、第十八节荷马自己拟定的墓志。铭文穿插出现在《竞赛》的散文叙述和诗歌吟诵中，成为一种特殊的文本，其刻于物品之上的不易朽坏的特点暗示出其文本的权威特性。在《竞赛》中，这几则铭文都与竞赛的核心主题"智慧"密切相关。阿尔戈斯人此处颂扬荷马文辞优美的智慧正是《竞赛》明暗铺陈中显现出的一种特质，与赫西奥德的道德教化的特性构成了诗性智慧的一体两面。

　　115　第十八节叙述了**荷马在提洛岛的最后创作**，以及**他在伊奥斯岛解谜失败后的死亡**。值得注意的是，《竞赛》从未让荷马前往小亚细亚的伊奥尼亚地区游历。

　　116　大概指五年一度的提洛节（Delia），一个泛伊奥尼亚的节日，崇拜提洛岛的阿波罗。这一节日后来中断了，直到公元前426年雅典人将其恢复。参见 *Hymn. Hom. Ap.* 146–155, Thuc. 3.104.

　　117　提洛岛的兽角祭坛（Κερατῶν，《竞赛》作 τòν κεράτινον βωμòν）位于阿尔忒弥斯神殿旁，岛上三座阿波罗神殿都面向此祭坛。卡利马科斯描绘了阿波罗用阿尔忒弥斯猎获的羊角筑造此祭坛的传说，见 Callm. *Ap.* 60–64.

　　118　*Hymn. Hom. Ap.* 1.

则把诗句刻在板上，在阿尔忒弥斯的神殿里将其奉献[119]。

大会解散后，诗人驶向伊奥斯岛去造访克瑞奥菲洛斯（Creophylus）[120]，并在那里打发时光，这时他年事已高。据说，当他坐在海边时，他询问一些捕鱼归来的孩童：

> 来自阿尔卡狄亚的猎人们，咱们有何收获？[121]

那些孩童答道：

> 我们把抓到的都留下了，没抓到的都带走了[122]。

他不明白他们所说的话，便问他们说的是什么。他们说自己在捕鱼时什么也没捉到，而是给自己捉了虱子。他们丢弃了捉到的虱子，并把没捉到的留在衣服里带走[123]。荷马回想起了那条说他人生大限已至的神谕，便为自己的坟墓创作了一首墓志诗。离开那里后，由于泥土湿滑，他从侧面摔倒，据说在第三天去世[124]。他被葬于伊奥斯。

119　巴西诺认为这也许反映了历史事实，因为提洛岛的阿尔忒弥斯神殿比三座阿波罗神殿都更古老，而且献给两位神明的祭品时常互换，见 Bassino 2018, p. 190。提洛岛的阿尔忒弥斯神殿改建自迈锡尼时代的建筑。

120　一般认为此人来自萨摩斯，据说他曾作史诗《俄凯里亚的陷落》（Οἰχαλίας Ἅλωσις），也有传说认为此诗是荷马送给他的礼物，见 Strab. 14.1.18=55 *HE*。围绕他和荷马还有许多其他传说，例如他接待荷马不周（Pl. *Resp.* 10.600b–c），或成为荷马的女婿（schol. Pl. *Resp.* 600b）；据说莱库古曾在伊奥尼亚聆听他的后代（Creophylei）吟诵荷马的诗歌，并将他们传承的荷马诗歌结集传播（Plut. *Vit. Lyc.* 41.4）。

121　这句诗在所有荷马传记传统中都无异文，但"来自阿尔卡狄亚"无法解释，因为阿尔卡狄亚是内陆地区。伊夫林－怀特根据克希利（Koechly）的修订把 ἀπ' Ἀρκαδίης 改为 ἄγρης ἁλίης【海中捕猎的】。

122　此诗不仅见载于各个荷马传记传统，还在庞培的"墓志诗之屋"（House of the Epigrams）中一幅描绘孩童挑战荷马的壁画上出现，见 *CIL* IV 3407, 5。

123　字面上显然指未捉到的虱子。关于这一谜题可能具有的深意，见 Bassino 2018, pp. 191–192。

124　在不同传记传统中，许多版本将荷马的死因归于解谜失败后的狼狈、抑郁或绝食（Ps.-Plut. *Vit. Hom.* 1.4, Procl. *Vit. Hom.* 5, Anom. *Vit. Hom.* 1.6, 2.3, 3.5），以对比斯芬克斯败给俄狄浦斯、卡尔卡斯败给摩普索斯（Mopsus）后的自杀。只有伪希罗多德版本（Ps.-Hdt. *Vit. Hom.* 36）强调荷马因生病而死，与解谜失败无关，也只有《竞赛》和普罗克洛斯（很可能参考了《竞赛》）在叙述荷马之死时提到了神谕。《竞赛》似乎更多地把荷马之死与神意联系起来，正如前文的赫西奥德之死。

墓志诗如下：

> 大地在此处掩埋了神圣的头颅，
> 英雄男子的装点者[125]，神样的荷马[126]。

---

[125] κοσμήτωρ 一般取 κόσμος 的两种含义，意为"领袖"或"点缀者"，但此处 κοσμήτωρ 也许可取 κόσμος 的另一重含义，即为史诗英雄创建神话秩序之人。

[126] 这首墓志诗在韵律上并不是挽歌体，而是典型的六步格史诗格律，荷马的六步格史诗墓志和赫西奥德的挽歌体墓志诗事实上也构成文体上的对比。在安菲达马斯的葬礼结束后，实际上荷马和赫西奥德的竞赛以另一种形式依旧在继续，具体表现在他们的作品、游历地区以及对待命运的态度：文中并未提到赫西奥德在葬礼之后创作了任何作品，却明确提到荷马创作了四部史诗和一首颂诗；文中只提到赫西奥德在葬礼后去过德尔斐神庙、俄诺厄两个地方，却说荷马先后来到雅典、科林斯、阿尔戈斯等著名城市表演并获得了极大的荣誉；赫西奥德在德尔斐求得神谕后自作聪明地刻意避开了伯罗奔尼撒地区，以为可以逃脱神谕中所说的命运，但最终人算不如天算，落得惨死的境地，而反观荷马，在功成名就步入老年之后，主动去往神谕中提到的伊奥斯，并坦然接受自己大限将至的事实。译者认为上述三点都在向读者暗示阿尔基达马斯或/和罗马时期编订者的倾向：识机知命的荷马在智慧（σοφία）和美名（κλέος）方面都要更胜一筹。

荷马与赫西奥德的竞赛[*]

马丁·韦斯特

（彭 川 译）

在过去的一百年里，很多学者的工作都有助于理解我们简称为《荷马与赫西奥德的竞赛》这篇文章的性质和起源[1]。目前的研究状况可以总结为以下几点。这部作品现存的形式可以追溯到安敦尼时期[2]，但文章绝大部分取自更早的材料[3]，一般认为是阿尔基达马斯的《缪斯集》（*Museum*）[4]。竞赛中问答的一些诗行甚至在更早的时候就

---

[*] Martin L. West, "The Contest of Homer and Hesiod", *The Classical Quarterly*, 17 (1967), pp. 433–450.（正文中古典文献为译者自译，并用方头括号括出，此外，原文脚注采用每页重新编号的格式，为求体例统一，译文改为连续编号。——译者按）

[1] 这个标题的希腊语和拉丁语的形式，皆为斯蒂芬努斯（H. Stephanus）对母本（Laur. 56.1）中的标题的缩写，本来的标题是《论荷马与赫西奥德及其世系与他们的竞赛》。

[2] ὅπερ δὲ ἀκηκόαμεν ἐπὶ τοῦ θειοτάτου αὐτοκράτορος Ἀδριανοῦ εἰρημένον【这是我们曾听过的在最神圣的皇帝哈德良的时代被讲述的故事】(§3, 32–33 Allen)，这个表述暗示哈德良已逝，但还是鲜活的记忆。Ἀδριανοῦ 是斯蒂芬努斯对 Ἀδιανοῦ 的校正。在引用《竞赛》的段落时，我会使用 Wilamowitz 的分节编号（*Vitae Homeri et Hesiodi*, 1916），Colonna 在他的版本中也采用了这个编号（*Hesiodi Opera et Dies*, 1959），以及艾伦的分行（*Homeri Opera*, v）。20世纪的各个校勘本中，Rzach 在赫西奥德详校本（1902）中的版本仍然提供了最全面、准确的不同抄本的读法；Allen 的版本流传最广泛，Wilamowitz 的最富才智，Colonna 的是最新的。Evelyn-white 的洛布本赫西奥德（1936年修订版）有时也会提及。抄本开头至第13节第214行有影印版，见于 R. Merkelbach and H. van Thiel, *Griechisches Leseheft*, 1965, pp. 6–10。

[3] 与 Flinders Petrie 纸草（P. Lit. lond. 191）的高度重合证明了这一点，纸草可以定年到公元前3世纪。措辞上的细微差异并不一定要归咎于安敦尼时期的编纂者，我同意 Wilamowitz 的判断：正如人们的预期，散文部分或多或少有些出入，而诗行则完全相符（*Die Ilias und Homer*, p. 400）。

[4] Nietzsche, *Rh. Mus.* xxv (1870), 536–540，论证了这一点，首先因为（转下页）

已经流行了[5]，还有一些学者推测这个竞赛故事可以追溯到公元前5、前6甚至前8世纪；但这一点现在受到很多质疑[6]。

在我看来，需要进一步澄清的问题是：

（1）阿尔基达马斯是否真的写了《竞赛》背后的叙事？如果确实如此，有多少细节是他自己创作的，有多少是已经存在的？他的作品的目的和性质是什么？

（2）编者还使用了多少其他材料，他是如何具体运用的，他的目标是什么？

I. 阿尔基达马斯

密歇根纸草的问题

两份纸草都是阿尔基达马斯《缪斯集》的抄本残篇，这一简单直接的观点于1950年突然受到柯克（G. S. Kirk）的驳斥[7]。他认为，密歇根纸草中和《竞赛》一致的部分，风格质朴、允许元音连续（hiatus）的存在，与接下去的句子（以及阿尔基达马斯残余文本的其他部分）大不相同，[8]这一部分与其余部分之间找不到思想上的联系，而它的语言在某些细节上类似于希腊共通语（koine）。他得出结论，这一部分是后来窜入阿尔基达马斯作品中的。随后多兹（E. R. Dodds）指出，通常认为是阿尔基达马斯作品尾声的那部分，更像是从开场白中截

（接上页）Stobaeus（iv. 52.22）引用了第78—79两行诗，说是出自《缪斯集》，其次因为《竞赛》自身（第14节，第240行）引用了《缪斯集》来提供赫西奥德之死的另一版本。他的假说得到证据支持，一是Flinders Petrie纸草，纸草表明对这场竞赛的描述至少可以追溯到希腊化时期或者更早，二是密歇根纸草 inv. 2754（ii–iii A. D., ed. J. G. Winter, *TAPA* lvi [1925], 120 ff.），纸草叙述的结尾和《竞赛》相似，其后是看起来像尾声的部分和 "]δαμαντος περι ομηρου" 的下款。但这个说法还存在疑点，须立即讨论。

5　78-79（这两行和Stobaeus 归于阿尔基达马斯的诗行相同）＝特奥格尼斯 425/7（Stobaeus 在同一节的后面部分 [ἔπαινος θάνατου, iv. 52. 30] 援引了特奥格尼斯的诗句及其五音步格律）；107–108 ＝ Ar. *Pax* 1282–1283，二者有一些无关紧要的不同之处。

6　E. Vogt, *Rh. Mus.* cii (1959), 193–221; K. Hess, *Der Agon zwischen Homer und Hesiod*, Diss. Zürich, 1960.

7　*C. Q.* xliv (1950), 149ff.

8　A. Körte, *Arch. f. Pap.* viii (1927), 263, 曾经提出这一看法，他认为阿尔基达马斯引用了更早的作品。

取的片段。取代柯克的窜入假说，他提出我们面对的文本是一系列 περὶ Ὁμήρου【讨论荷马的】片段合集，其中最后一条来自阿尔基达马斯，编者把这条"作为对荷马研究动机的有价值描述"，并以此结束他编选的作品[9]。如果柯克和多兹的观点被接受，那么情况将重述如下：

阿尔基达马斯在创作《缪斯集》的过程中，讲述了赫西奥德之死的故事，同时在这部作品中的另一处，出于我们不清楚的目的，他引用了两行六音步诗句，它们也出现于《竞赛》中，由荷马说出。这仅仅是一个巧合。

《竞赛》的编者大量采用了一个存在于希腊化时期的竞赛叙事，该叙事不是出自《缪斯集》，也不是由阿尔基达马斯所作。

但是，这位编者的确知道阿尔基达马斯的《缪斯集》，并引用了其中赫西奥德之死的情节。

这个希腊化时期的竞赛叙事的部分内容，与我们认为是阿尔基达马斯《缪斯集》的残篇的内容，出现在同一份纸草上，是又一个巧合，尽管没有外部证据表明二者不属于同一个文本。

这些巧合是令人怀疑的，而且还有其他需要进一步思考的情况。

（i）在《竞赛》的第五节（第54行），作者显然从一个材料换到了另一个，从荷马的生平转到竞赛叙事。据说，荷马当时居住在希腊中部，因为他曾到过德尔斐，在那里他获得一个神谕，警告他会被埋葬在伊奥斯岛，还要小心男孩们的谜语；所以他远离伊奥斯。这显然是为第18节第321行及以下数行叙述他的死亡做铺垫，在那里，男孩用谜语考验他，令他回想起这个神谕。因此，尽管编者在叙事的靠后部分（竞赛比出结果之后）可能已经采用了其他的材料，但荷马之死的情节还是以这种或类似的形式出现在竞赛叙事中。那么，如果竞赛叙事包括荷马之死的情节，就很有可能也包括赫西奥德之死的情节，并用相同的方式铺垫，即通过一个使得赫西奥德远离某个地方的神谕，并且同样以墓志铭结束。"竞赛——赫西奥德之死——荷马之

9　*C. Q. N. S.* ii (1952), 187 f.; Körte, p. 264, 已经表明自己不可能相信"像阿尔基达马斯这样有教养的作家以结结巴巴的句子结束对荷马的书写"，并认为内容被粗心的抄袭者缩短了。

死"的扭结,赋予《竞赛》结构上的紧凑,因此可以追溯到原先的竞赛叙事[10]。那么,为什么编者在给我们展示赫西奥德之死的两种版本时,分别将之归于阿尔基达马斯和埃拉托色尼?难道他不是在转述他创作之前既存的竞赛叙事里的内容?[11]还是此前的竞赛叙事已经把阿尔基达马斯作为权威来引用?"ὥς φησιν Ἀλκιδάμας ἐν Μουσείῳ"【正如阿尔基达马斯在他的《缪斯集》里说的那样】(第14节,第239—240行)这些词语好像是后来添加的,在故事的第一个版本刚结束、埃拉托色尼即将出现之处,当我们观察到这一点,看起来就更像是编者在此之前照搬了一个简单的叙事,并且没有提及出处,这时他记起埃拉托色尼,于是就按照保萨尼亚斯(Pausanias)和阿忒那奥斯(Athenaeus)时代的方式,援引另一个权威人物,借机炫学。这迫使编者公开第一个权威的身份,他在第5节第54行用τινες【某些人】将之隐匿,伪装成智术师类型的雅致作家,用另一种口吻说话[12]。

(ii)柯克-多兹方法有个麻烦的特点,它要求我们特殊看待密歇根纸草。对于柯克来说,这是一本阿尔基达马斯的书,讲述了完整的荷马之死的故事,但在结尾部分窜入了一部分荷马传记中的内容。多兹认为这个假说过于大胆,但是他自己的解决办法也无法令人完全信服。一本关于荷马的摘录集锦是合理的。但如果这位摘录者想要甩掉选集的文学形式的束缚以便出版,他一定会写一篇前言放在开头,而不是从别人为另一部相当不同的作品所写的序言里抄一个不合适的片段放在结尾。此外,我们还必须认为这个抄袭者粗心大意到将"ΑΛΚΙΔΑΜΑΤΟΣ ΠΕΡΙ ΟΜΗΡΟΥ"【阿尔基达马斯论荷马】以大写字母的形式写在下方,假装自己只抄了一部阿尔基达马斯的

10　Vogt, pp. 199 ff.也如此认为。另一种可能是,安敦尼时代的作家在竞赛开始前添加了荷马的神谕这部分内容,但这种观点预设的艺术技巧,在我看来与汇编中的不协调是不相容的。

11　Nietzsche, p. 538证明了这一点。

12　他的两种角色(personae)的对比曾引起Allen的注意,*Homer, The Origins and the Transmission*, p. 21:"阿波罗尼乌斯(Apollonius)与赫罗狄安(Herodian)的朴素是不容怀疑的,这本书在形式上太博学,不可能出自智术师之手……这一博学与修辞的结合……"但是他关于作者可能是波尔菲里(Porphyry)的假设是不可能成立的。波尔菲里说赫西奥德比荷马晚100年(*Suda s.v. Ἡσίοδος*, cf. s.v. Ὅμηρος),这一看法除了与竞赛故事不相符以外,也没有在前面的部分提及。

作品。

困难越来越多。我试图通过回归简单的想法来回避它们，即认为密歇根纸草就是阿尔基达马斯的作品，包括荷马之死与所有其他内容，同时这本书的靠前部分呈现了赫西奥德之死的情节，并且与《竞赛》第13—14节，即第215—239行高度相似，再往前有对竞赛的叙述，又和《竞赛》第5—13节，即第54—214行高度相似。我必须首先反驳 "χωρίζοντες"【分离派】的论点。

（1）纸草文本两部分之间的风格差异是不可避免的。一部分是叙事，另一部分是宣言（manifesto）：阿尔基达马斯认为适合第二部分的风格，仅仅是不适用于第一部分。我们只有证明他绝不会选择直接的叙事，才能说他在此处不会使用直接的叙事风格；然后我们必须说明他是如何处理赫西奥德之死的。

（2）叙事中有一处语言怪异值得注意：ἀναμνησθεὶς δὲ τοῦ μαντείου, [ὅτι] ἡ καταστροφὴ αὐτῷ τοῦ βίου ἧκεν, π[οι]εῖ εἰς ἑαυτὸν ἐπίγραμμα τόδε.【回想起了那一神谕，神谕说自己生命的终点已至，因此他为自己创作了墓志诗】《竞赛》中与之对应的句子是：ἀναμνησθεὶς δὲ τοῦ μαντείου, ὅτι τὸ τέλος αὐτοῦ (αὐτῷ Westermann) ἥκοι τοῦ βίου, ποιεῖ τὸ τοῦ τάφου αὐτοῦ ἐπίγραμμα.【回想起了那条说他人生大限已至的神谕，便为自己的坟墓创作了一首墓志诗】"回想起神谕" 和 "他的人生大限已至" 的联结是牵强的；人们可能会猜测 ὅτι ἡ καταστροφὴ αὐτῷ τοῦ βίου ἧκεν【自己生命的终点已至】，或者不管本来的用词是什么，是抄工所添加的解释，他认为前面提到的神谕似乎相隔太远，很难马上回想起来。假设这句话在编者编辑《竞赛》时就存在于文本中，并无任何困难。

将这七个单词移除，就一举去掉了纸草叙事中七个元音连续中的四个，如果我们考察剩下来的三个，便会发现每一个在《竞赛》中都有不同的措辞，其中元音连续或消失或出现在其他地方。

纸草：

4—5　οἱ δ' ἔφασαν ἐφ' ἁλιείαν οἰχό-
　　　μενο[ι ἀγρ]εῦσαι μὲν οὐδέν.

《竞赛》：

329—330　οἱ δέ φασιν ἐν ἁλείᾳ
　　　　　μὲν　ἀγρεῦσαι μηδέν.

10 ποιεῖ εἰς ἑαυτὸν ἐπίγραμμα τόδε.	333 ποιεῖ τὸ τοῦ τάφου αὐτοῦ ἐπίγραμμα.
13—14 καὶ ἀναχωρῶν πηλοῦ ὄντος ὀλισθάνει καὶ πεσὼν ἐπὶ πλευρὰν οὕτως, φασίν, ἐτελεύτησεν.	334—335 ἀναχωρῶν δ᾽ ἐκεῖθεν ὄντος πηλοῦ ὀλισθὼν καὶ πεσὼν ἐπὶ τὴν πλευρὰν τριταῖος ὥς φασι τελευτᾷ.

当然，这并不意味着原稿不存在元音连续。这其实是说，像这样一个文本的流传在措辞和词序的细节上太不准确，以至于我们不能从少数明显的例子中进行论证。《竞赛》中被认为出自阿尔基达马斯作品的部分，实际上确实也出现了一些元音连续，但比其他部分少（见下文，第54页）。

（3）柯克（Kirk, p. 154）举出以下数个单词作为出自希腊化时期的证据[13]。

（a）"即兴创作"用 σχεδιάζω，而不是 αὐτοσχεδιάζω。指出这一点的同时也要指出，即使存在文本损坏，αὐτοσχεδιάζω 也不太可能紧接在 αὐτόν 一词后使用[14]，柯克自己的回答是：尽管阿尔基达马斯在他的《论书面演讲稿撰写者》（περὶ τῶν τοὺς γραπτοὺς λόγους γραφόντων，简称 Soph.《论智术师》）中频繁使用 αὐτοσχεδιάζω，但在这里 αὐτόν 一词可以是他使用 σχεδιάζω 的充分理由。这个词在公元前4世纪可考的使用有三次：P. Hibeh 13.i.12，是说粗率的论证；Anaxandrides fr.15.3，是说用乐器进行即兴创作；托名柏拉图的《西西弗斯》（Sisyphus），是说即兴演讲[15]。无法证明阿尔基达马斯不会使用这个词来修饰那些遇见荷马并一时兴起给他出谜语的男孩们。如果我们更愿意不相信这个词是原文，那我们也不需要相信，因为这个

---

[13] 他这里是反对 Körte 的理论，即荷马之死的内容是阿尔基达马斯从更早的作品中引用的。看起来，他的论证更反对的是公元前5世纪的创作定年，而不是公元前4世纪。

[14] 阿尔基达马斯实际允许这样的表述出现于自己的作品中：τὴν αὐτὴν κατ᾽ αὐτῶν，Soph. 27.

[15] "这部托名柏拉图的作品很可能是在亚里士多德时代或之后不久创作的。" J. Souilhé，见 Budé Platon, xiii (3), p. 65。

词语没有出现在《竞赛》的版本中，而且对句意的理解来说并非关键。

（b）ἁλιεία. 这个词在亚里士多德的作品中出现过两次，而且是与规则的阿提卡方言词 ἁλιεύομαι, ἁλιεύς 对应的名词。没有理由说阿尔基达马斯不应该使用它。

（c）φθειρίζομαι. 这个词也被亚里士多德使用过，而且在此之前 φθειριστική 已经出现在柏拉图《智者篇》227B。阿尔基达马斯本就更可能使用此词，而非赫拉克利特笨拙的 φθρεῖρας κατακτείνω。

（d）"第14行的 οὕτως, φασίν, ἐτελεύτησεν 中的 φασίν 颇有后亚历山大里亚学派的意味。"

（4）另一个论点是，宣言不适合作为作品的结尾，并且明显缺少与前文叙事的联系。于此存在理解上的困难，给我们造成了障碍。其内容如下：

περι τουτου μεν ουν ποιεισθαι την αρετην ποι   15
ησομεν μαλιστα δ' ορων τους ιστορικους θαυ
μαζομενους οδη ̣ ̣ος γουν δια τουτο και ζων
και αποθανων τετιμηται παρα πασιν ανθρω
ποις ταυτη[ν] ουν αυτω της παιδιας χαριν α
ποδιδο[……]ενος αυτου και την αλλη[ν] ποι   20
ησιν δια[…]ειας μνημης τοις βουλομε
νοις φι[λοκαλ]ειν των Ελληνων εις το κοινον
παραδω[ ]

[Αλκι]δαμαντος
περι Ομηρου   25

我查看了刊登在以下期刊的照片：*TAPA* lvi (1925), pl. A 和 *Rh. Mus.* cii (1959), p. 210 对页。   17 Ὅμηρος Winter. "我在微缩胶片上很清楚地看到 μ", Vogt p. 210, 但我认为，对照 *TAPA* 上的照片，这很难让人接受。   19 παιδιας = παιδείας (Körte).   20]ενος: 字母 ε 的读法见 C. H. Roberts, 在 Dodds p. 187。   21 δια 后面有一个成角的笔画，转弯处笔画更粗（β，或可能是 α 或 φ），或者是竖直笔画末

端的衬线（如：γ,κ,τ）。 22 由 Hunt 补全。

第一行不知所云，所有人都认为存在损坏，除了首位编者，他将之翻译为"至于这一点，那么，我们要实现它为自己赢得荣誉"，于是他需要把 ορων 改成 ὁρῶντες。科特（Körte）正确地否定了上述翻译，并提出删掉 ποιεῖσθαι，翻译为"让我们向他证明我们的技艺（杰出）"。佩奇（Page）将 ποιησομεν 改成 πειρασόμεθα："在这个话题上，我们必须竭力获取声名。"多兹将 ποιεῖσθαι 修改为 πονεῖσθαι[16]，将 ορων 改为 ὁρῶ："那么，在这个问题上，我们将把劳动作为我们的特别服务。"[17] 我认为以上方案都无法让人信服，因为他们都默许了这绝无仅有的表达：τὴν ἀρετὴν ποιῶ 或 ποιοῦμαι，还涉及改变 ὁρῶν。我认为似乎有什么遗漏了，特别是这里没有什么需要用 μάλιστα δέ 作答。遗漏的部分，示例如次：περὶ τούτου μὲν οὖν ποιεῖσθαι <δεῖν ἡγοῦμαι τὴν ἐπιμέλειαν, ἀφ' οὗ Μούσαις φίλην> τὴν ἀρετὴν ποιήσομεν, μάλιστα δ' ὁρῶν τοὺς ἱστορικοὺς θαυμαζομένους。

  下一行如果我们采用 Ὅμηρος 这一修正——鉴于后面的内容很难不这样修正，那么意思就很明了了。"荷马给我展示了赢取荣耀的方式。"[18] 下一句的开头与这个观点存在逻辑勾连："我给他这个作为他教授的回报。"好了，我们又遭遇到第二个困难。建议的增补是 ἀποδιδο[ὺς（或者是 -ό[ντες）τὸ γ]ένος αὐτοῦ καὶ τὴν ἄλλην ποίησιν δι' ἀκ[ριβ]είας μνήμης … παραδῶ（或 παραδῶμεν）[19]。但 ἀκριβείας 如果用作形容词（我们也认为应该是形容词），是不合适的：它应该是 ἀκριβοῦς[20]。τὸ γένος 也并不令人满意，因为它仍让我们疑惑 τὴν ἄλλην ποίησιν 是指

16　但是主动态更为常见。Alcidamas, *Soph.* 30 就是如此。

17　他还建议用 ποιήσομαι 代替 ποιήσομεν。

18　ἱστορία 的重要性，参考 *Soph.* 1; Blass, *Die attische Beredsamkeit*, ii², 47–50, 347。荷马赢取荣耀的论点可以与 *Soph.* 9 比较：τοὺς δὲ λέγοντας ὡς ἰσόθεον τὴν γνώμην ἔχοντας ὑπὸ τῶν ἄλλων τιμωμένους ὁρῶμεν.【而我们看到那些言说的人，受到其他人的尊敬，仿佛他们拥有神样的智慧】

19　Page, Dodds. 可供选择的 ἀγ]ῶνος 和 ἀγ[χιστ]είας（Winter）没有意义；前者似乎也与字迹不合。

20　关于这一点，阿尔基达马斯与其他希腊人的用法一致：*Soph.* 18 ποιεῖσθαι τὴν μνήμην καὶ τὴν μάθησιν ἀκριβῆ。

什么[21]。看起来似乎只有两种可能，要么]ενος 隐藏着对荷马诗歌创作的某个部分的指涉，但是我找不到符合要求的词；要么 τὴν ἄλλην ποίησιν 指的是 "其余的诗歌"，不是荷马所作的诗歌，因为它出现在提到荷马之后[22]。这肯定是答案；增补会类似 ταύτη[ν] οὖν αὐτῷ τῆς παιδείας χάριν ἀποδιδο[ύς, ἀφέμ]ενος αὐτοῦ καὶ τὴν ἄλλη[ν] ποίησιν διὰ β[ραχ]είας μνήμης ... παραδώ[σω。【因而，这样回报他的教授以后，我将搁置他并继续以一种便利而简要的纪念方式，让其他诗人也被渴望尚美的希腊人知道】。

阿尔基达马斯的《缪斯集》经常被认为包括了数位诗人[23]，并且纸草上的 "περὶ Ὁμήρου"【论荷马】的下款标志着作品某一部分的结束。如果我的论证正确，这两种假设都得到了证实。我们现在看到的是荷马部分的结尾，至少是以荷马开头和结尾的一部分，尽管它也涉及赫西奥德。整个部分近似其他部分的序言，这也解释了多兹发现的序言性语言风格。

柯克和多兹的观点现已遭到反驳，我们不需要再相信他们假设的特殊巧合，可以回到这一观点：阿尔基达马斯是《竞赛》背后的 "竞赛—赫西奥德之死—荷马之死" 这个扭结的缔造者。

阿尔基达马斯材料的出处

有迹象表明，关于诗人之死的故事在阿尔基达马斯的时代之前就存在了[24]。他可能稍微敷演了一番，但并不是由他创造的。那竞赛故事呢？这个问题更加困难。我们至少可以驳斥贝克（Bergk）[25] 和艾伦（Allen）[26] 的说法，他们认为竞赛的故事可以追溯到史诗诗系诗人

21　"他的出身和他的其他诗歌"，Page；"他来自哪里，他还创作了什么"，Dodds，参见 Kirk, p. 153 的批评。

22　这几乎无须说明；不过可比较 Isoc. 12.33 περὶ δὲ τῆς Ὁμήρου καὶ τῆς Ἡσιόδου καὶ τῆς τῶν ἄλλων ποιήσεως【关于荷马与赫西奥德及其他人的诗歌】。

23　Μουσεῖον 的含义之一是 "藏书的地方"。就像后代作者如 Diodorus 还有神话编撰者 Apollodorus 称他们的作品为 Βιβλιοθήκη【书库】。因为它们给出的信息丰富，如果没有它就可能需要一整个书籍仓库，阿尔基达马斯将作品取名为《缪斯集》，因为其中包括了各种各样的诗人。Callimachus 也有一部《缪斯集》（Suda; i. xcv, ii. 339 Pf.）。

24　荷马之死见 Heraclitus fr. 56，赫西奥德之死见 Thuc. 3.96。

25　Griech. Literaturgeschichte, ii. 66.

26　Op. cit., pp. 25 ff.

勒斯基斯（Lesches）的传记诗。这个观点基于普鲁塔克《七哲宴集》
（*Sept. Sap. Conu.* 153F）中的一段话，原文如下：

> ἀκούομεν γὰρ ὅτι καὶ πρὸς τὰς Ἀμφιδάμαντος ταφὰς εἰς
> Χαλκίδα τῶν τότε σοφῶν οἱ δοκιμώτατοι [ποιηταὶ] συνῆλθον …
> ἐπεὶ δὲ τὰ παρεσκευασμένα τοῖς ποιηταῖς ἔπη χαλεπὴν καὶ
> δύσκολον ἐποίει τὴν κρίσιν διὰ τὸ ἐφάμιλλον, ἥ τε δόξα τῶν
> ἀγωνιστῶν [Ὁμήρου καὶ Ἡσιόδου] πολλὴν ἀπορίαν μετὰ αἰδοῦς
> τοῖς κρίνουσι παρεῖχεν, ἐτράποντο πρὸς τοιαύτας ἐρωτήσεις, καὶ
> προύβαλε μὲν ὥς φασι Λέσχης
> > Μοῦσά μοι ἔννεπε κεῖνα τὰ μήτ’ ἐγένοντο πάροιθεν
> > μήτ’ ἔσται μετόπισθεν·
> ἀπεκρίνατο δ’ Ἡσίοδος ἐκ τοῦ παρατυχόντος·
> > ἀλλ’ ὅταν ἀμφὶ Διὸς τύμβῳ καναχήποδες ἵπποι
> > ἅρματα συντρίψουσιν ἐπειγόμενοι περὶ νίκης·
> καὶ διὰ τοῦτο λέγεται μάλιστα θαυμασθεὶς τοῦ τρίποδος τυχεῖν.

【大意：因为我们听说当时有智慧的人中最著名的［诗人］
一起去到卡尔基斯，参加安菲达马斯的葬礼。安菲达马斯是一
位战士，在给埃雷特里亚人带去了很多麻烦之后，死于勒兰托斯
战争，由于诗人们准备的诗歌棋逢对手，让评判变得困难而麻
烦，选手［荷马与赫西奥德］的声望，更是使裁判充满敬意，也让
他们很是棘手。于是，他们转向了以下类型的问题，正如勒斯基
斯所说：
> 缪斯，请告诉我，那些过去没有发生，
> 将来也不会发生的事情。

赫西奥德随口回答说：
> 当宙斯的坟墓周围有蹄声鼎沸的战马将战车
> 粉碎，渴望着胜利。

据说，因着这个说法，赫西奥德深受敬仰，获得了三足鼎。】

这些诗行对应《竞赛》第97行及以下，普鲁塔克改变了说话者的顺

序:《竞赛》中这个谜语由赫西奥德提出,荷马回答。普鲁塔克必须做出调换,因为他把这个谜语设置为竞赛结果的决定环节,出现在吟诵完准备好的史诗(παρεσκευασμένα ἔπη)之后。《竞赛》则是由后者决定竞赛的结果,谜语出现在前面部分。

贝克及艾伦根据某个抄本选择了 ὥς φησι Λέσχης【据勒斯基斯说】的读法,于是勒斯基斯就出乎意料地成为被引用的权威了。但这从佩里安德(Periander)嘴里说出是不妥当的;而且一首勒斯基斯的竞赛诗存在于普鲁塔克的时代或者任何时代,都是难以置信的。我们已知古风时期有相当数量的早期六音步诗歌,但没有一首是关于后黑暗时代的人物的。就我们所知,"传记"诗并不存在;也没有任何证据表明,普鲁塔克或其他提到竞赛故事的帝国作者是从阿尔基达马斯以外的来源知道这个故事的[27]。

维拉莫维茨的读法是 φασι【他们说】,这个读法有更多的抄本支持[28],于是勒斯基斯替代荷马成为赫西奥德的对手;他在 ἀγωνιστῶν【竞赛者】后用括号括上了 Ὁμήρου καὶ Ἡσιόδου【荷马与赫西奥德】[29]。此处明显存在窜入的文字,但普鲁塔克一定是在谈论荷马和赫西奥德,即便他没有同时说出两者的名字。他在谈论安菲达马斯葬礼的竞技赛,那正是荷马与赫西奥德的著名竞赛发生的场合,不仅是《竞赛》,菲罗斯特拉托斯(Philostratus)、忒弥修斯(Themistius),还有普鲁塔克自己的其他著作(Quaest. Conv. 674F)都有引述。赫西奥德和勒斯基斯的竞赛则未见于记载,从内在逻辑来说也是不可能的[30]。同样,勒斯基斯不可能扮演荷马与赫西奥德竞赛的裁判:竞赛是由安菲达马斯的亲属组织的,而安菲达马斯的兄弟则是那位著名的裁判[31]。如果这儿硬要与勒斯基斯产生什么联系的话,我认为唯一

---

27 A. Kirchhoff, *S. B. preuss. Ak.* 1892, pp. 865–891.

28 见 Kirk, p. 150 n. 1。

29 首先发表于 *Hermes* xiv (1879), 161 = *Kl. Schr.* iv. 1。

30 虚构勒斯基斯与阿克提努斯之间的竞争(Phaenias ap. Clem. *Strom.* 1.131.6)更有意义。他们是与史诗诗系联系最密切的两位诗人。

31 阿尔基达马斯(Petrie 纸草); Philostratus, *Heroic.* p. 318; Tz. *vit. Hes.*; Apostolius 14.11 (*Paroem. Gr.* ii. 606. 20) Πανίδου ψῆφος· ἐπὶ τῶν ἀμαθῶς ψηφιζομένων.【帕诺伊德斯的石块:投票不高明的人】

的可能就是有人由这些诗行记起了他：

> Μοῦσά μοι ἔννεπε κεῖνα τὰ μήτ᾽ ἐγένοντο πάροιθεν
> μήτ᾽ ἔσται μετόπισθεν.[32]
> 缪斯啊，请告诉我，那些过去没有发生
> 将来也不会发生的事。

《竞赛》中的版本（97—98）是这样的：

> Μοῦσ᾽ ἄγε μοι, τά τ᾽ ἐόντα τά τ᾽ ἐσσόμενα πρό τ᾽ ἐόντα,
> τῶν μὲν μηδὲν ἄειδε, σὺ δ᾽ ἄλλης μνῆσαι ἀοιδῆς.
> 缪斯啊，那些当下在，将在或曾在的事物
> 不要对我歌咏它们；请你回想其他的诗篇。

通过把词组 τά τ᾽ ἐόντα τά τ᾽ ἐσσόμενα πρό τ᾽ ἐόντα 否定，谜语得以产生，这个短语在早期诗歌中也曾使用，特别与缪斯的神力有关[33]。归于勒斯基斯的某首诗（《小伊利亚特》或《伊利昂的陷落》[Ilius Persis]）可能在召唤缪斯时用了这个短语或与之类似的表达。有位读者在普鲁塔克作品的一个抄本边缘草草记下了 Λέσχης【勒斯基斯】，由于离 προύβαλε μέν, ὥς φασιν, Ὅμηρος 这些词很近，就导致一个名字替换了另一个[34]。

证明前阿尔基达马斯时代存在竞赛故事的另外的零星可疑证据，是斐洛科鲁斯（328 F 212）于品达《尼米亚凯歌》的古代注疏（schol. Pind. *Nem.* 2.1 [iii.31.7 Dr]）中引用的赫西奥德的诗歌残篇，引用这段是为了支持 ῥαψῳδός【游吟诗人】一词来自 ῥάπτειν τὴν ᾠδήν【编织诗歌】的说法：

32　人们可能会推测原版作 ἔννεπε ἔργα，与 *h. Aphr.* 1 一样。
33　Hes. *Th.* 38, 第32行有这个表达的简化形式；可比较 *Il.* 1.70, [Hes.] fr. 204.113 M.-W., orac. ap. Diod. 9.3.2, Solon 3.15, Eur. *Hel.* 14。
34　Bergk, *Analecta Alexandrina* (1846), i. 22 n 提出过类似的建议。

ἐν Δήλῳ τότε πρῶτον ἐγὼ καὶ Ὅμηρος ἀοιδοὶ

μέλπομεν, ἐν νεαροῖς ὕμνοις ῥάψαντες ἀοιδήν,

Φοῖβον Ἀπόλλωνα χρυσάορον ὃν τέκε Λητώ.

那时在提洛岛，我与荷马，两位吟游诗人，

首次将我们的诗歌编织成新的颂诗，歌唱

持金箭的福波斯阿波罗，他由勒托所生。

(Hes. fr. 357 M.-W.)

这里赫西奥德谈到了与荷马的竞赛，不是在卡尔基斯，而是在提洛岛，他们各自对阿波罗吟唱了一首颂诗。τότε πρῶτον【在那时首次】（或按照鲍尔森[Paulson]的读法，τὸ πρῶτον【首次】）暗示了之后在另一个地方还有一场比赛。这个残篇的出处很难确定。它不可能来自通常认为是赫西奥德所作的诗歌，否则就不会有哪位诗人年代更早的争论，而这场提洛岛的竞赛也会广为人知。想必阿尔基达马斯不知道这一诗篇，否则他可以将竞赛地点定于提洛岛，而不是基于《劳作与时日》的段落（650—660），这个段落并没有提到荷马。斐洛科鲁斯看见的这首诗似乎完全是当时新造的伪作，其中赫西奥德谈到两次竞赛（这和《劳作与时日》相抵触：他说除了前往卡尔基斯，他从未跨越大海）：前一次在提洛岛，荷马用《致阿波罗颂诗》打败了他，根据《竞赛》第18节第320行，这首颂诗被刻在一块石板（λεύκωμα）上献祭给阿尔忒弥斯的神庙；后一次在卡尔基斯，赫西奥德在这里复仇，还将著名的铭文三足鼎献给了缪斯。这首诗似乎从未广泛流传，而且很早就失传了。我们没有理由认为它存在于阿尔基达马斯的时代之前[35]。

还剩下的是阿里斯托芬《和平》（1282—1283）对这两行诙谐诗句的引用：

35　短语 ῥάψαντες ἀοιδήν 可能有一种古早的味道，但不如说是一个诗意的仿古，等同于 ῥαψῳδεῖν，如在《竞赛》第5节，第55—56行：ποιήσαντα γὰρ τὸν Μαργίτην Ὅμηρον περιέρχεσθαι κατὰ πόλιν ῥαψῳδοῦντα【荷马在创作了《马尔吉特斯》后周游各城邦吟诵诗歌】；以及第17节，第286—287行：ἐκεῖθεν δὲ παραγενόμενος εἰς Κόρινθον ἐρραψῴδει τὰ ποιήματα【他从那里前往科林斯并吟诵了自己的诗作】。

ὣς οἱ μὲν δαίνυντο βοῶν κρέα καὐχένας ἵππων
ἔκλυον ἱδρώοντας ἐπεὶ πολέμου ἐκόρεσθεν.
于是,他们吃了牛肉和马脖子
解除了马轭,浑身冒汗,因为他们饱尝战争之苦。

它们出现在《竞赛》第107—108行(有两处异文),作为一系列对句或三联句的第一组,其中赫西奥德吟诵一行荒诞不经的诗句,荷马则必须答以适宜的下句使之合理。这可能是一种公认的聚会游戏;但这类谜语更可能是照搬的而非原创,如果阿尔基达马斯原创了荷马与赫西奥德之间的竞赛,那么对他来说,使用那些已经流行的谜语也是很自然的。没有证据表明阿里斯托芬把这几行诗与荷马和赫西奥德联系起来。而有另一个迹象表明,阿尔基达马斯在这一部分使用了业已存在的诗行,并将其置于新语境。在他的叙事中,赫西奥德设置谜面,荷马解答。但借助一个误解,他还加入了一些双向谜语(double riddles),其中两位说话人都需要解谜。

121-123 A.   δεῖπνον δειπνήσαντες ἐνὶ σποδῷ αἰθαλοέσσῃ
         B.   σύλλεγον ὀστέα λευκὰ Διὸς κατατεθνηῶτος
         A(或 C).   παιδὸς ὑπερθύμου Σαρπηδόνος ἀντιθέοιο.
124-126 A.   ἡμεῖς δ᾽ ἂμ πεδίον Σιμοέντιον ἥμενοι αὔτως
         B.   ἴομεν ἐκ νηῶν ὁδὸν ἀμφ᾽ ὤμοισιν ἔχοντες[36]
         A(或 C).   φάσγανα κωπήεντα καὶ αἰγανέας δολιχαύλους.
133-137 A.   τοῖσιν δ᾽ Ἀτρείδης μεγάλ᾽ εὔχετο πᾶσιν ὀλέσθαι
         B.   μηδέποτ᾽ ἐν πόντῳ καὶ φωνήσας ἔπος ηὔδα·
                ἐσθίετ᾽ ὦ ξεῖνοι καὶ πίνετε, μηδέ τις ὑμῶν
                οἴκαδε νοστήσειε φίλην ἐς πατρίδα γαῖαν
         A(或 C).   πημανθείς, ἀλλ᾽ αὖτις ἀπήμονες οἴκαδ᾽ ἵκοισθε.

---

[36] 我不理解这句。ἂμ πεδίον需要一个运动动词,以造成第124行的悖论;但是第125行未能解释ἥμενοι αὔτως(οὔτως cod.)。Barnes推测第124行之后脱落了一行。

121–123	A.	在烟雾缭绕的灰烬间享用宴席后，
	B.	他们收殓逝者的白骨，它属于宙斯
	A(或 C).	之子，高傲的、神样的萨耳佩冬。
124–126	A.	我们坐在西摩伊斯平原上，这般
	B.	自船只出发走向道路，肩头所扛
	A(或 C).	乃带柄的刀剑和长颈投枪。
133–137	A.	阿特柔斯之子郑重祈祷，希望他们全体遇难
	B.	永不在海上，并张口说出诗句：
		"吃吧，客人们，喝吧！愿你们中无人
		归返家园回到亲爱的乡土
	A(或 C).	时负伤，愿你们毫发无损地回归家乡。"

显然，阿尔基达马斯认为这些三联句只有最后一行包含答案，即使第105—106行的导语 ἔστιν οὖν ὁ μὲν πρῶτος (στίχος) Ἡσιόδου, ὁ δὲ ἑξῆς Ὁμήρου, ἐνίοτε δὲ καὶ διὰ δύο στίχων τὴν ἐπερώτησιν ποιουμένου τοῦ Ἡσιόδου【第一行是赫西奥德的，接下来的一行是荷马的，不过赫西奥德有时也用两行诗来创设谜题】不应该归于他的版本。尤为重要的是上面引用的第三个谜语，原诗的第133—137行。它是这个谜语系列的最后一个，接下去的叙事是 πρὸς πάντα δὲ τοῦ Ὁμήρου καλῶς ἀπαντήσαντος πάλιν φησὶν ὁ Ἡσίοδος κλτ【鉴于荷马完美地解答了所有的谜题，赫西奥德又说道……】。据此看，第137行必须归于荷马，而第134—136行是赫西奥德的；但第133行也必须归属于赫西奥德[37]。因此，在只有一位诗人被考问的情节中，阿尔基达马斯使用了不适合这种情境的诗句。

没有证据可以表明，在阿尔基达马斯之前还有关于荷马与赫西奥德竞赛的更早记载。诗人、先知等群体内的竞赛母题，是历史悠久的；我们已知的有托名赫西奥德的诗歌《梅朗普斯之歌》(*Melampodia*, fr.

---

[37] Rzach 同此。只有 Busse 的版本与此不同（*Rh. Mus.* Lxiv [1909], 115 n. 1），他的分法是：第133行属于 A，第134行的 μηδέποτ' ἐν πόντῳ 属于 B，καὶ φωνήσας 到第136行属于 A，第137行属于 B。但是一行诗有两位说话者这一分法无疑是无法接受的。第一个悖论必须至少用完整的一行诗来回答。

278 M.-W.) 记载的卡尔克斯 (Calchas) 与莫普索斯 (Mopsus) 之间的竞赛，还有埃斯库罗斯与欧里庇得斯在《蛙》中的竞赛[38]。荷马与赫西奥德作为早期史诗体诗歌的两位伟大人物，创造一场他们二人之间的竞赛是自然而然的。但是谁创造的呢？喜剧作家也许是一个答案。但埃斯库罗斯与欧里庇得斯在《蛙》中的例子具有主题相关性，这是荷马与赫西奥德的作品比较不具备的，更不用说喜剧的常规戏仿对象是悲剧，不是史诗。艾伦与柯克提出可能是荷马后人 (Homeridae)，后者理所当然地讲述荷马生平的故事[39]。但是这种观点有一处硬伤，那就是诸多《荷马传》的终极来源必然是这些故事，但它们无一提到荷马与赫西奥德的竞赛；荷马后人也不可能传播荷马被其他诗人打败的故事。欧斯塔提奥斯 (Eustathius) 或他的材料来源在写下如下内容 (*Hom.*, p. 4.38) 时，也许指的就是《荷马传》: εἰ δὲ καὶ ἤρισεν Ὅμηρος Ἡσιόδῳ τῷ Ἀσκραίῳ καὶ ἡττήθη, ὅπερ ὄκνος τοῖς Ὁμηρίδαις καὶ λέγειν.【荷马是否也曾与阿斯克拉人赫西奥德竞比并被击败，荷马后人甚至都不愿提及】这些人选都不对，很难想象还有什么人比智术师更有可能去创造这场竞赛。

帕诺伊德斯的评判

现在需分析竞赛内容，以确定阿尔基达马斯的目的。赫西奥德首先问荷马: τί φέρτατόν ἐστι βροτοῖσι.【什么对凡人来说最佳】荷马以这两行诗作答:

> ἀρχὴν μὲν μὴ φῦναι ἐπιχθονίοισιν ἄριστον,
> φύντα δ' ὅπως ὤκιστα πύλας Ἀίδαο περῆσαι,
> 对地上的人来说，最好是一开始就不要出生，
> 抑或出生后不论如何尽快跨越哈德斯的门扉。

斯托拜乌 (Stobaeus) 也引用了这两行诗，并说出处是阿尔基达马斯

38　比较 Rohde, *Kl. Schr.* i 103f.; Radermacher, *Aristophanes' Frösche* (*S.B. Wien. Ak.* 198/4, 1921), p. 30; Dornseiff, *Gnomon* xx (1944), 139。

39　Pl. *Rep.* 599E, Isoc. 10.65.

的《缪斯集》，不过这两行诗与特奥格尼斯诗集中的五音步诗行一同出现，说明这两行无疑相当古老[40]。其后，赫西奥德又提出了几乎相同的问题：τί θνητοῖς κάλλιστον.【什么对凡人来说最美】（纸草中也是如此；有的抄本或作 τί θνητοῖσιν ἄριστον）荷马以《奥德赛》9.6-11处奥德修斯的话语回应。这是第一回合，基于旧诗作。接下来，赫西奥德要求荷马歌唱一首关于过去、现在和将来都不会发生的事情的诗歌，荷马用如下巧妙的消极预言（negative prophecy）来回答：

οὐδέποτ' ἀμφὶ Διὸς τύμβῳ καναχήποδες ἵπποι
ἄρματα συντρίψουσιν ἐρίζοντες περὶ νίκης.
蹄声响亮的马群从未在宙斯墓旁
因努力竞比争胜而损坏车舆。

这可能是一道传统的谜题，就像我上文已经提到的，赫西奥德第三回合说出的模棱两可的诗行。第四回合，他问有多少希腊人跟随阿伽门农前往特洛伊，荷马回答的诗句应该来自一部史诗诗系作品[41]。到目前为止，阿尔基达马斯让荷马面对一堆杂七杂八的测试和谜题，所有这些都可能是有传统的，而且好像除了闹着玩没有任何目的。变化即刻产生。赫西奥德再一次提出类似"对凡人来说最好的是什么"这一问题。但这次是一系列问题，共八个，而且问题和答案都更加诡辩；它们散发出公元前5世纪晚期到前4世纪早期的气息，可能是阿尔基达马斯自己的创造。竞赛变得更为严肃。现在，观众为荷马的表现喝彩，强烈要求授予他胜利者的桂冠，于是帕诺伊德斯介入并设置最后一关——决定性的考验：每位诗人吟诵自己诗歌的最好片段（τὸ κάλλιστον）。阿尔基达马斯挑选的诗节

40　阿尔基达马斯写过一篇文章赞美死亡（Cic. *Tusc.* 1. 116, Menander Rhet. iii. 346. 17 Sp., Tz. *Chil.* 11. 745ff.），这些诗行可能给他留下了深刻的印象。

41　这些诗句和 *Il.* 2. 123 ff., [Hes.] fr. 304 M.-W. 属于同一类。在抄本中紧跟着些不相干的笔记，τοῦτο δὲ εὑρίσκεται πλῆθος ἄπιστον κτλ.【这被认为是不可信的数字……】，显然是窜入的。它的结尾不完整，可能是因为它写在靠近页脚的边缘处，被损毁了。

（*Op.* 383 ff.[42]；*Il.* 13.126–133 + 339–344）确实很好；但是它们被选中很明显是为了体现他想表现的两位诗人的独特性。荷马回答的"智术师式"（sophistic）的问题暗示了一个观点，即判断诗人要基于他对社群的贡献；比如，他被这样问道：

πῶς ἂν ἄριστ᾽ οἰκοῖντο πόλεις καὶ ἐν ἤθεσι ποίοις;[43]
城邦怎样会被治理得最好，要采取何种风俗？

阿里斯托芬已借埃斯库罗斯之口言明赫西奥德与荷马的优点是什么（《蛙》1032—1036）：

Ὀρφεὺς μὲν γὰρ τελετάς θ᾽ ἡμῖν κατέδειξε φόνων τ᾽ ἀπέχεσθαι,
Μουσαῖος δ᾽ ἐξακέσεις τε νόσων καὶ χρησμούς, Ἡσίοδος δὲ

42　在抄本中，引语在第392行戛然而止，止于 γυμνὸν δ᾽ ἀμάειν, ὅταν ὥρια πάντα πέλωνται，而此处赫西奥德的实际文本如下：γυμνὸν δ᾽ ἀμάειν εἴ χ᾽ ὥρια πάντ᾽ ἐθέλησθα / ἔργα κομίζεσθαι Δημήτερος κλτ. 不过这个摘录原本可能持续到第404行，因为 Philostratus, *Heroic.*, p. 318 说：ἐπὶ Ὅμηρόν τέ φασι καὶ Ἡσίοδον, ὅτε δὴ ᾆσαι ἄμφω ἐν Χαλκίδι τὸν μὲν τὰ ἑπτὰ (?) ἔπη τὰ περὶ τοῖν Αἰάντοιν καὶ ὡς αἱ φάλαγγες αὐτοῖς ἀραρυῖαί τε ἦσαν καὶ καρτεραί, τὸν δὲ τὰ πρὸς τὸν ἀδελφὸν τὸν ἑαυτοῦ Πέρσην, ἐν οἷς αὐτὸν ἔργων τε ἐκέλευσεν ἅπτεσθαι καὶ γεωργίᾳ προσκεῖσθαι, ὡς μὴ δέοιτο ἑτέρων μηδὲ πεινῴη.【大意：另外一些人说，特洛伊之后，一百六十年过去才到荷马和赫西奥德的时代，他们一起在卡尔基斯吟诵：一是关于两个埃阿斯的七行史诗，讲述了战阵是如何紧凑而强大的，而另一个是关于他弟弟佩尔塞斯的诗歌，他鼓励佩尔塞斯去工作，投身农业，这样就不需要别人的帮助，也不用挨饿】这看起来不是对《劳作与时日》内容的模糊叙述，而是对以下诗行的准确引用：

ἐργάζευ, νήπιε Πέρση,
ἔργα, τά τ᾽ ἀνθρώποισι θεοὶ διετεκμήραντο,
μή ποτε σὺν παίδεσσι γυναικί τε θυμὸν ἀχεύων
ζητεύῃς βίοτον κατὰ γείτονας, οἱ δ᾽ ἀμελῶσι.
.... ἀλλά σ᾽ ἄνωγα
φράζεσθαι χρειῶν τε λύσιν λιμοῦ τ᾽ ἀλεωρήν.

(397—404)

【大意：愚蠢的佩尔塞斯！去做诸神为人类安排的活计，免得你的妻子儿女心中悲苦，在邻居中乞讨，而他们不会听你的。……你所说的一切都是徒劳】比较 Tzetzes, *Vit. Hes.*, p. 49.6 Wil. Ἡσίοδος δὲ τῶν Πληιάδων Ἀτλαγενέων ἐπιτελλομενάων ἀπάρχεται καὶ ὁμοίως Ὁμήρῳ προβαίνει μέχρι πολλοῦ τῶν ἐπῶν【但是，赫西奥德从这句诗开始："阿特拉斯生养的普勒阿得斯在天空升起时"，之后就像荷马一样继续吟诵了很多诗句】，及 Nietzsche, pp. 530, 532。

43　关于艺术的这一标准，比较 Ar. *Ran.* 1420 ff., Alcid. *Soph.* 9.26, 27, Isoc. 2.43。

γῆς ἐργασίας, καρπῶν ὥρας, ἀρότους· ὁ δὲ θεῖος Ὅμηρος
ἀπὸ τοῦ τιμὴν καὶ κλέος ἔσχεν πλὴν τοῦδ' ὅτι χρήστ' ἐδίδαξεν,
τάξεις ἀρετὰς ὁπλίσεις ἀνδρῶν;

因为俄耳甫斯教会我们秘仪以远离杀戮，

缪赛奥斯则教导疾病的治疗与神谕，还有赫西奥德

指导农工，收获及耕种；那么神圣的荷马

从哪里获取光荣与荣耀？无非是在这里教授有用之事：

用兵之道、男子气概、人类武装。

这些也正是阿尔基达马斯所挑出的。帕诺伊德斯评判的实质是，在和平与战争之间做选择。观众被荷马的诗歌娱悦，而国王却将胜利的桂冠奖给赫西奥德。

　　沃格特（Vogt）认为[44]，对这场竞赛的描述显示出对荷马明显的偏爱；在这一点上，他发现了阿尔基达马斯偏好即兴创作，而不是提前思索好的发言，如《论智术师》所示[45]。我认为这种解读是不正确的。整个叙事并没有暗示荷马与赫西奥德作为即兴诗人与刻苦钻研者形成对照，而《论智术师》也没有提到荷马。是赫西奥德，而不是荷马赢得了大奖，说赫西奥德赢得这个奖项仅因为裁判的反常行为（Vogt, pp. 199, 201, al.）是无效的；没有一个词表明这个决定是不公正的[46]。这个类型的故事深受希腊人喜爱，即某人的行为与预期相反，但他用新颖而绝非不值一提的情境分析来证明自己的正确，并以隽语的形式（epigrammatic form）表达。的确，以其他任何标准来衡量，荷马都应该获胜。除了最后一题，其他题目荷马都通过了。但这并不意味着叙述者真的希望荷马赢。这是在为最后惊人的裁决做铺垫，正如观众为荷马喝彩，都是为了使最后的评判更加生动。

　　赫西奥德是吟诵和平的诗人；因此，根据阿尔基达马斯的说法，

44　*Rh. Mus.* cii (1959), pp. 199, 201, al.

45　尼采已经这么认为，见Nietzsche, 539 f.。

46　Lucian (*Vera hist.* 2.22)，Philostratus 及 Apostolius 那里有表明判决不公正的用语，但与此都不相关。忽视故事原本的要义，是第二期智术师的典型表现。Apostolius记录的这句话可能来自那个时期的某个作家，而不是像一些人认为的那样来自Philostratus的篇章。

荷马必须将胜利拱手相让。古代另有一人也用相同的对立来刻画荷马与赫西奥德,但是对他们的价值的评估是相反的。据普鲁塔克所说[47],Κλεομένης ὁ Ἀναξανδρίδεω τὸν μὲν Ὅμηρον Λακεδαιμονίων εἶναι ποιητὴν ἔφη, τὸν δὲ Ἡσίοδον τῶν εἱλωτῶν· τὸν μὲν γὰρ ὡς πολεμεῖν, τὸν δὲ ὡς χρὴ γεωργεῖν παρηγγελκέναι【克里奥门尼斯,阿那克桑德里斯之子,说荷马是斯巴达的诗人,而赫西奥德是黑劳士的诗人;因为荷马给战斗提供必要的指导,而赫西奥德指导的是农事】。公元前360年以降,阿尔基达马斯支持美塞尼亚的独立与和平,而其他人则认为斯巴达通过战争重新奴役他们是可以得到辩护的[48]。上述对荷马与赫西奥德评价的分歧,与这些历史事实无关吗?克里奥门尼斯的观点看起来很像对阿尔基达马斯的回应。

II.编者

这位安敦尼时代的编者从阿尔基达马斯处挪用的叙事包括:
(1)荷马获得的神谕。
(2)竞赛。
(3)赫西奥德获得的神谕。
(4)赫西奥德之死。
(5)荷马之死。
在阿尔基达马斯那里,这是一篇论荷马文章的主要部分,而这篇文章是一部讨论几位不同诗人的文集的引言。编者抛弃了修辞框架,把这里的叙事与其他来源的材料综合了起来。

第1节,第1—8行:导言
文章第一句话是:Ὅμηρον καὶ Ἡσίοδον τοὺς θειοτάτους ποιητὰς πάντες ἄνθρωποι πολίτας ἰδίους εὔχονται λέγεσθαι.【所有人都希望最

47　*Apophth. Lac.* 223A;比较 Ael. *VH* 13.19。
48　比较 Busse, p. 119; Dornseiff, p. 137。亚里士多德不止一次提及《美塞尼亚演说》(Μεσσηνιακὸς λόγος),似乎这是阿尔基达马斯最重要的作品之一。

神圣的诗人荷马和赫西奥德被称作自己的公民同胞。】这对于赫西奥德来说显然不相宜,以至于人们怀疑这位编者是借鉴了某部《荷马传》中的句子,Ὅμηρον τὸν θειότατον ποιητὴν πάντες ἄνθρωποι πολίτην ἴδιον εὔχονται λέγεσθαι【所有人都希望最神圣的诗人荷马被称作自己的公民同胞】,然后简单地改写进自己的作品[49]。紧接着,他又自相矛盾地写下 ἀλλ' Ἡσίοδος μὲν τὴν ἰδίαν ὀνομάσας πατρίδα πάντας τῆς φιλονικίας ἀπήλλαξεν εἰπὼν ὡς ὁ πατὴρ αὐτοῦ【但赫西奥德曾提及家乡的名字,这足以平息一切争论,因为他说他自己的父亲】

> εἴσατο δ' ἄγχ' Ἑλικῶνος οἰζυρῇ ἐνὶ κώμῃ,
> Ἄσκρῃ, χεῖμα κακῇ, θέρει ἀργαλέῃ, οὐδέποτ' ἐσθλῇ.
> 【定居在赫利孔山附近的凄凉村庄,
> 阿斯克拉,凛冬苦夏,没有好年光】

Ὅμηρον δὲ πᾶσαι ὡς εἰπεῖν αἱ πόλεις καὶ οἱ ἔποικοι αὐτῶν παρ' ἑαυτοῖς γεγενῆσθαι λέγουσιν.【至于荷马,几乎所有的城邦及其居民都宣称他出生在他们当中】这可以直接追溯到更早的来源,从它与维莱乌斯 1.7.1(Hesiodus)的一致可见端倪,即 qui uitauit ne in id quod Homerus incideret, patriamque et parentes testatus est【他避免了荷马的错误,给我们证实了他的家乡和父母】。普罗克洛斯也在《荷马传》第4—8行说过类似的话:Ὅμηρος μὲν οὖν τίνων γονέων ἢ ποίας ἐγένετο πατρίδος οὐ ῥάδιον ἀποφήνασθαι· οὔτε γὰρ αὐτός τι λελάληκεν, ἀλλ' οὐδὲ οἱ περὶ αὐτοῦ εἰπόντες συμπεφωνήκασιν, ἀλλ' ἐκ τοῦ μηδὲν ῥητῶς ἐμφαίνειν περὶ τούτων τὴν ποίησιν αὐτοῦ μετὰ πολλῆς ἀδείας ἕκαστος οἷς ἐβούλετο ἐχαρίσατο.【就荷马而言,要证明他的世系和乡土是不容易的,因为他自己没有提及,那些谈论的人也莫衷一是;而且由于他的诗歌没有就这个话题给出明确的表述,所以其他人也都没有限制地按照自己的偏好进行选择】[50]维莱乌斯和普罗克洛斯的论述还有

---

[49] θεῖος 专门用于荷马:《竞赛》第214、309、338行, Ar. *Ran.* 1033, [Plut.] *Cons. Apoll.* 104D, Tz. *Exeg. in Il.*, p. 7.26, etc。

[50] 比较 [Plut.] *Vita I*, Eust. in Hom., p. 4.18。

其他重合点[51]，两者的背后显然是同一个来源。我们也许可以认为《竞赛》的编者也使用了它。

第 2 节，第 8—17 行：荷马的出生地

接下来的一节必须假定与上文出处不同，编者给出了荷马的三个诞生地，即士麦拿、基俄斯、克罗丰，对每一个诞生地都有论证。没有提到任何作者的名字；只写道 Σμυρναῖοι…φασί…Χῖοι δὲ πάλιν…Κολοφώνιοι δέ…【士麦拿人……说……继而基俄斯人……而克罗丰人……】，但所有说法应该都见于书面材料[52]。没有提及伊奥斯（亚里士多德）、雅典（阿里斯塔克斯），以及大量出现在一些《荷马传》中的五花八门的次要说法，暗示了一种相当早的，可能可以追溯到公元前4世纪的来源。这种展现方式使人想到该来源是一位历史学家[53]。维莱乌斯和普罗克洛斯的材料似乎比较晚近，因为两者都包含了一些公元前 2 世纪学者的年表。此外，他们的材料都提到诗人失明时把名字改为荷马（曾名 Melesigenes［墨勒西格涅斯］）[54]。

第 3 节，第 18—43 行：荷马的世系

这部分的开头很古怪："关于他的父母同样是众说纷纭。赫拉尼科斯和克勒安特斯说［他的父亲］是迈翁，欧盖昂说是墨勒斯"，等

51　Vell. 1.5.3 "如果有人坚持认为荷马生来就是瞎子，那他自己就是完全缺乏理智的"，见 Procl. lines 47–49（另比较 Luc. *Vera hist.* 2.20）; Vell. ibid. "荷马所处的年代距离他所写的特洛伊战争时期要遥远得多，因为他活跃于大约950年前，而他从出生到现在还不到一千年"，见 Procl. lines 59–63; Vell. 1.7.1 "这段时期属于赫西奥德，与荷马的年龄相差约120岁"，见 Procl. lines 50–57。Velleius 的编年框架通过 Nepos 的中介，来自 Apollodorus: Jacoby, *Apollodors Chronik*, pp. 101ff.; Dihle, *RE* viiiA 642 f.。比较 Rohde, *Rh. Mus.* xxxvi (1881), 551–2 = *Kl. Schr.* i. 87–88。

52　士麦拿人的故事——荷马是在失明后改为这个名字的——来自 Ephorus (70 F1)，他创造了一个塞浦路斯血统的荷马，但出生在士麦拿。基俄斯人根据他们中的荷马后人提出的主张，可能来自 Hellanicus (4 F 20)；尽管 Roman Life, p. 30. 24 Wil. 在提到荷马是基俄斯人这一说法的出处时，没有举出他的名字，但列举了 Damastes (5 F 11), Anaximenes (72 F 30), Pindar (fr.264)，还有 Theocritus 在他的隽语诗中提到（原文为 ἄλλος ὁ Χῖος【另一位基俄斯人】; 参见 *Idyll* 7.47）。克罗丰人的宣称源于克罗丰人 Antimachus 和 Nicander。

53　不太可能是阿尔达马斯。他曾在某处谈及荷马不是基俄斯人 (Arist. *Rhet.* 1398[b]12)，而竞赛之前荷马得到的神谕说伊奥斯是他母亲的家乡。

54　普罗克洛斯引用了这个说法，但是位于他所作传记的较早部分，源于不同的出处。

等。这是一份只有父亲名字的清单，大部分都同时有权威人士的名字。接着是，"有的人说他的母亲是墨提斯"，等等，这份名单没有权威人士的名字。事实上，如果我们将两份名单并列，可以发现母亲与父亲是相匹配的。

	权威人士	父亲	母亲
1	赫拉尼科斯、克勒安特斯（或尼特斯[Neanthes]）	迈翁	墨提斯
2	欧盖昂	墨勒斯	克瑞特伊斯
3	卡利克勒斯	†马萨戈拉斯	特弥斯特（Themiste）
4	特洛曾的德谟克尼斯（Democrines）	阿勒蒙（Alemon）	希尔勒托（Hyrnetho）
5	"某些人"	塔米拉斯	某个被腓尼基人卖掉的伊塔卡妇女
6	"埃及人"	墨涅马科斯	卡利奥佩
7	"某些人"	特勒马科斯	波吕卡斯特

1. 参阅 *Suda* iii. 525.2 Adler ὡς δὲ Χάραξ ὁ ἱστορικός【正如历史学家卡拉克斯所说】(103 F 62)，Μαίονος καὶ Εὐμήτιδος [ἢ Μήτιος] μητρός.【迈翁与母亲欧墨提斯[或墨提斯]】(抄本里 ἢ Μητίου［原文如此］在 καὶ Εὐμ. 之前，W 将之删除，我将之修正。)

2. 在所有的《荷马传》中，河神墨勒斯与 Κρηθηῒς νύμφη【宁芙克瑞特伊斯】都是一对。

3. 卡利克勒斯记述的荷马是一位从萨拉米斯来的塞浦路斯人（*Vita Romana*, p. 31.1 Wil.）；声称荷马属于他们的塞浦路斯人称他的母亲是特弥斯特（Themisto）(Paus. 10.24.3)。比较 *FGrHist* 758 F13，至于父亲的名字，见 Gow-Page, *Hellenistic Epigrams*, ii. 27。

4. 这一行所有的名字都是根据其他材料修正的；抄本中作 Δημόκριτος【德谟克里托斯】，Δαήμονα【达厄谟纳】，Εὐγνηθώ【欧格涅托】。我没有找到希尔勒托是阿勒蒙的妻子的直接证据。

5/6. 两位母亲的名字被调换了。墨涅马科斯被描述为

ἱερογραμματεύς【书吏】。欧斯塔提奥斯说荷马来自埃及，但父母的名字与此处不同（Eust. *Od.* p. 1713. 17ff.），他声称帕福斯的亚历山大（身份不明）是他的信息来源。

7. 最后一组与哈德良求得的神谕相一致，编者记录在了更后面。很清楚，在原始出处中，父亲和母亲是同时出现的：περὶ δὲ τῶν γονέων αὐτοῦ…Ἑλλάνικος μὲν γὰρ καὶ Κλεάνθης Μαίονα λέγουσι καὶ Μῆτιν, Εὐγαίων δὲ Μέλητα καὶ Κρηθηίδα νύμφην【关于他的父母……赫拉尼科斯和克勒安特斯说是迈翁和墨提斯，欧盖昂说是墨勒斯与宁芙克瑞特伊斯】，等等。编者将父母的名字分开，大概是因为两个名单看起来比仅有一个更博学，并且没有在第一句用"父亲"替代"父母"来掩盖他的思路。

这一节的材料来源知道哪些人把荷马说成是塞浦路斯人、埃及人或伊塔卡人，因此与第2节的出处不同。由于它与普罗克洛斯的《荷马传》几乎没有任何雷同之处，所以它似乎与第1节的出处也不同。那么，第3节的出处很可能就是它的首句所取材的那部《荷马传》，因为编者不太可能只从这个来源摘取一句话就不再使用它，而我们无法找到其他可以归于这一出处的小节。本小节的内容也充分符合首句的预示。同一材料来源可能也提供了父母清单之后的内容，即第27—32行：关于墨勒西格涅斯的信息和改名原因，或者是因为荷马被塞浦路斯人作为人质（应该是对卡利克勒斯说法的解释），或者是因为他失明了（埃弗鲁斯[Ephorus]）。之后，编者自己加上了给哈德良的神谕这一部分（第32—43行）。

第4—14节，第44—253行：荷马与赫西奥德的关系；竞赛；赫西奥德之死

赫西奥德再次回归视野。ἔνιοι μὲν οὖν αὐτὸν προγενέστερον Ἡσιόδου φασὶν εἶναι, τινὲς δὲ νεώτερον καὶ συγγενῆ. γενεαλογοῦσι δὲ οὕτως.【一些人说他比赫西奥德更早出生，而另一些人说他［比赫西奥德］更年轻且是近亲。他们这样描述［他们的］谱系】后文接续了那一世系的一个版本，从阿波罗到利诺斯、俄耳甫斯，最后是荷马与赫西奥德，其间包含的人物在数个《荷马传》中各不相同，这些传记被归于斯特辛布罗图斯

(Stesimbrotus)、赫拉尼科斯、斐里基德斯(Pherecydes)、达马斯特斯
(Damastes)、埃弗鲁斯,还有卡拉克斯名下[55]。《竞赛》与苏达辞书的版本
最为接近,苏达辞书称援引自卡拉克斯。我们目前假定的三种来源中,
维莱乌斯–普罗克洛斯的版本明确认为荷马早于赫西奥德,而且否认两
人有亲戚关系(Proclus, lines 50–53 S.),因此似乎被排除了。

编者现在转向阿尔基达马斯的叙事。这当然预设了赫西奥德和
荷马是同时代人。于是他以这句话开头:τινὲς δὲ συνακμάσαι φασὶν
αὐτοὺς ὥστε καὶ ἀγωνίσασθαι ὁμόσε ἐν Αὐλίδι τῆς Βοιωτίας.【然而,有
些人说他们活跃于同一时期,甚至共赴彼奥提亚的奥利斯进行竞赛】
阿尔基达马斯的叙事一直持续到第14节,第239行,[56]此后增加了埃
拉托色尼记载的赫西奥德之死。

第15—18,第254—338行:荷马的余生

最后一部分是关于荷马的叙事,一部分源自阿尔基达马斯(荷马
之死:密歇根纸草),然而更多内容来自其他地方。荷马周游希腊,
并吟诵他的诗歌,从《忒拜纪》(*Thebais*)和《后辈英雄纪》(*Epigoni*)
开始[57]。除了诗题,还非常奇怪地加上了取自一份图书馆书目的细
节:每首诗的行数(不是按照通常情况那样写的卷数,可能因为卷数
在这个语境中不合适)以及首行诗。弥达斯(Midas)的两位儿子对
这些作品印象深刻,因此邀请荷马为他们的父亲撰写墓志铭,荷马照
做了。他们奖给荷马一尊银杯作为回报,荷马将银杯献祭给德尔斐
的阿波罗,并创作了合适的铭文。这个故事与赫西奥德的三足鼎相
类似(已故国王之子的邀请、奖品、献祭、铭文),因此可能是阿尔基达
马斯的叙事,他倾向于将荷马和赫西奥德装进类似的故事模式(神
谕、死亡、墓志铭)中,这一点已经为人所注意。同样的故事不久后出

---

[55] Allen, op. cit., 第32页对此有阐述。比较 Rohde, *Rh. Mus.* xxxvi (1881), 385ff. = *Kl. Schr.* i. 6ff.。

[56] 在这个过程中,他透露了一些他自己关于诗人出身的想法,这与第1—4节中的信息不一致。赫西奥德是狄奥斯的儿子(156),正如 Ephorus-Charax 的谱系所示,但荷马是墨勒斯的儿子(75,151),还有一位来自伊奥斯的母亲(59)。

[57] 他在竞赛前已经完成了《马尔吉特斯》,见第55行。第260行的 φασὶ γάρ τινες καὶ ταῦτα Ὁμήρου εἶναι【因为有些人说这些诗行也是荷马的】显然是窜入的。它们不可能出自一个刚刚声称荷马确实从他的诗歌中吟诵了这些的人。

现在托名希罗多德的《荷马传》中。

之后，荷马又创作了《奥德赛》(12 000行)，此前已经创作了《伊利亚特》(15 500行)。——将之用如此奇怪的方式呈现出来，我想，是因为荷马已经在竞赛中吟诵了《伊利亚特》。但是如果阿尔基达马斯在他的叙述中提到《伊利亚特》和《奥德赛》的创作，他肯定不会处理得这么毫无技巧。似乎是编者在这里进行了改编。

《竞赛》接下来的内容是荷马停驻的几个地方。

雅典。受到国王墨冬(Medon)的款待。创作了铭体诗13 ἀνδρὸς μὲν στέφανος【男人的冠冕】[58]。

科林斯。吟诵诗歌且备受尊崇[59]。

阿尔戈斯。吟诵了关于阿尔戈斯的舰船名录中的诗行(第560行及以下)而且备受尊崇：除了其他一些活动，每五年还要到基俄斯举行一场献祭[60]。

提洛岛。吟诵了《致阿波罗颂诗》(再次用它的首句标识)。伊奥尼亚人让他成为自己的πολίτην κοινός【公民同胞】，而且颂诗被刻在板上并敬献给阿尔忒弥斯的神庙。

可以发现，这些地点都不在小亚细亚。但也没有暗示荷马不是伊奥尼亚人(阿尔戈斯的部分其实暗示了他来自基俄斯，把提洛岛的颂诗包括进来也是如此)。相反，这部分的要点是解释荷马诗歌中提到的一些特点与内容，它们与一位来自伊奥尼亚的诗人格格不入，同时把一些已知诗歌的创作缘由放进去。托名希罗多德的《荷马传》显示了类似的倾向，尽管它包含了更完整的偶成诗歌的集合，并对荷马的行动轨迹给出了不同的说法：他从未抵达希腊大陆，而是在去

58　在托名希罗多德的《荷马传》以及《苏达辞书》中，这首诗作于萨摩斯。

59　对这次平淡无奇的到访的解释似乎如下：Aristarchus被荷马除了使用更"早"的名字Ἐφύρη，还使用Κόρινθος这一点给弄糊涂了，觉得有必要给学生解释荷马用这个词是ἐκ τοῦ ἰδίου προσώπου，即以他自己的身份说话(sch.^A Il. 2.570，比较6.152, 210, 13.301)。甚至柯莱乌斯也认为这值得一说，见1.3.3。根据这样的解释，荷马之所以被描述为曾去过科林斯，仅仅是为了确保他熟悉这个地方。

60　荷马对阿尔戈斯人的揄扬早就引人注意了。西库昂的克里斯提尼因此禁止西库昂吟诵荷马诗歌(Hdt. 5.67.1)。托名希罗多德的《荷马传》(§28, line 378, Allen)中，荷马从伊奥尼前往希腊大陆之前，意识到自己曾频繁颂阿尔戈斯而不是雅典，因此插入了几段来赞美雅典。实际上，Philochorus说荷马是阿尔戈斯人(329 F 209)，可能就是因为荷马对阿尔戈斯的频繁提及(Jacoby ad loc.)。

雅典的路上生病了，不得不停留在伊奥斯岛上。

很难理解为什么阿尔基达马斯会对这样的练习感兴趣，还有一些因素会影响我们认为他是这节内容的来源：生硬地提到《伊利亚特》和《奥德赛》的创作（前文已述）；对这首诗书目式的描绘；把荷马说成是基俄斯人，但阿尔基达马斯说荷马不是[61]。这个结论的后果令人满意：弥达斯的儿子这一情节之后，留给阿尔基达马斯的全部内容就是有关荷马之死的最后一节，这就完成了荷马和赫西奥德个人经历的相似叙事。每位诗人从已故国王的儿子那里获得奖品并题词献祭之后，在神谕所预言的地方死去，墓碑上有恰当的墓志铭。

剩余的部分源自一部《荷马传》，属于墨守陈说的托名希罗多德《荷马传》式的传记，而不属于提供其他可能性的类型，因此与第2—3节中使用的来源都不同。它也不能被认定为第一节中引用的维莱乌斯–普罗克洛斯来源，因为这一来源否认荷马是眼盲的，那就必然否认了提洛岛颂诗的作者是他[62]。它可能与第4节谱系的出处相同[63]；那一出处一定对荷马的出身做了一定的说明，而编者似乎将手头所有的资源都用上了。以下事实可以支持该假设：紧跟第4节之后，在加入竞赛叙事的地方，我们发现荷马在游吟《马尔吉特斯》；正是因为他在"巡回表演"，所以他才有机会抵达德尔菲。这个细节与第15—18节内容类似，并对后者做了补充，似乎来自同一材料；它不可能来自阿尔基达马斯，据我们所知，他没有说过荷马还创作了哪些其他诗歌，又是在何种场合创作的。这位编者的做法看起来如下文所示。他在此处使用的两种材料提供了以下信息：

《荷马传》	阿尔基达马斯
荷马是赫西奥德的一位年轻亲戚，河神墨勒斯之子。他四处游走吟诵《马尔吉特斯》（在小亚细亚？），之后是《忒拜纪》《后辈英雄纪》，等等	赫西奥德和荷马曾经在奥利斯相遇，荷马刚去过德尔菲祈问他的出身（《竞赛》）

61　见上文第47页注53。

62　这是 Cynaethus 强加给他的说法（sch. Pind. *Nem*. 2.1），可能源于此或相关的来源。

63　除非这一节肯定荷马在基俄斯出生——前文的谱系暗示他出生于士麦拿。

编者将它们综合成如下情节：

> 一些人说荷马是赫西奥德的一位年轻亲戚……另一些人说他们是同时代的人，而且曾经在奥利斯相遇。荷马四处游历并吟唱《马尔吉特斯》，之后到达德尔菲，在这里他祈问他的出身……（竞赛）……被击败之后，荷马周游诸地吟诵他的诗歌，首先是《忒拜纪》和《后辈英雄纪》，等等。

第54—62行的间接引语（oratio obliqua）是编者自己的话，比如用περιΐστασθαι来表达"避免"之义，这是较晚的用法。

概要

《竞赛》的来源现在可以暂定如下。

A.	第1—2、18—32行	某部《荷马传》
B.	第2—8行	一个共同出处（communis locus），源自阿利斯塔克学派的一部文学史作品，也被维莱乌斯和普罗克洛斯使用
C.	第8—17行	一位公元前4世纪的历史学家？
D.	第32—43行	编者自己的认知
E.	第44—56、255—259、275—321行	某部《荷马传》
F.	第54—239、247—255、260—274、322—338行	阿尔基达马斯《缪斯集》
G.	第240—247行	埃拉托色尼《赫西奥德》（*Hesiodus*）

B、C、D和G相对不重要，它们只提供了零星素材。因而主要的来源有三种：阿尔基达马斯《缪斯集》，还有两部不同的《荷马传》。一部是百科全书式的，另一部通常被称为传奇故事（romance），但更好的说法是想象的重构。没有任何证据表明用到了《赫西奥德传》（除非

把埃拉托色尼的诗歌算上)。

　　这位编者试图达到什么目的？他的取材暗示了他的目的是要用竞赛这个故事(竞赛是阿尔基达马斯叙事的突出特点，也是一般的《荷马传》所缺少的)，结合一些阿尔基达马斯没有提供但诸《荷马传》涉及的细节，拼凑出一部荷马传记。引用阿尔基达马斯的作品涉及相当多的有关赫西奥德的叙事，但编者并没有尝试填补他的生活细节。在其他部分，他也没有使他的材料遵循一个连贯的构思。他不顾艺术或严谨的考虑，从相互矛盾的材料里摘出片段杂糅在一起。我们不知道编者给他的创作取了什么标题，如果不是像 περὶ Ὁμήρου καὶ Ἡσιόδου καὶ τοῦ γένους καὶ ἀγῶνος αὐτῶν【《论荷马与赫西奥德及其世系与他们的竞赛》】这样繁复，也就无法如此准确。

附录：元音连续（Hiatus）

　　在讨论阿尔基达马斯对《竞赛》的贡献时，元音连续出现的情况起到了一定的作用，我研究了它在作品各个小节的散文部分出现的频率。由随附的表格可知，第一行的字母 A 到 G 表示如上文所分析的来源不同的各个部分；G 被记入 D，因为用语不像是来自某个材料，而是编者自己的(除非我们假设有中介)。最后一列给出所有部分的总和除了 F，F 是阿尔基达马斯的叙事。在计算元音连续的情况时，我包括了那些在 καί 或定冠词后面的例子，还有出现于一个分句结尾处的元音连续，并单独计算(在确定分句的结尾在哪里时，我遵循自己的判断)。"行数"一栏的数字表示艾伦文本中每个部分的散文行数。

		A	B	C	DG	E	F	ABCDGE
元音连续	在 καί 或定冠词之后	—	2	—	2	8	20	12
	分句结尾处	3	—	1	1	3	7	8
	其他	5	1	1	6	12	15	25
行数		17	6	9	14	32	82	78

前四列代表的文本部分过于简短，所以统计数字没有多大意义，尽管也列出了不同的情况。比较 E 和 F 的内容会更有意义。在正式散文中更容易接受的两种元音连续类型在 E 和 F 两个部分的出现频率非常相似；其他元音连续在 F 中比在 E 中少得多。如果把数字简化为每100行出现的平均频率，就会更清楚：

	E	F
跟随 καί 或定冠词	25	24.4
分句结尾处	9.4	8.5
其他	37.5	18.3

A、B、C、D、G、E 的总数与 E 的相似，除了在 καί 或冠词之后的元音连续比纯叙事的部分更少。

这些数据暗示阿尔基达马斯确实极少容许真正的元音连续，尽管《缪斯集》的平和叙事不像《论智术师》那样严格。其中一些或所有明显的例子也许是由于语序的变化和文本流传中的其他意外造成的。我没有发现任何一个元音连续难以消除[64]。

（译者单位：复旦大学历史学系在读博士生）

---

[64] 我只提出两处，理校可能会为文本提供积极的改进。第14节，第228行：ὁ γὰρ τόπος οὗτος ἅπας ἐκαλεῖτο Διὸς Νεμείου [ἱερόν]. 第6节，第64—66行：πάντας τοὺς [ἐπισήμους ἄνδρας] οὐ ῥώμῃ καὶ τάχει μόνον ἀλλὰ καὶ σοφίᾳ <διαφέροντας> ἐπὶ τὸν ἀγῶνα ... συνεκάλεσεν.

荷马与赫西奥德的竞赛与
阿尔基达马斯的《缪斯集》[*]

尼古拉斯·理查森

（孙东生 译）

一、阿尔基达马斯的作用

是阿尔基达马斯虚构了荷马和赫西奥德的竞赛吗？马丁·韦斯特（Martin West）是如此论证的（*CQ* N.S. 17 [1967], 433 ff.），但我想有若干理由认为这个结论是不大可能的。

在阿尔基达马斯之前，荷马和赫西奥德之死的故事已经有其传统。赫拉克利特知道荷马之死以及与其相关的虱子谜语（*Vors.* 22 B 56），而赫西奥德之死更是在修昔底德（3.96）时期就已经广为流传。已知的第一位试图记述荷马生平的人是雷吉乌姆的特阿革涅斯（Theagenes of Rhegium），那是在约公元前6世纪晚期（*Vors.* 8. 1）。

* Nicholas J. Richardson, "The Context of Homer and Hesiod and Alcidamas' *Mouseion.*" *The Classical Quarterly* 31 (1981), pp. 1–10. 首先我要着重感谢理查德·扬科（Richard Janko）博士，我撰写此文的初衷就来自他关于早期希腊史诗年代的讨论，我从他的见解中受益良多。我同样要感谢肯尼斯·多弗（Kenneth Dover）爵士、多琳·伊涅丝（Doreen Innes）博士、玛丽·莱夫科维茨（Mary Lefkowitz）教授以及马丁·韦斯特教授，他们提供了非常有用的评语和富于建设性的不同观点。罗西（Rossi）教授于1979年秋季第一学期在牛津大学开设的论希腊会饮诗系列讲座饶有趣味，也填补了本文第一部分所讨论诸问题的某一方面的背景知识。（本文出现了不少希腊文原文，有些径直译出，另一些希腊文因为原作者需要使用希腊文之间的细微差别来说明他的观点，译文无法体现这些细微差别，因此保留希腊文原文不予译出。——译者按）

到那时为止，可能已经存在大量关于早期诗人的传说[1]。托名希罗多德的《荷马传》（*Herodotean Life of Homer*）中的六音步长短短格诗作大概可以追溯至公元前500年以前，其中一些表明，作者对古风时期的士麦那一带所知甚详。

在讲述诗人之死的故事时，阿尔基达马斯所做的是记录 ἱστορία【探究】的结果，他在密歇根纸草2754号中也暗示了这一点（参见 West op. cit. 437［见本辑第32页——译者按］）。韦斯特的观点要求人们假定，阿尔基达马斯把这些传统吸收进他虚构的竞赛故事中。我个人认为这违背了我们通常对阿尔基达马斯这样的智术师的活动的认识。尽管他们有创造神话的能力（如普罗迪库斯[Prodicus]所作的《赫拉克勒斯的选择》[*Choice of Heracles*]），但是没有证据证明他们会虚构关于早期历史人物的故事，他们更倾向于收集关于这些人的流行传说，并按照自身的目的去使用这些故事[2]。的确，举例而言，克里提阿斯（Critias）曾用阿尔基洛科斯（Archilochus）本人的诗歌作为证据得出一些关于他生平的结论（*Vors.* 88 B 44）[3]。但是，从无到有地虚构一个故事并不是同一回事。单单是赫西奥德自己对于他的诗歌胜利的证词（*Op.* 650 ff.），也就是他与荷马竞赛的传说的最初起点，就不支持这样的推论。这个传说更像是在对于这些早期诗人生平的猜测已经变成一种常态后，更早时期大众渲染想象的产物。

这一整体考量可能并没有多少分量，但其他证据似乎表明公元前6世纪是竞赛故事更可能的确定年代。

赫拉克利特也知道荷马之死的故事，该故事的中心是他没能解开儿童们的谜语，这一点很重要。如他所言，荷马"比所有希腊人都智慧"。荷马和赫西奥德作为"智者"（σοφοί）的身份是赫拉克利特和塞诺芬尼的主要攻击目标。解出谜语，回答困难问题的能力通常

1　参见 W. Schadewaldt, *Legende von Homer dem fahrenden Sänger,* Leipzig, 1942。

2　参见 R. Pfeiffer, *History of Classical Scholarship* i. 51 ff.。此书中关于西庇阿斯（Hippias）和克里提阿斯（Critias）的部分，在这方面可以和阿尔基达马斯形成对照。雷吉乌姆的格劳科斯（Glaucos）的作品《论早期诗人和音乐家》（περὶ τῶν ἀρχαίων ποιητῶν καὶ μουσικῶν）和西革乌姆的达玛斯忒斯（Damastes of Sigeum）的《论诗人与智术师》（περὶ ποιητῶν καὶ σοφιστῶν）都大约作于这个时期，可以在这一语境中作为例证。

3　参见 M. Lefkowitz, "Fictions in Literary Biography: The New Poem and the Archilochus Legend", *Arethusa* 9, 1976, 181 ff.。

被认为是这种智慧（σοφία）的重要方面，就像先知之间（如 Hesiod fr. 278 M.-W.）、七哲之间以及俄狄浦斯和斯芬克斯之间的竞赛故事所表明的那样。这类"谜题"（ἀπορίαι）在我们现存的荷马与赫西奥德的竞赛版本中扮演重要角色，所以有理由认为这个故事是产生了荷马之死传说的年代的产物。赫西奥德同样死于对神谕的误读，这又是另一种传统的智力测试（《竞赛》215 ff., pp. 233 ff. Allen）。此外，游吟诗人的智慧竞赛取代体育竞赛的观点（参见《竞赛》64 ff.），属于塞诺芬尼的时代，他本人就是四处旅行的游吟诗人，并且明确地声明他的观点，即运动员的勇气对于集体来说不像卓越的智力那样有价值，也不该受到那么高的尊崇（fr. 2 West）。"谜题"在普鲁塔克的竞赛故事版本（《道德论集》153 F ff.）中扮演尤为突出的角色。该文记事的顺序和我们现在讨论的文本不同。普鲁塔克的叙述开始于诗篇背诵，接着竞赛的结果取决于一个谜题，最终赫西奥德解决了这个谜题。这可能反映了这个故事的早期版本[4]。支持这种说法的一个可能论证是，普鲁塔克的这种安排和阿里斯托芬的《蛙》中顺序相似（从讨论准备好的篇章开始，之后才是城邦问题和解谜竞赛），这种情节安排如果以一个已经存在的荷马和赫西奥德的竞赛故事为背景，会更有意义，而不是相反[5]。这样一来，阿里斯托芬所做的就是选取人们熟悉的主题——诗人竞赛，并用原创性的手法赋予它新的生机。

这便令人忍不住推论，是阿尔基达马斯颠倒了故事的顺序，使得赫西奥德凭借背诵准备好的诗篇获得胜利，而那一诗篇揭示了赫西奥德是和平的诗人而非战争的诗人。但进一步的考量似乎反对这个结论[6]。《竞赛》中的一个谜题（107 f.）也出现于阿里斯托芬的《和平》

---

[4] 参见 M. J. Milne, "A Study in Alcidamas and his relation to contemporary Sophistic", Diss. Bryn Mawr, 1924, 57 f.。Milne 提出这才是这个故事的原始版本。普鲁塔克的版本为什么会提及莱斯基斯（Lesches）仍是一个谜。韦斯特试图解释莱斯基斯的出现，但显然是搪塞其词。Milne 的解释则更有吸引力，他认为莱斯基斯的名字在希腊化或者更晚的时期取代了荷马，因为说荷马和赫西奥德是同时期的人存在年代问题。

[5] 参见 Milne op. cit. 60, F. Dornseiff, *Gnomon* 20, 1944, 136 f.。

[6] 注意韦斯特不得不改变关于斯巴达国王克列欧美涅斯一世的一则逸闻，据说这个国王曾说荷马是斯巴达的诗人，赫西奥德是黑劳士的诗人，因为荷马颂扬战争而赫西奥德歌唱农耕（Plut. *Mor.* 223A, Aelian *VH* 13.19）。韦斯特（443）随意地将这则逸闻归于阿尔基达马斯的某个未知对手。实际上这个区分也存在于 Ar. *Ran.* 1033-6 中，其中说荷马是传授战略的老师，而赫西奥德传授农耕。

（1282 f.），而后者大约于公元前421年上演。正如韦斯特（440 f.）所说，这个孤证并不能证明竞赛故事在当时已经流传，但是《和平》似乎也回应了这场竞赛，这当然是具有重要意义的。当拉马科斯（Lamachus）之子吟诵战争史诗时，特律盖奥斯（Trygaeus）十分讶异，并告诉拉马科斯之子要歌颂宴饮来庆祝重获和平[7]。他接着提出谜题"于是，他们分食牛肉"（ὡς οἱ μὲν δαίνυντο βοῶν κρέα）云云作为一个例子。除了谜题以外，这里还有两个主题也出现在《竞赛》中，反对战争诗歌，赞颂宴饮（《竞赛》80 ff.）。《阿凯亚人》的结尾也提出类似的看法，即宴饮与和平胜过战争与搏斗。如果某人认为是阿尔基达马斯首创了竞赛故事，那么他必须证明，或者所有这些相似之处都是巧合，或者阿尔基达马斯版本的竞赛写于公元前421年之前。第二种可能和阿尔基达马斯的年表不符。第一种是可能的，但可能性很小。

这些主题（赞颂宴饮而反对战争诗歌）在当时并不新鲜。它符合公元前6世纪会饮诗歌的整体背景。在《和平》（775 ff.）的会饮语境中，我们看到有些诗行被视作对斯特西克鲁斯（Stesichorus）《奥瑞斯提亚》（fr. 210 Page）的模仿，那里缪斯被要求歌唱宴饮而不是战争。塞诺芬尼批评会饮时吟诵关于提坦、巨人或半人马的战争，或者关于"激烈纷争"（στάσιας σφεδανάς）的诗歌（fr. 1 West），而阿那克里翁则不喜欢任何在此类场合歌唱"令人洒泪的不和与战争"（νείκεα καὶ πόλεμον δακρυόεντα）的人。

因此，由于荷马颂扬宴饮是"对凡人而言最好的事情"而赞美他，完全与那个时代相符。同样，赫西奥德以和平诗人而不是战争诗人的身份获得意外的胜利，在那时也并非不合时宜。

韦斯特认为《竞赛》中的伦理和政治问题有智术师的味道，也就意味着作品的年代向后推移。这当然有可能是阿尔基达马斯的原因。但我怀疑人们是否能够如此教条地断言这些问题绝不会出现于公元前6世纪。其他学者也并不总是持此种观点[8]。

---

[7] 参见 M. Lefkowitz, *CQ* N. S. 28 (1978), 468（尽管她在文章中更倾向于竞赛的文本形成于公元前4世纪）。

[8] 参见 Schadewaldt, op. cit. 64 ff., K. Hess, "Der Agon zwischen Homer und Hesiod", Diss. Zürich, 1960, 7 ff.。

最后，还有一个小问题，即"赫西奥德"的一个残篇(fr. 357 M.- W)，其中诗人回忆了他和荷马各自为提洛岛的阿波罗进献一首颂诗的场合。韦斯特认为如果阿尔基达马斯知道这一点，他会把比赛场所设置在提洛岛，所以这个残篇应当晚于阿尔基达马斯。没有理由如此假设。相反，无论如何没有必要将这个残篇与竞赛故事联系起来，对这个问题应该不予考虑[9]。

如果阿尔基达马斯没有发明这个故事，那就有理由考虑是什么样的动机促使他使用这个故事，以及他出于自身的目的有可能强调这个故事的哪些方面。对密歇根纸草末尾处的重新审视，可能会使我们对这些问题获得一些理解。

二、密歇根纸草[10]

这份纸草的最后几行非常难懂。

περι τουτου μεν ουν ποιεισθαι την αρετην ποι   15
ησομεν μαλιστα δ ορων τους ιστορικους θαυ
μαζομενους οδη. ος γουν δια τουτο και ζων
και αποθανων τετιμηται παρα πασιν ανθρω
ποις ταυτη[.]ουν αυτω της παιδιας χαριν α
ποδιδο[......]ενος αυτου και την αλλη[ν] ποι   20
ησιν δια . [...]ειας μνημης τοις βουλομε

9　R. Janko认为(在他未发表的博士论文"Studies in the Langauge of the Homeric Hymns; the Dating of Early Greek Epic Poetry", pp. 128ff.)，这可能与二人联合创作《致阿波罗的荷马颂诗》有关，颂诗的第一部分归于荷马，第二部分归于赫西奥德。这个版本可能创作于波吕克刺忒斯(Polycrates)在提洛岛组织阿波罗节时，他当时在争论这个节日究竟应该被称为"皮托的"还是"提洛的"。关于这一传统，参见H. W. Parke, *CQ* 40 (1946), 105 ff. 和 W. Burkert, *Arktouros,* Hellenic Studies presented to B. M. W. Knox, Berlin, 1979, 58 f.。

10　除了韦斯特的文章，这份纸草也可在以下文章中见到：R. Renehan, *HSCP* 75, 1971, 85, ff., G. L. Koniaris, *HSCP* 75, 1971, 107 ff., Renehan, *Studies in Greek Texts, Hypomnemata* 43, 1976, 144 ff.

νοις φι[.....]ειν των Ελληνων εις το κοινον
παραδω[ ]

    [Ἀλκι]δαμαντος

        περι Ομηρου   25

15 lacunam post ποιεῖσθαι statuit West   17 Ὅμηρος Winter   19
ταύτη[ν] Winter: ταύτη[ς] Koniaris παιδ<ε>ίας Körte 19 f.
ἀποδιδο[ύς, ἀφέμ]ενος West   20 διὰ β[ραχ]είας West   22
φι[λοκαλ]εῖν Hunt: φι[λοδοξ]εῖν Richardson   23 παραδώ[σω West
24 [Ἀλκι]δάμαντος Winter

对于第15行及下一行的解释不明确，韦斯特认为这里有脱字可能是正确的。关于 περὶ τούτου 指的是什么，完全无从得知，而 ποιεῖσθαι τὴν ἀρετήν 很难解释，不过或许可以解释为"赢得某人的名誉"。参见《奥德赛》第2卷第126行，μέγα μὲν κλέος αὐτῇ ποιεῖτ(αι)[11]。ἀρετή 的意思是"因勇猛获得的荣耀"，如柏拉图《会饮》208 D，我们将看到该片段与阿尔基达马斯这里的主题相关。如布拉斯（Blass）所指出的，ποιεῖσθαι τὴν ἀρετήν 是阿尔基达马斯尤其喜欢使用的迂说法[12]。ποιήσομεν 更有可能应该校正为 πονήσομεν（参见 *Soph.* 30），尽管这个词在其他地方没有和不定式一起使用过。韦斯特将 τοὺς ἱστορικούς 和 *Soph.* 1中的 ἱστορία 进行对比。有趣的是，ἱστορικός 一词最早出现于此处和柏拉图的《智术师》267E，后者把它当作一个新词或刚创造不久的词。对 ἱστορικοί 的赞赏和赋予荷马的荣誉很可以使用《竞赛》的语言，如第66、71行（θαυμαστῶς），第90行及以下（θαυμασθῆναι），第176行及下一行，第205行及以下（θαυμάσαντες），也许还有提到荷马后来获得的荣誉的部分（271 ff., 276 ff., 286 f.,

---

11 阿尔基达马斯对史诗语言颇有兴趣（Arist. *Rhet.* 1406a6ff.）。

12 *Die Attische Beredsamkeit* ii. 2.356 f. 关于 ποιεῖσθαι 一词，参见 *Soph.* 17, 20。布拉斯发现阿尔基达马斯尤其喜欢在句子的结尾使用 παραδίδωσιν 的迂说法结尾（*Soph.* 15, 26, 27–8两次），参见 Mich. pap. 2754.23，用 παραδώ[σω（West）作为结尾。

302 ff., 319 ff.），如果这些属于阿尔基达马斯的版本[13]。赋予荷马和其他智识分子荣誉这一主题，在亚里士多德《修辞学》（1398b10ff.）引用的阿尔基达马斯那里，以类似的语言重复出现：

καὶ ὡς Ἀλκιδάμας, ὅτι πάντες τοὺς σοφοὺς τιμῶσιν· Πάριοι γοῦν Ἀρχίλοχον καίπερ βλάσφημον ὄντα τετιμήκασι, καὶ Χῖοι Ὅμηρον οὐκ ὄντα πολίτην (etc.)[14]

为了证明所有人都尊崇智慧的人，阿尔基达马斯如是说：“帕罗斯岛的人尊崇阿尔基洛科斯，尽管他言语刻薄；开俄斯岛的人尊崇荷马，尽管他并非城邦的公民。”

参见密歇根纸草2754号第16行及以下：

μάλιστα δ' ὁρῶν τοὺς ἱστορικοὺς θαυμαζομένους· Ὅμηρος γοῦν διὰ τοῦτο καὶ ζῶν καὶ ἀποθανὼν τετίμηται παρὰ πᾶσιν ἀνθρώποις.

尤其是看到那些“探究者”为人们所惊服；至少荷马因此而在生前与死后都受到所有人的尊崇。

---

[13] E. Bethe, *Der hom. Apollonhymnos und das Prooimion* 3 ff.，认为这些内容的大部分都具有希腊化时期的特征，韦斯特认为第260—274行属于阿尔基达马斯，但第275—321行不是（op. cit. 446 ff.）。

[14] 尽管韦斯特断言这里与《竞赛》第305行及以下矛盾（448），但并不必然如此。阿尔基达马斯完全可以说荷马是开俄斯的居民，但不是出生在那里的公民，就像有些《荷马传》所说的那样。

这段阿尔基达马斯引文继续提到赋予萨福、喀隆（Chilon）、毕达哥拉斯和阿那克萨戈拉的荣誉，然后是梭伦和莱库古的立法以及忒拜的优秀领袖带来的益处。这是精心构思的，有三组例子，每组又包含三个例子。还包括12个元音连续的例子。人们已经注意到，最后提到忒拜的哲学家领袖，以及他们所带来的繁荣（用了过去时），表明这段文字应该晚于佩罗庇达斯和伊帕米农达斯之死，两人分别死于公元前364年和前362年（参见 J. Vahlen, *Gesammelte Philologische Schriften* i. 128 ff.）。它可能来自阿尔基达马斯的《美塞尼亚演说》（*Messenian Speech*），此文也包含元音连续（参见 Arist. *Rhet.* 1397a11f. εἰ γὰρ ὁ πόλεμος αἴτιος τῶν παρόντων κακῶν, μετὰ τῆς εἰρήνης δεῖ ἐπανορθώσασθαι）。Renehan 提出这段引文来自《缪斯集》，因此《缪斯集》的写作时间应该晚于公元前362年（*Studies in Greek Texts* 154）。由于下文将要提到的理由，我不会将《缪斯集》的年份定得这么晚。

荷马不仅在生前被人尊崇，死后仍受礼遇，这一点与《竞赛》第254—321行的整体主题吻合。据我们现在所知，这个主题可以上溯至塞诺芬尼。但伊索克拉底的《泛希腊集会辞》（*Panegyricus*）开篇也引人注目地出现了这一主题。这篇演说辞的背景同样是泛希腊竞赛。伊索克拉底震惊于运动员的非凡本领被如此慷慨地嘉奖，而这样的荣誉不会授予以智力服务城邦的人[15]。阿尔基达马斯和伊索克拉底都是高尔吉亚的追随者，但二人互为对手，阿尔基达马斯在《论智术师》中抨击那些提前准备稿子的演说家，通常被认为其实是针对伊索克拉底的[16]。伊索克拉底被认为在发表于公元前380年的《泛希腊集会辞》（11）中回应了阿尔基达马斯的批评[17]。无论如何，这两个作品之间有着很紧密的联系。《竞赛》中也有内容和伊索克拉底的演说辞惊人地相似[18]。阿尔基达马斯在其他地方提到汗水和地峡赛会（*Rhet.* 1406a20–22），也可能发生在体力和智慧才能的对比的语境中[19]。

人们经常注意到，《竞赛》中的即兴创作主题与阿尔基达马斯的《论智术师》有很强的联系，也与伊索克拉底对这一主题的评点有关。柏拉图《斐德若》结尾处的讨论（274C ff.）表明，那一时期这个问题是多么被人关注，而这从公元前5世纪晚期和前4世纪时重点自口头表达转向书面文字便可以料想得到[20]。

阿尔基达马斯对竞赛故事感兴趣，似乎不仅因为它突出了即兴创作的价值，还因为它回应了塞诺芬尼和伊索克拉底提出的那类批

15　*Paneg.* 1（以及45）。

16　参见 Vahlen, op. cit. 140 ff., Blass op. cit. 353 ff., W. Steidle, *Hermes* 80, 1952, 285 ff.。

17　Blass op. cit. 353.

18　*Cert.* 64 ff. πάντας τοὺς ἐπισήμους ἄνδρας οὐ <u>μόνον ῥώμῃ καὶ τάχει, ἀλλὰ καὶ σοφίᾳ</u> ἐπὶ τὸν ἀγῶνα μεγάλαις δωρεαῖς τιμῶν συνεκάλεσεν ~ *Paneg.* 1 <u>τὰς μὲν τῶν σωμάτων εὐτυχίας</u> <u>οὕτω μεγάλων δωρεῶν</u> ἠξίωσαν (etc.), *Paneg.* 45 <u>ἀγῶνας μὴ μονον τάχους καὶ ῥώμης, ἀλλὰ</u> <u>καὶ λόγων καὶ γνώμης …καὶ τούτων ἆθλα μέγιστα</u>. 还可以参见 Gorgias 82B 6, P. 286. 2, 6 D- K, 可能已经存在相似之处。

19　参见 F. Solmsen, *Hermes* 67 (1932), 138 f. (= *Kl. Schr.* ii. 134 f.), 也比较了阿尔基达马斯的短语 δρομαίᾳ τῇ τῆς ψυχῆς ὁρμῇ (Arist. *Rhet.* 1406a23f.)。

20　参见 W. C. Greene, *HSCP* 60 (1951), 23 ff., P. Friedländer, *Plato*（英译本）i. 110 ff., Pfeiffer op. cit. 25 ff.。

评，也就是希腊人不赋予智慧应得的荣誉[21]。在亚里士多德的引文中，阿尔基达马斯称荷马和其他诗人确实被给予了很高的荣誉，哲学家和立法者也一样。这个主题在柏拉图的《会饮》中得到了回应（上文已提及），狄奥提玛（Diotima）"像完美的智术师那样"（ὥσπερ οἱ τέλεοι σοφισταί, 208C）论述了人对荣誉的渴望（φιλοτιμία），并且援引诗人和政治领袖为例，如荷马和赫西奥德，莱库古和梭伦，来展示他们的精神创造以及他们成就的美德（ἀρετή），是如何为他们赢得声名甚至宗教上的尊崇（208E—209E）的。这些人"周游四方"，寻找高贵的心灵以倾灌他们的智慧，同时尝试教育这些人（209BC）。

也是在这个意义上，阿尔基达马斯记录下自己为了其他同样热爱荣誉的希腊人而进行的"探究"（ἱστορία）的结果，从而感谢了荷马给予的"教育"（παιδεία）（Mich. Pap. 2754. 19 ff.）。第20行的读法不是很确定。我倾向于认同科尼阿里斯（Koniaris）对韦斯特的校订ἀποδιδο[ύς, ἀφέμ] ενος的批评[22]。我们弄不清楚，阿尔基达马斯说的是他会继续讨论其他被认为是荷马所作的诗作，还是其他诗人的作品。不过，根据韦斯特（438[见本辑第33—34页——译者按]）给出的理由，后者乍看上去更有可能。这与下款契合，下款表明阿尔基达马斯已经完成了荷马部分的写作。在第21—23行中，我认为应该读作τοῖς βουλομένοις φι[λοδοξ] εῖν τῶν Ἑλλήνων εἰς τὸ κοινὸν παραδώ[σω]。φιλοδοξεῖν相比φιλοκαλεῖν更清楚地在继续谈论荣誉的主题。φιλοδοξεῖν εἰς τὸ κοινόν在后来的希腊语中成为一个习语，这些词语同时在这里出现并非不可能[23]。

---

[21] 另参见Gorgias, Vors. 82B 8，其中τόλμα和σοφία之间的竞赛形成对照。如果接受这里抄本的读法：σοφίας δὲ τὸ αἴνιγμα γνῶναι，那么《竞赛》是高尔吉亚式"智慧"的非常好的例子！高尔吉亚是即兴回答的大师，不论是长篇的回答还是简短的回答（82A 1, 1a, Pl. Gorg. 447C, 449BC, Phdr. 267A, Arist. Rhet. 1418a34）。整体上另见W. K. C. Guthrie, History of Greek Philosophy iii. 42 ff.。

[22] HSCP 75 (1971), 124. 如果空间允许，可以读作ἀρξάμενος αὐτοῦ吗？参见如Pl. Rep. 600E，在这一上下文中，柏拉图可能想到了阿尔基达马斯的《论荷马》（Περὶ Ὁμήρου）（见下文第四节）。

[23] 用例另见Isocr. Paneg. 1 τοῖς ὑπὲρ τῶν κοινῶν ἰδίᾳ πονήσασι，提到智力服务。

三、阿尔基达马斯的《缪斯集》

如果阿尔基达马斯关于荷马的部分确实是从他的《缪斯集》中摘录出来的，而且他在《缪斯集》中还讨论了其他诗人的生平和作品，那么我们就要考虑他这样做的总体用意。可以确定，《缪斯集》（《竞赛》239f.）提到了赫西奥德之死，对杀死他的凶手的处置和他的尸体奇迹般的归来[24]，能够清晰地展现神圣惩罚中的道德教训。我们还可以看出，赋予两位诗人的荣誉对阿尔基达马斯而言同样重要，以及他将二人视为后来的智术师（sophists）和演说家（orators）的先驱，且互为对手。但是阿尔基达马斯首先考虑的是荷马作为教育者的价值。在这一背景下，阿尔基达马斯用"探究者"（ἱστορικός）来形容荷马，这一点引人注目。[25]这个词也许意味着，他认为荷马要么是传统的忠实记录者，要么是生活的精确观察者。在《伊利亚特》里他首先是前者，在《奥德赛》中则是后者。事实上，阿尔基达马斯对《奥德赛》的著名描述就是"人类生活的明镜"（καλὸν ἀνθρωπίνου βίου κάτοπτρον, Arist. *Rhet.* 1406b12f.）。他还将《奥德赛》第六卷第128—129行奥德修斯和瑙西卡见面的场景改写成具有他自己风格的句子："用森林的树枝掩住身体之羞"（τοῖς τῆς ὕλης κλάδοις τὴν τοῦ σώματος αἰσχύνην παρήμπισχεν, *Rhet.* 1406a27-29）。就我所知，没有其他人注意到另一处引文（1406a1f.），即"充满热情的灵魂，火色的面貌"（μένους μὲν τὴν ψυχὴν πληρουμένην, πυρίχρων δὲ τὴν ὄψιν γιγνομένην），是对《伊利亚特》第一卷第103—104行的改写，后者描述了阿伽门农的愤怒：

> μένεος δὲ μέγα φρένες ἀμφὶ μέλαιναι
> πίμπλαντ᾽, ὄσσε δέ οἱ πύρι λαμπετόωντε ἐΐκτην.
> 阴暗的心里充满愤怒，

24　参见 Vahlen, op. cit. 128.

25　ἱστορία 和 παιδεία 两个词都可以参见阿尔基达马斯的《论智术师》，其中"一些所谓的智术师"被指控忽视了二者。另参见3-4, 13, 15。

眼睛像发亮的火焰。

另外一些引文或者提到荷马，或者提到荷马的篇章，当然这更难以确定。"蔚蓝色的海底"（κυανόχρων τὸ τῆς θαλάττης ἔδαφος）可能受到荷马的"酒色的大海"的启发（*Rhet.* 1406a4f.）。阿尔基达马斯还使用过像 ἄθυρμα【玩物】和 ἀτασθαλία【鲁莽】这样的史诗语言（1406 a8f., b13f.）。有人曾提出，在提到《奥德赛》后紧跟着出现的引文，即"这样的玩物不会带来创造"（οὐδὲν τοιοῦτον ἄθυρμα τῇ ποιήσει προσφέρων），是将荷马作为"严肃诗人"（σπουδαῖος ποιητής）和其他不那么严肃的诗人形成对比[26]。其他残篇与高尔吉亚对于演说术和诗歌力量的观点高度相似。索尔姆森（Solmsen）提出，亚里士多德《修辞学》第33章的所有阿尔基达马斯引文都来自同一部作品（就像《修辞学》3.9—11几乎全部引文都来自伊索克拉底的《泛希腊集会辞》），而且这部作品讨论了诗歌和演说术所具有的文明教化力量[27]。索尔姆森有一个很冒险的观点，认为这些引用都来自《缪斯集》的前言部分。这种假设虽然很有吸引力，但难以证实。不过这些只言片语仍然可以让我们很好地了解阿尔基达马斯关于文学的基本看法。首先，阿尔基达马斯将《奥德赛》称为"人类生活的明镜"，他所想到的并不仅仅是它在模仿（μίμησις）意义上的现实主义，也想到了这种现实主义刻画的伦理价值[28]。演说家莱库古

---

[26]　H. E. Foss, *De Gorgia*, Halle, 1828, 83, Vahlen op. cit. 126.

[27]　*Hermes* 67 (1932), 133 ff. (=*Kl. Schr.* ii. 129 ff.)

[28]　阿尔基达马斯对"模仿"很有兴趣，参见短语 ἀντίμιμον τὴν τῆς ψυχῆς ἐπιθυμίαν【欲念是灵魂的逼真模仿】（*Rhet.* 1406a29f.），尤其在 *Soph.* 27f. 中，书面 λόγοι【语言】被描述为 εἴδωλα καὶ σχήματα καὶ μιμήματα λόγων【说话的影像、外在表现和模仿】，就像雕塑和绘画是对人体的 μιμήματα【模仿】一样，而即兴演讲是活生生的，并且 τοῖς ἀληθέσιν ἀφωμοίωται σώμασιν【就像声音的真正形体】；在32中（尽管有这些批评），书面作品作为纪念物有其用处，因为有可能"看着书面文字，就像从镜子里看到思维的前进"（εἰς τὰ γεγραμμένα κατιδόντας ὥσπερ ἐν κατόπτρῳ θεωρῆσαι τὰς τῆς ψυχῆς ἐπιδόσεις）。在《斐德若》(276D) 中，柏拉图将书面作品比作无声的、静止的画，可能就是受到阿尔基达马斯的影响。这和 Isocr. *Soph.* 12 也有些许相似之处，而这部作品有可能早于阿尔基达马斯的《论智术师》（参见 Steidle op. cit. 290 f.）。值得注意的是，在《斐德若》中，柏拉图两次使用 μουσεῖον（一处在267B，提及波鲁斯 [Polus] 时，他像阿尔基达马斯一样，是高尔吉亚的追随者，另一处在278B，提及宁芙时使用）。另见 Milne op.cit.，他尝试处理伊索克拉底的《驳智术师》、阿尔基达马斯和《斐德若》之间的关系，虽然不甚令人满意。

也呼应了阿尔基达马斯的观点，他赞美了在泛雅典娜节上吟诵荷马诗歌的传统，并将此作为荷马的诗歌受到雅典人重视的证据。他说他们这样做是正确的，因为法律太过简短，只能发出命令，而无法教育人民：

> οἱ δέ ποιηταὶ μιμούμενοι τὸν ἀνθρώπινον βίον, τὰ κάλλιστα τῶν ἔργων ἐκλεξάμενοι, μετὰ λόγου καὶ ἀποδείξεως τοὺς ἀνθρώπους συμπείθουσιν. (*In Leocratem* 102)[29]
>
> 诗人描绘人类的生活，选择最善的行为，并且通过言语和示范改变人心。

《奥德赛》的"伦理"特征，既是现实主义的，也具有"道德训诫"的作用（比照ἦθος），为后世批评家所承认（Arist. *Poet.* 1459b15，"Loginus" 9. 15）。喜剧是其后继者（*Poet.* 1453a30 ff.），有着相似的作用。米南德本人也许是在表现一位智慧的父亲，当他这样给他的儿子出谋划策道：

> Inspicere tamquam in speculum in vitas omnium
> Iubeo atque ex aliis sumere exemplum sibi. (Ter. *Ad.* 415 f.)
> 我让他看看人们的生活，就像透过镜子一样，
> 拿其他人为自己树立榜样。

类似的段落也可以在贺拉斯提及自己所受的教育时看到（*Sat.* 1. 4. 105 ff.）。西塞罗将喜剧称为"人生的模仿、传统的镜子、现实的投影"（imitationem vitae, speculum consuetudinis, imaginem veritatis, ap. Donatus *de com.* 5. 1），而对于凯基利乌斯（Caecilius）从米南德那里借来的一个场景，他又说：

---

[29] Vahlen（op. cit. 125 f.）也注意到了这一相似性。参见伊索克拉底在 *Paneg.* 159 中提及泛雅典娜节的规则，他引用这个规则也是为了证明"在音乐竞赛和青少年教育方面"赋予荷马诗歌的荣誉，证明他作为道德模范的价值。

haec conficta arbitror esse a poetis ut effictos nostros mores in alienis personis expressamque imaginem vitae cotidianae videremus. (*Pro Rosc. Amer.* 47)[30]

我想这些东西都是诗人发明的，目的是为了借陌生的角色让我们看到自己的习俗和品性的再现以及日常生活的栩栩如生的摹仿。

同样的（再回到《奥德赛》），贺拉斯总结了在他的时代已经司空见惯的观点，他说明了尤利西斯何以在美德和智慧两个方面都可以是有用的榜样（*Ep.* 1. 2. 17 ff.）。

但是文学作为生活的镜子的观点在阿尔基达马斯的时代并不常见，这从亚里士多德对他使用隐喻的指摘中可以看出[31]。这绝不是阿尔基达马斯看起来是创新者的唯一一处，他创造和发展了一些后来变得常见而通用的概念。我们已经注意到阿尔基达马斯很早就使用了"探究者"一词，柏拉图认为该词是一个新造词（*Soph.* 267E），突出的是他还在"探究性的模仿"（ἱστορικήν τινα μίμησιν）这一表达中使用了这个词。人们可能还会注意到，阿尔基达马斯可能是第一个在文学意义上使用 οἰκονομία【安置】一词的人（τὴν τῶν ὀνομάτων οἰκονομίαν【名词的安置】*Soph.* 25.）[32]。他还说，一部书面作品也可能产生"某些惊愕的情绪"（τινας ἐκπλήξεις），就像艺术品一样（*Soph.* 28）[33]。此外，他也清晰地划分了主题、结构和语言的区别（*Soph.* 33），尽管可能不是首创[34]。

30　关于这些段落，参见 Eduard Fraenkel, *Aeschylus Agamemnon* ii. 386。

31　不过这个隐喻已经在诗歌中出现过：参见 Pindar *N.* 7.14，说诗歌本身是 ἔργοις καλοῖς ἔσοπτρον【高贵行为的镜子】。这一处也和许多地方一样，品达预示了后来的文学批评语言。

32　参见阿尔基达马斯在一个演说术语境中对 οἰκονόμος 一词隐喻性的使用（*Rhet.* 1406a26f.），可能指的是某种风格。布拉斯在 *Soph.* 25 把这个词读作 οἰκοδομίαν，认为这个词与动词 διαλύειν καὶ συνερείπειν【损毁和拆除】能更好地搭配，而这个隐喻确实被后来的文学批评所使用（如 Dion. Hal. *CV* 6, p. 28 U-R）。

33　这个术语在文学批评中的情况，参见 Ar. *Ran.* 962, Pl. *Ion* 535B, Arist. *Poet.* 1454a4, 55a17 等。

34　参见 Isocr. *Soph.* 16，以及 Pl. *Phaedrus* 234E, 236A。

阿尔基达马斯显得是这些方面的首创者，也许部分由于巧合，因为我们所拥有的关于早期修辞学理论发展的资料实在太少。我们现在还拥有的他的作品只能使人重复布拉斯的遗憾之语——大部分都佚失了[35]。

四、阿尔基达马斯与柏拉图的《理想国》

根据我们所看到的阿尔基达马斯对荷马的看法，以及他的部分观点与柏拉图的呼应，再来看看这种诗歌讨论对《理想国》的影响是很有趣的。当柏拉图在《理想国》的结尾重新攻击艺术时，他的论调已经和狄奥提玛"智术师式的"演讲完全不一样了。他先是思考"模仿"（μίμησις）的本质是什么（595C ff.），同时值得注意的是，阿尔基达马斯的镜子比喻也用在了这里（596D）[36]。绘画和诗歌"和真实之间隔着三层"的观点可能就受到了阿尔基达马斯的影响，他谴责书面文字是对"说话的影像、外在表现和模仿"（εἴδωλα καὶ σχήματα καὶ μιμήματα λόγων），而口头的（或说真实的）话语才"像真实的东西"（Soph. 27 f.），尽管柏拉图在此当然没有区分口头和书写，两者都是事物的再现，又是现实的影像。柏拉图进而处理荷马和悲剧作家是所有知识的执掌者这种说法（598D ff.）。这使得我们回想起荷马和赫西奥德之间的竞赛整体上就是"智慧"（σοφία）的竞赛。竞赛的重点之一就是荷马回答各种问题的能力，以及解决所有"谜题"（ἀπορίαι）和难题的能力。在这个方面，诗人当然是智术师的榜样。柏拉图攻击这种观点的理由是，如果一个人"具有真知"（ἐπιστήμων），那么他就会试图留下自己"善行"（καλὰ ἔργα）的记忆，而不仅仅是"模仿"（μιμήματα），并会希望自己成为被赞美的对象，而不是赞美诗的作者（599B）。从这个角度来说，在《会饮》中与其他手工艺人（δημιουργοί）和立法者相联系的诗人，就与他们区别开了。当谈及

35　op. cit. 359.

36　参见 Solmsen op. cit. 143。

"教育"（παιδεία）时，柏拉图说没有任何证据说明哪个城市因荷马的影响而进步，如那些伟大的立法者，或者他对作战策略或科学做出什么贡献，或者建立一个学派，追随者按照他的方式生活，如毕达哥拉斯。相反，他生前受到了极大的忽视，即便是他的同伴克里欧菲罗斯（Creophylus）在这个方面也没有任何帮助（599C—600B；参看《竞赛》321 ff.）。伟大的智术师有众多门生并且被极度推崇，但是荷马和赫西奥德却"作为游吟诗人四处流浪"（参见《竞赛》56, 255），即无人追随地从一个地方到另一个地方。所以我们应该假设，荷马以来的所有诗人都只是美德（ἀρετή）的影像的模仿者，而不是真理的模仿者（600C—601A）。因此，模仿（μίμησις）是儿戏（παιδιά）而不是严肃的追求（σπουδή）（这个对比参看阿尔基达马斯《论智术师》34 f.：即兴演说是真正严肃且有用的，写作则是在童年时期[ἐν παιδιᾷ]练习的）[37]。

在这个段落里，柏拉图摧毁了阿尔基达马斯诗歌观的基础，以及《竞赛》的基本主题，也就是荷马、赫西奥德和其他诗人在他们生前和死后都享有应得的荣誉。当然，我们不能确定在《竞赛》中关于特定群体赋予荷马荣誉的内容有多少可以追溯到阿尔基达马斯。其中的一部分甚至可能是后人试图反驳柏拉图的攻击的结果。但我们应该注意到，柏拉图实际上没有与《竞赛》本身的证据相矛盾。柏拉图说荷马和赫西奥德四处吟诵，没有追随者，这就是《竞赛》所描绘的画面。他还说没有哪个城市承认荷马为立法者，但他也没有说荷马和赫西奥德没有受到个别群体的尊崇。他提到克里欧菲罗斯以及荷马遭受的忽视，仍然符合《竞赛》的故事，《竞赛》里年老的荷马在伊奥斯岛上和克里欧菲罗斯待在一起，并死在那里。他不光彩的死亡（没有解出孩子们的谜题，滑入粪堆）无疑证实了柏拉图的控诉，那就是克里欧菲罗斯并没有照顾好他的主人！

柏拉图继续谴责艺术性的模仿，因为它会为人的情感带来危险

37　另见 Pl. *Phdr*. 276B ff., Gorgias 82B 11.21, Isocr. *Hel*. 11, 整体上见 Friedländer, loc. cit.。

的影响，它所制造的愉悦令人怀疑（603C ff.）。再一次，对比亚里士多德的阿尔基达马斯引文对我们很有吸引力，后者也与这个主题相关，如："所有公民的恩惠制造者"（πανδήμου χάριτος δημιουργός）和"听众快感的管家"（οἰκονόμος τῆς τῶν ἀκουόντων ἡδονῆς）（对比 Pl. *Gorgias* 453A），或许还有"灵魂的满面愁容的忧虑"（σκυθρωπὸν τὴν φροντίδα τῆς ψυχῆς）（即 ἐκλύει？ Solmsen）以及"欲念是灵魂的逼真模仿"（ἀντίμιμον τὴν τῆς ψυχῆς ἐπιθυμίαν）[38]。

因此，当柏拉图在结束时提及那些"赞美荷马的人"（Ὁμήρου ἐπαινέται），他们说荷马是全希腊的教育者，他值得被当作"人类事务的管理和教育"【πρὸς διοίκησίν τε καὶ παιδείαν τῶν ἀνθρωπίνων πραγμάτων】的指导者（606E），我们也许有理由认为，柏拉图的脑海里首先想到的正是阿尔基达马斯的《缪斯集》。

五、《缪斯集》与《论智术师》

如果柏拉图确实想到了《缪斯集》，那么他同时对阿尔基达马斯的《论智术师》有所回应就是有意义的。在这篇文章中，阿尔基达马斯为他明显的不合逻辑之处进行了辩护，他谴责书写，而同时他自己又经由书写的中介"准备在希腊人中赢得名声"（εὐδοκιμεῖν παρασκευάζεται παρὰ τοῖς Ἕλλησιν）；他赞扬即兴创作及随机的灵感胜过预先的筹划和准备，同时又练习哲学（29）。最自然的推测便是，《论智术师》是一个更长的哲学作品的序言，阿尔基达马斯相信他会凭借这部作品获得声名[39]。再考虑到其他提及"探究"和"教育"的内容，这会让人们认为，那部更长的作品就是《缪斯集》本身，阿尔基达马斯在其中从荷马和赫西奥德的传说讲起，进一步阐述即兴创作的价值和史诗诗人作为教育者的重要性。我们无法确定亚里士多德

---

[38] 参见 Solmsen op. cit. 尤见 136 f.（亦比较了 Gorgias 82B11.8）。

[39] 另见 32：ἔτι δὲ καὶ μνημεῖα καταλιπεῖν ἡμῶν αὐτῶν σπουδάζοντες καὶ τῇ φιλοτιμίᾳ χαριζόμενοι λόγους γράφειν ἐπιχειροῦμεν.【既然我渴望在我身后留下纪念，也出于对名声的热爱，我把这篇演说辞写下来】

《修辞学》3.3中有多少其他内容出自这同一作品,但是根据《论智术师》对于演说术,以及它与哲学和生活的总体关系的关注,发现《缪斯集》其实(像索尔姆森认为的那样)就是其他引文的来源,也就并不意外了[40]。

（译者单位：复旦大学历史学系在读博士生）

---

[40] Milne, op. cit. 61 f.(从不同的角度进行研究)也认为《论智术师》是《缪斯集》的前言。她也注意到柏拉图和阿尔基达马斯之间可能存在关联的另一点:弥达斯的箴言,《竞赛》第260行及以下将之归为荷马所作,也被《斐德若》(264D)引用。

当然,理论上讲,我所讨论的阿尔基达马斯和柏拉图之间的相似之处有可能来自相反的影响方向。如果接受Renehan对《缪斯集》创作于公元前362年之后的定年(loc. cit. 见上 n. 14),就会得出这样的结论。但是(1)如果情况如此,那么阿尔基达马斯似乎没有尝试更好地回答柏拉图在《理想国》中的控诉(关于荷马和赫西奥德最终没能拥有任何追随者,也没有产生真正的"善行",而仅仅只是"模仿",还关于艺术性模仿带来的糟糕的情感影响),就显得奇怪了;(2)如果《论智术师》作于伊索克拉底《泛希腊集会辞》(380 B. C.)之前,而且确实是《缪斯集》的前言,那么这种可能性无论如何也要排除了。

智慧的竞赛[*]

芭芭拉·格拉齐奥西

（于明睿 译）

　　这篇论文和一则著名故事有关：荷马与赫西奥德在σοφία【智慧】方面的竞赛。我们有很多理由认为这是一则有趣的故事，特别是因为它将智慧与竞争性关联起来。在目前的学术环境下，这种关联很可能会立刻引发共鸣并唤起熟悉的忧虑。尽管一方面，人们或许会说像智慧（wisdom）或聪明（cleverness，在古希腊语中两者都可以用σοφία表示）这种抽象的品质无法得到量化，因此也不可能衡量出究竟谁是"最有智慧的"或"最聪明的"；另一方面，我们又都对当下精确衡量这类精神品质的尝试十分熟悉。例如，在英国的高校里，研究资金的分配一般基于不同院系之间的竞争，该竞争旨在评估它们相较其他院系"在研究方面的出色程度"。这个被称作英国科研评鉴（Research Assessment Exercise）的竞争是一个"零和博弈"的典型例子：一个院系所失去的会被另一个院系获得，而整体分配给例如古典学研究的资金总数在评鉴前后并无变化。在一篇写给高校古典学系委员会（Council of University Classical Departments）的文章

---

　　[*]　Barbara Graziosi, "Competition in wisdom", in F. Budelmann and P. Michelakis (eds.), *Homer, Tragedy and Beyond. Essays in Honour of P.E. Easterling*, London: Society for the Promotion of Hellenic Studies, 2001, pp. 57–74.（《荷马与赫西奥德的竞赛》[*Certamen Homeri et Hesiodi*]的中译文遵照"古希腊语原著研读班"的译注统合稿，本文中出现的其他古典诗文皆为译者直接译自古希腊语，而非根据文中的英译文转译——译者按）

里，帕特·伊斯特林（Pat Easterling）十分雄辩地展示了这类院系间的竞争是多么不明智：她认为从中产生的张力"很可能会威胁到创造性"[1]。根据当代经验，智力成就方面的竞争案例不难找到，而同时这类竞争事实上也可能会威胁到它们本该衡量的成就本身。我们在这里勾勒出的现代忧虑展现了智慧与竞争之间的张力，这种忧虑可以作为梳理荷马和赫西奥德竞赛故事的出发点。我认为，对这篇文本及其文化背景展开详细的分析是可取的，主要是因为这会吸引人们去关注有关希腊人竞争性的现代假设的一些缺陷。例如，人们通常认为零和竞争是古希腊社会的特征。马克·格里菲斯（Mark Griffith）很好地总结了这一观点："希腊普遍存在的竞争冲动，以及随之而来的心理和社会效应，已经得到了很好的记载和研究。在其最纯粹的形式（例如战争或田径比赛）之下，他们的'竞赛体系'就是一种'零和博弈'，在这个体系中，一个人只有在另一个人或其他几个人失败的时候才算获胜。……在某种程度上，所有的社会都具有这种自我肯定和竞争的个体冲动；但自古以来，这种冲动似乎就在希腊人中间显得异常强烈。"[2]不过，对《竞赛》（*Certamen*）的解读无疑表明，并非所有的希腊竞赛都是零和博弈。

颇具讽刺意味的是，"希腊人的竞争性"反过来经常被追溯现代资本主义和自由市场经济起源的作品所征引。如此一来，希腊人，尤其是公元前5世纪的雅典人，经常被视作英国科研评鉴核心意识形态的前辈[3]。然而，一旦我们仔细分析希腊人对于竞争的说法，我们就会发现古代和现代的概念之间存在重要差异。甚至格里菲斯所征引的竞争"最纯粹的形式"在古希腊文本中也很少以零和博弈的面貌出现。就战争而言，双方失去的人数和经济资源通常要比得到的多，因此声称一方所得即另一方所失是错误的：《伊利亚特》深刻地体现

---

[1] Easterling (1997), 27.

[2] Griffith (1990) , 188. 另参见 Lloyd (1996) 与 Cartledge (1997)。

[3] 将公元前5世纪的雅典人描绘成自由市场精神先驱的尝试，参考 Moore and Lewis (1999)，其中讨论了希腊人，尤其是雅典人所扮演的角色。我们可以将这项研究看作为当前的经济理论与实践制造崇高前身的一种尝试。关于现代经济主义中一些核心原则的起源，参见 Jarvis (1999) 更加扎实且更具启发性的分析。

了这一点⁴。至于田径比赛,我们的铭文证据表明平局也值得勒石记录⁵。现代将希腊竞赛体系描述为一种基于得失等价的系统,就古代的音乐、诗歌或其他任何种类的智慧竞赛而言,这显然是有失偏颇的⁶。例如,古尔德纳(Gouldner)同时声称:(a)希腊人通常在"口才与智慧"方面竞争,参见第46页;(b)"智慧与节制"无法成为零和竞争的宗旨,参见第51页;(c)希腊的竞赛体系是基于零和博弈的,参见第49—51页⁷。为了避免陷入这类矛盾境地,有用的做法是具体考察特定的希腊竞赛,并去理解智慧与竞争性之间的关系在古希腊文本中是如何被概念化的。当然,接下来对《竞赛》的分析称不上是对希腊竞争精神的一个整体理解,但仍可以为一幅更宏大的图景贡献尺寸之功。

遗憾的是,《荷马与赫西奥德的竞赛》的文本充满了令人疑惑之处,这便影响到了其解读路径。因此,在移步讨论它描述竞赛的方式以前,有必要简单介绍一下该文本的性质以及人们在试图确定其历史背景时遇到的困难。在提出各种问题之后,对于《竞赛》中"竞赛部分"的详细分析,比如本文提供的分析显然能够帮助解决其中的一些问题。我使用"竞赛部分"这个表达,来指代《竞赛》第62—214行⁸,因为该文本在内容上并没有严格遵照其题目,仅仅向我们讲述荷马与赫西奥德竞赛的故事。它在开头描述了两位诗人的乡梓、世系和相对齿序,而后讲述了一则关于荷马之死的神谕、竞赛的故事,一则关于赫西奥德之死的神谕以及他随后的死亡,接着它讲述了荷马的余生,并以他在伊奥斯(Ios)的死亡收尾。

该文本仅保存在一份佛罗伦萨抄本之中,并有一段有趣的历史。当时发现它的尼采立刻就看出该文本的不同部分来源于不同时期:

4　比如可参见Macleod (1982)。

5　柯尼希(J. König)提醒我注意这个细节。比如可参见《希腊语铭文集成》(*Corpus Inscriptionum Graecarum*), 4380g;《希腊语铭文增补》(*Supplementum epigraphicum Graecum*), xli 1352;比较Milner (1991), 34f.。

6　零和博弈的核心观点是得失相等, Jarvis (1999) 追溯了这种观点与基督教传统中的几个流派,尤其是詹森主义(Jansenism)之间的联系。

7　Gouldner (1965)。

8　《竞赛》的所有引文均引自Allen (1912)。尽管Wilamowitz (1916)在很多方面上都更可取,但并不经常容易获得。

引言部分的第33行提到了哈德良皇帝，从而给出了一个明确的时代上限。然而，文本的一些部分在哈德良时代之前就已为人熟知。斯托拜乌斯(Stobaeus)征引了第78行及其后一行，并将它们归于阿尔基达马斯(Alcidamas)的《缪斯集》(*Museum*)，后者是公元前4世纪的一位智术师，高尔吉亚(Gorgias)的学生。此外，《竞赛》本身在讲述有关赫西奥德之死的一种传说时，征引了《缪斯集》作为其来源。基于这两个细节，尼采将《竞赛》的核心部分归于阿尔基达马斯的《缪斯集》[9]。他的猜想被后来发现的两份纸草所证实。弗林德斯·皮特里(Flinders Petrie)纸草上的文本于1891年首次出版[10]，与《竞赛》中描述竞赛开始的部分(大概是第68—104行)非常相似：鉴于这份纸草可以追溯到公元前3世纪，我们就得到了《竞赛》中那一部分的时代下限。第二份纸草于1925年首次出版，它与《竞赛》的结尾部分非常相似，并在底部写有αλκι]δαμαντος περι ομηρου【阿尔基达马斯著，关于荷马 】的字样[11]。尽管在确定这份纸草和《竞赛》之间关系的方面还存在一些问题[12]，但有一点很清楚：尼采提出《竞赛》的核心部分取自《缪斯集》，该见解是正确的。目前学界公认，抄本中荷马的神谕、竞赛、赫西奥德的神谕以及两位诗人之死的叙述部分均取自阿尔基达马斯的作品[13]。

目前，争议尤其集中在竞赛的故事上，这也是本文的主要关注点。我们尚不清楚阿尔基达马斯在多大程度上汇集了和诗人们有关的早期故事和传统。赫拉克利特(*fr.* 22 B 56 DK)已经知道荷马因无法解开儿童的谜语而死，而关于赫西奥德之死的传说在修昔底德时代以前就已流行(3.96)：因此，在这两种情况下，我们知道阿尔基达马斯并未杜撰他所讲述的故事。出现在"竞赛部分"中的个别诗行也流行于公元前4世纪以前，例如第78行及其后一行出现在《特奥格尼斯诗集》(*Theognidea*)中的第425和427行[14]，而第107行及其后

9　Nietzsche (1870).
10　首次出版于Mahaffy (1891), no. 25；现在的编号为*P. Lit. Lond.* 191。
11　Michigan papyrus inv. 2754，首次出版于Winter (1925)。
12　参见Kirk (1950)和Dodds (1952)。
13　参见West (1967), 444。(参见本辑第45页。——译者按)
14　对《特奥格尼斯诗集》第425—428行的讨论，参见Campbell (1982) 366。

一行与阿里斯托芬的《和平》第1282行及其后一行相同。然而,学者们对这些相似之处提出了不同的解释。韦斯特(West)坚称,阿尔基达马斯杜撰了荷马和赫西奥德竞赛的故事,但他使用了一些耳熟能详的诗句[15]。换句话说,虽然竞赛部分的很多诗行都是从前流传下来的,但在他看来,是阿尔基达马斯首次将它们归于荷马和赫西奥德名下。

理查森(Richardson)依据各种理由来批判韦斯特的说法[16]。首先,他指出有关荷马和赫西奥德的轶事在公元前6世纪就已经很普遍。其次,他注意到一场塞诺芬尼(Xenophanes)想象的智慧竞赛,而且无论如何,诗歌与谜语的竞赛都代表了一种早期的形式[17]。除了这些更宽泛的考察,他还增添了一些关于《竞赛》和阿里斯托芬的《和平》之间关系的具体论点,他认为该喜剧中的情形不仅与《竞赛》中那两行孤立的诗句相呼应,而且还呼应了后者的两个主题:对战争诗歌的排斥和对宴饮的赞颂[18]。韦斯特假设阿尔基达马斯杜撰了竞赛的故事,但在其他各方面都遵循了传统,在理查森看来,该假设没有任何证据支撑,而综合各种考量,荷马与赫西奥德竞赛的故事在公元前5世纪就已广为人知,根据理查森的说法,甚至可以追溯到公元前6世纪。本文的讨论与这两种观点都能协调,尽管下文的各种观察都表明《竞赛》中的竞赛部分非常符合公元前5世纪雅典的背景。在该方面,这些观察为理查森的观点提供了一些支持。

竞赛的故事从第62行及其后数行开始,据说荷马和赫西奥德很有可能是在奥利斯(Aulis)偶然相遇的[19],他们一起前往卡尔基斯(Chalcis),并在安菲达马斯(Amphidamas)的葬礼赛会上进行了智慧竞赛。文本告诉我们,裁判是已故国王的兄弟帕诺伊德斯(Panedes)。故事的设定基于《劳作与时日》的第648—659行,赫西奥德夸耀自己能够提出与航海有关的明智建议,并讲述了他唯一的一次跨海之旅:

15　West (1967).(参见本辑第26—55页——译者按)

16　Richardson (1981).(参见本辑第56—72页——译者按)

17　关于最后一点,另参见Rohde (1901), 1.103f.。

18　Richardson (1981) 2ff.(参见本辑第58—59页——译者按)

19　参见Erbse (1996)。

δείξω δή τοι μέτρα πολυφλοίσβοιο θαλάσσης,
οὔτε τι ναυτιλίης σεσοφισμένος οὔτε τι νηῶν.
οὐ γάρ πώ ποτε νηὶ [γ᾽] ἐπέπλων εὐρέα πόντον,
εἰ μὴ ἐς Εὔβοιαν ἐξ Αὐλίδος, ἧ ποτ᾽ Ἀχαιοὶ
μείναντες χειμῶνα πολὺν σὺν λαὸν ἄγειραν
Ἑλλάδος ἐξ ἱερῆς Τροίην ἐς καλλιγύναικα.
ἔνθα δ᾽ ἐγὼν ἐπ᾽ ἄεθλα δαΐφρονος Ἀμφιδάμαντος
Χαλκίδα [τ᾽] εἰσεπέρησα· τὰ δὲ προπεφραδμένα πολλὰ
ἄεθλ᾽ ἔθεσαν παῖδες μεγαλήτορες· ἔνθα μέ φημι
ὕμνῳ νικήσαντα φέρειν τρίποδ᾽ ὠτώεντα.
τὸν μὲν ἐγὼ Μούσῃσ᾽ Ἑλικωνιάδεσσ᾽ ἀνέθηκα
ἔνθα με τὸ πρῶτον λιγυρῆς ἐπέβησαν ἀοιδῆς.

我将会向你展示汹涌大海的节律，
尽管我在航海和舰船方面没有什么经验。
因为我从未乘船在宽广的大海上航行，
除了从优卑亚到过奥利斯，阿凯亚人曾经在那里
过冬，并募集来自神圣的希腊的军队
以对抗盛产美女的特洛伊。
我穿过那里去参加好战的卡尔基斯人
安菲达马斯的（葬礼）赛会，他慷慨大度的儿子
宣布并颁发了大量的奖品。在那里我唱了
一首颂诗而取得胜利并带走了一尊带耳三足鼎。
我把它献给了赫利孔山的缪斯女神，
正是在那里她们首次将我领进了清唱的世界。[20]

（《劳作与时日》，第648—659行）

赫西奥德描述其旅程的方式显示出他与英雄史诗相竞赛的立场。赫西奥德指出，奥利斯是阿凯亚人从希腊航行到特洛伊之前曾

20　英译文：West (1988), 56。

经停留或等待（μείναντες）的地方[21]。与赫西奥德不同，阿凯亚人不知道何时是适宜的航行时间。我们也可以通过其他方式来感知赫西奥德的竞争性立场。对整个特洛伊远征的概括只占了不到三行的篇幅，这个概括极其精悍。在《伊利亚特》中，饰词καλλιγύναιξ【盛产美女的】总是与希腊联系在一起，而ἱερή【神圣的】则通常用于特洛伊：赫西奥德颠倒了这个惯例。他用καλλιγύναιξ来描述海伦居住的城市特洛伊，而用ἱερή去描述希腊，这种用法仅此一见，但也并非没有意义[22]。与荷马笔下漂洋过海追逐一位女子的希腊人不同，赫西奥德这个著名的厌女主义者留在了神圣的希腊。他用ἐπέπλων εὐρέα πόντον【在宽广的大海上航行】这个表达史诗般地描述了其旅程，但该旅程只需跨越从奥利斯到优卑亚的海峡。赫西奥德比荷马更具真知。

接下来我们得知他在一场诗歌竞赛中获胜。但他没有告诉我们他的对手是谁。《竞赛》所依据的传统提供了其对手的名字：荷马。考虑到前面的诗行，这种猜想不乏才思[23]。通常，传记故事可以被视作对文本的解释[24]。意味深长的是，《竞赛》第54行及其后一行说这两位诗人ἐν Αὐλίδι τῆς Βοιωτίας【在彼奥提亚的奥利斯】进行竞赛，也就是说，正是赫西奥德的活动路径与荷马诗歌中所提到的路线交叉重合的地方。尼采修订为ἐν Χαλκίδι τῆς Εὐβοίας【在优卑亚的卡尔基斯】，但在我看来，传世文本的第54行及其后一行可以被视为对《劳

21　Griffith (1983), 62正确地指出，第646—662行旨在确立赫西奥德作为诗人的资质，并指出奥利斯在该语境中的重要性：“（他前往诗歌竞赛的旅途）开始并结束于奥利斯，那里作为史诗中特洛伊远征的起点而闻名于世。”

22　比较Edwards (1971) 80：“人们更倾向于认为赫西奥德的幽默感在这里起到了作用，因为他故意选择了‘错误的’饰词，他本可以轻易地说，‘Ἴλιον εἰς ἱερήν ἐξ Ἑλλάδος εὐρυχόροιο’【从宽敞的希腊到神圣的伊里昂】（比较《伊利亚特》第7卷第20行与第9卷第478行）。此外还可能有另一种简单的解释：在对饰词的选择上，赫西奥德受饰词含义的影响要小于受他熟悉的短语的影响。”我认为赫西奥德的选择既非出于幽默亦非出于无能，而是源自与史诗传统竞争的立场。

23　赫西奥德击败荷马的传统具有一定的影响力，这一点从它以其特有的方式融入文本本身即可见一斑，第657行的异文即为一例。《劳作与时日》第657行的古注告诉我们：ἄλλοι γράφουσιν·ὕμνῳ νικήσαντ’ ἐν Χαλκίδι θεῖον Ὅμηρον【其他抄本写作：在卡尔基斯用诗歌打败了神样的荷马】。现代校订者在校勘记中给出了这另一种读法。

24　Fairweather (1974)和Lefkowitz (1981)都强调诗人的生平故事通常来源于他们的作品，而我则认为这类生平故事往往说明了古人对这些诗歌的有趣解读。

作与时日》第651—653行的深刻解读,并且正如埃尔布泽(Erbse)所指出的那样,无论如何它都与《竞赛》的第67行及其后一行兼容:συμβαλόντες ἀλλήλοις ἦλθον εἰς τὴν Χαλκίδα【他们在偶然地会面之后前往卡尔基斯】[25]。

就《竞赛》而言,有一件事从一开始就很清楚:赫西奥德将会赢得为纪念安菲达马斯葬礼而在卡尔基斯举行的诗歌比赛。事实上,《竞赛》中的竞赛部分在结尾处称赫西奥德将他赢得的三足鼎献给了缪斯女神,并在上面刻写了以下对句:

> Ἡσίοδος Μούσαις Ἑλικωνίσι τόνδ᾽ ἀνέθηκεν
> ὕμνῳ νικήσας ἐν Χαλκίδι θεῖον Ὅμηρον.
> 赫西奥德将此物敬献给赫利孔山的缪斯,
> 他在卡尔基斯用诗歌打败了神样的荷马。

(《竞赛》,第213—214行)

这段文字与《劳作与时日》中第658和657行的分别对应之处十分明显。但《竞赛》究竟如何呈现赫西奥德的胜利还有待观察。

两位诗人之间的竞赛可以被分为几个不同的阶段。首先,赫西奥德向荷马提出了两个关于生命中最佳之事的宏大问题。这样的问题在早期的希腊诗歌中很常见,并且一定是会饮的一个标准特征[26]。荷马回答说,生命中最好的事情是永不出生或英年早逝,从而表达出希腊思想中一个根深蒂固的观点[27]。这种观点无法在荷马的诗歌中找到,但它可能很早就被归到他的名下,只是因为这种思想众所周知,而荷马恰恰又代表着古希腊诗歌的最高权威。荷马的第二个回答征引了《奥德赛》第9卷的第6—11行:生活中最美好的事情就是坐在宴会上倾听一位伟大的游吟诗人。《竞赛》的文本继续讲道,这些诗

25　Erbse (1996).

26　参见 Simonides *fr.* 651 Page; *carm. conv. fr.* 890 Page;比较 Tyrtaeus *fr.* 12 West, Sappho *fr.* 16 Voigt; Xenophanes *fr.* 2 West, *Theogn.* 1063-1068。

27　《竞赛》第78行及其后一行与《特奥格尼斯诗集》的第425、427行几乎相同,这种思想亦见于别处,比如可参考 Bacchylides 5.160-162 和 Sophocles *O.C.* 1225。Campbell (1982), 366猜想特奥格尼斯是在征引两行众所周知的诗句。

行非常有名,以至于它们被冠以"黄金"之名,并且"直至今日"在会饮开始时还会被吟诵(无论那可能意味着什么)。古注(scholia)间接地证实了这种说法:他们强调这些诗行不应该脱离语境解读,并且荷马并非真的相信生活中最好的事情是宴饮,奥德修斯这样说是为了取悦费埃克斯人(Phaeacians)[28]。虽然荷马给出的两个答案大相径庭,但它们都代表了希腊文化中固有的观点,因此很可能是听众青睐的回答。那么,赫西奥德迅速转向一个更加困难的挑战也就不足为奇了:

> ὁ δὲ Ἡσίοδος ἀχθεσθεὶς ἐπὶ Ὁμήρου εὐημερίᾳ ἐπὶ τὴν τῶν
> ἀπόρων ὥρμησεν ἐπερώτησιν καί φησι τούσδε τοὺς στίχους·
>   Μοῦσ' ἄγε μοι τά τ' ἐόντα τά τ' ἐσσόμενα πρό τ' ἐόντα
>   τῶν μὲν μηδὲν ἄειδε, σὺ δ' ἄλλης μνῆσαι ἀοιδῆς.
> ὁ δὲ Ὅμηρος βουλόμενος ἀκολούθως τὸ ἄπορον λῦσαι φησίν·
>   οὐδέποτ' ἀμφὶ Διὸς τύμβῳ καναχήποδες ἵπποι
>   ἄρματα συντρίψουσιν ἐρίζοντες περὶ νίκης.

> 赫西奥德对荷马的成功感到不快,他开始提出难解的谜题,并说出如下诗行:
>   缪斯啊,那些当下在,将在或曾在的事物
>   不要对我歌咏它们;请你回想其他的诗篇。
> 荷马有意解开难解的谜题,他相应说道:
>   蹄声响亮的马群从未在宙斯墓旁
>   因努力竞比争胜而损坏车舆。

(《竞赛》,第94—101行)

ἀπορία【难题】自此成为威胁。从现在开始,荷马可能根本无法作答。如果我们将赫西奥德的挑战与《神谱》第31行及其后一行进行比较,我们就会意识到赫西奥德是在要求荷马不要侵犯缪斯授予

28　Scholia T *ad* 9.14. 尤斯塔修斯(Eustathius)在他对《奥德赛》的评注里进一步阐释了这几点,见 I 318f. (Stallbaum)。

他的特殊礼物——诗歌领域：歌唱过去、现在和将来一切的能力[29]。
此外，赫西奥德还使用了一个传统的程式化用语来发起这项挑战：
σὺ δ᾽ ἄλλης μνῆσαι ἀοιδῆς【请你回想其他的诗篇】[30]。出现在颂诗结
尾处的相同表达很可能标志着由颂诗向英雄史诗的过渡[31]。然而，在
此这句话的语境排除了这种可能性：荷马无法歌唱他的全部诗篇，
除非他愿意承认他歌唱的是一个从未存在过的世界。[32]可以理解的
是，他避免提出任何此类说法，但却找到了一种展示其智慧的方法。
他告诉我们竞赛在何种情况下是不可能的：宙斯是不死的，永远不
可能有为他举行的葬礼赛会。宙斯和安菲达马斯之间存在一个重要
的区别。

　　因此，赫西奥德必须找到更困难的挑战，在接下来的部分中，他
以荒诞不经或意思不当的诗行刁难荷马。荷马需要为赫西奥德给出
的那行诗句补出第二行，从而摆脱困局。这项挑战极其有趣，因为它
依赖于早期希腊六音步诗歌的一些风格特征。最明显的是，第107—
137行的整个回合都仰仗跨行连续（enjambment）：首先赫西奥德表
达出一种意涵，而后荷马在下一行对其进行改动。

　　正如许多学者指出的那样，跨行连续是荷马诗歌的一个显著特
征，但我们看到，它在《竞赛》中的使用非同寻常。让我们从荷马诗
歌中的跨行连续开始。米尔曼·帕里（Milman Parry）在一篇1929年
首次发表的重要文章中已经指出，荷马的诗句倾向于表达一种完整
的意涵，并且这种意涵接着可能会在以跨行连续开头的下一行中被重
新强调、延展或限定[33]。我们不难想到这种"非圆周句的"（unperiodic）
跨行连续（姑且使用帕里的术语）的例子：

　　　　　Μῆνιν ἄειδε, θεά, Πηληιάδεω Ἀχιλῆος,

29　比较《伊利亚特》1.70，在这行诗中，那种能力被归于先知卡尔卡斯（Calchas）。

30　例如比较 Homeric Hymns, 2.495, 3.546, 4.580, 6.21, 10.6, 19.49, 28.18, 30.19。

31　参见 Bremer (1981), 212【

32　诗人说谎的可能性很早就已经被考虑过了：比如可参见 Hesiod, Th. 24-8 和 Solon
fr. 29 West；这是柏拉图的荷马批评指出的一个重要特征，相关内容参见 Murray (1996)，
19-24。

33　Parry (1929). 后来许多学者都研究了荷马作品中的跨行连续，并在原先帕里直觉
的基础上补充了很多内容。最近的研究包括 Bakker (1997) 和 Clark (1997)。

οὐλομένην, ἣ μυρί᾽ Ἀχαιοῖς ἄλγε᾽ ἔθηκε

缪斯啊,请歌唱佩琉斯之子阿喀琉斯的愤怒,

那受到诅咒的愤怒给阿凯亚人带来了无穷的苦难。

(《伊利亚特》,第 1—2 行)

《伊利亚特》的首行无疑表达了一个完整的意涵,而跨行连续中以 οὐλομένην【受到诅咒的】开头的下一行进一步限定了这种意涵:它是一种破坏性的愤怒,造成了很多痛苦。柯克(Kirk)将这种"非圆周句的"或他更喜欢称之为"渐进式"类型的跨行连续与荷马诗歌中一个更基本的特征联系起来:"行文受到荷马风格的基本规则约束,这种风格的意涵与表达总是或在多数情况下是**线性的**(linear)和**渐进的**(progressive);它不会否定自身,也不会推迟或重新人为地调整重要的意涵元素。……诗人从一点到另一点的行文顺序是渐进的,并且符合简单的逻辑;这种顺序只能让他写出既不复杂也没有反转的长句子。"[34] 人们肯定能够想出这一总体规则的例外情况,但大体来说它是正确的[35]。

　　与之相对,在《竞赛》的第 107—137 行中,赫西奥德所说的每一行的含义都被荷马在下一行中颠覆或否定。荷马即兴创作的技艺受到了检验:他不被允许随性地进一步阐述原本的意涵,他必须当场修正一个差劲的开头。让我们来看一些例子。赫西奥德以下面这行诗开头:

δεῖπνον ἔπειθ᾽ εἵλοντο βοῶν κρέα καὐχένας ἵππων

然后他们享用牛肉大餐以及马的脖颈……

(《竞赛》,第 107 行)

　　赫西奥德用一个不恰当的暗示来挑衅荷马。我们知道英雄的饮

34　Kirk (1985) 31.

35　有一些有趣的诗行可以作为例证,它们纠正了前文提到的潜在的意思不当,纠正的方式与《竞赛》类似: *Il.* 5.340; *Od.* 11.602; Hesiod *fr.* 23a21 Merkelbach-West。

食是备受关注的谈论对象[36]，而马颈自然不包括在内。荷马用下面的
方式完成诗行以避开这种暗示：

> δεῖπνον ἔπειθ' εἵλοντο βοῶν κρέα καὐχένας ἵππων
> ἔκλυον ἱδρώοντας, ἐπεὶ πολέμου ἐκορέσθην.
> 然后他们享用牛肉大餐以及马的脖颈
> 上汗湿的轭被他们解下，因为饱尝战事。

（《竞赛》，第 107—108 行）

荷马完成这句话之后，我们便可以看到"马的脖颈"完全从属于一个不同的从句，这个从句描述了饭前发生的事情。换句话说，为了解决这个问题，荷马使用了跨行连续与 ὕστερον πρότερον【逆序法】，并顺便开了一个小玩笑：英雄们饱尝战事，而非食物。

现在，如果我们回到对荷马风格的观察上来，我们会看到《竞赛》既依靠其传统特征，又完全颠覆了它们。第 107 行确实可以被认为包含一个"完整的意涵"。然而，考虑到意涵的性质，这行诗又构成一个问题。因此，如果用柯克的话来说，荷马被迫创作了一个复杂的句子，这句话的确"否定了自身"，"推迟"并且"重新人为地调整了重要的意义元素"。

在阿里斯托芬的《和平》当中，当特吕该欧斯（Trygaeus）鼓励男孩背诵这些诗句时，他在问题开始之前就停了下来。换句话说，他并没有要求男孩即兴作答：

> Π.　ἀλλὰ τί δῆτ' ᾄσω; σὺ γὰρ εἰπέ μοι οἷστισι χαίρεις.
> Τρ.　"ὡς οἱ μὲν δαίνυντο βοῶν κρέα", καὶ τὰ τοιαυτί·
> 　　　"ἄριστον προτίθεντο καὶ ἄσσ' ἥδιστα πάσασθαι."
> Π.　"ὡς οἱ μὲν δαίνυντο βοῶν κρέα, καὐχένας ἵππων
> 　　　ἔκλυον ἱδρώοντας, ἐπεὶ πολέμου ἐκορέσθεν."

36　Montanari (1995), 13–19 追踪了欧布洛斯（Eubulus）（*fr.* 118 Kassel-Austin）和柏拉图（*Rep.* 3 404b）对英雄饮食的兴趣。

Τρ.　εἶεν· ἐκόρεσθεν τοῦ πολέμου κᾆτ᾽ ἤσθιον.

　　ταῦτ᾽ ᾆδε, ταῦθ᾽, ὡς ἤσθιον κεκορημένοι.

拉马库斯之子：但是我应该歌唱什么呢？你来告诉我那些
　　　　　　让你满意的诗行。

特吕该欧斯："接着他们享用了牛肉"，就像这样的诗行。
　　　　　　"他们提供了早餐以及各种美味佳肴。"

拉马库斯之子："接着他们享用了牛肉以及马的脖颈
　　　　　　上汗湿的轭被他们解下，因为饱尝战事。"

特吕该欧斯：很好。他们饱尝战事，而后进餐。
　　　　　　请你歌唱这些关于他们在饱尝战事之后如
　　何吃饭的事情。

　　　　　　　　　（阿里斯托芬《和平》，第1279—1285行）

阿里斯托芬淡化了由跨行连续带来的问题，而延伸了有关饱尝战事的玩笑。和韦斯特及理查森一样，我们可能也想知道这些诗行是否与《竞赛》相呼应，抑或后者是否基于阿里斯托芬的作品。在我看来，《和平》中的措辞强烈地暗示了这些诗行是众所周知的：直至此时那个男孩一直在背诵名句，并且这些诗句被当作引文。我也看不出这些诗行为何不应该与荷马联系起来：到目前为止，男孩一直在背诵归于荷马的诗句[37]。因此，阿里斯托芬似乎最有可能是在征引与荷马和赫西奥德有关且创作于阿尔基达马斯《缪斯集》之前的诗行[38]。

　　在结束与英雄饮食有关的首项挑战之后，赫西奥德毫不客气地使用其他潜在意思不当的诗句来刁难荷马，例如：

αὐτὰρ ἐπεὶ δμήθη γάμῳ Ἄρτεμις ἰοχέαιρα

---

[37] Platnauer (1964)评论第1280—1283行："这些诗行借自《荷马与赫西奥德的竞赛》。"总的来说，我同意他的看法，即这些诗行是从某处借来的，且最有可能借自竞赛故事的某个版本。

[38] 这个观察支持Richardson (1981), 2ff.（参见本辑第58—59页——译者按），而非West (1967) 440ff.（参见本辑第39页——译者按）。

射猎女神阿尔忒弥斯,屈从于婚姻……

（《竞赛》,第 117 行）

这当然是一种亵渎神明的暗示：对于阿尔忒弥斯来说，根本就不可能有婚后的生活，因为理论上她是一位童贞女神。该暗示甚至比英雄食马颈那个还要棘手。荷马再次使用跨行连续和我们称之为"不同断句"的方法来挽救局面：

αὐτὰρ ἐπεὶ δμήθη γάμῳ Ἄρτεμις ἰοχέαιρα
Καλλιστὼ κατέπεφνεν ἀπ' ἀργυρέοιο βιοῖο.
射猎女神阿尔忒弥斯,屈从于婚姻
的卡利斯托是她用银弓射杀。

（《竞赛》,第 117—118 行）

意思的恰当性得到了恢复。荷马借助阿尔忒弥斯的传统饰词演绎了他的故事："弓箭手"杀死了她那背弃信仰、屈从于婚姻的密友。似乎在公元前 5 世纪，这些荷马式的诗行可以有不同的断句方式[39]。这里出现的断句操作与该背景吻合。

我们的下一个例子也涉及公元前 5 世纪早期对荷马式语言的关注。赫西奥德以此开头：

οὗτος ἀνὴρ ἀνδρός τ' ἀγαθοῦ καὶ ἀνάλκιδός ἐστι
这个男人的父亲高贵而懦弱……

（《竞赛》,第 113 行）

问题是这里存在明显的矛盾之处：高贵之人不会是懦弱的。荷马修正道：

οὗτος ἀνὴρ ἀνδρός τ' ἀγαθοῦ καὶ ἀνάλκιδός ἐστι

39　参见 Democritus *fr.* 68 B 22 Diels-Kranz = Porphyry, *Quaest. hom.* 1.274, 9 Schrad。

μητρός, ἐπεὶ πόλεμος χαλεπὸς πάσῃσι γυναιξίν.

这个男人的父亲高贵而懦弱

的是他母亲，因战争对所有女人来说都艰难。

（《竞赛》，第 113—114 行）

这个文字游戏使用了二尾形容词（two-termination adjectives）。这里也许可以提出形容词 ἀνάλκις【懦弱的】应当是阴性的。我们知道普罗塔戈拉抱怨过名词 μῆνις【愤怒】在荷马的作品中是阴性的，尽管从其意思上来看应该是阳性的[40]。荷马在这里被展现为一个恰当运用语言的人："懦弱"是一个阴性形容词。

赫西奥德用更多的胡言乱语、语义矛盾和意思不当来发难，但随后它们总能被荷马出色地化解，因此赫西奥德改变了策略。下一项挑战与数字有关：

πρὸς πάντα δὲ τοῦ Ὁμήρου καλῶς ἀπαντήσαντος πάλιν φησὶν ὁ Ἡσίοδος·
    τοῦτό τι δή μοι μοῦνον ἐειρομένῳ κατάλεξον,
    πόσσοι ἅμ' Ἀτρείδῃσιν ἐς Ἴλιον ἦλθον Ἀχαιοί;
ὁ δὲ διὰ λογιστικοῦ προβλήματος ἀποκρίνεται οὕτως·
    πεντήκοντ' ἦσαν πυρὸς ἐσχάραι, ἐν δὲ ἑκάστῃ
    πεντήκοντ' ὀβελοί, περὶ δὲ κρέα πεντήκοντα·
    τρὶς δὲ τριηκόσιοι περὶ ἓν κρέας ἦσαν Ἀχαιοί.
τοῦτο δὲ εὑρίσκεται πλῆθος ἄπιστον· τῶν γὰρ ἐσχαρῶν οὐσῶν πεντήκοντα ὀβελίσκοι γίνονται πεντακόσιοι καὶ χιλιάδες β´ κρεῶν δὲ δεκαδύο μυριάδες, καὶ χιλιάδες ε´...

鉴于荷马完美地解答了所有的谜题，赫西奥德又说道：

你只需详细回答我问的这个小问题：

多少阿凯亚人曾随阿特柔斯的两子前往伊利昂？

他便以算术问题这般作答：

40　Protagoras, *fr.* 80 A 28 Diels-Kranz = Aristotle, *Soph. el.* 14.173b 17.

> 生火的炉灶有五十座,其中每处有
>
> 五十根肉签,在每根签旁有五十块肉;
>
> 每块肉边的阿凯亚人有三乘三百个。
>
> 但这会得到一个难以置信的数目:若有五十处灶,就有两
> 千五百根签,十二万五千块肉……

(《竞赛》,第138—148行)

前去特洛伊的阿凯亚人数量问题在公元前5世纪再次引发争论。众所周知,修昔底德根据船只数量和每艘船上阿凯亚人的平均数量(1.10.4f.),计算出他们的人数一定很少。如果我们结合修昔底德的计算来阅读这段文字,这看起来就像是一个旨在给荷马解围的戏谑回答:阿凯亚人要比人们一直以来想象的多。

　　紧接着数字谜题的是一些关于人类状况的更宏大的问题,正如韦斯特指出的那样,这些问题似乎不那么传统,大概只能追溯到阿尔基达马斯所在的时代[41]。在此之后,竞赛的第一部分就结束了。这时,主持竞赛的国王帕诺伊德斯开启了一个新的竞赛领域:

> ῥηθέντων δὲ καὶ τούτων, οἱ μὲν Ἕλληνες πάντες τὸν Ὅμηρον ἐκέλευον στεφανοῦν, ὁ δὲ βασιλεὺς Πανήδης ἐκέλευσεν ἕκαστον τὸ κάλλιστον ἐκ τῶν ἰδίων ποιημάτων εἰπεῖν.
>
> 这些诗句被言说之后,所有希腊人都要求给荷马授予桂冠。但国王帕诺伊德斯要求双方都吟诵自己诗作中最出色的篇章。

(《竞赛》,第176—179行)

　　在我们进入竞赛的最后阶段之前,停下来进行一些整体性的思考可能会有所裨益。首先,我们可能会问,到目前为止我们讨论的部分描述了一种怎样的竞赛。例如,我们可能会注意到,作为观众的"所有希腊人"以及作为裁判的"国王帕诺伊德斯"都并非什么重要角色:在第176行及其后数行提到他们之前,我们几乎已经忘记他们

41　West (1967), 442.(参见本辑第41—43页——译者按)

的存在。如果其中一位诗人设法让另一位无话可说，想必他就会成为胜利者，而不需要第三方的裁决。至于竞赛的价值，很明显，如果其中一位诗人提问或回答失败，我们就无缘见到一些可能的诗行以及智慧的范例。因此，竞赛的成功取决于参赛者双方延长竞赛时间的能力。实际上，荷马和赫西奥德都努力创作出了意涵丰富的诗行。回到开头讨论的一般竞赛模型，我们现在可以肯定地说，《竞赛》并未描绘一场零和博弈性质的竞赛，其目的并非分配现成的物质奖励。参赛双方在这样一场竞赛的结尾都获得了更多的荣耀，并且为了施展自己的才智，他们都依赖彼此的能力。实际上，我们偶尔会遇到双重谜题，此时两位选手都要解决一个谜题：这些例子进一步强调了由这种竞赛所建立起来的相互依赖关系[42]。参赛者越是势均力敌，就越是能施展他们的才智，让静默的观众大饱耳福。在这一方面，此处所描述的竞赛不仅很类似于古希腊先知之间的唱和[43]，而且也类似于更古老的《奥义书》(Upaniṣads)中所描述的竞赛：智者们互相提问，令对方无话可说的人获胜[44]。这种谜题竞赛的形式非常古老。

然而，我们也看到似乎很多文段都回应了公元前5世纪备受关注的问题。它们与阿里斯托芬、普罗塔戈拉、德谟克利特和修昔底德作品中有关部分的相似之处已经得到关注。《竞赛》的倾向是恢复荷马的声誉，对抗智术师和其他的攻击：荷马回答了就神而言什么是适宜的；他无法容忍有关英雄饮食的影射；他声称特洛伊远征军规模庞大；并且，他适当地运用语言，无论普罗塔戈拉可能会对此说些什么。如果我们自问究竟是何人热衷于为荷马辩护，我们可能会想到公元前5世纪荷马诗歌的表演者：吟游诗人(rhapsodes)[45]。这个假设之所以有吸引力，至少有两个原因：首先，吟游诗人的生计和声誉直接取决于他们维护荷马权威的能力。其次，我们已经看到荷马与赫西奥德之间的唱和显露出对荷马式六音步诗歌创作的深入认

42　参见 *Certamen* 121-123; 124-126 和 133-137。

43　比较 Hesiod *fr.* 278 Merkelbach-West。

44　《奥义书》的成书时间甚至可能比《竞赛》更难确定：保守地说，可以追溯到公元前6世纪，但除此之外几乎没什么是可以确定的。进一步的讨论，参见 Lloyd (1979) 60f.。

45　对一位公元前5世纪著名的吟游诗人并不赞许却提供了许多信息的描绘，参见柏拉图的《伊翁》。

识。正如帕里和其他人所指出的那样,荷马的观众有一种期望,即一行六音步诗包含一个完整的意涵,但《竞赛》戏弄了这种期望。布尔克特(Burkert)论证了吟游诗人致力于维护荷马的权威地位,以应对早在公元前6世纪就已出现的新潮攻击[46]。在我看来,《竞赛》最有可能证实了一种持续的解谜传统,这种传统能够将针对智术师攻击的新回应纳入其中。

轮到帕诺伊德斯发言时,他要求诗人们朗诵自己诗歌中最美妙的段落,之后事情便发生了巨大的变化。首先,裁判承担了一个完全不同的角色。与之前通过解谜进行智慧竞赛的模式不同,现在的模式似乎是诗歌竞赛,就如同大酒神节(Great Dionysia)上举行的那种。诗人们表演他们的诗歌,裁判或观众裁决谁更出色。我们似乎越来越接近一场零和竞赛,因为这两位诗人不再为了创作意涵深刻的诗行而进行合作。每个人都独自展示其作品的片段并等待裁决:要么胜利要么失败。然而,在这种情况下,情形也并未像乍看上去那么明晰。

就个人最佳的诗篇而言,赫西奥德选择了所谓"农夫的农时",即《劳作与时日》第383—392行;而荷马则吟诵了《伊利亚特》第13卷的两段节选,分别是第126—133行和第339—344行,这两段其实非常接近于在描述重装步兵的战斗场面。这两个选择都让现代学者感到困惑[47]。就赫西奥德而言,他对《劳作与时日》的偏好胜过《神谱》,这令人费解;而来自《伊利亚特》的诗行则被现代的一些校订者认为是伪作,因为荷马诗歌一般只颂扬个体间的战斗,应当对重装步兵的战术一无所知[48]。然而,如果我们将《竞赛》与阿里斯托芬《蛙》中的第1033—1036行进行比较,我们会再次看到,荷马与赫西奥德之间的竞赛其实展现了公元前5世纪人们对这两位诗人的普遍看法[49]。

在诗歌吟诵结束之后,我们得知听众最终的反应:

46　Burkert (1987).

47　Arrighetti (1987) 168;比较 Dover (1997) *ad* 1033 和 1036。

48　见前注,关于荷马,另见 Janko (1992), *ad* 13.126–35。

49　实质上,Xenophon, *Memorabilia* 1.2.56–58 也表达了对两位诗人相同的观点。

θαυμάσαντες δὲ καὶ ἐν τούτῳ τὸν Ὅμηρον οἱ Ἕλληνες
ἐπήνουν, ὡς παρὰ τὸ προσῆκον γεγονότων τῶν ἐπῶν, καὶ ἐκέλευον
διδόναι τὴν νίκην. ὁ δὲ βασιλεὺς τὸν Ἡσίοδον ἐστεφάνωσεν εἰπὼν
δίκαιον εἶναι τὸν ἐπὶ γεωργίαν καὶ εἰρήνην προκαλούμενον νικᾶν,
οὐ τὸν πολέμους καὶ σφαγὰς διεξιόντα. τῆς μὲν οὖν νίκης οὕτω
φασὶ τυχεῖν τὸν Ἡσίοδον καὶ λαβόντα τρίποδα χαλκοῦν ἀναθεῖναι
ταῖς Μούσαις ἐπιγράψαντα·

Ἡσίοδος Μούσαις Ἑλικωνίσι τόνδ' ἀνέθηκεν

ὕμνῳ νικήσας ἐν Χαλκίδι θεῖον Ὅμηρον.

希腊人在这一回合感到惊异，他们对荷马赞叹不已，因为这
些诗行异乎寻常。他们又要求将胜利授予荷马。国王却向赫西
奥德授予桂冠，宣称让呼唤劳作与和平之人，而非细述战争和杀
戮之人获胜才是正当的。据说赫西奥德就是这样获胜的。他得
到了一只三足铜鼎，随后将其献给缪斯，并刻下这样的铭文：

赫西奥德将此物敬献给赫利孔山的缪斯，

他在卡尔基斯凭诗歌打败了神样的荷马。

(《竞赛》，第205—214行)

现在我们以惊人的速度得到了我们知道注定会发生的结果：赫
西奥德赢得了三足鼎并将其献给了赫利孔山的缪斯。但在其他方
面，最终裁决及其表达方式都是难以预料的。

首先，值得注意的是，裁判和观众的意见不一：虽然希腊人普遍
(参见第176行)想要授予荷马桂冠，但国王却选择支持赫西奥德。
现在重点是那些听众，他们的裁决是否与竞赛者的智慧相称还有待
观察。其次，两位诗人引发的反应截然不同：希腊人十分惊叹
(θαυμάσαντες)，而帕诺伊德斯则关心什么是正当的(δίκαιον)。仔细
考察，两位诗人所吸引的听众以及他们引起的反应分别折射出他们
各自诗歌的一些重要特征。《劳作与时日》的开头就抱怨国王做出的
不公正裁决[50]。至于荷马，他并没有得到一个公正的裁决，但激发了一

---

[50] *Op.* 38f.

种即时的普遍反应：θαῦμα【惊异】。这种效果不仅与荷马诗歌中描述的对诗歌及叙事的反应相似，而且也和吟游诗人伊翁（Ion）所引发的反应类似[51]。荷马的诗歌强烈地吸引着听众。

两边旗鼓相当：荷马激发起所有希腊人的惊叹，赫西奥德则引发国王对正当性的关注。这种僵局很容易让人产生一种难题的感觉，因此我们所有的注意力都转向了帕诺伊德斯颁布的最终裁决。唯有打动人心且有说服力的裁决才能够解决困境。帕诺伊德斯能够胜任这项挑战，他用自己的机智表达来处理两位智者之间的竞赛：和平胜过战争。帕诺伊德斯的裁决令人惊讶，主要是因为到目前为止荷马一直占据上风。然而，我并不赞同福格特（Vogt）的说法，他将其描述为一个武断且任性的裁决[52]。恰恰相反，正如韦斯特指出的那样，帕诺伊德斯"对该情境"做出了"一个新颖且绝非不值一提的分析"[53]，这个分析试图解决评判赫西奥德和荷马高低的难题。

到此为止，我已经强调了竞赛两个阶段之间的差异。首先，赫西奥德直接挑战荷马，但在第177—179行，设定发生了变化：第三方将在两者之间做出裁决。但是两部分之间的一致性也值得一提。在每个节点，竞赛都存在着以难题收尾的威胁：荷马不断面对看似无解的诗行的挑战。但他设法找到了解决之道，从而展现出他的智慧。而在最后关头，帕诺伊德斯面临的问题与荷马在竞赛第一部分所要应对的问题类似。他必须决断出什么是最佳的，而且他面临的处境很容易以难题收尾[54]。他用以回应的妙语与荷马所言一样令人印象深刻。

回到我们开头提到的更宏大的问题，我认为可以从本文对《竞赛》的解读中得出一些简要结论。在最基本的层面上，荷马和赫西奥德之间的竞赛显然不是一场零和博弈。从多个角度来看，在竞赛结束时有明显输赢的说法颇具误导性。然而，即使我们打算强调赫

---

[51]　关于荷马诗歌中对于诗歌反应的描写，参见 Macleod (1983)，2–15，特别是6ff。关于伊翁夸耀荷马诗歌在其观众中产生的反响，参见 *Ion* 535e。

[52]　Vogt (1959), 199, 201.

[53]　West (1967)，443（参见本辑第43—44页——译者按）。

[54]　在普鲁塔克的竞赛故事版本中，我们清楚地得知裁判们受到了难题的困扰，请参考 *Septem sap. convivium*, 153f2–154a5。

西奥德获胜（毕竟他确实赢得了三足鼎），但同样也要看到荷马有充分的机会展示他的非凡才华，并捍卫自己的智慧声名，该行为不仅针对赫西奥德，而且正如我们所见，也针对其他攻击。从头到尾的重点并不是通过损害竞争对手而取得胜利。恰恰相反，在竞赛的第一部分，诗人联袂创作了许多寓教于乐的对句：如果把每位诗人各自创作的部分单独拿出来，就显得毫无意义。在第二部分，我们看到一位裁判的智慧是如何做到与竞赛选手的智慧相称的。

正如我们所见，"希腊人的竞争性"经常出现在研究自由市场和英语国家资本主义社会的起源的作品中[55]。但我们不应过分强调他们的相似之处。《竞赛》帮助我们聚焦于希腊竞争性的某些方面，这些方面可能会被现代读者所忽视。在这篇文本中，竞争没有被视作一种将物质奖励或荣耀都分配给胜利者而让失败者一无所获的手段，而是一种展示智慧并将其传达给观众的方式。

参考书目

Allen, T. W. (ed.) (1912), *Homeri opera*, vol. 5 (Oxford).

Arrighetti, G. (1987), *Poeti, eruditi e biografi: momenti della riflessione dei Greci sulla letteratura* (Pisa).

Bakker, E. J. (1997), *Poetry in Speech: Orality and Homeric Discourse* (Ithaca and London).

Bremer, J. M. (1981), "Greek hymns", in H.S. Versnel (ed.), *Faith, Hope and Worship: Aspects of Religious Mentality in the Ancient World* (Leiden) 193–215.

Burkert, W. (1987), "The making of Homer in the sixth century BC: rhapsodes versus Stesichorus", in D. von Bothmer (ed.), *Papers on the Amasis Painter and his World* (Malibu) 43–62.

Campbell, D. A. (1982), *Greek Lyric Poetry* (2nd edn., Bristol).

Cartledge, P. (1997), "Deep plays: theatre as process in Greek civic life", in P. E.

55　例如，Moore and Lewis (1999), 160和164："雅典在公元前5世纪中叶达到其势力和繁荣的巅峰。历史上第一个自由市场大都市孕育了第一个公民主导的民主城市文化"，"雅典的经济可谓是未来英语国家资本主义模型的先驱"。

Easterling (ed.), *The Cambridge Companion to Greek Tragedy* (Cambridge) 3–35.

Clark, M. (1997), *Out of Line: Homeric Composition beyond the Hexameter* (Lanham).

Dodds, E. R. (1952), "The Alcidamas-papyrus again", *CQ* 2: 187–188.

Dover, K. J. (1997), *Aristophanes: Frogs* (student edition, Oxford).

Easterling, P. E. (1997), "Research Assessment Exercise: report of Panel 57", *CUCD* 26: 25–28.

Edwards, G. P. (1971), *The Language of Hesiod in its Traditional Context* (Oxford).

Erbse, H. (1996), "Homer und Hesiod in Chalkis", *RM* 139: 308–315.

Fairweather, J. (1974), "Fiction in the biographies of ancient writers", *AS* 5: 234–255.

Gouldner, A. (1965), *Enter Plato: Classical Greece and the Origins of Social Theory* (London).

Griffith, M. (1983), "Personality in Hesiod", *CA* 2: 37–65.

— (1990), "Contest and contradiction in early Greek poetry", in M. Griffith and D. Mastronarde (eds.), *The Cabinet of the Muses: Essays on Classical and Comparative Literature in Honour of Thomas. G. Rosenmeyer* (Atlanta) 185–207.

Janko, R. (1992), *The Iliad: A Commentary*, vol. 4: *Books 13–16* (Cambridge).

Jarvis, S. (1999), "The gift in theory", *Dionysius* 17: 201–222.

Kirk, G. S. (1950), "The Michigan Alcidamas-Papyrus; Heraclitus Fr. 56D: the riddle of the Lice", *CQ* 44: 149–167.

— (ed.) (1985), *The Iliad: A Commentary*, vol. 1: *Books 1–4* (Cambridge).

Lefkowitz, M. R. (1981), *The Lives of the Greek Poets* (London).

Lloyd, G. E. R. (1979), *Magic, Reason and Experience: Studies in the Origins and Development of Greek Science* (Cambridge).

— (1996), *Adversaries and Authorities: Investigations into Ancient Greek and Chinese Science* (Cambridge).

Macleod, C. (ed.) (1982), *Homer: Iliad, Book 24* (Cambridge).

— (1983), "Homer on poetry and the poetry of Homer", in *Collected Essays* (Oxford) 1–15.

Mahaffy, J. P. (ed.) (1891), *Flinders Petrie Papyri* (Dublin).

Milner, N. P. (1991), "Victors in the Meleagria and the Balbouran élite", *Anatolian Studies* 41: 23–62.

Montanari, F. (1995), *Studi di filologia omerica antica*, vol. 2 (Pisa).

Moore, K. and Lewis, D. (1999), *Birth of the Multinational. 2000 Years of Ancient Business History – From Ashur to Augustus* (Copenhagen).

Murray, P. (ed.) (1996), *Plato on Poetry* (Cambridge).

Nietzsche, F. (1870), "Der Florentinische Tractat über Homer und Hesiod, ihr

Geschlecht und ihren Wettkampf", *RM* 25: 528–540.

Parry, M. (1929), "The distinctive character of enjambement in Homeric verse", *TAPA* 60, 200–20, repr. in M. Parry, *The Making of Homeric Verse* (Oxford) 251–265.

Platnauer, M. (ed.) (1964), *Aristophanes: Peace* (Oxford).

Richardson, N. J. (1981), "The contest of Homer and Hesiod and Alcidamas' *Museion*", *CQ* 31: 1–10.

Rohde, E. (1901), *Kleine Schriften* (Tübingen and Leipzig), repr. 1969 (Hildesheim and New York).

Sommerstein, A. H. (ed.) (1996), *Aristophanes: Frogs* (Warminster).

Vogt, E. (1959), "Die Schrift vom Wettkampf Homers und Hesiods", *RM* 102: 193–221.

West, M. L. (1967), "The Contest of Homer and Hesiod", *CQ* 17: 433–450.

— (1988), *Hesiod: Theogony and Works and Days, translated with an introduction and notes* (Oxford).

Wilamowitz-Moellendorff, U. von (ed.) (1916), *Vitae Homeri et Hesiodi* (Bonn).

Winter, J. G. (1925), "A new fragment on the life of Homer", *TAPA* 56: 120–129.

（译者单位：复旦大学历史学系在读硕士生）

论建设性的斗争与破坏性的和平：
《荷马与赫西奥德的竞赛》[*]

保拉·巴西诺
（何　炜　译）

古希腊的听众很早就开始通过思考史诗的作者来反思史诗经典。受一段赫西奥德诗篇（*Op.* 648-662）的启发，他们将荷马和赫西奥德的诗歌之间的差异改编为剧本，让两位诗人来到优卑亚的卡尔基斯，在安菲达马斯国王的葬礼赛会上公开竞赛。这种通过传记的形式来解读不同史诗传统的方法很流行：荷马和赫西奥德之间的竞赛故事被写入数部文学作品，而且从古代直到拜占庭时代，它不断地被创造性地重新讲述，以表达对荷马和赫西奥德诗歌的不同看法[1]。

今天，《荷马与赫西奥德的竞赛》是两位诗人之间竞赛的最著名版本。它是现存唯一一部专门讲述这个故事的作品，其独特的历史和文本的分层结构引起了学者们的极大关注[2]。《竞赛》通过一个孤本

[*]　Paola Bassino, "On Constructive Conflict and Disruptive Peace: *The Certamen Homeri et Hesiodi*", in Paola Bassino, Lilah Grace Canevaro, Barbara Graziosi eds, *Conflict and Consensus in Early Greek Hexameter Poetry*, Cambridge: Cambridge University Press, 2017, pp. 190–207. 本文研究的最后阶段是在一个大型跨学科项目的支持下进行的，该项目由杜伦大学的芭芭拉·格拉齐奥西（Barbara Graziosi）教授指导，由欧洲科学研究委员会慷慨资助，名为"活的诗人：古代诗歌研究的新方法"（www.livingpoets.dur.ac.uk）。

[1]　最近 Koning (2010), 266 列出了有关荷马和赫西奥德竞赛的古代片段。

[2]　近来的《竞赛》研究（包括对过往研究的讨论）参看：Graziosi (2001)（参见本辑第73—95页——译者按）以及(2002), 168-180; Beecroft (2010), 61-105; Kivilo (2000) 及 (2010), 7- 61; Koning (2010), 239–268; Debiasi (2012)。

流传至今,这个抄本现存于佛罗伦萨(Biblioteca Medicea Laurenziana, Plut. 56.1)[3]。佛罗伦萨抄本中留存的《竞赛》文本提到了2世纪的哈德良皇帝(33[译按:指行数,下同]),因此这一文本的年代得以确定[4]。然而,该文本的第一位现代校勘者尼采指出,作者必定使用了大量更早时期的材料,特别是阿尔基达马斯(公元前4世纪)现已失传的《缪斯集》(*Museum*)[5]。一些在尼采死后发现的纸草残片证实了他的猜测[6]。同时,阿尔基达马斯的作品肯定也囊括了在更早的几个世纪里流传的材料,例如荷马无法解开谜语的故事(321—338)在公元前6世纪就已经为赫拉克利特所知[7]。

由于《竞赛》借鉴了数百年来建立起来的书面和口传传统,它为早期希腊史诗的接受进程和正典化过程提供了独特的见解,特别是提供了对斗争主题,以及该主题如何塑造史诗传统和史诗接受的分析。在本文中,笔者探究了《竞赛》的一些段落如何描述我们可称之为"建设性的斗争"的一系列方法,其中诗歌竞赛似乎是史诗创作和表演背后的强大动力。随后,笔者将论证《竞赛》提供了有关斗争与

---

3 1492年雅努斯·拉斯卡利斯(Janus Lascaris)代表洛伦佐·德·美第奇(Lorenzo de' Medici)在克里特岛购买了这个抄本,并将其带到佛罗伦萨,从而成为美第奇图书馆收藏的一部分。它是一部由多人抄写的杂糅抄本,时间在12世纪和14世纪之间。抄本主要包含修辞学作品,可能供学校使用。《竞赛》抄写在抄本的15 v–19 r处。Fryde (1996)对该抄本的已知信息做了详尽的总结,特别是第784页,以及该页中的各种交叉引注。

4 行数依据Allen (1912)。

5 《竞赛》第240行提到了阿尔基达马斯的《缪斯集》,将其作为赫西奥德之死故事的来源之一。尼采认为《缪斯集》也是《竞赛》中竞赛部分的来源,理由是第78—79行中荷马说出的诗句曾被斯托拜乌(Stobaeus, 4.52.22)引用,后者说它ἐκ Ἀλκιδάμαντος Μουσείου【出自阿尔基达马斯的《缪斯集》】(见Nietzsche [1870])。尼采在很多方面都是现代《竞赛》研究的第一人。他还根据对斯特法努斯(Stephanus)首印本(*Homeri et Hesiodi Certamen. Matronis et aliorum parodiae. Homericorum heroum epitaphia. Excudebat Henr. Stephanus*, Geneva, 1573)之后的抄本的检查,出版了《竞赛》的第一个校勘本(Nietzsche [1871])。关于尼采的《竞赛》研究的影响,见最近的Latacz (2014),12–19。

6 最早出版于Mahaffy (1891)的P. Petr. I 25 (1)含有一段与《竞赛》第69—102行相同的文本,因而表明《竞赛》的一些诗行,包括被斯托拜乌归于阿尔基达马斯的对句(见注5),至少在公元前3世纪时就与荷马和赫西奥德竞赛的故事相互联系、共同流传了。最早出版于Winter (1925)的P. Mich. inv. 2754(2世纪)在第1—14行有一段关于荷马之死的叙述,这一版本与《竞赛》第327—338行相似,而且在第15—23行的一段赞美荷马的未知文本之后,有一条跋识(*subscriptio*)将这段文本归于阿尔基达马斯。关于这些内容,以及其他与《竞赛》有关的纸草,见Bassino (2012)。

7 Heraclit. 22 B 56 DK.

神性之诗学的广泛思索，它区分了斗争的经验和对斗争经验的再现，同时也探索了和平在一部史诗诗作里具有的破坏潜力。

斗争与史诗表演

在《竞赛》中，荷马和赫西奥德展开了多种多样的诗歌比赛。竞赛的前两轮，赫西奥德问荷马，什么是对凡人来说最佳、最美的（75—89）；随后他提出了一个"谜题"（ἄπορον），即一个看似没有答案的问题（97—101）；接着是一系列不合理的诗行，荷马必须对它们做出回答（107—137）。在一个算术问题（140—145）之后，比赛发展为一系列的哲学问题（151—175），并以两位诗人自认为是各自作品中最出色段落的表演结束（180—204）。这些诗句表明，"建设性的竞赛"的概念对于许多参与史诗创作和表演的人来说至关重要，他们当中包括诗人和传统的游吟诗人（rhapsodes），以及具有智术师倾向的新型"荷马专家"。

赫西奥德现存作品中的一些段落是自传性和元诗学（metapoetic）的陈述，诗人通过这些陈述塑造了自己在艺术上的声音和身份[8]。荷马与赫西奥德竞赛的故事源于《劳作与时日》的第648—662行，当中赫西奥德夸耀了他在诗歌竞赛中的胜利：

> 我将向你展示浪涛汹涌的大海的节律。我对航海和船只都没有任何专业知识，因为我从未乘船在广阔的海面上航行，除了从奥利斯到优卑亚；阿凯亚人曾在奥利斯越冬，聚集了一大批人，从神圣的希腊航向美女所在的特洛伊。在优卑亚，我自己渡海到卡尔基斯，参加英勇的安菲达马斯的葬礼赛会，这位勇武之人的儿子们已宣布并设立了许多奖项。我要说，我在那里凭借一首颂诗获得胜利，并赢得了一只带把手的三足鼎。这只鼎我献给了赫利孔山的缪斯，她们在这山上第一次引导我走上了优

---

[8] 其中一些内容在Canevaro（2017）中得到阐发。

美诗歌的道路。我关于多钉子的船只的经验就这么多；即便如此，我也要说出提神盾的宙斯的心思，因为缪斯们教我唱出一首不可思议的颂歌。

——赫西奥德《劳作与时日》第648—662行 [9]

这些诗行包含一个纲领性的声明：赫西奥德宣称，在缪斯女神的帮助下，尽管他的航海经验极少，但他有能力指导航海事业，这样便宣示了自己作为教谕诗人的权威。然而，证实赫西奥德具有诗人权威的主张的，是他提到自己在卡尔基斯的竞赛中取得的胜利。这表明，在确立一个人的诗人资格的种种手段中，竞赛具有中心地位。为了证明自己的诗人权威，赫西奥德将自己的权威与其他诗人和诗歌传统的权威进行对比。虽然赫西奥德没有明确提及他在比赛中的对手（们），但根据这些诗行针对英雄史诗的竞争姿态，我们也可以补出荷马的名字 [10]。

因此，《竞赛》讲述的故事受到了赫西奥德诗篇的启发，在这段诗篇中，史诗传统之间的竞争被设想为关键因素，它能够塑造一位古风时期诗人的艺术身份。然而，在古风时期主要诗歌创作背后发挥作用的过程，除了在《劳作与时日》中得到体现外，也在我们这个文本的一些章节，特别是那些描绘赫西奥德形象的部分中得到了反映。在《竞赛》中，总是赫西奥德提出问题，荷马则成功作答并得到公众的普遍认可。例如，在荷马回答完第一回合的问题后，我们读到：

> 据说，当这些诗句得到吟咏后，它们是如此令希腊人惊异，以至于被称为"黄金的"，而且甚至在今天所有人在公共献祭时

9　本文引用的《劳作与时日》原文及译文皆出自Most (2006)。（凡遇巴西诺在正文中同时引用古典文献的原文和英译文时，除《竞赛》以外，中译文直接从巴西诺使用的英译文译出，下同。此处英译文为散文体，中译文保留。——译者按）

10　学者们已经指出，赫西奥德在这段话中对英雄史诗传统表现出了竞争的态度，而在卡尔基斯竞赛故事中，荷马被呈现为英雄史诗的卓越代表。通过展示对最佳航海时机的认识，赫西奥德将自己与那些在从奥利斯航向特洛伊之前必须等待的史诗英雄们区分开来。不仅如此，通过与英雄史诗形成对比，带有史诗饰词καλιγύναιξ和ἱερή的程式化用语被反转。参见Rosen (1990) 及 Rosen (1997), 478-479, Graziosi (2002), 169-170。

也还要于进餐和奠酒前念诵。

——《竞赛》第90—94行 [11]

荷马的成功促使赫西奥德提出更难的问题。因此，他转向了更复杂也更精彩的提问形式：

> 赫西奥德对荷马的成功感到不快，他开始提出难解的谜题……

——《竞赛》第94—95行

之后，赫西奥德又转向一种更复杂的诗歌比赛，即所谓"模棱两可的主题"，这一点将在下文讨论。最后，出于嫉妒（φθονῶν），他向荷马提出了哲学问题：

> 因为荷马在所有问题上都占了上风，嫉妒不已的赫西奥德又说道……

——《竞赛》第149—150行

对手的成功是赫西奥德创造越来越难的诗歌挑战的主要动力，再加上对赫西奥德本人性格的刻画，这些元素让人想起《劳作与时日》对诗歌事业的描述。在距离诗歌开篇不远处，赫西奥德做出了著名的论断：

> ……而这位纷争女神对凡人有益。陶工向陶工生气，建筑工对建筑工生气，乞丐嫉妒乞丐，诗人嫉妒诗人。

——《劳作与时日》第24—26行

这段赫西奥德诗篇将 φθόνος 视作古风诗歌竞争中的重要元素。总体

11　本文使用的《竞赛》文本和翻译都出自笔者本人。（中译文采用了译者参与完成的新汉译版本，见本辑第3—25页——译者按）

而言，φθονῶν在《竞赛》第149行的出现反映了这一元素对史诗诗人而言具有的核心地位。与此同时，《竞赛》作者完全可能想到了赫西奥德的这段诗篇，并打算明确地引用它：《竞赛》的故事背景可能正来自对赫西奥德诗篇的深入解读，后者为读者留下了解释空间。在《劳作与时日》中，φθόνος与鼓励创造力和自我提升的"好的纷争女神"相关。因此，我们可以认为赫西奥德是在按照他自己的教导行事，因为他不断地受到对手成功的刺激，故而精益求精[12]。然而，在《竞赛》中，这种做法与荷马在整场竞赛中平静而成功的态度形成鲜明对比。读者可能会思考：当赫西奥德与荷马竞赛时，他是否正在赋予φθόνος消极的内涵，以此来质疑他自己的φθόνος概念？[13]

　　竞赛不仅对史诗诗人来说至关重要，对史诗的传统表演者即游吟诗人也是如此。正如柯林斯（Collins）所言[14]，《竞赛》中的诗句问答让我们了解到老练的游吟诗人在表演中会采用哪些类型的技巧。事实上，阿尔基达马斯——他在别处（《论智术师》第14章）表现出了对同时代游吟诗人的兴趣——似乎在这里"操纵着一个游吟诗人的框架"[15]，而《竞赛》中的诗句可能间接反映了游吟诗人实际的诗歌吟诵，正如我们从现存证据中了解到的那样。在泛雅典娜节上，游吟诗人们经常轮流表演，后一位表演者接续前一位表演者的吟诵，恰如荷马和赫西奥德在《竞赛》中所做的。根据柏拉图的解释，这一规则是由希帕科斯（Hipparchus）引入的：

　　　　[希帕科斯]是庇西特拉图（Pisistratus）的儿子中最年长、最聪明的一个，除了他展示的其他许多智慧之举外，他是第一个把荷马史诗带到这片地区的人，他要求泛雅典娜节的游吟诗人们

12　参见Koning (2010), 257-258等。

13　参见Clay (2003), 179关于赫西奥德在这里表现为"糟糕的参赛者"的论述。

14　Collins (2004), 特别是第三部分：*Epic Competition in Performance: Homer and the Rhapsodes* (167-222)。

15　Collins (2004), 189. 在这方面，应当注意《竞赛》中两次将动词ῥαψῳδέω与荷马联系起来使用：ποιήσαντα γὰρ τὸν Μαργίτην Ὅμηρον περιέρχεσθαι κατὰ πόλιν ῥαψῳδοῦντα (55-56："荷马在创作了《马尔吉特斯》后周游各城邦吟诵诗歌"）；ἐκεῖθεν δὲ παραγενόμενος εἰς Κόρινθον ἐρραψῴδει τὰ ποιήματα (286-287："他从那里前往科林斯并吟诵了自己的诗作"）。

轮流、连续地（ἐξ ὑπολήψεως ἐφεξῆς）表演荷马史诗，就像他们现在仍然做的那样。

——柏拉图《希帕科斯》228b5—c1[16]

正如柯林斯指出的那样，这种轮流吟诵可能允许展示各种即兴表演的技巧。表演者可以在下一个游吟诗人不易接续的地方停止朗诵，让对手难以找到与前一行诗或前一个场景能够适当联系的内容，以此构成对他的挑战[17]。我们可以举出《伊利亚特》中的一段来说明柯林斯的论点。狄奥墨得斯刚刚打伤了阿芙洛狄特：

……女神流出不朽的血液——

340　灵液，那是有福的诸神体内流淌的血液，
　　因为他们不吃面包也不喝晶莹的葡萄酒，
　　因此他们没有血，人们称他们为不朽者。

——《伊利亚特》5.339—342[18]

第一行诗声称，女神阿芙洛狄特像一个普通的凡人那样流着真正的血。虽然被定义为ἄμβροτον【不朽】，这种血液仍然形成一个问题，而这个问题接下来由下一行的跨行连续（enjambment）解决。我们被告知，这不是普通的血液，而是"灵液"（ἰχώρ），一种不同的、不朽的物质。

这个例子与《竞赛》中诗句问答的技巧有明显的相似之处。《竞赛》的第107—137行专门进行"模棱两可的主题"（102—103：ἀμφίβολοι γνῶμαι）的问答，赫西奥德用不合理的、大有问题的主张来挑战荷马，而荷马必须在恢复正常意义的前提下以另一行诗补全上一行。正如上引《伊利亚特》诗行表述了神学上的不妥之处，赫西奥

16　文本和译文来自笔者本人（Bassino [2013]）。
17　注意这类语言游戏和挑战不仅出现在游吟诗人的竞赛中，参看Collins (2004)关于悲剧中的对诗（verse-capping）、喜剧中的轮流对白（stichomythia）和挽歌中的会饮表演的论述。
18　本文所引《伊利亚特》文本来自van Thiel (1996)，译文来自Verity (2011)。

德的诗句或直接或间接地就一些对希腊人来说很重要的问题——例如英雄的行为和诸神的本质——提出了不妥的观点。荷马重新阐述了赫西奥德所表达的不恰当、不受欢迎的观点，并把它们转变为人们普遍持有的价值观。

《竞赛》的这一部分说明了游吟诗人们在传统史诗表演的语境下是如何相互影响的。与此同时，它也代表了分别由游吟诗人和智术师倡导的守旧和创新的史诗路径之间的对立。有学者已经指出，《竞赛》中的挑战内容反映了典型的智术师的关注点[19]。从句法上也可以看出智术师对文本的影响。通常情况下，六音步史诗的诗句（如荷马和赫西奥德史诗中的大部分六音步诗句）在语法上是独立的，表达独立的意义；跨行连续可以扩展这一意义，但很少对前一行的句法造成实质性的改变[20]。在《竞赛》中，赫西奥德的诗句在语法上也是独立的，它们表达了原则上可以设想的主题；但就像《伊利亚特》第5卷关于阿芙洛狄特之血的诗句那样，它们在内容层面上是有问题的。然而，与《伊利亚特》诗行不同的是，这里的不当之处是在句法层面上解决的。荷马的诗句跨行接续了赫西奥德的一个词汇，提出该词需要必要的跨行连接来重新解释它，从而赋予它新的句法结构。结果，每一个内容恰当的意义单元现在都由两行构成，而不是像荷马史诗的惯例那样由一行构成。《竞赛》中特殊的跨行连续用法，以及在散文中十分典型的复杂句法，似乎体现了传统游吟诗人和新的知识潮流之间的互动。

我们可以举几个例子。第113—114行处理的问题可称为对男女两性角色的适当划分：

赫：这个男人的父亲高贵而懦弱

荷：的是他母亲，因战争对所有女人来说都艰难。

——《竞赛》第113—114行

---

[19]　参看Graziosi (2001)［参见本辑第73—95页。——译者按］。

[20]　关于荷马的跨行连续，参看Kirk (1966), Parry (1971), Higbie (1990), Bakker (1990), Clark (1997)等。

赫西奥德对同一个人使用了两个相反的形容词：一位父亲被称为既高贵又懦弱，这是自相矛盾的。于是荷马将第二个形容词 ἀνάλκιδος【懦弱】与一个新的、阴性名词 μητρός【母亲】跨行连接。这个男人现在被称为一个高贵的男人和一个懦弱的母亲的儿子。荷马继续解释道，战争对女人来说是困难的。正如格拉齐奥西（Graziosi）所言，利用 ἄναλκις 既可作为阴性形容词又可作为阳性形容词的特性玩文字游戏，可能反映了公元前5世纪早期对荷马语言的关注[21]。例如，普罗塔戈拉（80 A 28-29 DK）说，《伊利亚特》第一行中的 μῆνιν【愤怒】一词应该是阳性的，尽管荷马把它当作阴性。在《竞赛》的这次问答中，荷马在纠正赫西奥德的语言，同时也改变了他的句法，因为 ἄναλκις 是一个用于女性的形容词[22]。当它应用于荷马史诗中的"高贵者"（ἀγαθὸς ἀνήρ）时，它总是用来责备此人缺乏 ἀλκή【力量】、无力发动战争，这解释了为什么荷马在《竞赛》中更愿意把形容词 ἄναλκις 与赫西奥德诗行里的"高贵者"分隔开[23]。

在另一次问答中，两位诗人分别给出了对神灵不当和恰当的认识的例子：

> 赫：射猎女神阿尔忒弥斯，屈从于婚姻
> 荷：的卡利斯托是她用银弓射杀。
>
> ——《竞赛》第117—118行

作为处女神，阿尔忒弥斯不可能像赫西奥德的诗句说的那样屈从于婚姻。因此，荷马将"屈从于婚姻"（δμήθη γάμῳ）与另一个主语"卡利斯托"（Καλλιστώ）连接起来。这样他便澄清了结婚的不是女神，而是卡利斯托。而由于卡利斯托曾发誓守贞以敬奉阿尔忒弥斯，女神便用箭矢射杀了她。这段对话也可以看作是公元前5世纪智术师对语言的关注的反映。荷马的回答通过在一组对句的两句内重新分

---

21 Graziosi (2001), 67.（参见本辑第86—87页——译者按）

22 例如 *Il.* 5.330 中 ἄναλκις 与阿芙洛狄特连用，以及 5.349-50。

23 也请参看 Kirk (1990), 97。关于 ἄναλκις 作为对战士的责备，并与 ἀπτόλεμος（"不好战的"）连用，见 *Il.* 2.201, 9.35, 9.41。

配单词来解决意义不当的问题，也就是说，将一个假想的逗号从诗行末尾移到 γάμῳ 之后。与此类似，德谟克利特的一个残篇（68 B 22 DK）论及荷马史诗中可选的各种断句方式[24]。因此，《竞赛》的这一部分展示了创作这些诗句的游吟诗人如何与新的知识发展进行建设性的对话，并发挥荷马史诗传统所固有的可能性——例如跨行连续——来回应智术师的挑战。

《竞赛》至少反映了史诗传统的三个不同方面，其中每一个都是由建设性的竞争所塑造的。这些方面包括：古风时期的主要诗歌的创作，如《劳作与时日》所示；吟诵诗歌片段的竞赛，游吟诗人们在竞赛中依次表演；古典时期新的知识发展与恢复传统史诗价值之间的竞赛。

作为史诗主题的斗争

在比赛末尾，当荷马完美地回答了赫西奥德提出的所有问题后，帕诺伊德斯国王要求两位诗人表演各自的诗作中自认为最出色的篇章（178）。对这些篇章所属作品的选择，对篇章本身的选择，以及最后的裁决，这三项选择都有效地建立并发展了诗歌中战争与和平、伦理与审美之间的对比。赫西奥德选择了《劳作与时日》第383—392行作为他最出色的篇章，这一段是农夫历法的开头部分：

> 阿特拉斯生养的普勒阿得斯在天空升起时
> 你要开始收割，她们落下时要开始耕种；
> 她们确实隐藏了四十个日日夜夜。
> 一年周而复始后，她们再次露面，
> 那时首先要做的是把铁农具磨砺。
> 这是平原的规律，对那些在海洋
> 附近居住者如此，对居住在远离

---

[24] Graziosi (2001), 66-67.（参见本辑第86页——译者按）

> 汹涌的海洋、土地肥沃的幽谷者
> 也如此。要光着身子耕耘、播种
> 和收获，每当万物合乎时令之时。
>
> ——《竞赛》第180—189行

荷马则通过缀合《伊利亚特》第13卷中的两个段落（126—133和339—344）描绘了一幅战斗场景：

> 强大的战阵在两个埃阿斯周围布起，
> 哪怕阿瑞斯或催人作战的雅典娜来了
> 也无可挑剔。被选出的最好的战士
> 等待着特洛伊人和神样的赫克托尔，
> 用长矛围着长矛，大盾连着大盾，
> 圆盾抵圆盾，头盔顶头盔，人挨人，
> 只要身子一倾，马鬃战盔的闪耀尖顶
> 便会相触；他们就这样互相依凭而立。
> 令人丧命的战场上长枪林立，
> 这些刺人的尖枪皆由他们手持。
> 耀眼的头盔、新擦的甲胄和闪亮的盾牌
> 发出铜色的光芒，亮光一同发来
> 令人目眩。谁若见此苦战不生哀叹
> 反倒欣喜，那可真是一副铁石心肠。
>
> ——《竞赛》第191—204行

在此之前，《竞赛》未提及《劳作与时日》和《伊利亚特》，而且从头到尾都没有谈及最出色的篇章来自这两部作品的事实[25]。但是，与保持竞赛情节所处的松散故事框架的前后一致相比，选择《劳作与时日》和《伊利亚特》作为诗人最出色篇章出处的叙事原因更为重要：选

25　文本声称荷马在竞赛结束后创作了《伊利亚特》和《奥德赛》（275—276），但从未提到赫西奥德的任何作品。

择这两部作品使《竞赛》能够处理并展开荷马和赫西奥德之间的传统对立，这种对立基于他们不同的诗歌主题，即战争与和平。这种对立在公元前5世纪就已形成。例如，阿里斯托芬就是这样描述两位诗人的：

> 赫西奥德谈论农业、作物的季节与耕种。如果不是在男人的战术、美德和武器方面给予良好的指导，神样的荷马还会在哪里获得尊敬和名声呢？
>
> ——阿里斯托芬《蛙》第1033—1036行[26]

为赫西奥德从《劳作与时日》选出一段，这个选择的理由是显而易见的。如前所述，正是在这部作品的第648—662行，赫西奥德做出了著名的宣告，即他在诗歌竞赛中的胜利。因此，在许多方面，选择《劳作与时日》第383—392行都是最适合文本语境的。在总体层面上，正如科宁（Koning）观察到的那样，《劳作与时日》中的这段话"独一无二地强调了赫西奥德热爱和平的农民诗人形象；在他的作品中很难找到另一段如此宁静祥和的文字"[27]。事实上，从《劳作与时日》中与佩尔塞斯（Perses）的争吵，到《神谱》中众神之间的斗争，赫西奥德作品中有不少涉及争斗的段落。然而，《竞赛》避免提及这类材料。事实上，恰好在提到诗人与他"愚蠢"的弟弟佩尔塞斯的争吵之前，赫西奥德的表演停止了。在那段争吵中，佩尔塞斯被警告不要再去他兄长家里乞求，因为后者不愿再给他任何帮助[28]。因此，《竞赛》

26　文本和译文来自Henderson (2002)。关于《蛙》和《竞赛》的关系，见下文注39。Graziosi (2002), 168—184和Koning (2010), 269—284讨论了其他的相关材料。

27　Koning (2010), 252.

28　《竞赛》似乎特意调整了赫西奥德的文本，略去了对佩尔塞斯的责备。《竞赛》中对赫西奥德的引用到 γυμνόν τ' ἀμάειν , ὅτ' ἂν ὥρια πάντα πέλωνται 就停止了，而在《劳作与时日》里，诗篇继续如下：γυμνόν δ' ἀμάειν , εἴ χ' ὥρια πάντ' ἐθέλησθα | ἔργα κομίζεσθαι Δήμητερος , ὥς τοι ἕκαστα | ὥρι' ἀέξηται , μή πως τὰ μέταζε χατίζων | πτώσσης ἀλλοτρίους οἴκους καὶ μηδὲν ἀνύσσεις - | ὡς καὶ νῦν ἐπ' ἔμ' ἤλθες· ἐγὼ δέ τοι οὐκ ἐπιδώσω | οὐδ' ἐπιμετρήσω· ἐργάζεο , νήπιε Πέρση...【光着身子收获，如果你想合乎时令地照顾好所有德墨忒尔的劳作，使每一棵庄稼都应季为你生长，免得你以后有需要时像乞丐一样到别人家去而一无所获——就像现在你到我这里来一样。但我不会再给你，也不会再量取东西给你。劳作吧，愚蠢的佩尔塞斯……】

的选段将赫西奥德诗歌的核心呈现为对普勒阿得斯——昴星团周期性升起的描述，这一星宿每年都以同样的方式指导人们进行农业生产。韦斯特（West）提出，在一个所谓的"原始"版本的竞赛故事中，赫西奥德可能会表演比《竞赛》中更长的选段，或许对佩尔塞斯的责备也会包含在内[29]。但是，撇开是否曾有其他版本流传这一问题不谈，关键是要注意，根据我们现有的《竞赛》文本，赫西奥德诗歌的核心是《劳作与时日》的第381—392行，其中不包括与佩尔塞斯的冲突；这个选段是为了适应这个版本的故事而精心剪裁的。《竞赛》的选择对赫西奥德来说极其合适，这一点可以从其他古代材料对这些诗行伦理价值的强调看出，这也令这些诗行与最后的裁决尤为相称。根据竞赛的裁决，赫西奥德获胜是正当的（208：δίκαιον），因为他歌唱和平和农业；而据《劳作与时日》第381—382行的古注，这些诗行鼓励农业生活和由此产生的正当（δίκαιον）收入[30]。

作为突出前述战争与和平对比的手段，当我们把荷马和赫西奥德选择的这两段文字放在一起对读时，这种选择的恰当性便显露无遗[31]。它们在一些细节上相互回应，这些细节在一种语境下被用作和平的象征，而在另一种语境下被用作描述战争的手段。两段诗篇都从非人类实体的形象展示开始，然后再聚焦于人类：赫西奥德提到调节农业生产周期的普勒阿得斯（180），而荷马则提到阿瑞斯和雅典娜两位神灵对战斗场面的喜悦（192—193）。赫西奥德笔下的人类为了确保生计而劳作，而荷马笔下的战士们则在"令人丧命的战场"（199：μάχη φθισίμβροτος）上奋战。在赫西奥德的诗篇中，铁器被磨砺以备收割（184），但荷马史诗中的ταμεσίχροας（200："刺人"）表明，金属在其他情况下可以成为致命的工具[32]。赫西奥德笔下的人类

29　West (1967): 442 n. 3.（参见本辑第43页注42——译者按）

30　Σ *Op*. 381–382 Pertusi: τὰ δὲ ῥηθησόμενα τῶν μὲν κακοπραγιῶν ἀπάγει τὸν ἀκροατήν, ἄγει δὲ ἐπὶ τὸν γεωργικὸν βίον καὶ τὸν ἐκ τούτου δίκαιον πόρον.【我的译文："将要讲述的内容使听众远离错误的行为，并使［他］更接近农业生活和由此产生的正当收入"】

31　关于这一点也请参看Hunter (2009), (2014), 302–315; Koning (2010), 253。

32　荷马的"刺人的尖枪"（199—200）不会是铁制成的，而是由铜制成的（在第201行处提到，与头盔、甲胄和盾牌相关）。但这两段诗篇相互关联之处在于提出了两种截然相反的活动，一种是生产性的，一种是破坏性的，人类在两种活动中都可以使用磨砺过的金属。值得注意的是，文本进行这种对比的方式是提到两种金属，而这两种金属对（转下页）

是赤身裸体的，这一点被强调并反复提及，而荷马史诗中的英雄则身披甲胄。荷马史诗中"手持长枪"的战斗画面（199—200：ἔφριξεν δὲ μάχη φθισίμβροτος ἐγχείησι | μακραῖς）让人回想起赫西奥德笔下的农田画面，也回应了赫西奥德最出色篇章中关于收割的文字。

与赫西奥德的诗歌表演一样，有人提出了"原始版本"的荷马表演是否比这里的表演更长的问题，特别是由于《竞赛》将《伊利亚特》第13卷中的两段诗篇拼接在一起，而这两段诗之间有大约200行的间隔，它们可能会被包含在《竞赛》的原材料或其他故事版本之中[33]。但在这一案例中，我们同样应该注意，无论有什么其他可能的版本流传，《竞赛》都将荷马史诗的核心定为现有的选段。我认为，被定为荷马最出色篇章的诗句之所以呈现为我们看到的模样，是为了向我们提供一种探索缪斯、诗人和听众之间关系的手段：诗人让听众分享神圣的目光，观看他们的人性在现实中不会选择目睹的事物——战争和死亡的景象。在荷马的诗篇中，我们看到了有关战争的两种视角——神灵的视角与人类的视角之间的细致比较。在开头的几行里，诸神被描述为享受战斗场面的看客（191—193）。在第二部分里，一个身处其中观看这一景象的凡人会有完全不同的反应：并非铁石心肠的人无法对此感到欣喜，因为对人类（包括人类观众和那些正在战斗的人）来说，战争意味着死亡（203—204），只有神——或聆听相关描述的荷马听众——才能享受它[34]。事实上，《竞赛》中的公众声称这些诗句是"异乎寻常"的：

> 希腊人在这一回合感到惊异，他们对荷马赞叹不已，因为这些诗行异乎寻常。他们又要求将胜利授予荷马。
>
> ——《竞赛》第205—207行

（接上页）两位诗人特别重要，是他们各自诗歌的代表：如上所述，铜是荷马史诗中制造武器所用的金属；铁在赫西奥德的《劳作与时日》中则标志着人类辛苦劳作的当代（174—201）。

33　Nietzsche (1870), 528-532提出了这一观点。

34　恰如Janko (1992), 89在他对《伊利亚特》这一段的评注中指出的那样，"假若我们亲眼观看这一场景，我们是无法像享受这段描述一样享受它的"。

这一场景的内部观众和外部观众的差异在于,前者完全冒着生命危险,而后者则身处安全的位置,并因此得以享受从壮丽场景中获得的审美愉悦——恰如阿瑞斯和雅典娜那样。经由诗人的中介,外部观众的地位达到诸神的地位。不仅如此,这段描述的力量强烈地冲击着读者的感情,致使他们接下来对自己在史诗表演中听到的内容进行反思。为了让这种反思成为对人性和苦难的有效反思,而不至于越界进入个人悲剧的领域,超脱是必不可少的[35]。

荷马史诗能够让人类安全地观看并体验斗争,从而让他们分享神灵的视角。通过把这一能力放在荷马史诗的中心位置,《竞赛》实际上是在对荷马史诗本身进行敏锐的解读。最近的研究表明,化听众为观众的能力是荷马诗歌的重要特征,而且这一特征在古代就已得到认可[36]。在造成这种变化的众多诗句中,《竞赛》里的诗行只是其中一例。例如,第17卷也有神对战争场景的反应,其中雅典娜和阿瑞斯被呈现为类似的战争场面的观众,而且与《竞赛》选段场景一模一样的是,他们对眼前的野蛮争斗毫无怨言:

> ……如此野蛮的一场鏖战围绕他
> 展开,不论催人作战的阿瑞斯或雅典娜
> 看了都无可挑剔,更不会对此大发雷霆。
>
> ——《伊利亚特》第17卷第397—399行

下面这段甚至更为相关:

> 那时再不会有参战之人对战事进行挑剔,
> 540　不会有未受箭矢与锋利铜剑伤害的人
> 走动在战场中央,帕拉斯雅典娜
> 携手引领,保卫他免受矢石攻击;
> 因为那日有那么多特洛伊人和阿凯亚人

35　这一点参见 Macleod (1983)。

36　特别要参考 Graziosi/Haubold (2010), 1–8; Clay (2011), 1–37。

相挨着摊开四肢,面朝下倒在尘土里。

——《伊利亚特》第 4 卷第 539—544 行

一个在神灵保护下进入战场的人将会享受战事的景象。《竞赛》中的选段阐明了对斗争的呈现和体验之间的区别——这种区别在几个世纪里一直很重要。尤斯塔提奥斯在注释上述段落时评论道,在安全的情况下观看战斗场面的人就是那些聆听诗人表演的公众:

> 这类观众会是那些聆听诗人的人,那些与战争的罪恶毫无关系,而是在脑海中欣赏战争叙述的壮美景象的人,他们游荡在战场上时也是安全的。
> ——欧斯塔提奥斯(Eustathius)《伊利亚特评注》506.6—8[37]

从根本上说,欧斯塔提奥斯这段话中的观众与《竞赛》中聆听荷马的听众处境相同;荷马扮演雅典娜的角色,牵着听众的手,带领他们穿越他们在其他情况下无法享受的地带[38]。

文本强调荷马而非赫西奥德的诗歌受到神的启示,因为它让听众体验到了诸神才能享受的事物。但在这之后,文本将胜利授予了赫西奥德:

> 希腊人在这一回合感到惊异,他们对荷马赞叹不已,因为这

---

[37] 文本来自 van der Valk (1971),笔者自译。

[38] 在《竞赛》最出色的篇章中,还有一处暗示了荷马独有的与神灵之间的联系,而且也与观看战争场面的可能性有关:尽管兵器的"亮光一同发来令人目眩"(200—201),荷马仍然能够观看战场并为我们描述它。古代荷马传记中的一段话明确将荷马的特殊视力表现为缪斯的礼物:ἐλθόντα γὰρ ἐπὶ τὸν Ἀχιλλέως τάφον εὔξασθαι θεάσασθαι τὸν ἥρωα τοιοῦτον ὁποῖος προῆλθεν ἐπὶ τὴν μάχην τοῖς δευτέροις ὅπλοις κεκοσμημένος· ὀφθέντος δὲ αὐτῷ τοῦ Ἀχιλλέως τυφλωθῆναι τὸν Ὅμηρον ὑπὸ τῆς τῶν ὅπλων αὐγῆς. ἐλεηθέντα δὲ ὑπὸ Θέτιδος καὶ Μουσῶν τιμηθῆναι πρὸς αὐτῶν τῇ ποιητικῇ.【当他来到阿基琉斯墓前时,他祈求能看到英雄身着第二套盔甲走上战场时的样子。当他看到阿基琉斯时,荷马被他的盔甲的光芒刺瞎了眼睛;但忒提斯和缪斯怜悯他,用诗歌作为礼物来荣耀他】(佚名《荷马传》6.5;文本和翻译来自 Bassino [2013])因此,荷马仰赖于缪斯才能在第 18 卷看到并为我们描述阿基琉斯的盔甲,第 13 卷的战斗亦然。在整篇《竞赛》中荷马都作为一位神启的诗人出现,其中我们两次看到程式化短语 θεῖος Ὅμηρος【神样的荷马】(第 309、338 行)。

些诗行异乎寻常，他们还要求将胜利授予荷马。国王却授予赫西奥德桂冠，宣称让提倡劳作与和平之人，而非细述战争和杀戮之人获胜才是正当的。

——《竞赛》第205—207行

帕诺伊德斯有争议的判决代表了文学批评的一种形式；更具体地说，它涉及一个复杂的问题，即我们应该根据诗歌的审美价值还是伦理价值来判断诗歌[39]。帕诺伊德斯决定重视农业与和平而非战争，从伦理的角度来看，很难不同意他的观点。但是，听众给出了审美的判决：他们考虑到了诗歌产生的 θαῦμα，通过分享神灵对人类有死性——亦即人类的杀戮——的注视得到的"惊异"。在赫西奥德的诗篇中没有任何内容可以产生这种反应；他的诗句描述了一个人类观众可以自行观看的东西，不需要神圣的指导或保护，也不会引发愉悦和恐惧的混合，而这正是荷马诗篇的伟大之处。诗人没有必要评论季节的固定周期并使其成为一首诗的对象，除非有两起斗争分别提供了适宜的场合：在赫西奥德诗歌中，由于兄弟之间的不和，加以佩尔塞斯无力完成应做之事，指导是必要的；在《竞赛》中，这段诗篇被吟诵则是由于诗人之间的斗争。事实上，帕诺伊德斯支持和平的判决会引发分歧，因为它与普遍的共识相悖[40]。从根本上说，《竞赛》

---

[39] 关于诗歌应该基于审美价值还是伦理价值来评判的争论，至少可以追溯到公元前5世纪，它也是"西方传统现存最早的一篇持续性的文学批评"（Sommerstein [1996]，14）的核心内容，亦即埃斯库罗斯和欧里庇得斯在阿里斯托芬《蛙》中的竞赛。在这部剧中，狄奥尼索斯做出了著名的选择，胜者是埃斯库罗斯，理由是他能够在雅典的困难时期为城邦提供有用的建议。这与荷马和赫西奥德的竞赛有着惊人的相似之处：两场竞赛都是以对共同体有利的诗人取胜而告终。然而，要想揭开这两段故事之间的正确关系并不容易。荷马与赫西奥德竞赛的传统肯定在阿里斯托芬的时代已经流传开来，而最后的裁决也必定偏向赫西奥德。因此，阿里斯托芬可能受到两个伟大史诗诗人之间竞赛的传统的启发。但帕诺伊德斯的形象在公元前3世纪（P. Petr. I 25 [1]）之前缺乏证据，因此不可能明确阿里斯托芬知道的是哪个版本的最后裁决。参见 Heldmann (1982)，O'Sullivan (1992), Sommerstein (1996), Cavalli (1999), Rosen (2004)。（参见本辑第116—145页——译者按）

[40] 在这里，《竞赛》似乎也从荷马史诗中获得了灵感。正如 Elmer (2013), 220 所指出的那样，整个情节"精心化用了《伊利亚特》对共识以及共识的不满的描述"：它回顾了《伊利亚特》的开幕集会，一个"不正义的例子、对社会规范的违反"，在集会上阿伽门农王"违背了集体意愿，支持自己的倾向"。

似乎暗示，虽然真正的艺术的目的在于创造和平与共识，但正如荷马的表演和公众一致的正面反应所体现的那样，支持和平作为艺术的对象破坏了审美上的欣赏。

征引书目[*]

Allen, T. W. (ed.) 1912. *Homeri Opera V: Hymnos Cyclum Fragmenta Margiten Batrachomyomachian Vitas Continens*. Oxford.

Bakker , E. J. 1990. "Homeric discourse and enjambment: a cognitive approach", *TAPhA* 120: 1–21.

Bassino, P. 2012. "*Certamen Homeri et Hesiodi*: nuovi spunti per una riconsiderazione delle testimonianze papiracee", *ZPE* 180: 38–42.

—. 2013. "Homer: A Guide to Selected Sources", *Living Poets* (Durham), http:// livingpoets.dur.ac.uk/w/Homer:_A_ Guide_to_Selected_Sources.

Beecroft, A. J. 2010. *Authorship and Cultural Identity in Early Greece and China: Patterns of Literary Circulation*. Cambridge.

Canevaro, L. G. 2017. "Fraternal Conflict in Hesiod's *Works and Days*", in P. Bassino, L. G. Canevaro, B. Graziosi (eds) *Conflict and Consensus in Early Greek Hexameter Poetry*. Cambridge, pp. 173–189.

Cavalli, M. 1999. "Le Rane di Aristofane: modelli tradizionali dell'agone fra Eschilo ed Euripide", in F. Conca (ed.) 1999. *Ricordando Raff aele Cantarella*. Milan, pp. 83–105.

Clark, M. 1997. *Out of Line: Homeric Composition beyond the Hexameter*. Lanham, MD.

Clay, J. S. 2003. *Hesiod's Cosmos*. Cambridge.

—. 2011. *Homer's Trojan Theater: Space, Vision, and Memory in the Iliad*. Cambridge.

Collins, D. 2004. *Master of the Game: Competition and Performance in Greek Poetry*. Cambridge, MA.

Debiasi, A. 2012. "Homer ἀγωνιστής in Chalcis", in F. Montanari, A. Rengakos, and C. Tsagalis (eds) 2009. *Brill's Companion to Hesiod*. Leiden, pp. 471–500.

Elmer, D. F. 2013. *The Poetics of Consent: Collective Decision Making and the*

---

[*] 以下书目根据作者在本文脚注中征引的文献，从全书的"征引书目"中提取出来，以便读者查阅。——译者注

Iliad. Baltimore.

Fryde, E. B. 1996. *Greek Manuscripts in the Private Library of the Medici, 1469–1510*, vol. II. Aberystwyth.

Graziosi, B. 2001. "Competition in wisdom", in F. Budelmann and T. R. Phillips (eds) in press. *Textual Events: Performance and the Lyric in Early Greece*. Oxford, pp. 57–74.

——. 2002. *Inventing Homer: The Early Reception of Epic*. Cambridge.

Graziosi, B. and Haubold, J. (eds) 2010. *Homer: Iliad Book VI*. Cambridge.

Heldmann, K. 1982. *Die Niederlage Homers im Dichterwettstreit mit Hesiod*. Göttingen.

Henderson, J. (ed.) 2002. *Aristophanes: Frogs. Assemblywomen. Wealth*. Cambridge, MA.

Higbie, C. 1990. *Measure and Music: Enjambement and Sentence Structure in the Iliad*. Oxford.

Hunter, R. 2009. "Hesiod's style: towards an ancient analysis", in F. Montanari, A. Rengakos, and C. Tsagalis (eds) 2009. *Brill's Companion to Hesiod*. Leiden, pp. 253–269.

——. 2014. *Hesiodic Voices: Studies in the Ancient Reception of Hesiod's* Works and Days. Cambridge.

Janko, R. 1992. *The Iliad: A Commentary*, vol. IV: *Books 13–16*. Cambridge.

Kirk, G. S. 1966. "Studies in some technical aspects of Homeric style", *YClS* 20: 73–152.

——. 1990. *The Iliad: A Commentary*, vol. II: *Books 5–8*. Cambridge.

Kivilo, M. 2000. "Certamen", *Studia Humaniora Tartuensia* 1: 1–5.

——. 2010. *Early Greek Poets' Lives: The Shaping of the Tradition*. Leiden.

Koning, H. H. 2010. *Hesiod: The Other Poet. Ancient Reception of a Cultural Icon*. Leiden.

Latacz, J. 2014. "On Nietzsche's philological beginnings", in A. K. Jensen and H. Heit (eds) *Nietzsche as a Scholar of Antiquity*. London, pp. 3–26.

Macleod, C. 1983. "Homer on poetry and the poetry of Homer", in B. Collins, (ed.). *Collected Essays*, Oxford, pp. 1–15.

Mahaffy, J. P. 1891. *The Flinders Petrie Papyri with Transcriptions, Commentaries and Index*. Dublin.

Most, G. W. (ed.) 2006. *Hesiod: Theogony. Works and Days. Testimonia*. Cambridge, MA.

Nietzsche, F. 1870. "Der Florentinische Tractat über Homer und Hesiod, ihr Geschlecht und ihren Wettkampf, 1–2", *RhM* 25: 528–540.

——. 1871. "Certamen quod dicitur Homeri et Hesiodi: e codice florentino post

Henricum Stephanum denuo edidit Fridericus Nietzsche Numburgensis", *Acta societatis philologae Lipsiensis* 1: 1–23.

O'Sullivan, N. 1992. *Alcidamas, Aristophanes and the Beginnings of Greek Stylistic Theory*. Stuttgart.

Parry, M. 1971. *The Making of Homeric Verse: The Collected Papers of Milman Parry, ed. A. Parry*. Oxford.

Rosen, R. M. 1990. "Poetry and sailing in Hesiod's *Works and Days*", *ClAnt* 9 (1): 99–113.

—. 1997. "Homer and Hesiod", in I. Morris and B. Powell (eds) 1997. *A New Companion to Homer*. Leiden, pp. 463–488.

—. 2004. "Aristophanes" *Frogs* and the *Contest of Homer and Hesiod*", *TAPhA* 134 (2): 295–322.

Sommerstein, A. 1996. *Aristophanes: Frogs*. Warminster.

van der Valk, M. (ed.) 1971. *Eustathii Archiepiscopi Thessalonicensis Commentarii ad Homeri Iliadem Pertinentes*, vol. I. Leiden.

van Thiel, H. (ed.) 1996. *Homeri Ilias*. Hildesheim.

Verity, A. (transl.) 2011. *Homer: The Iliad*. Oxford.

West, M. L. 1967. "The contest of Homer and Hesiod", *CQ* 17 (2): 433–450.

Winter, J. G. 1925. "A new fragment on the life of Homer", *TAPhA* 56: 120–129.

（译者单位：复旦大学历史学系在读博士生）

阿里斯托芬的《蛙》与《荷马与赫西奥德的竞赛》*

拉尔夫·罗森

（段盛雅 译）

献给 W. 杰弗里·阿诺特

阿里斯托芬的《蛙》引发了不少疑问，其中有一个问题最经久不衰，阐释影响极为广泛：戏剧结尾，为什么狄奥尼索斯决意带埃斯库罗斯返回雅典，而不是欧里庇得斯？狄奥尼索斯在戏剧开场昭然宣告，当他在船上读《安德洛墨达》（Andromeda）时（52—54［指《蛙》的行数——译者按］）对欧里庇得斯产生了一股强烈的"渴望"（53 πόθος），决定从冥府复活这位诗人，而非埃斯库罗斯。这之后的情节便是众所周知的了：当狄奥尼索斯到达冥府，他遇到了埃斯库罗斯和欧里庇得斯，发现就连冥府里也在争论谁才是更好的诗人，最终狄奥尼索斯为两人耗时已久的诗歌竞赛做了裁定。狄奥尼索斯评判诗人价值的标准从单纯的愉悦最终变为他们将如何拯救厌战、政治动荡的雅典城邦。当狄奥尼索斯将选择置于这样的框架中时，他觉得

* Ralph M. Rosen, "Aristophanes' *Frogs* and the *Contest of Homer and Hesiod*", *Transactions of the American Philological Association*. Vol. 134 (2014), pp. 295–322.（文中所涉希腊文引文，凡出自《论荷马与赫西奥德及其世系与他们的竞赛》皆取汉译统合稿，其余为译者自译——译者按）

必须选埃斯库罗斯而不是欧里庇得斯[1]。

近来许多学者主张,戏剧的结局反映出狄奥尼索斯从一个不负责任的享乐主义者成长为一个更成熟的、关心城邦事务的文化批评家(因此暗示阿里斯托芬支持埃斯库罗斯而非欧里庇得斯)[2],无论是否如此,人们都会同意竞赛的结果揭示了那个时代对诗人与观众间关系的复杂讨论。戏剧结尾,观众不仅必须消化狄奥尼索斯出人意料的决定,还有它在这一讨论的语境中更重大的意义。从始至终,一直存在一个简单的问题:阿里斯托芬真的只是希望我们认为埃斯库罗斯是一位比欧里庇得斯更优秀的诗人——在当时动荡的局势下对城邦更有益,更擅长为他的观众提供道德教诲——而欧里庇得斯创作的则是危害社会,甚至是不道德的戏剧?

虽然对这个问题没有完全达成共识,但大多数批评家觉得阿里斯托芬本人严肃地认为埃斯库罗斯和欧里庇得斯这样的诗人给观众提供了实际的道德劝诫,《蛙》的结尾积极倡导“埃斯库罗斯式的”而非“欧里庇得斯式的”生活方式[3]。戏剧结尾狄奥尼索斯出人意料的决定通常被视为这一道德轨迹发展的高潮。在本研究中我将试图证明,《蛙》的结尾在相当程度上比人们通常以为的更精妙,它实现了美学洞见与互文性意趣的奇妙结合,从根本上减轻了阿里斯托芬笔下埃斯库罗斯和欧里庇得斯长久以来被迫背负的教化负担。我提出这一观点是基于《蛙》与另一篇文学文本《荷马与赫西奥德的竞赛》(*Certamen Homeri et Hesiodi*)之间的关系,其主要内容也是一场备受瞩目的诗歌竞赛[4]。《竞赛》,或者更准确地说是一部与现存《竞

---

1 关于阿里斯托芬创作《蛙》时雅典的历史背景,见 Dover, 69–76 和 Sommerstein (1996), 1–9。人们常常注意到(如 MacDowell, 297),狄奥尼索斯宣称他决定复活埃斯库罗斯仍然是出于一种基本的享乐主义(他选择了“我的灵魂所喜爱的那个”,1468),但这只是在每位诗人都回答了他最后的政治问题以后,他觉得要赶快定下一个决策标准。对剧末狄奥尼索斯的举动有何意义的讨论见本文第三部分。

2 对这一观点有很多不同的演绎。例如,Bierl, 27–44, 尤见 41–43; Padilla, Bowie, 352(他视狄奥尼索斯的发展变化为一种厄琉西斯的过渡仪式); Sommerstein (1996), 18(“他的经历可以看作引导他……理解并内化戏剧的公众意义”),以及 Lada-Richards 在她对《蛙》中狄奥尼索斯和酒神元素的研究中,表明(9)“狄奥尼索斯旅程的不同阶段……是对神最初的降临以及在神话中融入雅典城邦的戏剧性重演”。

3 近期的讨论有 Hubbard, 213–219 和 von Möllendorff。

4 《竞赛》的希腊文本引自 Allen 的版本,《蛙》引自 Dover 的版本。

赛》非常相似的作品[5]，或许是《蛙》中竞赛（agōn）的样板。这一观点多年来一直被随意提及，但是这层联系对戏剧本身的阐释有何种影响却从未有人充分探究。正如我将在这篇文章中论述的那样，证据表明《竞赛》对《蛙》的影响比过去以为的要更为深刻和广泛，这有可能改变我们对于这部喜剧著名结尾的解读。

一、背景

维拉莫维茨校勘的《荷马与赫西奥德的传记》于1942年被沙德瓦尔特（Wolfgang Schadewaldt）译为德语，当1944年多恩赛夫（Franz Dornseiff）评述这个译本时，他惊讶于竟然从没有人将《竞赛》与《蛙》中的竞赛联系起来。他指出，除了拉德马赫尔（Ludwig Radermacher）曾在他1921年为《蛙》所做的评注本中简要提过这种关联，尚无人充分认识到这两部作品在结构和主题上惊人的相似性[6]。多恩赛夫在书评所讨论的范围内尽其所能地推进了这个话题，但他的这番讨论似乎并没有在那个时代产生多大影响。黑尔德曼（Konrad Heldmann）在他1982年关于《竞赛》的一本专著中，以多恩赛夫的意见为基础进一步讨论了这两部关于智慧竞赛（agōnes sophias）的文本在结构上的相似之处，但他无法撇开论述重心对《蛙》本身进行更多的讨论[7]。此外，尽管黑尔德曼确实假设了一个或许为阿里斯托芬所知的早期竞赛传统（他称之为"原初竞赛"［Urcertamen］），他认为现存《竞赛》文本中的许多细节都出自后来的异文或修订，因此对《竞赛》

5　文本的年代先后问题见本文第一部分。

6　Dornseiff, 136: "这两部作品结构上非常相似，阿里斯托芬因此捍卫了《竞赛》的传世文本的真实性。"

7　Heldmann指出，基于Plu. *Mor.* 153F-154A的引证，"原初竞赛"大概作于公元前5世纪，和《蛙》一样都是结尾处的谜语比赛决出了竞赛的胜利者。另见Richardson (1981), 2，他在黑尔德曼的专著问世前一年就指出，《蛙》中谜语场景的设置或许能够佐证普鲁塔克在记述中提到的一个早期《竞赛》版本："……阿里斯托芬《蛙》中竞赛的顺序与之类似（首先讨论准备好的选段，然后是政治相关的提问以及谜语解答），如果考虑到其背景是已经存在一个荷马和赫西奥德竞赛的故事，这一情景便会更好理解。"更多讨论请见下文注释25。

演变的考量限制了他对其与《蛙》之间关系的思考。奥沙利文（Neil O'Sullivan）在他1992年的研究《阿尔基达马斯、阿里斯托芬与希腊风格学理论的开端》(*Alcidamas, Aristophanes and the Beginnings of Greek Stylistic Theory*)中也曾指出《竞赛》和《蛙》之间的相似性，但没有对这个话题详细展开[8]。

尽管研究《竞赛》的一些学者对此有过一时的兴趣，认为这部作品曾这样或那样地影响过《蛙》，但他们的著作并没有在《蛙》的主流批评传统中产生太大影响[9]。这个观点值得更彻底的研究，尤其要关注《蛙》与《竞赛》文本（或竞赛传统）可能存在的联系如何能帮助我们理解阿里斯托芬的竞赛，从而更好地理解狄奥尼索斯的决定和埃斯库罗斯的胜利[10]。

人们花了很长时间才确认《蛙》与《竞赛》之间的联系，这当然与两个文本的年代先后问题有关。我们现有的《竞赛》版本无疑是一个2世纪的文本（通过文本一开始提到的哈德良皇帝可以确认，行33)[11]，显然不可能影响到阿里斯托芬。不过很多学者长期以来一直怀疑，这个现存版本反映了一个非常古老的传统。尼采在他1870年至1873年的一系列奠基性文章中勾勒了《竞赛》的早期历史，他认为我们现在最终看到的文本源头上出自阿尔基达马斯的《缪斯集》，

8　比较O'Sullivan, 87 n. 143和95 n. 183。正如下文所述，奥沙利文对公元前5世纪文学和修辞风格学（rhetorical stylistics）的讨论是本文论点的重要背景。Lardinois, 184在讨论《竞赛》中嵌入的荷马式格言（gnōmai）时，也简要地指出了《竞赛》和《蛙》之间的联系。另见Griffith, 189及n. 19。

9　例如最近的两位评注者Dover和Sommerstein都没有注意到这个观点。

10　Cavalli最近朝这一方向迈出了第一步。她认为是《竞赛》影响了《蛙》，尽管她对这一假设内含的年代先后问题的处理有些草率，但她对两个文本之间的具体联系做出了有用的详尽评述。不过，最终她认为《竞赛》对《蛙》的影响基本上是表面的。她写道："阿里斯托芬希望重现他的观众所熟知的古老的智慧主题和表现形式"，但她在《蛙》的最后一个场景中发现了两部作品间巨大的鸿沟，认为阿里斯托芬为建立《蛙》与《竞赛》的关系所付出的努力实际上只是突出了其本质上的无意义，《竞赛》对《蛙》来说，"与当下最紧迫、最真实的需求绝不匹配"。Cavalli关注《蛙》结尾的诗歌-伦理的模糊性是正确的，不过正如我在下面论述的那样，阿里斯托芬似乎发现这种文艺美学的问题在《竞赛》中得到了很好的阐述。Ford, 282也对《竞赛》和《蛙》之间的相似之处做了一些简短的评论。

11　32–34 ὅπερ δὲ ἀκηκόαμεν ἐπὶ τοῦ θειοτάτου αὐτοκράτορος Ἀδριανοῦ εἰρημένον ὑπὸ τῆς Πυθίας περὶ Ὁμήρου, ἐκθησόμεθα.【我们将要阐述的是我们已经在最神圣的皇帝哈德良的时代听说的、皮提亚女祭司所说的关于荷马的语句】

写于公元前4世纪[12]。现在普遍认为，随后几十年里发现的两份纸草证实了尼采的见解。正如奥沙利文所说，这一证据"这样解释最容易，即假设阿尔基达马斯在他的《缪斯集》中写过一个与现存《竞赛》基本内容一致的文本，发现的纸草就是这个文本的一部分"[13]。

阿尔基达马斯生活于公元前4世纪，从时间上看不可能对《蛙》产生影响，所以人们想知道这位智者本人是否在他自己的作品中吸收了更早的竞赛传统。有一些学者已经对这个前阿尔基达马斯传统进行过有力的论证了[14]，我们不必在此重提所有的论述，但其中几个基本观点会对我们接下来的讨论有所帮助。正如通常指出的，《竞赛》中体现的智慧竞赛这一组织原则与早期希腊文化有诸多共通之处，无疑有悠久的传统。这样的竞赛通常都包含智者（sophoi）之间的谜语比赛，就像我们在《竞赛》中看到的那样[15]。的确很难想象阿尔基达马斯不得不自己创造一个荷马与赫西奥德竞赛的故事，毕竟早在很久以前两位诗人就被认为是著名的智者了[16]。荷马和赫西奥德在公元前5世纪代表两种对立的文学风格和矛盾的世界观，奥沙利文对此进行了细致的讨论，这也正是阿尔基达马斯在他自己版本的《竞赛》中着意突出的话题[17]。很可能《竞赛》早已作为象征这种较量

---

[12] 在《竞赛》的结尾处，阿尔基达马斯作为赫西奥德之死的一个细节的来源被简要提及，这一点激起了尼采的兴趣。讨论尼采对《竞赛》的研究见 Porter, 239—241 和 318 n. 164，另见 Mariss, 21—24。

[13] O'Sullivan 64 总结了这一证据，并附上相关书目。O'Sullivan 的观点反映了一种普遍共识，尽管人们应该认识到，自尼采的时代以来，纸草的价值以及阿尔基达马斯是否创作过一部《竞赛》的问题就已是许多争论关心的话题了。如参见 Kirk, West, Koniaris 和 Renehan。另见 Mandilaras 对于最近发现的公元前1世纪纸草残篇的讨论，该残篇保存了《竞赛》中的十四行。

[14] 对此最清晰的阐述见 Richardson (1981)（参见本辑第56—60页。——译者按），他对 West 的观点（这个故事是阿尔基达马斯自己创造的）做出了回应。另见 Vogt, 219-221 以及最近的 Cavalli, 90—92。

[15] 见 Radermacher, 30 和 Griffith, 尤见 188-192。对于这一点，人们有时会引用摩普索斯（Mopsus）和卡尔卡斯（Calchas）的神话（值得注意的是赫西奥德似乎就这一问题亲自创作了一首诗，参见 frr. 278-279 Merkelbach-West）。这一神话有几个不同的版本，但故事都以卡尔卡斯之死结束，他或是死于无法解答摩普索斯的谜语，或是因为摩普索斯答出了卡尔卡斯的谜语，证明了自己是更好的先知。其他版本及来源参见 Gantz, 702。

[16] 赫拉克利特等人提供了充分的证据，证明荷马和赫西奥德早就被誉为智者（尽管赫拉克利特自己拒绝承认他们据说拥有的智慧），参见 frr. 22 B 40, 42, 56, 57, 105, 106 Diels-Kranz。

[17] O'Sullivan, 66—79 以及参见本文第二部分。

的文本出现了,而非出自阿尔基达马斯个人的虚构。最后,值得一提的是我们在阿里斯托芬《和平》(公元前421年)的第1282—1283行找到了现存版本《竞赛》中的两行诗(107—108)。很难理解为何会出现如此简短的引用,但这似乎让我们更容易设想是阿里斯托芬援引了一个早先存在的《竞赛》文本,而不是阿尔基达马斯为了在他的《缪斯集》中重新创作一个竞赛故事,从阿里斯托芬那里挪用了这些诗行[18]。

尽管我们不能确定《竞赛》的早期版本,但是我们似乎很容易在赫西奥德的《劳作与时日》(650—662)中辨别出这个故事的内核,诗人在此处暗示他在卡尔基斯参加了国王安菲达马斯葬礼赛会上的诗歌竞赛[19]。赫西奥德在这次竞赛中得了头奖,虽然他没有在诗中提及对手的名字,但是整段所用语言都被理解为赫西奥德视这次胜利为自己的诗歌风格对荷马史诗的胜利[20]。简言之,现有的证据似乎表明两位史诗诗人间正式竞赛的传统要早于公元前5世纪末《蛙》的创作。

在此对现存《竞赛》的简要概述可以作为接下来的论证的参照点。这部短小的作品(共338行)尽管传统题作"竞赛",事实上是由两位诗人的部分生平经历构成的。作品的开篇讨论他们各自的父母世系以及两人出生先后的问题,然后用最大篇幅呈现了两位诗人在卡尔基斯的竞赛,接着描绘两个人竞赛后的经历,一直到他们过世。整部作品只有不到一半的内容和竞赛本身相关,这一部分以赫西奥德胜过荷马告终。安菲达马斯的儿子伽尼克托尔举行体育和诗歌竞

---

[18]　West, 440—441(参见本辑第39—41页。——译者按)认为这些在阿尔基达马斯文本中重复出现的诗行是在重复他认为当时流行的谜语式的"宴饮游戏"中的一些句子。在West看来,没有任何证据表明阿里斯托芬把他的诗行同荷马和赫西奥德联系在一起,但Richardson, 2(参见本辑第59页。——译者按)对此做了很好的解释,他指出《和平》中的段落突出了两个与《竞赛》紧密相关的主题:在这两个文本中我们都可以找到"对战争诗歌的拒斥和对宴饮的赞美(Cert. 80ff.)"。另见Schadewaldt, 56 和66-67; Compton-Engle, 327-329, 以及Graziosi (2001), 66。

[19]　WD 654-657 ἔνθα δ᾽ ἐγὼν ἐπ᾽ ἄεθλα δαΐφρονος Ἀμφιδάμαντος | Χαλκίδα [τ᾽] εἰσεπέρησα · τὰ δὲ προπεφραδμένα πολλὰ | ἄεθλ᾽ ἔθεσαν παῖδες μεγαλήτορος · ἔνθα μέ φημι | ὕμνῳ νικήσαντα φέρειν τρίποδ᾽ ὠτώεντα. 这个段落对现存竞赛的重要性见 Arrighetti, 168; O'Sullivan, 96-105以及Graziosi (2002),168-174。

[20]　见Nagy, 66; Thalmann, 152-153以及Rosen。

赛来纪念父亲的逝世，荷马和赫西奥德因这一公开邀请来到卡尔基斯，显然他们进行了一场相当精彩的比赛（70—71, ἀμφοτέρων δὲ τῶν ποιητῶν θαυμαστῶς ἀγωνισαμένων,【两位诗人都以非凡技艺参赛】）。然而赫西奥德随后站出来对荷马提出了一系列考题，先问了两个一般性的问题（荷马以自己的诗行来回应），然后是一些本身没有意义的诗行，要求荷马必须补充完整，让其有意义。随后是一些既具体又一般的问题，赫西奥德再次提问，荷马成功地即兴作答。观众们判定荷马获胜（176—177）。但是国王帕诺伊德斯还不想就这样结束比赛，他要求他们两个背诵各自诗作中最出色的段落。观众再一次因荷马而惊异（205—206, θαυμάσαντες...τὸν Ὅμηρον οἱ Ἕλληνες ἐπῄνουν【希腊人在这一回合感到惊异，他们对荷马赞叹不已】），主张他拿奖。然而，接下来的文本是这样的（207—210）：

> ὁ δὲ βασιλεὺς τὸν Ἡσίοδον ἐστεφάνωσεν εἰπὼν δίκαιον εἶναι τὸν ἐπὶ γεωργίαν καὶ εἰρήνην προκαλούμενον νικᾶν, οὐ τὸν πολέμους καὶ σφαγὰς διεξιόντα.
>
> 国王却向赫西奥德授予桂冠，宣称让呼唤劳作与和平之人，而非细述战争和杀戮之人获胜才是正当的。

管他的民众意愿！

这部作品有许多有趣之处，无法在此一一讨论，但显然我们已经可以看出为什么之前的学者怀疑《竞赛》和《蛙》之间有联系。作为典型的智慧竞赛，这两部作品的结构都遵循同一个模式，有两位杰出的智者需要通过自我引用和谜语的双重测试，另有第三人做裁判[21]。《竞赛》中荷马和赫西奥德在国王帕诺伊德斯面前激烈角逐，就像《蛙》里埃斯库罗斯和欧里庇得斯在狄奥尼索斯面前竞争那样。此外，《竞赛》的最后一轮较量，即帕诺伊德斯要求加试一轮参赛者自己的诗行，无疑与《蛙》中最后一个场景十分相似，狄奥尼索斯直到听完两位诗人对阿尔西比亚德斯的评价后才做出决定。正如其他人

---

[21] 其他结构上的相似之处见 Heldmann, 59–63 和 Cavalli, 尤见 93–97。

注意到的那样，诸如此类的联系似乎足以表明阿里斯托芬是以类似于现存《竞赛》的文本作为《蛙》中竞赛的模板，但这种字面上的关联有何意义的问题还没有充分解决。因此，我们在此要关注的问题是，《竞赛》中对荷马和赫西奥德的描绘是否对阿里斯托芬在自己的作品中表现埃斯库罗斯和欧里庇得斯的方式以及如此表现的原因产生过什么具体影响。毫无疑问，这个问题回答起来很复杂，不仅因为我们唯一的《竞赛》文本时间上晚于《蛙》，而且我们首先还要确定荷马与赫西奥德的竞赛对于那个"原本的"作者阿尔基达马斯来说意味着什么，其次要确定这个故事在更早的公元前5世纪的形态中可能有怎样的文化价值。

奥沙利文提出了一个有力的说法，即阿尔基达马斯将他那一版《竞赛》收入自己的作品中，不仅因为它将荷马即兴、口传的风格——这也是阿尔基达马斯自己所采纳的风格，与赫西奥德更谨严、书面的风格相对照，也因为这个文本反映了其他相反的修辞策略之间的关系，他或许会对这些修辞策略感兴趣：比如简明扼要（βραχυλογία）与连篇累牍（μακρολογία），或是"时机"（καιρός）的概念。此外，奥沙利文表明，用荷马和赫西奥德的对立构成风格的两极几乎不可能是阿尔基达马斯自己的发明，而是公元前5世纪智者们的遗产，他们当时就已经开始利用这两位诗人展开自己的文学、教育和修辞方面的论战了 [22]。因此我们可以得出结论，无论诗歌的、伦理的，还是形而上学的，荷马和赫西奥德之间这些支撑着《竞赛》的特定联系，是阿里斯托芬可以利用的，而且更为重要的是他可以把它们视为他在《蛙》中戏剧化的那种文学论争的组成部分。

二、《竞赛》与《蛙》

有了这一背景，我们可以回到最初的问题，狄奥尼索斯在《蛙》中为何改变主意。为什么当我们以为是欧里庇得斯的时候，他却选

22　尤见 O'Sullivan, 66—95。

了埃斯库罗斯？有一个简单但不能带来什么启发的回答，即《竞赛》结尾也有一个类似的出人意料的转变，同样是比赛裁判造成的。尽管荷马整场比赛表现出色且得到观众的普遍支持，帕诺伊德斯在最后一刻强行违背民众的意愿，将胜利授予赫西奥德。从故事本身的上下文来看，他找的借口似乎与我们在《蛙》中两位悲剧家的竞赛里所看到的一样牵强、有失偏颇。事实上，《竞赛》自始至终都传达出这种含混的信息：一开始，赫西奥德掌控全局，暗示叙事"偏爱"他，但当荷马凭才华和谦逊成功应对了所有挑战以后，赫西奥德急躁起来，天平倒向荷马。叙述者两次告诉读者，人们认为荷马是赢家，但帕诺伊德斯决不同意。对于帕诺伊德斯的理由，叙述者没有做出评论，仿佛他也被说服了，认为述说和平的诗人要比描绘战争的诗人更优秀。但问题并没有就此解决，在讨论诗人死亡的结尾部分，正如莱夫科维茨（Mary R. Lefkowitz）所指出的，"这给我们一种印象，两位诗人中赫西奥德稍显逊色，因为作者对荷马着墨更多"[23]。奥沙利文解释道，"……赫西奥德（在竞赛结束之后）三言两语就被打发了，也没有写下更多的诗作……而且《竞赛》中引述的那个出自阿尔基达马斯《缪斯集》的赫西奥德之死是不光彩的"（他被人杀死后扔进了海里）[24]。奥沙利文意识到阿尔基达马斯的困境：他希望荷马成为《竞赛》的主角，但竞赛故事本身源于前面提到的《劳作与时日》中的片段，这规定了赫西奥德才是胜利者。因此，阿尔基达马斯无法改写赫西奥德的胜利，但他至少可以尽力淡化赫西奥德胜利的意义或价值[25]。

我说《竞赛》和《蛙》关系密切的意思是，在阿尔基达马斯之前

---

23 Lefkowitz, 7–8.

24 O'Sullivan, 98.

25 见 Vogt 199 对叙述者的描述："他表现出对荷马特别的喜爱，且似乎更乐意让这位伟大的即兴诗人获胜，但另一方面，他又被竞赛结果的既有传统约束，这一结果以《劳作与时日》第654行及以下为基础。" West, 443（参见本辑第44页。——译者按）对此提出了强烈反驳，但没有太多说服力："得奖的是赫西奥德，而非荷马，说他获胜只是因为裁判的反常，这是行不通的……文中没有任何一个词显示这个决策是不公正的。" 的确，叙述者本人从未明确宣称帕诺伊德斯的裁判是不公正的，但他对荷马夺目的表现表示出的震惊却不难察觉，他还让人们普遍的赞美和帕诺伊德斯对此的否认形成对比，他到底支持哪一方其实并没有什么悬念。见 Graziosi 的讨论（2002），168–184，尤见 173–174。

的《竞赛》中就有一个帕诺伊德斯的形象。这一形象的起源和他在故事中发挥的作用,研究者一直存在一些争议,但一份公元前3世纪的纸草让大多数人确信帕诺伊德斯这个形象出现得相当早,在阿尔基达马斯的版本中就出现过[26]。如果说帕诺伊德斯或这样一个难以捉摸的判官角色比公元前5世纪那个版本的《竞赛》出现得还要早,问题就更复杂了,因为这引发了一个更大的问题——《竞赛》对阿尔基达马斯之前的希腊观众来说意味着什么。比如,他们认为赫西奥德战胜荷马不成问题吗?倘若如此,就不需要一个帕诺伊德斯这样的角色出现,以少数人的决定否定民众的意见,赫西奥德可以直接凭他的诗歌艺术被民众和裁判授予冠军。当然,这总是有可能的,但考虑到竞赛故事的重点其实在于荷马深远持久的文化资产与赫西奥德获胜这一无法回避的事实之间的张力,这种可能性又是微乎其微的。赫西奥德虽然很有地位,但与荷马相比就不算什么了[27]。相反,比赛的结局出现了一个令人兴奋的转折:赫西奥德的胜利是如此成问题,以至于只有像帕诺伊德斯这样出乎意料的局外人,一个显然出离于公众对荷马的态度之外的人才能解释它。事实上,如果不是裁判做出这个出乎意料、不受欢迎的决定,我敢说事实上就不会有《竞赛》这个文本。出于这些原因,阿里斯托芬很可能在公元前5世纪末就知道有帕诺伊德斯这样一个角色了。

现在回到《蛙》中狄奥尼索斯的决定这个问题上:狄奥尼索斯是否只是在扮演帕诺伊德斯的角色?当然,狄奥尼索斯的举动并非完全是帕诺伊德斯的精确翻版(帕诺伊德斯推翻了公众的决定,狄奥尼索斯则是推翻了他自己早先的决定),但我们很容易像马丁·韦斯特(Martin West)对《竞赛》的评价那样,将《蛙》中的竞赛看作一种故事类型,它"深受希腊人喜欢,其中一个人做了违背预期的事情,

---

26　弗林德斯-佩特林纸草,见 Allen, 225。第1—4行写着 [ ]τρο[πον | [ ]απαντων | [ ] των κριτων | [π]ανηδου。考虑到与第3行的 κριτων 相连,下一行对 π]ανηδου 的补充(即给出一位裁判的名字)能够令人信服。相反,Heldmann, 12-14 和 85-90 认为帕诺伊德斯这一情节是现存文本同时代的后人添加的内容,最初竞赛结果不是由一位国王决定的。对 Heldmann 论文的批评见 Richardson (1984)。

27　关于赫西奥德为何必须获胜,见上文注释19。另见 Graziosi (2002), 101-110,她提出了赫西奥德必须赢得比赛的另一个原因:古人认为他生活的年代早于荷马。

并以一套新颖且绝非不值一提的情境分析为自己辩护"[28]。我认为阿里斯托芬创作《蛙》时，脑海中已经很熟悉《竞赛》故事的形式，这种联系至少可以部分解释狄奥尼索斯为何在结尾改变心意。但这个解释本身并没有解决更深层的问题，即阿里斯托芬为什么要让他笔下的竞赛模仿《竞赛》故事。也就是说，在他构思埃斯库罗斯和欧里庇得斯之间的竞赛时，荷马和赫西奥德竞赛中的哪些元素可能会引起他的共鸣？这些问题是本研究接下来要关注的，我将在此论证，《竞赛》背后风格的论争和诗歌-伦理的论争被阿里斯托芬以不同的方式调用，以达成他自己的目的。当然，他在《蛙》结尾的"目的"究竟是什么，长久以来无论内容上还是方法论上都饱受争议，但正如我下面将要指出的那样，充分理解该剧与《竞赛》的关系，对于澄清其中许多问题有很大帮助。

虽然我们或许永远搞不清《竞赛》最初的故事灵感从何而来，但它的历史表明这个故事往往被用来对比荷马和赫西奥德两种不同的诗歌风格。如我们所见，赫西奥德赢了比赛，但荷马表现出色，作品本身也呈现了要决定他们孰优孰劣的内在困境[29]。同样，埃斯库罗斯和欧里庇得斯之间的竞争也明显被塑造为风格的差异，并试图确定谁才是"更好的"诗人。当然，《蛙》是一部喜剧，没有哪位诗人能免于讥讽，但剧中两位诗人也都有自己的闪耀时刻，这是以牺牲对方为代价。狄奥尼索斯在全剧结尾那广为人知的困境就足以证明，尽管两位诗人中必须有一人获胜，但在他们各自的风格间做选择并非易事。

《蛙》结尾处狄奥尼索斯的裁判和带来这一结果的风格论争似

28　West 443（参见本辑第44页。——译者按），然而，他是在论证叙述者认为帕诺伊德斯的决定无可指责时提出的这一点（见此前一段的讨论）。诚然，无论是《竞赛》中帕诺伊德斯的决定还是《蛙》中狄奥尼索斯的决定，本身都不能被准确地描述为"不值一提的"（毕竟每位裁判都为自己的决定提供了依据），但考虑到每场比赛中，"大众的"和"专制的"决定之间的张力都在慢慢加剧，最后的决定至少是有问题的。见 Graziosi (2002), 178-180，她认为《竞赛》反映了一个受欢迎的、"民主的"荷马（或许是特别考虑到了民主雅典）和一个更为帕诺伊德斯这样的国王所喜爱的赫西奥德之间的紧张关系。Ford, 277 认为相比"文学的精妙"，《竞赛》更关注"王权"，并将这种专制的方式与民主雅典所采取的方式进行对比（276—282）。

29　见 Graziosi (2001), 71-72（参见本辑第91—93页——译者按）中的讨论。

乎与《竞赛》和阿尔基达马斯感兴趣的风格论争有关[30]。在这一场景中，阿里斯托芬似乎毫不避讳地戏仿了《竞赛》，将《竞赛》中评价诗歌的标准及其对风格和道德的讨论一并融入他自己的竞赛，但却反转了做出最终决定的条件。可以这么说：《竞赛》中荷马显然是更受偏爱的诗人，却输给了赫西奥德，因为裁判帕诺伊德斯更青睐和平诗人而非战争诗人；《蛙》中狄奥尼索斯（尽管他承认难以抉择）选择了战争诗人埃斯库罗斯——诗人称自己的戏剧"充满了阿瑞斯"（1021），并主张召回阿尔西比亚德斯。另外，如我们所见，埃斯库罗斯从风格和对战争主题的喜爱上看都是一位与荷马关系密切的悲剧家。赫西奥德式的诗人欧里庇得斯在风格上没有那么崇高，他的教谕计划中包括了非常赫西奥德式的家政主题[31]，他必然会输。也就是说，每场比赛中被看好的诗人最终都会输掉比赛，但原因却是相反的。《竞赛》中，叙事从荷马移向赫西奥德，而在《蛙》中则相反，是从一个赫西奥德式人物（欧里庇得斯）转移到一个荷马式人物（埃斯库罗斯）。

两场竞赛的最后一个情景在结构上非常相似，这也进一步强化了两部作品之间的联系。从《蛙》第1378—1406行，两位诗人进行了著名的称重环节，每个人都对着天平吟诵了自己作品的一小段节选。第1407行，埃斯库罗斯表示自己已经受够了："我不要再一行一行地比了！"（καὶ μηκέτ᾽ ἔμοιγε κατ᾽ ἔπος）此时，比赛已经接近尾声，狄奥尼索斯马上就要定胜负，但他却感叹自己不愿疏远任何一位"朋友"（1411—1412, ἄνδρες φίλοι, κἀγὼ μὲν αὐτοὺς οὐ κρινῶ. | οὐ γὰρ δι᾽ ἔχθρας οὐδετέρῳ γενήσομαι·）。"因为，"他在第1413行说，"我认为他们一个很有智慧，另一个让我愉悦。"（τὸν μὲν γὰρ ἡγοῦμαι σοφόν, τῷ δ᾽ ἥδομαι）当然，这些著名的模棱两可的句子只有通过表

---

30 《竞赛》中荷马最终输掉了比赛，长久以来这让那些把阿尔基达马斯视为荷马诗风拥护者的人感到很困扰，对此的讨论见O'Sullivan, 96–105, 他强调作品中对赫西奥德的处理基本是负面的，与此同时对荷马的处理却是正向的，且花费笔墨颇多。另见上文注释27。

31 例如见《蛙》第971—977行：τοιαῦτα μέντοὐγὼ φρονεῖν | τούτοισιν εἰσηγησάμην, | λογισμὸν ἐνθεὶς τῇ τέχνῃ | καὶ σκέψιν, ὥστ᾽ ἤδη νοεῖν | ἄπαντα καὶ διειδέναι | τά τ᾽ ἄλλα καὶ τὰς οἰκίας | οἰκεῖν ἄμεινον ἢ πρὸ τοῦ...【我把这样的思考灌输给这些人，把推理和探查纳入艺术之中，因此他们现在可以观察一切、认识一切，特别是如何更好地管理家务事……】

演的姿态(如果有的话)才能被澄清[32],但至少可以看出,狄奥尼索斯过去对欧里庇得斯的推崇已经陷入混乱。无论我们如何对应 μὲν...δέ 这个句子的指涉对象,狄奥尼索斯选择上的迟疑令人吃惊,随之有效地营造了紧张感。正如佐默施泰因(Alan Sommerstein)所说([1996],283),"埃斯库罗斯每轮比赛都能争论到底,称重环节显然也赢了,观众当然希望听到他获胜;然而令他们惊讶的是,狄奥尼索斯拒绝做决定,当普路同因此打破漫长的沉默时……比赛意外进入第五回合"。这最后一回合,两位诗人需要回答一个简单的问题:"你有什么建议可以让雅典摆脱眼下的困境?"与之前的诗句称量不同,这一回合允许每位诗人对当下的热点问题,也就是阿尔西比亚德斯问题和目前雅典的军事战略问题表明立场。这一部分的文本自古代以来就引人困惑,尤其是根据流传下来的文本,这里似乎特别允许欧里庇得斯提出第二种主张,而不是像前面说的那样每人只提一个(1435—1436)。更重要的是,他的第二种主张似乎不无道理[33]。但就我们的目的而言,我们只需记住,直到最后,比赛的最终赢家是谁依然不明朗。佐默施泰因对此做了很好的总结([1996],289):"这场竞赛耗时已久,最后一轮竟然让欧里庇得斯这个注定会失败的一方提出了观众很可能觉得还不错的建议,这是始料未及的。"观众的心情如过山车一般,临近结尾我们一时间觉得欧里庇得斯很可能将被判为雅典最明智、最能解决当务之急的拯救者。然而,当埃斯库罗斯最后发言时,那个决定性的时刻才出现,他主张大力建设海军(1463—1465),因为这似乎才是狄奥尼索斯最终选择他的原因。故意拖延的决定,紧张又模棱两可的终极较量(其中每位诗人都给出了中肯的建议),以及无疑违背观众起初预期、很可能与听到埃斯库罗斯最后建议之前的预期也相违背的最终决定,《蛙》结尾所有这些元

---

[32]　对此的讨论见 del Corno, 241–247; Dover, 19; ad loc. p. 369; Sommerstein (1996), 283 ad loc。我倾向于认为 ἥδομαι 指的是欧里庇得斯,表明即便埃斯库罗斯现在因为一些其他原因变得有吸引力了,狄奥尼索斯对欧里庇得斯莫名的渴望却依然强烈;不可否认,这段话含混不清。

[33]　这里我支持将第1442—1450行归于欧里庇得斯(与Dover一致),他认为雅典人不再信任现任领袖,而是想让那些目前不受欢迎的人重新掌权。见 Sommerstein (1996), 289 ad loc。关于第1435—1466行的文本问题的讨论,见 Sommerstein (1996), 286–292 与 Dover, 373–378。

素都可以用《竞赛》中的类似事件来解释。

《竞赛》中当国王帕诺伊德斯第一次有机会在荷马和赫西奥德之间做出评判时，两位诗人刚刚结束第四个回合[34]的较量（行161—175），和《蛙》中的称重环节一样，这个场景也是两个人逐行对诗（赫西奥德首先提问，荷马以同样的格律回应）。第176行，叙述者明白地指出，在观众眼中荷马显然应该胜出：ῥηθέντων δὲ καὶ τούτων, οἱ μὲν Ἕλληνες πάντες τὸν Ὅμηρον ἐκέλευον στεφανοῦν【这些诗句被朗诵之后，所有在场的希腊人都要求给荷马授予桂冠】。国王显然对此感到不安，他对荷马有偏见，便要继续追问，他要求进行一场终极较量以推迟决定。每部作品中，都是"荷马式的"诗人（荷马、埃斯库罗斯）赢得了当前的比赛，但裁判却不信服，仍坚持自己预设的选择：帕诺伊德斯真心希望赫西奥德获胜；狄奥尼索斯支持欧里庇得斯。《竞赛》随后进行了与《蛙》中类似的终极对决。荷马和赫西奥德都可以朗诵一段他们心目中自己"最好的"段落；《蛙》中，我们已经看到，每位诗人都要为雅典提供一条最好的建议。和《蛙》一样，《竞赛》中荷马和赫西奥德的回应对于决出胜负没有什么特别的帮助。赫西奥德首先吟诵了《劳作与时日》中的十行（383—392）；这一段相当优美，但它涉及的是并不高贵的家庭农业话题，意在提供一些关于耕作、播种、收获的实用建议。我们很容易联想到欧里庇得斯在《蛙》中的说法（如971—979，见上文注释31所引），他的诗歌促进理性思考，并且提供实际建议。荷马用《伊利亚特》卷13（126—133，339—344）的两个片段回应。这部分描写了令人毛骨悚然的战争场面，听来更像是对战争的批评而非对战斗精神的赞美。如343—344：μάλα κεν θρασυκάρδιος εἴη | ὃς τότε γηθήσειεν ἰδὼν πόνον οὐδ' ἀκάχοιτο【谁若见此苦战不生哀叹反倒欣喜，那可真是一副铁石心肠】。但我们很快就发现，国王并不是这样理解这个段落的。

人们又一次选择了荷马，认为他的诗歌超乎寻常（205—207）：

---

[34] 这的确是一个惊人的巧合，无论《竞赛》还是《蛙》，诗人间决定性的较量都发生在第五回合（根据我们的解读，《竞赛》里的两位诗人刚刚结束的是第五回合的较量，而决定性的较量发生在第六回合——译者按）。当然，很难确定这不只是巧合。

θαυμάσαντες δὲ καὶ ἐν τούτῳ τὸν Ὅμηρον οἱ Ἕλληνες ἐπήνουν, ὡς παρὰ τὸ προσῆκον γεγονότων τῶν ἐπῶν, καὶ ἐκέλευον διδόναι τὴν νίκην.

希腊人在这一回合感到惊异,他们对荷马赞叹不已,因为这些诗行异乎寻常。他们又要求将胜利授予荷马。

这一场景的作用类似于《蛙》的结尾(1443—1444)欧里庇得斯提供了剧中的合唱队 "献诗"(parabasis)早已提到的建议,不少研究者都注意到了这点。"民众"即悲剧观众无疑对这个建议早有认同 35。然而,就像在《蛙》里一样,裁判做了一个出人意料的选择。帕诺伊德斯选择了赫西奥德而不是荷马,而他的理由从表面上看,就像《蛙》的结尾狄奥尼索斯所给出的理由一样缺乏说服力(207—210,见本文第一部分的引文)。因此,这两场竞赛的情节十分相似,但有一个差异可以带来启发。就每场竞赛都展示了诗歌风格间的竞争而言,可以说比赛的结果是相反的:在《蛙》中,埃斯库罗斯凭着我们前面讨论过的荷马式的思想,战胜了 "赫西奥德式" 的欧里庇得斯,而《竞赛》则认为赫西奥德以及赫西奥德风格的诗歌比荷马和荷马风格的诗歌 "更好"。

这一差异引发了一些有趣的问题。首先,最显而易见的问题就是:为什么阿里斯托芬的竞赛会以与其默认的范式相反的方式结束? 这是否是对《竞赛》本身的某种评论——比如对它背后的社会

35　第 1443 行的建议是说,去信任一群与现在不同的领导者(…ὅταν τὰ νῦν ἄπιστα πίσθ᾽ ἡγώμεθα),这诙谐的表达含义晦涩,但基本上与 "献诗" 部分(674—737)的建议一致;见 Sommerstein (1996) , 289 ad loc。雅典人支持合唱队的政治 "建议",这一点从《蛙》的第二次上演中可以看出,这次演出可能发生在第二年;见 Sommerstein (1996) , 21。有两则引证提到了该剧的重演,奇怪的是,这两则引证提到雅典人因 "献诗" 而赞美阿里斯托芬时,其措辞与《竞赛》中公开赞荷马时类似。Dover 在校勘本《蛙》的 Hypothesis Ic,引用狄凯阿库斯(Dicaearchus): οὗτω δὲ ἐθαυμάσθη τὸ δρᾶμα διὰ τὴν ἐν αὐτῷ παράβασιν ὥστε καὶ ἀνεδιδάχθη...【这部剧因为其中的献诗如此被赞赏,甚至被重演了……】,以及《阿里斯托芬传》(Aristophanes Test. 1.35 Kassel-Austin),其中也提到雅典人对合唱队 "献诗" 的赞美,阿里斯托芬被雅典人 "赞扬" 和 "加冕": …ἐπηνέθη καὶ ἐστεφανώθη; 比较 Certamen 205: θαυμάσαντες δὲ καὶ ἐν τούτῳ τὸν Ὅμηρον οἱ Ἕλληνες ἐπήνουν【希腊人在这一回合感到惊异,他们对荷马赞叹不已 】。但在这个故事中,当然是赫西奥德摘得了胜利的冠冕: ὁ δὲ βασιλεὺς τὸν Ἡσίοδον ἐστεφάνωσεν【国王却向赫西奥德授予桂冠 】。倘若公众 "普遍" 赞同阿里斯托芬在他的合唱队 "献诗" 中提出的建议,如果在剧作结尾处欧里庇得斯支持同样的观点,那么完全有理由认为欧里庇得斯在这里是采取了大众立场。

风尚或体现出的诗歌等级秩序的评论？也许对两部作品间的差异最简单的解读，就是认为阿里斯托芬反转了《竞赛》的结局，表明与传说中的故事相比，时代已经发生了巨大的变化，对当下公元前5世纪的雅典来说，正需要一位荷马那样好战的诗人。狄奥尼索斯或许不情愿在他欣赏的两位诗人中做出选择，但事实是必须得做个决定，他选择了一个似乎最能满足雅典当前政治需求的人。这个解读很容易理解，因为它提供了一个简单的道德解读，或多或少符合传统上对结局的解释。《竞赛》对比赛做出了相似的处理，那位被认为最能满足当下文化需求的诗人被选中了，但这个结局并不简单，因为这部分的叙事强烈暗示选错了人[36]。考虑到《竞赛》和《蛙》之间的诸多相似，阿里斯托芬在创作《蛙》的最后一个场景时，很有可能已经对帕诺伊德斯的决定产生的影响有了充分的了解。如果我们假设阿里斯托芬严格遵循了《竞赛》中帕诺伊德斯的决定，那么《蛙》的结尾就会比大多数解读（这类解读通常认为选择埃斯库罗斯从目的上来说是必要的）更加讽刺和棘手。

将这个关键问题最直接地提出就是：如果帕诺伊德斯是一个违背大众意愿的糟糕裁判，那么狄奥尼索斯在阿里斯托芬的竞赛里也是如此吗？正如我们所见，《竞赛》中荷马无疑深受民众喜爱，就连赫西奥德自己也清楚。叙述者两次描述他对荷马的成功感到恼火。第94行，赫西奥德为荷马出色的表演而“恼怒”（ἀχθεσθείς）；第149行，赫西奥德感到“嫉妒”（φθονῶν），因为荷马巧妙地回答了他第140—145行提出的数学问题。如我们所见，集会上的希腊人数次表达了他们对荷马的惊异（90、205），帕诺伊德斯选择赫西奥德（207）只能看作一个明显带有专制色彩的极少数意见。《蛙》的结尾狄奥尼索斯选择埃斯库罗斯是否也同样无视了主流意见呢？或者换句话说，如果“民众”要在欧里庇得斯和埃斯库罗斯之间做出选择，狄奥尼索斯最初想要带回欧里庇得斯的打算是否会更符合“民众”意愿呢？当然，这是个难以回答的问题，因为这涉及欧里庇得斯在公元前

36　古代晚期，帕诺伊德斯成了谚语中的一个“类型”，代表做出愚蠢决定的权贵；见O'Sullivan, 96。

5世纪的雅典的声誉,而且这种评定无可避免地要受到围绕他生成的复杂但很大程度上出自虚构的传记传统影响[37]。然而,莱夫科维茨的研究表明,尽管欧里庇得斯的传记中附带一些怀有恶意或十分荒谬的故事,但证据显示,至少早在公元前4世纪,欧里庇得斯实际上享有崇高的地位[38]。欧里庇得斯创作生涯中获得的胜利也许的确比索福克勒斯少,但由此便推断他不受欢迎却是很危险的[39]。只要我们不尽信传记中那些把欧里庇得斯塑造得古怪又怨愤的虚构,就很容易认识到他在当时是大受欢迎、很有影响力的。最明白不过的事实就是,阿里斯托芬至少有两部作品将欧里庇得斯的悲剧描述为某种社会"问题",虽然用的是喜剧的方式,但也足以证明观众确实被欧里庇得斯吸引了,并且有些人很担心他在潜移默化中败坏公众道德[40]。的确,狄奥尼索斯在戏剧开始谈到对欧里庇得斯的渴望(pothos),结束时表示自己因欧里庇得斯的诗而感到愉悦(hēdonē),他所用的词汇是一个真正的"粉丝"才会用的,他被诗人对主题的处理所吸引(这令埃斯库罗斯失望,他对此并不赞许;例如见第1039—1044行),即便在今天,这些话题依然对观众有着难以抗拒的吸引力,如乱伦、疯狂、窥私癖、异装癖,不一而足。

事实上,阿里斯托芬在《蛙》中很清楚地刻画了欧里庇得斯和埃斯库罗斯各自对声望的态度。第907行开始的场景中,欧里庇得斯一直把埃斯库罗斯描绘成沉默、阴郁、傲慢、任性、难以捉摸的人。正如欧里庇得斯嘲笑埃斯库罗斯塑造的阿基琉斯和尼俄柏时说的那

37　最早讨论如何评估欧里庇得斯传记证据问题的,见Stevens。他将传统上对欧里庇得斯的生平叙述总结为"……在雅典度过他生命中最后的25年……生活在日益孤立、不受欢迎、受迫害的氛围中",他认为这是严重的夸大,他比当时的大多数学者更明白,喜剧式的嘲讽(这也是我们了解雅典人对欧里庇得斯态度的主要来源)很少隐含对当事人的非难。尤见92—93。

38　见Lefkowitz, 88-104。她指出索福克勒斯和埃斯库罗的传记中也记录了一些不光彩的故事,它们似乎是文学家"英雄式"传记的组成部分。另见Stevens, 90。

39　见Lefkowitz, 103；Stevens, 92认为,欧里庇得斯似乎并未被拒绝授予合唱队,这一点很重要:"……如果我们考虑他的职业生涯中剧作是可以实际上演的,他至少三次甚至可能更多次获得二等奖,四次获得一等奖,我们能说这是失败吗?"关于戏剧比赛的评判流程,见Csapo和Slater, 157-160和Wilson, 101-102。

40　见Stevens, 92:"……如果从《蛙》中可以清楚地看出什么……那就是整部戏的背景设定就表明,索福克勒斯和欧里庇得斯无疑是当时所有剧作家中最杰出的。"

样,埃斯库罗斯笔下的角色象征着他本人和他的风格(911—913):

> πρώτιστα μὲν γὰρ ἕνα τιν᾽ ἂν καθῖσεν ἐγκαλύψας,
> Ἀχιλλέα τιν᾽ ἢ Νιόβην, τὸ πρόσωπον οὐχὶ δεικνύς,
> πρόσχημα τῆς τραγῳδίας, γρύζοντας οὐδὲ τουτί.
> 首先,他会把某个人罩起来,再让这人坐下,
> 比如阿基琉斯或尼俄柏,不让他露面,
> 一副悲剧的派头,而又一声不吭。

　　欧里庇得斯继续嘲笑埃斯库罗斯的语言晦涩难解(930 ...ἃ ξυμβαλεῖν οὐ ῥᾴδι᾽ ἦν)。对此狄奥尼索斯也不得不同意,因为他花了许多不眠之夜,试图弄清什么是"黄褐色的马鸡(一种前半身是马,后半身为鸡的神话生物——译者按)"(931—932)。与此对比鲜明的是欧里庇得斯广为人知的自我描述:他对待悲剧很节制,减少浮夸的辞藻和含混的表达,剧中每个人物都在说话,哪怕是妻子、奴隶、年轻女孩或老年妇女(948—950)。埃斯库罗斯认为这是在犯罪,但欧里庇得斯却认为他的策略是"民主的"(952, δημοκρατικὸν γὰρ αὔτ᾽ ἔδρων),在接下来第959—962行的著名演说中,他宣称正是他将家庭事务(οἰκεῖα πράγματα)带上舞台。这样,观众便明白他所有角色的台词,可以对他的艺术提出合理的批评(960—961, ξυνειδότες γὰρ οὗτοι | ἤλεγχον ἄν μου τὴν τέχνην)。埃斯库罗斯回应欧里庇得斯对他的描述时,也证实了他没有兴趣迎合大众,没有兴趣为了轻松获得大众的赞誉而在戏剧创作上妥协。难怪欧里庇得斯抵达冥府时引发了真正的骚动,普路同的奴隶在第771—778行描述,冥府里的恶棍在听了欧里庇得斯对于他戏剧的展示演说(epideixeis)后,全都为这个新来者疯狂了,认为他是所有人中最聪明的:

> ΟΙ. ὅτε δὴ κατῆλθ᾽ Εὐριπίδης, ἐπεδείκνυτο
> τοῖς λωποδύταις καὶ τοῖσι βαλλαντιοτόμοις
> καὶ τοῖσι πατραλοίαισι καὶ τοιχωρύχοις,
> ὅπερ ἔστ᾽ ἐν Ἅιδου πλῆθος. οἱ δ᾽ ἀκροώμενοι

τῶν ἀντιλογιῶν καὶ λυγισμῶν καὶ στροφῶν

ὑπερεμάνησαν κἀνόμισαν σοφώτατον·

κἄπειτ' ἐπαρθεὶς ἀντελάβετο τοῦ θρόνου,

ἵν' Αἰσχύλος καθῆστο.

仆人：当欧里庇得斯下来，表演给

那些偷衣服的人，扒手，

弑父者，强盗，

这些人是冥府里的主流，他们听到

他的反驳、诡辩和伎俩，

就完全疯狂了，认为他是最智慧的；

于是他便取而代之坐上了

埃斯库罗斯过去坐的那宝座。

很容易忽略的是，这场小冲突实际上为剧中的竞赛提供了托词[41]，应该注意，这个小插曲既是《竞赛》中结果的缩影，也预示着《蛙》中竞赛的结果。也就是说，"民众"（这里是指第772—773行提到的那些不值一提的罪人，他们被戏谑地称为[774]冥府中的主流 [πλῆθος]）为欧里庇得斯叫好[42]，但比赛结束时不那么受欢迎的那位却占了上风。事实上，当克桑西阿斯直白地问及埃斯库罗斯在冥府是否有支持者时（782），普路同的奴隶不得不承认，"善良的人"自然会站在他这边，尽管人数不多（ὀλίγον τὸ χρηστόν ἐστιν）。

可以这么说，《蛙》中的欧里庇得斯和《竞赛》中的荷马都是"民众的最爱"，但他们却都在各自的比赛中落败，表明比赛的最终结果都是对民众意愿的直接否定[43]。这种观念无疑给《蛙》造成了解释上的困境，如此看来，《蛙》的结尾远不如人们通常以为的那样牢靠。

41　见Ford, 282，他指出这一幕反映了竞赛背后潜藏着的"民粹主义的激情"，对艺术进行民主评判其实充满陷阱，这里或许也是一种温和的讽刺。

42　尽管欧里庇得斯在冥府的拥护者被描述为一群罪犯，但不必认为这是在评价现实世界中支持他的人。欧里庇得斯在雅典显然很受欢迎，阿里斯托芬在这里基本上把大多数雅典人都描述成了罪犯。但此处的戏谑并不特别，阿里斯托芬在其他地方也如此嘲弄观众，例如在《云》（1094—1097）中对驳的结尾，"不义"说服"正义"相信大多数观众都是"淫棍"（εὐρύπρωκτοι）。

43　见Graziosi (2002)，178—180以及上文注释27。

对狄奥尼索斯"不得人心"的决定直接、合理的解读，就是随着剧情的发展，他已经认识到"受欢迎"的东西未必道德，政治上也未必可取。他或许意识到，即使是民主政体中，有时一个领袖也必须自己掌权，为了城邦的利益违背大众的意愿。当然，站在雅典当时所处的历史时刻，阿里斯托芬笔下埃斯库罗斯的尚武及其保守的道德立场比欧里庇得斯的智识主义和话语中的妥协对社会更有用，尽管后者在审美上有着直接的诱惑。在这种解读下，或许可以认为阿里斯托芬让狄奥尼索斯纠正了帕诺伊德斯在《竞赛》中的决定，他选择了一个帕诺伊德斯应选（即是说如果帕诺伊德斯在《竞赛》的叙事中尊重了观众的意愿）却没选的"荷马式"人物。

这种直截了当的解释乍看起来很有吸引力，但如果我们假设阿里斯托芬是以《竞赛》为模板精心设计了《蛙》中的竞赛，那它就有些站不住脚了。例如，如果他打算忠实、合理地复制《竞赛》的结构和道德细节，那么狄奥尼索斯的决定很可能也会带上一些帕诺伊德斯那个决定的否定性色彩；而且，在这样一个再明显不过的互文性迁移中，阿里斯托芬对调了《竞赛》中的决定（选择荷马式的埃斯库罗斯，而帕诺伊德斯选择赫西奥德）以作为对该文本的一种修正性的评论。毕竟，狄奥尼索斯选择了"荷马式"诗人（埃斯库罗斯），而他本可以选择"赫西奥德式"诗人（欧里庇得斯）；帕诺伊德斯选择了赫西奥德，而他本可以选择荷马。换句话说，狄奥尼索斯为自己选择了帕诺伊德斯应该选择的诗人，但由于《竞赛》中帕诺伊德斯的形象是一个典型的"糟糕的裁判"，而且狄奥尼索斯在《蛙》中扮演了帕诺伊德斯的角色，这似乎意味着在阿里斯托芬眼中，帕诺伊德斯选了狄奥尼索斯应该选择的诗人（即赫西奥德式的诗人——欧里庇得斯）。这两个裁判都做了对自己的故事来说是错的，但对于对方来说却是正确的决定。

三、《蛙》与文学评价

如果这种互文性在《蛙》的最后一幕奏效，那么整部剧就会以一种恶作剧式的讽刺意味收束,而不是陷入批评家们经常归咎的那种道德说教。但是,有可能阿里斯托芬无意把埃斯库罗斯当成"优于"欧里庇得斯的诗人来推崇,同样在欧里庇得斯被大加挞伐后他也没有迫切地要为其"恢复声誉"。事实上,我相当怀疑他在剧中是否真的想要传达他对某一位真心的偏爱。如果严格从平实的字面意义考虑,阿里斯托芬的确为埃斯库罗斯被誉为雅典最好的"拯救者"提供了合理的理由。埃斯库罗斯调用了不少有传奇色彩的英雄人物,常常描绘他们在战争中的场面,而雅典需要的正是一套可靠的战争策略,最好是果断的、有侵略性的。但考虑到该剧与《竞赛》之间的关系,我认为阿里斯托芬其实无意影响公共政策、传达道德判断,他感兴趣的是设想一种荒谬的情况:两位迥然不同的伟大诗人可能会出离艺术的范畴,被看成是严肃的政治力量。这似乎是阿里斯托芬创作《蛙》的竞赛时从《竞赛》内化而来的基本观点。因为帕诺伊德斯的决定最终表明,在两位伟大诗人的较量中,若是试图以非诗歌的标准定夺优胜者,所做出的决定只能是任性无常的。荷马输掉了比赛,因为帕诺伊德斯脱离上下文评价他的诗,只考虑吟诵的选段是否符合社会价值观念,所以才认为荷马在为一种反社会的、尚武的精神背书。帕诺伊德斯没有试图理解选段与作品整体或直接背景间的关系,也没有从诗学的角度评价(例如:修辞或格律的技巧)。民众的想法与帕诺伊德斯的标准出现冲突只能说明他的决定在《竞赛》作者看来是多么有误导性,至少在评价诗歌技艺方面是如此[44]。这两场竞赛都声称考验的是智慧,但这个词语义丰富,裁判的决定难免带有主观性。

《蛙》中精心构思的竞赛使这一观点深入人心:阿里斯托芬的确让两位悲剧家在"诗学"的意义上竞争,但这一环节的竞争对最终结果来说无足轻重。两位诗人中没有谁可以说"赢了"那些比赛,狄奥尼索斯只是陶醉于他们的不同风格,听凭自己的心情欣赏他们的优点,谅解他们的不足,好像那只是快节奏的喜剧对答中的一部分。而

---

44 毫无疑问,用"诗的"标准评价诗就足够了吗?阿里斯托芬对此也抱有类似的疑虑。当然,《蛙》中直接的文学竞赛并没有让狄奥尼索斯在两位诗人之间的抉择变得更容易或是更有理有据。

且,智慧竞赛的最后一回合,题目与阿尔西比亚德斯和雅典的公共政策相关,与埃斯库罗斯和欧里庇得斯的诗学相去甚远,和他们的作品毫无关联。它的作用和帕诺伊德斯要求荷马和赫西奥德再比一局是完全一样的,因为那个场景中也隐含着一个类似于《蛙》中狄奥尼索斯问埃斯库罗斯和欧里庇得斯的问题,即:"你能表演的对当下社会最有益的东西是什么?"无论他们各自的作者是否充分认识到这一点,事实上这些情节的背后隐藏着对诗歌之用、对传统诗歌评价标准的微妙批评。《蛙》中,尽管埃斯库罗斯和欧里庇得斯满口说教,但阿里斯托芬似乎已经明白,要确切地表达诗歌这种复杂的艺术形式所要"教"的东西几乎是徒劳的,尤其当我们假设诗教的主题必须"有益于道德"时。

当然,我们没有理由把阿里斯托芬视作一个系统的文学理论家,但与此同时,《蛙》中狄奥尼索斯的美学困境(aesthetic dilemma)与一个文学理论中至今未有定论的重大问题密切相关,这个问题即"道德教益"是否是评价诗歌的正当标准。学者们传统上认为,阿里斯托芬在《蛙》的结尾通过狄奥尼索斯这个人物,迈出了陈述美学理论的第一步,而几十年后柏拉图在《理想国》中将其强有力地展现出来。就像柏拉图在他的《理想国》中对"不道德"诗歌的著名谴责(例如3.386—398)以及他严格要求诗歌只能反映真和善一样,埃斯库罗斯在《蛙》中的胜利通常也被认为充满了道德优越感[45]。和狄奥尼索斯一样,柏拉图本人也很清楚诗歌诱人但可能"不道德"的魅力(10.607c6—7)。有趣的是,他让苏格拉底将那些有争议的诗歌面临的美学困境定义为"哲学与诗的古老纷争"的一部分(607b5 παλαιὰ μέν τις διαφορὰ φιλοσοφίᾳ τε καὶ ποιητικῇ)。显然,他指的是一种更广泛的,文学阐释中的"形式主义"和"说教主义"之间的张力。在这种张力间,对一首诗的评价标准要么来自其突出的形式因素,要么来自无形的"思想"或主题。无论一首诗的形式如何迷人,柏拉图显然都不为所动。至少对他来说,一首诗如果不能为观众带来显而易

45　例如,见Hubbard, 216。"像埃斯库罗斯一样,(欧里庇得斯)宣称要以他的戏剧改造公民(1009—1010);然而他似乎并不关心他的戏剧对观众的影响,也不关心城邦公民未来的举止。"

见的道德教益,就不可能真的称得上是一首好诗[46]。然而,正如柏拉图暗示存在一场 παλαιὰ διαφορά(古老纷争),我们完全有理由相信有人对这个问题持反对意见。柏拉图并不是第一个对这场纷争做出评判的人,尽管公元前5世纪和前4世纪的雅典文化的主流观念里,诗歌在某种意义上就应该有教谕功能。

我们无从得知《竞赛》是否最初创作时就被当成文学理论来写,但荷马与赫西奥德之间的较量本身就预设了一个关乎文学价值的基本理论问题("如何评价不同的诗人并为他们排名?"),而国王帕诺伊德斯的决定无疑充满了理论色彩。他做决定的理由是赫西奥德的选段从主题上看比荷马的对社会来说更可取,这预示了柏拉图对诗歌的审查,狄奥尼索斯在《蛙》的结尾也是如此。但是正如我们所看到的,每场竞赛的结局都让人有些困扰,因为它与观众的预期背道而驰,于是每部作品似乎都涉及对什么是真正的"好"诗的论争。两部作品之间明显的互文关系让这场论争更加引人注目。

认为阿里斯托芬本人在《蛙》中对评价诗歌时过分强调说教的方法提出了批评,这也许令人颇感不安,特别是实际上公元前5世纪没有其他对这一"古代论争"持相同立场的代表人物流传下来。但也有相当多的证据表明,从希腊化时期开始,文学评价问题就被激烈地讨论,而且这一讨论的复杂演变足以使我们确信,它的历史至少可以追溯到公元前5世纪。论争的萌芽,即我们是否可以将诗歌的形式因素、结构与它的主题和思想区分开来,这在《蛙》中已经很明显,而后来的证据尽管很复杂,也都可以通过一条知识的谱系回溯到这种二分法。

这里应当引证一个希腊化时期的例子,因其表达了我认为在《蛙》和《竞赛》中也存在的文学批评态度。虽然这些后起的证据显然不能证明类似的观点之前就存在,但却让我们更容易相信它们出现过。菲洛得墨斯(Philodemus)对赫拉克利得斯(Heraclides of

---

46　柏拉图并非没有意识到诗歌形式的多样性和其形式所蕴含的力量,但他对形式因素的分析和评价通常都只是关注这些成分如何能提升诗歌的道德价值。例如3.392d-403c,苏格拉底主张不同的摹仿、节奏和音乐调式都有不同的道德色彩。403c中他总结了他们的讨论,只是说诗歌-音乐艺术(poetico-musical arts)永恒的目的便是对善的渴望(δεῖ δέ που τελευτᾶν τὰ μουσικὰ εἰς τὰ τοῦ καλοῦ ἐρωτικά.)。总体的解读见 Halliwell, 72–97。

Pontus）有一则批评，仿佛是《竞赛》中希腊观众对帕诺伊德斯的批评，是说如果坚持诗人一定要有道德教益，就可能会否定那些最杰出的诗人的作品（*On Poems*, Book 5, col. 4.10–18 Mangoni）。

> ...διότι τὰ κά[λ-
> λιστ[α] ποίηματα τῶν [δο-
> κιμ[ω]τάτων ποιητῶ[ν
> διὰ τὸ μηδ' ἡντινοῦν
> ὠφελίαν παρασκευ[ά-
> ζειν, ἐνίων δὲ καὶ [τὰ
> πλ[εῖ]στα, τινῶν δὲ πά[ν-
> τα [τ]ῆς ἀρετῆς ἐκρ[απ]ἐ-
> ζει.

> ……因此他将最负盛名的诗人们的绝妙佳作（某些诗人的绝大多数作品，一些诗人的全部作品）排除在卓越行列之外，因为它们没有提供助益。

　　除了用道德标尺衡量诗歌外，另一种与之相对的评价方法当属极端的"形式主义"。例如，对马洛斯的克拉特斯（Crates of Mallos）来说，"声音"（φωνή）是评价一首好诗的首要准则。但菲洛得墨斯也不赞成这种方法，他认为诗歌实际上能让听众获益，也能从中受害。他想要反对的似乎是把"道德教益"作为评价一个诗人好坏的唯一标准[47]。《论诗》（*On Poems*）第二卷的一则残篇写到在早期"希腊"（Hellas）很尊崇那些创作"邪恶"（ponēra）主题或形象的诗人。或许，他在这里是要说诗歌的评价标准还囊括了其他内容，不是只有特定作品中反映出来的人物、行动的道德品质而已（*P. Herc.* 1074 fr. F col. iii 1–12 Sbordone）。

---

[47] 见 Asmis（1995b）。正如 Asmis 所总结的那样（165），对菲洛得墨斯来说，"一首好诗便是以恰切的措辞表达合适的思想"。道德内涵对于他（与他的一些"对手"相反）是关键的一部分，但作为一个伊壁鸠鲁主义者，他会更看重诗歌是否能带来快乐，尽管这种快乐被视为意义、思想和表达三者的综合职能。另见 Asmis（1995a），以及 Sider 和 Poter。

> ...τὴν Ἑλ-
> λάδα. ἀλλ᾽ ἐξ᾽ ὅτου τὸν[48]
> Ἀρχίλοχον ἐθαύμαζε
> καὶ τὸν Ἱππώνακτα
> καὶ τὸν Σιμωνίδην,
> καὶ τῶν παρ᾽ Ὁμήρωι
> καὶ Εὐρειπίδει καὶ τοῖς
> ἄλλοις ποιηταῖς ἔνια,
> πονηροῖς προσώποις
> περικείμενα καὶ περὶ
> πονηρῶν πραγμάτων
> γεγραμμένα...

……希腊。但是从那时起［希腊人］就惊异于阿尔基洛科斯、希波纳克斯和西蒙尼得斯，并惊异于荷马、欧里庇得斯和其他的一些诗人的篇章，即有关邪恶人物和卑劣行径所写的东西……

这段话与《蛙》和《竞赛》中的比赛密切相关，因为它阐明了对最后富有争议的决定可能做出的回应，正如我所论证的，这种回应似乎蕴含在两场比赛相同的结构中。这两部作品都突出了评判诗人价值的过程以及凭严格的道德考量评价诗人可能会引发的不公正。我们无疑会认为《竞赛》中的希腊观众（类似于上述段落中菲洛得墨斯的"希腊人"）对赫西奥德比赛中的表现印象深刻，并视他为一个"好"诗人[49]。但这部作品也清楚地表明，他们对何为杰作的评价标准（相对于帕诺伊德斯）并非在于赫西奥德的作品是否对当下社会提供了

48　我用Degani对这个短语的读法替换了Sbordone的读法（ἔξω τούτων），见他为Hipponax所作的引证；比较Degani, 18, ad Test. 48。

49　当然，无论是阿里斯托芬笔下的狄奥尼索斯还是《竞赛》中的帕奥尼德斯，从来都没有明确表示输掉比赛的那个诗人是一个"坏"诗人，并且对于狄奥尼索斯来说，他显然是在两个他都喜欢并心怀尊重（出于不同原因）的诗人之间艰难地做出决定。然而，每个裁判最后都会将两位参赛者进行比较，并以社会教益为标准决定谁是"更好"的。菲洛得墨斯反对的显然不是将诗人的教谕作用纳入评价过程，而是反对将其作为评判诗人全部作品的决定性因素。

什么显然的"益处"。想象一下他们可能对帕诺伊德斯做出的回应，一定会让菲洛得墨斯这样的人欣悦。在这群人看来，有很多"至美"（παγκάλα）的诗歌"毫无益处"（ἀνωφελῆ）[50]。这也是狄奥尼索斯在《蛙》中的两难，他显然钟爱欧里庇得斯，但最终觉察到需要依据道德教益这一颇为专断的标准来评价他[51]。《蛙》中竞赛结束时可能没有希腊观众（同《竞赛》结尾一样）向狄奥尼索斯指出，他显然已经放弃了他在喜剧开场宣称评价好诗所必需的"非功利"标准[52]，但我们完全可以想象，那些在欧里庇得斯到达冥府（774—776）时以疯狂的热情迎接他的人群，会对狄奥尼索斯的决定颇有异议。

《蛙》并非文学理论作品，就像《云》也不是哲学著作，《马蜂》也不是法学著作，但没人能否认阿里斯托芬在这些领域以引人深思的方式讨论了这些抽象的概念。阿里斯托芬的时代，那些用来讨论文学价值的理论基础的术语还没有完全发展出来，但《蛙》的情节本身以及它核心的理论问题——如何决定两位诗人哪一个"更好"，表明这种美学讨论的基本用语已经确立。因为《蛙》结尾考察的是两位参赛者的教育意义，也因为阿里斯托芬如同大多数讽刺诗人一样，总是声称（无论多么缺少诚意）要给他的观众以指导，所以传统上批评家们认为狄奥尼索斯选择埃斯库罗斯，是以一种说教的夸饰结束整部戏[53]。但这场辩论的另一种观点显然呼之欲出，仅

---

[50]　见 cols, xxxii 9–17, 收入 Asmis (1995b), 154。

[51]　考虑到雅典当下的需求，狄奥尼索斯的标准（发觉埃斯库罗斯能提供更好的建议）当然不是"专断的"，但如将其严格视为评价诗人及其作品的机制，就的确很专断，特别是考虑到《蛙》的比赛从头到尾其他许多回合的较量都因这样一个"非诗歌"的标准被忽略掉了。

[52]　例如，在他与赫拉克勒斯的谈话中（53—105），狄奥尼索斯以完全个人化的语言描述了他对欧里庇得斯的喜爱。第97行也同样揭示了这一点，狄奥尼索斯强调，欧里庇得斯的伟大依靠的就是他能够"高歌高贵的言辞"（ὅστις ῥῆμα γενναῖον λάκοι）。狄奥尼索斯对诗歌表达的关注（相对于诗歌的思想）预示着希腊化时期的"euphony"概念，这一概念与克拉特斯（还有其他人）有关，并为菲洛得墨斯所批评。见 Sbordone 和 Asmis (1995b), 152。

[53]　总体上的讨论见 Sommerstein (1992), 27–30。他甚至表示写作旧喜剧的诗人中只有阿里斯托芬对教谕（didaxis）和规劝（paraenesis）感兴趣。Heiden 对这部剧的结尾提供了一个讽刺性的解读，我对此基本赞同，尽管我不会像 Heiden 暗示的那样，认为阿里斯托芬实际上对埃斯库罗斯和欧里庇得斯都不认同。"……阿里斯托芬并没有像大多数阐释者所认为的那样赞同埃斯库罗斯，他也不赞同欧里庇得斯，对于戏剧以及戏剧在城邦中有何种功能，他们每个人都发表了自己的看法，但这些看法与阿里斯托芬的旧喜剧之间有着深刻的对立。"

仅因为我们必须要等到希腊化时期的思想家将道德教益从审美价值中剥离出来,并不意味着阿里斯托芬不能运用这种方法。《蛙》的结尾很难说是对诗歌严肃、系统的理论探讨,但正如我在前文所论证的那样,它与《竞赛》的互文关系,使得我们更容易发现,埃斯库罗斯胜过欧里庇得斯所引发的关乎诗歌本质的问题和这一结局佯装解决的一样多[54]。

征引书目

Allen, T. W, ed. 1912. *Homeri opera. Vol. V.* Oxford.

Arrighetti, Graziano. 1987. *Poeti, eruditi e hiografi: Momenti della reflessione dei greci sulla letteratura.* Pisa.

Asmis, Elizabeth. 1995a. "Epicurean Poetics." In D. Obbink, ed., *Philodemus and Poetry.* Oxford. 15–34.

—. 1995b. "Philodemus on Censorship, Moral Utility, and Formalism in Poetry." In D. Obbink, ed., *Philodemus and Poetry.* Oxford. 148–177.

Bierl, A. F. H. 1991. *Dionysos und die griechische Tragödie: Politische und 'metatheatralische' Aspekte im Text.* Münchner Studien zür klassischen Philologie, vol. 1. Tübingen.

Bowie, A. M. 1993. *Aristophanes: Myth, Ritual and Comedy.* Cambridge.

Cavalli, Marina. 1999. "Le *Rane* di Aristofane: Modelli tradizionali dell'agone fra Eschilo ed Euripide." In F. Conca, ed., *Ricordando Raffaele Cantarella. Miscellanea di studi. Bologna.* 83–105.

Compton-Engle, Gwendolyn. 1999. "Aristophanes *Peace* 1265–1304: Food, Poetry, and the Comic Genre." *CP* 94: 324–328.

del Corno, D., ed. 1985. *Aristofane. Le Rane.* Milan.

Csapo, Eric, and William J. Slater. 1995. *The Context of Ancient Drama.* Ann Arbor.

Diels, H. 1956–59. *Die Fragmente der Vorsokratiker.* 8th ed. by W. Kranz. 3 vols.

---

54 本研究始于2000年11月在利兹大学举行的纪念W. Geoffrey Arnott研讨会上发表的一篇论文。我很高兴能将如今这个扩充后的版本献给他,这位学者半个世纪以来在许多方面激励着喜剧研究者。我衷心感谢本文的匿名评审以及诸多朋友、同事,谢谢他们对本文的原稿提供了很有帮助的评论和建议,特别是Barbara Graziosi, Richard Janko, André Lardinois, James I. Porter以及Alan Sommerstein。

Berlin.

Dornseiff, F. 1944. Rev. of Schadewaldt. *Gnomon* 20: 134–140.

Dover, K. J. 1993. *Aristophanes*. Frogs. Oxford.

Ford, Andrew. 2002. *The Origins of Criticism: Literary Culture and Poetic Theory in Classical Greece*. Princeton.

Gantz, Timothy. 1993. *Early Greek Myth: A Guide to Literary and Artistic Sources*. Baltimore.

Graziosi, Barbara. 2001. "Competition in Wisdom." In F. Budelmann and P. Michelakis, eds., *Homer, Tragedy and Beyond: Essays in Honour of P. E. Easterling*. London. 57–74.

—. 2002. *Inventing Homer: The Early Reception of Epic*. Cambridge.

Griffith, Mark. 1990. "Contest and Contradiction in Early Greek Poetry." In Mark Griffith and Donald J. Mastronarde, eds., *Cabinet of the Muses: Essays on Classical and Comparative Literature in Honor of Thomas G. Rosenmeyer*. Atlanta. 185–207.

Halliwell, Stephen. 2002. *The Aesthetics of Mimesis: Ancient Texts and Modern Problems*. Princeton.

Heiden, Bruce. 1991. "Tragedy and Comedy in the *Frogs* of Aristophanes." *Ramus* 20: 95–111.

Heldmann, Konrad. 1982. *Die Niederlage Homers im Dichterwettstreit mit Hesiod*. Hypomnemata 75. Göttingen.

Hubbard, T. K. 1991. *The Mask of Comedy: Aristophanes and the Intertextual Parabasis*. Ithaca.

Kassel, R., and C. Austin, eds. 1983–. *Poetae comici graeci*. Berlin.

Kirk, G. S. 1950. "The Michigan Alcidamas-papyrus; Heraclitus fr. 56D; The Riddle of the Lice." *CQ* 44: 149–167.

Koniaris, G. L. 1971. "Michigan Papyrus 2754 and the Certamen." *HSCP* 75: 107–129.

Lada-Richards, I. 1999. *Initiating Dionysus: Ritual and Theatre in Aristophanes' Frogs*. Oxford.

Lardinois, André. 1995. *Wisdom in Context: The Use of Gnomic Statements in Archaic Greek Poetry*. Ph.D. diss., Princeton University.

Lefkowitz, Mary R. 1981. *The Lives of the Greek Poets*. Baltimore.

MacDowell, Douglas M. 1995. *Aristophanes and Athens: An Introduction to the Plays*. Oxford.

Mandilaras, Basil. 1992. "*A New Papyrus Fragment of the Certamen Homeri et Hesiodi*." In M. Capasso, ed., *Papiri letterari greci e latini. Papyrologia lupiensia* 1. Galatina. 55–62.

Mariss, Ruth. 2002. *Alkidamas: Über diejenigen, die schriftliche Reden schreiben, oder über die Sophisten. Eine Sophistenrede aus dem 4. Jahrhundert v. Chr. eingeleitet und kommentiert.* Münster.

Merkelbach, R., and M. L. West, eds. 1990. *Fragmenta selecta.* With F. Solmsen, ed., *Hesiodi Theogonia, Opera et dies, Scutum.* 3rd ed. Oxford. 109–226.

von Möllendorff, Peter. 1996–97. "Αἰσχύλοω δ'αἱρήσομαι — de'neue Aischylos' in den *Fröschen* des Aristophanes." *WJA* n.s. 21:129–151.

Nagy, Gregory. 1982. "Hesiod." In T. J. Luce, ed., *Ancient Writers.* New York. 43–74.

Nietzsche, F. 1870 and 1873. "Die florentinische Tractat über Homer und Hesiod, ihr Geschlecht und ihren Wettkampf." *RhM* 25: 528–40 and 28: 211–249.

O'Sullivan, Neil. 1992. *Alcidamas, Aristophanes and the Beginnings of Greek Stylistic Theory.* Hermes Einzelschriften Heft 60. Stuttgart.

Padilla, M. 1992. "The Heraclean Dionysus: Theatrical and Social Renewal in Aristophanes' *Frogs.*" *Arethusa* 25: 359–384.

Porter, James 1.2000. *Nietzsche and the Philology of the Future.* Stanford.

Radermacher, Ludwig. 1954 (original publication 1921). *Aristophanes' Frösche.* 2nd ed. by W. Kraus. Vienna.

Renehan, Robert. 1971. "The Michigan Alcidamas-Papyrus: A Problem in Methodology." *HSCP* 75: 85–105.

Richardson, N. J. 1981. "The Contest of Homer and Hesiod and Alcidamas' *Mouseion*" *CQ* 31: 1–10.

—. 1984. Review of Heldmann. *CR* 98 n.s. 34: 308–309.

Rosen, Ralph M. 1990. "Poetry and Sailing in Hesiod's *Works and Days.*" *CA* 9: 99–113.

Sbordone, F. 1955. "Filodemo e la teorica dell'eufonia." *RAAN* 30: 25–51.

Schadewaldt, Wolfgang. 1942. *Legende von Homer dem fahrenden Sänger: Ein altgriechisches Volksbuch.* Leipzig.

Sider, David. 1995. "Epicurean Poetics. Response and Dialogue." In D. Obbink, ed., *Philodemus and Poetry.* Oxford. 35–41.

Sommerstein, Alan. 1992. "Old Comedians on Old Comedy." In B. Zimmermann, ed., *Antike Dramentheorien und ihre Rezeption.* Vol. 1 of Drama. *Beiträge zum antiken Drama und seiner Rezeption.* Stuttgart. 14–33.

—. 1996. *Aristophanes.* Frogs. Warminster.

Stevens, P. T. 1956. "Euripides and the Athenians." *JHS* 76: 87–94.

Thalmann, W. 1984. *Conventions of Form and Thought in Early Greek Epic Poetry.* Baltimore.

Vogt, Ernst. 1959. "Die Schrift vom Wettkampf Homers und Hesiods." *RhM* 102:

193–221.

West, M. L. 1967. "The Contest of Homer and Hesiod." *CQ* 17: 433–450.

Wilson, Peter. 2000. The Athenian Institution of the Khoregia. *The Chorus, the City and the Stage*. Cambridge.

（译者单位：复旦大学中国语言文学系在读博士生）

古史探微

Ancient History: New Approaches

【编者按】 1970年，米歇尔·福柯在法兰西学院的就职演说上做了以《话语的秩序》为主题的著名演讲。在演讲中，福柯强调了话语具备的超乎寻常的力量。他提到，话语的生产受到一系列"限制系统"的影响。其中，话语主体的限制系统的最表层是由一套"仪式"所构建的，这套仪式规定了言说个体必须具备的资格，规定了手势、举止、环境以及所有必须伴随话语的一整套符号集合，从而确定了言语的假定或强加的效力。在福柯看来，宗教、司法、政治话语等很难脱离这种仪式所施加的影响，后者决定了演说者主体的特定属性及其约定俗成的角色。

虽然作者并未提及福柯的这套理论，但读者即将读到的这篇文章正是从一个类似的视角切入，通过展示古罗马法庭开庭前的法律诉讼（legis actiones）程序，印证了福柯所谓的"言说的仪式化"（les rituels de parole）的合理之处。罗马法律讼词文本带有确凿、既定和不可变更的特点，给人一种不断重复、了无新意甚至枯燥乏味之感。然而，正是这种千篇一律、看似空洞无物的程式，赋予文本一种永恒的仪式感。法律的庄严和效力就此透过独特的言语充分呈现出来。对此，文章做了精彩而独到的分析与论证。

文章的作者墨里奇奥·贝蒂尼出生于1947年，是意大利知名的古典语文学家和人类学家。他于1970年毕业于比萨大学古典学系，自1985年起在锡耶纳大学担任希腊—拉丁文学教授。同时，贝蒂尼长期在美国加州大学伯克利分校的古典学系担任客座教授，并于2018年成为年度萨瑟讲席教授（Sather Professor of Classical Literature）。贝蒂尼的研究涉及古代地中海世界的语言、神话、宗教和亲族关系等，尤其擅长以人类学的视角和方法对上述领域进行分析。至今，他已发表近200篇学术论文，以及数十部专著，多本著作已被译成英、法、德等语言出版。其中，出版于1986年的《人类学与罗马文化》一书可视作他的代表作，该著将人类学方法运用于早期罗马文化多个领域的研究，在学界产生了很大的影响。（王忠孝）

Solemn Words: Ritual Performance in Roman Ancient Courts

Maurizio Bettini

In this paper I intend to highlight some peculiar aspects of Roman civil procedure, still capable of stimulating not only our wonder, but also our reflection: the civil procedure through the *legis actiones*. In the reciting of these legal formulas—in front of the magistrate—according to a rigid ceremonial protocol, the "spoken word" displays all the power of its ritual efficacy.

In the most ancient phases of Roman legal practice, the only way to take an action before the magistrate was to resort to some fixed formulas derived from the laws of the XII tables, called *legis actiones*. The entire matter of the dispute should be "compressed" within them. In particular, the legal action consisted in the *recitation* of these fixed formulas, the act of writing playing no role in it: *orality* governed the whole development of the action. The procedure carried out through the *legis actiones* was extremely rigid and made it very difficult for the parties to bring the real *complexity* of individual cases before the magistrate. Often this procedure resulted even in injustice. As we know from Gaius—the famous jurist of the second century AD, author of the *Institutiones*—the *legis actiones* were "immutable" (*immutabiles*) —that is rigid and fixed —to such an extent, that a citizen had lost the case because, acting on the cutting of some vines, in the relative *actio* had used the term "vine" (*vites*), while he should have used the term "trees" (*arbores*), because the law of the XII tables, to which the legal action referred, spoke of "cut trees" (and not of "cut vines")[1]. The intrusion of an external and contextual element — that is unrelated to the standardized statement to be used — had the power to undermine the efficacy of the *actio*. As Gaius says, this was the result of the "pedantic subtlety" with which the "ancients" used the *legis actiones* they had created, even a minimal error could cause the dispute to be lost. For this reason, continues Gaius, the *legis actiones* "gradually came to hatred" and two successive laws established that the legal action would take place in different, more open and flexible forms. But let us see the way in which Sextus Pomponius, a jurist of the II AD, describes the *legis actiones* in his *Enchiridion*, a 'booklet' on the history of Roman law that has been handed down through the *Digesta*[2]:

> *The* legis actiones *was given a fixed form conforming to the ritual* (certas sollemnesque)*, to prevent the people from using it at their own will.*

The *legis actiones* therefore consisted of non-modifiable expressions (*certas*), whose enunciation had a ritualized character (*sollemnes*): in order to perform the legal action it was necessary to use the same words in the same order, according to a prescribed scheme.

In other words, the *legis actiones* consisted of *certa verba*. Before proceeding in our analysis, we should consider that *verbum* — normally translated simply as "word" — can indicate a single word, an entire sentence, multiple sentences combined in a complex speech, or even an

---

[1] Gaius, *Institutiones*, 4.11.

[2] Pomponius, *Enchiridion* in *Digesta* 1.2.2.7; 1.2.2.36 (all the quotations are my translation, unless otherwise indicated).

exchange of utterances that takes place between two interlocutors. More exactly, *verbum* generally designates a "speech flow", which as such can have variable length, from a simple "word" to a more complex enunciative segment. Consequently, the expression *certa verba* does not mean "certain or fixed words" but "certain or fixed utterances", that is, those fixed expressions—necessarily repeated in the same form from one time to another—which in Rome recurred not only in the *legis actiones* but also in the statements of the praetor; in the formulas recited by the general on the occasion of the *devotio*, when he consecrated his life to the underworld gods in exchange for the victory over the enemy; in the formulas that the *augur* uttered in delimiting a ritual space (*templum*) by the power of his speech; and so on. They were all ritualized utterances, pronounced by a figure endowed with *authority*.

In addition to preventing the arbitrary manipulation of the utterances forming the *legis actiones*, as Pomponius affirms, their formal closure certainly had a second motivation, which can be easily inferred from the rest of the story:

> *However* (continues Pomponius) *both the interpretative science of* legis actiones *and the* legis actiones *themselves were assigned to the college of* pontifices *("pontiffs"), establishing who should take care of private actions each year.*

In other words, the *legis actiones* were not made public. As Cicero tells us referring to the *pontifices*[3],

> *those ancients who dedicated themselves to this discipline [of law], to*

---

[3] Cicero, *De oratore* 1.184; Valerius Maximus, *Factorum et dictorum memorabilium libri* 2.5.2; Festus, *De verborum significatu*, p. 200.2 ff. (Lindsay): «... pontifex maximus, quod iudex atque arbiter habetur rerum divinarum humanarumque»; Cicero, *De legibus* 2.19.47: «"sae⟨pe⟩" inquit Publi filius "ex patre audivi, pontificem bonum neminem esse, nisi qui ius civile cognosset"»; *De oratore* 3.33.136; *Brutus* 42.156; etc.

preserve and nourish their power did not want their science to be divulged.

Indeed, it is possible to assume that the *legis actiones* had not been expressly recorded in writing, given that, again from Pomponius, we learn the following[4]:

later, Appius Claudius having drawn up an exposition of these actions in a definite form, his scribe Gnaeus Flavius, son of a freedman, after having stolen the book, handed it over to the people.

The fact that Appius Claudius is recorded as drafting a "book" (in which the actions were presented in an orderly manner), suggests that up to that moment the writing had not yet organically intervened in the conservation, transmission and management of *legis actiones*. In other words, they had to constitute a patrimony of juridical statements not only unknown to the public, as jealously guarded by the college, but also administered in oral or semi-oral form by the priests. In the absence of a written text to refer to, it was therefore indispensable that the sentences of the *legis actiones*, which were concretely used to take legal action, should be fixed and defined in all respects. Only their nature of non-modifiable and ritualized sentences could preserve them from the wear and tear produced by use and time. Their *standardized* shape provided the *legis actiones* with the character of *permanence* that in other historical and cultural environments is carried out by writing.

Concretely, however, how could it be ensured that the *legis actiones* retained their *certus*, *sollemnis* and *immutabilis* character? In the first place by prescribing that the words of which they were

---

[4]   Pomponius, *Enchiridion*, *Digesta* 1.2.2.7; 1.2.2.36. Cf. Nepotianus, *Epitoma* 2.5.2: «verum Gn. Flavius scriba, natus a patre libertino, formulas sacras verbis apertioribus expedivit et in notitiam populi publicavit».

composed should be repeated each time identical and in the same order; but at the same time, preventing the utterances of which they were composed from being modified by the intrusion of *extraneous / contextual* elements. If we observe the texts of *legis actiones* handed down to us by Gaius (*legis actio sacramento, per iudicis arbitrive postulationem, per pignoris capionem, per manus iniectionem, per condictionem*)[5] we are struck by the absolute absence of any contextual reference external to the pronounced sentence (personal names, places, circumstances, etc.). Why excluding any contextual and external references? Because as such they would inevitably change the *certus, sollemnis* and *immutabilis* character of the utterance's wording, making it different from one time to another.

Some examples. If it is about claiming possession of someone, the person's name is not mentioned, but is evoked as *hunc hominem*, that is, identifying him / her only through the "empty" instrument of the deictic (HUNC EGO HOMINEM / EX IURE QUIRITIUM / MEUM ESSE AIO "I declare that this person belongs to me under the laws of the Quirites"). It is only the *concrete* standing on the trial scene of the unnamed person, that makes the sentence understandable, "filling" the deictic *hunc* with referential meaning. Similarly, the other part is evoked through a generic personal pronoun, *tu /* you, without any personal appellation (QUANDO TU INIURIA VINDICASTI ... "Since you reclaimed unjustly ..."); if it is a question of claiming a given sum *ex stipulatione*, the temporal or local circumstances in which the case would have occurred are not stated, but only its existence is mentioned. No contextual intrusion must disturb the *certus, sollemnis* and *immutabilis* character of the sentences, which must be repeated in the same form on every occasion. As Marie Therese Fögen brilliantly wrote, "the stereotypical diction of formulas limits the entry of life into law",

---

5   Gaius, *Institutiones* 4.16 ff.

but at the same time forces all life to enter into law[6].

We know that in general the recitation of standardized utterances, to be repeated in a consistent way from one time to another, makes use of certain "recall structures", as Jack Goody called them, i. e. nuclei of memory capable of resurrecting the formulas to the mind[7]. In the case of *legis actiones*, compositional forms inspired by the rhythmic principle of similarity could act as "recall structures": such as the "three-block" composition, each of which in turn is characterized by a tri-member articulation, recurring in *HUNC EGO HOMINEM / EX IURE QUIRITIUM / MEUM ESSE AIO* "I declare that this person / under the laws of the Quirites / belongs to me". This sentence is then followed by a sequence marked by the initial alliteration in -S-, SECUNDUM SUAM CAUSAM SICUT DIXI "According to its cause as I said". "Pre-modeled" rhythmic configurations such as the following could also act as "recall structures": ... *AIO DARE OPORTERE. ID POSTULO AIAS AN NEGAS. QUANDO TU NEGAS* ... "I say that he / she ought to be given. This I ask, if you assent or deny. Since you deny ..." The responsive nature of this linguistic configuration (AIAS AN NEGAS. *QUANDO TU NEGAS* ... "if you assent or deny. Since you deny ..."), on the part of the actor, ensured the correct resumption in the acting after the interruption by the opponent. At the same time, ritualized gestures of performative value, external but simultaneous to the recitation of the formulas, could concur as "recall structures" to guarantee the correct formulation of the utterance, such as the act of "grasping" (*adprehendere*) the thing or person whose possession is reclaimed, the recitation of the formula and the imposition of the "stalk" (*festuca*) on the person or thing to be claimed *simultaneously* (*simul*) with pronouncing the words of the *legis actio*

---

6 M. T. Fögen, *Römische Rechtsgeschichten. Über Ursprung und Evolution eines sozialen Systems*, Göttingen:Vandonhoeck & Ruprecht, 2002, 140.

7 J. Goody, *The Logic of Writing and the Organization of Society*, Cambridge: Cambridge University Press, 1986, 76 ff.

sacramenti, that is HUNC EGO HOMINEM … ECCE TIBI VINDICTAM IMPOSUI "on this person … behold, I impose the stalk, i. e. I reclaim ownership"; and even more the "mirror" repetition, by the opponent, of the same verbal formulation and of the same and simultaneous gestures ("grasping" the thing or man whose possession is claimed, imposing of the "stalk" on the person or thing to be claimed). The same can be said for the equally ritualized gesture with which in the *legis actio per manus iniectionem* the actor "took a part of the opponent's body" *simultaneously* (*simul*) with pronouncing the sentence MANUM INICIO "I lay my hands on him, her, it". Ritualizing each gesture and pronouncing *simultaneously* the prescribed words, certainly contributed to making each sentence more "memorable".

If there is something striking in the use of the *legis actiones* made by the Romans, it is not only their fixity or their "limiting the entry of life into law", as has been brilliantly written: it is above all the *efficacy* attributed to them. These standardized "words", so poor and dry, in fact had the power to produce even significant effects on the economic or social condition of individuals. Where does the source of the "force" emanating from this way of enunciating ultimately reside, as for all the legal Roman procedures consisting of verbal acts?

According to an interpretation still taken up by historians and scholars of Roman law, the efficacy of these formulas would originate from some intrinsic virtue of the "word" itself, whether this virtue has a magical, religious or "magical-religious" nature[8]. Better to say, the efficacy exercised by these linguistic acts would be based on the permanence (even in more advanced times) of some "primitive", if not

---

[8] Since P. Hubelin, "Magie et droit individual", *L'Année sociologique*, vol. X, 1905–1906, pp. 1–47. A. Magdelain, *Le ius archaique*, in Id., *Jus, imperium, auctoritas: études de droit romain*, Paris: De Boccard; Rome: École Française de Rome, pp. 34–98; M. Pierre, *Carmen. Etude d'une catégorie sonore romaine*, Paris: Les Belles Lettres, 2016, pp. 82–83.

even "mystical" traits, which in Rome would have characterized the origins of legal thought. We neglect the fact that general notions such as the "magic power of the word" should today be reviewed and abandoned in the light of most recent anthropological studies, showing how fragile and generic this formulation is. In any ritual process it is not so much the mystical efficacy of the *word*, in itself, that produces a certain effect, but its specific belonging to a particular type of language (from time to time sacred, archaic, incomprehensible: just think of the obscure words used in the *Carmina Saliaria*); as well as the contextual relationship of single utterances with narrating specific myths; the performance of codified gestures or prescribed actions; the interaction with specific objects necessary for action; and so on. All such elements take part in the process and only as a *whole* produce the ritual efficacy. As Stanley J. Tambiah wrote, "words become effective only if spoken within a very special context of other actions"[9]. Naturally, the fact that law and religion have been strongly linked in Roman experience, especially the most archaic one, remains out of the question — even if nothing authorizes us to place both in a "primitivistic" dimension not only indebted to obsolete anthropologies, but substantially foreign to Roman culture itself (as we know it). Beyond this, however, invoking a generic "magical-religious" force to explain the verbal efficacy in the field of law, in our opinion runs into two difficult obstacles to overcome.

First obstacle, such hypotheses do not take into account which was the *local*, *internal*, Roman perception regarding "verbal efficacy". On the contrary, it seems to us that "emic" observation (i. e. respectful of the point of view shared by the culture studied) is always essential for building a correct interpretation of the facts to be analysed. Now, in some famous paragraphs of his *Natural History* Pliny the Elder asks

---

[9] S. J. Tambiah, *Culture, Thought and Social Action. An Anthropological Perspective*, Cambridge (Mass.): Harvard University Press, 1985, 47 ff.

himself this fascinating and crucial question: "whether words (*verba*), charms and incantations (*incantamenta carminum*) are of any efficacy or not". Then Pliny continues:[10]

> *this power should be accepted by men without question: but the most cultivated people, individually, reject this belief, while life (vita) taken as a whole believes in it every moment, and does not realize it.*

Pliny appears to be an acute observer of the culture that surrounds him, clearly distinguishing between the opinions of "intellectuals" and those that circulate in widespread culture — but above all, what is even more interesting, he grasps the unaware nature of certain beliefs, consequently uniting "intellectuals" and ordinary people in a single group as both categories actually share similar opinions. What we intend to highlight in particular, however, is the nature of the *examples* that the author brings to support his thesis, that is the widespread persuasion (even of an unconscious nature) according to which "words (*verba*), charms and incantations (*incantamenta carminum*)" would be endowed of efficacy. The list is quite rich.

There are prayers or invocations pronounced by priests or Vestals; by generals who consecrate themselves to the gods through the *devotion*; by generals who practice the *evocatio*, i. e. reciting prayers to let the divinity protecting the enemy city come out of it; divinatory responses; real magic "spells" (the two mentioned in the XII tables, both the one used to "steal" crops from the neighbor fields, and the "malevolent chant" [*malum carmen*] hurled at someone); amatory "spells"; formulas used in curses (*defixiones*); "spells" against the fires written on the walls of the houses; "incomprehensible words" used in chants; and so on. In other words, the "statements" about the efficacy of which Pliny wonders,

---

10   Pliny the Elder, Natural History, 28.10 ff.

all have a *religious* or *magical* character. No juridical formula is ever remembered: not the *legis actiones*, not the "three words" (*tria verba*) that the magistrate solemnly pronounces and so on. In spite of the "power" unquestionably possessed by *verba* and legal formulas — since they can cause the punishment or death of an individual, change his / her condition, determine the belonging of a good, and so on — and their large sharing in Roman life, Pliny does not think of putting them in the same category as the "prayers and invocations" used in religious practice, much less in that of spells or magic words. Therefore, if we respect the internal Roman perception of the "power" possessed by *verba*, we can only exclude that the words of the law were considered "effective" as they participated in the religious, or "magical-religious" power frequently attributed to them by the moderns.

The second obstacle against which the "magical-religious" interpretations of legal formulas run up, is the following. Given that recourse to *legis actiones*, as well as to other juridical procedures based on the word, is active even in phases of Roman culture far from any primitiveness, the magical-religious interpretation of their force must necessarily hinge on a notion dear to nineteenth-century anthropologists such as Edward B. Tylor, who explicitly theorized it, or J. F. McLennan: that of "survival". This interpretative category took it for granted that (in the words of the celebrated Italian anthropologist Alberto Mario Cirese) "remains of previous cultural stages ... persist, more or less active, even in subsequent cultural stages, similarly to what happens in the biological evolution of the species in which organs or parts of the body that have lost their previous function (famous, among other things, the wisdom tooth or the trace of "tail" represented by the coccyx) "[11]. The "survival" therefore constitutes a notion that made sense within an episteme of a

---

[11]   A. M. Cirese, *Cultura egemonica e culture subalterne*, Palermo: Palumbo, 1973, 43 f.

markedly positivist, scientist, evolutionist character, but which clashes with the paradigms shared by more modern anthropology. However, there is not only a not insignificant question of methodological aging at stake. The fact is that the idea of "survival" seems in itself misleading.

When you come across a cultural phenomenon that does not seem to "square" with the rest of the context, dismissing it as an (inert) "survival" of the past simply prevents you from addressing the issue. What if it were just a prospective deception? The temporal distance, and above all the superimposition of our cultural categories on the original cultural context, can play tricks on us. If a certain culture acts according to principles that do not seem to us to be in harmony with the rest, this does not mean that traces of its presumed primitive past "survive" in it: simply, this culture may have given itself a different organization from what we expect, and which at first glance we fail to understand. In other words, faced with difficulties of this type, it is time to undertake the analysis, trying to identify which are the functional traits that can explain the presence of the "anomalous" element within the cultural system — not to block it, simply postulating the existence of some "survival". We therefore believe that even in the case of *legis actiones*, as well as in that of legal formulas in general, resorting to the survival of ancient "magical-religious" forms to explain their efficacy is (as we said) misleading: concentrating on the alleged "magical" virtue that they would drag with them from a distant (and equally presumed) past, prevents us from seeing the presence of a series of functional traits — absolutely verifiable, coeval, synchronic with respect to the application of the formulas themselves — which in our opinion are already able to justify the efficacy attributed in Rome to the spoken word in the legal field. Starting with the form that these utterances take in their recitation, ending with the context in which they are pronounced.

Let us briefly review the distinctive features of the *legis actiones* we have outlined so far, that is, the *certus, sollemnis* and *immutabilis* character of the utterances; the absence of external intrusions; the peculiarities of the syntactic forms used; parallelisms and phonic echoes; the simultaneity between pronunciation and ritualized gestures. These formal characteristics of the single utterances immediately reveal as exceptional the discourse articulated between the parties and the magistrate. And this simply because a linguistic interaction, let's say, ordinarily would never take place according to such assumptions — in everyday life no one would speak in this way. The same also applies to the predefined simultaneity between certain phrases and certain gestures, according to a behavior that is not part of the usual social interaction. As such, the characters of the performance further increase the binding nature of the words and actions required to successfully complete the legal action. Such exceptional linguistic and gestural procedures also presupposed an equally special temporal context, as they could only take place on days defined *fasti* "lawful" by the calendar, as opposed to others (called *nefasti*) that would not have been recognized as valid for taking legal action. Only in these days the *praetor* could pronounce the so called *tria verba*, "*do*" "*dico*" "*addico*", provided with immediate effectiveness[12]. Above all, however, we must keep in mind that the action could only take place in the presence of a specific figure, a magistrate provided with *imperium*, whose *auctoritas* was made explicit through the possession of particular *insignia*: a specific type of toga (*praetexta* "a toga with a purple border"), the *fasces* and the *sella curulis* ("curule chair"). The display of these attributes was so important in determining the legal efficacy of the procedure, that the law excluded

---

[12]   Varro, *De lingua latina* 6.4.30: «dies fasti, per quos praetoribus omnia verba sine piaculo licet fari ... contrarii horum vocantur dies nefasti, per quos dies nefas fari praetorem "do", "dico", "addico". itaque non potest agi: necesse est aliquo eorum uti verbo, cum lege quid peragitur»; 6.53: «hinc fasti dies, quibus verba certa legitima sine piaculo praetoribus licet fari». Ovid, *Fastorum libri* 1.47 ff.; Macrobius, *Saturnalia* 1.16.14: «fasti sunt quibus licet fari praetori tria verba sollemnia, do dico addico».

the blind man from the possibility of forwarding a request to the magistrate in place of another (*postulare pro aliis*) as "without sight in both eyes ... he cannot see and reverence the *insignia* of the magistrate."[13] Perhaps the most interesting aspect, however, of the Roman legal performance, is its spatial context. We know that the area dedicated, par excellence, to legal action corresponded to the *forum* — in Rome justice was administered "in the open" (*sub divo*). Even more interestingly the person of the *praetor* had the power to determine the legal place though his sheer presence. As stated in the *Digesta*[14]:

> *Wherever the praetor has decided to "exercise his jurisdiction" (ius dicere), without prejudice to the majesty of his own imperium and the customs of the ancestors, this place is correctly called ius.*

In the Roman juridical tradition, the same term, *ius*, designated both the "right" and the "place" in which justice was given. As stated in the *Digesta* (1, 1, 1, 11):

> *The term ius is used in many senses ... With another meaning, ius is defined as the place where it is administered, deriving its name from what happens there.*

Building the *ius* as the "juridical place" presupposed the erection of a wooden "tribune" (*tribunal*), whose location could vary, provided that it supported the *sella curulis* (owned by the *praetor*) on which he sat exhibiting his own *insignia*. The "sitting" position of the magistrate guaranteed his person a special dignity, while the placement of the "curule chair" in an elevated position still allowed him to dominate

---

[13] *Digesta* 3.1.1.5.
[14] *Digesta* 1.1.1.11.

those around him. This "vertical" privilege, attributed to the *praetor*, made the *maiestas* of his *imperium* further visible[15]. Ultimately, how can we not be fascinated by the meticulous solemnity, the exhibited refinement, of such a social performance, certainly deserving the definition of "ritual"? This complex architecture of words, gestures, people, *insignia*, times, places — which was repeated each time in the same way — produces a fundamental effect: we could define it as an expansion of the "horizons of speaking".

With this expression we define the active reference to elements that are in themselves extraneous to a given context (constituted by the specific place / time of the utterance and the particular persons of the speakers); but that somehow become part of it as they are rooted in wider contexts, present to the awareness of the actors at the moment of the single utterances[16]. In the case of *legis actiones* the "horizons of speaking" we are referring to correspond to the shared memory of the fact that, in the past of the City, the same verbal procedure has already been consumed countless other times, in identical form and in similar contexts; and has been registered by the cultural tradition under the label "this is how it is done" or "this is how it works". In conclusion, it is precisely the fixity of the formulas, the exceptionality of their linguistic and gestural closure, as well as the repetitiveness of the contexts within which they are pronounced from time to time, that found their efficacy. Repeating every single action according to the same linguistic, gestural and contextual script produces the awareness that it is a *timeless* act. Hence its "strength", to use Louis Gernet's term. Now we understand better, perhaps, why the Romans wanted to "limit the entry of life" into

---

[15]   On the places for the *ius* in Rome cf. F. De Angelis, *An Introduction*, in idem (ed.), *Spaces of Justice in the Roman World,* Leiden-Boston: Brill, 2010, pp. 1–25.

[16]   W. F. Hanks, *Context*, in J. Mey ed., *Encyclopedia of Language and Linguistics*, London: Elsevier, 2006.

the juridical formulas: because in doing so the fragments of life initially selected by the custom could be repeated identical from one time to another, thus building the bases of the authority and efficacy of legal formulas.

(Maurizio Bettini, Center for Anthropology and the Classics, University of Siena)

研究综述
Research Survey

Recent Homeric Research: A Postscript

Xian Ruobing

The present piece is to be understood as a postscript to my review article "Recent Homeric Research" published in the first volume of *Museum Sinicum*.[1] There, I discussed the current status of Homeric studies, regarding Homeric questions, *Kunstsprache*, literary interpretation, and the Near Eastern influence. In acknowledging the importance of the last two topics in contemporary criticism, my review article concluded with the following words: "While the studies resulting from a renewed interest in the epics' Near Eastern background have been shown as less fruitful, the cognitive approaches taken by recent critics could shed new light on our understanding of Homer's narrative technique."[2] I still think that this judgment is basically correct.

In what follows, I would like to concentrate on two things. First, I will argue that the comparison between Near Eastern materials and the Homeric epics, though a favored topic in contemporary criticism, can only make a limited contribution to our understanding of the *Iliad* and the *Odyssey*. Second, I will discuss some recent works on literary interpretation of the Homeric epics, with special reference to

---

[1] Xian (2018).
[2] Xian (2018), 230.

cognitivist approach[3].

I

Currently, there is no scholarly consensus on the relationship between Near Eastern literature and the Homeric epics in general and that between *Gilgamesh* and *Iliad* in particular.

Pioneering studies by Burkert and West focused mainly on two issues: to identify potential parallels and to reconstruct the model and process of transmission[4]. In emphasizing the role of wandering bards and magicians in the eighth and seventh centuries, they took a number of Homeric passages to be "borrowed" from Near Eastern materials, not least due to the fact that these passages were thought problematic in their Homeric context and only explainable by appealing to external sources. This approach has been duly criticized by Kelly (among others), who argued that under closer inspection, many examples, which were previously thought problematic in their Homeric context, could be clarified in terms of epic convention or typical scenes[5]. On the other hand, scholars such as Haubold and Clarke have decided for a more balanced approach, which reads both the Homeric epics and the earlier literature of the ancient Near East within a shared cultural context[6]. Clarke, though himself an advocate of intertextual reading between *Gilgamesh* and *Iliad* in terms of Currie's "Homer's allusive art"[7], has argued that "the search for localised avenues of cross-influence may be

---

[3] On cognitive studies and classical texts in general, see Meineck, Short & Devereaux (2019); Anderson, Cairns & Sprevak (2019).

[4] Burkert (1984); West (1997). Cf. West (2018), who unconvincingly argued that "a vanished oral Heracles epic" (278), composed by a bard familiar with Babylonian poems, provides the missing link between *Gilgamesh* and Homer.

[5] Cf. e.g. Kelly (2007; 2008).

[6] Haubold (2013); Clarke (2019).

[7] Currie (2016).

less fruitful than the open-ended experience of reading the two literatures alongside each other, using the one to shape the questions that we address to the other, and by the comparison entering (with luck) into a more nuanced and historically authentic reading of both"[8].

This new trend is insofar promising as it rightly emphasizes such important themes like "mortality and wisdom" (the subtitle of Clarke 2019) common to both Homeric and Near Eastern mythological traditions[9]. That being said, the contribution of this sort of comparatism to literary interpretation of the Homeric epics, I contend, is limited. Two issues are at stake. First, while scholars have pointed out a number of comparanda between Homer and Near Eastern materials both on a micro (verbal similarities) and on a macro (mythological themes) level, "it is worth emphasising how much even on the level of plot in the Homeric poems is without parallel in the Gilgamesh epic"[10]. Second, the similarities between early Greek and Near Eastern literature might be "evident, and fascinating, for us", but they "were quite unknown, and of no interest whatsoever, to the Greeks"[11]. To sum up, the similarities between Homer and Near Eastern materials should not be overemphasized, and the latter might be insignificant for literary interpretation of the former from the perspective of early reception. To my mind, Near Eastern materials can be paired with Indo-European

---

[8] Clarke (2019), 27. The parallel between the *Iliad* and Anatolian ritual substitutes as claimed by Clarke (2019) (among others), however, has been challenged by Rutherford (2021).

[9] Cf. also Ballesteros (2021); Kelly and Metcalf (2021).

[10] Rutherford (2019), 235, who continued "there is nothing in *Gilgamesh* that corresponds to the Trojan War itself, to the pivotal figure of Helen, to the wrath and withdrawal of Achilles, to his knowledge of his death at Troy, to the revenge sought for the death of Patroclus, or to the eventual ransoming of Hector. The way in which Enkidu dies is completely different from the death of Patroclus. Without minimising the significance of the parallels relating to the inevitability of death, it is hard to see the *Gilgamesh* epic as having a formative influence on the main plot of the *Iliad*".

[11] Most (2003), 385. Most recently, Currie (2021) tried to challenge this scholarly consensus.

heritage[12], both of which are helpful but have limited use for the interpretation of the Homeric epics when compared with other relevant materials. Recent studies have shown that in addition to Hesiod, Archilochus, and early elegists whose works could be near contemporary with the *Iliad* and the *Odyssey*[13], the epic cycle and ancient scholia, if properly interpreted, are far more relevant to our understanding of Homeric artistry, both in terms of mythology as well as in terms of narrative techniques[14].

II

In this section, I will single out some most recent monographs, which, in my view, advance literary criticism of the Homeric epics in innovative ways[15].

Zanker's book on 'Metaphor in Homer' is the first monograph, which examines Homer's presentation of time, speech, and thought from the perspective of conceptual metaphor theory (CMT)[16]. By "comparing the modern metaphors described by Lakoff and Johnson", Zanker convincingly shows that "Homeric conceptions of time, speech, and self were not radically divergent from our own": "where scholars such as

---

[12]   E.g. Watkins (1995); West (2007); Allen (2020).

[13]   Cf. West (2011).

[14]   The materials concerning the *Cypria* and the *Aethiopis* have been examined thoroughly by Davies (2016; 2019), while Sammons (2017) has convincingly shown that narrative techniques well-known to the Homerists such as 'narrative doublet', 'foreshadowing', the use of 'catalogue', and *paradeigmata* are also demonstrable in the epic cycle. On the scholia, see esp. Montanari et al. (2017); Schironi (2018); Beck, Kelly & Phillips (2021).

[15]   I myself argued that the representation of space in the *Odyssey* plays a much more significant role in the epic's narrative dynamics than has been hitherto recognized (Xian [2021a]). This study might be complemented by Gazis (2018), who argued for the poetics of Hades in the *Iliad* and the *Odyssey*.

[16]   Zanker (2019). On contemporary metaphor studies and classical texts in general, see Novokhatko (2021).

Fränkel and Snell found items of pronounced foreignness in the Homeric epics, we have seen that Homeric diction is not so alien to modern thought as it might appear"[17]. On the basis of Zanker's pioneering work, scholars are now encouraged to analyse "the conceptual metaphors lodged within a continuous block of Homeric text"[18] in order to shed new light on the epics from the perspective of characterization and plot.

Purves suggested a series of novel readings concerning Homer's presentation of gestures[19]. Drawing on dance theory and studies of motion, Purves' book has persuasively shown "how the poet structures his narrative in relation to the coordinates and positions of his characters' bodies"[20]. Though her interpretation of some examples such as Hephaestus' and Ares' respective *falling* in human time and Achilles and Agamemnon's *standing apart* seems to be less convincing, the overall project has proved to be fruitful. With regard to the *Iliad*, Priamos' *reaching* of Hector's body is a significant movement for the epic's closure[21]. With regard to the *Odyssey*, both Odysseus' *leaping* at the pivotal moment of the mnestrophonia and Penelope's recurrent *standing* besides the *stathmos* are central to the epic's narrative dynamics. Furthermore, as Purves herself rightly pointed out, her approach is insofar promising as to illuminate "two related areas in studies of Homer and the body", namely "the performative gestures of the Homeric rhapsode" and "the question, raised most notably by Bruno Snell, of how we can conceptualize the Homeric body as a fully

---

[17] Zanker (2019), 201.

[18] Zanker (2020), 95.

[19] Purves (2019). One might note that the importance of body language for our understanding of Homer has already been emphasized by Lateiner (1995).

[20] Purves (2019), 6.

[21] In a similar vein, Forte (2020) argued that "one can understand Homeric narrative not as composed of static structures, but in terms of physical action: a reaching (for). As the active consequence of extending one's hand towards an object, the sense of touch features as the necessary component of Odysseus's return and reunions as well as of the *Iliad*'s closural scenes" (1).

realizable and visible 'whole'"[22].

Two books devoted to the *Odyssey* are worth noting[23]. Christensen has argued that the *Odyssey* as a whole has a psychological function, which might be understood in terms of Narrative Therapy as articulated by Epston and White[24]. Admittedly, the idea is not entirely new. Scholars have since long recognized that Odysseus' experience on the island of Scheria offers the hero a therapeutic rehabilitation to regain his heroic identity, a process which culminates in the protagonist's telling and retelling of his own *nostos* in books 9–12[25]. That being said, Christensen's reading extends to the whole *Odyssey*, including some controversially discussed episodes such as the *Telemachie* and the ending of the poem. Loney's recent book entitled *The Ethics of Revenge and the Meanings of the* Odyssey is the first monograph which examines one pervasive motif of the epic that is central to its main plot: the motif of revenge in the worlds of mortals and immortals alike[26]. Loney's book situates itself within contemporary criticism on the *Odyssey*, which problematizes Odysseus' mnestrophonia from an ethical perspective. The question of how the hero's killing of the suitors can be justified entails a narrative anxiety, which is demonstrable in the poem itself as well as in its early reception[27].

---

[22]   Purves (2019), 29.

[23]   Regarding the *Iliad*, Myers (2019), though less original, offers a systematic examination of divine audience, while Pucci (2018) is less well organized in order to convince the reader of his novel reading of the Iliadic Zeus.

[24]   Christensen (2020).

[25]   See esp. Mattes (1958); cf. Race (2014) and Rösler (2022).

[26]   Loney (2019). For the revenge theme in the *Iliad*, see Wilson (2002).

[27]   Contemporary criticism is mainly sympathetic with the suitors. See Xian (2021b), 195–196: "There is no doubt that in the *Odyssey* the narrator takes sides with Odysseus and portrays the hero as a justified slayer of the suitors. In the course of the epic narrative, the poem describes the suitors in negative terms and suggests some of their evil deeds which might justify Odysseus' slaughter. Furthermore, the murder of the suitors, which is repeatedly anticipated by omens and oracles, is portrayed as a divine punishment designed by Athena and endorsed by Zeus. However, the epic itself knows alternative views about the hero's act, an anxiety which is identified as one of the poem's central problems" (cf. also Nagler [1990]; Burgess [2014]; Grethlein [2017], 213–227).

Conclusion

As shown above, there are a number of highly interesting publications on the interpretation of the Homeric epics, which appeared within a short time (2018–2021)[28]. In related fields such as Archaic elegiac, iambic, and lyric poetry, the progress is even more visible[29]. To conclude, I have written "Recent Homeric Research" as well as this postscript not least "in the hope of persuading such students that this is in fact an exciting time to be a Homerist"[30].

Bibliography

Allen, N. (2020) *Arjuna-Odysseus. Shared Heritage in Indian and Greek Epic*, New York.

Anderson, M., Cairns, D. & Sprevak, M. (eds.) (2019) *Distributed Cognition in Classical Antiquity*, Edinburgh.

Ballesteros, B. (2021) "On Gilgamesh and Homer: Ishtar, Aphrodite and the meaning of parallel", *CQ* 71, 1–21.

Beck, B., Kelly, A. & Phillips, T. (eds.) (2021) *The Ancient Scholia to Homer's Iliad: Exegesis and Interpretation*, Oxford.

Bernsdorff, H. (2020) *Anacreon of Teos: Testimonia and Fragments*. 2 vols, Oxford.

Bozzone, C. (2022) "Homeric Formulas and their Antiquity: A Constructional Study of ἀνδροτῆτα καὶ ἥβην", *Glotta* 98, 33–67.

Burgess, J. (2014) "Framing Odysseus. The Death of the Suitors", in: M. Christopoulos and M. Païzi-Apostolopoulou (eds.), *Crime and Punishment in Homeric and Archaic Epic. Proceedings of the 12th International Symposium on the Odyssey, Ithaca, September 3–7, 2013*, Ithaka, 337–354.

Burkert, W. (1984) *Die orientalisierende Epoche in der griechischen Religion und*

---

[28] In addition to the works discussed above, I would like to single out Forssman (2019; 2020), who offers a complete *Sammlung* of Homeric (verbal and nominal) forms. Interesting new works in the field of Homeric morphology include Ward (2021); Fries (2022); Bozzone (2022); Xian (2022).

[29] To name just a few: Swift (2019); Sider (2020); Bernsdorff (2020); Di Marzio (2020).

[30] Doherty (2009), 1.

Literatur, Heidelberg.

Christensen, J. (2020) *The Many-Minded Man. The* Odyssey*, Psychology, and the Therapy of Epic,* Ithaca.

Clarke, M. (2019) *Achilles beside Gilgamesh. Mortality and Wisdom in Early Epic Poetry*, Cambridge.

Currie, B. (2016). *Homer's allusive art*, Oxford.

Currie, B. (2021) "The birth of literary criticism (Herodotus 2.116–17) and the roots of Homeric neoanalysis", in: J. Price and R. Zelnick-Abramowitz (eds.), *Text and Intertext in Greek Epic and Drama. Essays in Honor of Margalit Finkelberg*, London/New York, 147–170.

Davies, M. (2016). *The Aethiopis: Neo-Neoanalysis Reanalyzed,* Cambridge MA.

Davies, M. (2019) *The Cypria*, Cambridge MA.

Di Marzio, M. (2020) *Bacchylidis Encomiorum et Eroticorum Fragmenta*, Roma.

Doherty, L. (2009) "Introduction", in: L. Doherty (ed.), *Oxford Readings in Classical Studies: Homer's Odyssey*, Oxford, 1–17.

Forssman, B. (2019) *Die homerischen Verbalformen*, Dettelbach.

Forssman, B. (2020) *Die homerischen Nominalformen*, Dettelbach.

Forte, A. (2020) "Reach and reunion in the *Odyssey*: An enactive narratology", *Helios* 47, 1–38.

Fries, S. (2022) "Über die Herkunft der langvokalischen Konjunktive des Typs hom. ἐθέλωμι, ἐθέλησθα, ἐθέλησι",*Glotta* 98, 148–173.

Gazis, G. (2018) *Homer and the Poetics of Hades*, Oxford.

Grethlein, J. (2017) *Die Odyssee. Homer und die Kunst des Erzählens*, München.

Haubold, J. (2013) *Greece and Mesopotamia: Dialogues in Literature*, Cambridge.

Kelly, A. (2007) "The Babylonian captivity of Homer: the case of the Dios Apate", *RhM* 151, 259–304.

Kelly, A. (2008) "AΨOPPOOY ΩKEANOIO — a Babylonian reminiscence?", *CQ* 57, 280–282.

Kelly, A. and Metcalf, C. (eds.) (2021) *Gods and Mortals in Early Greek and Near Eastern Mythology*, Oxford.

Lateiner, D. (1995) *Sardonic Smile: Nonverbal Behavior in Homeric Epic*, Ann Arbor.

Loney, A. (2019) *The Ethics of Revenge and the Meanings of the* Odyssey, Oxford/New York.

Mattes, W. (1958) *Odysseus bei den Phäaken*, Würzburg.

Meineck, P., Short, W. & Devereaux, J. (eds.) (2019) *The Routledge Handbook of Classics and Cognitive Theory*, London.

Montanari, F., Montana, F., Muratore, D., Pagani, L. (2017) "Towards a new critical edition of the scholia to the *Iliad*: a specimen", *Trends in Classics* 9, 1–21.

Most, G. (2003) "Violets in crucibles: translating, traducing, transmuting", *TAPA* 133, 381–390.

Myers, T. (2019) *Homer's Divine Audience. The* Iliad's *Reception on Mount Olympus*, Oxford.

Nagler, M. (1990) "Odysseus. The Proem and the Problem", *ClAnt* 9, 335–356.

Novokhatko, A. (2021) "Contemporary metaphor studies and classical texts", *Mnemosyne* 74, 682–703.

Pucci, P. (2018) *The* Iliad — *The Poem of Zeus*, Berlin.

Purves, A. (2019) *Homer and the Poetics of Gesture*, Oxford/New York.

Race, W. (2014) "Phaeacian therapy in Homer's *Odyssey*", in: P. Meineck and D. Konstan (eds.), *Combat Trauma and the Ancient Greek*, New York, 47–66.

Rösler, W. (2022) "Ares und Aphrodite — das Lied des Demodokos und seine Funktion in der *Odyssee*", *Hermes* 150, 5–19.

Rutherford, I. (2021) "Substitute, sacrifice and sidekick: a note on the comparative method and Homer", in: J. Price and R. Zelnick-Abramowitz (eds.), *Text and Intertext in Greek Epic and Drama. Essays in Honor of Margalit Finkelberg*, London/New York, 132–146.

Rutherford, R. (2019) *Homer,* Iliad *Book XVIII*, Cambridge.

Sammons, B. (2017) *Device and Composition in the Greek Epic Cycle*, Oxford/New York.

Schironi, F. (2018) *The Best of the Grammarians: Aristarchus of Samothrace on the* Iliad, Ann Arbor.

Sider, D. (2020) *Simonides. Epigrams and Elegies: Edited with an Introduction, Translation and Commentary*, Oxford.

Swift, L. (2019) *Archilochus: the Poems. Introduction, Text, Translation and Commentary*, Oxford.

Ward, M. (2021) "ΓΑΜΕΣΣΕΤΑΙ/ΓΕ ΜΑΣΣΕΤΑΙ: Homer *Iliad* 9.394 and the constitutive role irregularity", *JHS* 141, 224–240.

Watkins, C. (1995) *How to kill a Dragon: Aspects of Indo-European Poetics*, Oxford/New York.

West, M. (1997) *The East Face of Helicon: West Asiatic Elements in Greek Poetry and Myth*, Oxford.

West, M. (2007) *Indo-European Poetry and Myth*, Oxford.

West, M. (2011) "Echoes of Hesiod and elegy in the *Iliad*", in: *Hellenica, Volume I: Epic*, Oxford, 209–232.

West, M. (2018) "Gilgāmeš and Homer: the missing link?", in: L. Audley-Miller and B. Dignas (eds.), *Wandering Myths: Transcultural Uses of Myth in the Ancient*

World, Berlin, 265–280.

Wilson, D. (2002) *Ransom, Revenge, and Heroic Identity in the* Iliad, Cambridge.

Xian, R. (2018) "Recent Homeric Research", *Museum Sinicum* 1, 217–230.

Xian, R. (2021a) *Raum und Erzählung in der* Odyssee, Leiden.

Xian, R. (2021b) "Blameless Aegisthus revisited", *Mnemosyne* 74, 181–199.

Xian, R. (2022) "Homeric ΠΕΡΘΕΤΟ (*Il.* 12.15), ΠΕΡΘΟΜΕΝΗ (*Il.* 2.374 = 4.291 = 13.816), and ΠΕΡΘΑΙ (*Il.* 16.708)", *Glotta* 98, 313–320.

Zanker, A. (2019) *Metaphor in Homer. Time, Speech, and Thought*, Oxford.

Zanker, A. (2020) "Metaphor in the Speech of Achilles (*Iliad* 9.308–429)", *Yearbook of Ancient Greek Epic* 4, 95–121.

(Xian Ruobing, Department of History, Fudan University)

参考书架

Reference Books

《希腊人名词典》与希腊人名学研究

詹瑜松

史学研究以史料为基础，而史料则多种多样，最常规的是传世文献，除此之外还有许多其他类型的史料，其中铭文、档案、日记等早已为史学界所熟用。然而，有些类型的史料其价值不太明显，加之分布零散、利用不易，通常不为学界所关注，但实际上如果能够充分挖掘，则可获得非同寻常的洞见。人名就是这样一类史料，以人名为核心的研究就是所谓的人名学（anthroponomastics）。跟其他史学分支相比，人名学无疑要冷门得多。由于人名本身的特点，人名研究需要进行资料建设，其中最重要的便是要有人名词典。本文首先介绍《希腊人名词典》（*Lexicon of Greek Personal Names*，简称*LGPN*）的编修和使用方法，再评述该词典的学术价值和编修得失，同时也对目前的希腊人名学研究略加介绍。

一、《希腊人名词典》的编修过程

在西方古典学领域，大型工具书往往出自德国，德国学者在这方面的工作十分出色。毫不意外，最早的希腊人名词典也是德国学者编的。早在1842年，德国学者帕佩就出版了一部《希腊专名词典》[1]；

---

[1]　W. Pape (ed.), *Wörterbuch der Griechischen Eigennamen*, Braunschweig: F. Vieweg, 1884.

之后由本泽勒做了几次修订、扩充，成为此后一百多年里唯一的一部希腊专名词典[2]。该词典不仅包含历史人物的人名，还收录了地名、神话中的人名和神名。此后，一些学者开始了对希腊人名的研究，贝希特尔在1902年和1917年先后出版了《阿提卡女性人名》和《希腊历史人名》，主要内容是按字母顺序分析希腊人名的词根[3]。大约同时，兰贝茨出版《希腊奴隶人名》，总结了奴隶人名的不同类型[4]；西蒂希的《论希腊人的神义名》则以神义名（theophoric name）来探讨宗教崇拜的传播[5]。这些都是典型的人名学研究成果，主要围绕人名本身展开。

法国学者虽然没有编修人名词典，但却最早意识到人名可以用于历史研究。1851年，勒特罗纳发表了一篇长达139页的《关于可从希腊专名研究中获取对历史学和考古学益处的论文》[6]。然而，此后一百年里追随勒特罗纳脚步的学者似乎很少，一直到20世纪60年代罗贝尔才发表了一部比较有代表性的专著《希腊罗马时期小亚细亚的本地人名》[7]。罗贝尔通过人名考察小亚细亚的族群和历史，其分析表明很多人名看似是小亚细亚原住民的，但实际上是希腊人的名字；罗贝尔由此证明，人名学所涉及的不仅是人名目录，还有人名的历史，以及人名背后的历史（l'histoire par les noms）。

以上便是彼得·弗雷泽（Peter Fraser）提议编修《希腊人名词典》时的学术背景。弗雷泽有此提议跟前人的研究不无关系，因为他在研究希腊化的萨拉匹斯崇拜时也曾用神义名来论证该宗教的传

2　W. Pape and G. E. Benseler (ed.), *Wörterbuch der Griechischen Eigennamen*, 3rd edition, Braunschweig: F. Vieweg, 1870.

3　F. Bechtel, *Die Attischen Frauennamen: nach Ihrem Systeme Dargestellt*, Göttingen: Vandenhoeck & Ruprecht, 1902; F. Bechtel, *Die Historischen Personennamen des Griechischen: bis zur Kaiserzeit*, Halle: M. Niemeyer, 1917.

4　M. Lambertz, *Die Griechischen Sklavennamen*, Wien: K. K. Staatsgymnasium, 1907–1908.

5　E. Sittig, *De Graecorum Nominibus Theophoris*, Halis Saxonum: E. Karras, 1911.

6　A. Letronne, "Mémoire sur L'utilité Qu'on Peut Retirer de L'étude des Noms Propres Grecs, pour L'histoire et L'archéologie", *Mémoires de l'Institut de France*, vol. 19, no. 1, 1851, pp. 1–139.

7　L. Robert, *Noms Indigènes dans L'asie-Mineure Gréco-Romaine*, Amsterdam: Adolf M. Hakkert, 1963.

播。1972年,作为英国国家学术院(British Academy)院士、在牛津大学万灵学院工作的弗雷泽,正式向英国国家学术院建议编修一部新的人名词典,以便取代帕佩和本泽勒的《希腊专名词典》。当时,弗雷泽预计编修新词典大概不会超过十年;而学术院秘书艾伦(D. F. Allen)回应称,以他的经验看,项目总是会超期,需要仔细盘算,因为学术院不喜欢那些看不到头的项目[8]。这位秘书确实经验丰富,早就料到项目会超期,但是他的经验还不够丰富,没有料到项目竟会超期四五倍:整整五十年过去了,新词典还是没有完成。可能因为迟迟无法完成,所以1996年此项目转归牛津大学古典学院管理,现为牛津古典研究项目之一,同时也接受英国艺术与人文研究理事会、英国国家学术院、牛津大学约翰·费尔基金会和雅典科学院资助。

　　和帕佩的旧词典不同,新词典排除地名、神名和神话人物,亦不收录迈锡尼时期的人名,只囊括之后的历史人物,其统计年代从公元前8世纪一直到公元6世纪。新词典看似缩小了范围,但由于一百多年来的材料积累,新词典的规模远远超过了旧词典。按最初的计划,新词典的编修分为两个阶段,第一个阶段处理希腊人传统的活动范围,第二个阶段处理埃及、叙利亚、巴勒斯坦、两河流域等区域。经过彼得·弗雷泽、伊莲·马修斯(Elaine Matthews)等几代编者的努力,第一阶段的任务已经完成。新词典已出版5卷8册,其中第一卷涉及爱琴海岛屿、塞浦路斯和北非的库勒涅,第二卷是阿提卡(2007年修订),第三卷的两册是希腊中南部加上西西里和意大利,第四卷是希腊北部从马其顿一直到黑海北岸,第五卷的三册则是小亚细亚。这些已经涵盖了希腊人活动的大部分区域。第二阶段的任务也正在进行。词典的第六卷是从巴勒斯坦、叙利亚到幼发拉底河以东,预计今年(2022年)将会出版;同时,埃及地区的卷册也正在筹备之中[9]。如今我们可以确信,词典肯定能在十年之内完成,只是弗雷泽和马修斯这两位最重要的编者均已过世,无缘得见词典之大成。

　　当弗雷泽提议编修新词典时,计算机技术尚未发展起来,但从第

8　*LGPN* V.C, p. xxxi.
9　计划并非一成不变,比如小亚细亚内陆地区原打算放在第二阶段处理,但最终放到了第五卷里。

一卷出版（1987年）开始，编者已经非常前瞻地在考虑将词典数字化，做成网络数据库。目前，除了第五卷C分册以外，其余卷册已全部上线，各条目跟纸质词典没有区别，而且较之纸质词典，数据库增加了性别信息，还提供人名、地名、身份和职业的目录。词典原计划以第六卷为索引卷，方便查找每个人名在各卷中的位置，这一功能实际上已经由数据库实现了。在便利性方面，编者一直在不断努力。根据第一卷的书评反馈，词典从第二卷开始提供人名的末字母索引，官方网站也补充提供了第一卷的末字母索引。当然，最便利的是数据库完全免费公开，通常我们只需检索数据库即可，不必翻阅纸质词典。

　　词典的编修从一开始就是国际合作。弗雷泽最初计划对人名进行形态上的归类，如复合名、神义名，并分析人名的词源、词根，但一直没有实现。2015年，项目组和法国学者合作，设立了一个"希腊人名的词源和语义分析"项目（LGPN-Ling［Etymological and Semantic Analysis of Greek Personal Names］），旨在分析人名的词根、词缀，词根的意义，复合名的形式结构和最初的含义。相应的数据库预计将在2023年上线。

二、《希腊人名词典》的体例和使用方法

　　新词典跟旧词典在体例方面有相同之处，也有不同之处，其中最重要的是新词典只收历史人名。那么，所谓的希腊人名是指什么呢？按通常的理解，希腊人名自然是指希腊人的名字。这种理解不算错，但实际操作要复杂、棘手得多。弗雷泽在第一卷前言中介绍了词典的体例。根据他的解释，词典不收录地名，但如果有人将地名用作人名则会收录；神话和史诗中的人名，词典不收录，但如果它们跟某地区有特别的关系，比如说是某地的建城者，则会收录；文学作品里的人名也会收录，编者认为它们也是当时正常的人名，词典会将其年代归入作者本人的年代，同时标注fict(itious)（虚构的）；用非希腊字母——例如迈锡尼的线形文字、阿拉伯字母——书写的希腊人名，

词典不收录,但是用拉丁字母和塞浦路斯音节文字书写的希腊人名,则会收录;用希腊字母书写的非希腊人名,词典也会收录;钱币上缩写形式的人名、铭文中的残破人名,词典亦不收录,但如果能够肯定其完整的拼写形式则会收录,必要时还会标明复原的可靠程度。

可见,词典收录人名的标准相当复杂,后来也做了一些改变,像小亚细亚地区用非希腊字母书写的人名实际上也收录了。就我个人的理解而言,在新词典中,希腊人名指的是出现在希腊语强势地区且可以确认其希腊语形式的人名,要么是希腊语人名,要么是有希腊语形式的非希腊语人名,具体包括:(1)用希腊字母书写的希腊语人名;(2)用非希腊字母书写的希腊语人名;(3)用希腊字母书写的非希腊语人名;(4)用非希腊字母书写但可确定其希腊语形式的非希腊语人名。第一类完全收录,其他三类则未必。因此,存在这样一种情况:用拉丁字母书写的色雷斯人名,如果是在希腊语强势地区内则收录,如果是在拉丁语强势范围内则不收录。

词典累计已收录大约40万个人物,出自传世文献、碑铭、草纸、钱币、涂鸦、人工制品等,那么数量如此庞大的人名材料该如何编排呢?旧词典完全是按首字母顺序来编排的,其优点在于方便了解某个人名的整体情况而不必翻阅每一卷。弗雷泽起初也有此想法,但考虑到各种因素,词典最终遵循的是地理原则,即按地区来编排,必要时牺牲地区间族群或文化联系。大一点的岛屿通常单列,即使该岛与邻近的大陆联系极为密切。譬如伊奥尼亚的十二个城邦,有些在爱琴海的岛上,便归在第一卷;有些在小亚细亚西部,便归在第五卷。各卷册再以人名首字母顺序编排,人名之下的例证仍按地区来编排。不过这不是什么大问题,因为数据库已经能让我们方便地了解某个人名的整体情况。

真正麻烦的是人名的归属原则。主要有两种原则,一是属人原则,即某人是哪个城邦的人,人名就归入哪个城邦,无论人名是在哪里发现的;二是属地原则,某人常住哪个城邦就归入哪个城邦,或者人名是在哪个城邦发现的就归入哪个城邦。属人原则可能出现的麻烦是,某人名义上是米利都人,但他一辈子都在雅典居住,或者我们根本不知道他是哪里人;属地原则可能出现的麻烦是,同一个人名可能在不同地方出现。

新词典遵循的是属人原则，但有些情况需要特殊处理，具体来说：（1）如果某人可能是某城邦的本地人但又不完全确定，那就在地名后面加一个问号"?"；（2）如果某人活跃于某城邦但又难以确定他的归属，那就在地名后面加一个星号"*"。侨民（metics）如果能够确定其母邦，则归入其母邦并标明"侨民"。如果不能，则归入人名所在的城邦并标明"侨民"；如果带有父名，其父名则归入"其他"（Other）；（3）如果某人的母邦完全无法确定，那就会归入"其他"（Other）。来源不清的奴隶和获释奴亦是如此。对于拜占庭时期的主教，也默认他们不属于所在城市，也归入"其他"。起初，词典计划把"其他"人名单列一卷，但后来似乎放弃了。

编排原则确定后，剩下的便是词条的编写了。在新词典中，一个词条分为五个部分：人名、地点、年代、出处、补充信息（通常置于括号中）。其中人名和年代的处理比较复杂。首先，人名存在方言问题。根据体例，文献里的人名通常保持阿提卡形式或通用希腊语的形式，铭文等材料里的人名则保留或还原其本来的形式，不会将其阿提卡化。然而，两个人名的细微差异是源自方言还是源自正字法，这并不那么容易区分。

至于年代，通常就是文献、铭文等材料本身的年代。年代的精确程度差异极大：我们知道生卒年的人物，会标明确切的年代；不知生卒年但知道人物的活跃时间的，则标注一个年代范围，例如公元前某世纪；如果连材料本身的年代也不清楚，则根据铭文的字母形式等间接手段提供一个宽泛的年代，例如 hell（enistic）（即希腊化时期）、imp（erial）（即罗马帝国时期）；实在无法做出推测的，则标注 inc（ertum）（即年代不详）。

关于出处，铭文优先标注 *SEG*（《希腊铭文补遗》），出现在《大保利百科全书》（Pauly-Wissowa, *Realencyclopädie*）中的人物则优先标注 *RE*。补充信息通常是社会关系，偶尔也会标明身份和职业。社会关系只标明亲子关系，不标注夫妻、兄弟姐妹关系，例如儿子用"s."表示，如果存在收养关系，那么亲生的加注"nat."、收养的加注"ad."。身份和职业主要是那些带有世袭性质、跟人名有密切关联的,例如国王、奴隶、雕塑家或医生,但后来显然打破了这一体例。就数据库提供的目录来看,真正标注身份和职业的并不多。

了解体例之后,最重要的是使用词典。检索数据库自然要方便得多,其中特别方便的一个功能是可以按时间段来检索,只要在起、止时间的方框内输入阿拉伯数字即可(负整数代表公元前、正整数代表公元后)。数据库虽然有在谷歌地图上标注地点的功能,但实际并不好用。查找地点最好是配合《巴灵顿希腊罗马世界地图集》[10],和基于此地图集开发的"古代世界地图绘制中心"(Ancient World Mapping Center)网站,后者尤为便利。

下面我们来具体看看如何阅读词条,以第二卷的Αὐτοκράτης词条为例:

ATHENS: (1) **v/iv BC** Lys. fr. xxv (*PA* 2739); (2) ~ *PCG* 4 pp. 18 ff. (*PA* 2736); (3) **c. 411 BC** *IG* I³ 1190, 46 (*PA* 2737) (–**τες**); (4) **f. iv BC** *IG* II² 11961; 11962 (f. Λέων); (5) ~ [Lys.] viii 15 (*PA* 2738); (6) **m. iv BC** *IG* II² 1613, 99 ([Αὐ?]**τοκράτης**); (7) **c. 330–320 BC** ib. 1554 etc. = *SEG* XVIII 36 B, 232, 234, 237 (**s.** Ἀγ[–]);[11] (8) **c. 206 BC** *IG* VII 273, 5 = *IOrop* 172 (*PA* 2740) (**s. Νικοκλῆς**);[12]

——Daidalidai: (9) **iv/iii BC** *SEG* XIII 186 (Αὐτ[ο]κράτης)[13]

——Eleusis: (10) **c. 340–317 BC** *IG* II² 6028 (*PA* 2742) (**f. Αὐτοκλείδης**)

——Euonymon: (11) **ii BC** *IG* II² 6191 (*PA* 2743)

——Lamptrai: (12) **336/5 BC** *Ag.* XV 42, 52

——Paiania: (13) **s. iv BC** *IG* II² 478 = Reinmuth, *Ephebic Inscr.* 17, 37; *Ag.* XV 32, 16 (= *PA* 2744); *Ag.* XVII 259, 1 (**s.**

---

10   R. J. A. Talbert (ed.), *Barrington Atlas of the Greek and Roman World*, Princeton: Princeton University Press, 2000.

11   数据库中第7条为 "s. iv BC *SEMA* 2244",原第7条变为第8条,其后序号依次顺延。

12   数据库中此条为 "**iii/ii BC** *IOrop* 172, **3, 5**; = *PA* 2740 (s. Νικοκλῆς)"。

13   数据库中此条为 "**f. iii BC** *SEMA* 189 (Αὐτ[ο]κρά τ ης)"。

Αἰσχίνης)[14]

——Pithos: (14) 174/3 BC ib. XV 202, 2; *SEG* XXI 449, 3; *Hesp.* 16 (1947) p. 191 no. 95 [2] (**I f. Αὐτοκράτης II**);[15] (15) ~ *Ag.* XV 202, 2; *SEG* XXI 449, 3; *Hesp.* 16 (1947) p. 191 no. 95 2 (**II s. Αὐτοκράτης I**)[16]

——tribe Erechtheis: (16) **c. 430–405 BC** *IG* I³ 965 (*PA/APF* 2741) (f. Κλεισθένης)

ATHENS?: (17) **iv–iii BC** *IG* II² 10706 ([Ἀο]τοκράτης—lap.); (18) **s. iv BC** *CAT* 4.421;[17] (19) c. 250/49 BC *IG* II² 1534 B = Aleshire, *Asklepieion* Inv. V, 123 (Αὐ[τοκ]ράτης)

ATHENS*: (20) **f. iv BC** *IG* II² 2346, 54 ([Αὐ]τοκράτης: s. Καλλικράτης)

雅典：(1) 公元前425—前375年，吕西亚斯残篇第25号（《阿提卡人物志》第2739条）；(2) 同上，《希腊喜剧残篇》第4卷第18页及以下（《阿提卡人物志》第2736条）；(3) 约公元前411年，《希腊铭文集成》第一卷第3版，第1190条第46行（《阿提卡人物志》第2737条）（铭文中人名末尾的拼法为-τες）；(4) 公元前399—前350年，《希腊铭文集成》第二卷第2版第11961、11962条（列昂之父）；(5) 同上，[吕西亚斯]演说辞第15号（《阿提卡人物志》第2738条）；(6) 公元前375—前325年，《希腊铭文集成》第二卷第2版第1613条第99行（铭文残缺前两个字母，复原存疑）；(7) 约公元前330—前320年，同上，第1554条等 =《希腊铭文补遗》第18卷第36条B栏第232、234、237行（Ἀγ[–]之子，父名残缺）；(8) 约公元前206年，《希腊铭文集成》第七卷第273条第5行 =《奥洛波斯铭文集》第172条（《阿提卡

14　数据库中没有*Ag.* XVII 259, 1，而多了*SEMA* 508。

15　数据库中没有*SEG* XXI 449, 3; *Hesp.* 16 (1947) p. 191 no. 95 [2]，而多了*Ag.* XVI 281, 3; *Ag.* 282, 2; *Ag.* 283, [2]。

16　数据库中没有*SEG* XXI 449, 3; *Hesp.* 16 (1947) p. 191 no. 95 2，而多了*Ag.* XVI 281, 3; *Ag.* 282, 2; *Ag.* 283, [2]。

17　数据库中无此条。

人物志》第2740条)(尼科克勒斯之子)

——代达利代德莫:(9)公元前325—前275年,《希腊铭文补遗》第13卷第186条(铭文残缺第四个字母 o)

——埃琉西斯德莫:(10)约公元前340—前317年,《希腊铭文集成》第二卷第2版第6028条(《阿提卡人物志》第2742条)(奥托克莱德斯之父)

——欧奥尼蒙德莫:(11)公元前2世纪,《希腊铭文集成》第二卷第2版,第6191条(《阿提卡人物志》第2743条)

——兰普特莱德莫:(12)公元前336/335年,《雅典广场:美国驻雅典古典研究院发掘报告》第15卷第42条第52行

——派亚尼亚德莫:(13)公元前350—前300年,《希腊铭文集成》第二卷第2版第478条 = 赖因穆特:《公元前4世纪的青年铭文集》第17条第37行;《雅典广场:美国驻雅典古典研究院发掘报告》第15卷第32条第16行(《阿提卡人物志》第2744条);《雅典广场:美国驻雅典古典研究院发掘报告》第17卷第259条第1行(埃斯基涅斯之子)

——皮托斯德莫:(14)公元前174/173年,同上第15卷第202条第2行;《希腊铭文补遗》第21卷第449条第3行;《赫斯佩里亚》第16卷(1947年),第191页第95条[第2行](此为奥托克拉特斯一世,乃奥托克拉特斯二世之父);(15)同上,《雅典广场:美国驻雅典古典研究院发掘报告》第15卷第202条第2行;《希腊铭文补遗》第21卷第449条第3行;《赫斯佩里亚》第16卷(1947年)第191页第95条第2行(此为奥托克拉特斯二世,乃奥托克拉特斯一世之子)

——埃瑞克泰斯部落:(16)公元前430—前405年,《希腊铭文集成》第一卷第3版第965条(《阿提卡人物志》/《公元前600—前300年雅典有产家庭》,第2741行)(克莱斯特涅斯之父)

可能是雅典人:(17)公元前399—前200年,《希腊铭文集成》第二卷第2版第10706条(经核验原碑,前两个字母残缺,Ἀο是复原的);(18)公元前350—前300年,《古典时期的阿提卡墓碑》,4.421;(19)约公元前250/249年,《希腊铭文集成》第二卷第

2 版第 1534 条 B 栏＝阿利希尔：《雅典的阿斯克勒庇奥斯神庙：民众、奉献品和目录》第 5 目录第 123 行（铭文残缺，τοκ 是复原的）

可能是在雅典的侨民：（20）公元前 400—350 年，《希腊铭文集成》第二卷第 2 版第 2346 条第 54 行（铭文残缺，Aὐ 是复原的；此人为卡利克拉特斯之子）。

Aὐτοκράτης 是一个中等长度的词条，可以反映词典的一些体例（粗体为笔者所加），特别是时间的表示方法[18]。值得注意的是第 14、15 两例，二者是父子关系，标注的年代一样，都是铭文本身的年代，但现实中父亲的年代肯定更早一些。类似地，第 4 例的年代也是儿子列昂的年代，作为父亲 Aὐτοκράτης 的年代无疑也要更早。人名出处的年代不等于人物的年代，这点我们在使用时不可忽视。

因为词典第二卷出过修订版（数据库显然采用的是修订版的数据），所以有些信息发生了变动：有的是出处有变，有的是年代有变，更突出的是删除了一条同时又增加了另一条。可见，编者认为之前的一些判断有误。事实上，我之前在引用一些人名例证时，也认为词典所给的性别等个别信息有误。当然，错误是不可避免的，弗雷泽在前言中也并不讳言。因此，我们在使用时必须尽可能查证原文，对人名的相关信息要有自己的判断。然而，对国内研究者来说，最困难的正是查证原文。尽管现在网络电子资源已经大为丰富，但是大量的铭文、草纸文献等资料仍然不易获得，这是影响我们充分利用词典的最大障碍。

三、《希腊人名词典》的学术价值和编修得失

编修大型工具书是一件嘉惠学林的善举。新词典虽然尚未全部完成，但其学术价值已经显现出来了，有学者称之为自《希英大词

---

[18]　除了词条里的几种，还有 b.(efore)，例如 b. 212 BC 表示公元前 262—前 212 年；还有 a.(fter)，例如 a. 100 AD 表示公元 100—150 年。

典》(*Greek-English Lexicon*)出版以来,英国对古典学界最有意义的贡献。[19]

首先,新词典已经成为人名学研究的全新起点。以往我们对希腊人名只能有一些粗略的判断,而现在根据词典所提供的数据,我们可以确切知道希腊人名的一些基本特点,也能知道最流行的人名是哪些。第一卷至第五卷A分册共涉及300 582人,累计35 982个人名,平均每个人名约有8个例证[20]。和早年出版的卷册相比,第五卷的A、B两个分册还提供了进一步的统计数据:A分册中54%的人名仅有1个例证,即孤例名(hapax),最热门的三个人名分别是Ἀπολλώνιος(1 354例)、Διονύσιος(903例)和Δημήτριος(744例)[21];类似地,B分册中56%的人名仅有1个例证,少于10个例证的人名更是高达91%,最热门的三个人名和A分册一样,分别有977例、872例和793例[22]。然而,这三个人名并非在所有地区都同样流行,譬如在第三卷A分册中,就分别只有101例、304例、153例。从时间上看,不同时代流行的人名也并不相同,像前面引用的Αὐτοκράτης最晚的例证只到公元前2世纪,之后七个世纪里雅典就没什么人再取这个名字了。可见,希腊人名具有以下几个特点:(1)人名数量众多;(2)多数人名极少使用,热门人名重复率极高;(3)人名具有明显的时代性和地域性。这是泛希腊的特点,具体地区和城邦的情况可以根据词典做进一步的研究。

在人名学的研究方法上,新词典和数据库可以推动我们从定性研究走向定量研究。以前的研究多是分析人名的词根、词义,即使想做定量研究也不具备条件,但如今情况不同了,我们可以直接给出百分比,而不是模糊地说"很多""大量"。例如我们可以准确地说约97%的"亚历山大"(2 238例)出现在公元前3世纪及以后,其原因不

---

[19]　R. W. V. Catling and F. Marchand (ed.), *Onomatologos: Studies in Greek Personal Names Presented to Elaine Matthews*, Oxford: Oxbow Books, 2010, p. xi.

[20]　目前这个数据只统计到第5卷A分册,不含B和C分册。这两个分册的人数可以直接跟其他分册的相加,但人名数不能,因为会出现重复计算。就分册本身而言,B分册涉及44 748人,8 418个人名,每个人名平均仅5.3个例证;C分册涉及42 830人,7 328个人名,每个人名平均仅5.8个例证。

[21]　参见 *LGPN* V. A, pp. xvi–xviii。

[22]　参见 *LGPN* V. B, pp. xxx–xxxi。

言而喻。随着词典的编修逐渐完成,数据越来越全,定量研究也将越发接近历史事实。原先弗雷泽打算接受莫米利亚诺(Momigliano)的建议,对最常见的一些人名采用历史概述而非逐条收录的方式。幸好词典最终选择逐条收录的方式,否则这将会明显损害词典在定量研究方面的价值。

另外,有一个领域跟人名学非常相近,即人物志(prosopography)研究,人名学所需要的核心信息也是人物志研究必不可少的。同时,二者又有明显的不同:人名学的研究范围可大可小,可以所有人名为对象,也可以某组人名为对象,但要求的历史信息少;人物志的研究范围一般比较小,通常是以某个或某组人物为中心,但要求的历史信息多,包括婚姻、履历等各个方面,越多越好。人物志研究的往往是名人,大多数普通人留下的信息不足以支撑人物志研究,但他们作为一个整体却是人名学研究不可或缺的。对于要不要更多地体现人物志方面的信息,新词典的编者其实有些摇摆不定。不管怎样,词典收录了已知的绝大多数人物,虽然不能直接当作人物志,但至少也提供了最全面的人物线索。

其次,新词典拓展了我们的史料范畴,可以为其他领域提供新的材料和思路。新词典的官方网站上说人名可以揭示人群从哪里来,可以透露不同地区的文化联系,可以表明特定时期哪些神灵更加流行,甚至还可以表达政治理想。实际上,人名能发挥的作用远不止这些。近年来,基于新词典产生了五部论文集:《希腊人名:其作为史料的价值》《希腊专名学中的新旧世界》《专名学家:致敬伊莲·马修斯的希腊人名研究论文集》《古代安纳托利亚的人名》和《变化中的人名:古希腊专名学中的传统和创新》[23]。和早期的研究类似,这些论文中有一

23　E. Matthews and S. Hornblower (ed.), *Greek Personal Names: Their Value as Evidence*, Oxford: Oxford University Press, 2000; E. Matthews (ed.), *Old and New Worlds in Greek Onomastics*, Proceedings of the British Academy, Oxford: Oxford University Press, 2007; R. W. V. Catling and F. Marchand (ed.), *Onomatologos: Studies in Greek Personal Names Presented to Elaine Matthews*, Oxford: Oxbow Books, 2010; R. Parker (ed.), *Personal Names in Ancient Anatolia*, Oxford: Oxford University Press, 2013; R. Parker (ed.), *Changing Names: Tradition and Innovation in Ancient Greek Onomastics*, Oxford: Oxford University Press, 2019. 此外,还有专题研究: S. G. Byrne, *Roman Citizens of Athens*, Dudley: Peeters, 2003; P. M. Fraser, *Greek Ethnic Terminology*, Oxford: Oxford University Press, 2009。

部分也是分析人名本身,即人名分类、人名构成和含义等,有的还结合了语言学的研究;除了希腊人的人名,有些论文也涉及非希腊人,包括波斯人、犹太人。多数论文是定性研究,通过人名来分析族群、宗教等问题,但也有一些简单的定量研究。这些论文集的作者来源广泛,主题不一,方法各异,足以反映当前国外希腊人名学研究的前沿动态。正如第四部论文集的主编帕克所说,人名研究是多学科融合的范例,在这种研究中语言的历史和社会史融合在一起。

不过,新词典也并非尽善尽美,作为使用者,我认为有些地方词典处理得并不妥当。首先是人名的收录范围。排除地名是正确的,地名跟人名毕竟不同,而且《巴灵顿希腊罗马世界地图集》所附的电子文档已经具备了地名词典的一些功能,地名词典的工作由该团队去完成无疑更加合适。然而,如果文学作品里的虚构人名尚且收录,那么排除神话、史诗里的人名、神名就显得有些不合理。历史上,不仅是史诗中的英雄,甚至神灵的名字也是有人使用的。词典完全可以收录神话里的名字,然后标注 myth(神话)。再者,词典也不应该排除缩写或残缺的人名。暂时无法复原的人名以后也有可能通过其他方式复原出来,譬如发现了相似的完整铭文。即使无法复原,也不代表这些人名没有价值。例如"Σπαρ —"是个残缺的人名,但我们大概可以推断这是个非希腊语的人名;这类人名是研究族群交往、文化交流的重要材料,数据越多,对研究就越有益。词典最重要的是尽可能多地收集,特殊的人名可以单独一卷,复原工作可以让使用者自己去尝试。

其次是人名的归属问题。词典遵循的是属人原则,但没有解决属人原则可能出现的麻烦。词典把侨民归入其母邦,但是没有标注侨居地,比如在雅典出现的大量人名就被归入各自的母邦。这一方面容易使我们高估其母邦的常住人口,另一方面则使我们低估雅典的常住人口。实际上,第二卷的两位编者本身对此就存在分歧,妥协的结果是他们另外出版了一本《雅典的外来居民:〈希腊人名词典〉的一个附录》[24]。但是,其他人员辐辏、外来人口众多的城邦,则很难

---

[24]　M. J. Osborne and S. G. Byrne (ed.), *The Foreign Residents of Athens: An Annex to the* Lexicon of Greek Personal Names: Attica, Leuven: Peeters, 1996.

有一个单独的附录[25]。其实属人原则可以和属地原则结合起来,亦即在人名的出处标注所在地,如果是常住,再标注"侨民"(目前数据库中标注"侨民"的仅330例)。由此我们可以知道该人物曾经在哪些地方出现过,这对我们研究古代的人口流动和跨区域交流将是十分便利的,也能进一步提升新词典的学术价值。从技术角度说,标注人名出处的所在地不需要太多的主观判断,也不会使词典过分庞大。

当然,词典已经接近完成,这两个体例问题恐怕也难有改变。对于未来或许还可以有所期待,其中最迫切的是词典的更新和订正。第一卷1987年便已出版,收录的是1984年以前的人名。现在将近四十年过去了,新的人名必然又积累了很多。弗雷泽在前言中说后续的卷册会有相关的删除和增补部分,但到目前为止并未兑现。查阅历年*SEG*的索引是寻找新出人名的一个比较方便的办法,但也仅限于铭文。或许数据库可以在更新和订正方面发挥作用,以便研究者可以更有时效地获得最新的人名。

如果愿意,数据库其实还可以提供更大的便利。一个是关于人名的出处。查证原文是使用词典时可能遇到的最大问题,要求纸质词典直接给出人名出处的原文很不现实,因为这样会让词典变得过分臃肿,但数据库完全可以实现这一点。如果数据库可以提供原文,特别是那些绝版的、不易获取的材料,那自然是极好的。如果不能,哪怕只是提供相关网络资源的跳转链接,那也将大大节约使用者的时间。另一个是地点的查找。数据库所搭配的谷歌地图并不好用。如果可以和"古代世界地图绘制中心"网站合作,点击地点就可以直接跳转到地图上的准确位置,那将更加便利。如果合作再深入一些,还可以进行可视化分析,制作各类人名地图,甚至还可以和其他信息一起整合成一个历史地理信息系统。

(作者单位:安徽师范大学历史学院)

---

25 有一本《提洛铭文集》的索引可以起到类似的作用: J. Tréheux (ed.), *Inscriptions de Délos: Index, Tome 1: Les Étrangers, à L'exclusion des Athéniens de la Clérouchie et des Romains*, Paris: Diffusion de Boccard, 1992。

学术书评

Book Reviews

城邦视角下的亲属关系构建

——评《古代雅典的亲属关系：人类学的分析》

张新刚

雅典悲剧作家埃斯库罗斯曾用《奥瑞斯提亚》三部曲向观众展示了阿伽门农家族内部复仇与最后的政治性解决的过程。三部曲的剧情简单说来，就是阿伽门农当初为了远征特洛伊顺利进行，将自己的小女儿伊菲革尼亚杀了献祭。在他得胜归来之后，阿伽门农的妻子克里泰墨涅斯特拉杀了丈夫为女儿报仇，之后他们的儿子俄瑞斯泰斯杀了母亲为父亲报仇。在三部曲的终篇《复仇女神》中，戏剧冲突集中体现为一场激烈的价值冲突，这就是复仇女神要捍卫的母子血亲关系与雅典娜偏向的夫妻婚姻关系。虽然这场冲突最后通过雅典人投票的方式得以解决，但雅典法庭的投票结果却是1∶1，也就是说，有一半的人支持婚姻关系，而另一半人支持母子关系。埃斯库罗斯的剧作可以有很多种解释方式，但是将血亲关系和婚姻关系以极端对立的方式展示在舞台上，表明公元前5世纪的雅典人非常关心亲属关系的议题。亲属关系不仅仅体现为家庭中的伦常关系，而且还和共同体的构建高度相关。正因为如此，亲属关系的性质以及衍生秩序也成为后代学者理解古代城邦秩序逻辑的重要切入点。在这一方面，莎拉·汉弗莱斯撰写的近1 500页的《古代雅典的亲属关系：人类学的分析》[1]无疑是晚近学界极具分量的一部著作。

[1]　Sarah C. Humphreys, *Kinship in Ancient Athens: An Anthropological Analysis* (2 vols.). Oxford; New York: Oxford University Press, 2018, xxi + 1457.

汉弗莱斯本科在牛津大学学习古希腊语言、历史与哲学,并于1957年获得学士学位。在1960—1970年代,她先后在牛津和伦敦工作,曾和莫米利亚诺一起组织古代史研讨班,从1972年开始任教于伦敦大学学院,1985年前往密歇根大学担任古代史教授,现为该校荣休教授。汉弗莱斯的研究极具特色,她一直试图结合古代史与人类学研究范式,或者更准确地说,将人类学的方法引入古代史研究领域。汉弗莱斯的第一本著作是《人类学与希腊人》[2]。在该书中,汉弗莱斯就已显示出对人类学方法的自觉。她不仅讨论了人类学与古典学的关系,还对卡尔·波兰尼、路易·热尔内、涂尔干学派等做了精到的评析。除方法论的关切之外,在这首部专著中,汉弗莱斯展示了自己对于古代经济、宗教、亲属关系以及城邦结构的关注,这些话题也在她后续的著作中有更进一步的展开。1983年,汉弗莱斯发表了论文集《家庭、女性和死亡:比较研究》[3]。2004年,她出版了自己的第三部著作《诸神的陌生性》[4],这部书聚焦于雅典宗教解释传统与范式;晚近出版的《古代雅典的亲属关系:人类学的分析》一书从酝酿到成书前后用了35年的时间,是汇聚她学术关切的集大成之作。在这部巨著中,汉弗莱斯通过亲属关系讨论了雅典的家庭、经济、宗教、政治等种种组织形态。

一、(社会)人类学与古代社会研究

从书名副标题即可看出,汉弗莱斯非常注重人类学以及社会学方法的应用,这体现在她在序言中对本书由来的说明上。根据作者回忆,她最初接触到社会人类学是在1960年代的伦敦大学学院。这期间,她所了解到的社会人类学的核心议题就是亲属研究。如果追

---

[2] S. C. Humphreys, *Anthropology and the Greeks*, London: Routledge & Kegan Paul, 1978.

[3] S. C. Humphreys, *The Family, Women and Death: Comparative Studies*, London: Routledge & Kegan Paul, 1983.

[4] S. C. Humphreys, *The Strangeness of Gods: Historical Perspectives on the Interpretation of Athenian Religion*, Oxford: Oxford University Press, 2004.

溯学术史不难发现,19世纪像梅因、摩尔根等学者都是同时在人类学和早期历史研究中跨领域工作的,但由于后来人类学历经学科发展的剧变,古代史领域的学者与人类学家渐行渐远。于是,汉弗莱斯决心要写一本新的《古代城邦》(作为对库朗热著作的更新)。到1970年代,这个念头得到了芝加哥大学著名的社会学家爱德华·希尔斯(Edward Shils)的鼓励。这是该书得以形成的起源。

提到人类学,人们首先想到的往往是人类学家常年驻扎在某地进行田野调查,然后通过观察和访谈理解当地的社会关系和生活方式。甚至,人类学家还会试图对空间上相隔甚远的某些相对"原始"的村落进行田野调查,以增进对人类早期社会的理解。简言之,人类学是用空间来消解时间带来的理解隔阂的一门学问。这样一来,当人类学方法直接介入古代史研究时,就会面临一个棘手的问题,那就是人类学家如何对古代社会进行田野调查。汉弗莱斯对此的回应是,将历史人群学(prosopography)作为田野调查的替代,利用古代希腊城邦中材料最多的雅典为案例进行实践探索。所以汉弗莱斯的这一努力更像是实验性的,验证人类学方法究竟能在古代史领域走多远。

那么,我们应该对汉弗莱斯对古代雅典亲属关系的研究所采用的人类学方法做出何种定位呢?这就需要将她的研究放到整个20世纪人类学的亲属关系研究以及19世纪以来的古代亲属关系研究传统中加以把握。

我们先来看(社会)人类学对于亲属关系的研究流变。正如汉弗莱斯在1960年代就已意识到的那样,亲属关系的确曾是人类学研究的核心,因为亲属关系是社会中最为核心和基础性的关系,而家庭在绝大多数情况下也是社会结构的基础。但虽说如此,回顾自19世纪以来人类学家对亲属关系所做的研究,关于亲属关系的认知这个问题,却一直没有定论。涂尔干提出亲属关系是社会的,因为是社会认定的法律和道德构成了亲属关系,或者说血缘关系是生物性的,而亲属关系则是社会性的。20世纪上半叶,英国人类学家阿尔弗雷德·拉德克利夫-布朗则认为亲属关系与权利义务是不同性质的。他认为是社会把权利、义务和行为方式与亲属关系联系在一起。紧接着，法国人类学家列维-斯特劳斯提出了著名的亲属制度理论。他指出联姻关系构成亲属关系的基础。到了1970年代，亲属关系的研究遭遇危机，其中最具代表性的研究来自美国人类学家大卫·施耐德对亲属关系研究的批判。在施耐德看来，生物学意义上的血亲关系和血统并不能决定亲属关系，且世界范围内也并不存在文化上普适的血亲关系。进而，他认为亲属关系研究作为一个研究话题甚至并不成立。施耐德的批评使得亲属关系这一人类学研究的核心地位受到挑战。在这之后，亲属关系研究出现了严重分化。有的学者试图为亲属关系寻找新的、统一的界定，如马歇尔·萨林斯在《亲属关系是什么，不是什么》[5]一书中就提出，亲属关系不是基于生物学关系建立起来的，而是处于亲属关系中的人相互参与对方的存在。另有学者则试图通过以跨文化比较来具体理解不同文化语境中所构建的个别性亲属关系，特别是通过考察不同文化是如何具体构建权利义务关系以及行为方式的，来对亲缘关系进行描述性研究。他们不再试图用预设的普适定义来应用到不同族群上。近十年来，学者们将更多的精力投向一些新的议题，如捐精、代孕母亲、同性关系和婚姻等话题，这些新视角无疑给亲属关系理论带来新的挑战。

通过以上回溯，汉弗莱斯对古代雅典社会的亲属关系研究应该说属于传统的亲属研究范式，这一范式更为倚重婚姻和生育基础上的亲缘关系，进而强调生物学关系对于亲属关系的决定性作用。这并不是说，汉弗莱斯对1980年代以后的人类学亲属研究状况不了解。她自己在回应牛津大学出版社审稿人的意见时说，她并非故意不采用后殖民话语的分析方式，雅典帝国当然是古典希腊历史上的重要历史事件，但学者基本上没有足够材料来研究帝国对于希腊世界亲缘关系的影响。所以，汉弗莱斯的研究方法虽然比较传统，但它适用于古代雅典社会，因为对于前现代社会来说，用结构-功能主义范式来研究亲缘关系是极为有效的。

除了人类学研究传统外，古代亲属关系也是古代社会研究关注的重要议题之一。当下，很多关于亲属关系的议题和概念的讨论都

5　马歇尔·萨林斯：《亲属关系是什么，不是什么》，陈波译，商务印书馆，2018年。

源自19世纪学者对古代世界的分析，像摩尔根、梅因、库朗热等大师都特别关注古代世界的亲属关系体系，尤其是他们对罗马氏族的研究有着深厚的基础。一方面，氏族是父系社会的典型代表，而另一方面，氏族首领与贵族关系密切，这种范式不仅局限在对罗马早期社会的深入研究上，还被应用到雅典早期历史中。19世纪，对genos最为经典的界定来自格罗特（George Grote），他提出genos的要素包括宗教庆典、公共墓地、继承权利、相互间的义务、防卫与复仇、保障财产的同族联姻、公共财产等方面。Genos这一组织基于血缘，并且要延续血缘的传承。格罗特的这一界定影响了后来的库朗热、格罗茨、摩尔根等人的研究。这一学术传统后来在安德鲁斯为《剑桥古代史》撰写的"雅典国家的成长"[6]一章中得到集中体现。到1976年，对genos的这一认识传统被两位法国学者颠覆。菲利克斯·布里奥（Félix Bourriot）[7]和丹尼斯·鲁塞尔（Denis Roussel）[8]分别在独立研究中指出，古风时期的雅典并不存在一个从家族式的私人宗教权力向城邦中的贵族宗教权力发展的过程。布里奥提出，雅典的genos成员身份与精英身份之间并无关联。特别是公元前4世纪的材料表明，genos是城邦共同体的一个人为的次级组织，因此可以将genos视作德谟（deme）的前驱，而德谟是明确按照地理而非亲属关系确定的组织。在此之后，学界一般不再将雅典的genos与父系血缘关系绑定在一起，并且不认为genos建基于真实的血缘关系。经过半个多世纪的研究推进，学者们已经放弃将罗马氏族作为一种范式套用于其他古代社会或现代族群之上。

氏族理论的更新不止关系到对这一组织形态的理解，更关系到另一个宏大的主题，即城邦的演进。因为根据传统的城邦演进理论（如库朗热），城邦是从前国家状态的亲属关系主导的社会演进到国

6　A. Andrewes, "The Growth of the Athenian State", in J. Boardman & N. Hammond Eds., *The Cambridge Ancient History.* Vol. 3, Cambridge: Cambridge University Press, 1982, pp. 360–391.

7　Félix Bourriot, *Recherches sur la nature du "génos" : étude d'histoire sociale athénienne, périodes archaïque et classique.* Lille: Université de Lille III, 1976.

8　Roussel Denis, *Tribu et Cité. Études sur les groupes sociaux dans les cités grecques aux époques archaïque etclassique.* Besançon : Université de Franche-Comté, 1976.

家主导的社会，所以理解前国家亲属关系对于理解城邦的诞生至关重要。在传统理论中，早期希腊是部落亲属关系主导的社会，在这一社会中，一些强大的家族控制着土地和宗教权力，随着城邦逐步出现，这一国家形态的新共同体逐步取代家族亲属关系成为基础的组织形态。但随着对家族和部落理解的推进，城邦演进理论也逐步被批判和替代。汉弗莱斯就是批判传统城邦演进理论的代表性学者，但是，对传统家族与部落内涵的重新界定并不表示她否认从亲属关系到城邦关系的总体演变思路。与传统学者更为关心权力秩序转移的政治史研究进路相比，汉弗莱斯的研究将更多的精力投向了社会史，正是在这里，结构主义分析范式发挥了重要作用。因为在结构主义理论者看来，家庭与城邦共同体相对，构成了私与公、家与城、女与男的二元对立，这一预设实际留给了社会史研究巨大的空间。

除了人类学方法外，在《古代雅典的亲属关系》一书中，汉弗莱斯还特别提到两种影响她的社会学方法，分别是布鲁诺·拉图尔（Bruno Latour）和尼克拉斯·卢曼（Niklas Luhmann），而这也是读者在阅读全书之后往往最不确定的地方。汉弗莱斯提到自己试图采用拉图尔的"行动者网络理论"（Actor-network theory），即人以及非人都可以被视为行动者，每个行动者都是一个结点，结点之间相互联结，最后成为一个协调的行动网络。与传统以人为关照中心的理论相比，拉图尔理论的长处是将物质环境也纳入互动考量之中，甚至取消了人的中心地位，将所有的行为体看作处于相互依存又相互影响的网络关系之中。卢曼则为汉弗莱斯提供了系统理论来理解社会，即将社会视为由诸多沟通系统构成的，而借助于货币、法律等符号规则所进行的沟通，是一切社会系统产生和维持的基础。在汉弗莱斯看来，卢曼的这一理论对于理解古代雅典的文本材料，特别是理解事实与虚构、法律、修辞与行动等之间的关系非常有价值。不仅如此，卢曼的系统理论还将社会进一步分殊为诸多的子系统，特别是现代社会基于功能分殊而存在同质的诸多子系统（包括政治、经济、宗教、文化、教育、家庭、科学与军事等）。卢曼的这一分析被汉弗莱斯类比为雅典社会的诸多子系统（精英与平民、德谟、部族、祭祀群体等），并且汉弗莱斯希望将卢曼的洞见用在对这些子系统之间的交织与分殊以及历时性变化的分析上。需要指出的是,汉弗莱斯对卢曼系统理论的倚重表面上看非常有道理,但如果放到卢曼自身的理论框架中就略显尴尬了。因为卢曼的社会功能分殊理论是针对现代社会的,只有在现代社会才出现按照功能专业化进行的子系统分化,而前现代社会则是在社会分层基础上的社会分殊。以古希腊城邦为例,卢曼认为它主要是由家庭和家族的区隔构成的。简言之,汉弗莱斯对于卢曼理论的使用在一定程度上是非卢曼式的,当然这并不意味着这种使用方式是完全失效的。我们不能确定的是,汉弗莱斯对拉图尔和卢曼理论的使用是如何具体体现在浩繁的材料与议题分析之中的,因为检索全书会发现,她总共在四处注释中提及两人的名字和著作,所以只能将两人的理论作为这本1 500页巨著的总体引领性线索来加以把握了。

二、雅典社会网络的全景呈现

全书规模宏大,共分为6个部分,凡32章,主体内容有1 200页,参考文献列表近140页,使用的古代文本和铭文数量超过4 000种。汉弗莱斯考察的对象是雅典的亲属关系,时段从德拉古的立法(公元前620年)到米南德的戏剧作品(公元前300年)。在卷一中,汉弗莱斯从德拉古和梭伦立法开始讨论(第1章),之后对雅典亲属关系的具体类型和相关仪式、非正式与正式的政治群体做了全局性描绘和分析(第2—17章,第1—4部分)。从卷二开始的第五部分则聚焦克里斯提尼改革前后的雅典共同体变革(第18—21章)。至此,她的视野重新回到雅典政治共同体的形成这种宏观叙事。全书的最后一部分则是以440页的篇幅对雅典10个部落的已知德谟进行了穷尽式的列举分析(第22—32章)。

汉弗莱斯从德拉古的立法开始写起,一方面是因为德拉古立法是雅典早期最为明确的涉及亲属关系的成文立法,另一方面,从德拉古和梭伦可以看到雅典早期共同体形态的变迁,而这关系到理解城邦的兴起过程。上文已经提及,汉弗莱斯并不同意传统的演化理论,即认为城邦的兴起是个人逐步从家族关系中解放出来的过程,而是在早期法律的语境中考察亲属关系与公共秩序形成的复杂关系。汉弗莱斯提出，德拉古立法的主要背景是雅典精英群体之间的严重冲突，而立法可以被视为贵族家族间的一种和平条约。就亲属关系的主题来说，在德拉古立法中，权利和义务首次正式地与亲疏关系联系在一起。德拉古法律中体现出亲属关系的范式是相对简单的，个体处于亲疏程度差别的亲属和拟制亲属关系中，并且可以根据自己的需要来寻求亲属关系的帮助和支持。梭伦立法同样是为了应对危机，只不过这次危机是贵族与平民之间的冲突导致的。除了一系列具体的缓解冲突的措施外，作者认为梭伦将胞族（phratry）成员身份纳入处于演变中的公民身份界定中，并且构建了比德拉古更为细致的亲属关系范式。梭伦将血统关系作为测量亲疏关系的唯一标准。具体来说，这个标准就是：一个家庭的子女中，男性和男性后裔具有优先性，哪怕是来自更年轻一代的男性后裔也处于优先地位。这一标准的确立不仅是对亲属关系的规定，而且是对依附于亲属关系上的财产继承权利等的确定。这样的确定可以解决众多日常的财产纠纷。因此，梭伦通过立法的方式来规定和引导雅典人对于亲属关系以及与之相关的权利义务关系的认知。由于法律对于城邦的精英和平民是普遍适用的，这又促进了城邦的政治化过程，即以城邦官员和成文法的方式逐步替代了精英群体的裁判权力。

在重新厘清法律与亲属的关系之后，汉弗莱斯便通过古代众多的法庭案例来考察雅典是如何利用法律强化和规定收养、监护和族内婚姻等亲属关系纽带的。以收养为例，收养人与养子并无生理血缘关系，但通过收养可以建立一种拟制的亲属关系。最为重要的是，这种关系受到城邦法律的保护。家庭不仅仅是亲缘关系的共同体，而且还是财产的所有单位，财产的继承需要有子嗣，如果有多个男性子嗣，那么家产则需要在男性后代中均分。一个人如果没有子嗣，那么他所拥有的财产最后需要收回到他之前所属的家庭之中。所以，收养一个合适的养子来进行劳动和继承家产是非常自然且合理的事情。只不过，养子因为牵扯两个家庭的关系，所以需要对收养的权利和义务进行明确规定。为了让每个家庭都有子嗣，梭伦的立法规定，一旦被新的家庭收养，养子则完全进入一种新的亲属关系中，彻底摆脱与原生家庭的亲缘纽带关系；并且，养子不能再收养子嗣。但是，如果他生了儿子替代自己之后，他可以选择回到原生家庭中。收养人需要将养子介绍给他所在的胞族和德谟，以将养子正式纳入自己所在的共同体中。从梭伦的法律可以看出，收养制度主要是维护家庭财产权利的继承。可以合理设想，被收养人不可能完全切断和原生家庭的情感纽带，但是梭伦将这一拟制的亲属关系限定在法律关系上，而非生理情感意义上。

在第一部分剩下的篇幅中，汉弗莱斯通过详细考察雅典人生活的各个阶段，试图证明家庭中新一代人的出生以及结婚和生育是身份变化的关键节点。一个雅典人认同的建立需要出生后的一系列过程进行确认，特别是需要获得他/她所在的社会关系网络的确认，而亲属关系则在社会关系网络中扮演着实质性作用。认同问题也将研究带向了全书的下一个单元，即考察雅典人如何通过各类仪式来构建认同。在第二部分（第8—12章），汉弗莱斯考察了取名、人生各个阶段的仪式、葬礼和埋葬、悼念和宗教节日等在塑造雅典人认同中所发挥的作用。这一部分的内容涵盖了一个雅典人从生到死的所有大事，全面地展示了城邦公共关系之外亲属关系的社会经验。这部分所讨论的很多议题，我们也可以在其他类似主题的著作中读到，而其中最为独特和贡献最大的讨论当属对姓名的分析，一则学界对姓名材料的研究尚不充分，二来作者非常明显地使用了卢曼的系统理论，有必要做一简要评述。

汉弗莱斯利用《希腊人名词典》（*Lexicon of Greek Personal Names*）提供的丰富数据对雅典人的名字进行了详细研究[9]。作者将雅典人的名字视作一套"系统"，即通过名字可以判断人的身份。比如一个公民的名字会由三部分组成，即个人名字、父姓和德谟名；客籍民的名字不会有德谟名；奴隶的称呼主要是个人名字，以及主人的名字；女性除了自己的名字外，一般以她的父亲或者其他男性监护人（丈夫、兄弟或儿子）的名字来指称等。名字除了能够显示社会信息外，命名系统还会强化亲缘关系，因为在正常情况下，长子要以祖父名字命

9　关于这部工具书的编纂体例和使用方法，参见本辑第179—192页。

名,其他的孩子则可以用其他亲属的名字命名。比如,有材料显示次子可以用外祖父的名字命名。女性的命名虽没有如男性命名那么稳定的范式,但也能看到一些和男性相似的命名方式。再考虑到雅典人名还往往具有实质性的含义,这就使得雅典人的姓名成为一种重要的沟通方式。汉弗莱斯认为,给一个孩子取名就是进行沟通的行为。在取名仪式上,亲属和家庭朋友会直接见证孩子的命名,如果是男性婴儿,他的名字日后还会被同胞族、同德谟的成员,以及城邦的公民乃至其他城邦的人所知。在这个意义上,雅典人的"姓名"成了卢曼理论中与"货币""权力"和"真理"一样的普遍化沟通媒介。

在对雅典社会系统进行百科全书式的讨论之后,作者在第三、四部分(第13—17章)将目光转向了非正式与正式的政治活动与团体,考察亲属关系在政治活动中所扮演的角色,具体涉及年轻人的伙伴群体、政治婚姻、政治帮派、城邦官职以及议事会和公民大会等主题。与之前的全景式讨论相比,第三、四部分的内容更多的是依赖已有的材料性质进行的选择性的主题讨论。总体来说,作者在第一卷中以亲属关系为线索,向读者展示了雅典社会网络的复杂与特质。

三、雅典共同体的历史考察

在完成了对雅典社会全貌的描绘之后,汉弗莱斯在第二卷又回到城邦崛起的主题,接续了德拉古和梭伦立法所铺垫的城邦发展脉络,考察存在于家庭与城邦之间的共同体形式,包括部落(tribe)、三一区(trittye)、胞族(phratry)、家族(genos)和德谟(deme)等。汉弗莱斯认为亲属关系是这些共同体的构成性结构原则。如果说作者在第一卷中主要采用体系化方式讨论,展示雅典社会的亲属关系总体状况,那么在第二卷中则更多地采用历时性分析,考察不同共同体在雅典历史不同阶段的演变。

由于雅典城邦形成的一个重要节点是克里斯提尼的改革,所以汉弗莱斯在第五部分中以克里斯提尼改革前后的共同体演变作为关注点,以此探究城邦形成的过程。作者一贯的立场是拒绝简单的演化理论,而是认为雅典城邦最终的形成经历了一个渐进的过程,在此期间原来诸多拥有不同功能的共同体相互渗透,最终慢慢形成了一个统一而集中的系统。

汉弗莱斯重点考察了胞族和家族这两种共同体。胞族是雅典成年男性首要的共同体形式,胞族成员会在宗教庆典日聚集在一起,并在这些场合引介新的胞族成员,共同进行祭祀献祭等活动。同一胞族的成员在法律上有义务为被害人亲属诉讼凶手提供帮助,同时,胞族最初也承担着军事组织的任务。除此之外,早期的胞族很可能承担着组织各种宗教仪式的任务。胞族的成员身份一般通过父系家庭获得,而外族人也有可能通过联姻等方式获得新胞族的成员身份。在雅典城邦演变的过程中,胞族扮演着重要角色。汉弗莱斯提出,正是经由胞族这一组织,雅典人以及雅典公民最终得以与疆域结合在一起,这也将话题引向克里斯提尼的改革。在克里斯提尼改革后,德谟开始扮演重要作用,并与胞族呈现交错竞争之势。

汉弗莱斯对胞族性质的认定并没有太多突破,比如之前的学者已经提出胞族是雅典的早期机构(库朗热),与村庄和乡村节庆是联系在一起的(热尔内)。她的特殊贡献在于对雅典胞族的历史演变进行了非常细致而精彩的分析。她将公元前507年到前431年(即伯罗奔尼撒战争爆发)作为一个历史单元来进行考察,认为在这个阶段中,不同地区的胞族情况出现分化,乡村中的重要家族仍然住在当地,并在所属的胞族及德谟中发挥重要作用,而城区胞族中部分重要家族开始在城区和德谟中建构新的权力,而有一些家族则继续维系自己在胞族中的影响力。与此同时,有些地区的德谟快速取代了胞族承担起宗教仪式职能,而有些地区则仍由胞族来组织当地的宗教仪式,这一趋势在公元前431年被战争中断。伯罗奔尼撒战争爆发后,伯里克利将雅典人全部搬到城墙内居住,实质性地改变了人们的生活方式,特别是乡村地区的共同体组织方式。当乡村中的人搬入城区之后,胞族和德谟所受的影响并不相同,因为胞族的很多活动需要在当地的圣所或祭坛举行,而德谟则不受这一限制,德谟的事务只需在公共空间内就可进行。此外,在战争中,德谟所发挥的组织作用也远远大于胞族。在漫长的战争过程中,远离乡村故土的人们实际上已经无法按照原有的胞族来组织集体的宗教生活。战争结束后，随着雅典帝国的瓦解以及民主制的动荡，雅典民众对于寡头制以及拥有土地的精英群体抱有敌对态度，原来胞族中的重要家族影响力普遍受到威胁，大部分地区的胞族也将宗教仪式和圣所交给了德谟掌管。公元前378—前322年间，随着阿提卡局势的逐步稳定，雅典虽然恢复了部分海上力量，但帝国不再，年轻人也无法通过船上服役获得薪资，以土地为主的生产生活方式重新回归，在乡村地区，胞族模仿城邦公共生活中的一些举措重新成为当地公共生活的中心。到前322年，胞族和德谟都随着定居点的废弃而衰落。

在胞族之后，汉弗莱斯也对贵族家族（genos）进行了类似的历史分析。正如本文第一部分中已经提到的那样，genos自19世纪以来就成为学者们理解古代社会的重要出发点，但是晚近的研究已经将genos与父系血缘的联系切断。作者通过研究指出，genos最初是指阿提卡拥有祭司权力的贵族家族，自公元前7世纪开始引入选举官员机制后逐步确定下来的一个群体，因为只有互相认定为高贵出身的人才能成为官员的候选人。到梭伦改革后，这一群体从出身的限定逐渐扩展至财富的限定，并且财富成为出任公职的标准，但是贵族家族仍然在各自的胞族中拥有特权地位。到了公元前6世纪，草根阶层的宗教活动增多，同时人口迁移频繁。贵族和工匠搬到城区及城郊，到克里斯提尼改革前，这些贵族家族已经分散在阿提卡各处，克里斯提尼的改革对阿提卡地区进行了组织重组，目的之一就是防止贵族家族和其他地方性的宗教共同体再次造成地区间冲突。在此之后，雅典历史就和战争密不可分，无论是区域战争还是希波战争都使得城邦的公民大会和议事会在城邦中担任核心作用，其他形式的组织相对式微。希波战争之后，客蒙是最后一位想利用genos扩充自身实力的政治家，到了公元前5世纪后半期，genos宗教仪式已经成为人们对于战前乡村生活的乡愁式想象。总体来说，古典时期的贵族家族基本被吸纳和融入城邦其他共同体的日常运作之中。

在全书的最后一部分，汉弗莱斯将历时性分析用在德谟这一共同体上，并且还利用文献资料、考古材料和历史人群学材料对雅典10个部落的德谟进行了穷尽式的分析，堪称雅典德谟研究的集成。对于各个部落和德谟的具体情况,本文从略,但是对于作者呈现的德谟演变过程,则有必要进行重点评述。

雅典德谟体系是学者们关心的老话题,19世纪时就已经形成对德谟的传统看法。根据梅因、库朗热等学者的研究,克里斯提尼改革是雅典城邦组织原则变更的关键时刻,在此之前人们是按照亲属关系组织在一起的,而在改革后人们将地理空间作为社会组织原则。在这一框架之下,德谟被视为微缩版城邦的自治组织,公民们通过在德谟中的集体生活来演练并获得在城邦公共生活中的技能、习惯和价值。19世纪形成的对德谟的传统看法影响深远,一直到20世纪中叶,学者们仍将克里斯提尼改革创立的德谟体系理解为旨在削弱地方性宗教共同体或地方性庇护关系网络。自1960年代以来,随着新的考古发掘项目的开展,大量关于德谟的材料出土使得学者能够对德谟的格局有更为清楚的认知。汉弗莱斯注意到已有的德谟研究对不同时段的差别仍然关注不足,所以非常有必要对从公元前507年到前300年间雅典德谟的演变进行梳理,而这也是作者特别看重的工作。

根据汉弗莱斯的梳理,在克里斯提尼改革之前已经有地方性组织的基础,而在公元前507年改革之后,德谟体系也并非立即建立和完善起来。作者将公元前507年至前450年(克里斯提尼改革到伯里克利公民权法案)视为一个时段,这一阶段中各个地方性的定居点缓慢调适自身与德谟的关系,德谟成员也通过参与议事会、重装步兵方阵和划桨手等慢慢熟悉城邦的公共生活。汉弗莱斯特别提出,伯里克利的公民权法案对德谟的影响更为直接,因为法案要求公民身份的确定需要父母双方都是雅典公民。传统的研究往往重视这一法案对于贵族家庭的影响,但是汉弗莱斯指出,这一法案实际也对平民产生重大影响。因为要确立孩子的公民身份,很可能要重新依靠传统的胞族来确定双亲的公民身份,而这样带来的实际结果很可能是使得法案的具体实施并不十分严格。

德谟系统演变的下一个节点仍然是伯罗奔尼撒战争的爆发,特别是在战争最初十年,伯罗奔尼撒军队每年都要入侵阿提卡,蹂躏雅典城外的土地,住在雅典城外的居民全部搬进城内居住。当众多城外德谟的成员涌入城内后,必然四散开来,而不会按原有的德谟组织共同生产生活。再考虑到战争爆发不久便在城内出现了严重的瘟疫(公元前430—前426年),德谟这一组织形态必然遭到严重的冲击,德谟成员不得不在城内举行公共活动,并在战争和平的间歇期,即尼基阿斯和平达成时(公元前421年)立马回到乡村住所。伯罗奔尼撒战争后来的阶段对雅典的破坏更为严重,斯巴达将军阿吉斯驻扎在雅典东北部的德克雷亚,始终威胁着阿提卡地区的安全。雅典最终的失败给雅典内外局势带来剧变,帝国的丧失使得原来依靠帝国供养的雅典公民不再能从城邦的公共服务中获得薪资,他们必须回到百废待兴的乡村德谟从头开始谋划生计;同时相对于拥有大量土地的少数有钱人,一贫如洗的平民便开始借机对寡头群体展开攻击。但另一方面,战争期间在城区的生活经验也使得人们能够熟练地参与公民大会、议事会和各项军事组织,这些习得的政治经验在战争结束后被带回到乡村德谟中。所以公元前4世纪的雅典公民,首先是在德谟中接受公共生活的训练,也正是在这时德谟才能够成为一个微缩版的城邦。这个世纪中,经过更新后的德谟重新成为雅典的基础性组织,德谟也承担着众多政治、教育和宗教职能,并且还能颁布德谟的法律。德谟作为重要的共同体形式,前后持续了近两个世纪,到公元前3世纪才彻底退出历史舞台。

总体来说,汉弗莱斯在第二卷中对诸如胞族、贵族家族、德谟等共同体的历史分析给人留下深刻印象,她特别强调了希波战争期间以及之后的城邦公共生活对雅典公民的训练,伯罗奔尼撒战争期间乡村居民搬进城内后对各类共同体的根本性影响,以及雅典在失去帝国后将经过政治化训练的公民群体重新疏解安置回原来的乡村组织系统。汉弗莱斯成功地展示了不同类型共同体在历史进程中的更新、兴衰和相互作用,揭示出传统研究对雅典共同体的静态化或者范式化分析所看不到的丰富内容。

四、总结

由于全书缺乏主题导引性的序言和结论,导致读者在努力阅读全书之后也并不能立即从无数的文本细节和材料中抽身出来，进而对作者的著述意图有完整的把握。但是在综述了汉弗莱斯的研究方法以及两卷的内容后，需要对她的三十五年研究的成果进行总体性评价。笔者认为，最重要的贡献有以下两点：

首先，汉弗莱斯成功地证明古代雅典社会组织是建基于亲属关系之上的，从家庭内部的关系到城邦内各种共同体的人际关系，再到城邦公共的政治性关系，都需要在亲属关系的原则上加以理解。但是，汉弗莱斯所阐述的亲属关系与城邦的关联并不是自19世纪以来的传统演化论，即亲属关系被公共性的政治关系所压制和取代，而是二者相互交织。城邦在塑造和强化亲属关系，亲属关系又反过来成为城邦中公民关系和各种组织形态的基础。

其次，汉弗莱斯对雅典亲属关系的讨论做到了双重全面性。第一重是在第一卷中对雅典所有与亲属关系相关的社会网络进行了鸟瞰式分析。她不仅处理了成年男性在亲属关系中的位置，还细致讨论了妇女、儿童和各种拟制亲属关系；还有雅典人（男和女）从生到死的所有仪式性过程；以及各种正式与非正式的政治团体。第二重是在第二卷中对处于家庭和城邦之间的诸种共同体的历时性考察，将共同体的演变与雅典历史的进程密切联系在一起进行考察，涉及的时段和材料涵盖了雅典从古风时期到希腊化时期的全过程。

汉弗莱斯曾回顾自己的研究生涯始于1950年代的一次海上航行，当时她和朋友们乘船从马耳他驶向希腊。在爱琴海上，汉弗莱斯开始思考古时候希腊商船在这片海上航行的情形，这进一步激发了她思考前现代经济中的贸易问题。六十年后，汉弗莱斯为读者提供了海洋一般波澜壮阔的著作。虽然汉弗莱斯给出了人类学以及拉图尔和卢曼的方法论作为灯塔引路，然而，一旦进入这片海域，读者总还是不免在浩如烟海的文本细节中迷失方向。不过，好在海上的风景足够丰富，任何对希腊城邦"社会"感兴趣的读者必定能够从中获得直接的知识以及研究线索的启发。

（作者单位：山东大学历史文化学院）

长时段[1]视角下罗马意大利地区的政治生活

——评塔科玛《罗马政治文化：公元1—6世纪元老院与意大利城市议会个案研究七例》

温珊珊

在罗马史研究领域中，政治史研究的传统深厚。19世纪后半期，德国史学巨擘特奥多尔·蒙森（Theodor Mommsen）以罗马法律制度为核心，开创了制度史研究范式，为罗马政治史研究奠定了基础[2]。进入20世纪，许多罗马史家开始超越制度史视角，将关注焦点转向社会层面，聚焦政治生活中的具体人物、家族关系以及更广泛的社会网络，并通过研究视角下移，将社会中下层广大被统治群体纳入研究视野[3]。近几十年来，学者们继续拓展古罗马政治史的研究范围，将政治

1　本文中的"长时段"意指广义上的较长时段，不涉及年鉴学派的"长时段"理论。

2　蒙森对罗马政制的研究主要集中在其《罗马公法》（T. Mommsen, *Römisches Staatsrecht*, Leipzig: Hirzel, 1887–1888）中。蒙森之后，制度史研究的传统由后世学者继续发扬，涌现出如G. E. F. Chilver, "Augustus and the Roman Constitution 1939–50," *Historia: Zeitschrift für Alte Geschichte*, vol. 1, no. 3 (1950), pp. 408–435; Dieter Timpe, *Untersuchungen zur Kontinuität des frühen Prinzipats*, Wiesbaden: F. Steiner, 1962; V. Fadinger, *Die Begründung des Prinzipats: Quellenkritische und staatsrechtliche Untersuchungen zu Cassius Dio und der Parallelüberlieferung*, Berlin: Habelt, 1969; Andrew Lintott, *The Constitution of the Roman Republic*, Oxford: Oxford University Press, 1999; Karin Sion-Jenkis, *Von der Republik zum Prinzipat: Ursachen für den Verfassungswechsel in Rom im historischen Denken der Antike*, Stuttgart: Franz Steiner, 2000等研究成果。

3　代表性成果包括Matthias Gelzer, *Die Nobilität der römischen Republik*, Leipzig: Teubner, 1912 (*The Roman Nobility*, trans. Robin Seager, Oxford: Blackwell, 1969);（转下页）

生活置于更广阔的社会环境中,关注不同参与群体,着眼相关影响要素,考察"人—事件/历史情境—史料"之间的关系,探索古罗马政治史研究的新方向,将传统政治史研究发展为内涵更为广阔的政治文化研究[4]。

任教于荷兰莱顿大学古代史系的罗马史学者劳伦斯·塔科玛,于2020年由牛津大学出版社发表新作《罗马政治文化:公元1—6世纪元老院与意大利城市议会个案研究七例》[5],成为新近出版的专门聚焦"罗马政治文化"的重要成果。"政治文化"一词含义甚广,众多议题都可囊括其中加以研究。在罗马政治史研究中,共和时期的"政治文化"成为近年来学者们关注的一大焦点[6]。对于共和政制终结

(接上页) Friedrich Münzer, *Römische Adelsparteien und Adelsfamilien*, Stuttgart: Metzler, 1920 (*Roman Aristocratic Parties and Families*, trans. Thérèse Ridley, Baltimore: Johns Hopkins University Press, 1999); Ronald Syme, *The Roman Revolution*, Oxford: Oxford University Press, 1939; Claude Nicolet, *Le métier de citoyen dans la Rome républicaine*, Paris: Gallimard, 1976 (*The World of the Citizen in Republican Rome*, trans. P. S. Falla, London: Batsford, 1980); Fergus Millar, *The Crowd in Rome in the Late Republic*, Ann Arbor: The University of Michigan Press, 1998; H. Mouritsen, *Plebs and Politics in the Late Roman Republic*, Cambridge: Cambridge University Press, 2001; Robert Morstein-Marx, *Mass Oratory and Political Power in the Late Roman Republic*, Cambridge: Cambridge University Press, 2004等。

4　近20年来部分研究成果如下:K.-J. Hölkeskamp, *Senatus Populusque Romanus: Die politische Kultur der Republik — Dimensionen und Deutungen*, Stuttgart: Franz Steiner, 2004; K.-J. Hölkeskamp, *Reconstructing the Roman Republic: An Ancient Political Culture and Modern Research*, trans. H. Heitmann-Gordon, Princeton: Princeton University Press, 2010; K.-J. Hölkeskamp, *Libera Res Publica. Die politische Kultur des antiken Rom — Positionen und Perspektiven*, Stuttgart: Franz Steiner, 2017; Geoffrey Sumi, *Ceremony and Power: Performing Politics in Rome between Republic and Empire*, Ann Arbor: The University of Michigan Press, 2005; Carlos F. Noreña, *Imperial ideals in the Roman West: Representation, Circulation, Power*, Cambridge: Cambridge University Press, 2011; Cristina Rosillo-López, *Public Opinion and Politics in the Late Roman Republic*, Cambridge: Cambridge University Press, 2017; A. Angius, *La Repubblica delle opinioni: Informazione politica e partecipazione popolare a Roma tra II e I secolo a.C.*, Milano: Le Monnier, 2018; Valentina Arena and Jonathan Prag eds., *A Companion to the Political Culture of the Roman Republic*, Chichester: Wiley-Blackwell, 2022; Cristina Rosillo-López, *Political Conversations in Late Republican Rome*, Oxford: Oxford University Press, 2022. 有关罗马帝国早期政治史研究的学术史回顾,参见王忠孝:《从元首政制到王朝统治:罗马帝国早期政治史研究路径考察》,《世界历史》2020年第3期,第118—132页。

5　L. E. Tacoma, *Roman Political Culture: Seven Studies of the Senate and City Councils of Italy from the First to the Sixth Century AD*, Oxford: Oxford University Press, 2020. 下文简称*Roman Political Culture*(《罗马政治文化》)。

6　参见注释3相关成果。

后的罗马政治生活,鲜有学者从政治文化的角度进行专题式研究,帝国时期的"政治文化"似乎成为一个被普遍接受、拿来即用的概念[7]。然而当对元首制乃至古代晚期数百年间的"政治文化"加以审视,试图厘清"罗马政治文化"所指向的准确内容与概念边界时,便会发现与很多总括性的术语一样,对其下定义这一尝试本身便充满挑战。从这个意义上来说,塔科玛以"罗马政治文化"为研究主题,将公元1世纪后数百年间的"罗马政治文化"作为整体进行研究,无疑是突破性的尝试,对相关讨论大有增益。

一

在罗马政治史研究中,共和时期的政治体制常被用来与帝国时代对标。共和政制有其长期遵循的原则,比如精英的权势经由竞争得以确认,由获得象征荣誉(*honor*)的官职体现,官员通过人民大会选举产生,元老院与人民大会的权力在实践博弈中达成平衡[8]。元首制下,行政官员从人民大会选举发展到由皇帝直接任命,改变了传统的竞争模式。这种转变消除了人民大会的作用,消解了荣誉竞争的动力,在事实上剔除了罗马传统政治生活的核心内容。如果以共和国为参照,那么在元首制建立后的长时期内,罗马政制的内核已经不再,传统的政治机构逐渐成为形式上的存在。

帝国时期,元老院作为传统的政治机构继续存在,为皇帝统治的合法性服务。在数个世纪中,元老院和元老阶层历经数次变化,权威不断缩减。至罗马城失去特权地位、新的元老院在君士坦丁堡创建时,罗马元老院的地位更加沦落,俨然地方城市议会一般。在地方社会中,城市议会遵循与罗马元老院相似的组织原则。在很长时期内,

---

7 关于罗马共和国时期"政治文化"概念的探讨,参见 K.-J. Hölkeskamp, "Political Culture: Career of a Concept", in Valentina Arena and Jonathan Prag eds., *A Companion to the Political Culture of the Roman Republic*, Chichester: Wiley-Blackwell, 2022, pp. 4–19。

8 相关研究的详细综述,参见晏绍祥:《西方学界关于共和时代罗马人民政治作用的讨论》,《希罗多德的序言》(《西方古典学辑刊》第四辑),复旦大学出版社,2022年,第175—211页。

地方贵族也为当选行政官员互相竞争，官员选举同样依赖于地方城市的人民大会。两个机构虽然不同，却有很多相似之处。除了基于相似的原则建立和运作，元老院和市议会也成为精英贵族表达自身地位的媒介。然而从帝国早期开始，这两个机构的职权范围不断缩小，元老和市议会成员主要处理与自身有关的事务，如人员增补、荣誉授予、协调成员之间的关系等。

在《罗马政治文化》中，塔科玛将目光投向公元1世纪到6世纪间的元老院与意大利城市议会，选择七例相关个案进行研究。他提出在这一长时段内，意大利始终处于个人统治之下。在这一大背景下，元老院与意大利城市议会原有的中心地位逐渐衰落，沦为制度中的某种存在。然而，直到公元6世纪末，不管社会外部环境如何变化，不论这两个机构本身所拥有的权力和地位如何被削弱，它们在某种程度上仍在发挥作用。与此同时，罗马式的政治行为也仍在实际发生，如选举候选人的支持网络依然重要，荣誉竞争依然存在，贵族精英仍然为城市提供福利等。可以说，当社会经历变革时，意大利地区政治生活的内在结构并未发生颠覆性变化，不论是政治语言的形式，还是政治行为的模式，包括制度设置，都表现出很强的延续性。塔科玛认为，罗马元老院和意大利城市议会在数个世纪中一直存在，使意大利地区在几百年间形成了一种独特的政治文化形态。从长期来看，这两个机构的政治权力弱化，社会价值增强；机构内部成员既受到规范约束，也在其中找到可供自己发挥作用的空间，同时凭借元老或议员身份在社会中继续保持名望声誉、巩固已有地位。

对于聚焦意大利地区，塔科玛解释一方面是出于对七例个案所处历史情境在大背景下的连贯性考虑，另一方面则是因为意大利地区的政治文化更加稳固，相比行省存续时间更长，材料保存比其他地区更为完善。作者强调意大利参与罗马的征服扩张以及帝国统治，且在地方行政管理及权利地位方面长时期异于行省，特别是只有在意大利，元老院和城市议会才保留了在制度实践上如此长的延续性。作者认为，罗马政治生活中两个传统政治机构——罗马元老院与意大利地方城市议会——的长期存在，对意大利地区形成独特的政治文化产生了重要影响。

针对元首制时期至古代晚期的元老院和地方城市议会,学者们长久以来多从制度史的角度进行分析,讨论元老院和城市议会在政治制度中的地位、权力、构成、运作等方面;同时也关注它们的历时性变化,探讨元老院的变化对自身地位的影响,关注元老院与统治者之间的关系,包括对元老们进行人物志研究[9]。将目光投向地方城市议会的学者除了考察其组织方式、成员变化,还特别关注城市议会的衰落问题[10]。近年来,学者们将研究重点从元老院和地方议会转向贵族精英,关注精英之间及与其他群体的互动关系[11]。权力需要表达与确认,无论是统治者还是精英个体,都需要通过某种方式与各方协商沟通,需要社会仪式来展示与确认权力。地方贵族作为罗马帝国运转的关键要素,除了调适自身行为以适应帝国统治的需要外,也通过互相间的竞争赢得自己的地位。这些研究视角固然有助于我们了解元老院与地方城市议会的基本情况,认识到贵族精英如何在罗马社会中处理各方关系,但却不足以帮助我们理解元老院和地方城市议会为何能够长期存在。

---

[9] Richard Talbert, *The Senate of Imperial Rome*, Princeton: Princeton University Press, 1984; A. Chastagnol, *Le Sénat romain à l'époque impériale*, Paris: Les Belles Lettres, 1992; L. Cracco Ruggini, "Il senato fra due crisi (III–VI secolo)," in E. Gabba ed., *Il senato nella storia. Vol. 1. Il senato nell'età romana*, Rome: Istituto Poligrafico e Zecca dello Stato, 1998, pp. 223–375; F. Millar, *The Emperor in the Roman World (31 BC – AD 337)*, London: Duckworth, 1977; G. Alföldy, "Consuls and consulars under the Antonines: prosopography and history," *Ancient Society*, Vol. 7 (1976), pp. 263–299; T. P. Wiseman, *New Men in the Roman Senate 139 B.C.–A.D. 14*, Oxford: Oxford University Press, 1971.

[10] W. Langhammer, *Die rechtliche und soziale Stellung der Magistratus municipales und der Decuriones*, Wiesbaden: Steiner, 1973; H. Mouritsen, *Elections, Magistrates and Municipal Elites: Studies in Pompeian Epigraphy*, Rome: L'Erma di Bretschneider, 1988; H. Mouritsen, "The album of Canusium and the town councils of Roman Italy," *Chiron*, Vol. 28 (1998), pp. 229–254; L. E. Tacoma, "Roman elite mobility," in N. Fisher and H. van Wees eds., *'Aristocracy' in antiquity. Redefining Greek and Roman elites*, Swansea: The Classical Press of Wales, 2015, pp. 125–146; P. Garnsey, "Aspects of the decline of the urban aristocracy in the Empire," in P. Garnsey (ed. with addenda by W. Scheidel), *Cities, Peasants and Food in Classical Antiquity*, Cambridge: Cambridge University Press, 1998, pp. 3–27.

[11] A. Zuiderhoek, *The Politics of Munificence in the Roman Empire: Citizens, Elites and Benefactors in Asia Minor*, Cambridge: Cambridge University Press, 2009; S. Wen, *Communal Dining in the Roman West: Private Munificence Towards Cities and Associations in the First Three Centuries AD*, Leiden: Brill, 2022.

塔科玛在书中指出,在一人统治之下,罗马元老院与意大利城市议会有如此长的生命力,有两层含义。首先,两个机构能够长期存在,意味着它们对各自成员仍然有意义和价值,否则成员停止参与,机构也无法继续运转。元老院及地方议会的存在,帮助精英贵族作为整体区别于社会其他阶层,帮助内部成员确认并维持其在社会中的优势地位。其次,两个机构在如此长时段内保有生命力,意味着它们发挥作用的方式具有适应性。意大利地区在公元1—6世纪中经历了社会环境和权力关系的数次变化,从罗马帝国的核心地区,到地位下降几近与行省平级,而后在帝国分裂中成为西罗马帝国的一部分,直至受到东哥特王国统治。在这一长时段中,罗马元老院与意大利城市议会的政治影响力不断衰减,却在社会中保持了自身的优势地位[12]。两个机构在经济、宗教、公共事务等方面发挥着重要作用,其成员的声望、地位也借由不同方式和场合得以彰显,个人荣耀获得社会认可。

对于本书讨论的主题,作者很清楚其中涉及的概念有其棘手之处。塔科玛提到,"政治"一词具有迷惑性,人们很容易认为对它很熟悉,但若要精确说明该词到底包含什么内容,却非常困难。他提出在本书的研究范围内,"政治"是一种依托于正式设置的机制(Politics are defined here as the mechanisms in formalized settings ...),使其中的参与者能够做出决策以管理国家和组织社会。这些"正式设置"包含不同政治机构,它们被专门创设以便政治生活的参与者能够共聚讨论决策国事、解决利益分歧并投票表决[13]。作者提醒到,在这个定义中,关键点不在于政治机构的参与者由谁构成,而在于这些机构能够做出会对整个社会产生影响的决策。

对于如何理解"政治文化",塔科玛从政治学者们提供的解读入手。后者强调民众对政制的集体想法与态度,强调意识观念与价值体系,考察影响政治决策的因素时引入经济物质层面之外的考量。然而对政治文化基于现代视角的理解,对于古代社会并不完美适用。

---

12 *Roman Political Culture*, pp. 10–11.

13 *Roman Political Culture*, p. 2.

历史学家们提出应从关注选民对政治的态度转向关注政治生活参与者的表现,将关注中心转向参与者的行为及其社会意义。塔科玛明确表示,将政治文化理解为参与政治的方式,才契合本书对元老院和意大利城市议会的探究。他进而将政治文化定义为:政治机构中的成员内部之间及与外部世界相互作用的规范化模式[14]。政治机构的存在有助于协调其中的紧张关系,政治生活的参与者对惯例规则拥有共识并在实践中据此行动。

在本书中,政治文化被视为一种参与政治生活的方式,具体而言,是元老院和意大利城市议会的成员作为个体或集体的行为方式。塔科玛认为,罗马政治文化是贵族的,是为贵族服务的,也是由贵族展现出来的[15]。传统的政治机构为参与者提供了平台,供其协商处理政治生活中的张力关系和不确定性,而这些都与贵族自身的地位密切相关。对元老院和意大利城市议会而言,所作决策既基于自身,又受到外部影响;做出的决策既关乎内部成员,也对政治生活的其他参与者产生影响。

作者强调了定义(共和)政治的一个关键要素,即政治机构能够做出对社会产生广泛影响的决策。随着元首制的建立,传统的政治权力运作方式发生变化,元老院和地方市议会的决策权及影响力无疑从根本上受到影响。基于本书的研究目标,作者提出使用“政治文化”指代元首制及之后的时期,专门用于描述一人统治下的特定政治文化形态。随着政治权力被削弱,元老院与城市议会逐渐变成自我指向(self-referential)和自我定义(self-definitional)的机构[16]。公元1—6世纪期间,罗马政治文化的自我指向和自我定义的特点创造出一种独特的社会关系,其中包含许多张力与模糊之处,隐含在贵族精英的行为中[17]。元老与意大利城市议员的行为,尤其是其行为方式受到的影响与规范成为作者探究的焦点。

14　*Roman Political Culture*, p. 15.

15　*Roman Political Culture*, p. 17.

16　*Roman Political Culture*, p. 5.

17　*Roman Political Culture*, p. 18.

二

本书所讨论的七例个案横跨六个世纪,比一般的古代史研究所涉及的时段更长。将公元1—6世纪作为整体进行讨论,并不意味着在这漫长时段内没有发生任何变化。从元首制建立,帝国统治加强到衰败,直到东哥特人统治,意大利的政治环境并非静止不变。作者指出,从整体性的视角看待公元后的六个世纪,是因为在这一长时段内,罗马政治文化呈现出一些主要特征。作者在"导论"中阐明,在本研究中,罗马政治文化指向政治机构(元老院与意大利市议会)中成员的行为方式,尤其关注精英贵族在彰显自身地位时遇到的张力关系与模糊处境。接下来的正文部分由七章组成,每一章讨论一例个案。作者特别强调这些个案的排序不能互换,不仅因为它们是按照时代顺序来安排的,也因为这样的安排顺序内含了罗马政治文化的动态发展过程。

第一章以归在塞内卡名下的《神圣的克劳狄乌斯变瓜记》(*Apocolocyntosis*)为分析文本,探讨元老院的决策范围、权力大小以及辩论的自由度。文本所涉情境是一场神界元老院会议,神明们在议事厅讨论是否允许死后的克劳狄乌斯皇帝进入神界的问题。文本虽是虚构的,但塔科玛将其与现实世界中的罗马元老院相观照,指出元老院难免会商讨有关皇帝的议题。元老们看似可自由各抒己见,但在元首制下,这种自由讨论的空间无疑受到限制。元老的发言自由与皇权对讨论的干预构成一对张力关系,在元老院会议中,皇帝和元老双方对对方如何表现拥有心照不宣的共识。

第二章聚焦庞贝城房屋外墙上涂写的一系列竞选铭文(*programmata*),探讨精英竞争、庇护网络以及地方政治。作者主张竞选活动激活了候选人与支持者之间的庇护关系,然而这种社会关系网络并不稳固。候选人的支持者来源多样,除了直接受到保护的个人或团体,候选者的亲友近邻甚至不具投票权者也可能会表达对竞选人的支持,但候选人无法保证一定会得到最大限度的支持。竞选活动不仅与候选人的竞选策略有关,也涉及地方市议会内部的权力关系以及精英之间的竞争。尽管元首制的建立对官员选举与政治机构的决策权产生巨大影响，但在地方社会，竞选活动仍然意义重大。贵族精英虽然在等级结构中占优势地位，也依然需要通过获得民众支持以确认自己的统治权，地方精英与普通民众对彼此应如何表现同样抱有期待。

第三章关注小普林尼的两封书信，其中提到元老院选举时的无记名投票、选票上的玩笑话甚至污言秽语，以及选票上竞选人的名字被替换的问题。元老贵族在财富和地位上存在内部差异，选举不仅关乎竞选者，某种程度上更关乎其居于高位的支持者。作者从普林尼对玩弄选票的态度入手，讨论他对于共和与帝国时期的投票方式、对元老的行为以及对皇帝的影响的态度与看法，引发对选举本质的思考。作者指出，元老贵族的自我呈现方式与适宜得体的行为之间存在张力。投票选举既要有序也要有礼，在重要的政治场合，元老贵族应注意自身行为，遵循合适的礼仪规范，维护所在阶层的尊严。

第四章继续以元老院为中心，关注康茂德死后召开的元老院会议，相关记录保留在《奥古斯都传记汇编》(*Historia Augusta*)中。元老们在会议中采用集体呼喊的方式表达对已逝皇帝的巨大不满与憎恶，要求继位者对其"除名毁忆"。如第一章中所讨论的，元首制下的元老院在讨论涉及皇帝的议题时，很难正常进行自由讨论。作者提出，当元老试图表达意见、行使权力时，不可避免地会遇到名义上的权力与真实权力不一致的问题。而通过诉诸集体呼喊，元老们可以在集体名义的保护下有力地表达自己的情感态度。然而权力有限的元老院与拥有实权的统治者之间的张力关系仍然存在。新任元首即便承受巨大压力，仍然有权做出并坚持自己的决定。作者展现出元老院权力受限时，相关情境中权力关系的复杂性。

第五章讨论公元4世纪早期君士坦丁对翁布里亚城市希思贝鲁姆(Hispellum)的一份请愿回复。该城请求皇帝准许它以皇帝的名字重新命名，希望得到允许在城中举办节庆戏剧表演和角斗比赛，并希望向皇室家族敬献神庙。该城希望通过获得特权与荣誉提升自身的等级地位，其请求得到了皇帝的肯定答复。长久以来，城市间的竞争受到地方精英推动，通过参与其中，贵族精英们能够展示并确认他们在本地社会中的优势地位。然而专制统治改变了城市间竞争的实质,从精英间的竞争转向从皇帝处争夺特权和荣誉。作者指出,当竞争中的负担逐渐加重时,地方精英从主动赞助转为躲避逃离,寻求其他方式强化自身地位。

第六章对东哥特国王狄奥多里克统治时期国王与元老关于蓬蒂内沼泽排水工程的通信进行分析。为城市提供福利是罗马帝国贵族城市生活的重要组成部分,该个案中的书信往来发生在公元6世纪初期,不仅表明罗马式行为方式的持久性,也暗示了公益善行能够适应不同时代的需要。从理论上来说,贵族的善举出于自愿,然而在实际生活中,加诸其身的社会期待非常强烈。自发与被迫之间的张力内置于贵族为城市做出的善举中。在国王统治下,受迫的方式发生了变化,由过往城市居民对本城精英的恩泽期待转变为被迫接受统治者的要求,精英在何种程度上仍保有自主性难以言明。在这样的张力关系中,不论是统治者还是元老贵族,都对对方的行为以及自己该如何表现有着清晰的认知。

第七章聚焦拉文纳纸草文书,包含拉文纳和意大利其他城市市议会的一系列会议记录。在古典时代之后,意大利地区政治生活的图景发生变化。教会获得大量财富,开始取代城市议会的中心地位;地方精英的构成更加多样,议会议员不再是城市中唯一居于高位的群体;政治活动逐渐仪式化,城市议会的作用更多的在于帮助精英维护自己的身份与地位。城市议会尽管继续主张自己的核心地位,但事实上已逐渐边缘化,地方精英的地位也不再限于通过城市议会议员的身份来表达。作者指出,本例个案中的城市议会变化之大,使得本书所讨论的罗马政治文化几乎失去了存在的语境,加之教会逐渐发展为主导力量,可以说,本例个案中反映出的变化标志着罗马政治文化的终结。

这七例个案涵盖了政治生活的不同方面,参与者清楚自身所处的地位与实际拥有的权力,对其他参与者的行为方式抱有预期。他们既受限于自身的角色,也在一定程度上保有能动性。本书所探讨的政治文化,其关键特征便是这种有限度的行动空间。政治机构的权力受限,使其内部充满张力:政治机构既需要成员参与,又限制了参与者能够拥有的权力；权力受限的同时，参与者仍然保有一定程度的主动权；贵族精英受到相应规范的限制，但在许可范围内，仍然可以继续发挥作用。如我们所见，这些个案时间跨度大，涉及政治生活中的不同群体，通过不同史料载体得以留存。每一例个案都相对独立完整，作者提出的罗马政治文化中的张力关系和模糊处境包含其中，通过相关文本的分析阐释渐次呈现。

七例个案既独立，也互相关联，相同议题在不同个案中出现，如元老与皇帝之间的关系（个案一、三、四）、庇护制与社会网络关系（个案二、三）、贵族的自我展示方式（个案三、六）、荣誉竞争与社会期待（个案五、六）、贵族地位的确认方式（个案五、七）等。如作者所言，每一个个案都经过了审慎挑选，除了各自的独特性外，它们被视作能够在更广泛意义上反映罗马政治文化的特点。作者坦言候选案例有很多，但考虑到收益递减原则，他认为本书所选七例个案已能够撑起对罗马政治文化的研究。

塔科玛清楚地表示，将公元1—6世纪意大利地区的罗马政治文化视作整体进行研究，是基于主观建构。虽然研究所依据的每例个案都有自身特定的历史情境，然而如前所述，这些个案包含了罗马政治文化中的核心议题，展示出相似的特征。罗马政治文化创造出一种被普遍接受的话语体系，参与者可以进行自我表达，同时它相对清晰的边界也对参与者的行为起到规范作用。这种话语体系几乎成为一种独占力量，只有遵守其规定的行为才被允许并可接受。如七例个案所展示的那样，罗马政治文化帮助贵族精英确认身份地位、同时对他们的行为进行约束和规范。

当拥有的实际权力不断缩减时，罗马元老院和意大利城市议会为何能够在数世纪中持续存在？本书一再强调，两个政治机构得以长期存在意味着它们对于内部成员具有重要意义。换言之，元老院和地方市议会都在为贵族精英服务。在此基础上，作者引入路径依赖理论与社会均衡论进一步予以阐释。根据路径依赖理论，当社会向着特定方向发展，政治生活的参与者受制于过去的境况，对已经存在的政治机构会继续保留。正如我们所熟知的那样，元首制建立时元老院没有被裁撤，君士坦丁堡出现第二个元老院时，罗马元老院也没有被关闭。显然,政治生活的参与者们将政治机构和自身行为都锚定在了过去。元老院和城市议会在某种程度上被锁定在各自的路径中,不会被轻易终结。同时,如社会均衡论所指出的,社会系统总是趋向一种和谐均衡的状态。当贵族精英的地位持续得到巩固加强时,实际上强化了社会的稳定状态,更加难以改变他们所在政治机构的发展路径。

元老院与意大利城市议会长期存在,元老与地方议员也持续发挥作用。作者通过分析元老院讨论、地方竞选、元老投票行为、元老集体决策、城市的荣誉竞争、贵族善行以及城市议会的变化,展现出元老贵族与地方精英参与政治生活的种种方式及其行为所受到的影响与约束。塔科玛指出,罗马政治文化呈现出一种矛盾状态。一方面,它有很强的影响力,为政治生活的参与者提供一套行为规范;另一方面,它又十分脆弱,高度依赖于参与行为,只有当参与者愿意遵循其原则时,它才能够发挥作用[18]。

三

塔科玛很清楚自己所选研究对象的棘手之处与该课题面临的潜在挑战,也正因此,从某种程度上可以说,本书对罗马政治文化进行长时段主题式探究本身已颇具价值。从总体上来看,作者超越以往研究古罗马政治史所采用的时段划分方式,以共和时期为参照,将其之后的时段视为整体,用一种长时段的眼光考察罗马政治文化中的"变"与"不变"。对于承载延续性特征的两个传统政治机构——元老院与意大利城市议会,塔科玛脱离制度层面的探讨,关注机构内部参与者之间的关系及其与外部社会的交互,通过七例个案揭示出公元1—6世纪意大利地区罗马政治文化中的张力关系、适用原则以及主要特征。

长时段视角无疑是本书值得称道之处。在横跨六个世纪的长时

18　*Roman Political Culture*, p. 288.

段中,在元老院和意大利城市议会的不同情境中,政治生活的参与者在相互之间或与外界交互时,其行为方式呈现出一些相似的特征。若非拉长研究时段、突破某一特定时期的局限,很难观察到罗马政治文化中的某些特征跨越数世纪而存在。

当研究时段被特别拉长时,对研究主题的分析与对具体历史情境的考察,平衡好这两者之间的关系并非易事。塔科玛特别强调对罗马政治文化,尤其是对其中的张力关系和模糊之处进行探讨时,不能脱离具体情境。因此,在研究方法上,他选择个案研究。书中所选七例个案出自不同时期,涉及不同情境,使我们能够更加深入地理解在当时的元老院和城市议会中到底发生了什么。作者还提到,对罗马政治文化的分析非常依赖文本材料,不同情境中的张力关系通过具体文本得以呈现。不论是文学作品还是碑铭纸草,作者对个案文本的分析十分深入,同时引用其他关联文本进行对比印证。不仅对以往受到较少关注的文本进行细致探讨,对于已有较为充分研究的文本,也能结合本书主旨提出新的洞见。可以说,作者对每一个案的探讨既是本书的重要组成部分,也为基于每个个案的其他独立研究提供了新的解读视角。

本书跳脱出传统的时代界限划分,也在努力克服研究中的一些割裂做法,使所选七例个案能够放在一处进行探讨,而非零散、孤立地被看待和讨论。如作者所言,本书介于专题性的学术著作和松散的个案研究之间,在提供一系列详细的个案研究的同时,将这些个案置于一个整体的框架中[19]。可以说,本书不仅开创性地将共和国之后数世纪内的"罗马政治文化"作为特定对象进行研究,在研究方法上也进行了有益的探索。

个案研究法固然有其优点,但也有局限之处。这些个案或许只能展现出罗马政治文化的部分样貌,而我们对其全貌仍不得见。对此,塔科玛在书中使用了一个比喻,形象地说明了采用个案研究法会给我们带来什么。作者建议我们想象一座房子,在不同楼层和不同朝向都有窗户。当围绕这座房子从外向内看时,每一扇窗户都能让

---

19 *Roman Political Culture*, p. 19.

观察者看到房子的局部情况，每一扇窗户都从不同角度提供了关于这座房子的细节信息。这些房间看起来可能各不相同，其中也可能居住着不同房客。然而，观察者能够意识到这些房间和它们的居住者以不同的方式相互联系。尽管房子的某些部分无法被看到，但它们仍是房子整体的一部分。本书便是通过仔细观察选中的每一扇窗户，以探究罗马政治文化的样貌[20]。

此外，个案研究法也很难全面展示出时代变化。作者一再声明，本书并非要勾勒时代变化，部分原因在于史料本身零散细碎、分布不均，无法为罗马政治文化勾画出一幅延续的图景，无法对其发展进行连续性分析。同时，也因为罗马政治文化有其灵活性，能够在不同情境中做出调整适应，因而很难对其进行线性描述[21]。作者提出应该谨慎对待时代发展变化的线性叙述，这也可视作对研究罗马政治文化的学者们的善意提醒。

意大利是罗马帝国的核心地区，如作者所言，基于该地区所探讨的许多议题也适用于其他地区、其他政治机构、其他时段甚至古代世界的其他社会[22]。如果罗马—意大利政治文化中的行为或特点也在其他行省城市的政治生活中存在，那么是否存在一种可以被称为意大利类型的罗马政治文化？又或者说，在行省中是否存在更多种类型的罗马政治文化，其在权力分配方式及政治机构运作方面表现出很强的地区差异？这些问题有待学者们进一步探索，而塔科玛的《罗马政治文化》无疑为罗马政治史研究开辟出了一条新的路径。

（作者单位：上海师范大学人文学院世界史系）

---

[20] *Roman Political Culture*, p. 19.

[21] *Roman Political Culture*, p. 20.

[22] *Roman Political Culture*, p. 19.

比较研究

Comparative Studies

【**编者按**】 西方古典学术正式进入我国已近四十年，平心而论，尚处于为自己的发展和定位踌躇犹疑的阶段。进入中国的西方古典学术是作为西学的一支，如自然科学一般保持其西学的异域性和纯粹性，还是作为一种人文精神逐步融入中国文化的思想核心？这是问题的关键所在。

编者认为，西方古典学术倘要成为最优秀的中国学术之一部分，就必须与中国文化发生某种融合，常言所谓中西会通是也；而若欲会通，其前提条件便是比较，因为只有通过比较，方能明辨中西古典文化的异同，反思其共性和特性，洞察可兹会通之处，最终实现两者在当下中国文化情境里的会通。

比较之为方法，有隐性和显性之分。翻译、撮述、绍介等，皆属隐性的比较，而显性的比较，尤其是学术性的比较研究，或许更有助于奠定文化会通的稳固基础。近几十年来，此种比较研究正是西方古典学界一个方滋未艾的新兴领域，也是西方古典学术与中国学术结合的一个难得契机。国内古典学者虽偶有涉足，然即便与邻国日本和韩国学者相比，亦在少数，不禁令人汗颜。有鉴于此，本刊设立"比较研究"专栏，不定期推出相关研究成果。本辑率先刊布的三篇长文，分别对古希腊—中国、古罗马—中国和古埃及—中国的比较研究现状给出较为全面且细致的概览，旨在为有志于此的研究者提供全局性的指引。编者需要说明的有两点：其一，古埃及–中国比较研究虽不属于古典学术的范畴，却可以作为古希腊罗马—中国比较研究的重要参照，为此编者特别致谢李安敦（Anthony Barbieri-Low）教授的热情参与。其二，为求统一，三篇研究概览在此皆以英文首发，俟日后再精心译成汉语，既能令读者更感亲切，亦是一种显隐交织的中西比较之实践。（张巍）

Sino-Hellenic Studies: A Survey

ZHANG Wei

The comparison of ancient Greece and China entered a new stage around half a century ago in Western academia. It has hence been baptized Sino-Hellenic Studies. The defining features of this new field are threefold. First, whereas previous comparisons of the two ancient cultures were mostly done in passing or implicitly, such as the translation of classical Chinese texts into Western languages or the sinological works of sinologists educated in Greek and Roman classics, Sino-Hellenic studies is by nature explicit, that is to say, the two cultures are put to direct comparative study. Second and in addition to explicit comparison, the two cultures are placed on more or less equal terms. The lack of one culture's prominent features in the other culture is not to be lamented but to be explained, and sometimes also to be mended. Third, the comparison is designed for a deeper understanding of both cultures, by finding out what is common and universal, and what is distinctive and unique.

So far Sino-Hellenic studies has seen three general surveys of its current state[1]. With full acknowledgment of the fact that these surveys

---

[1] Tanner (2009) (still the most comprehensive and in-depth discussion), Beecroft (2016) (concentrating on reception history and comparative literature, skimming over science and philosophy) and Raphals (2018) (bibliographical entries with brief descriptions, including many more items than the previous two, to which the present survey is most indebted in terms of bibliographical guidance. In addition, I thank Lisa Raphals for critical comments on a draft of this survey).

have provided us with much guidance and insights, the present survey will differ from them and to some extent supplement them. It is broadly structured by the **aims and uses of comparison**, next by the **different disciplines or sub-fields to which the comparison belongs**, and finally by the **main topics or problems the comparison deals with**[2]. Given the fast-growing body of work published in this burgeoning field, the present survey does not strive to be exhaustive (which is beyond the scope of this survey and will anyhow soon be outdated), rather, it arranges the relevant output in terms of three distinct models (the cross-cultural, the transcultural, and the cultural critical[3]) and gives a representative and reasonably comprehensive overview of work done in each[4]. By laying out the aims and uses of these three models and presenting Sino-Hellenic Studies with all its breadth and variety, our goal is to demonstrate that this blooming field is ripe for Chinese scholars to enter and to participate, and to jointly shape its future[5].

1. Cross-cultural Comparison

Three models of Sino-Hellenic studies have emerged so far. All

---

[2]   This is the format of the by far longest first section; the second and third sections are structured by main topics or problems. Of course, such a division into disciplines, sub-fields and main topics or problems cannot be too rigid, when applied to individual monographs and essays and more so to collected volumes, I have therefore chosen the overarching topic of each work (each essay in the case of collected volumes of a miscellaneous nature) to categorize it, with cross-references where necessary.

[3]   I adapt these terms from Tanner (2009), who, however, uses the term "intercultural" for what I designate as "transcultural". Tanner limits them to three approaches within comparative Sino-Hellenic philosophy, but I apply them to the entire field to delineate three distinct and vital models. Cf. also Ralph Weber's theoretical discussion of the four approaches to comparative philosophy (Weber [2013], 3–7), but he does not name them.

[4]   This survey does not engage in explication of comparative methodology or criticism of individual works, which would make it even longer than it already is.

[5]   In the spirit of consistency with the other two surveys, I have made the hard choice of writing this one in English, but hope to use Chinese to an Chinese audience on other occasions.

three models, being comparative, are **based on the identification and description of commonalities and differences, leading to the explanation and interpretation of these commonalities and differences**. But the explanation and interpretation serve different purposes and have different uses for the comparer. In the first model, which is usually called the cross-cultural comparison, ancient Greece and China are kept apart and compared as two unrelated entities. It problematizes analysis confined to one of these cultures only, and uses evidences from the other culture to test the theory developed from one culture, to come up with more systematic, persuasive and comprehensive explanations, and explanations that give better causal analysis of historical phenomena. Though starting from one culture (the primary culture), its overall goal is not to serve only the study of the primary culture, but to achieve a better understanding of both cultures, by historically contextualized and mutually illuminating comparison. This type of cross-cultural analysis is believed to be capable of de-parochializing ourselves who are always born into one culture, that is, to question the presumptions and the categories that we are born with, to put ourselves into perspective and to be more self-critical. Furthermore, it can help avoid the hyper-specialization that is pestering present-day academic training, and combat exceptionalism and essentialism of the culture in which one specializes.

Comparative work done on this model, like Sino-Hellenic studies in general, started with and is still largely dominated by intellectual history of various aspects of thought and knowledge. It received a dual impetus in the 1950's and 60's, and two events can be singled out symbolically as founding events. As early as 1938, Joseph Needham, the preeminent British sinologist embarked on an unprecedented venture to study the entire history of the sciences and technology in China, and started to publish his work since the 1950's under the title *Science and Civilisation in China*. This monumental work is inherently comparative, especially the important second volume on the history of scientific thought which came out in 1956. As the driving force of his life's work, Needham formulated the hugely influential question nowadays named after him (see below 1.a). A few years later in Paris, a group of young scholars, each specializing in a different ancient culture, gathered to do comparative work under the leadership of Jean-Pierre Vernant. The Center for the Comparative Study of Ancient Civilizations (*Centre de Recherches Comparées sur les Sociétés Anciennes*) was established in 1965 to be a meeting place for their collaborative work. Vernant, who was influenced by Marxism and structuralism, had already conducted an exemplary dialogue with the renowned French sinologist, Jacques Gernet, adopting a comparative perspective to examine the economic, social and political contexts of the rise and evolution of rational thought in ancient Greece and China. The dialogue was organized by the Association Guillaume Budé on November 22, 1963 and published in the *Bulletin* of the Association in the following year[6], which subsequently exerted a profound impact on the Sino-Hellenic study of intellectual history[7].

These two examples set the agenda for the cross-cultural comparison. **The main concern is the identification and explanation of the salient characteristics of ancient Greek and Chinese thought, their distinguishing features and principal differences. This concern leads to the comparative investigation into the origins, the formative stages and the further development of ancient Greek and Chinese thought, as well as the various manifestations of these characteristics and differences in religion, literature, philosophy, the sciences and so on.**

Given its methodological self-awareness and ideological timeliness,

---

[6]   Vernant & Gernet (1964).

[7]   For instance, Geoffrey Lloyd, perhaps the most distinguished living voice in this field (see below 1.a) was deeply inspired by it and often evoked it as a stimulating example.

this model has attracted by far the most followers throughout the academic world. It is therefore the most developed one, greatly overshadowing the other two. The following survey gives it the fullest attention to reflect the current situation, but by doing so, we do not imply that it is without question the most desirable or the most effective model. The advantages and insights of the other two models must speak for themselves, as will be seen.

a. Science

The most conspicuous difference between ancient Greek and Chinese thought that has caught the attention of not only the Sino-Hellenic comparativists but also the general public pertains to science. This difference, as mentioned above, was incisively formulated by Joseph Needham as follows:

> Why did modern science, the mathematization of hypotheses about Nature, with all its implications for advanced technology, take its meteoric rise only in the West at the time of Galileo? This is the most obvious question which many have asked but few have answered. Yet there is another which is of quite equal importance. Why was it that between the second century B.C. and the sixteenth century A.D. East Asian culture was much more efficient than the European West in applying human knowledge of Nature to useful purposes?[8]

The "**Needham Question**" is in fact a two-prolonged question. Not only

---

[8] Needham 1969: 16 (this essay entitled "Poverties and Triumphs of the Chinese Scientific Tradition" was first published in 1963). The "Needham Question" is repeated several times in this collection of previously published essays, e.g. at the beginning of "Thoughts on the Social Relations of Science and Technology in China" (1953) and "Science and Society in East and West" (1964). The latter was revised and reprinted as the first essay of Vol. 7 part 2 of *Science and Civilisation in China*; see also Needham & Robinson 2004, p. 1 for the "Needham Question" in slightly different wording.

does it ask why modern science *did not* rise in China, but also why for most of the time before the modern age ancient China *did* stride ahead of the West in the applications of scientific knowledge. Expectedly, such a complicated question required detailed and sophisticated research, to which Needham devoted his life. While his own investigations remained mostly within the sinological framework and only inherently comparative, he sparked a comparative interest that was soon to bear fruit. It called for a full-scale comparison of ancient Greek and Chinese sciences that was taken up most effectively by the British classicist Geoffrey Lloyd and the American sinologist Nathan Sivin.

As a classicist, Lloyd started his research on Aristotle, but went gradually back in time, to the beginnings of Greek sciences and medicine. In this early phase of his career, Lloyd already adopted the approaches of cultural anthropology and sociology to look for explanations in the social and political contexts of ancient Greece[9]. He felt more and more the need to test his hypotheses concerning the rise of ancient Greek science against another major ancient civilization with no direct contact with it, a Great Other, as it were. The turning point came in 1987 on a visit to lecture in Beijing, when he decided to learn classical Chinese. Previously, the dialogue between Vernant and Gernet had already set an inspiring example for him, which he repeatedly acknowledged. Since then Lloyd has embarked on a wide-ranging comparison between the **beginnings of science and scientific thought in Greece and China**, producing a series of monographs by himself[10]. Just like his earlier work on the rise of Greek science, he conducts the comparative project by going between the intellectual history of

---

[9]   See, for example, Lloyd (1979; 1983; 1987).

[10]   Lloyd has published more than a dozen single-authored books in the past thirty years, see the bibliography entries under his name since 1990. The publications that specifically compare ancient Greek and Chinese science begin with the last chapter of Lloyd (1990), followed by Lloyd (1996; 2002; 2004; 2006 and 2012).

knowledge and the sociology of knowledge. The sociology of knowledge is defined as an "inquiry into the conditions under which knowledge, or what passed for it, was produced, and the conditions under which those who claimed to do the producing worked"[11]. China proved to be an ideal test-case to combine intellectual history with the sociology of knowledge.

This approach culminated in his collaboration with Nathan Sivin the renowned American historian of Chinese science, exemplified by their co-authored book *The Way and the Word: Science and Medicine in Early China and Greece* (2002)[12]. For their project, they criticize the "Needham Question" as misleading and distracting, since it has increasingly been acknowledged by historians of science that no culture, Greek or Chinese, aimed toward modern science, which could be traced only to medieval Europe. What interests Lloyd and Sivin is to compare ancient Greek and Chinese science in their own historical contexts. To achieve this goal, they reject the comparing of concepts or factors one at a time, and insist that:

> *The most fruitful comparisons begin not with individual concepts or methods but with complexes of thought and activity seen in their original circumstances. Whether it is a matter of studying the stars, or the human body, or harmonies, or the cosmos as a whole, the first step is to analyze what the ancient investigators themselves say they were trying to do — their conception of their subject matter, their aims and goals.*[13]

Starting from this emic approach, the investigation then proceeds in two stages. The first part of the book is devoted to the sociology of

---

[11] Lloyd (1996), 16.

[12] Lloyd & Sivin (2002). This book, by the way, is dedicated to Gernet and Vernant, a testimony to the example their dialogue set for Lloyd and Sivin.

[13] Ibid., 6.

knowledge, studying the social and institutional framework of Chinese and Greek science, respectively. The social factors considered include the training and education, the livelihood of the ancient inquirers, what bonds connect those inquirers who do the same work, how they communicate to each other and to outsiders, their relation to authority, and their employment and patronage. The second part focuses on intellectual history, examining the fundamental issues of Greek and Chinese science. These issues consist of the problems asked by the inquirers, their aims of inquiry, the concepts and assumptions they rely on, their modes of reasoning and persuasion, and their use of evidences.

These two parts form what they call "the cultural manifold", which comprises politics, society, institutions, practices, knowledge, and theories. By going from the social end to the intellectual end of the manifold, Lloyd and Sivin do not imply that the social factors determine thought (or vice versa), but stress the interactions between these ends for a deeper understanding of complex historical phenomena. Based on the previous parallel analyses, the conclusion then submits Chinese and Greek science to direct comparison. After summarizing the important similarities and differences between the Chinese and Greek "cultural manifolds" in which science developed under seven headings, they come to the following general conclusion:

> The dominant, but not the only, Greek way was through the search for foundations, the demand for demonstration, for incontrovertibility. Its great strengths lay in the ideals of clarity and deductive rigor. Its corresponding weaknesses were a zest for disagreement that inhibited even the beginnings of a consensus, and a habit of casting doubt on every preconception. The principal (though not the sole) Chinese approach was to find and explore correspondences, resonances, interconnections. Such an approach favored the formation of syntheses unifying widely divergent fields of inquiry. Conversely, it inspired a reluctance to confront

established positions with radical alternatives.[14]

This conclusion, endeavoring to do justice to ancient Greek and Chinese scientific thought within their own historical contexts, while at the same time bringing out their salient characteristics and pinpointing the distinguishing features and principal differences, is typical of the cross-cultural comparison. A better understanding of both scientific cultures is believed to be achieved historically by such a mutually illuminating comparison.

Lloyd himself as well as in collaboration with Sivin has covered a wide range of topics in the history of science (and further afield, historiography notably, as we will see below 1.e), inspiring other scholars to make further explorations. Good examples are the three specialist studies published in the collected volume to celebrate the eightieth birthday of Lloyd[15]. Two of these studies concern **mathematics**. The French historian of mathematics Karine Chemla examines "Abstraction as a Value in the Historiography of Mathematics in Ancient Greece and China"[16]. The first part of the paper discusses the distinct views among 19th century missionaries about the use of abstraction in ancient China, but the second part turns to the ancient Chinese view on "abstraction", its expression and its function in mathematical practice, as formulated in commentaries on *The Nine Chapters* (《九章算术》), and the paper concludes with a brief comparison with the structure of Euclid's *Elements*. The Israeli historian of Greek mathematics and specialist on Archimedes Reviel Netz compares how Archimedes and Liu Hui employ a similar method to account for the Box-Lid—the figure produced by the intersection of two cylinders circumscribed within the same cube—and stresses the importance of

---

[14] Ibid., 250.
[15] Lloyd & Zhao, eds. (2018), Part IV.
[16] Chemla (2018).

fine-grained, mathematical detail, not broad cultural contrasts[17].

The other contribution, jointly by Vivienne Lo and Eleanor Re'em concerns **Medicine**, but it deals with a subject often neglected by historians of medicine, namely aphrodisia. These products and practices that induced sexual pleasure are studied to compare the gathering of medical knowledge in ancient Greece and China, Many categories, definitions, concepts and techniques of the sexual arts were shared, while the key differences "include the overarching reproductive aims of Greco-Roman aphrodisiac recipes, and the unique Chinese use of self-experimentation in the sexual arts as a cornerstone of a new medicine"[18].

Medicine is also the subject of a vivacious comparative study by the Japanese scholar Shigehisa Kuriyama[19]. Its title *The Expressiveness of the Body and the Divergence of Greek and Chinese Medicine* implies that ancient Greek and Chinese medicine set out from similar beginnings or parallel origins, but then diverged into different traditions. Indeed, historical change and factors that caused the divergence are the main concern of the comparison. Conceptions of the structure and workings of the human body such as the pulse, blood, breath, and "wind" are used as concrete illustrations to study comparatively the specific histories of these cultural constructions. The specific histories will in turn contribute to a reassessed understanding of the cultural distinctiveness, as manifested in the Greek and later Western fixation on anatomic view of the body and musculature on the one hand, and the Chinese obsession with the microcosmic view of the body and acupuncture on the other. What is more, Kuriyama's comparative inquiry into the history of the body, by stressing the inseparability of perceptions of the body and conceptions of personhood, invites us to reassess our own habits of feeling and

---

[17] Netz (2018).
[18] Lo & Re'em (2018) (the quote on p.348).
[19] Kuriyama (1999).

perceiving[20]. This is a clear statement of the use of cross-cultural comparison for the comparer mentioned above.

b. Philosophy

Along with science philosophy is a form of rational thought that has early on received very intensive comparative study. Indeed, many scholars believe that philosophy is *the* form of rational thought out of which science emerged, and moreover, it is in philosophy that the most salient characteristics of the origins, the formative stages and the further development of ancient Greek and Chinese thought can be identified and explained. A strong impetus to this belief is the highly influential idea of "axial age" put forward by the German philosopher Karl Jaspers in the Second World War[21]. Since then, ancient Greece and China have figured prominently in the intellectual achievements of mankind during the first millennium before the common era. While historians and archaeologists remain skeptical about this "speculation" and demand its verification by concrete historical details, philosophers and philologists tend to be more favorable to the grand framework under which comparative work can proceed.

Accordingly, the comparison of the **mainstream schools of Greek and Chinese philosophy** has taken the lead. By the mainstream schools, I refer specifically to the Greek tradition founded by the triad Socrates, Plato and Aristotle and the Chinese tradition founded by the triad, Confucius, Mencius and Xunzi. Among these triads, the comparison of **Socrates and Confucius** has enjoyed iconic status, since the two philosophers are considered the icons of ancient Greek (and Western) and Chinese (and sometimes Eastern) philosophy or indeed entire civilization. Jaspers himself played no small part in this. He substantiated

---

[20]   Ibid., 272.
[21]   Jaspers (1949).

the idea of "axial age" with philosophical study of the life and thought of Socrates and Confucius. These two figures are selected, along with Jesus and the Buddha, as the definitive men (*die maßgebenden Menschen*) of their respective culture, and also great philosophers deserving to be studied side by side[22].

Ethics or moral philosophy has so far occupied the center of much comparative work done on the mainstream schools of Greek and Chinese philosophy. It is investigated predominantly from the perspective of modern virtue ethics, focusing on **Aristotelian (and less often, Platonic) and Confucian ethics**. I give some examples from recent publications to illustrate the range of topics and especially the different configurations of the comparanda. The "doctrine of the mean", often held to be a marked point of intersection between Greek and Chinese moral philosophy, is closely examined by Andrew Plaks through a comparative reading of Aristotle's ethical writings and the Confucian treatise known as the *Zhongyong* (《中庸》). His systematic investigation of the precise shape of the argument in these two unrelated sources both brings out the most striking points of common conception and expression, and sheds light on certain significant divergences in philosophical assumptions and modes of argumentation[23]. The same topic is treated by two essays published in a special issue on comparative Greek and Chinese ethics in the *Journal of Chinese Philosophy*. One of them is by Kenneth Dorter, who compares the concept of the Mean in Confucius and Plato by turning to a number of Plato's dialogues and the Confucian literature[24]. The other essay penned by Yu Jiyuan scrutinizes the Aristotelian Mean and the Confucian Mean, and compares these two

---

[22] Jaspers (1964) (reprint of the first part of *Die großen Philosophen* published in 1957).

[23] Plaks (2002).

[24] Dorter (2002).

doctrines of the mean, treating each as a mirror for the other[25]. We may mention that this special journal issue also contains a study on the moral reasoning of Aristotle and another Confucian, namely, Xunzi by Eric L. Hutton, who, through a close analysis of Book VI of the *Nicomachean Ethics* and the *Jiebi*（《解蔽》）Chapter of *Xunzi*, argues that a certain way of understanding Aristotle's conception of moral reasoning provides unexpected insights to make sense of Xunzi's view of moral judgment[26].

Scholars have also compared specific virtues of the two moral philosophical traditions. Tim Conolly focuses on two virtues central to relational ethics, the Aristotelian idea of *philia* (friendship) and the early Ruist idea of *xiao* (filiality) and examines their origins and philosophical justifications. He argues that the Aristotelian and early Confucian accounts, while different in focus, share many of the same tensions in their attempts to balance hierarchical and familial associations with those between friends who are on the same footing[27]. Lisa Raphals discusses gendered virtues, especially the claim that women differ from men in intellectual and ethical capacities, including capacities for moral reasoning and political and ethical judgment. This claim originates from Plato's *Republic* and the *Laws* and Aristotle's *Politics* in the Greek tradition, and from the *Analects* in the Chinese tradition, which are analyzed for comparison. She demonstrates that arguments about gendered virtue and debates about the relative ability of women and men to make intellectual and ethical judgments are not the property of any one "tradition"[28].

The ongoing workshops of comparative ancient Greek and Chinese ethics held in Munich and Glasgow, organized by the historian of Greek

---

[25] Yu Jiyuan (2002). For his book-length study which includes this essay and others to compare various aspects of Aristotle's and Confucius' "virtue ethics", see Yu Jiyuan (2007), discussed below 2.c. See also the monograph by May Sim (Sim [2007]) discussed there.

[26] Hutton (2002).

[27] Conolly (2012).

[28] Raphals (2002a).

philosophy Richard King, have produced two collected volumes that deal with a variety of topics. The first volume, entitled *How Should One Live? Comparing Ethics in Ancient China and Greco-Roman Antiquity* (2011), contains four sections: introductory papers on fundamental questions about the nature and methodology of comparing ethics are followed by specialist papers on core issues (harmony, virtue, friendship, knowledge, the relation of ethics to morality, relativism) in each of the traditions, and the volume concludes with comparative studies on emotions (Geoffrey Lloyd), prediction (Lisa Raphals), complexity and simplicity in Aristotle and early Daoist thought (David B. Wong), being and unity in the metaphysics and ethics of Aristotle and Liezi (May Sim)[29]. The second volume with the same format turns to the ideas of "good life"[30]. The comparative section covers topics such as autonomy, fate and divination (Lisa Raphals), the virtue of equanimity (Lee Yearley), the Stoic notion of *oikeiosis* and Mencius' idea of *tui* (extension) (Richard King).

It is remarkable that three of the comparative papers included in these two volumes make unusual juxtaposition of the *comparada*: Aristotle with early Daoism, with the Daoist philosopher Liezi, and Mencius with the Stoics. This may raise some eyebrows as to the choice of what is comparable. Intellectual affinity is a good reason to compare, but sometimes sharp contrast may be a more stimulating cause for comparison. At any rate, it is salutary to bring the **non-mainstream or marginal schools of philosophy** into comparison so that a more complicated and variegated picture of both Chinese and Greek philosophy can take shape.

The Daoist school of philosophy, represented by the Daoist triad Laozi, Zhuangzi and Liezi, is often opposed to the mainstream school of

---

[29] King & Schilling, eds. (2011).
[30] King ed. (2015).

Confucianism. Take Zhuangzi as an example of comparandum. **Zhuangzian philosophy has been compared with the Hellenistic schools of stoicism and skepticism**. A collection of essays on skepticism, relativism and ethics in the *Zhuangzi* is headed by two comparative studies[31]. Paul Kjiellberg's lead essay compares Zhuangzi's skepticism to that of Empiricus Sextus. He demonstrates their similarity in drawing knowledge into question to produce a state of uncertainty, and argues that while the goal of Sextus' skepticism is *ataraxia* or relief from the anxiety caused by commitment to unverifiable assumptions, Zhuangzi prescribes skepticism as a means of living in accord with nature not mediated by human representation[32]. Then follows Lisa Raphals' essay which compares the arguments in Zhuangzi's *Qi Wu Lun* (《齐物论》) and Plato's *Theaetetus* to distinguish three versions of skepticism: skepticism as a thesis or doctrine denying the possibility of true knowledge, as an attitude or a recommendation to live with a certain attitude of doubt, and as a method of questioning and inquiry that leads the practitioner to doubt. By way of careful analysis, she argues that Zhuangzi and Plato alike employ skeptical methods and implicitly recommend skeptical attitudes but that they carefully refrain from committing themselves to skeptical theses and thus avoid self-refutation[33].

Zhuangzi resembles the Stoics also in their views on "following nature." These views are submitted to closer comparative analysis by a number of scholars. David Machek has published two essays on this topic. One of them treats their similar distinction of emotions, showing that both Zhuangzi and the Stoics differentiated "natural" emotions — feelings emerging by themselves, not involving evaluative judgments or desires — from "passions" that do involve judgements or desires. The other

---

[31] Ivanhoe & Kjellberg (1996).

[32] Kjiellberg (1996).

[33] Raphals (1996).

essay extends the comparison of emotional detachment into their ideas of freedom, understood by both Zhuangzi and the Stoics to be the ability to do only the necessary things[34]. The idea of freedom is also the topic of comparison between Zhuangzi and Epictetus made by Richard King. He argues that both understand it as living without impediment, but in Epictetus' stoicism, this lack of impediment is associated with reason, for Zhuangzi it is associated with practices which align one with Tian or Dao[35].

Besides the Stoics and the Skeptics, **Daoism merits comparison with other schools of Greek philosophy, for example, with Aristotle**[36]. David Machek compares the notion of craft analogy in the thought of Zhuangzi and Aristotle, showing that both philosophers have ambiguous view on this analogy and their divergence owes to some central cosmological and ontological commitments that undergird their theories of action[37]. In the comparative part of the collected volume *How Should One Live?* David Wong juxtaposes selected passages of Aristotle's *Nichomachean Ethics* and of the early Daoists, mainly the *Daodejing* and the *Zhuangzi* to compare what he calls the value of complexity and simplicity in living[38]. The same volume includes a paper by May Sim, who compares the notion of being and unity in the metaphysics and ethics of Aristotle and another Daoist, namely Liezi[39]. The author shows that the differences in Aristotle's and Liezi's ethical views are based on their differences with respect to the first principle[40].

---

[34] Machek (2015) and (2018).

[35] King (2018). Note also Coleman (2002) who approaches the comparative analysis of Stoic and Daoist (including Zhuangzi and Laozi) ethics from a less familiar but intriguing perspective, that of aesthetics.

[36] For transcultural comparison with Plato, see below 2.a.

[37] Machek (2011).

[38] Wong (2011).

[39] Sim (2011).

[40] It is worth mentioning that the second collected volume contains an essay by Richard King, who compares the Stoic notion of *oikeiosis* and Mencius' idea of *tui* (extension). The stoics and Menius are an unusual choice of comparanda that is to be commended.

To sum up, we agree with Lisa Raphals' call for further work in this field so as to break away from the predominant focus on Confucianism and virtue ethics. In a brief survey on Daoism and Greek philosophy, she identifies three areas that promise rigorous, informed and evenhanded comparison: explicit concepts such as "truth" and "nature", methods of knowing, reasoning and inquiry, and recommendations for how to live in the original sense of *philosophia*[41]. Comparative work in all these areas can contribute to an enriched understanding of Chinese and Greek philosophy that should by no means be confined to Confucian and Aristotelian ethics.

For example, a marginal school of philosophy, the school of Names (名家), represented by Deng Xi, Hui Shi and Gongsun Long, reveals a dimension of Chinese philosophy hardly touched upon by Confucianism. **These so-called Chinese sophists have easily found the Greek sophists of the 5th century BC. as their counterparts**. Jean-Paul Reding's substantial monograph, *Les fondements philosophiques de la rhétorique chez les sophistes grecs et chez les sophistes chinois* compares their philosophy of rhetoric[42]. After a thorough discussion of comparative methodology in the first part, the second part lays the philosophical foundation of the comparison: was sophistry a stage in the intellectual history of rational thought and what philosophical problems did it strive to resolve? The next two parts prepare for the answer by way of detailed doxographical and philological study, one of them analyzing the problem of names and the philosophy of rhetoric among the Greek sophists, while the other collecting, translating and interpreting the fragments of Hui Shi and Gongsun Long. The final part returns to the questions raised in the second part, based on the examination of the texts.

---

[41] Raphals (2015b).
[42] Reding (1985).

The comparison of sophists brings us to a crucial aspect of cross-cultural comparison between ancient Greek and Chinese philosophy that has received special attention, i.e. the **relation of language to thought**. One main question is linguistic relativism. Does Greek philosophy ultimately derive from linguistic features characteristic of and peculiar to the Greek language (and Chinese philosophy likewise)? Two illustrating examples are Aristotle's categories and the Greek metaphysical concept of Being. Both are systematically examined by Reding. His essay "Greek and Chinese categories: A Reexamination of the Problem of Linguistic Relativism" addresses the first example, using classical Chinese philosophy as a lens to revaluate Aristotle's categories and asks whether they are truly universal[43]. Another essay "'To Be' in Greece and China" turns to the second example and starts with the question: if ancient China had neither a verb "to be" comparable to the Greek *einai* nor a theory of being comparable to what Aristotle and Plato had constructed, does it follow that ontology simply could not arise in China?[44]

The first example is also the subject of a monograph by Robert Wardy, who approaches it from a different perspective, i.e. the reception of Aristotle's *Categories* in 17th century China[45]. The monograph begins with a philosophical discussion of linguistic relativism, referring specifically to the Chinese case. Wardy attacks the hypothesis that Classical Chinese was a language ill-suited for the development of logic and deductive reasoning. The second part is devoted to a reading of the 名理探 ("The Investigation of the Theory of Names"), which is a seventeenth-century translation of part of Johannes Argyropulos' Latin translation of Aristotle's *Categories* into Classical Chinese jointly made by the Jesuit

---

[43] Reding (2004), 65–92 (first published in the journal *Philosophy East and West* 36, 1986, 349–374).

[44] Ibid., 167–194. For Reding's broader aim of transcultural comparison, see 2.b below.

[45] Wardy (2000).

missionary Francisco Furtado and the Chinese literatus Li Zhi Zao. The reading serves as a test to demonstrate that Classical Chinese, if deployed by skillful translators, was not only able to render Aristotle's categories adequately, but in certain cases could even be superior to Latin.

In this regard, Christopher Harbsmeier's magisterial survey of Chinese language and logic, though not an explicitly comparative work, has to be mentioned[46]. Belonging to the *Science and Civilization in China* series, it studies the foundations of science in China, making constant comparison with the Greek language and thought processes. For instance, translations from Plato's works into classical Chinese are compared with the original and the English translation to analyze the ability of the Chinese language to serve as a medium of logical discourse in terms of clarity and complexity[47]. With reference to the founding father of Greek logic, Aristotle, the index shows 14 sub-entries with numerous discussions.

Explicitly comparative is Reding's investigation into the origin of logic in China from the perspective of language. He argues that logic operated differently in ancient China, favoring analogical reasoning, as opposed to syllogistic reasoning in Greece. He demonstrates that the Later Mohists, unlike their Greek contemporaries, did not discover formal logic and grammar, probably because Chinese is logically more transparent than Indo-European languages. The first Greek philosophers, for their part, had to fight against a language that seems to be much more hostile to logical reasoning than classical Chinese and as a consequence developed formal logic and grammar[48]. The logical notion of contradiction in early Greek and Chinese philosophy is another subject of comparative analysis by Reding. He reaches the conclusion that with this notion we do not move in two totally different and incommensurable

---

[46] Harbsmeier (1998).

[47] Ibid., 164–170.

[48] Reding (2004), 31–48.

philosophical universes, but the theories proposed are the result of choosing one solution rather than another within one and the same pool of possibilities. In ancient Greece, the notion of contradiction had been discovered within the framework of epistemology and ontology, whereas the notion had been conceptualized from a quite different direction in ancient China, namely from that of human action[49].

Other scholars have compared the ancient philosophers' own understanding of their language. Anthony Yu, for example, compares the *Cratylus* of Plato and the chapter "On the Right Use of Names" (《正名》) in *Xunzi* with regard to three issues: the meaning of names, the purpose of names, and the maker of names[50].

Another aspect of the relation of language to thought is **how the use of language in philosophical rhetoric informs thought**. Metaphor, for instance, is such a use of language not infrequently made by philosophers with profound meaning for their thought. Reding, again, raises fundamental questions about the philosophical uses of metaphor in China and in Greece[51]. Ancient Greek philosophers, he submits, generally adopt a pessimistic attitude to the cognitive powers of language, a mistrust counterbalanced by an "inflation of metaphor", which explains the fact that although metaphors are theoretically banned from philosophical discourse, Plato, the Presocratics, and even Aristotle rely very heavily on metaphorical expressions. The ancient Chinese philosophers, on the other hand, adhere to an epistemological optimism concerning language and therefore, although the metaphorical way of arguing was approved, metaphors are actually sparingly used and reflections or theories on them are hardly found. The supposedly Western root metaphors of the light and the mirror are then used as examples of metaphoric philosophical discourse.

---

49   Ibid., 17–30.
50   Yu (2002).
51   Reding (2004), 127–166.

Root metaphors have also attracted the attention of other scholars. Those dealing with mind-body dualism are compared by Lisa Raphals. She surveys three comparable sets (1) mind and body as an amalgam, (2) body as a container of mind, and (3) mind (or soul or spirit) as ruler of the body, to study early Chinese and Greek representations of the self and their account of the relations among body, mind, and soul or spirit[52]. In another essay, she compares the root metaphors used to describe fate in philosophical texts, *Zhuangzi* and *Xunzi* on the Chinese side, Parmenides and Plato on the Greek side[53]. An apparent semantic similarity between *ming* (命) and *moira* (both words use a root metaphor of division and allotment) is shown to mask important semantic, metaphoric and philosophical differences[54].

Rina Camus focuses on shared metaphors between Confucian and Aristotelian texts, taking archery metaphors in the *Analects* and the *Nicomachean Ethics* as a case study. After establishing the respective backgrounds and meanings of archery imagery in these texts and drawing out the disparities and convergences that come to light through the metaphor, she demonstrates that shared metaphors can serve both as hermeneutic tools for reading early texts and as focal points for comparing views of different traditions[55].

Similar to metaphor, symbols can be deployed to shape arguments through analogies and examples. This is the subject of David Schaberg's study on what he calls the "logic of signs"— arguments from signs and from examples — which he suggests provided early Warring States writers, including historiographers and philosophers such as Mencius and Xunzi, with some of their fundamental rhetorical tools[56]. His study starts from

---

[52] Raphals (2015c).
[53] Raphals (2002b). Note also the enlarged version published as Raphals (2003).
[54] Ibid., 226.
[55] Camus (2017).
[56] Schaberg (2002).

an Aristotelian perspective, clarifying Aristotle's theoretic analysis of the sign in the *Prior Analytics* and the *Rhetoric*, and then examines its uses in *Zuozhuan* rhetoric and in philosophical reasoning, especially Mencius' arguments by analogies and examples from the *Book of Songs* and Xunzi's arguments by "analogy" (比类) and "analogical projection" (推类). The comparison reaches the conclusion that "(t)he logic of signs does not permit a wholesale distinction of 'Chinese' modes of argumentation from 'Greek' modes; but it does account for certain continuities in pre-Qin historiographical and philosophical texts"[57].

c. Religion

To fully understand the rise of philosophy and science in ancient Greece and China, comparative work must necessarily probe into religion, where many of the salient characteristics of ancient Greek and Chinese thought that the comparativists look for are already displayed. Regrettably, no comprehensive study comparing Greek and Chinese religion has emerged so far. Recent work tends to focus on particular aspects. Lisa Raphals, one of the leading scholars in this area, conveniently identifies three of them that are both of significant interest and suitable for comparison: first, cosmogony and cosmology, including macrocosm-microcosm analogies; second, relations and distinctions among humans, animals, and gods; third, the scope and nature of mantic practices such as divination and prediction[58].

The last topic — **mantic practices** — is the subject of a pioneering systematic comparison undertaken by Raphals herself. Her *Divination and Prediction in Early China and Ancient Greece* provides side by side account and analysis of the sources, theories, practitioners, methods, questions, consultors, mantic narratives and hermeneutics, as well as the

---

[57] Ibid., 181.

[58] Raphals (2015a).

relations of divination and prediction to the development of systematic thought in both traditions.[59] Drawing on the work of Jean-Pierre Vernant to study the rationality of divination and his method to examine it from the dual aspects of intellectual and social operations, the book starts with the contexts for the comparative study of Chinese and Greek divination (chapters 2–3 on the sources, the theorizing of divination in both Classical and Sinological scholarship), and moves from the social and institutional aspects (chapters 4–7 on practitioners and their methods, topics, questions and responses, the consultors and their access to divination) to the intellectual aspects (chapters 8–9 on mantic narratives as a genre and their hermeneutics, the contributions of divination to systematic inquiry). The commonalities and differences are summarized in the conclusions under five headings of "social and institutional comparables" and three facets of "intellectual operations". Both Chinese and Greek divination are shown to share a form of rationality and have contributed to systematic thought, but in different ways: "Chinese notions of symmetry, number, and abstract patterns of change were central to the development of systematic medicine, astronomy, and cosmology. Greek debates about divination were central to the development of skepticism, logic, and theories of causation."[60]

The second topic — **relations and distinctions among humans, animals and gods** — has not been studied systematically. Only specific topics are treated. Michael Puett, for instance, examines the theme of "self-divinization" in early China and Greece[61]. According to his observation, beginning around the same time in 5th and 4th centuries BCE, similar debates concerning the potential of humans to achieve divine powers developed in Greece and China against the traditional views about the nature of divinities and humans and the proper

---

[59] Raphals (2013).
[60] Ibid., 385.
[61] Puett (2002b).

demarcation that should exist between the two. Focusing on Empedocles for Greece, and for China on self-cultivation literature of the Warring States period such as the "Neiye" chapter (《內业》) of the *Guanzi*, Puett studies the causes for the emergence of these self-divinization movements. He argues that the material at hand should force us to rethink the model of explanation that emphasizes the contrastive cosmologies of the two cultures (see below), and the debates concerning self-divination are comparable in terms of their motivating concerns and tensions. Comparative study is well-positioned to discover how and why the debates worked out historically in the two cultures.

Apart from the philosophical texts, mythology is an important source for ancient views on the relations among humans, animals and gods, especially between humans and gods. Unlike the more or less systematic accounts of Greek mythology, early Chinese mythology exists in a fragmentary state. The best known English compilation and translation of Chinese mythology, the one by Anne Birrell, contains some 300 myth narratives selected from over 100 classical texts, and these scattered narratives are not organized by any indigenous principles, but according to themes and motif classes common to world mythology[62]. Yet, these narratives offer good material for comparative mythology. They cover a wide range of themes, such as cosmogony, creation, etiology, divine birth, metamorphoses, strange places, peoples, plants, birds, and animals, the primeval and the lesser gods, and founding heroes. The comparison with Greek mythology is natural to an English audience, as Birrell states, and she duly points out a good many of such parallels[63].

---

[62] Birrell (1993).

[63] Ibid., 13. The index entry "Greco-Roman myth" has the following sub-entries: creation, culture bearer, fire, foundation, fraternal rivalry, grain deity, love, metamorphosis, sacred beast, separation of sky and earth, star, sun and moon, violence. All these references to parallels may bear fruit under comparative study.

The relations between humans and gods come to full view in myths about the most outstanding humans, i.e. the heroes. David Keightley is one of the first scholars to study Chinese and Greek mythology of the heroes comparatively. His examination of the representations of heroes in early Chinese texts (the *Book of Songs*, the *Book of Documents* and the *Zuozhuan*) and Greek epics (Homer and Hesiod) as well as in art, covers their typology, their morality and mortality. With regard to the relations between the heroes and the gods, he makes the following remark:

> (T)he themes that attracted early Chinese mythologists were social order and social morality; stories of dying and death were not emphasized. The general harmony that pervades the relations of the Chinese to their gods contrasts strongly with the heroic and adversarial universe of early Greece, in which warrior gods and goddesses like Apollo, Artemis, and Pallas Athena involve themselves in the lives of mortals like Achilles or Hector. Early Chinese society was dominated by kinship ties, the royal ancestors representing the most senior members of the kinship unit in heaven. There was little discord between gods and men. Obedience and filiality ruled on earth as they did in Heaven.[64]

Keightley draws our attention to opposing views with important consequences for the representations of heroes in these two cultures: while the ancient Greeks considered gods and humans as radically separate and distinct beings, the ancient Chinese saw humans and gods (spirits) as inherently linked, correlating to each other and subject to the same processes of nature. This telling contrast presupposes a cosmological framework that relates to the first topic — **cosmogony and cosmology**. This is a topic that reverberates widely in almost every

---

[64] Keightley (2014, first published in 1993), 271.

aspect of intellectual history, not only in religion, but also in philosophy, science, literature and so on. The most important secondary scholarship is extensively reviewed by Michael Puett in the introduction to his monograph *To Become a God. Cosmology, Sacrifice and Self-Divinization in Early China* from the sinological perspective[65]. His comparativist essay cited above gives a more succinct summary:

> *One of the commonly made contrasts between Greece and China concerns the purported differences in the respective cosmologies of the two cultures. In contrast to the so-called tragic cosmology of the Greeks, wherein an inherently agonistic relationship was seen to exist between humans and gods, scholars often emphasize the degree to which early Chinese cosmology emphasized continuity between the human and divine realms.*[66]

Understandably, much recent work aims to revise and play down this contrast between "tragic cosmology" and "continuous cosmology". Puett himself is one of the specialists on ancient Chinese religion opposed to such a sharp contrast. His essay on "self-divinization" asserts that the cosmological statements found in ancient Greek text such as Empedocles and ancient Chinese text such as the "Neiye" chapter of the *Guanzi*, which are usually held to be unmistakable evidence for "tragic cosmology" and "continuous cosmology" respectively, are claims being made within larger political and cultural conflicts. As a matter of fact, these claims imply the existence of opposite ones, and a contextual and historical reading must ask why such claims were being made and who such claims were being made against[67].

---

[65] Puett (2002a), 5–21.
[66] Puett (2002b), 56.
[67] Ibid., 72.

d. Literature

With literature we enter a vast field of dynamic comparative research, similar to what we saw in the case of philosophy. Both ancient Greece and China produced a large amount of high-quality literary works (just as philosophical works) that exert profound impact till this day. The comparison of these works is regularly conducted in more established disciplines such as comparative literature and world literature. Sino-Hellenic cross-cultural comparativists readily adopt many of the theories and methods developed there, and strive to go deeper into the cultural and historical contexts when comparing these literary works.

Since literature in ancient Greece and China began with **the Homeric Epics and the *Book of Songs*** respectively, we start our survey in this area with a conference held at Beijing University in 2014, the papers of which were later published under the title *The Homeric Epics and the Chinese* Book of Songs: *Foundational Texts Compared*[68]. As the conference organizer and book editor Fritz-Heiner Mutschler states, unlike earlier comparative studies focused on specific problems which used the Homeric epics and the *Book of Songs* as "source materials"[69], this study engages in direct and systematic comparisons of the two as the dominant poetic classics in Western and Chinese culture. The comparisons are predicated on the most basic commonality between the Homeric epics and the Chinese *Book of Songs*, namely, "foundational texts" of each culture, and revolve around two main subjects. First, the history of the texts are discussed, and their formation, their philological reception and cultural roles are compared to bring out "the historic

---

[68]   Mutschler, ed. (2018).

[69]   For example, part one of Shankman & Durran (2000) is devoted exclusively to a comparison of the *Odyssey* with *Book of Songs* to search for the intimations of intentionality and participation in each culture, see 2.a below.

embedding of the texts"; second, the texts are read as poetry, and their form and structure, their contents and their values are compared to underline "the basic poetic features". Comparisons in the first subject lay the groundwork for comparisons in the second, which bring into focus "the basic poetic features" that characterize these "foundational texts". The overall aim is to read the two text corpora against each other in their own contexts, so as to go beyond commonalities and to look for significant cultural differences shaping and shaped by them. These commonalities and differences are well summarized by the editor at the end of the book[70].

Of particular interest are the essays in the first two sections of Part II, which compare the form, structure and contents of the Homeric epics and the *Book of Songs*. Form (meter, language, formulas, set phrases, type scenes, speeches) and structure (static vs. dynamic structure, macro- vs. micro-structure, unity) of the former are analyzed by Fritz-Heiner Mutschler and Ernst A. Schmidt, of the latter by Chen Zhi and Nick M. Williams, and they are compared by Zhang Wei[71]. The contents (subject matter, recurrent themes, characters, heroes and gods, nature) of the Homeric epics are disucussed by Øivind Andersen, and those of the *Book of Songs* by Wai-yee Li, followed by the comparative remarks of Fritz-Heiner Mutschler, and a brief comparison of heroes and gods by Andrew Plaks[72]. Admittedly, these comparisons are conducted only on the level of the basics, but they amount to the first systematic examination of the poetic elements of these foundational texts side by side[73]. Such direct comparison of their poetic features and literary values will no doubt contribute to a deeper understanding of the literary

---

[70] Mutschler, ed. (2018), 451–465.

[71] Ibid., 229–296.

[72] Ibid., 299–378.

[73] The commonalities and differences are recapitulated in Mutschler's summary on pp. 454–457.

tradition they founded[74].

The Homeric Epics and the *Book of Songs* are not only the origin of ancient Greek and Chinese literature, but also inaugurated a long history of literary thought for their respective culture. Most importantly, they had a formative influence on what each culture believed to be the nature, function and value of poetry (and literature in general), which we designate with the term **poetics**. The later philological and philosophical tradition that gave rise to an explicit poetics often revolved around the exegesis and hermeneutics of these texts. Such explicit poetics was put to comparative study by Earl Miner, a scholar of Japanese literature, with the goal to develop a theory of cross-cultural poetics. Drawing on the evidences from Aristotle's *Poetics* (and Plato's *Republic*) and the *Major Preface* to Mao's recension and exegesis of the *Book of Songs*, he proposed that at their origin Chinese poetics is lyric-based and hence affective-expressive in character while Greek poetics is drama-based and hence mimetic or mimetic-affective[75].

But we must be cautious when following later philologists or philosophers to impose explicit poetics on these texts. The immanent poetics of the Homeric Epics and the *Book of Songs*, as well as the implicit poetics of other early traditions concerning their formation and performance must be taken into consideration to give us a more balanced picture of the salient characteristics of ancient Greek and Chinese poetics. One attempt at comparing the implicit poetics has been fruitfully made by Alexander Beecroft. He chooses what he calls "the

---

[74] For an attempt to situate this comparative approach within contemporary Chinese receptions of the Homeric epics with reference to the *Book of Songs*, see my analysis in Zhang Wei (2021).

[75] Miner (1990). Miner claims further that affective-expressive poetics is the dominant one worldwide, while the mimetic poetics of the West is a minority one, the odd one out (p. 8). Cai (2002), 113–141 puts the philosophical poetics of Plato and Confucius to a direct comparison on the scale of what he calls the "Microcosmic Textures of Western and Chinese Poetics", and he affirms the "mimetic theories of literature in the West and nonmimetic theories of literature in China" (p. 141).

scenes of authorship" as found in poetic biographies such as the *Lives of Homer* and the *Zuozhuan*, and in the works of other philosophical and historical authors such as Plato, Aristotle, Herodotus, Confucius, and Sima Qian. These narrative episodes or anecdotes are examined to compare "the development of the concept of authorship in early Greece and China, specifically with reference to Homer and Archaic lyric on the Greek side and to the *Canon of Songs*, or *Shi Jing* on the Chinese side"[76]. The comparative study of these often-neglected stories leads not only to important conclusions about the function of authorship for the cultural identity of the early Greek and Chinese worlds, but also to a major revision of the bipolar opposition between Greek mimetic and Chinese affective-expressive poetics. The poetics implicit in the biographical anecdotes of poets and the descriptions of poetic performances makes the picture more blurred and more complicated. The differences are in degree and in emphasis, not in kind, and one may easily discern the expressive dimension of Greek poetry and the mimetic dimension of Chinese poetry[77]. Beecroft concludes that these different models of poetics in Greece and China "emerged from similar contexts, in which a variety of similar ideas coexisted, with one approach gradually becoming dominant for historically contigent reasons"[78].

Besides poetics, another area of literary thought that deserves to be compared is **rhetoric**. Lü Xing's survey of *Rhetoric in Ancient China Fifth to Third Century B.C.E.* is also an attempt at making broad comparisons with ancient Greek rhetoric, hence its subtitle *A Comparison with Classical Greek Rhetoric*[79]. As a survey of Chinese rhetorical theory and practice, the book first studies Chinese terminology of rhetoric, its key terms and their linguistic meanings, and the evolution of

---

[76] Beecroft (2010), 1.

[77] Ibid., 278–282.

[78] Ibid., 282.

[79] Lü Xing (1998).

vocabulary concerning speech and persuasive discourse in Pre-Chin China. The author puts forward Ming Bian (名辩) as the Chinese equivalent to Greek Rhetoric. He then goes on to study rhetorical features and persuasive styles in selected historical and literary texts, including the *Book of Songs*, the *Book of Documents*, *Zuozhuan*, *Guoyu* and *Zhanguoce*. The bulk of the survey consists of examinations of philosophical views and rhetorical perspectives articulated by individual thinkers from five major philosophical schools, the Mingjia ("Sophists"), Confucianism, Mohism, Daoism and Han Fei Zi. Comparisons with ancient Greek rhetoric are scattered in these chapters, and summarized in the conclusions. The similarities and the differences between Greek Rhetoric and Chinese Ming Bian are each discussed under five headings, the former including the art of persuasion, ethical emphasis, rational engagement, psychological activity, and evolutionary nature, the latter including the role of language, mode of inquiry, treatment of emotions, the domain of rationality, and rhetorical education. Through the identification of these similarities and differences the author aspires to the understanding and construction of a multicultural rhetoric which recognizes both culturally specific and transcultural elements of rhetoric.

Lü's general survey may be used as a basis for more fine-grained comparisons on specific topics. Another interesting survey that goes from the opposite direction, as it were, may also contribute to such comparisons. This is Ulrich Unger's *Rhetorik des klassischen Chinesisch*, which selects some fifty mostly Greek rhetorical concepts from Heinrich Lausberg's systematic handbook of Greco-Roman rhetoric (*Handbuch der literarischen Rhetorik*) and applies them to passages culled from pre-Han texts[80]. These concepts are divided into large categories of synonyms, tropes, figures, citation and allusion, acoustic means. Under each Greek (or Latin) rhetorical concept, a brief definition is first given and then a few

---

[80] Unger (1994).

examples are provided to demonstrate how it works in classical Chinese. This is not an uncontroversial exercise, but it is an exercise which could easily instigate further comparative research.

Literary texts have also been compared for **the ideas** they convey. I give a few examples that compare the Homeric epics with the *Book of Songs* and/or other Chinese literary texts to explore specific ideas. One of the pioneering scholars to do so is Lisa Raphals with her *Knowing Words: Wisdom and Cunning in the Classical Traditions of Greece and China*[81]. Its subject is to study the possible Chinese equivalents to Greek *mētis* ("cunning intelligence"), which, following the seminal work of Jean-Pierre Vernant and Marcel Detienne, Raphals understands as an independent mode of intelligence with its own logic and methods, typically applied to shifting, ambiguous situations that are not amenable to rigorous logic or calculation. This type of "metic intelligence", as she puts it, is typically associated with Athena and Odysseus in ancient Greek culture, but is believed to be universal. Consequently, she applies it to early China, and the first part of her book (chapters 1–5) examines its manifestations and configurations in early Chinese philosophical, military and historical texts, focusing on the range of meanings of the Chinese word *zhi* (智). The second part of the book (chapters 6–9) then turns to cross-cultural analysis, comparing the two Homeric epics not with the *Book of Songs*, but with two novels of the Ming dynasty, the *The Romance of the Three Kingdoms* (《三国演义》) and the *The Journey to the West* (《西游记》). After showing the centrality of metic intelligence to the construction of these novels, and how both novels feature metic characters (primarily Zhu Geliang in the former and the Monkey in the latter) and illustrate characteristic modes of action of metic individuals, Raphals compares them with the Homeric epics, arguing that metic intelligence informs five broad themes common to all these texts: force

---

[81] Raphals (1992).

and guile, kings and kingmakers, representation of the hero, designing women, and like-mindedness.

A similar topic is treated by David Keightley in his essay "Epistemology in Context: Disguise and Deception in early China and early Greece"[82]. He compares the *Odyssey* with the *Shiji* and a number of Chinese historiographical and philosophical texts to study different Greek and Chinese attitudes toward disguise and deception. The essay begins with the simple observation that disguise played a significant role in early Greek literature, most notably in the *Odyssey*, but it played no significant role in early Chinese literature. The explanation for these striking differences of attitudes are to be sought in epistemology, and Keightley states his insight right away:

> ... the interest in disguise, manifested in early Greek literature, may be correlated with the uncertainties about the nature of reality and about man's ability to know reality with confidence present in early Greek philosophy and that the lack of interest in disguise in early Chinese narratives may be correlated equally well with the metaphysical and epistemological optimism that underlies much early Chinese philosophy.[83]

Thus, it is an epistemological pessimism that accounts for the deceptive gods and the deceptive heroes such as Odysseus in the Homeric epics, while an epistemological optimism turns the attention of early Chinese literature and philosophy away from the realm of knowledge and reality to that of action and morality.

More recently, a pair of articles in the aforementioned *The Homeric*

---

[82] Keightley (2014b, originally published in 2001).

[83] Keightley (2014b), 283. Another essay by Keightley (2014a, originally published in 1993), discussed earlier (1.c) also compares the Homeric epics and Hesiod's *Theogony* with the *Book of Songs*, the *Book of Documents* and the *Zuozhuan* to study their representations of heroes and heroic action.

Epics and the Chinese Book of Songs analyze their moral and political values with special reference to the virtues of kingship or leaders, the former treated by Douglas Cairns, the latter by Zhou Yiqun, and these values are compared by Huang Yang and Yan Shaoxiang[84]. Despite the vastly different social-political structures reflected in the two sets of texts, commonalities of the ideals of kingship, exemplified by Nestor and Odysseus for the Homeric world and King Wen for the Zhou empire, can be easily identified. However, the differences are numerous, and the most striking one is that military prowess and warrior qualities are central to the Homeric leaders, which remain marginal for the Zhou kings, who distinguish themselves by moral superiority. This and other differences are related to the different functions of "glory" and "good fame", since "glory" is considered by the Homeric leaders, who are heroes par excellence, as the highest value they aspire to and compete for, whereas "good fame" is only a means to an end, that of moral exemplarity, for the Zhou leaders.

e. Historiography

Historiography is a special type of literary text with its distinct traits. On the one hand, it shares many common features with other prominent genres of the literary tradition within which it emerged, while on the other hand, it has truth-claim to the past and to social reality that it must constantly maintain. These two sides are reflected in the comparative study of Greek and Chinese historiography, but our survey will focus on the comparison of historiography as a genre, only touching on topics of social reality that are investigated using historiography as primary sources.

The Czech sinologist Jaroslav Průšek is often considered a pioneer of this field. In 1961 he read a paper entitled "History and Epics in

---

[84] Mutschler, ed. (2018), 381–450.

China and in the West: a study of differences in conception of the human story" at the International Council for Philosophy and Humanistic Studies in Tokyo[85]. This work is a first attempt to compare the **origins of Greek and Chinese historiography**. Starting with the close connections between Greek historiography (Herodotus and Thucydides as the prime examples) and literature, especially with the Homeric epics, he turns to the early examples of Chinese historiography, the *Zuozhuan* and Sima Qian's *Shiji*, and identifies their organization of material, structural principles, their literary classification and aims as differing widely from Greek historiography. Two causes are shown to be responsible for these divergent approaches to recording historical phenomena. The first one is the fact that Greek historiography emerged from a literary tradition dominated by the epic, while Chinese historiography did so from a literary tradition dominated by the lyric. As Průšek puts it:

> *Whereas in Greece literature begins with the epos, in China it begins with lyrical songs. In Greece historiography imitates the epic mode of expression; in China the categorization and systematization of facts by free linking of rough material reminds one of lyric methods[86].*

The second cause, Průšek explains, is different conceptions of the individual. The early Greek historians, under the profound influence of the two Homeric epics, had an intensive interest in the fate of the individual, in the extraordinary individual who stands out from his community as the "hero". The lyric tradition imprinted upon the early Chinese historians a prevailing concern with the general, the norm, the typical and the appropriate. The fate of the individual or the exceptional individual is not an object of study in itself, but only to capture what is

---

[85] Published in *Diogenes* 42 (1963), 20–43, reprinted in Průšek 1970, 17–34.
[86] Průšek (1970), 31.

morally and politically appropriate and normative[87].

Průšek has paved the way for **a systematic study of Greek and Chinese historiography as such**, concerning not only the identification of other characteristics and differences, but also the explanation of the causes. One outstanding scholar who has followed his lead and produced a sequence of papers on this topic over some twenty years is Fritz-Heiner Mutschler[88]. As a Latinist, his interest is broad enough to bring Roman historiography into the comparison, and has consequently developed a method to compare the triad in a more nuanced way. He contends that given the wide divergences between Greek and Chinese historiography, the Roman tradition should not only be brought into the picture, but also be compared with the Chinese tradition in its own right, since these two appear to have more resemblances[89]. As for the comparison between Greco-Roman and Chinese historiography, Mutschler urges us to take account of the different characteristics of each of the three traditions with regard to different aspects of comparison. When the macrostructure, the subject matter, the microstructure or the horizons of perception are compared, the three traditions come into different constellations. It turns out that Greek and Chinese historiography stand in stark contrast to each other, much more so than Roman and Chinese historiography[90]. The causes for the contrast and the similarity are to be sought, besides what Průšek identified as the epic and the lyric tradition, also in the contexts of production. The practitioners of historiography, their audiences, their modes of communication, methods of argument and persuasion, etc, all of these factors had to be taken into consideration

---

[87] Ibid., 31–34.

[88] Mutschler (1997, 2003, 2006, 2007a, 2007b, 2008, 2015, 2016). For the Chinese reader these papers are conveniently collected in 穆启乐:《古代希腊罗马和古代中国史学：比较视野下的研究》,北京大学出版社,2018.

[89] For the comparison dealing exclusively with Roman and Chinese historiography, see Mutschler (2006, 2007a, 2008, 2016).

[90] Mutschler (1997, 2003), see also his summary in this journal, pp. 334–335.

for the explanation of causes.

Another scholar, the aforementioned Geoffrey Lloyd has also turned to history and historiography as part of his comparative project to study the rise of rational thought in Greece and China. For example, the first chapter ("Histories, annals, myths") of his book *Ambitions of Curiosity. Understanding the World in Ancient Greece and China* is a comparative study of the origins and the intellectual development of Greek and Chinese historiography as systematic inquiry into the past and how it related to other inquiries[91]. His contribution to Volume One of the *Oxford History of Historical Writing* summarizes in a few pages the diachronic developments of Greek and Chinese historiography[92]. First, he points out that the historical conception of the past originated in other forms of records, inscriptions on stone for the Greeks, inscriptions on turtle shells, ox bones, bronze vessels, as well on stone for the Chinese. Second, when historiography as such emerged, it had to define itself in contradistinction to other competing genres, such as scientific prose and rhetoric on the Greek side, court chronicles, almanacs and annals on the Chinese side. Third, the very concept of history, *historia* and *Shi* (史), each encompassed more than our history in their original contexts, and to compare what was within their purview sheds considerable light on the nature and function of Greek and Chinese historiography. Finally, the most conspicuous contrast that catches the eye is the "overt competitiveness" of the Greek historian who endeavored to define himself in competition with his predecessors, and the "covert criticalness" of the Chinese historian who appeared to be more respectful to his predecessors but could at the same time express critical opinion in a veiled and indirect way. The cause for such different strategies has often been ascribed to "agonistic" Greeks and "irenic"

---

[91] Lloyd (2002), 3–20.

[92] Llyod (2011), 601–619, esp. 609–616.

Chinese, but should be studied in more depth[93].

Lloyd's primary concern, however, has to do with the place of historiography in the intellectual history of the two cultures. By contrast, Mutschler pays closer attention to the canonical texts of Greco-Roman and Chinese historiography, that is Herodotus, Thucydides, Polybius on the Greek side, Sallust, Livy, Tacitus on the Roman side, and *Shangshu, Chunqiu, Zuozhuan* and *Shiji* on the Chinese side. He has also undertaken the comparison of the individual historians and their texts, especially between Tacitus and Sima Qian[94]. Within the parameters of Sino-Hellenic studies, the best known comparison of individual historians is no doubt that between **Herodotus** and **Sima Qian**, juxtaposed as "two fathers of history". To my knowledge, the earliest formulation of this label dates to a short introductory essay by S. Y. Teng published some sixty years ago. The author justifies the label by laying out their similarities in methods of research and their differences in techniques of synthesis and systematic presentation[95]. A more recent textbook with the eye-catching title *Herodotus and Sima Qian: The First Great Historians of Greece and China* also conducts this rudimentary type of comparison[96]. Its first part is an overview of the different settings and times in which the two historians worked, discussing how each man introduced interpretation and moral judgment into his writing. The second part contains accompanying documents with excerpts from Herodotus' *Histories* and Sima Qian's *Shiji*, which illustrate their approach to history-writing and their understanding of their own cultures.

More sophisticated comparison is conducted on the level of

---

[93] Lloyd (1996), 20–46 gives institutional explanations for this contrast. Durrant (2002) criticizes the contrast from the Chinese side using Sima Qian as an example.

[94] Mutschler (2006, 2007a, 2008).

[95] Teng (1961).

[96] Martin (2010). The book is admittedly aimed at beginning students.

representations of reality, social, political or cultural, using the two historians as primary sources. The Dutch scholar Siep Stuurman, for example, juxtaposes Herodotus and Sima Qian, focusing on the ethnographic parts of their histories, in particular Herodotus' description of the Scythians and Sima Qian's treatment of the Xiongnu, to examine their views of empire and cultural difference[97]. He finds the independent developments of historiography that reached their first culmination in these "two fathers of history" a fascinating comparative case. For him the ethnographies in the *Histories* and the *Shiji* are instances of what he calls the anthropological turn of history, where the two historians attempt to understand the "others" living in foreign lands "from within", and to investigate the functioning of other cultures as interlocking systems. More generally, both historians conceive of history as a critical, explanatory discourse about political power. Apart from these parallels and many others, Stuurman also highlights two main differences: first, the temporality underpinning their historical narrative and their relation to empire; second, their formulation of cultural relativism. He seeks to explain these differences by the geographical position and the political history of Greece and China, and by the peculiarities of Greek and Chinese intellectual history, rather than by essentialist conceptions of Greek, European, or Chinese identity.

Another notable example is the monograph by Kim Hyun-Jin, which takes Greek and Chinese **representations of the foreigner** as its subject[98]. Kim conducts a comparative analysis of archaic/classical Greek and early Chinese historical and ethnographic sources, focusing also on Herodotus and Sima Qian, choosing likewise the former's logos of the Scythians and the latter's chapter on the Xiongnu. The study consists of two parts. The first part surveys the historical and cultural

---

[97] Stuurman (2008).

[98] Kim (2009).

contexts of the subject: after the Introduction, Chapter 2 examines the beginnings of the images of the other in archaic Greece and in early China from the Shang to the Spring and Autumn Period, while Chapter 3 focuses on the representations of the barbarian in classical Greece and Warring States China. The second part is an in-depth comparison of Herodotus and Sima Qian: their intellectual milieu and general attitudes to foreigners (Chapter 4), their respective ethnographic accounts of the nomadic Scythians and the Xiongnu (Chapter 5), and their respective representations of the sedentary Lydians and the states of Joseon and Nan Yue (Chapter 6). Throughout the book, Kim shows that both ancient Greeks of the archaic/classical periods and the Chinese of the Han dynasty were assertive in claiming their ethnic superiority over foreigners, and shared the same breadth and variety of prejudices towards outsiders, but each chose to emphasize different categories of differentiation. While the Greeks could not claim radical difference of their material culture from those of other Eastern Mediterranean ethne, and therefore preoccupied with their martial and genetic superiority over the barbarian, the Chinese stressed precisely their differences and superiority in material culture. To explain the causes for the difference, he argues that Greece was an integral part of the wider Eastern Mediterranean and Near Eastern civilization and that this had a major impact on the ways in which the Greeks chose to represent foreigners in their literature, while in the world of early China, although neighboring cultures posed military threats, the Chinese were able for some time to act on the assumption of cultural and material superiority to all the cultures in their purview.

Other ancient historians have also been fruitfully compared for their representations of social reality. For example, David Schaberg chooses Thucydides the historian of Athenian imperialism and Sima Qian the historian of imperial Han Dynasty, and compares in particular the Melian dialogue in Thucydides and the scenes of confrontations with the Xiongnu in the *Shiji* to study their representation and criticism of imperial power[99]. The comparison is based on the shared "water metaphor", the idea that "for both writers, and indeed for both traditions, imperial ways of knowing had their roots in archaic models of circulation: the circulation of water on the surface of the earth, of travelers, adventurers, traders and administrators along the rivers and seas, and of language and knowledge along the same routes"[100]. Thucydides' account of the Melian dialogue is then connected to the watery return of Odysseus in the *Odyssey*, and the tale of Zhonghang Shuo (中行说) in Sima Qian's chapter on the Xiongnu to the myth of water-worker Yu (禹), to demonstrate that metaphors of circulation underlie both the representation and the criticism of imperial power in the passages of the two historians compared.

f. Philology

A special discipline studying the literary, philosophical and historiographical texts discussed above and cultivated by both ancient Greek and Chinese intellectuals is **classical philology**. It is indeed remarkable that a huge amount of philological scholarship was produced on written texts, especially on the classics, in both cultures. To take again the prime example of the Homeric epics and the *Book of Songs*. The ancient philological work done on these two foundational texts in their formative stages is reviewed by Barbara Graziosi and Achim Mittag respectively, and then submitted to comparison by Gao Fengfeng and Liu Chun in the pathbreaking collection *The Homeric Epics and the Chinese Book of Songs: Foundational Texts Compared*[101]. The comparison shows that while the two text corpora were at first freely discussed, reflected and commented on, they both ended up being state-sponsored

---

99   Schaberg (1999). Shankman & Durrant (2000) also pairs the two, see below 2.a.

100   Ibid., 154–155.

101   Mutschler, ed. (2018), 87–160.

enterprises, the one under the Hellenistic kings, the other under the Han emperors. They were both taken care of by state-employed philologists and scholars, the royal librarians in Alexandria and Pergamum for the transmission and interpretation of the Homeric epics, and the three official chairs established by the Western Han emperors Wendi and Jingdi for the transmission and interpretation of the *Book of Songs*. However, there is a remarkable difference concerning the degree of closeness to political authority in the actual scholarship: while the royal librarians did not feel obliged to serve specific political interests imposed by the Hellenistic kings, the holders of the official chairs were expected to fulfil specific ethico-political aims and to endorse the state ideology.

Another, somewhat related example is a contribution entitled "On Libraries and Manuscript Culture in Western Han Chang'an and Alexandria" made by Michael Nylan to the collected volume to honor Geoffrey Lloyd[102]. This rich study compares the Great Library at Alexandria probably founded by Ptolemy II (r. 285–246 BCE) with the set of palace libraries assembled, edited and catalogued from 26 to 6 BCE in the capital of Chang'an under the Western Han emperor Chengdi (r. 33–7 BCE). Following the lead of Lloyd to attend to "cultural manifolds", the author conducts the comparison on the institutional, intellectual and political levels, using the comparative material to examine the emergence of authorship, manuscript culture, book depositories, erudite learning and textual criticism in these two widely separate institutions.

Aside from ancient classical philology, it should at least be mentioned that the comparison of **modern classical philology** is also on the way, although this area lies outside the time limits of our survey. Modern classical philology that began in the second half of the 18th

---

[102]   Nylan (2018).

century and flourished throughout the 19th century, especially in Germany, coincided intriguingly with the emergence and proliferation of the evidential scholarship around the same period in Qing Dynasty China. They can be compared at many levels that will eventually contribute to the nascent field of comparative and global classics.

g. History

Unlike the other disciplines surveyed above, history was previously studied by comparativists to explain intellectual phenomena, not for its own sake. But with the current rise of world history and global history, there has been in the recent years a trend to compare ancient Greek and Chinese history on their own terms, and this trend will no doubt continue. Here it is only possible to give a few recent examples relating to **social and political history**[103].

A monograph authored by Zhou Yiqun examines **gender relations** in the two ancient societies as reflected in convivial contexts such as family banquets, public festivals, and religious feasts, and aims to illuminate the different sociopolitical mechanisms, value systems, and human bonds in the two classical civilizations[104]. Zhou's analysis is based on a wide range of sources, including epic and lyric poetry, historical and philosophical texts, as well as bronze inscriptions. In order to encompass the various types of gender relations, the study is divided into three parts: Part 1 is devoted to an examination of the sociable relationships among men, Part 2 to the interaction among women and between men and women in various sociable contexts, and Part 3 to a search for a female perspective and an analysis of the relationship between female experience and male imagination. The conclusion

---

103 The comparative study of the cultural history of Greek and Chinese art, to name another area, has been undertaken most notably by Jeremy Tanner, see Tanner (2013, 2017 and 2018).

104 Zhou (2010).

summarizes the two patterns of gender and sociability, which are interpreted in terms of two different dialectics of affinity and conflict.

Zhou has also ventured to compare the **representations of women**. In a stimulating essay on *femmes fatales*, Helen on the Greek side, Mo Xi, Da Ji and Bao Si on the Chinese side are taken to be the prime examples of such women in each civilization[105]. These examples are analyzed through close readings of literary texts to illustrate the contrast between the coexistence of variegated and oftentimes conflicting views of Helen in the Greek sources and the invariably negative judgments passed on the three Chinese women in Chinese sources. The article also attempts to explain why the two ancient societies engaged their common suspicion, anxiety and fear about iconically beautiful and attractive women in strikingly different ways.

The **social use of food** is the object of a short article entitled "From the Harvest to the Meal in Prehistoric China and Greece: A Comparative Approach to the Social Context of Food"[106]. Drawing on the anthropological insights of Jack Goody on the enduring features of culinary practice in Europe, Asia and Sub-Sahara Africa, the three authors examine the food patterns observable in archaeological records from China and Greece as well as in early written texts, to explore the origins of unequal access to food.

A new volume edited by Hans Beck and Griet Vankeerberghen takes "the cultural and political dynamics between the rulers and the ruled in ancient China, Greece, and Rome" as its overarching theme[107]. Besides the introduction co-authored by the two editors which provides a survey of the meanings of the people, *demos* in Greece, *populus* in

---

[105] Zhou (2018). An earlier article by Michael Nylan compares the representations of elite women in the two great empires of Achaemenid Persia and Han China, drawing mostly on Herodotus for the former, see Nylan (2002).

[106] Liu, Magaritis & Jones (2018).

[107] Beck & Vankeergerghen, eds. (2021).

Rome, *min* (民) in China, and Hans Beck's piece on the registers of the "people" in these three cultures, only the last pair of articles explicitly compare ancient Greek and Chinese ideas of ethnic identity and the "barbarian"[108]. The one by Huang Yang traces the early development of the dichotomy between self and Other in China in comparison to early Greece, to examine its role in shaping the self-perceptions of the "Chinese" and the "Greeks," and the outlooks of their respective societies[109]. The other one by Hyun Jin Kim summarizes the Greek and Chinese representations of the foreigner and their distinguishing features, recapitulating some of the main ideas of his book discussed above (1.e)[110].

2. Transcultural Comparison

On the whole, cross-cultural comparison adopts a strictly historical method to keep ancient Greece and China apart as two unrelated cultural entities. The current trend is against previous, often simplistic attempts to construct dichotomies. Instead, differences between the two cultures identified and described in any given area or subject of study are more cautiously taken to be differences in emphasis, not in kind. Apart from the mainstream of one culture, one is advised to look for counter- and under-currents, which may be the mainstream of the other culture, and the dominance of the mainstream in one culture is better explained as the result of historical contingencies, not of inevitable *mentalité* that

---

[108] For the majority of articles comparing Rome and China, see Mutschler's discussion below pp. 306–309.

[109] Huang Yang (2021).

[110] Kim (2021). One may also take notice of Wooyeal & Bell (2004), which compares state-sponsored physical education in ancient Greece and China, explaining the divergent outcomes with reference to the idea of citizen. Still relevant is the earlier study by Karen Turner (Turner [1990]) on ancient Chinese and Greek law.

inhered as essence of that culture. The cross-cultural model of Sino-Hellenic studies that hold onto these tenets can be conceived as part of global cross-cultural studies. The comparátive study of each of the discipline or sub-field surveyed above, be it history of science, philosophy, religion, literature or history, is only a tributary to its corresponding global cross-cultural study with an ultimately universal scope.

But can the achievements of these two towering cultures confront each other to enable us better solve problems that are still facing us? Can we take into account all available ancient resources, and if this is not feasible, at least the resources from these two paradigmatic cultures when we examine the origins of these problems? Some of the Sino-Hellenic comparativists have thought so, and practice what may be called the transcultural model of comparison. **Transcultural comparison no longer keeps ancient Greece and China apart to confine them in their historical contexts, but invites the two cultures to meet each other in the present moment. It lays less emphasis on causal explanations of the commonalties and differences, but focuses more on those commonalties and differences that transcend their specific cultural backgrounds and contexts, and on how the commonalities may build a shared framework to allow the differences to complement each other, and thereby enriching our approach to the problems that matter most to us.** Its uses for the comparer are more positive than the cultural relativism that the cross-cultural comparison seems inevitably to end up. The transcultural comparer starts from problems that Western or Chinese culture is facing, goes to and fro in the two cultures, and aims at "transcultural truth" (not "transcendental truth") that helps one cope better with the perils of the contemporary world, whether one lives in the West or in China.

As can be expected, transcultural comparison finds its adherents more readily in the field of philosophy and literature, and in the following I will give examples pertaining to these two fields under the heading of the main problem that the comparison deals with. It has to be pointed out at this juncture that the transcultural model sometimes overlaps with the cross-cultural (hence some of the examples below also appear in the first section). But there is at least a degree of emphasis: the transcultural model stresses the solution to the problem itself for the here and now, rather than the historical causal explanations for how the ancients tackled the problem. This emphasis has caused criticisms from the followers of the cross-cultural model, but I believe their criticisms can be met firstly by attending more closely to the original problem-context (rather than the contingent historical context) to which the philosophical and literary texts addressed, and secondly by replying that the embeddedness of these texts in the assumptions of their tradition brings difficulty not only to the transcultural comparativist, but also to anyone who studies another culture, especially an ancient culture.

a. Recovering wisdom

The collaborative work of the American classicist Steven Shankman and sinologist Stephen Durrant bears fruit in their book *The Siren and the Sage: Knowledge and Wisdom in Ancient Greece and China*[111]. The title of this comparative literary study invokes the image of the Siren on the Greek side, who stands for knowledge, equated with "the ideal of encyclopedic comprehensiveness"[112], and the image of the Sage on the Chinese side, who embodies wisdom, associated with the experience that allows "a person to participate in the oneness that is the *dao*"[113]. The tension between knowledge and wisdom is attributed to that between two modes of consciousness, intentionalist and participatory. The main problem the two authors set for their

---

[111] Shankman & Durrant (2000).

[112] Ibid., 9.

[113] Ibid., 10.

comparative study is one that still profoundly matters to us: how can we recover a participatory consciousness and thereby gain access to wisdom in a world overwhelmed by intentionalist quest for knowledge? Or in their own words:

> *We all desire to know, and yet the intensity of this very desire to know and to control reality can cause a serious imbalance in the human psyche. We may forget that this desire to know takes place within a comprehensive structure of reality (dao) of which the human consciousness is itself a part and which can never be mastered. In our desire to know, we may forfeit the wisdom of the sage. Knowledge and wisdom will be at odds.*[114]

The reconciliation of the tension between knowledge and wisdom, between intentionality and participation is the goal of their transcultural comparison. Using the method of philologically grounded close-reading, they turn to the origins of the tension and explore comparatively how the tension is intimated, expressed, articulated and recovered in Greek and Chinese classical texts of poetry, historiography and philosophy. The first part starts with two poetical texts, the *Odyssey* and the *Book of Songs*; the second part moves on to historiography, taking as examples Thucydides' history and Sima Qian's *Shiji*; the third and final part compares the Chinese philosophical texts of Confucius, Laozi and Zhuangzi with Plato's *Symposium*. When put to comparison, the Greek poets, historians and philosophers appear often to stress intentionality, while their Chinese counterparts are more responsive to participation. At the same time, the comparison uncovers an intentionalist strain in China and a participationist tradition in Greece, and examines how the dominant trend responded to the opposing strain. With all these factors in mind, the two trans-cultural comparativists are able to carefully join

---

[114]   Ibid., 11.

the forces of the participatory mode, culminating in the wisdom of the Chinese Sages Laozi and Zhuangzi and the wisdom of the Greek Sage Plato (the *Symposium* in particular), to counterbalance the intentionalist mode radicalized in our world as the comprehensive and absolute knowledge of the Siren[115].

b. Out of linguistic determinism

A few seminal essays by the Swiss scholar Jean-Paul Reding dealing with the problem of the relation of language to thought have already been discussed above (1.b). They are collected along with other pieces under the title *Comparative Essays in Early Greek and Chinese Rational Thought* [116]. The introduction to the volume elaborates Reding's methodology, subject and purpose of study, which formulates a transcultural model for the overarching project undertaken by these essays. What lies behind the project is the central question: is philosophy a purely European phenomenon, incommensurable with the thought of other cultures? This is a thesis put forward by Hegel and Heidegger, and assumed by other eminent philosophers such as Husserl and Gadamer[117]. Moreover, Hegel and Heidegger believe that Greek (and German, which to their mind is closest to Greek) is the natural language of philosophy, through its connection of truth and knowledge which gives birth to epistemology and its connection of reality and existence which brings forth ontology and metaphysics.

Yet, viewed from another perspective, this thesis and belief amounts to saying that philosophy is imprinted but also constrained by the structure of the Greek (and German) language. How might we go out

---

[115] This thought-provoking comparison between the Chinese Daoists (Laozi and Zhuangzi) with Plato is recapitulated in Steven Shankman's essay with the telling title "These three come forth together, but are differently named: Laozi, Zhuangzi, Plato" (Shankman & Durrant, eds. [2002], 75–92).

[116] Reding (2004).

[117] Ibid., note 9.

of such a linguistic determinism of philosophy? Only by a comparison of the beginnings and the formative stages of philosophical thinking in two independent and linguistically unrelated ancient cultures such as Greece and China. Reding insists that such a comparison must be methodologically rigorous by philosophical standards. Drawing on the principles of comparative historical linguistics, he formulates a comparative method to study the "diverging evolutionary chains", on the assumption of "supposed common ancestor" (such as PIE for the Indo-European languages). The "supposed common ancestor" of Greek and Chinese philosophy is of course a metaphor, denoting "the basic unity of rational thinking". On this assumption, the comparativist should ask why Greek and Chinese philosophy are not *the same*, instead of why they are *different*. In other words, one should examine why "the basic unity of rational thinking" started to branch off, and should isolate the parameters that caused these two "evolutionary chains" to diverge and become different.

Reding focuses essentially on two such parameters: the difference in the starting-points of philosophy and the difference in language. It is with the second one that he tackles the central question raised above in a non-relativistic way. Against the thesis that philosophy is entrapped in language, or indeed in the Greek (and German) language, he sets out the following program:

> *What is needed, then, in order to go beyond this crude type of linguistic relativism? From the philosophical point of view, it would be enough to show that there are cognitive structures that are independent of language, which is, of course, very difficult, because these structures always have to be expressed within language. Nevertheless, there is another way of conducting the experiment, if we reverse the terms of the problem. Instead of starting with different cognitive contents, we shall try to demonstrate that one and the same cognitive insight can be expressed*

through the medium of structurally very different languages.[118]

The comparative essays on argumentation, logic, categories, metaphor and ontology etc. are concrete examples to show that Greek and Chinese rational thinking are different facets of one and the same phenomenon. There is not a kind of Chinese or Greek rationality, but simply rationality in China or Greece. In the final analysis, the Chinese and Greek philosophers are not entrapped in their native language, but the same cognitive insight can be expressed in either ancient Chinese or Greek, even though, due to the different starting points of philosophy, it "may turn up as a philosophical theory in one culture and as a grammatical rule or a semantic structure in another"[119].

By focusing on the neglected facets of rational and logical thinking in ancient Chinese philosophers such as the Later Mohists, Zhuangzi and the School of Names, Reding uncovers domains he believes to be most suitable and most fruitful for comparisons with the central interests of the ancient Greek philosophers, such as epistemology and ontology. This is perhaps ample proof that philosophy does not have to speak Greek (or German).

c. Toward a transcultural virtue ethics

After its revival in contemporary philosophy, virtue ethics is very much alive today. As we saw above (1.b), many Sino-Hellenists have compared different aspects of the moral philosophy of Aristotle and Confucius on the cross-cultural model. However, two monographs appearing in the same year of 2007 and claiming to be the first book-length scholarly comparison of the ethics of Aristotle and Confucius, target at different aims[120].

---

[118] Ibid., 12–13.
[119] Ibid., 13.
[120] Yu Jiyuan (2007) and Sim (2007).

Yu Jiyuan's monograph *The Ethics of Confucius and Aristotle* is subtitled *Mirrors of Virtue*, which refers to one of the two methods that Yu derives from Aristotle's ethics and applies to the comparison, namely, "the friend as mirror" thesis. Aristotelian and Confucian ethics are thus conceived as mirrors for each other, Within the framework of this friendly relationship, the author then applies the second method, that is, the method of "saving the phenomena" to the actual comparison, and the goal is to save the truth in the congruence and contrast of Aristotelian ethics and Confucian ethics taken as comparable phenomena[121].

The "truth" that Yu aims at is not some transcendental truth, but transcultural truth, truth that emerges from an imagined friendly conversation between Aristotle and Confucius in the present moment. To maintain their intellectual friendship, they have to transcend cultural boundaries and come to an agreement on terms that are not culturally bound, reaching a better understanding of virtue and its role in human perfection.

The individual chapters of the monograph puts this goal into practice. Yu demonstrates how the key concepts of *dao, de, ren* in Confucius' thought and the related issues of human nature and its fulfillment, the doctrine of the mean, the role of social customs and traditions, self-cultivation and moral education, love, family, virtue politics, moral emotion, moral reasoning, family are also the central themes in Aristotle's theory of virtue. By these studies, he uncovers how their overall frameworks are strikingly parallel, and what philosophical significance we can draw from their similarities and differences to contribute to present-day discussions on virtue ethics.

Likewise, May Sim stages an imagined dialogue between these two pivotal figures on the topics that still interest contemporary virtue ethics in her monograph *Remastering Morals with Aristotle and Confucius*.

---

[121]   Yu Jiyuan (2007), 5.

Her aim, however, is more ambitious, since she claims "to involve these authors [i.e. Aristotle and Confucius as 'authors' of ethical writings] in each other's problems and to engage both in reconsidering the contemporary difficulties to which they speak with surprising frequency in one voice, or at least in genuine harmony"[122]. Moreover, she takes the bold step toward an "evaluative comparison", outlined and defended in these words, which deserve to be quoted at length:

> *My claim is that evaluative comparison is difficult but not impossible, and I aim to bring Aristotle and Confucius head-to-head, where the strengths and weaknesses of their ethics are revealed and each can suggest remedies for the other's deficiencies. In particular, I shall make the case that while Aristotle's ethics makes social training central and leaves room for cultural variation within the perimeters of shared natural function, Aristotelians can learn much from Confucians about the nature and ethical pertinence of ceremony and decorum. In other words, Confucian aestheticism provides resources for Aristotelian theoreticism. Reciprocally, Confucian traditions can learn from Aristotle a form of first philosophy that grounds talk of our common humanity without neglecting cultural or individual differences and roots ethics in a practical rationality that does not claim mathematical exactness or exceptionless legislation. Aristotelian metaphysics provides resources for Confucian parochialism.*[123]

The topics treated in the actual comparison include the "doctrine of the mean" and its relation with harmony, the nature of the self and its best life, virtue and family or politics, friendship in the cultivation of virtue and for the cohesion of society. How much she succeeds in achieving her stated goal I leave others to judge. Here I wish to point out that

---

[122] Sim (2007), 1–2.
[123] Ibid., 2–3.

"evaluative comparison" could be conducive to the synthesis of a transcultural virtue ethics, which, building on the strengths of both Aristotle and Confucius, with their weaknesses mitigated or remedied, may go a long way toward elucidation of many moral problems that are still with us.

3. Cultural Critical Comparison

Like the transcultural model, the third model, the cultural critical comparison also foregrounds the here and now of the comparative moment. The cultural critic identifies a major deficiency of one culture (usually, if not always, the culture into which he or she was born) in the light of the other, and uses the other to criticize the self. This was the practice, for example, of the Neo-Humanist classicists in early 19th century Germany. Classical Greece was held to be the other of contemporary Christianity into which these humanists were born. One after another cultural characteristic of Classical Greece that differentiated it from Christianity was celebrated as the remedy and cure for what they saw as deficient in contemporary culture.

Today, the contrast between Classical Greece and Christianity no longer satisfies the critics of Western culture, largely for the reason that these two strains have been too closely entangled with each other within Western tradition. These critics seek a Great Other, which they find most paradigmatically in ancient China. **The differences between Ancient Greece and China, in particular those transcend their specific cultural contexts interest the cultural-critics most, which they believe can be deployed in an enlightening and constructive way to criticize the cultural deficiency they have diagnosed. The cultural critic valorizes precisely these differences in kind. They are not to be explained away by the historicism which undermines the self-critical** use of cross-cultural comparison, but must retain their power to extract oneself critically from one's culture, so as to stand outside or on the margin of it, where rigorous cultural criticism can be launched to begin with.

Currently, the cultural critical model of Sino-Hellenic comparison is championed almost single-handedly by François Jullien the French philosopher and sinologist (or better, sinologizing philosopher). Hence I shall take him as the sole example in this section and give him more air space to explicate this model. It has to be stressed that comparative work done on this model does not have to be confined to philosophy (Jullien's work, though focusing on philosophy, includes also literary criticism, poetics, rhetoric and art). Any cultural phenomenon that can be traced back to ancient Greek or Chinese ways of thinking may fall under the purview of cultural critical comparison.

Access through Detour

Jullien decidedly adopts the notion of heterotopy from Michel Foucault, and maintains that only a heterotopic position will allow Western philosophy (and Western culture in general) to be as radically self-critical as possible. The gaze upon ourselves from without is the only way to diagnose and to find remedy for the deficiencies in our culture. To attain this heterotopic position, China emerges as the only choice for three reasons. First, to get outside the Indo-European zone, especially the Indo-European languages with which Western philosophy is closely entangled. Second, to find a culture that has no historical relationship with the Indo-European zone, at least at its origin and in its formative stages and for a long period of its development. Third, to find a culture that preserves very early on its ways of thinking in texts. Ancient China, rather than, say India or Japan, meets these requirements and presents herself as the very embodiment of heterotopy.

Therefore, the appropriation of Chinese ways of thinking with other possible modes of intelligibility is for Jullien an instrument to probe the implicit prejudices of European reason, or in his words "to think the un-thought of in our thought"[124]. These prejudices are exemplified by entrenched Western modes of intelligibility such as cause and effect, theory and practice, the notion of Being, and the idea of God. By their persistence, other ways of thinking have sunken into the rupture or rift of European reason and thought.

Since his student years in China during the last phase of the Cultural Revolution, Jullien delved into Chinese culture, both ancient and modern, to look for other ways of thinking, which he has discovered abundantly. His early works treat topics such as the allusive quality in Chinese literary tradition, the logic of propensity, the conception of efficacy, the notions of process, blandess and immanence, and the strategies of meaning[125]. The last one is the main topic of his best known book, *Detour and Access: Strategies of Meaning in China, in Greece,* which is also the most manifestly comparative[126].

The object of this comparison is what the subtitle calls the "strategies of meaning" in China, i.e. those indirect, oblique, allusive or subtle ways of conveying meaning, and they are related to patterns of thought that pervade all aspects of Chinese culture. Jullien begins with the indirectness and subtlety of contemporary Chinese political discourse, of which he was an eyewitness (Chapter I). He then launches a series of comparisons between ancient China and Greece. In the domain of military strategy, where the ancient Chinese favored oblique

---

[124] Jullien has thus been accused of instrumentalizing China by his bad comparative philosophy and worse sinology, notably in Billeter (2006). For an assessment of the controversy, see Weber (2014).

[125] After some 40 years, Jullien's oeuvre is now immense, see de Boever (2020) for a recent English introduction.

[126] Jullien (1995 [2000]), cf. Reding's review (Reding [1996]). One may note that the subtitle of the English translation by Sophie Hawkes adds the conjunction "and" to join China and Greece, which are subtly separated in the French original by the comma, apparently to mirror the detour and access strategy of the book itself.

attack in stark contrast to the classical Greek model of war, the frontal clash of phalanges. The Greek model of war also manifests itself in the agonistic debate at the theater, the law court, and the assembly, whereas the Chinese avoided such contentious disputation and preferred indirect verbal confrontation veiled in oblique speech (Chapter II). The comparison then turns to the domain of the Chinese classics. The insinuous and oblique way of reading the *Book of Songs* is contrasted with the allegorical reading of Homer: the former reads poetry as oblique speech for political efficacy, while the latter reads poetry as indirect speech for metaphysical truth (Chapter III). The political use of poetry is also displayed in diplomatic quotations of poetry in the *Zuozhuan* (Chapter IV). The same reading strategy is applied by *Zuozhuan* as an explanatory commentary on the *Spring and Autumn*, which is treated as a highly insinuating text (Chapter V). The comparison then moves onto Chinese and Greek poetics. The poetical incitement (兴) is an indirect projection of one's inner feelings on the world, but the Greek mimesis through poetry gives a direct representation of the world (Chapter VI). The figurative meaning of Chinese poetry does not refer to another higher, spiritual level, as Greek symbolism does, but to the ethical and political level (Chapter VII). The next group of comparisons finally comes to philosophy. Confucius' method of modulation and generality is opposed to Socrates' method of definition and globality (Chapters IX–X); Mencius' insistence on avoiding philosophical discussions as the road to wisdom stands in sharp contrast to Greek philosophers' predilection for endless debates (Chapter XI). The Neo-Taoist Wang Bi's commentary on Laozi is read against the Neo-Platonist Plotinus on how to indicate the ineffable (Chapter XII), and Zhuangzi's metaphor of the net and fish is compared with the Western metaphor of the veil or cloak on how to gain access to nature (Chapter XIII). The book ends with discussion of typically Chinese approach to literary criticism, how the literary critic highlights the indirectness of literary texts. Jin Shengtan's commentary on the drama *Western Chamber* focuses almost exclusively on literary sinuosity (Chapter XIV), and his commentary on Du Fu's poetry pays special attention to the displacement between the poem and its title. The conclusion summarizes what Jullien is able to bring home after this long detour, laying out the benefits of indirectness for "the un-thought of" in Western thought. Remarkably, he also points out what the benefits of directness are for Chinese culture[127].

Jullien is fully aware that China does not have a monopoly on the indirect and the allusive strategy of meaning. The Greeks also developed various areas of cunning intelligence (*mētis*), the oblique way of communication exemplified by the Delphic oracle, the allegorical and symbolic reading of poetry, etc. However, the indirect "strategies of meaning" that are systematically thought out and pervasively dominant in almost every domain of Chinese culture amounts to an "alterity" in Chinese ways of thinking, as striking as the Greek direct confrontational way of thinking would appear to the traditional Chinese mind.

The title of the book thus epitomizes Jullien's entire project: it is a Sino-Hellenic comparison based on the cultural critical model, which can be summed up as "access through detour". Before setting out, the detour via China aims at a return, i.e. a better access to Greek philosophy at the origin of Western thought. For the cultural critic, sinology serves to guide the detour. If this detour would not end up in no return, it has to keep comparing, especially with ancient Greece. Jullien makes this point provocatively clear during an interview:

> ... this means that Western sinology does not have to be the double of
> Chinese sinology — a very pale double indeed, since we always began too

---

127 Jullien does not shrink from performing the role of the cultural critic on both sides. Witness his explicit criticism of the political price of subtlety in Chapter VI, since such subtlety endangers the very existence of the cultural critic whose mission Jullien takes on for himself.

late and will never know enough — but that it can actively and positively
*be Western by finding the reasons for its fecundity in its outside position, if
it reflects on the latter.*[128]

Conversely, we may wonder, what is the use of Chinese "Helladology" (to coin a corresponding new term), if not to engage in Sino-Hellenic comparison, to make it a detour and thereby gaining access to "the un-thought of" in Chinese culture?

4. Sino-Hellenic Studies in China

From Geoffrey Lloyd to François Jullien we have traversed the vast terrain of Sino-Hellenic studies. As of today, these two names may stand for the extreme poles that set the boundaries of this new field in Western academia. The tension between their approaches, between the cross-cultural and the cultural critical model (with the transcultural model lying somewhere in the middle), is high, but I believe salutary for the vitality of Sino-Hellenic studies.

When we turn to the hidden side of the story, as it were, that is, to Chinese academia, this new field tends to be considered a latest branch of Western studies (西学), which is exterior to Chinese culture and by its exteriority often causes uneasiness, if not rejection. Therefore to conclude this survey, I raise (but do not attempt to answer here) the question: what is the role of Chinese scholars to play in Sino-Hellenic studies?

As a matter of fact, now and then a handful of eminent Chinese scholars did venture into the comparison of ancient China and Greece, but what they did was mostly on a random and secluded basis. The three

---

[128] Jullien (1999), 116.

models of Sino-Hellenic studies, as we saw, have been developed in a self-reflective and systematic way by Western comparativists. Using these models and measured by their different goals and uses, we are enabled to shed light on previous work done by these few Chinese scholars. Just to give some notable examples. The historian of Greek philosophy Yan Qun (严群, 1907–1985) compared the ethics of Aristotle and Confucius (the "Doctrine of the Mean" in particular), intending a mutual understanding that may bring about an encounter between Western and Chinese philosophy. His approach is clearly transcultural. Also favoring the transcultural approach is the world-renowned scholar of comparative literature, Qian Zhongshu (钱锺书, 1910–1998). Although he did not specialize in ancient Greece, the comparative comments scattered throughout his works on Chinese literature, poetics and philosophy bristle with insights on similarities to ancient Greece, which to his mind enrich the understanding of each, pointing to a transcultural literary sensitivity. More legendary is the economist Gu Zhun (顾准, 1915–1974), who, during the heat of the Cultural Revolution, cool-headedly turned to a surreptitious study of ancient Greek history and compared it with ancient Chinese history, hoping to find a way out of the plights he saw the socialist nation was plunging into. The comparative study was abruptly stopped by his untimely death, but his cultural critical approach to the comparison of ancient Greece and China caused a sensation when the posthumous papers finally came to light in the 1990's.

These are only a few well-known examples. If we look aside from the academic world, we will meet the thronged group of the journal *Critical Review* (《学衡》) under the leadership of the comparative literature scholar Wu Mi (吴宓, 1894–1978), who advocated the "comparison" of ancient Greek classics to defend the traditional values of Confucian classics. Or, the solitary figure of Zhou Zuoren (周作人, 1885–1967), the foremost translator of ancient Greek literature and essayist on ancient Greek culture in modern China, who turned to the comparison with Greece to draw profound insights for his cultural criticism of traditional and contemporary China. With all these (and still other) previous examples in mind, it is time to contemplate what Chinese scholars can contribute to Sino-Hellenic studies in the future, what are the specific merits of each model for the self-understanding and the reinvigoration of Chinese culture, especially at a time when both Western and Chinese classics are bombing concurrently in China.

Bibliography

Beck, H. & G. Vankeerberghen, eds. 2021. *Rulers and Ruled in Ancient Greece, Rome, and China*. Cambridge, UK: Cambridge University Press.

Beecroft, A. 2010. *Authorship and Cultural Identity in Early Greece and China*. Cambridge, UK: Cambridge University Press.

Beecroft, A. 2016. "Comparisons of Greece and China." in *Oxford Handbooks Online*. New York: Oxford University Press.

Billeter, J. F. 2006. *Contre François Jullien*. Paris: Allia.

Birell, A. 1993. *Chinese Mythology: An Introduction*. Baltimore, MD.: The Johns Hopkins University Press.

Cai, Z. 2002. *Configurations of Comparative Poetics Three Perspectives on Western and Chinese Literary Criticism*. Honolulu: University of Hwai'i Press.

Camus, R. M. 2017. "Comparison by Metaphor: Archery in Confucius and Aristotle."*Dao* 16: 165–185.

Chemla, K. 2018. "Abstraction as a Value in the Historiography of Mathematics in Ancient Greece and China: A Historical Approach to Comparative History of Mathematics." in Lloyd & Zhao, eds. 2018: 290–325.

Coleman, E. J. 2002. "Aesthetic Commonalities in the Ethics of Daoism and Stoicism." *Journal of Chinese Philosophy* 29: 385–395.

Conolly, T. 2012. "Friendship and Filial Piety: Relational Ethics in Aristotle and Early Confucianism." *Journal of Chinese Philosophy* 39: 71–88.

de Boever, A. 2020. *François Jullien's Unexceptional Thought: A Critical Introduction*. London: Rowman & Littlefield.

Dorter, K. 2002. "The Concept of the Mean in Confucius and Plato." *Journal of Chinese Philosophy* 29: 317–335.

Durrant, S. W. 2002. "Creating Tradition: Sima Qian *Agonistes*?" in Shankman, S. & S. W. Durrant. eds. 2002: 283–298.

Hall, D. L. & R. T. Ames. 1987. *Thinking through Confucius*. Albany, NY: State University of New York Press.

Hall, D. L. & R. T. Ames. 1995. *Anticipating China. Thinking through the Narratives of Chinese and Western Culture*. Albany, NY: State University of New York Press.

Hall, D. L. & R. T. Ames. 1998. *Thinking from the Han: Self, Truth and Transcendence in Chinese and Western Culture*. Albany, NY: State University of New York Press.

Harbsmeier, C. 1998. *Science and Civilisation in China. Vol. 7 Part I: Language and Logic*. Cambridge: Cambridge University Press.

Huang Yang 2021. "The Invention of the 'Barbarian' and Ethnic Identity in Early Greece and China." in Beck & Vankeerberghen, eds. 2021: 399–419.

Hutton, E. L. 2002. "Moral Reasoning in Aristotle and Xunzi." *Journal of Chinese Philosophy* 29: 355–384.

Ivanhoe, P. J. & P. Kjiellberg, eds. 1996. Essays on Skepticism, Relativism, and Ethics in the *Zhuangzi*. Albany, NY: State University of New York Press.

Jaspers, K. 1949. *Vom Ursprung und Ziel der Geschichte*. München: Piper Verlag.

Jaspers, K. 1964. *Die Maßgebenden Menschen. Sokrates, Buddha, Konfuzius, Jesus*. München: Piper Verlag.

Jullien, F. 1995. *Le Détour et l'Accès: Stratégies du sens en Chine, en Grèce*. Paris: Grasset. (English translation: *Detour and Access: Strategies of Meaning in China and Greece*. Trans. Sophie Hawkes. Cambridge, MA: MIT Press, 2000).

Jullien, F. 1999. "A Philosophical Use of China: An Interview with François Jullien." *Thesis Eleven* 57: 113–130.

Keightley, D. N. 2014a. "Clean hands and shining helmets: heroic action in early Chinese and Greek culture." in *These Bones Shall Rise Again: Selected Writings on Early China*. Edited by Henry Rosemont Jr. Albany: State University of New York Press, 253–281.

Keightley, D. N. 2014b. "Epistemology in Cultural Context: Disguise and Deception in Early China and Early Greece." in *These Bones Shall Rise Again: Selected Writings on Early China*. Edited by Henry Rosemont Jr. Albany: State University of New York Press, 283–310.

Kim, Hyun-Jin. 2009. *Ethnicity and Foreigners in Ancient Greece and China*. London: Duckworth.

Kim, Hyun-Jin. 2021. "Ethnic Identity and the 'Barbarian' in Classical Greece and Early China Its Origins and Distinctive Features." in Beck & Vankeerberghen, eds. 2021: 420–442.

King, R. A. H. & D. Schilling, eds. 2011. *How Should One Live? Comparing Ethics in Ancient China and Greco-Roman Antiquity*. Berlin: De Gruyter.

King, R. A. H., ed. 2015. *The Good Life and Conceptions of Life in Early China and Graeco-Roman Antiquity*. Berlin: De Gruyter.

King, R. A. H. 2018. "Freedom in Parts of the *Zhuangzi* and Epictetus." in Lloyd & Zhao, eds. 2018: 83-109.

Kjellberg, P. 1996. "Sextus Empiricus, Zhuangzi, and Xunzi on 'Why Be Skeptical?'" in P. J. Ivanhoe & Paul Kjellberg, eds. 1996:1-25.

Kuriyama, S. 1999. *The Expressiveness of the Body and the Divergence of Greek and Chinese Medicine*. New York: Zone.

Liu, X. E. Magaritis & M. Jones. 2018. "From the Harvest to the Meal in Prehistoric China and Greece: A Comparative Approach to the Social Context of Food." In Lloyd, G. E. R. & J. Zhao, eds. 2018: 355-372.

Lloyd, G. E. R. 1979. *Magic, Reason and Experience: Studies in the Origin and Development of Greek Science*. Cambridge: Cambridge University Press.

Lloyd, G. E. R. 1983. Science, Folklore and Ideology: Studies in the Life Sciences in Ancient Greece. Cambridge: Cambridge University Press.

Lloyd, G. E. R. 1987. *The Revolutions of Wisdom: Studies in the Claims and Practice of Ancient Greek Science*. Berkeley: University of California Press.

Lloyd, G. E. R. 1990. *Demystifying Mentalities* Cambridge: Cambridge University Press.

Lloyd, G. E. R. 1996. *Adversaries and Authorities: Investigations into Ancient Greek and Chinese Science*. Cambridge: Cambridge University Press.

Lloyd, G. E. R. 2002. *Ambitions of Curiosity: Understanding the World in Ancient Greece and Chia*. Cambridge: Cambridge University Press.

Lloyd, G. E. R. 2004. *Ancient Worlds, Modern Reflections: Philosophical Perspectives on Greek and Chinese Science and Culture*. Oxford: Oxford University Press.

Lloyd, G. E. R. 2005. *The Delusions of Invulnerability: Wisdom and Morality in Ancient Greece, China and Today*. London: Duckworth.

Lloyd, G. E. R. 2006. *Principles and Practices in Ancient Greek and Chinese Science*. Aldershot, UK: Ashgate.

Lloyd, G. E. R. 2007. *Cognitive Variations: Reflections on the Unity and Diversity of the Human Mind*. Oxford: Oxford University Press.

Lloyd, G. E. R. 2009. *Disciplines in the Making: Cross-Cultural Perspectives on Elites, Learning and Innovation*. Oxford: Oxford University Press.

Lloyd, G. E. R. 2011. "Epilogue." in A. Feldherr, G. Hardy & I. Hesketh, eds. *The Oxford History of Historical Writing Volume 1: Beginnings to AD 600*. Oxford: Oxford University Press, 601-619.

Lloyd, G. E. R. 2012. *Being, Humanity and Understanding*. Oxford: Oxford University Press.

Lloyd, G. E. R. 2014. *The Ideals of Inquiry*. Oxford: Oxford University Press.

Lloyd, G. E. R. 2015. *Analogical Investigations: Historical and Cross-Cultural Perspectives on Human Reasoning*. Cambridge: Cambridge University Press.

Lloyd, G. E. R. 2017. *The Ambivalences of Rationality: Ancient and Modern Cross-Cultural Explorations*, Cambridge University Press.

Lloyd, G. E. R. 2020. *Intelligence and Intelligibility: Cross-Cultural Studies of Human Cognitive Experience*, Oxford University Press.

Lloyd, G. E. R. & N. Sivin. 2002. *The Way and the Word: Science and Medicine in Early Greece and China*. New Haven, CT: Yale University Press.

Lloyd, G. E. R. & J. Zhao, eds. 2018. *Ancient Greece and China Compared: Interdisciplinary and Cross-Cultural Perspectives*. Cambridge: Cambridge University Press.

Lo, V. & E. Re'em. 2018. "Recipes for Love in the Ancient World." in Lloyd & Zhao, eds. 2018: 326–352.

Lü, Xing. 1998. *Rhetoric in Ancient China, Fifth to Third Century B.C.E.: A Comparison with Classical Greek Rhetoric*. Columbia, SC: University of South Carolina Press.

Martin, T. R. 2010. *Herodotus and Sima Qian: The First Great Historians of Greece and China. A Brief History with Documents*. Boston – New York: Macmillan Learning.

Miner, E. 1990. *Comparative Poetics. An Intercultural Essay on Theories of Literature*. Princeton: Princeton University Press.

Mutschler, F.-H. 1997. "Vergleichende Beobachtungen zur griechisch-römischen und altchinesischen Geschichtsschreibung."*Saeculum* 48, 213–54.

Mutschler, F.-H. 2003. "Zu Sinnhorizont und Funktion griechischer, römischer und altchinesischer Geschichtsschreibung", in K.-J. Hölkeskamp, J. Rüsen, E. Stein-Hölkeskamp, and H. T. Grütter (eds.). *Sinn (in) der Antike. Orientierungssysteme, Leitbilder und Wertkonzepte im Altertum*. Mainz: Zabern, 33–54.

Mutschler, F.-H. 2006. "Tacitus und Sima Qian: Eine Annäherung." *Philologus* 150, 115–135.

Mutschler, F.-H. 2007a. "Tacitus und Sima Qian: Persönliche Erfahrung und historiographische Perspektive." *Philologus* 151, 127–152.

Mutschler, F.-H. 2007b. "Sima Qian and his Western Colleagues: On Possible Categories of Description." *History & Theory* 46, 194–200.

Mutschler, F.-H. 2008. "Tacite (et Tite Live) et Sima Qian: La vision politique d'historiens latins et chinois." *Bulletin de l'Association Guillaume Budé* 2008.2, 123–155.

Mutschler, F.-H. 2015. "Ancient Historiographies Compared." in: Ch.-Ch. Huang / J. Rüsen (eds.), *Chinese Historical Thinking: An Intercultural Discussion*, Göttingen, 103–112.

Mutschler, F.-H. 2016. "The Connection between Deeds and Consequences (Tun-Ergehens-Zusammenhang) in Ancient Chinese and Roman Historiography." in: 《纪念雷海宗先生诞辰110周年——中国第四届世界古代史国际学术研讨会论文集》, Beijing: Zhonghua Shuju, 178–186.

Mutschler, F.-H. & W. Scheidel. 2017. "The Benefits of Comparison: A Call for the Comparative Study of Ancient Civilizations." *Journal of Ancient Civilizations* 32/1: 107–121.

Mutschler, F.-H. ed. 2018. *The Homeric Epics and the Chinese Book of Songs: Foundational Texts Compared*, Newcastle upon Tyne: Cambridge Scholars Press.

Needham, J. 1956. *Science and Civilisation in China. Vol. 2: History of Scientific Thought*. Cambridge: Cambridge University Press.

Needham, J. 1969. *The Grand Titration: Science and Society in East and West*. London: George Allen & Unwin Ltd.

Needham, J. & K. G. Robinson. 2004. *Science and Civilisation in China. Vol. 7 Part II: General Conclusions and Reflections*. Cambridge: Cambridge University Press.

Netz, R. 2018. "Divisions, Big and Small: Comparing Archimedes and Liu Hui." in Lloyd & Zhao, eds. 2018: 259–289.

Nylan, M. 2002. "Golden Spindles and Axes: Elite Women in the Achaemenid and Han Empires." in Shankman, S. & S. W. Durrant. eds. 2002: 251–281.

Plaks, A. 2002. "Means and Means: A Comparative Reading of Aristotle's *Ethics* and the *Zhongyong*." in S. Shankman & S. W. Durrant, eds. 2002: 187–206.

Puett, M. J. 2002a. *To Become a God: Cosmology, Sacrifice and Self-Divinization in Early China*. Cambridge, MA.: Harvard University Asia Center.

Puett, M. J. 2002b. "Humans and Gods: The Theme of Self-Divinization in Early China and Early Greece." in S. Shankman & S. W. Durrant, eds. 2002: 55–74.

Průšek, J. 1970. "History and epics in China and in the West: a study of differences in conception of the human story." in J. Průšek. *Chinese History and Literature: Collection of Studies*. Dordrecht: Academia, 17–34.

Raphals, L. 1992. *Knowing Words: Wisdom and Cunning in the Classical Traditions of Greece and China*. Ithaca, NY: Cornell University Press.

Raphals, L. 1996. "Skeptical Strategies in the *Zhuangzi* and *Theaetetus*." in P. J.

Ivanhoe & P. Kjellberg, eds. 1996: 26–49 (reprinted from *Philosophy East & West* 44 (1994): 501–526).

Raphals, L. 2002a. "Gender and Virtue in Greece and China." *Journal of Chinese Philosophy* 29: 415–336.

Raphals, L. 2002b. "Fatalism, Fate, and Stratagem in China and Greece." in Shankman, S. & S. W. Durrant. eds. 2002: 207–234.

Raphals, L. 2003. "Fate, Fortune, Chance and Luck in Chinese and Greek: A Comparative Semantic History." *Philosophy East and West* 53: 537–574.

Raphals, L. 2005. "Craft analogies in Chinese and Greek argumentation." in E. Ziolkowski (ed.). *Literature, Religion and East/West Comparison: Essays in Honour of Anthony C. Yu*. Cranbury, NJ: University of Delaware Press, 181–201.

Raphals, L. 2013. *Divination and Prediction in Early China and Ancient Greece*. Cambridge, UK: Cambridge University Press.

Raphals, L. 2015a. "China and Greece: Comparisons and Insights." in *The Oxford Handbook of Ancient Greek Religion*. Edited by Esther Eidinow and Julia Kindt, 651–665. Oxford University Press.

Raphals, L. 2015b. "Daoism and Greek Philosophy." in *Dao: Companion to Daoist Philosophy*. Edited by Liu Xiaogan, 527–538. Dordrecht, The Netherlands.

Raphals, L. 2015c. "Body and Mind in Early China and Greece." *Journal of Cognitive Historiography* 2: 132–182.

Raphals, L. 2018. "Sino-Hellenic Studies, Comparative Studies of Early China and Greece." in *Oxford Bibliographies Online*. New York: Oxford University Press.

Reding, J.-P. 1985. *Les fondements philosophiques de la rhétorique chez les sophistes grecs et chez les sophistes chinois*. New York: Peter Lang.

Reding, J.-P. 1996. "Review of François Jullien. *Le Détour et l'Accès: Stratégies du sens en Chine, en Grèce*." *China Review International* 3: 160–168.

Reding, J.-P. 2004. *Comparative Essays in Early Greek and Early Chinese Rational Thinking*. Aldershot: Ashgate.

Schaberg, D. 1999. "Travel, Geography, and the Imperial Imagination in Fifth-Century Athens and Han China." *Comparative Literature* 51: 152–191.

Schaberg, D. 2002. "The Logic of Signs in Early Chinese Rhetoric." in Shankman & Durrant. eds. 2002: 155–186.

Shankman, S. & S. W. Durrant. 2000. *The Siren and the Sage: Knowledge and Wisdom in Ancient Greece and China*. London: Cassell.

Shankman, S. & S. W. Durrant. eds. 2002. *Early China/Ancient Greece. Thinking through Comparisons*. Albany, NY.: State University of New York Press.

Sim, M. 2007. *Remastering Morals with Aristotle and Confucius*. Cambridge:

Cambridge University Press.

Tanner, J. 2009. "Ancient Greece, Early China: Sino-Hellenic Studies and Comparative Approaches to the Classical World: A Review Article." *Journal of Hellenic Studies* 129: 89–109.

Tanner, J. 2013. "Figuring Out Death: Sculpture and Agency at the Mausoleum of Halicarnassus and the Tomb of the First Emperor of China." in *Distributed Objects: Meaning and Mattering after Alfred Gell.* edited by Liana Chua and Mark Elliott, London: Berghahn: 58–87.

Tanner, J. 2017. "Narrative and Naturalism in Classical Greek and Early Imperial Chinese Art." in *Comparativism in Art History.* edited by Jaś Eslner, London: Routledge: 180–224.

Tanner, J. 2018. "Visual Art and Historical Representation in Ancient Greece and China." in Lloyd & Zhao, eds.: 189–233.

Teng, S.Y. 1961. "Herodotus and Ssu-ma Ch'ien: Two Fathers of History." *East and West* 12: 233–240.

Turner, K. 1990. "Sage kings and laws in the Chinese and Greek traditions." in P. S. Ropp, ed. *Heritage of China: Contemporary Perspectives on Chinese Civilization.* Berkeley: University of California Press, 1990: 86–111.

Unger, U. 1994. *Rhetorik des klassischen Chinesisch.* Wiesbaden: Harrassowitz Verlag.

Vernant, J.-P. & J. Gernet. 1964. "L'Évolution des idées en Chine et en Grèce, du VIe au IIe siècle avant notre ère." *Bulletin de l'Association Guillaume Budé* 3: 308–325. (English trans. "Social History and the Evolution of Ideas in China and Greece from the Sixth to the Second Centuries BC." in *Myth and Society in Ancient Greece.* Trans. Janet Lloyd. London: Methuen, 1974: 79–100.)

Wardy, R. 2000. *Aristotle in China: Language, Categories and Translation.* Cambridge, UK: Cambridge University Press.

Weber, R. 2013. "A Stick Which may be Grabbed on Either Side: Sino-Hellenic Studies in the Mirror of Comparative Philosophy." *International Journal of the Classical Tradition* 20: 1–14.

Weber, R. 2014. "Controversy over 'Jullien,' or Where and What is China, Philosophically Speaking?" *Journal of Chinese Philosophy* 41: 361–377.

Wooyeal, P. & D. A. Bell 2004. "Citizenship and State-Sponsored Physical Education: Ancient Greece and Ancient China." *Review of Politics* 66: 7–34.

Yu, A. C. 2002. "*Cratylus* and Xunzi on Names." in Shankman, S. & S. W. Durrant. eds. 2002: 235–250.

Yu, Jiyuan. 2002a. "Guest Editor's Introduction: Toward a Chinese-Greek Comparative Ethics." *Journal of Chinese Philosophy* 29: 313–316.

Yu, Jiyuan. 2002b. "The Aristotelian Mean and the Confucian Mean." *Journal of Chinese Philosophy* 29: 337–354.

Yu, Jiyuan. 2007. *The Ethics of Confucius and Aristotle: Mirrors of Virtue*. New York: Routledge.

Zhang Wei 2021. "Reading Homer in Contemporary China (From the 1980s until Today)", *International Journal of the Classical Tradition* 28: 353–379.

Zhou, Yiqun. 2010. *Festivals, Feasts, and Gender Relations in Ancient China and Greece*. Cambridge, UK: Cambridge University Press.

Zhou, Yiqun. 2018. "Helen and Chinese Femmes Fatales." in *In Ancient Greece and China Compared: Interdisciplinary and Cross-Cultural Perspectives*. Edited by G. E. R. Lloyd and Jenny Jing-yi Zhao: 234–256.

（ZHANG Wei, Department of History, Fudan University）

China and Rome Compared — a Report

Fritz-Heiner Mutschler

Sino-Roman studies have emerged as a distinct branch of research within the growing body of work concerned with the comparison of Chinese and Western antiquity. It arose after the related branch of Sino-Hellenic studies had already become established and has a different orientation from it in terms of subject matter.

Comparative observations concerning the development of Chinese and Greek civilization began to be presented on a larger scale in the middle of the last century with the work of Joseph Needham[1]. They were the explicit purpose of the common endeavor of Jean-Pierre Vernant and Jacques Gernet in the sixties[2], and they have been the focus of the multi-year investigative program by Geoffrey Lloyd, partly in cooperation with Nathan Sivin, since the nineties[3]. The subject of most of these studies was intellectual history, at first in particular science and philosophy, then also religion, myth, and literature.

Sino-Roman studies developed later. Stimulated by China's continuous ascent to the rank of a superpower — first economically and then also politically, second only to the USA, ancient historians started

---

[1] Cf. Zhang above, pp. 230–231.
[2] Cf. Zhang above, p. 231.
[3] Cf. Zhang above, pp. 233–236.

to put the dyad China–USA into perspective through comparative analysis of the Chinese and the Roman Empires, the two great Eurasian body politics of antiquity. But while the focus of Sino-Hellenic studies was on intellectual history, Sino-Roman studies, in accordance with the modern context, were first of all oriented towards the analysis of political and economic history. Only in recent years have other subjects, like religion, philosophy, and literature, attracted attention as well.

The subsequent survey will reflect this situation[4]. In the first part, I will characterize the work that has been devoted to the comparative analysis of the two empires: their political and administrative structures, their social and economic history, their underlying ideology etc. In the second part, I will report on the less numerous studies to date on religion, philosophy, historiography, and poetry, which treat their subject matter without primary regard to the question of empire. In a final third part, I will give a concise summary of what has been done so far and look ahead to what might be done in the future.

1. Empire Studies

1.1. Universal Studies

One of the earliest manifestations of a comprehensive interest in the historical phenomenon of empires came from the sociological side. This was Samuel Eisenstadt's first magnum opus *The Political Systems of Empires* (1963)[5]. Studying twenty-seven socio-political units from the 3rd millennium BCE to the 20th century CE that he qualified as "Historic Bureaucratic Societies" (HBS), Eisenstadt tried to develop categories of description that allowed for a comparative analysis of these

---

[4] For a brief survey focusing on methodological issues see Scheidel 2018, 48–55.

[5] Eisenstadt (1963).

polities: of the conditions of their coming into being, of the ways in which they functioned, and of the reasons for their downfall. The book met with as much acclaim for its choice of topic and its comprehensive approach as criticism concerning its argumentative validity and its language. As for our subject, the Chinese and Roman empires were, of course, among the HBS studied, but without receiving particular attention or being directly juxtaposed to each other.

This holds similarly for the great majority of trans-regional empire studies that have been published in the subsequent decades, most of them in the form of collective volumes[6], and it also holds for the two monumental works that can be said to represent the present state of the

---

[6] I restrict myself to short remarks concerning some of the works that appeared after the turn of the millennium. The volume edited by Susan Alcock et al., *Empires: Perspectives from Archeology and History* (2001), deals with the empires of the ancient Near East, of Rome and China, of India, of South- and Middle America and others. In spite of the—in principle—comparative approach of the undertaking, no real comparison takes place, and since there are no guiding questions structuring the volume as a whole the individual articles stand side by side more or less unconnected. In the first of two collections of essays edited by P.F. Bang and C.A. Bayly (2003), the one contribution (out of seven) that compares the Roman, the Mughal, and the Chinese empires deals with Tang (!) China. In the second collection (2011), the one comparative essay (out of fifteen) on the Roman empire and Qin/Han China discusses the problem of taxation (Scheidel [2011]). A volume on "War and Peace in the Ancient World" edited by K.A. Raaflaub (2007) contains, of course, articles on ancient China, Greece and Rome, and the editor's introduction offers comparative considerations, understandably however without attempting a direct juxtaposition of ancient China and Rome. Only in passing does China appear in P.F. Bang's monograph on "The Roman Bazaar" (2008), which in terms of comparison concentrates on the Roman and the Mughal empires. China is not taken into account in the volume edited by F. Hurlet (2008) *Les Empires: Antiquité et Moyen Age* or in the collection of essays *The Dynamics of Ancient Empires*, edited by I. Morris and W. Scheidel (2009). The volume *The Roman Empire in Context. Historical and Comparative Perspectives*, edited by the sociologist J.P. Arnason and the historian K.A. Raaflaub (2011), does contain a paper on early China, but explicitly comparative considerations about China and Rome are only found in Arnason's introduction. The idea of "Universal Empire" from the 10th century BCE to the 18th and 19th centuries CE in Eurasia as well as in the New World is the subject of a volume edited by P.F. Bang and D. Kołodziejczyk (2012) in which the (archaeological) article dedicated to ancient Rome discusses a relatively specific topic, and the article on China deals not with ancient China but with the Qing dynasty. In the volume *Cosmopolitism and Empire*, edited by M. Lavan, R.E. Payne and J. Weisweiler (2016), which opens a discussion on an interesting and potentially fruitful subject for the comparison of China and Rome, China is mentioned but not substantially dealt with.

art: one in German, edited by M. Gehler and R. Rollinger[7] with more than 1700 pages, and one in English, edited by P.F. Bang, C.A. Bayly, and W. Scheidel[8], with more than 1800 pages. Both contain, on the one hand, contributions that discuss theoretical aspects and, on the other hand, condensed discussions of an impressive number of individual empires from Pharaonic Egypt and the polities of the Ancient Near East to the dominant powers of the present. Ancient China and ancient Rome receive appropriate attention[9], but comparative observations that concern the two polities in particular are limited to parenthetical remarks[10]. All of this is not to say, however, that the direct juxtaposition of the Qin-Han empire and the Roman empire has not attracted more and more interest in recent decades. For this is indeed the case.

1.2. China-Rome Studies

The basis and stimulus for the particular juxtaposition of these two empires are obvious. They developed at around the same time into the most extended and most populated polities of the ancient world. They did so at the two ends of the Eurasian continent, i.e. under similar ecological circumstances, but independently from each other[11]. They were of similarly impressive durability before the one met its end, the other a temporary disintegration. On the other hand, there are also clear differences: the Roman empire developed around the Mediterranean

---

[7]   Gehler/Rollinger (2014).

[8]   Bang/Bayly/Scheidel (2021).

[9]   Gehler/Rollinger (2014): K. Ruffing, "Rom — das paradigmatische Imperium", 401–448; W.C. Schneider, "Das oströmische Imperium der Spätantike vom 4. bis zum 6. Jh. Das Imperium Justinians", 479–502; H. van Ess, "Chinesische Imperien", 515–536. Bang/Bayly/Scheidel (2021): M.E. Lewis, "The First East Asian Empires: Qin and Han", vol. 2, 218–239; P.F. Bang, "The Roman Empire", vol. 2, 240–289.

[10]   The editors of the first work even see a danger for general empire research in a possible concentration on these two—or other prototypical—empires, as it may lead to the erroneous and limiting inference that empire is only what resembles these particular formations (Gehler/Rollinger [2014], 15).

[11]   I.e. apart from certain indirect trading contacts.

Sea, whereas the Chinese empire represents the prototype of a land empire; and the Roman empire remained without a real successor in medieval and modern Europe while the Chinese empire was repeatedly reconstituted anew until the beginning of the 20th century. But, apart from these interest-evoking *historical* givens, there is evidently an additional reason for the increasing interest in the juxtaposition of Qin-Han China and imperial Rome: after the breakup of the Soviet Union, these two ancient empires can be seen as the predecessors of the two most powerful polities in the *present*-day world: the People's Republic of China and the "New Rome", the USA. Since even historians live in the present there is nothing wrong with such additional motivation as long as it does not impair the objectivity of description and analysis.

Before we look in more detail at the pertinent scholarly production of the last decades, a preliminary remark is required concerning the notion of "comparative studies." A few years ago, H.J. Kim published a programmatic plea for the comparative study of China and the Greco-Roman world[12]. Inter alia, he illustrated the usefulness of such studies with two examples. The first concerns the fall of the Roman Empire in the fifth century, in which, according to many interpreters, the Huns played a decisive role. In Kim's view, this remains incomprehensible as long as the Huns are considered "primitive, badly organized barbarians" (263) as ancient Western sources, like Ammianus Marcellinus, and modern scholarship in their wake have seen them. "This is where a comparative study of Central Asian Steppe empires as they are described in Chinese historiography becomes extremely helpful" (263). The "comparative material derived from the Chinese historical sources" makes it clear "that the Huns who entered Europe were a very well-organized military state that in no way resembled the primitive mob described by Ammianus" (265). In other words, it is the "proposed

---

[12]   Kim (2015).

comparative methodology [my emphasis]" that "allows us radically to reinterpret the nature of the Hunnic state and its impact on Late Roman history" (266). This sounds perfectly plausible, but it should be noted that we have here a very specific kind of "comparative" approach. The comparison that Kim seems to have in mind is simply the comprehensive examination and evaluation of all available sources that should be carried out as a matter of course — though admittedly is not always — whenever one wants to clarify a specific historical problem[13]. Kim is not concerned here with the comparison of the Chinese and Roman empires for the sake of comparison, i.e. for a more precise perception of the features they share and the peculiarities by which they differ, and thus for a deeper understanding of the two polities and their functioning[14]. This, however, is the focus of the research discussed in what follows.

---

[13]   Kim's second example confirms this impression. It concerns the representation of the Scythians in Herodotus' *Histories* and the Xiongnu in Sima Qian's *Shiji*. Kim starts out by stating that concerning "the earlier Classical period of the 5th and 4th centuries BC ... literary, socio-economic and political-military parallels or similarities rather than actual historical links are the more fruitful areas [of] comparative research" (267). But, a few lines later he claims that "a comparative approach can be far more useful if both textual traditions (Greek and Chinese) are shown to have treated the same or closely related phenomena or subject matter", and that in fact "the following second example demonstrates the treatment of the same subject matter by a Greek and Chinese writer and highlights the value of subjecting both (Greek and Chinese) material to comparative analysis" (267). This time, Kim's "comparative" research leads to the result that quite a number of Herodotus' assertions concerning the Scythians that modern scholars have considered products of fantasy are confirmed by what Sima Qian reports about the Xiongnu. This is to say that the two historians "provide us with verifiable ethnographic details from which we can with some confidence partially reconstruct the identity and lifestyle of early steppe peoples" (270). In this way, according to Kim, "the *comparative approach* [my emphasis] ... allows us to ... re-establish the value of Herodotus as an historical source" (270). Thus, once again we see that Kim is not interested in comparison for the sake of gaining a more distinct idea of the respective character and peculiarity of the polities or civilizations concerned, but simply pushes for a comprehensive taking into account of all available sources for the sake of clarifying a specific issue of historical research.

[14]   The same kind of argument is to be made concerning Teggart (1939). Teggart has deservedly been praised for having been one of the first to connect the study of Roman and Chinese history. But his aim too is not comparison in the sense defined above but simply the thorough analysis of a specific historical constellation.

1.2.1. Tentative Surveys

The first two relevant studies were published in the nineties of the last century and they were introductory in character. They pointed to the comparison of the Qin-Han empire and the Roman empire as a worthwhile task for future research and gave the first indications of how such research could proceed. Astonishingly, the beginning was made in a journal for Austrian history teachers with the paper "Das Imperium Romanum und das China der Han-Dynastie. Gedanken und Materialien zu einem Vergleich"[15]. This was motivated by the national curriculum for AHS (Allgemeinbildende Höhere Schulen: General Educational High Schools), which in the subject of history for 15-year-old students suddenly included a comparison between the *Imperium Romanum* and Han-China. In this paper, G. Lorenz, in cooperation with R. Trappl and P.W. Haider, undertook to provide teachers with a brief survey of similarities and differences between the two polities and their history, and with materials for the stipulated comparison. Although the paper, as Lorenz himself stated, was only "a first introduction into a fascinating topic" (9) it deserves respect as a pioneering effort.

A few years later, Chr. Gizewski, in one of the standard journals for academic research, offered a thoughtful and more detailed variation on the theme[16]. After reflecting on the difficulty of historical comparison in general and clarifying fundamental concepts like "society", "culture", "antiquity", "middle ages" etc., Gizewski designed a system of categories of description and a tentative parallel periodization for Chinese and Roman history as possible auxiliary frameworks for further comparative analysis.

A little more than a decade later, there followed a third article of the introductory kind when M. Dettenhofer presented a sketch of a

---

[15] Lorenz (1990).
[16] Gizewski (1994).

comprehensive general comparison of the two empires[17]. In the relatively limited scope of an article of less than twenty pages she pointed to a considerable number of structural commonalities of the polities without neglecting important differences.

1.2.2. Specialized Research

At the same time, more elaborate investigations were already being conducted. Given the evident necessity for multiple competencies, it is not surprising that most of these took place within the framework of joint projects and resulted in collective volumes. The first two appeared almost simultaneously in 2008 and 2009[18] and were followed by a still ongoing series of others[19]. As a first glance shows, these collections differ not only concerning their subject matter but also in degree of internal uniformity. Therefore, it could be rather confusing to present them volume by volume in simple chronological order together with the (not too numerous) independent articles and the (very few) monographs interspersed accordingly. For this reason, I will discuss the individual contributions according to *sub-fields* and *topics*, even though the assignment of each publication to a specific sub-field and topic is not always easy and in some cases may seem debatable.

1.2.2.1. Politics and Administration

Unsurprisingly, quite a number of contributions deal with the

---

[17] Dettenhofer (2006).

[18] Mutschler/Mittag (2008), Scheidel (2009).

[19] An interesting indication of the growing interest in comparison is the fact that even in works dealing with one of the two empires the other one is brought in as well. Thus, in Arnason and Raaflaub's volume on "The Roman Empire in Context" (2011) there appears also a contribution on early China. A volume edited at around the same time by M. Nylan and M. Loewe on "China's Early Empires: A Re-appraisal" (2010) contains a paper on imagined visits of travelers to ancient Rome and Changan. And in a volume edited by M. Nylan and G. Vankeerberghen (2015), which is specifically dedicated to Changan, the allusion to Rome appears already in the title *Chang'an 26 BCE: An* Augustan [my emphasis] *Age in China*, even though the volume contains only one explicitly comparative contribution, that by C.F. Noreña (see below).

political sphere: internal and external power relations, decision-making processes, administration etc. Three papers in the volume edited by Scheidel in 2009 belong to this category. First of all, there is the editor's introductory essay "From the 'Great Convergence' to the 'First Great Divergence'. Roman and Qin-Han State Formation and Its Aftermath"[20] in which he draws in broad strokes a comparative picture of the trajectories of state formation in the Western and Eastern parts of the Eurasian continent. According to Scheidel, in spite of undeniable differences — such as the unusual degree of centralization and bureaucratization of Qin and the much looser administrative structures of republican and early imperial Rome — we observe a "Great Convergence" for almost a millennium as the result of which "the mature Roman Empire of the fourth century C.E." closely "resembles the Han Empire both in institutional as well as practical terms" (17f.). The "Great Divergence" sets in later, when Sui- and Tang-China succeeds in reunification and the restoration of the bureaucratic state, whereas in the West, in spite of Justinian's attempt to reunify the Roman state, permanent political fragmentation is the outcome[21].

Concentrating on a more specific topic, N. Rosenstein investigates the influence of the nature, frequency, and intensity of the wars in which the two polities were involved on the development of their political and social structures[22]. Thus, he suggests that the continuity of existence-threatening wars in Warring States China was an important reason for the emergence of the highly rationalized and efficiently bureaucratized administrations of those states in general, and of Qin in particular. By

---

[20] Scheidel (2009a).

[21] In his contribution "Fiscal Regimes and the 'First Great Divergence' between Eastern and Western Eurasia," Scheidel (2011) supplements these reflections focusing on the problem of taxation.

[22] Rosenstein (2009), "War, State Formation, and the Evolution of Military Institutions in Ancient China and Rome". Already in 1980, I-tien Hsing in a PhD thesis (University of Hawai'i at Manoa) had dealt with a related topic: "Rome and China: The Role of the Armies in the Imperial Succession: A Comparative Study".

contrast, in the case of Rome, the absence of a similarly continuous and intense military threat after the 2nd Punic War was the precondition for the fact that "patronage and ideology along with a limited bureaucracy were adequate to the task of governing the empire" (50).

A very different component of the political sphere, namely the position of eunuchs and women at the imperial courts, forms the subject of M.H. Dettenhofer's paper[23]. There can be no doubt that the former group played a much less significant role in Roman than in Chinese history. But eunuchs did gain considerable importance in the fourth century CE in the East Roman court too, and at least a structural parallel can be seen between the collusion of eunuchs and women at the imperial court in China and that of freedmen and women at the imperial court in Rome.

In the second volume published by Scheidel, the emphasis on power structures is indicated by the title itself: *State Power in Ancient China and Rome*.[24] At least four of the eight contributions are strictly pertinent. They represent three different ways of how to do comparative studies that involve two distinct scholarly disciplines.

The first paper, on "Kingship and Elite Formation", is co-authored by the Romanist P.F. Bang and the sinologist K. Turner[25]. The authors are sceptical concerning alleged fundamental differences between the two polities, e.g. between *aristocratic* Rome and *bureaucratic* China, or Roman militarism and its supposed Chinese opposite. Instead, they stress commonalities, like the role of slaves, eunuchs and family members at court, the often precarious situation of high ranking members of the elite, the fostering of "elites with a strong military component" (17) at the beginning of the imperial period, and the later channeling of "elite ambition into a wider set of arenas for the display of

---

[23] Dettenhofer (2009).
[24] Scheidel (2015).
[25] Bang/Turner (2015).

social excellence" (23). According to Bang and Turner, "parallels" like these "reflect the logic of the situation: shared organizational constraints and broad similarities in the constitution of society, the structure of power, and processes of elite formation" (37).

T.C. Brennan, a Roman historian, is one of the scholars who venture beyond the borders of their principal field of expertise. The subject of his paper is decision-making processes in the Roman and Han empires[26]. In a series of case studies (most, though not all, from the late republican period in Rome and the Western Han period in China), he demonstrates the importance of advisory councils to those officially in charge in both polities, thus indicating another structural parallel.

The following two papers represent a third way of organizing comparative research: the juxtaposition of two papers, one from each side, dealing with the same topic. D.X. Zhao[27] and P. Eich[28] investigate the role of bureaucracy in the Han and Roman Empires. Both use Weberian categories of description — though differently accentuated — and both trace the development of the bureaucratic system through the centuries. In comparative remarks in the last part of his paper, Eich points to a high degree of similarity between the operational frameworks of the late Roman and the Han Empire: a "roughly equal ... number of basic administrative units", the division of leadership into "a civilian and military branch", the supervision of "operators on the ground" by "an administrative middle level" etc. (147). On the other hand, he stresses that bureaucratization in the Roman Empire commenced "much later" than in China and that its "bureaucratic structures, functions, and notions remained much less formalized, more flexible and more deeply embedded in older structural contexts" (148).

In H. Beck and G. Vankeerberghen's recent "Rulers and Ruled in

---

26 Brennan (2015).
27 Zhao (2015).
28 Eich (2015).

Greece, Rome, and China"[29], the emphasis is on China and Rome while Greece remains in the margin, despite the book's title. Several contributions concern the political sphere.

F. Pina Polo investigates the relation of "Rhetoric, Oratory, and People in Ancient Rome and Early China"[30]. As the author states, in republican Rome, *public* oratory always played a central role in politics, with the assemblies of the people as the most important venue, and the republican tradition continued to exert influence in the imperial period when the "communication and interaction with the populace through *contiones* became one of the chief characteristics of the good emperor" (141). In early China, by contrast, there was never a public venue for oratory. The use of rhetoric, often in written form, was restricted to "a narrow circle: the persuaders were usually ministers and statesmen, and their targets were rulers" (148). In other words, in China the Emperor could be the addressee of rhetorical persuasion, while in imperial Rome the Emperor — at least if he wished to be a good emperor — would still act as persuader, pretending to communicate as a citizen with co-citizens.

H. Beck's "Registers of 'the People' in Greece, Rome, and China"[31] is the only paper to present a balanced comparison of the *three* polities. Not surprisingly, it reveals commonalities and differences. In all three cases, the registers were connected with taxation, military service, and territorial subdivisions, and in all three cases, in addition to their technical functions, they also fulfilled a symbolic function. On the other hand, there were differences. The registration system of the Han Empire was far more developed in terms of information than the systems in Greece and Rome (209–210); the Roman *census* and the registers of the Greek *poleis* were based on the idea of *citizenship*, whereas in China the

---

[29] Beck/Vankeerberghen (2021).
[30] Pina Polo (2021).
[31] Beck (2021).

registration targeted the people as *subjects*; and the ritualistic context of the registration emphasized in China the "loyalty between the emperor and his subjects" (203), in Athens the reception of the eighteen-year-old boy into the citizenry (213–214), and in Rome the highly expedient organization of the citizen body (218).

A. Yacobson's "Augustus, the Roman Plebs and the Dictatorship: 22 BCE and Beyond,"[32] as the title indicates, is a paper on a special issue in *Roman* history. Its aim is to analyze and interpret Augustus' refusal to accept the dictatorship offered to him by the people during the food crisis of 22 BCE. Apparent Chinese parallels are discussed only marginally (271–273) and with the understanding that, in "diametrical opposition" to such cases in Rome, they do not "reflect any uneasiness with monarchy as such" (271) but "represent efforts to legitimate the transfer of monarchical power to different dynastic houses" (273).

D. Engels in "Historical Necessity or Biographical Singularity? Some Aspects in the Biographies of C. Iulius Caesar and Qin Shi Huangdi"[33] is less interested in *static* parallels than in the parallel *dynamics* he sees in the unification process of the Chinese empire and the transition from republic to monarchy in Rome. Thus, in the main sections of the paper (332–344), he attempts to show that beneath the superficial differences "fascinating subliminal parallels" (333) exist between China and Rome in general, and Qin Shi Huangdi and Caesar in particular. Still more important for Engels, however, are the "parallel dynamics linking Augustus to Caesar and Han Gaozu to Qin Shi Huangdi" (345). For him, they indicate that in these processes it was not simply individuals, i.e. the protagonists, that were at work but structural necessities (347–348).

Finally, in "Employing Knowledge: A Case Study in Calendar

---

[32] Yakobson (2021).

[33] Engels (2021a).

Reforms in the Early Han and Roman Empires"[34], R. Robinson investigates and compares the calendar reforms by Emperor Wu and Julius Caesar and their reflection in the historiographical traditions. In both cases, the reform is undertaken out of the necessity to bring the civic calendar into accord with astronomical givens, is carried out with the help of scientific specialists from outside the traditional elites, and serves not least the political purposes of its initiator (369–378). As for their representation in the historical traditions, both Roman and Chinese texts relate the reforms to achievements of sage rulers of the past, but while the individual Roman writers agree in their praise of the reform, in China, Sima Qian and Ban Gu differ greatly in their evaluation of it (378–382).

1.2.2.2. Social Structures and Practices

In addition to politics and administration, social structures and practices have also attracted scholarly attention. Pertinent contributions cover a considerable spectrum of topics.

In Scheidel 2009, M.E. Lewis provides an analysis of the role of gift circulation and charity as a source of political and social authority[35]. As to China, he distinguishes eight types of imperial beneficence. Some of these can also be observed in Rome, which does not, however, exclude considerable differences in the direction and form of the emperor's generosity. Bang and Turner in "Kingship and Elite Formation," discussed above[36], demonstrate the intersecting of the political and the social spheres. Similarly, the overlap between administrative, economic, and social issues becomes evident in Scheidel's paper on "Slavery and Forced Labor in Early China and the Roman World" in yet another edited volume[37]. The author here again treats an important aspect of the workings of the two

---

34 Robinson (2021).
35 Lewis (2009).
36 See above pp. 305–306.
37 Scheidel (2017).

empires and in this case determines the main difference to be that in the Roman economy "slave labor" played a decisive role in the *private* sector whereas in China it was the *state* that relied heavily on "forced labor".

Further topics concerning the social sphere are discussed in several contributions to Beck/Vankeerberghen 2021. Vankeerberghen herself compares nobles of the post-Emperor Wu period in China with their counterparts in late republican Rome[38]. She observes striking parallels. Most importantly, like the Roman nobles, the Chinese nobles competed intensely with one another and with potential newcomers for offices, especially for spots at the top of the political and military hierarchy, and in this competition activities that enhanced their genealogical profile, like the burial of family members in family tombs and cemeteries, the exploration of family histories and their presentation in various media, played a decisive role. The undeniable differences in terms of political, social, and ideological environment make these parallels all the more noteworthy.

Dealing with the same social layer as Vankeerberghen are M. Brown and Zh. Zhang in their article "A Tale of Stones: Social Memory in Roman Greece and Han China"[39]. Like Vankeerberghen the authors point to astonishing parallels, in this case between inscriptions accompanying Greek honorary statues of the Roman period and inscriptions on steles of Han times. Closer investigation, however, of the inscriptions' *Who*, *When*, *Where*, *How*, and *Why* reveals a fundamental divergence. In the Greco-Roman case, "social memory", and thus the phenomenon of honorary statues, "was inextricable from the polis" (76), whereas the "Han steles reflected the importance of expansive personal networks, networks that connected people in various localities to

---

[38] Vankeerberghen (2021), "Of Gold and Purple in Western Han China and Republican Rome".

[39] Brown/Zhang (2021).

officials and office-holding clans in the capital" (77).

C.F. Noreña's "Private Associations and Urban Experience in the Han and Roman Empires" concentrates on the urban middle stratum, the craftsmen, shopkeepers, merchants etc., in the two empires[40]. The central point is the observation that in the Roman Empire the members of this stratum were widely organized in private associations through which they were active in the public sphere whereas no real equivalent to this phenomenon can be found in the Han Empire (108). The second part of the paper is dedicated to the explanation of this discrepancy, which the author, in his final analysis, sees as a repercussion of the different relationship between the central regime and local elites in each case (115).

A rather special topic is treated in M.L. Kim's "Welfare, Food, and Feasts in Qin/Han China and in Rome"[41]. Against the backdrop of the expectable general difference between the diet of the rich and powerful and that of the commoners and the poor, the author shows that both in China and in Rome, even though in varying concrete forms, general welfare distributions of food in times of crisis as well as particular food distributions on the occasion of public — but partly also private — feasts "provided practical solutions to the problems of how to adequately feed people at every level of the social hierarchy" (256).

1.2.2.3. Law and Jurisdiction

Law and jurisdiction are important factors of social life. A number of articles are dedicated to this field. In Scheidel 2009, K. Turner discusses the role of "Law and Punishment in the Formation of Empire"[42]. She deals with a great variety of topics, e.g. pertinent theoretical considerations in the classics, the role of emperors in the law-making process, critical assessments of legal and judiciary practices, the treatment of treason, and the forms and functions of torture and physical

---

[40] Noreña (2021).
[41] Kim (2021).
[42] Turner (2009).

punishment. The paper ends with brief reflections on the legacies of antiquity in China and the West (79–82).

The collective volume "Law and Empire. Ideas, Practices, Actors"[43] covers the time period from mid 1st millennium BCE to the 19th century CE. In terms of political geography, it shows a certain emphasis on Western Europe and China. Ancient Rome and ancient China are dealt with in J. Harries' "Roman Law from City State to World Empire"[44] and K. Turner's article "Laws, Bureaucrats, and Imperial Women in China's Early Empires"[45]. Both papers are survey articles, with Harris examining the time from the early republic to late antiquity, and Turner concentrating on the Qin and Western Han Empires against the backdrop of earlier thought. There are no explicit comparative statements in either article, but in the juxtaposition of the two papers certain differences come to the fore, for example, that in Rome the idea of law from the beginning was and always remained connected with the idea of the citizen "with a civic identity, obligations and rights" (61) while in China things were to a greater extent dependent on the emperors, the experts at court, and a few imperial women.

Finally, a much more specific topic was recently examined by R.D.S. Yates in "Female Commoners and the Law in Early Imperial China: Evidence from Recently Recovered Documents with Some Comparisons with Classical Rome"[46]. In this paper, the author uses a wealth of new source material to draw an initial picture of the status and rights of commoner women in the Qin and Han periods. As it turns out, women could "register as household heads", "had the right to own and inherit property", "held the same rank as their husbands", and "were

---

[43] Duindam/Harries/Humfress/Hurvitz (2013).
[44] Harries (2013).
[45] Turner (2013).
[46] Yates (2021). The space dedicated to the description of the Roman situation is limited to ca. 1½ out of the 21 pages of the main text.

protected to a certain extent from violence inflicted by their spouses" (176). This evidence leads Yates to the thesis that "Roman society was apparently much more 'patriarchal' than early Chinese society" (176).

1.2.2.4. Economics

Economic issues are often closely intertwined with political, social, and legal ones. There are several papers dedicated to relevant topics. In Scheidel 2009, P.F. Bang discusses the development of trade and commerce and its interaction with empire formation[47]. He interprets both the Chinese and the Roman empires as tributary empires on an agricultural basis, which controlled and distributed wealth on a large scale and which were successful because they were able to keep their administrations lean and the costs of hegemony low.

Scheidel himself compares "The Monetary Systems of the Han and Roman Empires"[48]. Apart from many concrete commonalities and differences, he presents on a general level the suggestion that the opposition between a "fiduciary" (Chinese) and a "metallistic" (Roman) system is exaggerated and should be replaced by the insight that both systems worked in a similar fashion on the basis of a combination of intrinsic metal value and the willingness of the people to accept the coinage at its nominal value (188)[49].

Scheidel deals with the direct relation of politics and economy in "State Revenue and Expenditure in the Han and Roman Empires"[50], where he focuses on the late Western Han empire and the Roman empire of the 2nd century CE. According to his "guesstimates", the scale of state revenue and expenditure in the two empires was similar, and in both cases relatively limited. To put it differently, "both (empires) were,

---

[47] Bang (2009).

[48] Scheidel (2009b).

[49] For a complementary paper on coin quality, coin quantity, and coin value see Scheidel (2010).

[50] Scheidel (2015).

or became, essentially 'low-tax regimes' benefiting from the lack of peer competitors that could have exerted serious pressure" (178). The differences concern the distribution of "agency costs" — "top officials were dramatically better compensated by the Roman emperor than by his Han counterpart" (168) — and the distribution of "protection costs" — the Roman empire spent significantly more on its military than its Chinese counterpart, whereas in the Han empire the subsidies paid to foreign peoples in order to avert open conflict amounted to a much larger share of "defense spending" than in Rome (174–176).

1.2.2.5. Urbanism

In both East and West, the city was an important material and institutional framework for political, social, and economic activities. Therefore, it is with good reason that the urban environment has been the object of several investigations. This concerns the capitals first of all. Thus, part of each of the two papers on art and architecture in Mutschler/ Mittag 2008 is devoted to the layout of the respective capitals. R.M. Schneider[51] presents Rome as a "civic" city, which, to be sure, already under Augustus did become more emperor-oriented but in which, nevertheless, the urbanistic projects of the *princeps* created new *public* spaces or were integrated into existing ones (270–278). M. Pirazzoli-t'Serstevens[52] interprets Changan as the paradigm of a "palatial" city with five palaces and a huge arsenal occupying large parts of the area *intra muros*, strictly separated from the space where the population lived (307–309).

A little later, interest in the character of the capitals found playful expression in a paper by T.C. Brennan and I-tien Hsing "The Eternal City and the City of Eternal Peace"[53]. The two authors follow a Chinese visitor to the Eternal City in the 1st century BCE and

---

[51] Schneider (2008), "Image and Empire: The Shaping of Augustan Rome."
[52] Pirazzoli-t'Serstevens (2008), "Imperial Aura and the Image of the Other in Han Art."
[53] Brennan/Hsing (2010).

Cicero traveling east and walking through the streets of the City of Eternal Peace.

In 2015, the comparison of the two capitals was again taken up in C.F. Noreña's "Chang'an and Rome: Structural Parallels and the Logics of Urban Form" in a volume specifically dedicated to Changan[54]. In this article, the author, without denying the original differences between the "palatial" city Changan and the "civic" city Rome, shows how the "overhaul of the city by Augustus and his successors" in the imperial period led to the "emergence of a more coherent and univalent urban form", which in the end "overlapped" in many respects "neatly with that of Western Han Chang'an" (93). In his contribution to Scheidel 2015, Noreña extends the scope of his research to the role of urban systems in general[55]. His aim is "to assess the extent to which cities were the product of ... state power... and whether or not they served as effective instruments of social control" (181). With respect to both questions Noreña tends to stress the contrasts between the two cases. He points out that Changan was built from scratch by the first Han emperor as an instrument and symbol of imperial power, whereas Rome grew over centuries and was given the appearance of a truly imperial capital only under Augustus. He also contrasts the firm control that the Han Empire exercised over its cities through centrally appointed officials with the relative autonomy of the local elites in the Roman empire.

Continuing this line of research, in the same volume M.E. Lewis investigates the physical organization of the cities and its connection with the interaction of their inhabitants[56]. Taking for granted basic similarities between the functions of cities in the two empires, Lewis, too, focuses mainly on differences: Roman cities were characterized by

---

[54] Noreña (2015a).

[55] Noreña (2015b), "Urban Systems in the Han and Roman Empires: State Power and Social Control."

[56] Lewis (2015), "Public Spaces in Cities in the Roman and Han Empires".

spaces and building complexes that served as venues for social activities and public entertainments, while in Chinese cities "public" buildings were reserved for state agents and accessible to outsiders only in cases of official business. As for the capitals, Rome filled its public spaces with monuments commemorating historical events and personalities, with military achievements playing a particularly important role. The Qin-Han capitals Changan and Luoyang, on the other hand, presented themselves as brand new structures, symbols of the dynasty's imposition of peace, order and hierarchy — without historical commemorations and triumphal monuments.

1.2.2.6. Ideas of Empire

The research surveyed up to now has concerned, to a large extent, components of what one could call the *hardware* of the two polities under consideration. But their *software* has also been examined. Concepts of empire and imperial rulership, the relation between empire and belief or value systems, and the role played in this context by different media of symbolization have been the subject of scholarly analysis[57].

Thus, the volume "Conceiving the Empire. China and Rome Compared," edited by Mutschler and Mittag[58], has as its core subject the idea of empire as it developed in ancient China and Rome. The contributions by A. Dihle[59], Weizheng Zhu[60], and M. Nylan[61] survey this development from early literary reflections on the theme to extended texts of the 1st and 2nd centuries CE. In the Greco-Roman West, the idea of empire as divinely legitimized monarchic rule over a large

---

[57] Obviously the dividing line between "hardware" and "software" is fluid. A good example is the (just discussed) design of the capitals, which has both a concrete-practical and an abstract-symbolic side. As an instrument of analysis the distinction seems useful nevertheless.

[58] Mutschler/Mittag (2008).

[59] Dihle (2008), "City and Empire".

[60] Zhu (2008), "Interlude: Kingship and Empire".

[61] Nylan (2008), "The Rhetoric of 'Empire' in the Classical Era in China".

territory, the binding force of which could be observed in Egypt and the Near East, always remains in tension with the idea of the city as the self-governing community of free citizens under the rule of their own laws. This tension can be felt even after the (former city-) state of Rome has successfully established its empire and, for the sake of expediency, adopted the monarchic form of government. In China, on the other hand, the monarchic form of government is always taken for granted concerning both All under Heaven (*Tianxia*) and the individual territorial states. Discussions of the best government do not concern its form (monarchic, aristocratic, democratic) but the conduct of the ruler or the efficiency of administrative measures etc.

The pair of papers by Y. Pines[62] and Y. Huang and F.-H. Mutschler[63] deals with (mostly historiographical) texts from the period immediately before and during the emergence of the imperial order in 3rd-century BCE China and 1st-century BCE Rome. One difference brought out by the papers is the fact that in China the idea of unified rule providing peace and order to the world already plays a distinct role in texts prior to the unification under the Qin and Han, while in Rome such an idea develops only gradually alongside the empire's actual emergence, and it is interestingly a Greek outsider (Polybius) who first speaks unequivocally of Rome's dominion over "the inhabited world".

The contributions by Mutschler[64] and Mittag[65] continue the discussion of historiographical texts for the period of the firmly established empires. On the Chinese side, it can be observed that the monarchic form of government is taken for granted as before, while the esteem for the ideal

---

[62] Pines (2008), "Imagining the Empire? Concepts of 'Primeval Unity' in Pre-Imperial Historiographic Tradition."

[63] Huang/Mutschler (2008), "The Emergence of Empire: Rome and the Surrounding World in Historical Narratives from the Late Third Century BC to the Early First Century AD".

[64] Mutschler (2008b), "The Problem of 'Imperial Historiography' in Rome".

[65] Mittag (2008), "Forging Legacy: The Pact between Empire and Historiography in Ancient China".

of "Great Peace" and the tendency towards a cyclical view of history intensify. As for Rome, grand (i.e. senatorial) historiography retains its scepticism towards monarchy and views the alleged limitation of military expansion under the first emperors with regret, while other texts by non-senatorial authors show greater acknowledgement of the emperors' achievements, in particular of the restoration of peace and prosperity.

A final pair of papers on historiographical texts deals with the critical periods from the 3rd to the 5th century CE in Rome and from the 3rd to the 6th century in China. As the contribution by H.A. Gärtner and M. Ye shows[66], in Roman historiography there develop different discourses implying different interpretations of the historical situation, with the traditional Roman this-worldly and optimistic approach and the strictly otherworldly Christian view representing the opposite ends of the spectrum. In China too, as A. Mittag and M. Ye demonstrate[67], different works offer different interpretations of the course of history, but all of them retain the belief that the united empire is still a possibility and an aim that must be pursued.

Concomitant with the investigations of concepts of empire in historiographical texts are two pairs of papers that discuss the reflection of these and related concepts in geographical works and cartography[68], and in art and architecture[69]. Not surprisingly, the geographical texts and maps in both China and Rome present the world as an ordered whole oriented towards a center. On the other hand, all the Chinese texts belong in a state-related context whereas the most important "Roman"

---

[66] Gärtner/Ye (2008), "The Impact of the Empire's Crises on Historiography and Historical Thinking in Late Antiquity."

[67] Mittag/Ye (2008), "Empire on the Brink: Chinese Historiography in the Post-Han Period".

[68] Schmidt-Glintzer (2008), "Diagram (*tu*) and Text (*wen*): Mapping the Chinese World" and Clarke (2008), "Text and Image: Mapping the Roman World".

[69] Schneider (2008), Pirazzli-t'Serstevens (2008) and above p. 314.

text is the result of private (Greek) scholarship, and while most of the maps on both the Chinese and the Roman sides serve administrative or military purposes, the most famous Roman map was displayed in public to show the Roman people that they had conquered the world. As for art and architecture, the contrast between the "civic" city of Rome and the "palatial" cities of Changan and Luoyang has already been mentioned[70]. It can be supplemented by the observation that though the cosmic dimension of empire found comparable artistic and architectural expression in both polities, this took place on the Chinese side within the segregated district of Qin Shi Huangdi's palace and mausoleum whereas in Rome it was orchestrated on the Campus Martius, i.e. in public, before the eyes of the people.

Subsequent research has pursued the topic further. The relationship between the idea of empire and universalistic ideas has been the subject of two papers. In "Empire and Humankind: Historical Universalism in Ancient China and Rome", Mittag and Mutschler ask when "the world" at large begins to play a role in the sources and how these sources view the relationship between the respective polity/empire and the world[71]. It seems that in China ideas such as All-under-Heaven (*Tianxia*) develop relatively early in connection with the doctrine of Heaven's Mandate (*Tianming*), whereas for a long time the Roman texts see the surrounding world primarily as the object of Roman conquest. Later on, however, one observes a convergence insofar as in both cases the achievement of imperial rule is located in the establishment of peace and order and the spread of civilization and culture in "the world." T.T. Chin, in "What is Imperial Cosmopolitanism? Revisiting *Kosmopolitēs* and *Mundanus*"[72], discusses the complex relationship between ideas of empire and ideas of cosmopolitanism in Hellenistic, Roman, and ancient Chinese texts. She

---

[70] See above p. 314.
[71] Mittag/Mutschler (2010).
[72] Chin (2016).

works out the varying meaning of the pertinent notions and their accordingly varying relationship, and contextualizes both within the social structures of the empires and within the frameworks of intercultural contact.

The recent collective volume *Empire and Politics in the Eastern and Western Civilizations: Searching for a "Respublica Romanosinica"*[73] contains another paper dealing with the idea of empire. In his essay "Empire and Politics in Eastern and Western Civilizations," M.N.S. Sellers strongly — and perhaps a little too unqualifiedly — emphasizes the congruence between Chinese and Roman perceptions and ideas, and finds the reason for this congruence in the universality of human nature[74]. As he puts it, according to the shared view "politics should seek the common good, and ... empires and emperors are only legitimate, when they serve the welfare of all those subject to their rule" (170). Thus, "all the cardinal virtues and concepts of Roman and Chinese empires and politics find correspondences in the parallel culture" and though "these correspondences are not exact ... they are close enough that each can sharpen and improve its meaning and self-understanding by attending to the other" (173).

1.2.2.7. Concepts of Rulership

Closely related to concepts of empire are concepts of rulership. A group of fundamental primary texts concerning this topic — the epigraphic self-representations of Qin Shi Huangdi and Augustus — are preserved and have been analyzed several times in recent years.

In Mutschler/Mittag 2008, M. Kern and Ch. Witschel devote parallel papers to "The Stele Inscriptions of the Qin first Emperor"[75] and "The *Res Gestae Divi Augusti*"[76]. Their analyses reveal commonalities

---

[73] Balbo/Ahn/Kim (2022).
[74] Sellers (2022).
[75] Kern (2008).
[76] Witschel (2008).

and differences. For example, in both cases the communicative context is different: The self-descriptions of the Chinese First Emperor were put up on the peaks of holy mountains serving the communication with Heaven, whereas Augustus' *Res Gestae* were put up in front of his mausoleum, i.e. in public, to be seen by the citizens. In terms of contents, both parallels and divergences strike the eye. The claim to have established peace and order and to have taken care of the needs of the populace is an important point in both cases. On the other hand, the stele inscriptions describe the achievements of Qin Shi Huangdi in the third person and in rather abstract terms, stressing the re-establishment of unity and order after a period of division and chaos, and presenting the subdued opponents less as enemies than as criminals and rebels, and as punished rather than conquered. Augustus' *Res Gestae*, in contrast, are formulated in the first person; they start by documenting the quasi "republican" legitimacy of Augustus' position as *princeps*, then record his merits in re-establishing peace and order, before describing in the final part, extensively and in concrete detail, his uniquely successful efforts in expanding the empire through military conquest.

In an Australian MA thesis, Dan Qing Zhao investigates Augustus' and Qin Shi Huangdi's self-image and propaganda in the context of their portrayals of foreigners and barbarians[77]. Against the backdrop of pre-imperial attitudes towards warfare and foreigners in Rome and China, Zhao tries to show that, despite differences in accentuation, both emperors, in their propaganda, not only emphasized their military prowess but "also manipulated the representation of foreigners" in such a way as "to highlight their [own] morality and their special connection to the divine" (136).

Reference has already been made to D. Engels' extensive study of

---

[77] Zhao (2018).

Qin Shi Huangdi (and Gaozu) and Caesar (and Augustus)[78]. Although its orientation is different, it also offers some material concerning conceptions of rulership. In a further paper, Engels discusses specifically "'Reinheit' als Herrscherqualität im ideologischen Narrativ der großen Universalherrscher der alten Welt: Rom, China, Indien und Iran"[79]. He sees in all four cases the development from a formalistic to a moralistic understanding of "purity", which is followed later by a return to a more traditionalist view, partly in connection with an unprecedented elevation of the figure of the ruler. At the same time, in each case specific givens of social, intellectual, and religious history lead to varying configurations of the fundamental ideas.

G. Malinowski deals with the concept of a "highest universal divine ruler" in world history[80]. His main interest is in the title of the Roman emperor: "Imperator (Caesar Augustus)". He reconstructs in detail its coming into being and its meaning and relates it to other denotations for the supreme ruler from 3rd-millennium BCE Sumer to 15th-cent CE Mesoamerica. His main conclusion is that the Roman title is unique insofar as it "originated in the republican milieu ... hostile to kingship" while in most other cultures "the designations for universal rulers" utilize "the word 'king'" (22), which applies also for the Chinese title/word/character "huangdi" 皇帝 .

In "*Pax Romana* and *Pax Sinica*: Some Historical Aspects," W. Kim and K. Kim undertake to demonstrate that the establishment and preservation of peace and order plays an important role not only in the Chinese and Roman ideology of empire in general but also in the justification of the personal rule and the praise of the achievements of Augustus and Emperor Wu in particular[81].

---

[78] See above 308.

[79] Engels (2020).

[80] Malinowski (2022).

[81] Kim & Kim (2022).

1.2.2.8. Belief Systems

Another topic that has attracted interest in the last one and a half decades is the relation between empire and belief systems. This relation gained particular significance in the final centuries of the Western Roman and the Han empires. Accordingly, in Mutschler/Mittag 2008 the ideological developments in this period were surveyed by G. O'Daly[82] and T. Jansen[83]. The two papers bring to the fore striking commonalities, such as a discourse deploring decadence and the loss of traditional values, an increasing emphasis on the "souci de soi", and the emergence of new religious groups and esoteric cults. On the other hand, they also reveal decisive differences, such as the one between religions that allow for a relatively unproblematic integration into the imperial system (Daoism and Buddhism) and a monotheistic, radically otherworldly religion (Christianity) that in the end transformed the city of Romulus and Remus into the city of Peter and Paul.

The topic was taken up from a wider chronological perspective in M. Puett's paper "Ghosts, Gods, and the Coming Apocalypse: Empire and Religion in Early China and Ancient Rome"[84]. Puett focusses very much on the Chinese side, for which he distinguishes different models of "political theology": (a) an older tradition that derives aristocratic power from ancestral spirits, (b) concepts of divine rulership based on a direct linkage with Heaven, and (c) doctrines of self-divinization connected with millenarian movements. References to Rome are scarce, but Puett does point out that there too the idea of divine rulership gained significance in times of political crisis and that later on a millenarian movement, i.e. Christianity, was "appropriated by the state and transformed into a new imperial ideology" (257).

---

[82] O'Daly (2008), "New Tendencies, Religious and Philosophical, in the Roman Empire of the Third to Early Fifth Centuries."

[83] Jansen (2008), "New Tendencies, Religious and Philosophical in the Chinese World of the Third through Sixth Centuries."

[84] Puett (2015).

S. Lieu's study of "The Serpent from Persia. Manichaeism in Rome and China," in the volume edited by Kim, Vervaert and Adali, can also be said to deal with the theme of empire and religion[85]. But, although Rome and China are juxtaposed in the article's title, Lieu's main interest — and merit — lies not in the *comparison* of the role of Manichaeism in the two empires but in the analysis of the conditions and mechanisms of a two-sided (or even three-sided, if one includes Sassanian Persia) case of contact and exchange.

1.2.2.9. Value Systems

Related to the theme of empire and belief systems is that of empire and values. Two papers in the volume just referred to are concerned with it as they investigate the significance of "Honour and Shame in the Roman Republic" (F. Vervaet)[86] and "Honour and Shame in Han China" (M. Lewis)[87]. The approach of the two authors differs insofar as Vervaet pursues synchronic treatment, analyzing in three sections the circumstances in the Roman family, the Roman senate, and the Roman military, while Lewis puts more emphasis on the historical development, from the period of the Warring states up to and then within the Han-period. Although neither author carries out an explicit comparison, it becomes evident that a fruitful topic for comparison is here at hand. In both cases, honor and shame play an important role in social and political life, and points of agreement and difference are of interest for an understanding of the workings of the two polities[88].

---

[85]   Lieu (2017).

[86]   Vervaet (2017).

[87]   Lewis (2017).

[88]   To give only one example: Originally, the connection of honor and shame with military achievement and failure is close, both in Rome and in China. But in Han China, not least under the influence of "the emergent philosophical traditions", "the military focus of honour/shame largely disappeared" (129), whereas in imperial Rome even a non-soldierly nature like Augustus decided "to convert the public triumph from a republican aristocratic ritual into a strictly observed imperial monopoly" (107) in order to reserve the public demonstration of military success for himself and his successors.

Contemporaneously with the papers on honor and shame, an article was published by D. Engels in which he provided a quadruple comparison of the Roman, Chinese, Sassanian and Fatimid empires concerning the development of their value systems in general[89]. According to Engels, this development is strikingly similar in all four cases. After a period of political, religious, and intellectual unrest in which the validity of the traditional norms is called into question, there follows a decisive historical phase — in China the period of Qin Shi Huangdi and Han Gaozu in Rome the Augustan period — in which "a new authoritarian power centralist and charismatic" is able to put an end to the political turmoil and to establish a new normative framework together with peace and order. This, in turn, is characterized by numerous references to "ancestral" norms, often reinvented rather than revived, and the canonization of an identity-creating idealized historical and mythical past (71f.).

Under the heading of "empire and values" in a wider sense, we may finally take account of Engel's most recent paper in which he analyzes the critical impact of utopias in Chinese and Greco-Roman antiquity[90]. The main subject of his analysis is Tao Yuanming's "Peach Blossom Source" but references to images of the Golden Age in Homer, Hesiod, Euhemerus, Virgil, Horace, Ovid, the *Historia Augusta* and Boethius, open up a comparative perspective. More significant than the differences — such as the fact that, in contrast with the pragmatist and empiricist Chinese thinkers, most Greco-Roman authors imagine their utopian society with links to the gods — is the coincidence that basically all the texts value such "goods as abundance, peace, beauty, good health or social harmony as highest goals of history" (293) and use this yardstick for the critical evaluation of political reality especially in its

---

[89] Engels (2017).
[90] Engels (2021b).

imperial form.

1.2.2.10. Worldviews and Policies

In a Leiden dissertation of 2015, Zh. Wang analyzes the interplay between worldviews and policies with respect to a decisive component of empire building: war and expansion[91]. The study is divided into three parts, each of which consists of a chapter on Rome and a chapter on China that includes a comparative section. In chapters 1 and 2, Wang traces the formation of the idea of world dominion in pre-imperial Rome and China. Although central notions like *orbis terrarium* and *tianxia* seem rather similar at first glance, closer analysis shows that, actually, "an open, externally orientated and all-inclusive worldview" (Rome) and "a far more closed, inwardly orientated and exclusive view of the world" (China) are opposed to each other (58). Accordingly, the Roman idea of "a never ending process of centrifugal expansion" culminating in *imperium sine fine* (61) has no counterpart on the Chinese side where we find instead the idea of the successful protection of a civilized center of the world, surrounded by barbarian margins. In chapters 3 and 4, Wang seeks to demonstrate that different military policies correspond to these different worldviews. As he points out: "Although the rhythm of Roman expansion did slow down in the later years of the reign of Augustus, various later emperors still thought it necessary to embark on ambitious military campaigns" (131), whereas "the vast majority of Qin and Han emperors showed little interest in foreign wars and military conquest" (137). Chapters 5 and 6 investigate the emperors' roles still further. The conclusion is obvious: "Because of social and cultural expectations Roman emperors were under pressure to seek military honours, preferably by leading the army in person", while "in stark contrast to their Roman counterparts the emperors of the Qin and Han dynasties were not expected to play any

---

[91] Wang (2015).

military role after the decision to start a particular war had been taken" (206). Wang's dissertation is now being prepared for publication in book form.

1.2.3. Comprehensive History

As the previous pages have shown, there have been numerous studies comparing important aspects of the Chinese and Roman empires. These studies have been carried out by specialists in the different scholarly disciplines involved, and they have broadened and deepened our understanding of the subject considerably. Perhaps understandably, however, from the specialists' side no attempt has been made so far to present a *comprehensive comparative history* of the two empires. The task is daunting. Thus, it may need the ingenuousness of an outsider to take it up. S.Y. Auyang has had the courage to do so[92]. After her retirement as a professor of physics, she began to work on a comprehensive comparative study of the Chinese and Roman empires from the time of the Zhou dynasty and the foundation of Rome to their downfall in the 4th and 5th centuries CE, which she published in 2014 under the title *The Dragon and the Eagle*. Given the magnitude of the endeavor and the book's length of only 320 pages, it cannot be a surprise that Auyang's account is rather general and tends to over-simplify de facto complex matters. It is also understandable that a single author, especially if he or she is coming from outside the pertinent disciplines, is not in full control of the latest scholarship on each of the many research problems involved. *The Dragon and the Eagle* has been criticized for these kinds of weakness[93]. But it is my feeling that the author should be respected for having made the first attempt at undertaking a task that is and will be worth undertaking.

---

[92] Auyang (2014).
[93] Rosenstein (2016).

2. Studies on Intellectual and Literary History

When we turn from empire studies to studies on intellectual and literary history, two preliminary remarks are appropriate. The first concerns the assignment of studies to one or the other category. As said before, this assignment is not always unambiguous. Thus, the distinction between studies dealing with the political "software" of the two empires and studies dealing with intellectual and literary history is sometimes a mere question of degree, that is, the degree to which political issues shape the material investigated, whether they dominate it or are only of a circumstantial nature. In order to mitigate the problem, it is advisable when dealing with studies one has assigned to one category not to lose sight of related studies one has assigned to the other.

The second remark concerns the role of Greece. With respect to political history, it is unproblematic to consider Rome as an entity in its own right, independent from Greece, and, as we have seen, this has frequently been done. For intellectual and literary history, the situation is different. In these areas, Rome was under the formative influence of Greece to such an extent that Greek tradition almost always comes into the picture when Roman achievement is discussed. Thus, the China–Rome comparison appears quite often as part of a triple comparison between China, Rome, and Greece. And more seriously, as we will see, in a field like philosophy, the comparison of China with Greece has attracted so much attention that the possible comparison of China with Rome has been either neglected or greatly overshadowed.

2.1. Religion

As we have seen, in Mutschler/Mittag 2008, G. O'Daly and Th. Jansen examined *inter alia* the intellectual, spiritual, political and social significance of the arrival and development of Christianity in the Roman empire and of Buddhism in the Chinese empire of the first centuries CE[94]. The interaction of these two belief systems with the established religious and cultural traditions is also the subject of a collective volume *Old Society, New Belief: Religious Transformation of China and Rome, ca. 1st–6th Centuries*, edited by Mu-chou Poo, H. A. Drake, and Lisa Raphals[95]. As Poo and Drake state in their introduction, this "is a large topic, and one that can easily become drowned in generalities"[96]. And they continue: "To avoid that fate we asked specialists in the history of both traditions to provide *concrete examples* [my emphasis] that show *in some detail* [my emphasis] the obstacles each religion faced and how each succeeded in surmounting them"[97]. The editors' concern is understandable, but the drawback of their strategy is also obvious. The volume contains fifteen contributions by specialists, each on a topic concerning *one* of the two traditions. Thus the envisaged *comparison* of the *two* "old societies" and the *two* "new beliefs" comes up rather short. It is limited to complementary remarks in some of the articles, implicitly contained in a few others, and eventually brought into focus in Lisa Raphals' conclusion. I restrict my report to contributions in which the comparative aspect is at least touched upon.

In "'Buddhism Enters China' in Early Medieval China," R.F. Campany examines five "narratives that depict the influx of Buddhism ... into China" (14) [98]. The result of the examination is that in these narratives "Buddhism's early arrival and impact narrated in the first few centuries in China ... weren't one big thing; they were a lot of little things — little things of many different kinds" (33). H.A. Drake in "Christianity in Rome. A Study in Power Relationships" follows a comparable strategy by

---

[94] See above 323.
[95] Poo/Drake/Raphals (2017).
[96] Loc. cit. 2.
[97] Loc. cit. 2.
[98] Campany (2017).

focusing *inter alia* on Lactantius' and Eusebius' reports of Constantine's dream and his vision of the cross before the Battle of the Milvian Bridge[99]. As a general difference between the situations in China and in Rome, Drake observes that in China Buddhists were never able to monopolize access to the divine, whereas the Roman state became Christian and enforced exclusive Christian worship and belief (37f.).

H.J. Kim discusses different "Christian Reactions to Encounters with Greco-Roman Culture and Imperial Prosecution"[100]. His examples are Justin Martyr's *First Apology* and Tatian's *Oratio ad Graecos*. Looking ahead to the following paper on Buddhism in China by Zongli Lu[101], Kim addresses and interprets a number of parallels — as the partial indigenization of a foreign religion in both cases — and differences — as the non-occurrence of a persecution of Buddhists in China like that of Christians in Rome.

Papers 9 and 10 are each focused on *one* of the two cases, but can be considered as implicitly comparative given their similar subject matter. Sze-kar Wan presents a survey of Greco-Roman daimonology, paying particular attention to the process by which the "broad, ambiguous *daimōn*" of early Greece became "an evil demon" for Christian thinkers like Augustine (148)[102]. Mu-chou Poo shows how translations of Buddhist texts used the traditional Chinese terms for "ghost" and "spirit", allowing "the readers to have a certain sense of familiarity", but on the other hand, reproduced the individual names in phonetic transliteration and thus created "a sense of awe and respect for their sutras" (172)[103]. In the second part, Poo analyzes practical actions that the Buddhists propagated — often in competition with indigenous

---

[99]   Drake (2017).

[100]   Kim (2017).

[101]   Lu (2017).

[102]   Wan (2017), "Colonizing the Supernatural. How *Daimōn* Became Demonized in Late Antiquity".

[103]   Poo (2017), "The Taming of Ghosts in Early Chinese Buddhism".

belief systems — to exorcize ghosts and demons (172–179).

Papers 12 and 13, too, can be said to form a pair insofar as both deal with material culture. P. Chatterjee in "Ancient Statues, Christian City: Constantinople and the *Parastaseis Syntomoi Chronikai*" uses the analysis of this text to suggest that pagan statues "plotted an alternative historical trajectory to the Orthodox markers of salvation in the cityscape ... one that underwrote the longevity of the Queen of Cities, its imperial dynasties and of Romania itself" (215)[104]. Yin Zhou in "Adaptation and Assimilation of Buddhism in China as Reflected in Monastic Architecture" traces how Indian monastic architecture in the course of time accommodated itself to the local environment and its traditional way of building, until in the end a unique style of *Chinese* Buddhist architecture had developed[105].

The volume ends with a "Conclusion. Comparative Perspectives on China and Rome" by L. Raphals, organized under three headings: "(In)tolerance and Religious Violence" (259–263), "Fate, Justice, and Retribution" (263–268), and "Changing and Interacting Genres" (268–271)[106]. In summary, Raphals states that "the chapters in this book show that the process by which Christianity and Buddhism became established in their respective regions was much more complex than the language of conquest or triumph would suggest" and that "over centuries of interaction and dialogue, the old societies changed the new religions as much as the religions changed the old societies" (271).

2.2. Philosophy

Together with the sciences, philosophy has been the subject of intensive comparative activities, but these have been almost exclusively concerned with China and *Greece*. Given the quality and quantity of

---

[104] Chatterjee (2017).
[105] Zhou (2017).
[106] Raphals (2017).

preserved Greek philosophical texts, this is understandable, but the fact that publications dealing with China and Rome are almost totally lacking is nonetheless regrettable. The few studies that include Rome are the following.

Concerning late antiquity, the socio-political role not only of religion but also of philosophy in China and Rome has been discussed in a general way in the aforementioned contributions by O'Daly and Jansen [107]. The articles in the volume *How One Should live? Comparing Ethics in Ancient China and Greco*-Roman [my emphasis] *Antiquity*, edited by R.A.H. King and D. Schilling, are more specific, but on the Western side — in spite of the volume's subtitle — more or less exclusively concerned with Greek authors and texts[108].

Thus, the first work dealing specifically with Chinese and *Roman* philosophy is the collection of essays *Confucius and Cicero: Old Ideas for a New World, New Ideas for an Old World*, edited by A. Balbo and J. Ahn[109]. The volume contains three groups of papers. Two papers continue the ongoing comparison of Chinese and Greek philosophy and thus present a kind of background for the comparison of Confucius and Cicero[110]. Two papers deal with Latin translations by Jesuits of Confucian Classics, and look at the role of Ciceronian Latin in this process[111]. Finally, there are five *comparative* studies. In the volume's introductory paper, F.-H. Mutschler discusses the "Problems and

---

[107]　See above 323.

[108]　King/Schilling (2011). No article has a Roman author or text as an explicit subject, and even the *Index Locorum* lists only three Cicero passages and one Seneca passage (no Lucretius passage).

[109]　Balbo/Ahn (2019).

[110]　T. Bai, "The Private and the Public in the *Republic* and in the *Analects*" (29–42); G. Parkes, "Confucian and Daoist, Stoic and Epicurean. Some Parallels in Ways of Living" (43–58). J. Yum's paper "Mind and Heaven, and Ritual in the *Xunzi*" (59–70) focuses exclusively on a Chinese text.

[111]　M. Ferrero, "The Latin Translations of Confucius' *Dialogues* (Lun Yu). A Comparison of Key Concepts" (73–108); J. Ahn, "Is Confucius a Sinicus Cicero?" (109–125).

Possibilities" of the envisaged comparison[112]. In spite of difficulties such as the strikingly different source situation, possible subjects of comparison do exist, for example, the conception and role of moral qualities in Confucius' *Analects* and Cicero's *De officiis*, or the meaning of Confucian *ren* (仁) and Ciceronian *humanitas* and their significance in the two men's ethical thought. In the concluding paper, Y. Takada sketches the dissimilarities between the socio-political frameworks within which Confucius and Cicero underwent their intellectual formation and built their philosophical, as well as political, careers[113]. These dissimilarities have the effect that the relative closeness in the ethical positions of the "undogmatic Stoic" Cicero and the Confucius of the "ten thousand things" represents only a "similitude in disguise" (197–198). The three remaining contributions deal with key concepts of Ciceronian and Confucian thought. The papers by C. Høgel and St. Mercier on Ciceronian *humanitas* and Confucian *ren* are implicitly comparative[114]. Høgel describes the broad usage of *humanitas* by Cicero, which can denote *inter alia* "mankind", "education", and "kindness", and traces the meaning and significance of the term in later writers such as Lactantius and Erasmus. Correspondingly, Mercier studies the role of *ren* in the *Analects*, and then analyzes the use of the term by the Korean Christian convert Yi Byeok in his exposition of the Christian doctrine. Finally, K. Kim investigates the role of *pietas* in Cicero's *Pro Roscio* and then, prompted by Korean, Chinese, and Japanese translations of the speech, which all use the character 孝 to render *pietas*, he analyzes the meaning of 孝 (xiao) in the Confucian "Classic of Filial Piety", the 孝经 (Xiaojing)[115].

---

[112] Mutschler (2019).
[113] Takada (2019).
[114] Høgel (2019) and Mercier (2019).
[115] Kim (2019).

2.3. Historiography

Though Roman material is not lacking, in the case of historiography too, comparison with Chinese works was for a long time exclusively concentrated on Greek texts, with the juxtaposition of the alleged "fathers of history", Herodotus and Sima Qian, receiving special attention[116]. This interest in the comparison of Chinese with *Greek* material in particular can still be observed in Volume One of *The Oxford History of Historical Writing*, which covers the period from the "Beginnings to AD 600"[117]. In the individual — non-comparative — contributions, Chinese, Greek, and Roman historiography receive equal consideration, but in the epilogue, the comparison of Chinese and *Greek* historiography is intensely discussed on three pages while *Roman* historiography is dispensed with in a few lines (609–611).

But things have begun to change. In 1997 and 2003, F.-H. Mutschler published two papers in which he attempted a comparison of ancient Chinese, Greek, and Roman historiography, taking the classics of each tradition as the basis of his analysis[118]. It emerges from these studies that the three traditions appear in different constellations depending on the aspect chosen. Regarding macrostructure and subject matter, the segmentation of the Chinese works and their broad thematic interest, not least in peace-time matters, are in contrast with the continuous narrative of the Greek and Roman works and their particular interest in war. On the other hand, Chinese and Roman historiography are strikingly close to each other and different from Greek historiography in their emphasis on the moral dimension of events and a narrative microstructure which

---

[116] Cf. Zhang above, pp. 265–267.

[117] Feldherr/Hardy (2011).

[118] Mutschler (1997, 2003). *Shangshu, Chunqiu, Zuozhuan,* and *Shiji* serve as representatives of Chinese historiography, Herodotus, Thucydides, and Polybius of Greek historiography, Sallust, Livy, and Tacitus of Roman historiography.

aims less at factual connectivity than at the repeated conveyance of (moral) meaning (Mutschler 1997). With respect to the horizons of perception, the constellation changes once again, with each tradition preserving a character of its own: In the Greek works, the horizon of perception includes the whole of human history with its unending ups and downs; in the Roman works, it is the restricted horizon of "national" history seen as a movement from humble beginnings to the mastery of the world; in Chinese texts, it is the horizon of the one realm, which from early on is conceived of as "All under Heaven", and within which history runs its course in different cycles (Mutschler 2003).

Three subsequent papers by Mutschler deal with Chinese and exclusively *Roman* historiography, in particular with Sima Qian and Tacitus. Taking the representations of emperor Wendi in the *Shiji* and emperor Tiberius in the *Annals* as its starting point, the first paper discusses the basic political ideas of the two authors, their ways of representing persons, and the structure of their works[119]. The second paper analyzes the influence of the painful personal experiences the two authors underwent under emperors Wudi and Domitian on their historiographical practice, in particular on their representations of Wendi and Tiberius[120]. The third paper includes Livy in the comparison and extends the textual analysis to the depictions of the earliest periods of Chinese and Roman history[121].

At least in passing the reader should be reminded that in the collective volume "Conceiving the Empire", discussed above, the contribution of Chinese and Roman historiography to the self-understanding of the two empires is analyzed in three pairs of papers

---

[119] Mutschler (2006).

[120] Mutschler (2007a).

[121] Mutschler (2008a). In two shorter papers, Mutschler discusses theoretical issues connected with the intercultural comparison of ancient historiographies (Mutschler [2007b and 2015]).

dealing with the periods of the emerging empires, the flourishing empires, and the empires in crisis[122].

While in F. Marsili's article on "The Ghosts of Monotheism: Heaven, Fortune, and Universalism in Early Chinese and Greco-Roman Historiography," the comparative counterpart to — once again — Sima Qian's *Shiji* is not a Roman work but Polybius' *Histories*[123], the juxtaposition of Chinese and *Roman* historical texts has continued as well. In a graduate thesis of 2016, D. Zhao analyzes the representation of barbarians in Sima Qian and Tacitus and shows that in both cases the apparent contradiction between a positive presentation of the "noble barbarian" and a principally imperialistic view, implying the assumption of the center's general superiority, disappears if one understands that the author intends the depiction of the barbarians less as an objective commentary on them than as a selective critique of the imperial center[124].

A very specific topic is treated in J. Walter's paper on "*terrae motus* and *dizhen* (地震) ... in historical works from the Roman Empire and Ancient China."[125] As the author states, at first sight, the Chinese sources seem to document the events less subjectively and more accurately than the western works, but closer examination shows that in both cases the decisive goal of the chronicler is the integration of the event into a socio-political or cosmic-religious context, helping those concerned to come to terms with what has happened and to derive some guidance for their conduct in the future.

In 2020, R.B. Ford dedicated a substantial monograph to the question of how the barbarian states that were able to establish themselves for a certain period on Chinese and Roman ground are

---

[122] See above 317–318.
[123] Marsili (2013/4).
[124] Zhao (2016).
[125] Walter (2016).

represented and evaluated in Procopius's *Wars* and the *Jinshu*, the *History of the Jin-Dyansty*[126]. Since Procopius, though writing in Greek, is after all an (East-)Roman historian, it makes sense to include Ford's book in this section of the report. After an extensive sketch of the development of the image of the barbarian in the Greco-Roman and Chinese historiographical and ethnographical traditions, Ford provides a detailed analysis of the two texts. He focuses on (a) the usage of the categories and points of view of predecessors, (b) the manner of presentation of barbarian rulers, and (c) the discussion of the legitimacy of the barbarian states, especially in inserted speeches. One of his findings is that Procopius, who is often considered tradition-oriented and conservative, describes and evaluates the Vandals and the Goths (i.e. the most important barbarian agents) with a high degree of impartiality and open-mindedness, whereas the author of the *Jinshu*, which stems from the supposedly cosmopolitan Tang-period, treats the barbarian tribes throughout as reincarnations of a traditional "other", essentially distinct from and inferior to the Chinese ethnos.

The latest pertinent publications return to the "classical" period. For D. Engels' comparative analysis of the self-representations, and also the historiographical representations of Qin Shi Huangdi and Caesar, Gaozu and Augustus, see above[127]. G.P. Olberding, in "Liberation as Burlesque: The Death of the Tyrant," seeks to demonstrate that Sima Qian's account of Jing Ke's attempt to assassinate the king of Qin (*Shiji* 86) is "not a philippic against tyranny but a satiric critique of political imbroglios and their general triviality" (301)[128]. Similar tendencies in Sima Qian's representations of Chen She and Liu Bang, "the two most celebrated rebels against the Qin regime" (315), and the similarly ironic description of "'liberators' of whatever ilk or station" (317) in

---

[126] Ford (2020).
[127] See above 308 and 322.
[128] Olberding (2021).

Roman historiography serve as important elements in Olberding's argumentation.

2.4. Poetry

In spite of the intensive comparative activity dealing with the cultural achievements of ancient China and ancient Greece, poetry has only recently become the subject of pertinent studies[129]. This should not cause surprise since it is even more difficult in this field than in others to find counterparts for which comparison makes immediate sense. Concerning Chinese and *Roman* poetry, the process is just starting.

As a kind of prelude, a few years ago W. Denecke presented a groundbreaking comparative study of Roman and *Japanese* poetical texts[130]. Since one of the prerequisites that made this comparison plausible is the fact that both Roman and Japanese literatures are "derived" literatures (with Roman literature building on Greek literature and Japanese literature building on Chinese literature), Denecke also set some *Roman* and *Chinese* texts in an, at least, *indirect* relation to each other[131].

The first *direct* comparisons of Roman and Chinese poetry, however, are emerging only now. As we have seen, Tao Yuanming's "Peach Blossom Source" has just been compared by D. Engels to passages not only in Homer and Hesiod, but also in Vergil, Horace, Ovid, and Boethius[132]. The paper is certainly relevant, but its author's interest is not in the texts as poetry but in their, so to speak, ideological content. This is different in the following case.

In 2017, one of the conferences to commemorate the 2000th anniversary of Ovid's death took place in Shanghai. It was organized

---

[129] Cf. Zhang above, 254–256.
[130] Denecke (2014).
[131] Such as Roman and Chinese exile poetry: Denecke (2014), 203–233.
[132] See above 325.

within the framework of an amazing project based at Shanghai Normal University: the undertaking of a complete translation of Ovid's works into Chinese. The conference was well attended by international and domestic participants, and it led to two major publications, one in Chinese[133] and one in English[134]. Whereas the first one deals with a great variety of traditional Ovidian topics, the second concentrates to a large extent on the reception of Ovid in China. But it also contains four studies that *compare* Ovidian with Chinese texts. Like most of the contributions, the articles are by members of the translation project and reflect the work of their authors on the Ovidian texts they are translating.

In "Writing in Misfortune: Ovid's *Heroides* in Light of Chinese Poetic Perspectives," Chun Liu juxtaposes Ovid's *Heroides* and parts of his exile poetry with a relatively wide range of Chinese poetry and Chinese theoretical statements about poetry[135]. She concentrates on two topics: the plaintive utterances of women formulated by male poets, and the relationship between misfortune in life and writing poetry. Regarding the first topic, Liu observes a considerable degree of agreement between the Ovidian and Chinese texts in terms of motifs, imagery, and psychology. On the other hand, she also states that "Ovid's heroines are diverse and individually portrayed and offer more interpretative possibilities than the nameless women in the Chinese plaintive poems" (161). Another contrast is more ostensible than real and points ahead to the second topic. While "in the Chinese tradition, the love-sick women are often delineated metaphorically to represent the male poet's unfulfilled ambition or setbacks in life", it appears that "Ovid is not using his heroines to air his own grievances" (161). On the other hand, there is definitely "a correspondence between the heroines' letters and Ovid's 'sad songs' in exile" (161). Accordingly, the latter part of Liu's

---

[133] Liu (2021).
[134] Sienkewicz/Liu (2022).
[135] Liu (2022).

paper is dedicated to the comparison of passages in Ovidian and Chinese texts that discuss the intricate "relationship between suffering and poetry writing" (162).

Ying Xiong's article on "themes of women's vengeance" combines reception study and comparison[136]. In the first part of her paper, Xiong traces the reproduction (translation and compilation) of the myths of Procne and Medea in 20th-century China. In the second half, she compares the treatment of female vengeance and filicide in Chinese literature with Ovid's handling of the two myths in the *Metamorphoses*. In traditional Chinese literature (i.e. literature before the middle of the 19th century), "women came to the fore as agents of vengeance only when there were no male members of the family to do so. It was not for the wrongs they themselves suffered that they took vengeance, but for those suffered by their family" (248), "filicide" was "considered as symbol of utmost cruelty" (149), and "revenge for betrayed love was despised" (251). In the modern period this changed: "Women's vengeance against her unfaithful lover ... now began to appear more frequently and took on more positive meanings" (252). The vengeance theme in general became more popular, and, in view of the frequent humiliation of China by western powers, a growing number of Chinese intellectuals "believed that it was softness of mind that prevented Chinese people from seeking national salvation" and "through vengeance stories in their translation or their own writing, they hoped to encourage their compatriots" (253). Thus "Medea" became "a strong symbol. ... She epitomized a recalcitrant and rebellious spirit in an age calling for both individual and national rejuvenation" (256).

A relatively "odd couple", as the author herself admits (277), is compared by Heng Du: Ovid's *Fasti* and the first part of the *Lüshi*

---

[136]   Xiong (2022).

Chunqiu, the "Spring and Autumn Annals of Master Lü"[137]. In contrast with Ovid's poem, the *Lüshi Chunqiu* is an encyclopedic work, mostly in prose and compiled from other texts by the merchant, politician and philosopher Lü Buwei. Its first part, however, consists of twelve books, which correspond to the months of the year and list seasonal activities, and thus offer the possibility of comparison with Ovid's poetic calendar. In accordance with Du's interest in understanding the two texts in their analogous historical environment — i.e. "the early and transitional stages of their respective empires, during the time of territorial expansion and institutional shift" (278) — the comparison is carried out on a rather abstract level, with "special attention" paid "to manifestations of multilingualism as a proxy for the 'internal diversity' of empires" and their interaction "with the universalist visions associated with the calendar and astronomy" (279). Du's textual analyses lead her to the conclusion that, "while both works bear traces of the centrifugal regionalism across the empire, the astronomical discourse associated with the solar cycle introduces or imposes a countervailing universalist vision" (289).

A comparative study of a more traditional kind is Chenye Shi's paper on the exile poetry of Ovid and the Song-dynasty poet Su Shi (1037–1101 CE), like Ovid, one of the truly greats of his literary tradition[138]. After introducing the Chinese poet to the Western reader, Chenye Shi first examines the significance of *philosophical* consolation for the exiled poets. The result of his comparison is rather surprising. Traditionally, quite differently from Ovid the ever plaintive weakling, Su Shi is seen as the steadfast man who in misery finds comfort in the teachings of philosophy. But Chenye Shi shows that although "philosophical comfort" can "reconcile Su Shi with his immediate

---

[137] Du (2022).
[138] Shi (2022).

environment", "when reflecting on his fate more generally, the Chinese poet succumbed to compulsively revisiting and bemoaning his fate like Ovid" (329). And the parallel can be taken even further since for both poets *poetic* consolation fails too. In their attempts to conjure up missing persons such as their wives in their poems, both Ovid and Su Shi realize that the externalization in writing of their internalized memories leads only to the confirmation of the losses from which they suffer.

3. Acta and Agenda

3.1. Acta

The above report can be summarized in the following way.

In the numerous works on empires in general, the Roman and Chinese cases are almost always taken into account, and the particular analyses devoted to them are substantial elements of the empirical basis on which the resulting general conclusions and theories are formulated. On the other hand, direct comparison of Rome with China in these works has been restricted to parenthetical remarks.

This limitation, however, is more than compensated by the fact that the publications specifically devoted to this comparison have continuously increased in number. In addition to the early publications, which juxtaposed the historical development of the two empires in general, and thereby outlined a task worth pursuing, there are now numerous comparative studies on more specific issues. Taken together, they have significantly advanced our understanding of "the working" of the two empires and of the factors influencing the course of their histories.

In comparison with studies directly or indirectly concerned with the phenomenon of empire, studies on intellectual and literary history per se have been relatively few. There has been a certain number of papers on historiography, but work on religious issues, philosophy, and poetry has only just started. As it seems, with regard to the cultural sphere, comparison of ancient China with ancient Greece has absorbed most scholarly energy.

3.2. Agenda

In my concluding remarks about possible agenda for future research I will take account of the situation just described[139]. As to empire studies, I will restrict myself to a few general remarks, while I will be more detailed with regard to possible topics in the sphere of intellectual and literary history. As will be seen, the political sphere, in particular issues concerning the imperial "software", will repeatedly come into play nonetheless.

3.2.1. Empire Studies

As we have seen, the comparison of the ancient Chinese and Roman empires is in full swing, and it can be expected that it will continue and even intensify in the years to come. To a large extent, this will happen along the established lines, i.e. with concentration on the analysis of the particular components that enabled and determined the functioning of the imperial systems, and on the description and explanation of the ups and downs in the development of the two realms. It is both desirable and to be expected that further topics will be investigated in addition to those already dealt with[140], and that, in view of the increasing number of studies of specific topics, there will also be comprehensive descriptions of certain fields and then also of the structure and history of the two empires *in toto*.

---

[139] For a voice which cautions against possible pitfalls of comparison see Günther (2017).

[140] For a survey of the "tasks, questions, and fields" of future empire research in general cf. Gehler/Rollinger (2014), 26–28, for the suggestion of "subjects and problems" suitable for comparative Sino-Roman studies cf. Loewe (2018), 414–419.

3.2.2. Intellectual and Literary History

Up to now, comparative studies on China and Rome have been devoted, for the most part, to the political sphere. As a consequence, it is particularly the cultural sphere that offers hitherto unexplored research opportunities. That in part they will reach into the field of Empire studies is only natural.

This applies, for example, to *religion*, though one realizes here first of all that it is the period *before* the establishment of the empires which deserves interest. Thus, early ideas about superhuman powers and the means and ways to find out about their will (divination) and to influence their interventions (ritual and prayer) await comparative study, as do the qualification and organization of the relevant personnel[141]. Concerning the empire period, the interaction between traditional beliefs and the new religions Christianity and Buddhism should be further investigated, perhaps with emphasis on the handling of the new religions by the imperial state. As we have seen above, previous research has already examined a number of broader themes and thus created a context for more narrowly defined investigations that can lead to more concrete results.

In the related area of *philosophy*, almost everything remains to be done, since the comparison of ancient Chinese with ancient Greek philosophy has overshadowed the fact that possibilities for a productive juxtaposition of Chinese and Roman texts are not lacking. I give a few examples. A comparison of the theories of the state and of the laws as worked out in the *Hanfeizi* (at the end of the Warring States period) and in Cicero's *De re publica* and *De legibus* (in the final years of the Roman republic) could open up interesting perspectives on ancient Chinese and Roman political thought. By the same token, the side by

---

[141] The topic would be well suited for an expanded comparison including ancient Greece and Egypt.

side analysis of cosmological theories and the ethics of rulership in the thinking of Dong Zhongshu, Han Wudi's court ideologist, could be compared with the similarly simultaneous interest of Seneca, emperor Nero's teacher and advisor, in individual and political ethics and in the natural sciences. Eventually, on a more general level, an investigation of the relation between tradition and reason in Chinese, (Greek,) and Roman thought could contribute to a deeper understanding of the two (three) cultures.

As the report has shown, in the **literary** field, **historiography** has already received relatively much attention. Nevertheless, there is still enough to do. Particularly important as a next step is the systematic inclusion of biography in the comparative analysis. Thus, Suetonius' *Lives of the Caesars* represent the obvious object of comparison with the biographies of the Qin-Han emperors in Sima Qian's *Shiji* and Ban Gu's *Hanshu*, and Nepos' biographies of the generals invite comparison with the biographical sketches of military personnel in these two Chinese works. Furthermore, it is worth noting that anecdotal literature belongs in this context too, and that the relationship between historiography, biography, and anecdotal literature in the two traditions would form a rewarding topic for a general study.

As for **poetry**, a comparative survey of genres and their social contexts could provide a helpful framework for more detailed studies of individual authors and works. As possible objects of concrete comparison, the following come to mind: for the early period, the *Shijing* and the poetry of Livius Andronicus, Naevius, and Ennius, although the fragmentary transmission of the latter makes things difficult; for the period of the established empire, the works and the cultural and socio-political roles of Sima Xiangru, who has been called the "court poet" of Wudi, and of Virgil and Horace, the Augustan poets par excellence; for the period of late antiquity, the poetry and social attitude of men like Tao Yuanming and his contemporary Prudentius. As a closely connected or complementary project, a comparative analysis of concepts and categories of literary criticism, as it developed both here and there, suggests itself.

In addition, I would like to point to a field that, concerning China and Rome, has thus far remained almost entirely without attention: the field of *language* and *script*. It is of interest from the political as well as from the cultural point of view. The substantial role of the standardization of the script in China's unification by the First Emperor is a commonly accepted given[142]; and in the most recent history of Latin, the relation between the spread of the Latin language and the development of the Roman empire forms the subject of the second largest chapter[143]. Thus, it could be a rewarding task to juxtapose the two histories of the relationship between language, script and power, and to observe and interpret their commonalities and differences. But the significance of language and script extends beyond politics. Language and, in special cases, also script tend to be important factors in shaping a community's views of world and life, and so a comparative analysis of Chinese and Latin languages and scripts may, on a very fundamental level, lead to interesting insights concerning the character of Chinese and Roman cultures[144].

Postscriptum: Beyond the "Crosscultural"

Apart from the different amount of effort devoted to intellectual and literary history in one case and to political history in the other, the two reports on Sino-Hellenic and Sino-Roman studies have revealed, at least implicitly, a second difference between the two fields of

---

[142] Cf. Twitchett/Loewe (1986), 56–58.

[143] Cf. Leonhardt (2013), 41–121: Chapter 2 "The Language of the Empire".

[144] For a survey of studies of the relationship between Chinese language and Chinese thought in contrast with the Indo-European situation, see Roetz (2006). For initial comparative reflections regarding the Chinese and the Western way of writing, see Ledderose (2021).

research.

The report on Sino-Hellenic research distinguishes between three types of study. First, there are "crosscultural" studies, which compare the two ancient cultures, describe and explain commonalities and differences, and in this way aim at a better, because de-parochialized, historical understanding. Second, there are "transcultural" studies and third, "cultural critical" studies. What distinguishes the second and third type together from the first is that they are both concerned with the contemporary world insofar as by looking back and analyzing what happened in the past they hope to contribute to the mitigation or solution of problems that trouble the respective cultures in the present.

The report on Sino-Roman studies does not apply this differentiation. A look at the discussion of the individual publications makes clear why. While already among the Sino-Hellenic studies those of the first type are overwhelmingly more numerous than those of the second and third type, the Sino-Roman studies can be said to be exclusively "cross-cultural" in the sense defined above.

It would be interesting to reflect about the reasons for this situation, but such discussion must wait for another occasion. What should be considered, however, is the question whether any consequences for future Sino-Roman studies might emerge from the present state of affairs. It seems to me that this is the case. The "transcultural" and the "cultural critical" approaches open new dimensions for comparative studies of ancient cultures, and therefore it is worth considering the possibility that they can be fruitfully applied to the comparison of ancient China and Rome as well.

According to Zhang, "transcultural comparison no longer keeps ancient Greece and China apart to confine them in their historical contexts, but invites the two cultures to meet each other in the present moment. ... The transcultural comparer ... goes to and fro in the two cultures, and aims at 'transcultural truth' that helps one cope better with the perils of the contemporary world"[145]. As Zhang notes "transcultural comparison finds its adherents more readily in the fields of philosophy and literature"[146] and the examples he gives pertain to these two fields. One is the comparative analysis of Confucian and Aristotelian ethics functioning as a contribution to contemporary virtue ethics[147]. It is not difficult to see that as representative of a third tradition, namely the Roman, Ciceronian ethics could be brought in easily and with profit, enriching the current approaches to the problems. But transcultural comparison is also imaginable between China and Rome exclusively, especially in the field of political history, which has not played any role in the transcultural comparison of China and Greece. Looking back at the agenda formulated above, one can see for some of them an easy transfer from the "cross-cultural" into the "transcultural" mode[148]. This holds, for example, for the relation between state and religion, which played a highly important role in some periods of the history of both the Chinese and the Roman Empire. A comparative analysis of the different ways it was handled in Roman and Chinese antiquity might very well be of interest for those who have to deal with it in the contemporary world. For other topics, as the relation between civic participation and efficient state organization, we can assume the same.

Concerning the "cultural critical" comparison, things are less clear. The cultural critic "identifies a major deficiency of one culture (usually, if not always, the culture into which he or she was born) in the light of the other, and uses the other to criticize the self"[149]. In the one example that Zhang presents, it is Western culture that is criticized in the light of

---

[145] See above p. 273.

[146] See above p. 273.

[147] See above pp. 278–281.

[148] The fact that both models sometimes overlap is stated by Zhang (see above p. 274). What remains is a difference in emphasis (loc.cit.): "the transcultural model stresses the solution to the problem for the here and now, rather than the causal explanations for how the ancients tackled the problem."

[149] See above p. 281.

Chinese culture, and Greek and Chinese antiquity come in to demonstrate that the problematic trait of Western culture and the Chinese alternative are deeply imbedded in their respective traditions[150].

Given the generality of this approach, it is difficult to imagine how reference to Roman culture can play an independent role in such a comparison. Of course, Rome can be referred to as part of the Western tradition, and this may strengthen the case being made. But this would only be a supporting role. The possibility that remains is to look for traits in Western culture that one would trace back to ancient Rome rather than to ancient Greece, and to which an alternative would be found not in Greece but in China. That such traits exist cannot be denied a priori. What can be said is that they are not obvious at first sight.

Bibliography

Alcock, S.E. / D'Altroy, T.N. / Morrison, K.D. / Snoopily, C.M. (eds.) 2001, *Empires: Perspectives from Archaeology and History*, Cambridge.

Arnason, J.P. / Raaflaub, K.A. (eds.) 2011, *The Roman Empire in Context. Historical and Comparative Perspectives*, Oxford.

Auyang, S.Y. 2014, *The Dragon and the Eagle: The Rise and Fall of the Chinese and Roman Empires*, New York.

Balbo, A. / Ahn, J. (eds.) 2019, *Confucius and Cicero: Old Ideas for a New World, New Ideas for an Old World*, (= Roma Sinica 1), Berlin-Boston.

Balbo, A. / Ahn, J. / Kim, K. (eds.) 2022, *Empire and Politics in the Eastern and Western Civilizations: Searching for a "Respublica Romanosinica"*, (= Roma Sinica 2), Berlin-Boston.

Bang, P.F. 2008, *The Roman Bazaar: A Comparative Study of Trade and Markets in a Tributary Empire*, Cambridge.

Bang, P.F. 2009, "Commanding and Consuming the World: Empire, Tribute, and Trade in Roman and Chinese History", in: W. Scheidel (ed.) 2009, 100–120.

Bang, P.F. / Bayly, C.A. (eds.) 2003, "Comparing Pre-Modern Empires", *The Medieval History Journal*, Vol. 6.2 (special issue).

---

[150] See above pp. 282–286.

Bang, P.F. / Bayly, C.A. (eds.) 2011, *Tributary Empires in Global History*, Basingstoke.

Bang, P.F. / Bayly, C.A. / Scheidel, W. (eds.) 2021, *The Oxford World History of Empire*, 2 vols., Oxford.

Bang, P.F. / Kołodziejczyk, D. (eds.) 2012, *Universal Empire: A Comparative Approach to Imperial Culture and Representation in Eurasian History*, Cambridge.

Bang, P.F. / Turner, K. 2015, "Kingship and Elite-Formation", in: W. Scheidel (ed.) 2015, 11−38.

Beck, H. 2021, "Registers of 'the People' in Greece, Rome, and China", in: H. Beck / G. Vankeerberghen (eds.) 2021, 193−224.

Beck, H. / Vankeerberghen, G. (eds.) 2021, *Rulers and Ruled in Ancient Greece, Rome and China*, Cambridge.

Brennan, T.C. 2015, "Toward a Comparative Understanding of the Executive Decision-Making Process in China and Rome", in: W. Scheidel (ed.) 2015, 39−55.

Brennan, T.C. / Hsing, I. 2010, "The Eternal City and the City of Eternal Peace", in: M. Nylan / M. Loewe (eds.) 2010, 186−212.

Brown, M. / Zhang, Zh. 2021, "A Tale of Two Stones: Social Memory in Roman Greece and Han China", in: H. Beck / G. Vankeerberghen (eds.) 2021, 70−101.

Campany, R.F. 2017, "'Buddhism enters China' in Early Medieval China", in: M.-Ch. Poo / H.A. Drake / L. Raphals (eds.) 2017, 13−34.

Chatterjee, P. 2017, "Ancient Statues, Christian City: Constantinople and the *Parastaseis Syntomoi Chronikai*", in: M.-Ch. Poo / H.A. Drake / L. Raphals (eds.) 2017, 203−215.

Chin, T.T. 2016, "What is Imperial Cosmopolitanism? Revisiting *Kosmopolitēs* and *Mundanus*", in: M. Lavan / R.E. Payne / J. Weisweiler (eds.) 2016, 129−151.

Clarke, K. 2008, "Text and Image: Mapping the Roman World", in: F.-H. Mutschler / A. Mittag (eds.) 2008, 195−214.

Denecke, W. 2014, *Classical World Literatures: Sino-Japanese and Greco-Roman Comparisons*, Oxford.

Dettenhofer, M.H. 2006, "Das römische Imperium und das China der Han-Zeit: Ansätze zu einer historischen Komparatistik", *Latomus* 65, 879−897.

Dettenhofer, M.H. 2009, "Eunuchs, Women, and Imperial Courts", in: W. Scheidel (ed.) 2009, 83−99.

Dihle, A. 2008, "City and Empire", in: F.-H. Mutschler / A. Mittag (eds.) 2008, 5−28.

Drake, H.A. 2017, "Christianity and Rome: A Study in Power Relationships", in:

M.-Ch. Poo / H.A. Drake / L. Raphals (eds.) 2017, 35–52.

Du, H. 2022, "Translating Time: Writing the Calendar in Early China and Ancient Rome", in: T.J. Sienkewicz / J. Liu (eds.) 2022, 272–296.

Duindam, J. / Harries, J. / Humfress, C. / Hurvitz, N. (eds.) 2013, *Law and Empire. Ideas, Practices, Actors*, Leiden-Boston.

Eich, P. 2015, "The Common Denominator: Late Roman Imperial Bureaucracy from a Comparative Perspective", in: W. Scheidel (ed.) 2015, 90–149.

Eisenstadt, S.N. 1963, *The Political Systems of Empires*, New York.

Engels, D. 2017, "Construction de normes et morphologie culturelle. Empire romain, chinois, sassanide et fatimide — une comparison historique", in: T. Itgenshorst / P. Le Doze (eds.), *La Norme sous la République et le Haut-Empire Romains: Élaboration, Diffusion et Contournements*, Bordeaux (Scripta Antiqua 96), 53–74.

Engels, D. 2020, "'Reinheit' als Herrscherqualität im ideologischen Narrativ der großen Universalherrscher der alten Welt: Rom, China, Indien und Iran", in: B. Eckhardt / C. Leonhard / K. Zimmermann (eds.), *Reinheit und Autorität in den Kulturen des antiken Mittelmeerraumes*, Baden-Baden (Religion und Politik 21), 19–54.

Engels, D. 2021a, "Historical Necessity or Biographical Singularity: Some Aspects in the Biographies of C. Iulius Caesar and Qin Shi Huangdi", in: H. Beck / G. Vankeerberghen (eds.) 2021, 328–368.

Engels, D. 2021b, "Tao Yuanming's 'Peach Blossom Source' and the Ideal of the 'Golden Age' in Classical Antiquity: Utopias in Ancient China and Classical Antiquity", in: P. Destrée / J. Opsomer / G. Roskam (eds.),*Utopias in Ancient Thought*, Berlin-Boston (Beiträge zur Altertumskunde 395), 275–301.

Feldherr, A. / Hardy, G. (eds.) 2011, *The Oxford History of Historical Writing.Vol. 1: Beginnings to AD 600*, Oxford.

Ford, R.B. 2020, *Rome, China, and the Barbarians: Ethnographic Traditions and the Transformation of Empires*, Cambridge.

Gärtner, H.A. / Ye, M. 2008, "The Impact of the Empire's Crises on Historiography and Historical Thinking in Late Antiquity", in: F.-H. Mutschler / A. Mittag (eds.) 2008, 323–345.

Gehler, M. / Rollinger, R. (eds.) 2014, *Imperien und Reiche in der Weltgeschichte. Epochenübergreifende und globalhistorische Vergleiche*, 2 vols., Wiesbaden.

Gizewski, C. 1994, "Römische und alte chinesische Geschichte im Vergleich: Zur Möglichkeit eines gemeinsamen Altertumsbegriffs", *Klio* 76, 271–302.

Günther, S. 2017, "*Ad diversas historias comparandas*? A First, Short and Droysenbased Reply to Mutschler and Scheidel", *Journal of Ancient Civilizations*

32/1,123−126.

Harries, J. 2013, "Roman Law from City State to World Empire", in: J. Duindam / J. Harries / C. Humfress / N. Hurvitz (eds.) 2013, 45−61.

Høgel, C. 2019, "*Humanitas*: Universalism, Equivocation, and Basic Criterion", in: A. Balbo / J. Ahn (eds.) 2019, 129−139.

Hsing, I. 1980, "Rome and China: The Role of the Armies in the Imperial Succession: A Comparative Study", PhD thesis, University of Hawai'i at Manoa.

Huang, Y. / Mutschler, F.-H. 2008, "The Emergence of Empire: Rome and the Surrounding World in Historical Narratives from the Late Third Century BC to the Early First Century AD", in: F.-H. Mutschler / A. Mittag (eds.) 2008, 91−114.

Hurlet, F. (ed.) 2008, *Les Empires: Antiquité et Moyen Age. Analyse Comparée*, Rennes.

Jansen, Th. 2008, "New Tendencies, Religious and Philosophical, in the Chinese World of the Third through Sixth Centuries", in: F.-H. Mutschler / A. Mittag (eds.) 2008, 397−419.

Kern, M. 2008, "Announcements from the Mountains: the Stele Inscriptions of the Qin First Emperor", in: F.-H. Mutschler / A. Mittag (eds.) 2008, 217−240.

Kim, H.J. 2015, "Ancient History and the Classics from a Comparative Perspective: China and the Greco-Roman World", *Ancient West & East* 14, 253−274.

Kim, H.J. 2017, "Justin Martyr and Tatian: Christian Reactions to Encounters with Greco-Roman Culture and Imperial Persecution", in: M.-Ch. Poo / H.A. Drake / L. Raphals (eds.) 2017, 69−79.

Kim, H.J. / Vervaet, F.J. / Adali, S.F. (eds.) 2017, *Eurasian Empires in Antiquity and the Early Middle Ages. Contact and Exchange between the Graeco-Roman World, Inner Asia and China*, Cambridge.

Kim, K. 2019, "*Pietas* in *pro Sexto Roscio* of Cicero and Confucian 孝 (*xiao*)", in: A. Balbo / J. Ahn (eds.) 2019, 155−169.

Kim, M.L. 2021, "Food Distribution for the People: Welfare, Food, and Feasts in Qin/Han China and in Rome", in: H. Beck / G. Vankeerberghen (eds.) 2021, 225−265.

Kim, W. / Kim, K. 2022, "*Pax Romana* and *Pax Sinica*: Some Historical Aspects", in: A. Balbo / J. Ahn / K. Kim (eds.) 2022, 177−190.

King, R.A.H. / Schilling, D. (eds.) 2011, *How One Should live? Comparing Ethics in Ancient China and Greco-Roman Antiquity*, Berlin-Boston.

Lavan, M. / Payne, R.E. / Weisweiler, J. (eds.) 2016, *Cosmopolitanism and Empire. Universal Rulers, Local Elites, and Cultural Integration in the Ancient Near East and Mediterranean*, Oxford.

Ledderose, L. 2021, *China Schreibt Anders*, Stuttgart.

Leonhardt, J. 2013, *Latin. Story of a World Language*, Cambridge (Mass.) – London (originally *Latein: Geschichte einer Weltsprache*, München 2009).

Lewis, M.E. 2009, "Gift Circulation and Charity in the Han and Roman Empires", in: W. Scheidel (ed.) 2009, 121–136.

Lewis, M.E. 2015, "Public Spaces in Cities in the Roman and Han Empires", in: W. Scheidel (ed.) 2015, 204–229.

Lewis, M.E. 2017, "Honour and Shame in Han China", in: H.J. Kim / F.J. Vervaet / S.F. Adah (eds.) 2017, 110–132.

Lieu, S.N.C. 2017, "The Serpent from Persia: Manicheism in Rome and China", in: H.J. Kim / F.J. Vervaet / S.F. Adah (eds.) 2017, 174–202.

Liu, Ch. 2022, "Writing in Misfortune: Ovid's *Heroides* in Light of Chinese Poetic Perspectives", in: T.J. Sienkewicz / J. Liu (eds.) 2022, 155–176.

Liu, J.Y. (ed.) 2021, Quan qiu shi ye xia de gu luo ma shi ren ao wei de yan jiu qian yan (*New Frontiers of Research on Ovid in a Global Context*), Peking [Xifang gudianxue yanjiu xilie congshu (Studies in Western Classics Series)].

Lloyd, G.E.R. / Zhao, J.J. (eds.) 2018, *Ancient Greece and China Compared*, Oxford.

Loewe, M. 2018, "Afterword", in: G.E.R. Lloyd / J.J. Zhao (eds.) 2018, 410–419.

Lorenz, G. 1990, "Das Imperium Romanum und das China der Han-Dynastie. Gedanken und Materialien zu einem Vergleich", *Informationen für Geschichtslehrer zur postuniversitären Fortbildung* 12, 1990, 9–60.

Lu, Z. 2017, "When Buddhism Meets the *Chen-Wei* Prophetic and Apocryphal Discourse: A Religious Encounter in Early Medieval China", in: M.-Ch. Poo / H.A. Drake / L. Raphals (eds.) 2017, 81–89.

Malinowski, G. 2022, "*Imperator-Huangdi*: The Idea of the Highest Universal Divine Ruler in the West and China", in: A. Balbo / J. Ahn / K. Kim (eds.) 2022, 5–22.

Marsili, F. 2013/4, "The Ghosts of Monotheism: Heaven, Fortune, and Universalism in Early Chinese and Greco-Roman Historiography", *Fragments* 3, 43–77.

Martin, T.R. 2010, *Herodotus and Sima Qian: The First Great Historians of Greece and China. A Brief History with Documents*, Boston–New York.

Mercier, St. 2019, "Becoming human(e): Confucius' Way to 仁 and the Imitation of Christ in Yi Byeok's *Essence of Sacred Doctrine* (圣教要旨; *Seonggyo yoji*)", in: A. Balbo / J. Ahn (eds.) 2019, 141–153.

Mittag, A. 2008, "Forging Legacy: The Pact between Empire and Historiography in Ancient China", in: F.-H. Mutschler / A. Mittag (eds.) 2008, 143–165.

Mittag, A. / Mutschler, F.-H. 2010, "Empire and Humankind: Historical Universalism in Ancient China and Rome", *Journal of Chinese Philosophy* 4,

2010, 527–555.

Mittag, A. / Ye, M. 2008, "Empire on the Brink: Chinese Historiography in the Post-Han Period", in: F.-H. Mutschler / A. Mittag (eds.) 2008, 347–369.

Morris, I. / Scheidel, W. (eds.) 2009, *The Dynamics of Ancient Empires: State Power from Assyria to Byzantium*, New York.

Mutschler, F.-H. 1997, "Vergleichende Beobachtungen zur griechisch-römischen und altchinesischen Geschichtsschreibung", *Saeculum* 48, 213–153.

Mutschler, F.-H. 2003, "Zu Sinnhorizont und Funktion griechischer, römischer und altchinesischer Geschichtsschreibung", in: K.J. Hölkeskamp et al. (eds.), *Sinn (in) der Antike*, Mainz, 33–54.

Mutschler, F.-H. 2006, "Tacitus und Sima Qian: Eine Annäherung", *Philologus* 150, 115–135.

Mutschler, F.-H. 2007a, "Tacitus und Sima Qian: Persönliche Erfahrung und historiographische Perspektive", *Philologus* 151, 127–152.

Mutschler, F.-H. 2007b, "Sima Qian and his Western Colleagues: On Possible Categories of Description", *History & Theory* 46, 194–200.

Mutschler, F.-H. 2008a, "Tacite (et Tite Live) et Sima Qian: La vision politique d'historiens latins et chinois", *Bulletin de l'Association Guillaume Budé* 2008.2, 123–155.

Mutschler, F.-H. 2008b, "The Problem of Imperial Historiography in Rome", in: F.-H. Mutschler / A. Mittag (eds.) 2008, 119–141.

Mutschler, F.-H. 2015, "Ancient Historiographies Compared", in: Ch.-Ch. Huang / J. Rüsen (eds.), *Chinese Historical Thinking: An Intercultural Discussion*, Göttingen, 103–112.

Mutschler, F.-H. 2019, "Comparing Confucius and Cicero: Problems and Possibilities", in: A. Balbo / J. Ahn (eds.) 2019, 7–25.

Mutschler, F.-H. / Mittag, A. (eds.) 2008, *Conceiving the Empire: China and Rome Compared*, Oxford.

Mutschler, F.-H. / Mittag, A. 2010, "Empire and Humankind: Historical Universalism in Ancient China and Rome", *Journal of Chinese Philosophy* 37.4, 527–555.

Noreña, C.F. 2015a, "Chang'an and Rome: Structural Parallels and the Logics of Urban Forms", in: M. Nylan / G. Vankeerberghen (eds.) 2015, 75–97.

Noreña, C.F. 2015b, "Urban Systems in the Han and Roman Empires: State Power and Social Control", in W. Scheidel (ed.) 2015, 181–203.

Noreña, C.F. 2021, "Private Associations and Urban Experience in the Han and Roman Empires", in: H. Beck / G. Vankeerberghen (eds.) 2021, 102–132.

Nylan, M. 2008, "The Rhetoric of 'Empire' in the Classical Era in China", in: F.-H. Mutschler / A. Mittag (eds.) 2008, 39–64.

Nylan, M. / Loewe, M. (eds.) 2010, *China's Early Empires: A Re-appraisal*, Cambridge.

Nylan, M. / Vankeerberghen, G. (eds.) 2015, *Chang'an 26 BCE. An Augustan Age in China*, Seattle.

O'Daly, G. 2008, "New Tendencies, Religious and Philosophical, in the Roman Empire of the Third to Early Fifth Centuries", in: F.-H. Mutschler / A. Mittag (eds.) 2008, 373–396.

Olberding, G.P. 2021, "Liberation as Burlesque: The Death of the Tyrant", in: H. Beck / G. Vankeerberghen (eds.) 2021, 300–327.

Pina Polo, F. 2021, "Rhetoric, Oratory, and People in Ancient Rome and Early China", in: H. Beck / G. Vankeerberghen (eds.) 2021, 133–155.

Pines, Y. 2008, "Imagining the Empire? Concepts of 'Primeval Unity' in Pre-Imperial Historiographic Tradition", in: F.-H. Mutschler / A. Mittag (eds.) 2008, 67–90.

Pirazzoli-t'Serstevens, M. 2008, "Imperial Aura and the Image of the Other in Han Art", in: F.-H. Mutschler / A. Mittag (eds.) 2008, 299–317.

Poo, M.-Ch. 2017, "The Taming of Ghosts in Early Chinese Buddhism", in: M.-Ch. Poo / H.A. Drake, / L. Raphals (eds.) 2017, 165–181.

Poo, M.-Ch. / Drake, H.A. / Raphals, L. (eds.) 2017, *Old Society, New Belief*, Oxford.

Puett, M. 2015, "Ghosts, Gods, and the Coming Apocalypse: Empire and Religion in Early China and Ancient Rome", in: W. Scheidel (ed.) 2015, 230–259.

Raaflaub, K.A. (ed.) 2007, *War and Peace in the Ancient World*, Oxford.

Raphals, L. 2017, "Conclusion: Comparative Perspectives on China and Rome", in: M.-Ch. Poo / H.A. Drake / L. Raphals (eds.) 2017, 257–271.

Robinson, R. 2021, "Employing Knowledge: A Case Study in Calendar Reforms in the Early Han and Roman Empires", in: H. Beck / G. Vankeerberghen (eds.) 2021, 369–396.

Roetz, H. 2006, "Die chinesische Sprache und das chinesische Denken. Positionen einer Debatte", *Bochumer Jahrbuch zur Ostasienforschung* 30, 9–37.

Rosenstein, N. 2009, "War, State Formation, and the Evolution of Military Institutions in Ancient China and Rome", in: W. Scheidel (ed.) 2009, 24–51.

Rosenstein, N. 2016, "Review of S.Y. Auyang, *The Dragon and the Eagle*", *American Journal of Philology* 137, 740–743.

Scheidel, W. (ed.) 2009, *Rome and China: Comparative Perspectives on Ancient World Empires*, Oxford.

Scheidel, W. 2009a, "From the 'Great Convergence' to the 'First Great Divergence': Roman and Qin-Han State Formation and Its Aftermath", in: W. Scheidel (ed.)

2009, 11–23.

Scheidel, W. 2009b, "The Monetary Systems of the Han and Roman Empires", in: W. Scheidel (ed.) 2009, 137–207.

Scheidel, W. 2010, "Coin Quality, Coin Quantity, and Coin Value in Early China and the Roman World", *American Journal of Numismatics* 22, 93–118.

Scheidel, W. 2011, "Fiscal Regimes and the 'First Great Divergence' between Eastern and Western Eurasia", in: P.F. Bang / C.A. Bayly (eds.) 2011, 193–204.

Scheidel, W. (ed.) 2015, *State Power in Ancient China and Rome*, Oxford.

Scheidel, W. 2015a, "State Revenue and Expenditure in the Han and Roman Empires", in: W. Scheidel (ed.) 2015, 150–180.

Scheidel, W. 2017, "Slavery and Forced Labor in Early China and the Roman World", in: H.J. Kim / F.J. Vervaet / S.F. Adali (eds.) 2017, 133–150.

Scheidel, W. 2018, Comparing Comparisons, in: G.E.R. Lloyd / J.J. Zhao (eds.), 2018, 40–58.

Schmidt-Glintzer, H. 2008, Diagram (*tu*) and Text (*wen*): Mapping the Chinese World, in: F.-H. Mutschler / A. Mittag (eds.) 2008, 169–193.

Schneider, R.M. 2008, "Image and Empire. The Shaping of Augustan Rome", in: F.-H. Mutschler / A. Mittag (eds.) 2008, 269–298.

Sellers, M.N.S. 2022, "Empire and Politics in Eastern and Western Civilizations", in: A. Balbo / J. Ahn / K. Kim (eds.) 2022, 165–175.

Shankman, S. / Durrant, S. 2000, *The Siren and the Sage: Knowledge and Wisdom in Ancient Greece and China*, London–New York.

Shi, Ch. 2022, "Reading Two Exiles in Rome and China: Philosophical Comfort, Literary Consolation, and the Impossible Mourning", in: T.J. Sienkewicz / J. Liu (eds.) 2022, 320–343.

Sienkewicz, T.J. / Liu, J. (eds.) 2022, *Ovid in China. Reception, Translation, and Comparison*, Berlin-Boston.

Takada, Y. 2019, "Cicero and Confucius: Similitude in Disguise", in: A. Balbo / J. Ahn (eds.) 2019, 189–199.

Teggart, F.J. 1939, *Rome and China. A Study of Correlations in Historical Events*, Berkeley.

Turner, K. 2009, "Law and Punishment in the Formation of Empire", in: W. Scheidel (ed.) 2009, 52–82.

Turner, K.G. 2013, "Laws, Bureaucrats, and Imperial Women in China's Early Empires", in: J. Duindam / J. Harries / C. Humfress / N. Hurvitz (eds.) 2013, 63–85.

Twitchett, D. / Loewe, M. 1986, *The Cambridge History of China, Volume I: The Ch'in and Han Empires, 221 B.C.–A.D. 220*, Cambridge.

Vankeerberghen, G. 2021, "Of Gold and Purple: Nobles in Western Han China and Republican Rome", in: H. Beck / G. Vankeerberghen (eds.) 2021, 25‒69.

Vervaet, F.J. 2017, "Honour and Shame in the Roman Republic", in: H.J. Kim / F.J. Vervaet / S.F. Adah (eds.) 2017, 85‒109.

Walter, J. 2016, "*terrae motus* und *dizhen* (地震) — Alles anders am anderen Ende der Welt? Vergleichende Betrachtungen zum Umgang mit Erdbeben in Geschichtswerken aus dem Römischen Reich und dem Alten China", in: J. Borsch / L. Carrara (eds.), *Erdbeben in der Antike: Deutungen–Folgen–Repräsentationen*, Tübingen, 249‒260.

Wan, Sz.-k. 2017, "Colonizing the Supernatural: How *Daimōn* became Demonized in Late Antiquity", in: M.-Ch. Poo / H.A. Drake / L. Raphals (eds.) 2017, 147‒164.

Wang, Zh. 2015, "World Views and Military Policies in the Early Roman and Western Han Empires", Diss. Leiden.

Witschel, Chr. 2008, "The *Res Gestae Divi Augusti* and the Roman Empire", in: F.-H. Mutschler / A. Mittag (eds.) 2008, 241‒266.

Xiong, Y. 2022, "Themes of Women's Vengeance and Filicide in Ovid's *Metamorphoses*: Reception and Comparison in Modern Chinese Literature", in: T.J. Sienkewicz / J. Liu (eds.) 2022, 237‒260.

Yacobson, A. 2021, "Augustus, the Roman Plebs and the Dictatorship: 22 BCE and Beyond", in: H. Beck / G. Vankeerberghen (eds.) 2021, 269‒299.

Yates, R.D.S. 2021, "Female Commoners and the Law in Early Imperial China: Evidence from Recently Recovered Documents with Some Comparisons with Classical Rome", in: H. Beck / G. Vankeerberghen (eds.) 2021, 156‒192.

Zhao, D. 2015, "The Han Bureaucracy: Its Origin, Nature, and Development", in: W. Scheidel (ed.) 2015, 56‒89.

Zhao, D.Q. 2016, "Barbarians in Rome and China: A Comparative Analysis of Sima Qian and Tacitus", Graduate thesis, University of Melbourne.

Zhao, D.Q. 2018, "Foreigners and Propaganda: War and Peace in the Imperial Images of Augustus and Qin Shi Huangdi", MA thesis, University of Melbourne.

Zhou, Y. 2017, "Adaptation and Assimilation of Buddhism in China as reflected in Monastic Architecture", in: M.-Ch. Poo / H.A. Drake, / L. Raphals (eds.) 2017, 217‒230.

Zhu, W. 2008, "Interlude: Kingship and Empire", in: F.-H. Mutschler / A. Mittag (eds.) 2008, 29‒37.

(Fritz-Heiner Mutschler, Professor Emeritus, Technische Universität Dresden)

Comparative Studies of Ancient Egypt and Early China

Anthony Barbieri-Low

In sharp contrast with the recent voluminous scholarship comparing Early China to either Classical Greece or the Roman Empire (see reviews by Zhang Wei and Fritz-Heiner Mutschler in this issue), the body of work drawing comparative insights between Ancient Egypt and Early China is relatively meager. This is quite unfortunate, since the two venerable and long-enduring civilizations share some compelling structural similarities and abound with potential subjects for comparison that could lead to critical new insights into the nature and history of both.

We can point to several possibilities as to why the field of Egypt/ China comparisons remains underdeveloped in contrast to the burgeoning field of China/Greco-Roman studies. First, both Egyptology and the Early China field are relatively small. There are less than sixty PhD granting programs in Egyptology worldwide with only ten in North America[1]. By my informal count, there are just over two dozen university faculty in North America who specialize in Early China, with a lower number in Europe. This contrasts with the over five hundred

---

[1] https://egypt.fitz.ms/institutions.html.

faculty positions in Greco-Roman studies, just at English-speaking institutions. Second, the two fields have traditionally been quite insular. Until recently, and with a few notable exceptions, most Egyptologists have focused on philology, archaeology, and art history, believing that the best way to understand Egypt is to study only ancient Egypt, rather than looking at insights gained from a broader comparative study of ancient civilizations[2]. A recent issue of the *Journal of Egyptian History,* dedicated to global history in Egyptology, signals a sharp and welcome reversal in this traditional orientation[3]. The Early China field has also been traditionally quite parochial, focusing on philosophy, philology, and art and archaeology, but thanks to the instigation of scholars coming from the Greco-Roman fields, more China scholars are now publishing comparative scholarship in edited volumes or joining research institutes on Global Antiquity. But once again, Ancient Egypt is usually left out of the party.

A third reason for the lack of comparative engagement with Egypt on the part of Early China scholars involves challenging linguistic barriers. While several Early China scholars have a decent familiarity with the Greek or Latin languages, and others have an adequate grounding in ancient Mediterranean history, only a few have any training in Egyptian language or any other aspect of Egyptology. Some scholars with native Chinese linguistic ability who have trained in PhD programs in Egyptology have demonstrated the ability to read texts from both traditions.

Another possible reason for the paucity of studies comparing Ancient Egypt with Early China involves the types of surviving textual materials from each civilization. The "classical" texts from Middle Kingdom Egypt include ritual texts, wisdom literature, admonitions,

---

[2]   Trigger (1993), 2.
[3]   Moreno García, Morris, and Miniaci (2020).

long-form poetry, and some narrative tales and personal letters. Similar texts survive from the New Kingdom, in addition to various official documents related to royal tomb construction or legal administration. However, based on current evidence, there appears to have been no tradition in Ancient Egypt of narrative history, beyond simple chronicles or narrations of specific battles. This is in sharp contrast to the voluminous histories composed in early China, such as the *Historical Records* (Shiji 史記) of Sima Qian 司馬遷 or the *History of the Former Han* (Han shu 漢書) of Ban Gu 班固, or the writings of the so-called "hundred schools" of philosophy. Therefore, those scholars interested in comparative historiography or comparative philosophy are attracted to comparison with Greece or Rome, where similar written traditions developed. For comprehensive reviews of this scholarship, see the appropriate subsections in the articles by Zhang Wei and Fritz-Heiner Mutschler in this issue.

There is also the sense among many China scholars that Ancient Egypt is not a valid pair for comparison with Early China, because the peak of each civilization occurred at a different point in time on an absolute chronological scale. The New Kingdom of Egypt reached its peak in the 14th century BCE, while the first extensive territorial empire in China was only founded by the First Emperor of Qin in 221 BCE. These skeptical scholars also view Ancient Egypt as a primitive or archaic state that holds almost nothing in common with a developed imperial bureaucratic state like the Qin or Han empires. This is a mistaken view born of old Orientalist assumptions about the mystical ancient Egyptians and from an unfamiliarity with details about the powerful and complex New Kingdom Egyptian state.

An unspoken assumption behind these judgments appears to be a misguided concern for contemporaneity, insisting that two cultures must be roughly contemporary to be comparable. It seems more suitable to them to compare Classical Greece (ca. 510−323 BCE) and Warring

States China (ca. 453–221 BCE), especially in areas like comparative philosophy, historiography, or literature, since both cultures not only shared the phenomenon of a splintered multi-state political system, but also because they occupied nearly the same time period on an absolute chronological scale. The same assumption also underlines comparisons between the Roman Empire (27 BCE–476 CE) with the Han empire (202 BCE–220 CE) of China. Contemporaneity is completely irrelevant for solid comparative study. The two societies only need to share some similar underlying structural features to be comparable; the time period of their fluorescence is immaterial.

In Figure 1, reproduced from Barbieri-Low (2021), I show the customary comparative dyads for China-Greece and China-Rome comparisons, and suggest that the New Kingdom of Egypt and the Qin and Han empires of China is a compelling pair from similar stages of civilizational development. Bruce G. Trigger (2003) also suggests that the Old Kingdom of Egypt and the late Shang Dynasty at Anyang (ca. 1250–1045 BCE) is another suitable pair, and looking to an earlier stage, John Baines (2014) argues that the late Predynastic Period in Egypt (Dynasty 0, 3200–3050 BCE) and the Erligang Period in China (ca. 1500–1300 BCE) would also be at a comparable stage (not depicted in Figure 1).

Some of the first rudimentary comparisons between Ancient Egypt and Early China occurred in the nineteenth century and mostly revolved around the nature and evolution of the Chinese writing system. Some early superficial studies claimed that Chinese writing was derived from Egyptian hieroglyphs. Remarkably, it was actually an insight drawn from the Chinese *fanqie* 反切 systems for sounding out words, including those of foreign origin, that indirectly helped lead to the decipherment of the Rosetta Stone by Jean-François

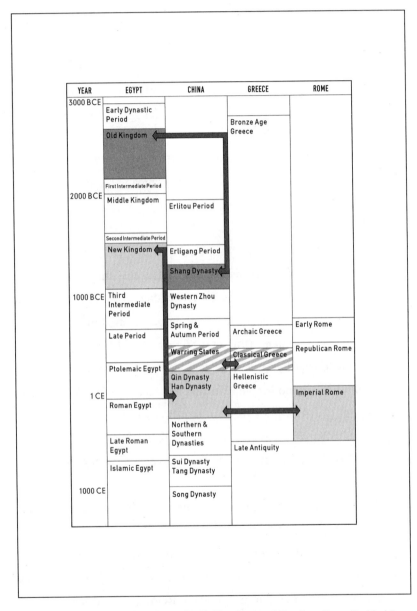

Figure 1: Comparative Pairs for Early Civilizations and Empires. From Barbieri-Low 2021, 14 fig. I.1

Champollion[4].

In their surveys of Sino-Hellenic studies and Rome-China comparative work, Zhang Wei and Fritz Heiner Mutschler (this issue) were presented with such a plentiful amount of earlier scholarship, that they were able to organize their overviews by themes, topical areas, and theoretical approaches. Since the scholarship comparing Ancient Egypt and Early China is not so plentiful at present, I will survey this work in chronological order by author. For the purposes of this review article, I will divide previous studies into two groupings, those broadly comparative works published during the first three-quarters of the twentieth century and those more detailed studies published since the early 1970s.

Earlier Comparative Studies Incorporating Ancient Egypt and Early China

Karl A. Wittfogel

In the first half of the twentieth century, the comparative study of Egypt and China was central to the formulation of the theory of "hydraulic civilization" in historical sociologist Karl Wittfogel's (1938, 1956, 1957) work and the more developed anthropological theories of cultural evolution it influenced, such as Julian Steward's (1949) "Cultural Causality and Law." Over two decades from the 1930s to the 1950s, Wittfogel developed his influential and controversial theory. For

---

[4]   Pope (1999), 65–66, 71, 75–76. The first French Sinologist, Jean-Pierre Abel-Rémusat, had remarked on the *fanqie* 反切 spelling system in his 1811 work *Essai sur la Langue et la Litérature chinoises*, and this influenced his teacher, the Orientalist Silvestre de Sacy, who later that year suggested that the names in the cartouches of the Rosetta Stone must have been spelling out foreign names (which in that case at least, they were). De Sacy was also the teacher of Champollion, who used this insight, and the later writings of Abel-Rémusat (1822) which stated that the majority of Chinese characters have a phonetic (not ideographic) value, in his eventual solution to the basic phonetic nature of the Egyptian writing system.

Wittfogel, the early hydraulic civilizations of Mesopotamia, Egypt, China, and highland Mexico were characterized by their setting in an arid or semiarid landscape next to a large body of water. He theorized that political centralization first arose in these areas to overcome a problem of labor organization, for he believed that only strong leadership could bring together the manpower needed to build and maintain the large-scale works of irrigation and flood control that could tame the bodies of water and make agriculture possible in these arid zones. Thus, water control was the "prime mover" that brought about the rise of the first states. Wittfogel further argued that the states that arose in these areas were fundamentally different in nature from those decentralized states that arose in places like Iron Age Europe, which did not practice irrigation agriculture on any scale during antiquity. The states in China and Egypt were "Oriental despotisms," characterized by dense populations, centralized political power, hierarchical social orders, elaborate bureaucracies, a command economy, and practical sciences, but lacking any internal checks on absolute power, such as autonomous churches, knighthoods, or guilds. He saw them as static civilizations (an idea drawn from the works of Hegel), without any kind of political evolution toward the type of democracy seen in places like Greece.

Wittfogel's theory was inspired by his work on later periods of Chinese history, when the state engineered massive waterworks like the Grand Canal and operated them through complex bureaucracies. He also studied the Early Dynastic period in Mesopotamia, where city-states maintained complex canal irrigation networks. However, when Wittfogel was writing, the archaeology of early states was in its nascent stages, and when his theories were later put to the test of the shovel by archaeologists, they did not fair very well. Archaeology in Mesopotamia, Mexico, China, India, and Egypt has revealed that intensive agriculture and state formation developed in those areas before any large-scale irrigation works were attempted. There is evidence in Egypt and China of some smaller-scale local or regional hydraulic works in the early dynastic periods, but nothing of the scale that would require the sort of massive labor organization or hydraulic-focused bureaucracies envisioned by Wittfogel. It thus appears that the larger works may have been more the result of the rise of the state rather than the cause. In addition, Wittfogel fundamentally misunderstood the nature of North China agriculture, which in the pre-modern period primarily relied on rainfall, supplemented by some well water. So, while irrigation canals like the third century BCE Zheng Guo canal 鄭國渠 of the Qin state were able to reclaim poor soils for agriculture and intensify production through massive hydraulic works, irrigation in general was not required to grow crops in North China.

Shmuel Noah Eisenstadt

In 1963 sociologist S.N. Eisenstadt (1923–2010) published his influential book, *The Political Systems of Empires*[5]. In this lengthy work, Eisenstadt conducts a comparative analysis of what he called "centralized historical bureaucratic empires." Expanding on a Weberian analysis, he defines these as an intermediate stage between earlier feudal or patrimonial states and more modern bureaucratic states, wherein there is relative autonomy of the political subsystem of society and in which the ruler has independent "political goals" which he seeks to accomplish by gaining access to "free-floating resources," like military conscription and direct taxation of the peasantry, and by utilizing a semi-autonomous bureaucracy in his political contention with established groups like the aristocracy. His study seeks to identify the factors that lead to the development and perpetuation of this type of state, and what conditions lead to its evolution or devolution into other forms. Eisenstadt identifies twenty-seven of these historical bureaucratic empires in his text and

---

[5] Eisenstadt (1963).

tables, including Ancient Egypt and imperial China, along with the Roman, Byzantine, and Ottoman empires, the Abbasid Caliphate, and even the Spanish empire in the Americas. In his introduction, he considers China to have constituted this type of state from the Han dynasty up until the end of the Qing dynasty, although in the elaborate tables in the back of his book, and in the narrative of the chapters, he only includes the Tang, Song, Yuan, Ming, and Qing dynasties. For Egypt, he surprisingly identifies the state which governed the Old Kingdom (ca. 2670–2168 BCE) through the Second Intermediate Period (ca. 1640–1548 BCE) as occupying this stage, omitting the much more convincing case of the New Kingdom (ca. 1548–1086 BCE). He considers that the centralized historical bureaucratic empire of Egypt evolved from an earlier patrimonial state and that the one in China developed from a feudal state (i.e., the Zhou)[6].

In his chapters, Eisenstadt refers to the bureaucratic state in China frequently, often in comparison to Rome, Byzantium, or early modern European states. For his sources, he relies mostly on translations and a broad range of secondary scholarship by leading Sinologists like Étienne Balázs, Derk Bodde, Edwin Pulleyblank, Wolfram Eberhard, William Theodore de Bary, Otto Franke, Joseph Levenson, Denis Twitchett, and Robert des Routours. Egypt shows up far less often in Eisenstadt's comparisons, and very rarely in direct comparison with China. His source base for the Egyptian state is also extremely meager, consisting of only a couple dozen works by Egyptologists like Henri Frankfort or John A. Wilson, but he does not even include the translated primary sources of James Henry Breasted. The comparison between pre-New Kingdom Egypt and middle-to-late imperial China is a very poor one, and Eisenstadt even admits it at one point[7]. Even by his own definition,

---

[6] Eisenstadt (1963), 11.

[7] Eisenstadt (1963), 108.

Egypt in the Old and Middle Kingdoms should not have been grouped with his centralized historical bureaucratic empires, since it was clearly still a patrimonial state with poor separation of the political subsystem, with an underdeveloped bureaucracy and no real channels for "political struggle." To compare the Old Kingdom of Egypt with the Ming or Qing dynasties of China makes no sense at all. At times, Eisenstadt is still under the spell of the illusory "Asiatic mode of production," and Wittfogel's "Oriental despotism," when he singles out the Chinese state as being a "predominantly agrarian-bureaucratic, Oriental society"[8].

Robert Carneiro

In 1970, anthropologist Robert Carneiro (1927–2020) published in the journal *Science* his concise and influential theory of primary state formation, called "A Theory of the Origin of the State"[9]. Since Egypt and China are considered to have been the home of two of the five (or six) "pristine states" in the Old and New Worlds, where state-level society arose without influence from another more complex society, any theory of state formation must consider the cases of both Egypt and China to be comprehensive. Later critics characterized Carneiro's theory as a "prime-mover" model (a phrase used by Carneiro himself in his article), since it posits a single overarching factor which drove the process of cultural evolution. For Carneiro, this prime mover was warfare, but not just any type of warfare, for armed conflict is found in all human societies. Specifically, Carneiro pointed to the practice of warfare over land in circumscribed environments that were experiencing population pressure. Since the losers of these conflicts could not flee, this then led to the conquest and subjugation of one group by another, resulting in a "supra-village" political organization, a layered social

---

[8] Eisenstadt (1963), 31.
[9] Carneiro (1970).

hierarchy, and a functional need for permanent leadership with an administrative structure to process tribute, taxes, and coerced labor.

Carneiro's model was originally designed to incorporate those same arid environments that Wittfogel considered, places like the Nile Valley, Indus Valley, Valley of Mexico, and Mesopotamia, where valuable and limited agricultural land was located near a reliable source of water but was bounded in by deserts or mountains that had no agricultural potential. The narrow coastal river valleys of Peru, where early states like the Moche arose, was another area that Carneiro knew well and which he believed fit his model perfectly. But the situation of the Yellow River in North China forced Carneiro to modify his model with two corollaries or "auxiliary hypotheses," since land on either side of the Yellow River was not hemmed in by deserts or mountains as was the case in Egypt or Mesopotamia. So, to take China into account, Carneiro added the first corollary of "resource concentration," in which there was a "steep ecological gradient" as one moved away from the river and the prime land, resulting in a type of bounded environment almost as limited as the hard line of the desert in Egypt. The second corollary, "social circumscription," added the suggestion that village groups in densely-populated core areas could be so hemmed in by other human groups that the restriction on out-migration was almost as severe as having a mountain or desert blocking one's exodus after losing a war. However, just like Wittfogel had done a few decades earlier, Carneiro's limited knowledge of the practice of agriculture in North China led him to assume that farmers must have relied on river-based irrigation from the dangerous Yellow River, and for that reason, they had to live near it. That may be true to a limited extent, since the fertile loess deposits from previous large-scale flooding would have been deposited near the river course and would have been attractive to new farmers. But North China agriculture in the period of state formation around 2000 BCE was almost exclusively based on rainfall and did not draw water from the mighty

Yellow River for irrigation. Carneiro also assumed severe population pressure on prime agricultural land in North China, leading to "social circumscription," but this is not supported by archaeological settlement or survey data.

Paul Wheatley

During the 1950s and 1960s the study of premodern urbanism was an exploding field in history, sociology, and anthropology, and in 1950, archaeologist V. Gordon Childe extended this debate into the ancient period when he formulated his famous ten criteria of the "Urban Revolution" in a classic article[10]. In 1966, Mesopotamian archaeologist Robert McC Adams, published his ground-breaking comparative study, *The Evolution of Urban Society,* which contained an in-depth comparison of the formation of cities in ancient Mesopotamia and pre-Columbian Mesoamerica[11]. Then, in 1971 geographer Paul Wheatley (1921–1999) responded to this scholarship, and to older and highly influential definitions of the city by Max Weber, with his monumental work *The Pivot of the Four Quarters*[12]. Wheatley was concerned that earlier studies of urban origins had been affected by the modern and Eurocentric biases of Max Weber (who based his formulation on the "free cities" of early modern Europe) and the materialist bias of Childe and had not fully taken the case of Shang and Zhou China into account.

Wheatley's study is a comparison of "primary urban generation" in seven pre-modern societies: Mesopotamia, Egypt, the Indus Valley, the North China Plain, Mesoamerica, the central Andes, and the Yoruba territories of Nigeria. These are almost the same seven societies later studied by Bruce G. Trigger (2003), but Trigger diverges sharply

---

[10]   Childe (1950).
[11]   Adams (1966).
[12]   Wheatley (1971).

from Wheatley's theories on urban origins.[13] In his introduction, Wheatley explains the benefits of the comparative method for studying this topic:

> *The evidence available in each of the other realms of nuclear urbanism is so meager, fragmented, and ambiguous that a comparative approach alone appears likely to provide fruitful insights into the dynamics of urban genesis. The Chinese evidence alone would prove inconclusive even were it very much more abundant than is in fact the case, but it assumes a completely new significance when viewed in light of the totality of materials available for study of the early history of urbanism.[14]*

This comparative method allowed Wheatley to arrive at a new theory of urban origins, testable by future archaeological excavations. His thesis is clearly stated at the outset of part two:

> *Whenever, in any of the seven regions of primary urban generation, we trace back the characteristic urban form to its beginnings, we arrive not at a settlement that is dominated by commercial relations, a primordial market, or at one that is focused on a citadel, an archetypal fortress, but rather at a ceremonial complex.[15]*

Briefly outlined, Wheatley's theory is that the primary integrating factor which superseded village level organization in the ancient world was a coalescing around a ceremonial center, a sacred shrine situated at

---

[13] Trigger (2003), 121. Trigger excludes the Indus Valley civilization, because of lack of sufficient evidence, and separates Mesoamerica into the Valley of Mexico and the lowland Maya civilization.

[14] Wheatley (1971), 6.

[15] Wheatley (1971), 225.

an *axis mundi* which was a node for heaven-earth communication and which modeled the human realm upon a cosmic order. This center then became the nexus of a redistributive economy which extracted an agricultural surplus from peasants and provided rations to full-time specialists like priests and later artisans and bureaucrats. While Wheatley acknowledges that warfare, trade, and irrigation might also be additional integrating factors towards urbanism, all of these could only operate after the umbrella of the divine legitimation was first provided to early leaders by their control of the ceremonial center.

Wheatley's theory was clearly inspired by the finds at places like the lowest levels at the Eridu site in Mesopotamia which showed a series of eighteen smaller and smaller ancient shrines underlying the later ziggurat at the city site, or the current state of Shang archaeology at Anyang, which seemed to reveal an urban formation primarily devoted to divination and sacrifice. Wheatley's theory was also a counterreaction to the over-emphasis on material factors in societal evolution and accords with his contemporary anthropologist Roy Rappaport's influential theory about the role of religion and the sacred in the rise of complex societies[16].

Numerous criticisms have been levelled at Wheatley's theory. It argues for a universal unilinear evolution of cities in the Old World and the New World. Rather than seeing massive cities like Teotihuacán as fundamentally divergent in character from less-densely populated places like Anyang, he just sees them as occupying different stages on the same evolutionary continuum. The role of Egypt and China in his comparison is also problematic. The study of Egyptian urbanism is still in its infancy, and was even more so in Wheatley's day, and the great majority of Egyptian towns are still buried under meters of Nile silt. There was a time not too long ago that Egyptologist John A. Wilson called Egypt

---

[16] Rappaport (1971).

before the 18th Dynasty "a civilization without cities", because of the dearth before the New Kingdom of the type of large, dense settlements like those seen at Uruk in Mesopotamia or Mohenjo Daro in the Indus Valley.[17] The only real evidence Wheatley can point to that early Egyptian cities were founded around ceremonial centers is the tradition that places like Hierakonpolis possessed a patron deity (Horus) with some remains of Predynastic shrines or later traditions about the founding of Memphis. For his Chinese evidence, Wheatley relied mostly on the ongoing publication of the Anyang excavations by Shi Zhangru 石璋如 (1902-2004), and the syntheses by Li Ji 李濟 (1896-1979) and Zhang Guangzhi 張光直 (K.C. Chang, 1931-2001), and the excavation reports of the Erligang period site at Zhengzhou 鄭州. At that time, the Shang "cities" at Yanshi 偃師 and Huanbei 洹北 had not yet been discovered, and the earlier site of Erlitou 二里頭 had not yet been published. Wheatley also uses later Chinese texts to formulate his cosmic picture of the Chinese city, including the *Shangshu* 尚書, the *Shijing* 詩經, and particularly the *Kaogong ji* 考工記, the compilation of which dates to the late Warring States period. Wheatley's theory is also heavily under the influence of Karl Polanyi's (1886-1964) work, which argues that ancient societies went through economic stages of reciprocity and redistribution and had no true price-setting markets until modern times. This has been proven incorrect many times over, as market elements already existed in most ancient societies, including in China, alongside structures of a command economy.

Xia Nai

One interesting standout during the mid-twentieth century, trained in Egyptology and Chinese archaeology, was the remarkable scholar Xia Nai 夏鼐 (1910-85), a protégé of Li Ji. Xia became the first Chinese

---

[17] Wilson (1951, 34; 1960).

citizen to obtain a PhD in Egyptology, at University College London (submitted 1943; granted 1946). He studied archaeology under Mortimer Wheeler and learned to read Egyptian (hieroglyphic, hieratic, and demotic) under Stephan Glanville and Alan Gardiner. He participated in the British dig in Armant, Egypt as well as another in Palestine and did dissertation research in the Cairo Museum for over a year. His dissertation on Egyptian beads in the Petrie Collection at UCL was quite important for its seriation typology and chronology, but it was not published until 2014[18]. When Xia returned to China in 1941, he switched fields to become an archaeologist of Early China. He became a leader of the archaeological field in China for the next several decades, and as Director of the Institute of Archaeology of the Chinese Academy of Sciences (1962–1982), he had a great influence on theory and methodology in the field[19]. He frequently relied on his experience working on digs in England and Egypt when analyzing prehistoric Chinese sites, though he published very little explicitly comparative work on Ancient Egypt and Early China. A curious short research note published by then doctoral candidate Xia Nai in 1938 does compare a similar idiom in the Chinese and Egyptian languages regarding the notion of "youth" and the smell of soured mother's milk on the breath[20]. In an interview with NHK in 1983, he also briefly compared the structure of the Chinese and Egyptian writing systems[21]. Even this amount of foreign experience and comparative work proved dangerous for Xia Nai, for during the Cultural Revolution, he was persecuted as a "capitalist roader" and spent long periods in labor and reeducation camps.

---

[18] Xia Nai (2014).
[19] Tian Tian (2017), 173–98.
[20] Shiah N. (Xia Nai) (1938).
[21] Xia Nai (1985), 91.

Recent Comparative Studies Incorporating Ancient Egypt and Early China

Bruce G. Trigger

The anthropologist Bruce G. Trigger could be considered the "bearer of the torch," the man who continued and refined comparative studies of ancient civilizations into the contemporary era. As the preeminent historian in the field of archaeological thought, Trigger was keenly aware of his position in the field[22]. Trigger acknowledged that theories of socio-cultural evolution and superficial comparative study of civilizations had been sharply criticized by post-processual archaeologists and those of the cultural relativist school of scholars like Clifford Geertz (1926–2006) since the 1970s. These critics argued that cultural traits cannot be extracted from their larger societal context and drawn out for comparison, and that every culture was unique and could only be understood on its own terms. Thus, they rejected the validity and utility of cross-cultural comparisons. But Trigger continued to engage in this field, because he believed that cultural comparison was at the core of the mission of anthropology.

His study was a couple decades in the making. A preliminary survey was published in 1993 as a series of lectures at the American University of Cairo he had given the previous year[23], and the final study was published a decade later in the more than 750-page tome, *Understanding Early Civilizations: A Comparative Study*[24]. His study compares what he calls "early civilizations", defined as the first "class-based societies"[25], in

---

[22] Trigger (2006).
[23] Trigger (1993).
[24] Trigger (2003).
[25] For his definition of what constitutes an "early civilization" and the notion of "classes", see Trigger (2003), 43–46.

seven areas in the Old World and New World, including Old and Middle Kingdom Egypt, Mesopotamia from Early Dynastic III to the Old Babylonian period, late Shang and early Western Zhou in China, the Aztec, the Classic Maya, the Inka kingdom, and the Yoruba people of West Africa (18th–19th centuries). These are almost the same civilizations studied by Wheatley (1971), except Trigger dropped the Indus Valley civilization, and separated his consideration of Mesoamerica to consider highland (Aztec) and lowland (Maya), separately. To qualify for his study, each civilization had to be "primary," meaning it had to be the first class-based society to develop in its area of the world and not have been "shaped by substantial dependance or control by other, more complex societies", even though some might have been a further elaboration on earlier state-level societies from the same area (such as with the Aztec and Maya)[26].

Trigger's core comparative methodology was to try and separate out similarities between the early civilizations that were brought about through "constraints" on human behavioral variation from the environment, functional limitations, rational economic calculations, or "practical reason" and "human nature", from those differences that arose idiosyncratically because of historical particularities and regional cultural practices. This is the methodology I chose to follow in my recent book on Ancient Egypt and Early China as well (Barbieri-Low 2021).

Unlike Wheatley, who chose to just look at the topic of urban generation in the early civilizations, and its relationship to religion and the economy, Trigger (2003) chose to look at three major areas of comparison, sociopolitical organization, economy, and cognitive and symbolic aspects, subdivided into twenty-three different chapters on comparable subjects like kingship, urbanism, administration, law, food

---

[26] Trigger (2003), 28–29.

production, land ownership, craft specialization, trade, cosmology, ritual, art, architecture, and literacy.

To defend against the critiques of the cultural anthropologists, Trigger tried to understand the workings of each civilization before he began to compare aspects of them. He insisted that "a detailed and independent understanding of each early civilization is a prerequisite for comparative study", because "using information about one early civilization to fill gaps in our knowledge of another inevitably creates the appearance of greater cross-cultural uniformity than was actually the case"[27]. Trigger was clearly thinking of Wittfogel (1957) and especially Wheatley (1971) when he was making this statement. He had a curious practice of reading nearly all the secondary literature on each civilization and only stopping when the books ceased to reveal new information to him, resulting in about one hundred books and numerous articles for each area[28].

Trigger hoped to understand *emic* terminology to comprehend culture on its own terms and to avoid the subjective bias of using translations of indigenous concepts. He also hoped to root out subjective elements in the original sources and in secondary literature[29]. However, Trigger only had intermediate-level training in one of the ancient languages of his study (Egyptian), which put him at the mercy of translators and their interpretations. This could have been mitigated by using a co-authored approach (or by limiting the number of cultures under comparison), but Trigger claimed that "multi-authored studies of early civilizations have their own pitfalls", and that "a single interpretative viewpoint" more than compensates for a "heavy reliance on secondary sources"[30].

---

27   Trigger (2003), 28–29.
28   Trigger (2003), 53.
29   Trigger (2003), 62–65.
30   Trigger (2003), xii.

Trigger's conclusions were surprising to even himself and have met with significant criticism. He had originally assumed, along with the materialist (Marxist) and ecological-evolutionary perspective, that societies at the same stage of development would be most similar in their economic institutions, relatively similar in their political arrangements, but completely different in the areas of religious beliefs. In contrast, Trigger found among his group of cultures only "one general form of class structure, only two main forms of sociopolitical organization, and one set of key religious beliefs"[31].

Unfortunately, in Trigger's grand comparative study, China is easily the weakest participant. Because he insisted on choosing what he considered the first class-based society in each civilizational tradition, he selected the Shang civilization as seen at Anyang (ca. 1300–1045 BCE) for his China component. While some reliable information could be obtained from the archaeology of the Shang temple, workshop, and royal burials around the Anyang site, or from the Shang oracle bones, this information pales in comparison to the detailed archaeological and textual information available for Mesopotamia and Egypt or the rich ethnographic accounts concerning the Inka and Aztecs that Trigger had at his disposal[32].

Examining his footnotes and his bibliographical essay on the Chinese material, we see that Trigger had to rely primarily on articles and syntheses in English by the most active interpreter of Chinese archaeology for the non-Chinese speaking world, K.C. Chang[33]. This

---

[31] Trigger (2003), 684.

[32] Trigger (2003, 117) acknowledges this deficiency, when he states, "Although numerous site reports, monographs, and papers relating to ancient China have been published in the Chinese language, the literature regarding this civilization published in English is probably less abundant than that relating to any other early civilization." He also states (Trigger 2003, 58) that "for Shang China, a similarly restricted range of written texts is combined with limited archaeological data, which are also skewed towards upper-class culture."

[33] K.C. Chang joined the anthropology department at Yale when Trigger was finishing up his PhD there, and the two became lifelong correspondents.

included the 1986 edition of Chang's *Archaeology of Ancient China* as well as his 1980 synthesis *Shang Civilization* [34]. Trigger also cites Ho Ping-ti's equally famous but contentious 1975 synthesis, *Cradle of the East,* and the structuralist interpretations of Sarah Allan's, *The Shape of the Turtle* from 1991[35]. For oracle bone scholarship, Trigger only had access to David Keightley's book, *Sources of Shang History,* and articles by Keightley or K.C. Chang on various aspects of the Shang as seen through oracle bones[36].

The hypotheses of K.C. Chang are not universally accepted by even a majority of Shang specialists, especially his disputed theory about the shamanistic nature of Shang kingship, most widely published in his 1983 book, *Art, Myth, and Ritual: The Path to Political Power in Ancient China,* which Trigger frequently cites[37]. Not being able to read Chinese, Trigger was unable to assess the archaeological reports or textual data for himself, but could only rely on these syntheses or a small subset of translated inscriptions. Therefore, he uncritically accepted the unproven hypotheses of the synthesizers and the interpretive worldview of the translators of ancient inscriptions. Because of these problems and biases, nearly every conclusion Trigger draws about the Shang economy, politics, or religion is highly problematic. Trigger's conclusion that the Shang state at Anyang was a territorial state like Egypt, rather than a hegemonic city-state, does not accord with the evidence from the oracle bones or the evidence for early walled settlement sites in north and south China.

Even if a scholar like Trigger had been able to read Chinese, the Shang period would still have been a poor choice for comparison with Near Eastern or New World civilizations. Even with the advances of the

---

[34] Chang (1980, 1986).

[35] Ho (1975); Allan (1991).

[36] Keightley (1978).

[37] Chang (1983).

last thirty years of Shang archaeology, most major aspects of Shang economy, politics, society, and religion are still very poorly understood. Despite some further advances and new discoveries, oracle bones are still a very limited source of information for anything outside of the divination ritual and its pantheon of recipients. As I argued in my book (Barbieri-Low 2021), it would have been far better to compare early imperial China with New Kingdom Egypt, since the robust source base for the Qin and Han periods makes the comparison so much richer and the conclusions more reliable.

Poo Mu-chou

A comparative study that was more focused than Trigger's work, and in my view more successful, was Poo Mu-chou's 2005 study, *Enemies of Civilization*[38]. This was the book that first inspired me to undertake comparative study of Egypt and China and showed the scholarly community the kind of fresh insights that could result from such careful work. Unlike Trigger's study of seven civilizations (work which Poo was aware of in its preliminary publication from Trigger [1993]), Poo Mu-chou's study focused on only three civilizations: Mesopotamia, Egypt, and China. And unlike Trigger, who was only competent at an intermediate level in one philological tradition, that of Egypt, Poo Mu-chou had earned a PhD in Egyptology at Johns Hopkins, with a secondary field in Near Eastern studies, and has worked as a Sinologist studying Early China for decades. Therefore, he was able to read the primary sources of his study in at least two of the three areas under his study, with some competency in the third as well. This helped to mitigate one of the major problems of Trigger's study, where he often fell under the spell of the interpretations of the translators or synthesizers, especially regarding the Chinese evidence. Poo Mu-chou

---

[38] Poo (2005).

excluded the civilization of India from his study because he lacked similar linguistic training in that area, and he decided to exclude Greek civilization as well, because he felt that adequate studies had already been published on the Greek view of foreigners.

Poo also focused his study on a single topic, the view of foreigners in each of the three civilizations, rather than look at the dozens of topics compared by Trigger (2003). The reason Poo chose this topic is that he hoped that by studying how each society viewed the "other", he could approach an understanding of the "cultural consciousness" of each civilization, which Poo defines as "the conceptions of the characteristics of a culture commonly shared and employed by its people to distinguish themselves from other cultures"[39]. The book is divided into an introduction, conclusion, and six topical chapters, such as "In Search of Cultural Identity," "Representations", "Relations and Attitudes", "Foreigners Within", and "The Transformation of the Barbarians".

The comparative method allowed Poo Mu-chou to arrive at some illuminating conclusions that would not have been possible if he had only studied Chinese or Egyptian civilization, thus justifying his use of the comparative method. First, he demonstrated that in each culture area there was an official elite discourse which decried the intractably uncivilized and evil nature of foreigners, even while private documents and mortuary remains suggests that the actual situation was more flexible and accommodating. Furthermore, he concludes that in all three civilizations, "foreigners were distinguished mainly on cultural rather than racial grounds", adding significant weight to the argument that racial constructions of difference are a very late, modern development[40]. The key difference between the three civilizations' view of foreigners was in their attitude toward assimilation. Though each culture shared the

---

[39] Poo (2005), 2.
[40] Poo (2005), 152.

feature of considering themselves superior to foreigners, Mesopotamians demonstrated no ideological imperative why foreigners should be assimilated to their superior culture, though in practice that is exactly what happened to Amorites, Kassites, and a number of other outsiders or invaders. In Egypt, there was also no ideological drive to assimilate foreigners, in fact the dual nature of *maat* (order) and *isfet* (chaos) basically required that the world must have barbarians in it, to fulfill the nature of the duality of the world order. In China, however, Confucians "posed the ideal of Sinicizing all the barbarians as one of the main goals in the political-cultural life of the nation"[41]. Poo suggested that this Chinese attitude was born more from a sense of insecurity or lack of confidence than anything else. Poo's study also helped to refine a definition of what a civilization actually was, concluding that civilization "should be seen not as a morally or aesthetically justified state of existence, but as a set of intricate strategies that presupposed a hegemonic order aimed at the continual survival of the community in opposition to the foreigners"[42].

Professor Poo was quite aware of the myriad problems inherent within his chosen topic and was quite modest in calling his work an "experiment" in comparative study. Throughout the study, it became apparent that the comparison was rendered more problematic by the uneven nature of the surviving sources for the different civilizations. For example, the chapter on representations of foreigners was certainly hampered by the lack of a tradition of representational art in China before the Warring States period, which makes it hard to compare visual representations of foreigners with traditions like that of Egypt, where Nubians and Syrians were depicted in meticulous, if stereotypical, detail. In addition, Poo falls into the same problem as Trigger by relying

---

[41] Poo (2005), 153.
[42] Poo (2005), 156.

on the textual records of the Shang, which are limited to the biased divination records of the Anyang period.

This brings up an even more important issue with Poo's study and that is the selection of time periods upon which he focuses. Because his study seeks to look at the entire traditions of these three "great civilizations", Poo spreads out a very broad chronological net. So, rather than just focus on a structurally comparable period like the "early civilization" of the Shang period in China and the Old Kingdom in Egypt as Trigger (2003) does, Poo extends his study within China all the way up to the early imperial period (ca. 1500 BCE–200 CE). For Egypt, his study draws on the entire pharaonic period, up until the Ptolemaic Period, so roughly 3000–300 BCE, and for Mesopotamia, he incorporates the entire tradition from the Uruk Period up until the Persian conquest (ca. 3000–550 BCE). He sees these cutoff dates as constituting a major break, termination, or revolutionary change in the character of each civilization, when they "entered into a new period of cultural metamorphosis"[43]. However, one cannot consider these broad periods of time as monolithic entities. There were vast changes in the society, economy, and religion over those spans, and one could hardly consider the Shang king and the First Emperor of Qin as residing in the same world or possessing an even remotely similar worldview. The same is true for Egypt, for the empire of the New Kingdom was almost as different from the archaic Old Kingdom in Egypt as any two disconnected cultures would be. While Poo does acknowledge that there were important changes in both Egypt and China regarding the view of foreigners over the timespan his study covers, this broad selection still leads to an unfortunate essentialization of each culture, though Poo's study is certainly far more nuanced and less essentializing than earlier studies such as those of either Wittfogel (1957), Eisenstadt (1963), or

---

[43] Poo (2005), 20.

Wheatley (1971).

Haicheng Wang

The most ambitious global comparative study since Trigger's book, which incorporates information from both Ancient Egypt and Early China, was art historian Haicheng's Wang 2014 book *Writing and the Ancient State*[44]. Wang's book investigates the use of writing to "create and maintain order in early states" and argues that the use of writing by state actors created a common body of knowledge that allowed people to recognize the existence of the state and imagine themselves as its subjects, especially through administrative procedures like census and taxation. Conversely, writing also allowed the state to better see its subjects, through standardization, mapping, and naming. Wang openly acknowledges that his work was inspired by the notion of "imagined communities" formulated by historian Benedict Anderson (1926–2015) to explain the origins of nationalism, in which the printed word and the attendant standardization of languages helped people in large countries conceive of belonging to one "nation"[45], and the concept of "legibility" to the state formulated by anthropologist James C. Scott, where modern states simplified, standardized, and homogenized land, resources, writing, and people in order to better count them, control them, and extract resources from them[46].

Haicheng Wang compares writing and record-keeping systems in six early state areas, Mesopotamia, Egypt, highland Mexico, the lowland Maya, the central Andes, and China. He expressly states that his study "aims to use our knowledge of other early states to help us take a fresh look at China"[47]. The book is structured into three parts (king lists,

---

[44] Wang (2014a).
[45] Anderson (1983).
[46] Scott (1998).
[47] Wang (2014a), 1.

administration, and scribal education), with each part consisting of two chapters. The first chapter examines some aspect of writing and literacy in the other five state areas, while the second chapter in each part looks only at China, but also draws explicit comparisons with the other areas just presented. Wang is a specialist in early Chinese material culture and texts, though he did undertake some basic training in Egyptology and Assyriology in graduate school before starting this comparative work. His work runs into some of the same chronological coverage issues as Poo Mu-chou's study, as he draws from written inscriptions and transmitted and excavated texts from China from the Shang period up until the Han and compares this with material from Mesopotamia from the Uruk period until the Babylonian period, and from Egypt from the Predynastic to the New Kingdom period.

Wang uses the comparative method to great effect, for it allows him to offer a fresh approach to the Chinese evidence and offer provocative new interpretations to old problems. For example, ever since the discovery of the oracle bones of the Shang from the site at Anyang, it has been recognized that the list of Shang kings recorded in the divinations is in almost complete agreement with the list of kings recorded by Sima Qian more than a thousand years later. Scholars had assumed that the Han historian somehow had access to the temple genealogy of the Warring States polity of Song, which was a state founded to continue sacrifice to the Shang ancestors after the Zhou reconquest following the Wu Geng rebellion. But the state of Song was annexed by Qi in 286 BCE, and this speculative theory has never had any textual basis. By looking at the long tradition of king lists in Mesopotamia and Egypt, Wang Haicheng is able to suggest that the traditional list of Shang kings was maintained for a millennium as a school text in a scribal tradition. He provocatively suggests that the Mandate of Heaven ideology, which Herrlee Creel and others attributed to the Duke of Zhou at the beginning of the Western Zhou, may have actually been formulated during the decline of the Western Zhou by high-ranking scribal officials employing the king lists of Xia and Shang to obtain leverage over kings who had wayward morals. Sima Qian used this king list in a very similar way to Near Eastern traditions, as it presented an unbroken line of legitimate kingship as decreed by Heaven[48].

The comparative method also enables Haicheng Wang to recharacterize certain canonical Chinese texts as originating in school exercises to teach scribes at the intermediate to advanced level[49]. In both Egypt and Mesopotamia, intermediate scribal students usually advanced from copying simple lists and categorically arranged primers to copying collections of maxims (i.e., wisdom texts like *The Teachings of Ptahhotep*) and short hymns. After demonstrating just such a wisdom text from the Warring States Chu tomb at Guodian, Haicheng Wang then daringly suggests that the famous *Analects of Confucius* (*Lunyu* 論語) and the *Classic of Filial Piety* (*Xiaojing* 孝經) both originated as school texts in the scribal tradition. There is certainly textual evidence from the Han to support their use in education. To this list, I would also include texts like the so-called "Weili zhi dao" 為吏之道 ("How to Be a Good Official") text from tomb no. 11 at Shuihudi, which should now be recognized as a school text.

Finally, Haicheng Wang's comparative method allows him to make a significant intervention in the long-running debate over the reasons behind the invention of writing in the Old World and the New World. The oracle bone script used to write Chinese during the Anyang period is already very advanced and is used to write connected speech. Elsewhere in the world, this stage is achieved several hundred years after the invention of writing. Proto-writing in places like Egypt usually

---

[48] Wang (2014a), 44–52.
[49] Wang (2014a), 286–289.

just records individual names of kings for display (like at tomb U-J at Abydos), or as in Mesopotamia attaches numbers to object names for administrative accounting (as in the proto-cuneiform tablets from Uruk). This stage is lost in China, due to the use of perishable materials for most writing but can be reconstructed by taking a fresh look at the oracle bones for signs of accountancy or list-making structures. Because the oracle bones are the earliest extant writing in China, and deal almost exclusively with divination and sacrifice, it has led to the persistent interpretation among scholars that writing was invented in China for the purpose of ritual communication, and not for royal display or accountancy as seems to be the case in Mesopotamia or Egypt. Haicheng Wang's comparative method allows him to offer a counterargument to this theory.

John Baines

One Egyptologist who has seriously engaged in comparative study with early China is John Baines of Oxford. In 2008, he participated in the symposium at Princeton University, "Art and Archaeology of the Erligang Civilization." His revised paper was eventually published in 2014 as "Civilizations and Empires: A Perspective on Erligang from Early Egypt"[50]. The paper serves as a complement to another paper by Haicheng Wang, which draws parallels between the Erligang expansion and comparable phenomenon in the Uruk period of Mesopotamia and in the Indus Valley and Olmec civilizations. Wang tentatively concluded that the Erligang civilization should be characterized as China's first colonizing empire, which demonstrated a uniform elite culture of bronze ritual vessels that was forcibly exported to outlying areas, but with various underlying local ceramic cultures that continued relatively

---

[50] Baines (2014), 99–119.

unchanged[51].

In Baines' paper, he suggests that the closest parallel period in Egyptian prehistory to the Erligang period of China is the Nagada IIIA-B periods (ca. 3300-3000 BCE) straddling the late Predynastic and Early Dynastic periods in Egypt. In Egyptology, the Nagada IIIB period is also called Dynasty 0, whose kings were buried in the cemetery at Abydos. According to Baines' analysis, the two periods in Egypt and China featured a "uniform character of its elite culture over a large geographical area and its position in a long view as a formative phase of a larger development", which allowed them to be comparable, but he also pointed out a key structural difference in that the Erligang state may have been a short-lived "colonizing empire", ruled from a dominant city-state (at Zhengzhou), whereas Dynasty 0 in Egypt was a "territorial state" that "briefly entertained something like imperial ambitions"[52]. Both periods lasted roughly two centuries.

Baines notes a strong continuity in elite culture and tradition from the late Predynastic in Egypt into the Early Dynastic period, while in China, there appears to have been a break in the continuity between the Erligang Period at Zhengzhou and the late Shang period state seen at Anyang. When comparing the expansion of the Erligang state and the Nagada IIIB state, Baines concludes that "shortly after the formation of the state, both Erligang and Egypt sought to dominate surrounding regions, but their strategies were different". He notes that while the Erligang state seems to have colonized outlying areas (like at the site of Panlongcheng), providing an overlay of elite material culture over a continuous local ceramic culture, whereas the Nagada IIIB state's expansion into Lower Nubia appears to have been more "destructive," seeking to eradicate or drive out the local population, more similar to the

---

[51] Wang (2014b).
[52] Baines (2014), 100.

European colonization of North America. The early Egyptian state's expansion into Palestine was of a different character still, mostly involving securing trade or gift-exchange in key import resources like timber and oil but not imposing colonial control (though there does appear to have been some Egyptian settlements) or influencing the local culture in any appreciable way. The Egyptian aim in Palestine was to "trade with the local elite rather than to replace or eliminate it"[53]. Baines suggests that while the Erligang state does probably reach the definition of a colonizing empire, the Nagada IIIB state's expansion does not fit the definition sufficiently, so the first true Egyptian imperial expansions would be those in the second millennium during the Middle Kingdom and New Kingdom. Baines also points to one further distinction, contrasting the period of decentralization following the collapse of the short-lived Erligang empire with the continuous strengthening of the territorial state in Egypt during the Early Dynastic and Old Kingdom periods.

Christian Langer

In 2018, Christian Langer, then a doctoral candidate at the Freie Universität in Berlin published a chapter in an edited volume called "The Concept of 'Frontier' in New Kingdom Egypt: A Comparative Approach to the Spatiality of Ideology"[54]. His chapter explored the concept of frontier in the New Kingdom empire, comparing the ideology of frontiers in Egypt, the colonial imperialism of early modern Europe, the Roman Empire, and Early China. The comparative study allowed Langer to extricate indigenous concepts of "frontier" from Egyptian, Roman, Chinese, and other contexts, even if one specific word could not be found to equate with "frontier".

---

[53] Baines (2014), 110.
[54] Langer (2018).

He begins by clarifying that a "border" is a hard line on a map that is "bilaterally agreed upon," whereas a "frontier" is a spatial-cultural division between a civilized domain and the barbarian void, a concept that is unilaterally defined by the civilized power, denoting an unequal relationship between societies. Thus, "frontiers are not only constructions of boundaries in space but also of boundaries between human beings", epistemological boundaries that differentiate "different ideologies and modes of knowledge production"[55].

In Egyptian political and religious thought, there is the idea that Egypt proper is the domain of *maat* (truth, justice, and order), whereas the lands beyond Egypt are the realm of *isfet* (chaos and disorder), inhabited by uncivilized peoples. The ideological imperative to conquer disorder and replace it with *maat* gave Egyptian armies a conquest ideology similar to the frontier concept of Euro-America. Ideologically, this was a clear-cut cultural boundary, with no gray area in between, even though in the real world, there existed hazy zones of contact between the two.

Langer then surveys the concept of frontiers from European early modern empires in the New World, which viewed the frontier as separating the economically vibrant Christian world from the economically backward infidels and pagans and thus justified imperial conquest as a civilizing mission. Looking at the case of the Roman Empire, Langer shows that while there is no Latin word precisely matching the word "frontier", a constellation of terms including *humanitas, imperium,* and *provinciae* constructed the unequal relationship between a civilized insider group and a barbarian outsider group, which could become Roman through conquest and assimilation within the "civilizing medium" of the provinces outside of the Italian peninsula. The case of the Sino-Barbarian (Hua-Yi 華夷) dichotomy was chosen in Langer's study,

---

[55] Langer (2018), 47–49.

because it "presents an othering narrative outside European contexts"[56]. Langer interprets a similar frontier ideology in the preimperial and imperial Chinese case, where the dichotomy between a civilized in-group and a barbarian out-group is given a spatial dimension and justification for conquest and assimilation at the frontier, for the barbarians could be converted to Chinese culture, thus expanding the realm of Zhongguo 中國 to become coterminous with the known world (Tianxia 天下). Despite the civilizing ideology found in Confucian texts, Langer finds that in real terms, Qin and Han governments did not explicitly carry out a "civilizing mission" of conversion in real practice. Therefore, Langer concludes that Early China did not really have the same concept of frontier as New Kingdom Egypt, European empires, or the Roman Empire[57]. And whereas the barbarians in the Roman and Chinese cases could acculturate and become civilized by adhering to in-group ethical norms, Egyptian discourse does not seem to have allowed barbarians to be fundamentally transformed into Egyptians. Their land could be conquered and incorporated into the Egyptian empire, but they would remain essentially foreign.

According to his website, Dr. Langer is currently a postdoctoral fellow at Peking University and is editing a volume called *Global Egyptology II*, which will include a chapter comparing the Yellow River and the Nile, co-authored by Di Shiru. The first volume of *Global Egyptology* that Dr. Langer edited did not contain any chapters with similar Egypt-China comparisons, but it does contain a brief history of the field of Egyptology in China by Tian Tian[58].

Yuri Pines and Juan Carlos Moreno García

The 2020 special issue of the *Journal of Egyptian History* (Moreno

---

[56] Langer (2018), 53.
[57] Langer (2018), 63-64.
[58] Tian Tian (2017).

García, Morris, and Miniaci 2020) was dedicated to the topic of "Egyptology and Global History", and contained one article specifically devoted to a comparison between Egypt and China[59]. In his introduction to the special issue, Egyptologist Juan Carlos Moreno García explains that the paradigm of global history encompasses both studies that explore the connections between cultures as well as those that conduct a rigorous comparative analysis between them. This trend in historical studies was in part a reaction to Eurocentric narratives with their imperialist and Orientalist viewpoints. These new studies have explored constructions like the "state" or "empires" or the nature of ancient economies from a comparative viewpoint, but Moreno García laments that it is "most regrettable that pharaonic Egypt has played a marginal role and contributed little or nothing to most of these inspiring debates". To begin to correct this inadequacy, this issue contains examples of both types of studies of Egypt within the field of global antiquity[60].

The special issue contains an excellent article comparing Ancient Egypt and Early China, co-authored by Juan Carlos Moreno García and Sinologist Yuri Pines called "*Maat* and *Tianxia:* Building World Orders in Ancient Egypt and China"[61]. In many ways, the article builds on the earlier piece by Langer (2018) as well as on recent work by Moreno García (2013, 2019) on the nature of the Egyptian state and administration and by Pines (2002, 2021) on changing conceptions of the phrase *tianxia.*

The article seeks to explore the impact of concepts of "world order" on the resiliency and longevity of the two great civilizations, both of which survived extended periods of fragmentation and foreign conquest.

---

[59] Moreno García and Pines (2020). This article was published too late for me to analyze or survey in my book *Ancient Egypt and Early China* (Barbieri-Low [2021]), though I did include it in my bibliography.

[60] Moreno García (2020), 5–10.

[61] Moreno García and Pines (2020).

For Egypt, the single term which signified "order, justice, harmony, and good government" was *maat*. The legitimation of the Egyptian ruler was in part founded on the principle that he was the "Lord of *maat*," who preserved order and justice in the world and kept the forces of chaos and injustice (*isfet*) at bay. The term also had a geographic connotation, for the land along the Nile was the domain where *maat* prevailed, whereas the barbarians and nomads of the desert were regarded as a dangerous "other" which could only be conquered, but never truly assimilated to the culture of the land of *maat*. In contrast, *tianxia* "all under Heaven" was primarily a spatial term which originally incorporated all the land under the vault of the sky. Thus, it theoretically incorporated the land of the barbarians as well as the Chinese. During the Spring and Autumn period, it came to represent a "cultural unified *oikumene*, the realm of shared values, shared public opinion of the elites, shared cultural orientations". By the Warring States period (453−221 BCE), it came to represent a "supra-territorial realm" which encompassed all the various states and should ideally be "unified" or "settled" under one monarch[62]. By extension, *tianxia* also had some sense of a moral and political order, for it was supposed to be ruled with humanity and righteousness by the "son of Heaven", the clan leader chosen by the sky god to justly rule the world. The strongest similarity the authors identify between the two concepts is that they both encouraged a world order in which "political disintegration was considered anomalous and most unwelcome"[63]. Both concepts were also idealistic conceptions, and when confronted with real-world situations such as powerful neighbors (Hittites or Xiongnu) or the immigration and incorporation of foreign peoples, there was great tension between the rhetorical ideal and the political situation on the ground.

---

[62] Moreno García and Pines (2020), 232.
[63] Moreno García and Pines (2020), 245.

This stimulating article also prompts us to consider two methodological issues. The first involves the working methods of comparativists. In comparative work on China and Greece or China and Rome, the three most prominent writing styles of comparison have been single-authored articles or books, where the primary author may or may not have linguistic competence in each culture under study, co-authored pieces where one specialist from each area work together, or parallel articles or book chapters by two authors, writing about the same subject in each of their areas of specialization. This co-authored article by Moreno García and Pines reveals clear seams in the writing, where the full exposition on Egyptian *maat* or Chinese *tianxia* were written by the two authors separately, and the comparative analysis is mostly saved for the introduction and the conclusion.

The other methodological issue centers on the notion of translatability. The two authors admit early in the article that there is no exact Chinese equivalent to the Egyptian term *maat*, which has geographical, political, social, and ethical connotations, whereas *tianxia* is mostly a geographic designation, and only rarely is it used with an extended meaning suggesting a "regime of value". As the authors point out, the core meanings of the Egyptian *maat* are spread over several partially-overlapping Chinese terms, including *de* 德 (virtue/charismatic power), *yi* 義 (righteousness/justice), *zhi* 治 (orderly rule), and *li* 禮 (ritual propriety)[64]. This discussion shows the difficulty of comparing *emic* terms which are deeply embedded in the cultures that are being compared and of finding common ground for the translatability of core concepts.

This comparative analysis of *maat* and *tianxia* did enable the authors to pose a novel and challenging question for further research at the conclusion of the article, pondering whether the more universalistic,

---

[64] Moreno García and Pines (2020), 239–240.

inclusive and "elastic" nature of *tianxia* contributed to the "greater resilience of Chinese civilization", wherein conquest dynasties like the Mongol-led Yuan (1261–1368) and Manchu-led Qing (1644–1912) could claim rulership over *tianxia,* even though they came from areas outside the geographic core of China, turning them into "defenders rather than destroyers", who actually revitalized and territorially-expanded Chinese civilization.

Art Historical Studies

In the field of art history, there have been very few attempts to seriously compare the temple and palace architecture, mural paintings, stone and brick reliefs, bronze vessels and statuary, jewelry, or ceramic and wooden funerary figurines of Ancient Egypt and Early China, despite a wealth of surviving materials and some compelling comparative opportunities.

Before the detailed study of funerary models and figurines from both cultures that I published in my book (Barbieri-Low 2021), there was an exhibition and catalog from the Metropolitan Museum of Art in New York in 2015, which was primarily focused on architectural funerary models from the ancient Americas, primarily from Mexico and the Andes, but which brought in architectural models from both Egypt and China in the Met collections as comparative pieces in a short section called "Architectural Models from Other Traditions". Unfortunately, this section yielded only one sentence of direct comparison between the models of Egypt and China, noting that, "As with the wood examples from Egypt, the Eastern Han models were designed to emulate full-scale architecture and serve as stand-ins for the real thing, ensuring the comfort of the elite deceased"[65].

In 2017, the Ägyptisches Museum und Papyrussammlung in

---

[65] Pillsbury, Sarro, Doyle, and Wiersema (2015), 6–11.

Berlin held a major Exhibition called *China und Ägypten: Wiegen der Welt* (China and Egypt: Cradles of World Civilization), which directly juxtaposed the art of Egypt and China in the same galleries, including numerous loans from the Shanghai Museum and Xuzhou Museum[66]. The exhibition catalog was divided into sections by theme and by media. Some of the sections included: "The Living World", "Writing", "Death and the Afterlife", "The World of Beliefs", and "Kingship and Administration". This allowed the curators to juxtapose Middle Kingdom Egyptian funerary models with Han dynasty Chinese models, New Kingdom glass containers with Warring States, Qin and Han lacquer vessels, Old Kingdom copper vessels with Shang dynasty bronze ritual vessels, Western Zhou bronze bells with Egyptian Late Period *sistrum* and flutes, New Kingdom steles and Shang oracle bones, Egyptian scribal kits and Han inkstones and brushes, Egyptian mummy masks and anthropomorphic sarcophagi alongside a Han dynasty royal jade suit, and various Egyptian and Chinese seals.

Unfortunately, other than grouping analogous items from Egypt and China under the same headings by function or media, there was only minimal comparative analysis of the form, function, or cultural significance of the many objects in the exhibition within the introductory essays of each section. Only in the sections on writing systems or on the types of tombs in each culture was there even an attempt at comparison, and those were in fact very superficial. This was a tremendous lost opportunity, for so much more could have been accomplished in this exhibition.

Anthony Barbieri-Low

When I was working on my dissertation on the origins of mass production in ancient China during the late 1990s, I was encouraged by

---

[66] Kampp-Seyfried and Jung (2017).

my advisor Robert W. Bagley to follow a comparative approach, looking at similar or divergent production techniques in Egypt, Greece, and Rome. Bagley also strongly encouraged me to read all the works of Bruce G. Trigger. Using this comparative approached helped me to uncover the parallel factors which might have led to a fine division of workshop labor in any pre-modern culture, not just in Early China. However, I only touched upon these comparative aspects in the introduction and conclusion to my dissertation (Barbieri-Low 2001). I certainly did not feel confident enough to include very much of this comparative study in my book *Artisans in Early Imperial China* (Barbieri-Low 2007), since I could not read the source texts and inscriptions in the original languages.

As a young assistant professor, I eagerly read Trigger's magnum opus, *Understanding Early Civilizations* (Trigger 2003), and was impressed at his exhaustive comparison of the seven societies in his study, but I was dismayed at his treatment of Shang China. While Trigger had certainly read and absorbed nearly all the secondary literature on Shang China in European languages, he was not able to read the inscriptions in the original languages and also had to rely on synthesizers of Chinese archaeology like K.C. Chang, instead of reading the original archaeological reports. In fact, Trigger was not really an expert in the language of any of the cultures in his massive study, which was a serious handicap. Relying solely on translations of primary sources is quite dangerous, since the translation of an ancient text is an interpretative exercise, and those using those translations unconsciously adopt the interpretation and worldview of the translator.

But then I read Poo Mo-chou's *Enemies of Civilization* (Poo 2005), which came out around the same time. This inspired me further and demonstrated that a comparative study that focused on a single topic across two or three ancient civilizations could be quite illuminating and more manageable. It also demonstrated the increased fidelity and persuasiveness of a study conducted by an author who had training in the languages of the majority of his primary sources.

When the opportunity presented itself in 2013 for me to retrain myself in a second field, I quickly decided to undertake the study of Egyptology, so that I could advance the comparative study of Egypt and China. During my three-year course of study at UCLA, I outlined an ambitious book comparing the "Black Land" of ancient Egypt and the "All under Heaven" of early China. I determined that my study would combine the methodology of Bruce G. Trigger (2003), separating out shared structural traits from historical particularities, the linguistic competency of Poo Mu-chou (2005), relying on my own readings of all the Egyptian and Chinese texts in my study, and the case-study approach of the Rome and China volumes edited by Walter Scheidel (2009, 2015). The result was *Ancient Egypt and Early China: State, Society, and Culture*, which was published in 2021[67].

Avoiding Bruce Trigger's poorly selected comparison of Shang dynasty China with Old and Middle Kingdom Egypt, I chose to compare the Western Han and Wang Mang periods (202 BCE–23 CE) of China with New Kingdom Egypt (ca. 1548–1086 BCE). Despite the thirteen hundred years that separated them on an absolute chronological scale, I considered this to be an appropriate pair for comparison, based on apparent structural parallels and their similar placement on a scale of socio-cultural and political development. Specifically, these two state-level societies represent intensive agricultural infrastructure located near a major flood-prone river, ruled over by a patrilineal monarchy legitimated by divine sanction and administered by highly-trained scribes, which had both conquered territories beyond their traditional political and cultural boundaries to form a far-flung tributary empire.

The study is divided into seven mostly discrete case studies, with

---

[67]   Barbieri-Low (2021).

each focusing on a comparison of analogous phenomenon from the two cultures, but the studies are also grouped into two major parts, based on thematic considerations and source material. The first part, from chapter one to the beginning of chapter five, focuses on the above-ground world of the environment, empire, politics, administration, law, and society. Chapter one is a comparison of the Nile and the Yellow River, framed as a survey of the physical landscape of the rivers and their relationship to agriculture, the political landscape that tied the legitimation of the ruler and fortunes of the dynasty to the flooding of the river, and a ritual landscape which mirrored the contours of the hydrological system in the creation of river deities and their sacrificial systems.

Chapter two compares the empires formed by New Kingdom Egypt in the Levant and that of Han China in the Western Regions of Central Asia. While both empires were originally founded to serve as buffers against foreign aggression, they also served to provide import of tributary luxury goods and export of metropolitan elite culture (i.e., civilization). In both empires, these distant territories were not directly administered but relied on a system of vassal states combined with strategically-placed military garrisons. I also comparatively explore the forms of written diplomacy conducted with these vassal states and with other major powers, including the practice of marriage diplomacy.

Chapter three is an experimental comparison of two notorious figures, Akhenaten, the "heretic king" of Egypt, and Wang Mang, the promoter of Confucianism and the villainous "usurper" of the Han throne. Rather than focus on old problems such as the monotheistic character of Akhenaten's new religion or Wang Mang's supposed insincerity, I reorient the framework to look at the similar role that both "fundamentalist" monarchs played in unsuccessful attempts to reform a troubled, aging empire in which significant resources were jealously guarded by entrenched interest groups.

Chapter four is a comparison of the legal principles of each state, as seen through a side-by-side comparison of analogous legal cases. I examine parallel cases of infringement on sacred property and compare those to cases of simple robbery, and then I look at cases of fornication and adultery. Finally, I examine the practice and enforcement of testamentary wills. Legal principles reveal the values upon which a state is based, and the power and scope of the administration of justice reveals the extent to which that state is able to penetrate into local society or the family.

Chapter five is an in-depth comparison of scribes and scribal culture in Ancient Egypt and Early China. Professional scribes played a crucial role in both cultures, ensuring the day-to-day functioning of the state and its financial stability. This chapter expands the inquiry into scribes by looking at their group identity as expressed through material culture, scribal curricular materials, literary aspirations, and the mortuary assemblages from the tombs of scribes. To personalize this comparison, I select two individual scribes for which we have detailed biographical information and uncover fascinating parallels in how they used connections within their bureaucratic network to enhance their status and wealth.

The second part of the book, which begins in the latter portion of chapter five (on scribes' tombs) changes focus towards funerary culture and the afterlife, a fertile subject for comparative study of Egypt and China, since each culture had constructed elaborate textual, visual, and mortuary representations of afterlife realms. Chapter six explores the parallel practice in Egypt and China of placing into the tomb three-dimensional models that depict production of food and clothing, transport vehicles, domestic architecture, servants, entertainers, and guardians. The study uncovers striking similarities in the function and range of models as well as the class of owners who employed them in their tombs. An examination of the materiality of the models further reveals key similarities and subtle differences in value hierarchies and ritual expression between the two cultures.

Chapter seven explores a comparison of the notion of post-mortem paradises in Egypt and China, looking at textual and visual representations of the "Marsh of Reeds" that is mentioned in Egyptian ritual texts since the Old Kingdom and the paradise of the Queen Mother of the West on Mount Kunlun from the Han period. I suggest that both cultures had developed a notion of an afterlife paradise which was open to the pure of heart, the worthy, or the ritually initiated, and not just to the monarch and his family. This chapter also explores the striking parallel development, whereby one could gain access to these paradisaical realms through playing certain boardgames, *liubo* in China and *senet* for Egypt.

And while the seven case studies were meant to be mostly self-contained, I do reach one broader conclusion in a closing epilogue. I found that the early imperial Chinese state was far more effective at projecting its power into the environment, the society, and the economy than was the New Kingdom Egyptian state, representing a more centralized and intrusive form of totalitarian, bureaucratic monarchy. Rather than explain this difference by persistent cultural factors (i.e., cultural essentialism), I point to the prolonged interstate competition of the Warring States period as the main factor leading to the greater centralized power of the Chinese state, along with Qin innovations like the creation of an abstract notion of the "bureaucratic state," separate from the dynasty.

In the conclusion to the book, I also made some suggestions of areas where scholars could fruitfully compare the two civilizations. Let me review some of those suggestions here. One obvious area for comparison would be the ideology of kingship/emperorship in Egypt and early imperial China, since both civilizations were ruled by a patrilineal monarchy which claimed a universal dominion that was legitimated by divine sanction. Such a study could be combined with a comparative analysis of monumental royal tombs which proclaimed that ideology in physical form.

In the area of politics, ideology, and identity, it would be fascinating to have a cross-cultural study of so-called "conquest dynasties," in which a ruling class from an outsider ethnic group conquered the former imperial core and established their own state. One could compare the Xianbei-led Northern Wei dynasty (386–534 CE) in China with the Libyan Twenty-Second and Twenty-Third Dynasties in Egypt (962–725 BCE) or the Nubian-led Twenty-Fifth Dynasty (770–656 BCE).

Even though Paul Wheatley and Bruce G. Trigger have made comparisons between early Egyptian and Chinese cities and urban formation, given the advances in recent archaeology, a much more detailed comparison of urbanism, as well as of outlying suburban settlements and villages, could certainly be undertaken.

In the area of social history, there are numerous comparable features that could be explored. First, given the fortuitous amount of textual and archaeological material available from the site of Deir el Medina in Egypt, where the craftsmen who constructed the tomb of the New Kingdom pharaohs lived, one could undertake a major comparative study of the lives, careers, and methods of artisans in Egypt and China. In fact, my first book, *Artisans in Early Imperial China* (Barbieri-Low 2007) was originally inspired by the studies I had been reading about Deir el Medina artisans by scholars like Jaroslav Černý (1973), Morris Bierbrier (1989), and Andrea McDowell (1999).

A second area of social history that just begs for comparative study is the realm of coerced labor. Comparative slavery is a major field of study in academia, but the various forms of coerced labor in early China, including conscripts, convicts, indentures, bondservants, and chattel slaves would make an interesting comparison with the numerous types of coerced labor in pharaonic Egypt.

Another vast area of social history open for comparison would be studies of gender and sexuality. These fields are well developed within Egyptology and Sinology separately, but they have never been brought into conversation. In a related area, both royal courts maintained sizeable harems, which were often the location of palace intrigues and assassinations, another fascinating topic for comparative study.

Although some past and planned studies by Poo Mu-chou have compared aspects of Egyptian and Chinese religion and ritual, there are still numerous areas available for comparison. One compelling case study of interest I see is in the area of divination practices.

No serious comparative studies of Egyptian and Chinese literature have yet been undertaken, but there are numerous suitable areas for comparison, including modes of narrative, love poetry, the genre of wisdom literature, and the influence of orality on written genres to name a few.

The field of history of technology is very well developed for both Egyptian and Chinese civilizations, but they are only brought into comparison in passing, in works on the history of metallurgy, nautical technology, or wheeled vehicles. There is certainly room for a more sustained engagement. Some other promising areas for potential work in this area include the nature of the natural and artificial pigments used in artistic creations, or a comparison of the body preservation methods employed in mumification in Ancient Egypt and Early China.

Works Cited

Abel-Rémusat, Jean-Pierre. 1811. *Essai sur la langue et la littérature chinoises.* Paris: Treuttel et Wurtz.

Abel-Rémusat, Jean-Pierre. 1822. *Élémens de la grammaire chinoise, ou, Principes généraux du kou-wen ou style antique: et du kouan-hoa c'est-à-dire, de la langue commune généralement usitée dans l'Empire chinois.* Paris: Imprimerie Royale.

Adams, Robert McCormick. 1966. *The Evolution of Urban Society: Early Mesopotamia and Prehispanic Mexico.* Chicago: Aldine Publishing Company.

Allan, Sarah. 1991. *The Shape of the Turtle: Myth, Art, and the Cosmos in Early China.* Albany: SUNY Press.

Anderson, Benedict. 1983. *Imagined Communities: Reflections on the Origin and Spread of Nationalism.* London: Verso.

Baines, John. 2014. "Civilizations and Empires: A Perspective from Erligang." In *Art and Archaeology of the Erligang Civilization,* edited by Kyle Steinke and Dora C.Y. Ching, 99–119. Princeton: Tang Center for East Asian Art.

Barbieri-Low, Anthony J. 2001. "The Organization of Workshops during the Han Dynasty." PhD diss., Princeton University.

Barbieri-Low, Anthony J. 2007. *Artisans in Early Imperial China.* Seattle: University of Washington Press.

Barbieri-Low, Anthony J. 2021. *Ancient Egypt and Early China: State, Society, and Culture.* Seattle: University of Washington Press.

Bierbrier, Morris. 1989. *The Tomb-Builders of the Pharaohs.* Cairo: American University in Cairo Press.

Carneiro, Robert L. 1970. "A Theory of the Origin of the State." *Science* 169 (3947): 733–738.

Cerný, Jaroslav. 1973. *A Community of Workmen at Thebes in the Ramesside Period.* Cairo: IFAO.

Chang, K.C. 1980. *Shang Civilization.* New Haven: Yale University Press.

Chang, K.C. 1983. *Art, Myth, and Ritual: The Path to Political Authority in Ancient China.* Cambridge: Harvard University Press.

Chang, K.C. 1986. *The Archaeology of Ancient China.* 4th ed. New Haven: Yale University Press.

Childe, V. Gordon. 1950. "The Urban Revolution." *The Town Planning Review* 21 (1–3): 3–17.

Eisenstadt, S. N. 1963. *The Political Systems of Empires.* New York: The Free Press.

Ho, Ping-ti. 1975. *The Cradle of the East: An Inquiry into the Indigenous Origins of Techniques and Ideas of Neolithic and Early Historic China, 5000–1000 BCE.* Chicago: University of Chicago Press.

Kampp-Seyfried, Friederike and Mariana Jung. 2017. *China und Ägypten: Wiegen Der Welt* Munich: Prestel.

Keightley, David N. 1978. *Sources of Shang History: The Oracle Bone Inscriptions of Bronze Age China*. Berkeley: University of California Press.

Langer, Christian. 2018. "The Concept of 'Frontier' in New Kingdom Egypt: A Comparative Approach to the Spatiality of Ideology." In *Time and Space at Issue in Ancient Egypt*, edited by Gaëlle Chantrain and Jean Winand, 47−69. Hamburg: Widmaier Verlag.

McDowell, Andrea. 1999. *Village Life in Ancient Egypt: Laundry Lists and Love Songs*. Oxford: Oxford University Press.

Moreno García, Juan Carlos, ed. 2013. *Ancient Egyptian Administration*. Leiden: Brill.

Moreno García, Juan Carlos. 2019. *The State in Ancient Egypt: Power, Challenges, and Dynamics*. London: Bloomsbury.

Moreno García, Juan Carlos. 2020. "Egyptology and Global History: An Introduction." *Journal of Egyptian History* 13 (1−2): 5−10.

Moreno García, Juan Carlos and Yuri Pines. 2020. "*Maat* and *Tianxia:* Building World Orders in Ancient Egypt and China."*Journal of Egyptian History* 13 (1−2): 227−270.

Moreno García, Juan Carlos, Ellen Morris, and Gianluca Miniaci, eds. 2020. "Egyptology and Global History." Special issue, *Journal of Egyptian History* 13, no. 1−2.

Pillsbury, Joanne, Patricia Joan Sarro, James A. Doyle, and Juliet B. Wiersema. 2015. *Design for Eternity: Architectural Models from the Ancient Americas*. New York: Metropolitan Museum of Art.

Pines, Yuri. 2002. "Changing Views of *Tianxia* in Pre-imperial Discourse."*Oriens Extremus* 43: 101−116.

Pines, Yuri. 2021. "Limits of All-under Heaven Ideology and Praxis of 'Great Unity' in Early Chinese Empire." In *The Limits of Universal Rule: Eurasian Empires Compared,* edited by Yuri Pines, M. Biran, and J. Rüpke, 79−110. Cambridge: Cambridge University Press.

Poo, Mu-chou. 2005. *Enemies of Civilization: Attitudes toward Foreigners in Ancient Mesopotamia, Egypt, and China*. Albany: SUNY Press.

Pope, Maurice. 1999. *The Story of Decipherment*. rev. ed. London: Thames and Hudson.

Rappaport, Roy A. 1971. "The Sacred in Human Evolution." *Annual Review of Ecology and Systematics* 2: 23−44.

Scheidel, Walter, ed. 2009. *Rome and China: Comparative Perspectives on Ancient World Empires*. Oxford: Oxford University Press.

Scheidel, Walter, ed. 2015. *State Power in Ancient China and Rome*. Oxford: Oxford University Press.

Scott, James C. 1998. *Seeing Like a State: How Certain Schemes to Improve the Human Condition Have Failed.* New Haven: Yale University Press.

Steward, Julian H. 1949. "Cultural Causality and Law: A Trial Formulation of the Development of Early Civilizations." *American Anthropologist* 51, no. 1 (January–March): 1–27.

Tian Tian. 2017. "Budding Lotus: Egyptology in China from the 1840's to Today." In *Global Egyptology: Negotiations in the Production of Knowledges on Ancient Egypt in Global Context*, edited by Christian Langer, 173–198. London: Golden House.

Trigger, Bruce G. 1993. *Ancient Civilizations: Ancient Egypt in Context.* Cairo: AUC Press.

Trigger, Bruce G. 2003. *Understanding Early Civilizations: A Comparative Study.* Cambridge: Cambridge University Press.

Trigger, Bruce G. 2006. *A History of Archaeological Thought.* 2nd ed. Cambridge: Cambridge University Press.

Wang, Haicheng. 2014a. *Writing and the Ancient State: Early China in Comparative Perspective.* Cambridge: Cambridge University Press.

Wang, Haicheng. 2014b. "China's First Empire? Interpreting the Material Record of the Erligang Expansion." In *Art and Archaeology of the Erligang Civilization,* edited by Kyle Steinke and Dora C.Y. Ching, 67–97. Princeton: Tang Center for East Asian Art.

Wheatley, Paul. 1971. *The Pivot of the Four Quarters: A Preliminary Enquiry into the Origins and Character of the Ancient Chinese City.* Chicago: Aldine.

Wilson, John A. 1951. *The Burden of Egypt: An Interpretation of Ancient Egyptian Culture.* Chicago: University of Chicago Press.

Wilson, John A. 1960. "Egypt through the New Kingdom: Civilization without Cities." In *City Invincible: A Symposium on Urbanization and Cultural Development in the Ancient Near East,* edited by C.H. Kraeling and Robert McC Adams, 124–164. Chicago: University of Chicago Press.

Wittfogel, Karl August. 1938. "Die Theorie der orientalischen Gesellschaft." *Zeitschrift für Sozialforschung* 7 (1938): 90–122.

Wittfogel, Karl August. 1956. "The Hydraulic Civilizations." In *Man's Role in Changing the Face of the Earth*, edited by William L. Thomas, 152–164. Chicago: University of Chicago Press.

Wittfogel, Karl August. 1957. *Oriental Despotism: A Comparative Study of Total Power.* New Haven: Yale University Press.

Xia Nai. 1938. "A Chinese Parallel to an Egyptian Idiom." *The Journal of Egyptian Archaeology* 24, no. 1 (December): 127–128.

Xia Nai 夏鼐. 1985. *Zhongguo wenming de qiyuan* 中國文明的起源. Beijing: Wenwu Chubanshe.

Xia Nai. 2014. *Ancient Egyptian Beads*. London: Springer.

（Anthony Barbieri-Low, Department of History, University of California, Santa Barbara）

图书在版编目(CIP)数据

荷马与赫西奥德的竞赛/张巍主编.—上海：复旦大学出版社，2023.5
（西方古典学辑刊. 第五辑）
ISBN 978-7-309-16691-0

Ⅰ.①荷…　Ⅱ.①张…　Ⅲ.①史诗-诗歌研究-古希腊　Ⅳ.①I545.072

中国国家版本馆 CIP 数据核字(2023)第 015025 号

荷马与赫西奥德的竞赛

张　巍　主编
责任编辑/史立丽

复旦大学出版社有限公司出版发行
上海市国权路 579 号　邮编：200433
网址：fupnet@ fudanpress. com　http://www. fudanpress. com
门市零售：86-21-65102580　　团体订购：86-21-65104505
出版部电话：86-21-65642845
上海四维数字图文有限公司

开本 787×960　1/16　印张 26　字数 373 千
2023 年 5 月第 1 版
2023 年 5 月第 1 版第 1 次印刷

ISBN 978-7-309-16691-0/I·1345
定价：75.00 元